W9-AGK-727

LUSTY WIND
FOR CAROLINA

In the fourth thrilling novel of Inglis Fletcher's famous Carolina Chronicles, three unforgettable stories entwine:

The sacrifice and triumph of the Fountaine party as they challenge the uncharted swamps and forests of Cape Fear River in search of a promised land.

Brawling battles at sea, and the love of Roger Mainwairing for a lady buccaneer whose heart longs only for plunder.

The scandalous passion of mistress and servant, of fiery Gabrielle Fountaine and David Moray, never more enslaved than in the world they called free.

ADVENTURE, ROMANCE AND PERIL IN A LAND WHERE DREAMS WERE THE PRIZE OF VALOR

Bantam Books by Inglis Fletcher
Ask your bookseller for the books you have missed

BENNETT'S WELCOME
LUSTY WIND FOR CAROLINA
MEN OF ALBEMARLE
ROANOKE HUNDRED
ROGUE'S HARBOR

Lusty Wind
for Carolina

Inglis Fletcher

*This low-priced Bantam Book
has been completely reset in a type face
designed for easy reading, and was printed
from new plates. It contains the complete
text of the original hard-cover edition.*
NOT ONE WORD HAS BEEN OMITTED.

LUSTY WIND FOR CAROLINA
*A Bantam Book / published by arrangement with
Bobbs-Merrill Company, Inc.*

PRINTING HISTORY
Bobbs-Merrill edition published 1944

Bantam edition / January 1971

2nd printing .... April 1971	5th printing ...... January 1974
3rd printing .... March 1972	6th printing .... February 1976
4th printing .... March 1972	7th printing .. September 1976
8th printing .... October 1980	

*All rights reserved.
Copyright 1944 by The Bobbs-Merrill Company.
Cover art copyright © 1980 by Bantam Books.
This book may not be reproduced in whole or in part, by
mimeograph or any other means, without permission.
For information address: The Bobbs-Merrill Company,
4 West 58th Street, New York, New York 10019.*

ISBN 0–553–13393–4

Published simultaneously in the United States and Canada

Bantam Books are published by Bantam Books, Inc. Its trademark, consisting of the words "Bantam Books" and the portrayal of a bantam, is Registered in U.S. Patent and Trademark Office and in other countries. Marca Registrada. Bantam Books, Inc., 666 Fifth Avenue, New York, New York 10103.

PRINTED IN THE UNITED STATES OF AMERICA

17 16 15 14 13 12 11 10 9 8

DEDICATED TO

VILHJALMUR STEFANSSON

who, in our time, has thought beyond known horizons.
In common with the great sea captains of the past,
he ventured uncharted seas and unmapped
land, to advance knowledge.

CONTENTS

BOOK I

BOOK II

ACKNOWLEDGMENT

This is the third in a series of novels of Colonial Carolina. It deals with the struggle to maintain free trade routes, from American Plantations to world markets. The period 1718 to 1725 has been compressed for reasons that concern the swifter movement of the story. But the important and immovable dates have been observed. Regarding the settlement of the Cape Fear River, I have drawn on the two attempted seatings that antedated the permanent settlement of 1725.

After the Peace of Utrecht in 1713, the merchants of Britain endeavoured to restore trade to all the known seas; to bring back the days of Elizabeth and her great sea captains; and build up, through trade, the much-needed prosperity of the Island Kingdom.

The Lords of Trade and Plantations, sitting in London, held the key. Their records tell the story of all the Plantations in America. The Carolinas and the West Indian Plantations presented a particular problem, because of the pirate hordes that infested the Caribbean waters and the long outer Banks that guard the coast of Carolina.

The book had its beginnings at Nassau, on the island of New Providence, which was once a rendezvous of pirates, comparable with Madagascar. From here their ships lay across the trade routes north and south, east and west.

The Nassau Library, housed in an old octagonal building, with walls several feet thick, was a powder magazine in colonial times. From the balcony atop the building one looks over the harbour, which once sheltered the pirate captains and their ships. It is easy to dream up stories of the past in these surroundings.

The story was completed in the Library of Congress, in Washington. Here in the Rare Book Room I had access to an exhaustive collection of books on pirates and early colonial trade. In the Manuscript Division there were the photostat copies of Calendars of State Papers and the British Trade and Plantation Journals, dealing with the West Indies and Carolina and Virginia Plantations.

I wish to acknowledge the enthusiastic help of Miss Emma Woodward, Librarian of the Wilmington, North Carolina, Public Library, and Miss Sue Hardin, Assistant Librarian. In the collection of North Caroliniana, in the North Carolina Room of the Wilmington Library, I found many interesting fragments of the history of the Cape Fear River and the Carolina Banks.

I wish to acknowledge my indebtedness to Mrs. Devereaux Lippitt, of Wilmington, North Carolina. For almost a year we lived on her beautiful plantation, Clarendon, on the Cape Fear River, the locale of a section of this story.

Other sources of historical information were:

Chowan County Courthouse, Edenton, North Carolina.

Cupola House Museum, Edenton, North Carolina.

The State Historical Commission, Raleigh, North Carolina, for Edward Moseley Map and Pollock Letters.

For Ships of the period:

United States Naval Academy Library, Annapolis, Maryland.

Mariners' Museum, Newport News, Virginia.

My sincere thanks to the many descendants of the colonial planters in the Carolinas, who have given me valuable information concerning the social history and the lives of the people of the period.

INGLIS FLETCHER

Lusty Wind
for Carolina

BOOK ONE

Chapter 1

MEG'S LANE

The rambling Elizabethan cottage stood at the dead end of Meg's Lane in the old city of Bristol, a few blocks from the docks and well within sight of the tall masts of the ships that lay at anchor off Kingroad. The house had an air of comfortable homeliness. The leaded windows were bright with the reflection of the fading sun, twinkling and beckoning to the passer-by as if to say: "Behind this tall hedge, within this old garden and this timbered house, dwell decent folk who love their home." There was an air of serenity and peace. The blustering winds of February made for a skeleton garden, with naked branches of trees and shrubs silhouetted against the yellow west, but the paths were new-raked and the brown earth overturned for early setting.

A young girl walked swiftly down the lane, her wide skirts flying and whirling from the windy gusts that blew off the water. Her crimson cloak fitted closely to her narrow waist and three little capes snugged to her shoulder, a style that had been in vogue since King George had come over from Hanover, four years before, to rule England. A little hat of red beaver laced with silver sat jauntily on her dark hair and her cheeks were bright from the whip of the wind. At close view she was not a beautiful girl, but there was something about the composure of her oval face that gave confidence at first glance. Her large dark eyes carried an expression of thoughtfulness. Her brows were strong dark lines. Her curved mouth was sensitive, but purpose was in the strong line of her jaw and her high-bridged nose. Behind her, carrying a laden basket, walked a porter, dressed in a sombre grey woollen suit. He held the picket gate open for the girl to enter, then hurried down the path to the rear entrance of the cottage, aware that he was late, and that the cook had an uneven temper.

The girl moved slowly, looking closely at the trim geometrical bed set in borders of boxwood. At the sight of slender green sprouts pushing up through the brown earth, she

3

stopped. Stripping off her furred gloves, she knelt in the path, her slender, sensitive fingers making little mounds of earth over the venturesome leaves.

"You are too early, you poor silly little things," she murmured, "much too early for little crocuses to venture out of your deep warm bed of earth."

"That's what I have been telling them all this day long, Mistress Fountaine. They should know that frost in February will nip them hard. I thought I had blanketed them all, but I missed these."

Gabrielle Fountaine rose slowly to her feet and dusted her hands as the gardener spoke. The young bondman stood leaning on his rake, his eyes on her instead of on the flower-beds. Something in his gaze disturbed her vaguely. She had noticed before that he spoke too carelessly, that his eyes were too bold for a bondman, yet nothing he said could offend. But she preferred servants to speak when they were spoken to, not to address her so freely. She ignored his comment about the young crocuses.

"You are working late, Moray," she said. "Cook will be wanting you. She doesn't like the servants' tea kept waiting."

"So I have found, Mistress." He did not move away but continued looking at her. He stood high, a head above her and she was tall for a girl. His red-brown eyes had an inscrutable expression. His hand, brown with earth, with nails black-rimmed, pushed back a straggling lock of reddish-brown hair. "I have finished the seed-beds and mended the heater in the potting-room," he said. Gabrielle did not look at him again but something in the tone of his voice made her think he was secretly laughing. She felt annoyed without having a real reason for annoyance. Why should a bondman be laughing, always laughing at some secret thought? Yet she could not say that he was disrespectful. She gave him a quick upward glance through her long dark lashes. His face was solemn, too solemn, she thought, almost as if he forced solemnity on lips that were set to laughter, which even the pointed Stuart beard could not hide. She touched the little earth mound about the crocus with the tip of her red-heeled shoe, angry at herself because she sought pretence to linger. To justify herself she said, "Please do not transplant the purple fleur-de-lis until I bid you. It is possible that we may be leaving for the American Plantations this spring, and if we do, I shall take all the young bulbs with me."

The young gardener took a step nearer. He had laid the

rake against the barrow, turning his deerstalker cap in his hands.

"It was of the American Plantations I wished to speak," he said hurriedly. There was no hint of laughter in his voice now, only earnest purpose. "Mistress Gabrielle, if you would be so gracious as to speak to the Master—I would go to America with him when he goes. I——"

Gabrielle interrupted: "I do not know that my father has determined on this move; at any rate he will not take you with him. He intends to turn your bond to the Duchess of Kendal. She is on the lookout for tall young men to wear her livery."

The bondman's face grew brick-red. He spoke harshly. "Before I'd be one of that beldame's grenadiers, I'd throw myself into the Channel. I have no wish to have the favour of the Hanoverian King's mistress."

"I do not imagine that you will be consulted in the matter," Gabrielle said primly, in her most grown-up manner. She was angered that the fellow should speak so openly about the Duchess, although everyone knew that the King had brought Madam Schulemberg from Hanover with him and made her an English duchess. He perhaps is a Jacobite, she thought as she walked quickly up the path. That was it. He was a Jacobite. Well, that served him right for following the fortunes of the Stuarts. Her father had often told her not to make judgements on political matters, but she didn't like rebels, and Jacobites were rebels to the Crown, as well as serving Rome.

The gardener overtook her as she was about to open the front door, her furred gloves in his hand. "Pardon, Mistress, your gloves." He held them out over the back of one hand as if he were presenting the hilt of a sword. The old annoying amusement lightened his changeable red-brown eyes. "Thank you, Moray," she said sedately.

When she had closed the door, Gabrielle stood for a moment before she took off her outer wraps. She was annoyed with herself that she should be disturbed by the words and actions of a servant. The parlourmaid came from the back hall and took her cloak and hat. With the familiarity of an old servant she scolded, "You are late, Miss Gabrielle. The Master has been asking for you. He wants that you should come to his workroom at once."

"Is Miss Molly with him? Are they having tea?"

"Your father had his chocolate early." Her expression

5

spoke her disapproval of the beverage. Barton had never given way to that uncivilized thick chocolate drink, when a body could have a grand dish of strong China tea.

"I'll go right in," Gabrielle said.

"There is a gentleman visitor," Barton informed her, "a fine figger of a gentleman."

Gabrielle turned to the mirror to smooth a lock of hair into the knot at the nape of her neck. "A foreign gentleman, Miss Gabrielle, from the Carolina Plantations."

Gabrielle turned from the mirror. "A young man? Is it a young man, Barton?"

Barton allowed a vestige of a smile to break across her prim lips. "Well, Miss Gabrielle, not as you would call young, perhaps, but as I would call young. Middling is what he be, but a pleasant and fine set-up gentleman as you would want. Mr. Ma'n'ring is the name he gave—Mr. Ma'n'ring. 'E said it nice and clear for me to announce to the Master."

"Oh, Mr. Mainwairing! Why didn't you tell me before, Barton?" Gabrielle started down the hall, then turned to call over her shoulder, "Please find Miss Molly and tell her I'll have tea in the salon with her later."

"Yes, Miss Gabrielle, but I wish you wouldn't run. Your legs are too long and you are too old. You look like a gawky colt."

Gabrielle's laugh floated back. "But I am gawky and there isn't anything to do about it, so I may as well run if I feel like it." Barton shook her head disapprovingly as she hung the red cloak in a walnut press in the lower hall. Her good Scotch soul was tormented many times by her young Huguenot charge. After ten years' service she still could not understand the rise and fall of the Gallic temperament. Although the Fountaines called themselves Presbyterians and went to kirk, in Barton's mind the Huguenot family was foreign, and remained so in spite of her deep attachment to them.

Gabrielle stood before the door of her father's workroom, her hand poised a moment before she gave the little staccato tap which had been her signal since she was a small child. She was thinking of the blustery night last December, when a stormbound stranger stopped at their door and asked shelter; how her father had hesitated to unlatch the door to the strong peremptory knock. Too often—in his native France and again, not so long ago, in Ireland—visitors that came

6

late in the night had been the symbol of disaster to Robert Fountaine.

The tall blond gentleman who stood at the door that rainy December night had not brought disaster, but something far different. He was what he appeared to be, a stormbound traveller from the New World. He told a tale of the fabulous Carolina Plantations on the rim of the Western Ocean. A land of abundance, a land where one could live in security now that peace had been made with the Indian tribes. That was the first time Gabrielle had thought of Carolina as a place to live. Before, it had seemed a place for a bold man's adventure. But she had thought of it often since, waking and in her dreams. Roger Mainwairing had opened a door through which she saw delightful vistas of a new world.

The two men were standing near the loom. As she entered the room her father laid on a bench a length of the new woollens he had designed, and held out his hands to Gabrielle. The way his sad, dark eyes lightened and a warm smile came to his lips showed his love for his young daughter. "You remember my little Gabrielle, Mr. Mainwairing?"

The tall blond gentleman bowed, lifting Gabrielle's hand to his lips. "Indeed yes. Only yesterday I was speaking of you both to my wife. In truth we have spoken of you often, Mr. Fountaine, ever since your letter came to me, inquiring about the prospects of a Carolina venture. My wife hopes you will decide to come. 'We need French blood,' was her comment. 'We need their gaiety and their imagination and their pleasant ways.' My wife came over last winter so that our second child would be born in England." He laughed a little. "That is Rhoda's idea, not mine. I think a man is English wherever he is born, so long as he has English parents."

"I agree with you, Mr. Mainwairing. I am sure I shall always be French no matter where I live. This little one will be French even though she was born in England."

Gabrielle looked up at her father, surprised at what he was saying. "But you tell us we must behave as the English, and speak only English," she exclaimed.

Fountaine smiled as he stroked her dark hair. "So I do, my dear, but I talk now of the soul, of the personality." He turned to his visitor. "I have thought often that a marriage between France and England would be good. We French are feminine and you English are so very masculine—but instead of marriage we continue to make wars."

"It is our rulers, not our people, who make wars, Mr.

7

Fountaine," Mainwairing said soberly. "But to return to Carolina and the question you asked me: 'Have the Carolinians tolerance?' I think I may safely say yes to that. A few years ago the answer would have been different, but the Quaker rebellion is over and our people see the folly of it. That is what our new land is for, peoples to dwell amicably together. There is an abundance of everything in the Carolinas—vast forests, streams abounding in fish, game birds and game animals that provide food; and every plant thrives there." A smile lightened his lean, bronzed face. "It is indeed the Golden Land. I wish you could see it as I saw it first in its lush greenness of spring, then see it in its golden autumn."

Fountaine motioned his guest to a seat and sat down on a bench, his arm across Gabrielle's shoulder.

"I am a Huguenot, Mr. Mainwairing," Robert Fountaine said, in his slow, precise English. "I have known bitter persecution, both in France and later in Ireland, where we sought refuge. I have seen my father and my mother perish by the yellow-caped Dragonade. Sometimes I think that our only hope of freedom is in a new land, where hates have not become established and hereditary hates are dimmed." His eyes sought the floor and his face took on the sombre tragic look that Gabrielle had come to dread.

"I do not often speak of those terrible days that followed the Revocation of the Edict of Nantes, Mr. Mainwairing, but I want you to understand the reason for my question about tolerance. My affianced wife and her family and I escaped from our home in Lorient, to seek haven under King Charles's proclamation to the French refugees. I was young then and bolder than I am now. The day after my arrival I walked through the streets of London. My heart was singing with thankfulness for our freedom. Suddenly I came on a square near the Tower. Here I saw men executed, their heads and quarters exposed on Tower gates and at the crossroads. All because the Duke of Monmouth, the King's nephew, had led a rebellion. The square was a butchers' shambles. I shook with fear for I saw the shadow of intolerance swaying above a scaffold.

"I was told that many of them were not rebels to the Crown. They had committed no other crime than that of being Presbyterians. I ran home in alarm, to warn my people. A few days later we fled to Ireland." He sat for a moment staring at the floor. "I cannot forget that sight, my welcome to your England."

"But for the Grace of God you would have seen my head and body exposed on the Tower gate." Mainwairing's face was grim. "I was one of Monmouth's luckless followers. I was sixteen when I ran away from Oxford to join the Duke's men. The judge who sentenced the leaders gave the young boys the choice—to die or be sold to the West Indies Plantations. Bloody Jeffreys, they called him. I chose to be a bondman. In the end it was a good choice. I was sent to St. Kitts and learned planting. I had a kind master who, after I had served a portion of my bond, sent me to the Carolinas. That was the best day of my life, Mr. Fountaine: the day I sailed up the great Albemarle Sound and landed at the little village on Queen Anne's Creek."

Gabrielle watched the changing expression of the planter's face, fascinated. Mr. Mainwairing must have been of her father's age, yet he had the vigour and health of a young man. His strong, straight body was as lean as a leopard's at the Garden, while her father was stooped and his dear face pale and lined and thin.

"But please continue, Mr. Fountaine," Mainwairing said.

"Then there is my wife." Fountaine's voice dropped. "Her health was seriously impaired in Ireland. In France it was the habit of her family to spend the winters in the south, on the Mediterranean, where they had a villa. The English winter is long and the cold penetrates the bones. The doctor says that she needs mild weather if there is to be a cure."

"You will find Carolina mild," Mainwairing said. "In the Albemarle we have only a little frost. Snow once in a long time. The breezes are soft—" he laughed suddenly—"unless a hurricane blows in from the Caribbean."

Gabrielle leaned forward. "Oh, Mr. Mainwairing, do please persuade my father to your way of thinking! I so much want to go to the Plantations."

Mainwairing looked doubtful. "I hesitate to persuade any man to take so drastic a step. I do not know whether a young girl like you would be satisfied in our Carolina. There is no London with opera and masquerades and balls. No society."

"But I don't want society or London gaiety, if my mother can be well again." Tears clouded her dark eyes and she could not say more.

Roger looked away to give the girl opportunity to recover her composure.

"Our young people have pleasant gatherings at the plantations along the Sound and up Chowan River; picnics and oyster roasts at Bath, a day's journey away. Their friends from Williamsburg and Suffolk come for visits. They sail and hunt and have deer drives in the forests across the Sound in the autumn, or go duck shooting in the pocosins. Every man can shoot and most of the women. Women and girls can handle their own sailboats." He smiled as he watched her eager face. "You can see, Miss Gabrielle, that plantation life is quite different from your life here in England."

"You mistake us, Mr. Mainwairing. We are not folk who go to London for the season. We are alien people, living quietly as middle-class folk live in a provincial city. I wish I might go to your New World. What you tell me makes me think that your people must be the most fortunate in the world. If we could only live in your way!" She spoke wistfully, her great dark eyes fixed on her father's face. "Would it be so hard to uproot ourselves, Father? Surely we have not grown deep in the soil of England in this short time."

Fountaine patted the hand which lay on his arm. "We will consider, my child. There are many things to consider in so great a change."

Mainwairing said, "I hope you will decide in favour of the Albemarle, if you come to Carolina. I know Charles Town will want you and your settlers. My friend Légare the goldsmith came over on the same ship I sailed on. He told me that the plantations of the Huguenot settlers on Goose Creek and the Ashley are in excellent condition. The Ravenels and Frenzards and Peronneays are well established in Charles Town, as are the Laurents, the Gauillards and the Papons."

"I know them all," Fountaine said, his eyes brightening for a moment. "Only last post I had a letter from my friend Armond Huger from Charles Town." He walked to the carved walnut desk and took a letter from a drawer. It was a long letter, made up of a number of closely written pages. "'I implore you, Robert, to come out here, when my family comes back, and take an estate near one I have on the Ashley River. You will be deep in our little group of Huguenots. Many are from Lorient and the island of Ré. We have our little temple in Charles Town and a good devout minister. Our vineyards and our orchards do well but we have no fine weavers or hatters and your people could take over that work. You would do well and prosper in our colony, and we need you."

10

He folded the letter and put it back into the desk before Roger spoke. "He makes a good case, this Huger. His words are those of wisdom; he speaks well of his community."

Fountaine smiled one of his rare smiles. "You can say the same of your Edenton, and your plantations on Albemarle Sound, wholeheartedly?"

Roger had the grace to redden. "Not entirely. We have no colony of Frenchmen. A few, not many, live along the creeks. But there are many in Virginia. What I was going to point out was that we have no good weavers either, and we also want men who make goods for us to trade with the Indies and with the other colonies. But I suppose it would be hard to convince you that Northern Carolina held some advantages over the southern end of the province. It is natural that you should wish to be with your own people."

Fountaine reflected a moment. "I am not so sure of that, Mr. Mainwairing. I have given thought to these things. Much thought. I have come to the conclusion that it is not well to live as a little group of foreigners, within another government. It is better to assimilate—no?—as much as may be, for one can learn how to live outside his own country. His mind then takes up the problems of the country where he lives, not all the while turns back to the old life. No, I think I must choose a new environment and cut from the old. A sword severs and leaves nothing behind."

The Huguenot spoke slowly. It was evident to Roger and to Gabrielle that he had pondered long over this matter. It was not easy for him to translate his thoughts into words, but Roger realized what he left unsaid. He wanted a new life under new conditions for Gabrielle and his two boys.

Roger rose to his feet and took up his travelling cape which lay on a bench on the far side of the great loom. It was dusk now; shadows lay on the room. Gabrielle lighted a taper from the fire that blazed on the hearth, and touched it to the candles.

Fountaine held open the door. Gabrielle, carrying a candle, walked ahead to light their guest to the front door. She heard her father say, "I must think this over very carefully, Mr. Mainwairing. It is serious, this transplanting of a whole family and all the household goods to the New World. It requires careful thought."

Mainwairing agreed to that. He turned to Gabrielle, smiling down at her from his overshadowing height.

"I am going to have my bookseller send you a book on

11

Carolina. It was written by John Lawson, our first Surveyor General. He knew Carolina more intimately than any other man. He loved the country. I should like you to see it through his eyes."

Gabrielle's face lightened with a charming smile. "Oh, thank you. Thank you very, very much, Mr. Mainwairing. But it is you who have opened my eyes to Carolina. I shall always think of it as you have showed it to us by your words."

Roger took her hand and held it a moment in both of his. "You will forget my feeble words when you read John Lawson's book. He loved every tree, every flower, every beast; he even loved every Indian tribe, though Indians murdered him for all his kindness to them."

There was consternation in Gabrielle's face and in her wide dark eyes.

"The Indians killed him?"

"Yes, they killed him." Realizing the impression his words made on the sensitive imagination of the young girl, he added hastily, "But this happened some years ago. Before the Tuscarora war. Now we have signed peace treaties with King Blont, as their chief is named. Have no fears, my dear child. The Indians are conquered in the north of Carolina."

They stood for a moment at the heavy wooden door that opened to the street. The planter took up a subject which he and the Huguenot had been discussing before Gabrielle joined them.

"I am sure you will get immediate attention from Lord Carteret, if you decide to write to him. Since he has been Palatine of the Lords Proprietors, we in the province have fared better. Carteret is a farseeing man. He understands government, from his own experience in Ireland. He knows the worth of the charter by which they own the Carolinas."

Fountaine said, "I had occasion to seek an interview with my Lord Carteret in Ireland. He was kind. Very kind and considerate to a humble refugee weaver."

"Perhaps Lord Carteret did not see you as a humble weaver. Perhaps he thought of you as an unfortunate gentleman who had lost his country and his home."

"My Lord has been most kind to the Huguenots," Fountaine said.

Mainwairing shook his host's hand warmly. "Perhaps I shall have the pleasure of seeing you in London before I leave for America. I am trying to make arrangements to sail with Captain Woodes Rogers when he goes out in April to take over the office of Governor of the Bahamas."

Fountaine shielded the candle from the wind that came in the open door. "I heard on the Exchange that Captain Woodes Rogers had leased the Bahama Islands and would take out a colony of six hundred or more from this county and from Devon."

"Yes, he will have three ships. The *Delicia* is his flagship—a stout vessel, and I would be very glad to sail in her."

"Oh, Father! It is the *Delicia* that is being fitted now. I've seen her at the dock. I can see her from my window. She is so beautiful! Oh, Father, if only we could sail across the Western Ocean on the *Delicia!*"

Robert put his arm over his daughter's shoulder. "Always so impetuous, my girl. We must consider these things carefully."

Roger raised Gabrielle's hand to his lips. "Fare you well, my dear child. Let us hope your wish may be fulfilled." He slipped the long woollen cape over his brocaded coat and buttoned the heavy braid frogs. "I must be moving on. My man is at the Fox and Grapes, holding our places on the London coach."

Gabrielle pressed forward to the open door. "Oh, please have a care, Mr. Mainwairing. That is the coach that the highwaymen have robbed so often of late. My brothers were so frightened, when Jack Sheppard himself delayed the coach they were on, when they were travelling to school at Bedford."

"Jack Sheppard, eh? I should really deem it a pleasure to be robbed by the infamous Jack Sheppard."

" 'Tis no laughing thing, Mr. Mainwairing. He is a bloodthirsty fellow. 'Tis said he slits people's noses and hacks off ears, just as a pleasure before he slashes their throats or shoots them through the heart."

"Gabrielle, what is it you are saying?" Her father's voice expressed his astonishment at her words.

The girl's eyes were sparkling. "Molly told me. She says all London is terrified of Jack Sheppard. Please be careful, Mr. Mainwairing."

"I will speak to Molly. This is unsuitable talk for young ladies," her father admonished.

Roger was smiling broadly. "Do not worry that pretty head of yours, Mistress Gabrielle. I have a brace of pistols and—" his hand rested for a moment on the hilt of his slender blade—"I will be alert, no fear."

Father and daughter watched Mainwairing stride down the lane in the gathering dusk. The last streak of yellow in the western sky glowed behind the masts of ships that rose above the heavy shadow of close-lying hulls beyond the wharves.

"He is straight and tall, like the pine trees of his country. A tall, straight pine tree that has grown in a vast forest under a kind blue sky and a warm sun. I like him, Father. When I am with him I think of the sea and the hills and the fresh warm earth."

Fountaine shielded the candle from the wind. It sent a bright reflection into the girl's eyes, making them glow with little flames of light. "Your imagination will run away with you, my dear. Mr. Mainwairing is a fine man, but I don't see him as a pine tree."

Gabrielle caught her father's hand and nestled close to his shoulder as they walked down the hall.

"He must have been wonderful when he was young." The worried lines on Robert's face smoothed out at his daughter's words. Girls had been known to fall in love with older men. He must not let that happen to Gabrielle. He had betrothed her some years past to Paul Balarand, son of his old friend Pierre. Of this he had never spoken to Gabrielle. He was saving the announcement until her eighteenth birthday. The papers had been drawn, and the dot agreed upon. But the two fathers had thought best to wait before they told the young folk until Paul was twenty-one. The idea came across his mind, as they stood at the door of the salon, that it might be well to apprise the young people now, within a short time, particularly if he should decide to go to America. Another time he would give this consideration. Not now.

He kissed Gabrielle lightly on her white brow. "I will go to your mother now," he said.

"May I come with you?" She spoke eagerly. "I did not see her yesterday. Perhaps she will be well enough to see me today."

"Wait. Wait until I have talked to Celestine. After you have had your tea. No doubt Molly is waiting for you now. Run along, my child."

Chapter 2

HUGUENOT FAMILY

Gabrielle watched her father walk slowly up the stairs on the way to her mother's room. By the stoop of his shoulders she realized his discouragement. If only her mother could be well again! Her beautiful gay mother, whom she remembered so happily. She would like to have gone with him. But these twilight visits to his wife's bedside were always made alone.

If the outside of the cottage was English, the little salon which Gabrielle entered was all French—the curved, brocaded elbow chairs, the little seats with the soft down pillows, the blue and rose damask curtains and the highly polished fender and andirons. The candles were not lighted. The fire in the grate burned brightly, casting soft mellowed shadows. Little flames of fire danced on the polished floor and gave life to the quiet room. A tea table was drawn up near the fire in front of the curved seat. A tea-kettle, with a lighted spirit lamp underneath, purred gently.

The window that gave on the garden was swinging open. Gabrielle crossed the room to close it. Glancing out into the garden, she saw her cousin Molly talking animatedly with David the gardener. She had thrown Gabrielle's crimson cloak over her shoulders and her golden-blonde curls were blowing in the wind. The gardener was leaning negligently against the door of the potting-shed, looking down at the bright upturned face of Molly Lepel. Gabrielle's first inclination was to call out. David was not behaving as a gardener ought to behave. He should be standing, cap in hand, listening deferentially. Instead, his cap lay in the barrow and his brown hair was blowing across his face. It gave him a dark, almost sinister look in spite of the smile on his curved lips.

Molly was so impulsive. Although Molly was eighteen, a year older, Gabrielle sometimes felt herself ten years older than her vivacious cousin. She had the habit of mothering Molly—softening her bold tongue and protecting her when she talked too much of the social world of London to suit

15

Robert Fountaine. Molly spent part of the year with her father's half-sister, whom she called Aunt Lepel, acting as governess to some younger children. The Lepels were of the great world, although they did not have a fortune.

Gabrielle called to Molly. Something of her impatience sounded in her voice. Molly moved swiftly away from the gardener and said in a loud voice that Gabrielle could hear, "Be sure and wrap the Irish rose plants separately when you make up the box. My Aunt Lepel is particularly fond of good roses in her glasshouse. I want to take them when I go up to London on Wednesday."

"Very good, miss," she heard the gardener reply. "I will have the cuttings ready for you on Wednesday."

Gabrielle stood looking out into the bare garden, wondering whether another spring would find them in the Meg's Lane cottage. It made her sad. They had been quiet here, almost happy after the terrible days in Ireland and her mother's illness. Almost happy. Not quite. She, sensitive to her father's moods and thoughts, knew that he worried. It wasn't the shop, for it was doing well. It was the new cloth they were making. Men had come once or twice to see the woollen and had asked questions of Robert Fountaine. How much did he weave a month of the woollen? Did he sell at home or abroad? Where did he get the chamois skin that he dyed for men's breeches, doeskin so soft and pliable as to be mistaken for satin? Would it not interfere with woollen trade to make skin breeches?

After these visits her father would shut himself into his workroom and she would hear the clink of the loom far into the night. Some men smoked or drank when they worried deeply; her father went to his loom. Something in the rhythmic movement of his hands cleared his thoughts. It might be the Guild that worried him. That trouble had come up once before. They pressed him to join the association, until they found he was a foreigner. Then they said that it was not permitted for a foreigner to hold a Guild membership.

She walked across the room and pulled a bell cord. Barton would be waiting to serve the tea. She was petulant, always, when the tea was not served at the moment. The gentry always had their tea at the proper time, she often told Gabrielle.

Gabrielle wished that her father would be satisfied to make cloth of the same quality as that which the other weavers made. That was the trouble: the new cloth was better than

16

any weaver in Bristol turned from the loom and this aroused jealousy. It was useless to speak to him about it. He would have perfection or nothing, for that was his character. She glanced up at that moment and noticed she had not drawn the damask curtain at the long window. As she crossed the room she was aware of a face close to the glass, and the gardener's bold eyes looked directly into hers. She snatched the cord and drew the curtain quickly. A shiver passed over her. She was glad that her father was determined to sell the bondman. He was too strange, too secretive. She walked quickly across the room to the table. When Molly entered, she was seated at the table pouring tea into delicate Sèvres cups.

Molly Lepel came into the room like an east wind, her blue-green eyes shining, her tawny hair ruffled by the wind. Gabrielle's word of caution sent her halfway across the room to catch the door before it banged, but she was too late. She stood for a moment, her bright provocative face showing her contrition, her eyes turned towards the ceiling. "Oh, Gabrielle, do you think I disturbed your mother? I am so thoughtless." Gabrielle said nothing. She knew that the moment Molly had spoken her distress it was off her mind.

Molly tossed Gabrielle's crimson cloak on a near-by chair and went to the glass above the mantel board to arrange her hair. She smiled back at her own reflection and ran her hands carelessly over her curved breasts and her slender waist, smoothing her striped silk bodice into place. She took a lace-trimmed handkerchief from the square-cut neck of her bodice, glancing mischievously at Gabrielle as she dusted her face with it. "It's not real French *poudre*," she said. "It's powdered orris. It gives an enchanting fragrance to the skin in case one is kissed by a handsome gallant."

"Or to ward off the odour of the barnyard," Gabrielle returned dryly, thinking of the gardener. A delicate flush covered Molly's fair skin.

"You say the crudest things, Gabrielle," she cried, flinging herself on the little blue satin sofa. "For a well-bred girl you are sometimes quite vulgar."

Gabrielle laughed at Molly's petulance. "If I am too frank," she said, "at least I am truthful."

"There is such a thing as being too truthful. It gets you into trouble to tell the truth," Molly said, her anger subsiding as quickly as it rose. "Where were you all this afternoon and yesterday afternoon? You disappear at three o'clock and don't come home until teatime. What are you doing all those hours when you should be getting a beauty sleep? Meeting a lover?" Gabrielle opened her lips to reply, but Molly lifted a slim, languid hand, suddenly the great lady. "No, miss, don't answer. I swear if you deny having met a lover I shall not believe you. Or if I do believe you I shall be bored with your answer. A miss of eighteen who hasn't a lover is doomed to spinsterhood."

"Then I am doomed, for I haven't any lover and you know it."

"True, true," Molly sighed, sipping her tea delicately. "I will attend to that. You must come up to London. I shall ask Aunt Lepel to invite you." She let her cool eyes run over Gabrielle as if she had never seen her before. "Not too bad, for the Junoesque type," she said appraisingly. "That's the fashion now, with some of the gallants. Lord Peterborough's Mrs. Robinson is as tall as you—and ages older—and my cousin, the other Mary Lepel, is the tallest girl among the Princess' ladies, save Mrs. Howard, and half the town is mad for her." She reached for a currant cake and sank her small white teeth into it. "If Aunt Lepel could only be induced to take an interest," she said speculatively, "she might manage a good marriage for you. How much of a dot will Uncle settle on you?"

"Molly, stop this nonsensical talk."

Molly did not heed. She was enthralled with her new idea of taking Gabrielle to London and marrying her off. "No," she said, after a moment's reflection. "No, it's no good to ask Aunt Lepel. She has got Mary to think of first. She's angling for Lord John Hervey for my cousin, but he's head over heels in love with Lady Mary Wortley Montagu. I can't see why. Maybe she is handsome, but she's got a voice like a man's and she walks like a man, and they say she has a dreadful temper." Her voice dwindled off.

Gabrielle poured a second cup of tea for herself and filled the cup her cousin held out. She always felt uneasy when Molly began talking about London and the fashionable world of her family. Molly herself was the little poor relation who made her home with her Uncle Lepel's widow. They were kind to her and in return she taught French and Italian to her cousins, and served as amanuensis for her aunt. It was unfortunate, she found, that she had the same name as her older and more beautiful cousin, Mary Lepel; for that reason she was always Molly in that household.

She came often to them at Meg's Lane. Robert Fountaine was one of her guardians. He had been a lifelong friend of her father and he felt his responsibility for Molly's spiritual welfare. He hoped, in his quiet way, to counteract the worldliness in her nature, a worldliness that was intensified by her life in the Lepel household. Robert felt that Gabrielle was a steadying influence. It did not occur to him that Molly might conceivably influence the more serious Gabrielle. He was so sure of his daughter.

Molly was like a richly colored butterfly that paused for a moment before it took flight into the unknown blue. She brought life and colour into their austere existence. Gabrielle listened to her light gay prattle, her gossip of the great world of London, with an eagerness that rose above her disapproval of the worldly existence that Molly so loved. Unconsciously she fed on Molly's gay life, her tales of lords and ladies and the great people who made up the Hanoverian's Court. The fact that much of Molly's gossip came second-hand through her cousin Mary Lepel did not make it any the less exciting. Mary Lepel was a lady-in-waiting to the Princess. Therefore she knew everything that went on in the two courts.

Even Robert Fountaine relaxed under Molly's gayness, not troubling to reprove her for little tales that would have brought rebuke had they come from Gabrielle's lips.

Molly put her cup on the table and leaned back on the sofa. She flicked a long curl over her shoulder, patting it into place, then smoothed her slim white hands along her silk-covered knees, so that the folds of her gown clung closely to her thighs and legs, for all the world like an amber cat, flexing and unflexing its rippling muscles, taking its ease. But her eyes could become narrow and her claws unsheathe if she desired. Gabrielle had seen her change in an instant. She didn't like Molly in such a mood, when malicious words issued from her red, curved lips.

Molly glanced at Gabrielle now. Her glance was speculative, and she returned to her earlier question.

"So you have no lover with whom to keep an assignation. How dull, how very dull of you, Gaby! I had quite made up my mind that you were going to the lodgings of some handsome gentleman every day for tea."

Gabrielle blushed furiously. Angry that she should appear so guilty, she spoke more vehemently than was her wont.

"You know quite well that I would never do such an

unmannerly thing, Molly. If you must know, I go to walk along the wharves on Kingroad to see the ships at anchor."

Molly sparkled. She directed her glance above Gabrielle's head. "Ah! Now I have it! She goes to meet a handsome sea captain! His ship has just come up the Channel. He has brought her wines from Madeira, Spanish shawls from Cadiz, perfumes and spices from the Indies! How romantic, how vastly romantic!"

Gabrielle laughed in spite of herself at Molly's whimsy. "Molly, you are incorrigible."

Molly was not listening to her companion. She leaned back, her hair like pale amber against the blue satin sofa, humming a gay little French song.

"If you disclaim the sea captain, my dear, I shall think it is that handsome planter from the American colonies."

"Mr. Mainwairing?" exclaimed Gabrielle, really laughing now. "Why, he is an old man, as old as my father! Besides, he is married and has children."

"Marry an old man and sleep with a young one," Molly said. She shook with laughter at the sight of Gabrielle's face. "My love! You are naïve as any country milkmaid. Don't you know that all the fine ladies take on lovers? 'Tis the custom. An affair of the heart is nothing. No one voices disapproval—if a woman is married. That's why I am going to marry young. Then I can do as I want."

"Molly, you are a very wicked girl. I am sure——"

"My Uncle Robert would disapprove? Of a certainty. But he too is as innocent as a lamb, the old darling. We Londoners belong to a different age. Yet there must be hundreds of clandestine affairs going on here in this good provincial town of Bristol, if one only peeped behind the scenes. Don't pretend such innocence, miss. The King brought over two mistresses from Hanover when he came. The avaricious Schulemberg and the fat lazy Kielmansegge, to say nothing of the fair maids Mr. Secretary Craggs takes to his cabinet by the back stairs. Like king, like court and on down to the commoners."

"Molly Lepel, I will not listen to your horrid gossip."

"Laws, my Gaby, you like it although you pretend to be so shocked."

Gabrielle did not reply, for there was some truth in Molly's words. She made things so amusing. That was her gift, to turn small unimportant happenings into swift laughter.

"My Gabrielle! It is surely time you went to London and

had a glimpse of the world of fashion." She slid her slim legs forward, half reclining, her hands clasped behind her head. She is beautiful, Gabrielle thought, so very beautiful. It is a great pity she has no one to train her to be more decorous.

Molly leaned forward, a wicked little glint in her eyes. "Gaby, if you swear not to tell anyone, anyone at all, I'll tell you a secret. I had an adventure, a real adventure, when I was staying with my aunt in the Midlands last autumn. But you must raise your hand above your heart and swear."

"Oh, I couldn't do that. It is wrong to swear; it is against God's will."

Molly clicked her tongue against her teeth. "Oh, Lordy, I'd forgotten how religious you are, Gaby. Well, promise not to tell."

"I promise," Gabrielle said, knowing to do so was a weakness to encourage her cousin. But she did want to hear about the adventure. Molly was right. Her own life, since she had come to Bristol, was dull and uneventful.

"It was the time Aunt Lepel had the big house party for the hunting season in November. I wish you could have seen the fine ladies. Miss Martha and Miss Teresa Blount of Mapledurham and that funny little Mr. Pope who writes poetry to them—and Lady Mary Montagu, you know she is just back from Turkey. They talked all the time about the new preventive for smallpox she brought back. She even had her little son scratched, so he wouldn't have the real pox. Lord Peterborough was there, and Lord John Carteret, without his plump wife. You've no idea how handsome and distinguished he is! Then, two young men from the colonies. One was Mr. Tom Chapman from Jamaica and the other—" she paused for emphasis—"Mr. Michael Cary from Nassau." She waited a moment to create suspense before she went on, without further mention of Mr. Michael Cary. This did not fool Gabrielle. She knew he was the man of the adventure. Molly liked her own way of working up to a dramatic climax.

"Lord Hervey was staying near by and he paid so much court to Lady Mary Montagu that Cousin Mary was in tears, and her eyes were so red that my Aunt Lepel asked me to go down and sit in her place for dinner. She even let me wear on of my cousin's elegant satin dresses and had her maid dress my hair London-fashion. I had a wonderful time at dinner!"

She leaned back, a reminiscent little smile on her curved

red lips. "I must have looked vastly attractive," she said with amazing frankness. "I sat between Lord Peterborough and Mr. Michael Cary. They both paid strict attention to their partners on the other side but each of them had a hand on one of my knees. It made me laugh. Suppose the hands got wandering and either one of them discovered the other!"

"Molly Lepel, you are outrageous!"

The smile broadened. "It would have served old Peterborough right. He's madly in love with that opera woman, Mrs. Robinson, and they say he has set up a wonderful place for her near Twickenham. And as for Mr. Michael Cary, I vowed I would make him suffer for not turning his eyes to me, instead of that quiet little Blount. I can't see why she is called a beauty—and Michael was young and so thrillingly masculine. He made poor Lord Hervey look very queer. Do you know he paints his face, like a woman? Some people call him Lord Fanny. He gives me the creeps. I can't for my life see why my cousin would weep over him."

"Perhaps she was weeping over the son of the Earl of Bristol," Gabrielle said with unexpected shrewdness.

Molly stared at her. "Sometimes you are almost wordly, my sweet. What you say may be true of my aunt. She has an eye to a title, but I believe Mary actually likes the man. But to return to my adventure: Lord Peterborough got me to walk on the terrace, cool as it was, but I kept in sight of the drawing-room windows, after he had run his hands over my bare shoulders when he helped with my wrap. He is a woman lover, they say, and he runs after all ages from sixteen to sixty, trying to get new sensations."

"Molly, you are very, very remiss to talk so, or to know these things. Why, you . . . talk . . . "

Molly interrupted her. "Laws, that is nothing at all, my sweet. You should have seen some of the men sneaking down the corridors to their mistresses' rooms late at night, carrying their bed candles! If Aunt Lepel had known, she would have turned them all out." Molly grinned. "She is almost as innocent as you are, Gaby."

She got up and walked about the room, pausing at the closed door. "Shh!" she said. "It is time for Barton to come for the tray. I'll tell you the rest of the adventure after she carries away the tea-things."

Gabrielle breathed, "Surely there was no more?"

"Indeed yes, about Michael. I made Tom Chapman tell me about him. Tom says Michael is unhappy about a girl. That's

22

what makes him so reckless. The girl's mother is someone quite high. She doesn't like Michael and she has carried her daughter over to France to take her away from Michael."

"Oh, Molly, how unfortunate for you!"

Molly laughed. "Don't say 'Oh, Molly' to me, my dear. Many a heart has been caught on the rebound, even if the man is married."

"Married? Molly, you must be careful. How do you know this strange man's thoughts are honourable?" Molly's laugh sounded a little forced. She got up swiftly and went to the harpsichord. A gay little tune flowed from her lips:

> "Why should a foolish marriage vow
> Which long ago was made
> Oblige us to each other now
> When passion has decayed?
> We lov'd—and we lov'd, as long as we could,
> Till our love was lov'd out in us both,
> But our marriage is dead, when the pleasure is fled:
> 'Twas pleasure first made it an oath."

"You think lightly of sinful things, Molly Lepel. I don't understand how you can speak so frivolously of anything as sacred as marriage."

"Marriage sacred? You don't know London. Marriage is an excuse for sin." Her slim, white fingers slid along the yellowed keys. "Sometimes I wonder about sin, Gabrielle. There must be something rather nice in sinning. So many nice people are called sinners."

Gabrielle had no answer. She was without words to check Molly's worldliness. Her eyes rested for a moment on her companion's lovely face, marred now by the expression of the soft mouth. Petulant and a little cruel. She is still a child, thought Gabrielle; she only repeats what she has overheard in her aunt's drawing-room. She wants to impress me. I shall not let her see how shocked I am.

Barton came in and cleared away the tea-things. Molly got up from the harpsichord and went again to the mirror above the mantel board. She stroked her hair into place, rearranging her curls. She placed her hands at her waist, drawing them slowly upwards with a caressing movement until her firm round little breasts showed half their contour above the square of her bodice, above her tucker.

"This is the way I looked in Mary's gown," she said, moving her head first on one side, then on the other, to get the effect. "It had a yellow sack, a lovely soft yellow brocade, perfect with my hair."

She pressed her waist in closely. "I pulled in my stays until I could scarcely draw a full breath. Men like tiny waists with a bulge above," she continued artlessly. "They must, because they look and look, making excuses to lean forward, even the old ones." She laughed slyly.

"Oh, you are wicked, wicked!" The words burst through Gabrielle's lips.

"Don't be a prude, Gaby; I'm no different from any fine London lady from duchess to lady-in-waiting. You'll never know about life if you keep such country ways. I intend to be a worldly woman. I shall have lovers. As for kissing—well, I can tell you kissing is nice, very nice indeed. A little sly kiss in the garden, your hand pressed ardently in a country dance . . ."

She performed a deep curtsy to an imaginary partner, and extended her hand to be kissed. She had such twinkling gaiety in her piquant face that Gabrielle's disapproval faded.

"You've no idea how a gallant can make love in a dance, squeezing your hand, allowing his shoulder to brush against your bosom as your pass together under the drawn swords. Really, it is very enlivening." She sighed loudly. "Only it happens so seldom. I tell you, Gaby, I shall marry the first man who asks me, provided he has enough money. It is only after a girl marries that she can have fun and as many men friends as she wants. Yes, and lovers. It must be exciting to wear a vizard over one's face, take one's serving woman and go to one of the warehouse meeting rooms."

"What are you talking about?" Curiosity got the better of Gabrielle.

"Everybody does."

"Does what?"

"Why, goes to meet a friend at one of the big warehouses down on the river. The East India is the nicest—with great bales of mysterious merchandise and the smell of spices and perfumes. You sit in a dusky corner and drink tea from Canton ware and have sweet nothings whispered in your ear by your escort. Why, I . . ." She stopped and looked at Gaby under her half-closed lids, wondering just how far it would be wise to go with her cousin.

"You talk a great deal of nonsense, Molly," Gabrielle said.

"Do I? So you don't think I'm fascinating?"

"Silly girl!"

A little wicked gleam came in Molly's blue-green eyes. "You may not, but your handsome gardener does. You should see the admiring glances he casts at me. I know when a man's losing himself. I know all the signs, my dear."

Gabrielle rose quickly. "I won't hear another word. To demean oneself . . . a gardener, a bondman——"

"But handsome, devastatingly handsome—if only he didn't wear that disguising beard," mocked Molly. "Why, your cheeks are red. I do believe you are jealous that he looks at me."

Gabrielle struggled a moment to keep her composure. She rose to her feet and left the room, walking smoothly, her tall body erect, moving easily.

Chapter 3

THE COUNCILMAN MAKES A VISIT

Gabrielle walked up the steep stairs, her thoughts in a turmoil. She was annoyed that Molly could, by her light words, disturb her so deeply. She lingered a few moments, hoping that Celestine, her mother's nurse, would come into the hall on her way to the servants' tea. She had not waited long when the bulky peasant figure filled the doorway. Closing the door carefully behind her, the old Frenchwoman raised her plump finger to her lips and tiptoed to the narrow leaded-paned window at the end of the hall. Gabrielle followed, taking care that her wooden heels did not tap the worn floor boards too loudly.

"Madame sleeps." Celestine spoke in the low subdued voice of the sickroom. "The day has been a weary one so the doctor mixed a potion for my lady and she sleeps."

"May I not even look in, Celestine?" Gabrielle's voice was pleading. "Sometimes I find comfort looking at her dear face as she sleeps."

Celestine shook her head—a short turn of her round fat neck that gave the appearance of a turtle reaching from its shell. *"Non!* It is not permitted. When the Master sits with Madame, no one may enter. Tomorrow, my child, after a night of repose."

There was no expression in her dark opaque eyes. She moved off, her step surprisingly light for a heavy person. Gabrielle watched her going down the stairs, a squat figure seen from above, the part in her sleek black hair as exact and precise as the woman herself.

Gabrielle was always a little fearful of Celestine. She was so remote, so calm and unflurried, yet how patient she had been throughout her mother's long illness! Almost three years since the terrible day when the uncouth mob of Irish weavers forced their way into Robert Fountaine's house and destroyed the looms. But she was not to think of it. How often her father had said to her to let the past erase itself in the

26

present and hope of the future! To throw one's mind forward, not back, was the part of wisdom.

She went on to the back of the hall to her bedroom, a large low room under the sloping roof, lighted by four little dormer windows that looked out on the Channel, Kingroad and the "long roadway of ships."

Sitting down on the padded window seat, she watched the great ball of the sun go down in crimson glory, lining the murk of fog drifting in from the Channel. Daylight was fading slowly, as if it wanted to linger and greet the thin crescent of the moon. Tall masts of ships would soon separate themselves from the street of ships that made Bristol Harbour. Each ship would find its way to the sea, each in its own time sail to some far destination. And where would they go? To far Cathay, or fabulous India; the Strait of Dampier and the Solomons; or to the Azores and the new Plantations across the Western Ocean? Someday, someday she would walk the deck of a gallant ship as it ploughed its way through the green waves, feel the dash of spume against her cheeks and the salt spray on her lips. She knew it as truly as she had life within her veins, she knew it. Even now she could hear the flap of canvas and the wind sliding, wailing down the rigging in a storm. She came back to herself with a start. The dreams of the sea and of ships would be her undoing. She thought again of the ship she had seen on her afternoon walk—the *Delicia*, flagship of Captain Woodes Rogers, the great navigator who had carried the flag of Britain and the goods of Bristol merchants around the world. How beautiful she was with her curved bow and her high waist and her flapping sails that drooped with the dying wind. Beautiful and well named.

The prolonged ringing of the dressing bell brought the girl to her feet. She must hurry; she had only a half-hour until supper. To bathe and dress, yes, and mend the torn ruffle on the sleeve of her flowered silk would take all of the time. Gabrielle never kept her father waiting. A quiet, gentle man, he had certain set rules she must adhere to, and punctuality was one.

There was a light tap on the door. Barton came in carrying a shining brass jug of hot water for Gabrielle's toilette.

"Thank you, Barton," she mumbled, her dress turned over her head. Barton helped her untangle a long lock of black hair from the lacings of her bodice. "Thank you. Will you please bring my wrapper and lay out the flowered silk? Oh

27

yes, and a thread and needle. I forgot to mend the lace in the sleeve."

"I mended it last night, though I shouldn't have. It will teach you laziness, not to do for yourself, Miss Gabrielle." Her tone was disapproving. Gabrielle dropped her frock on the floor and sat down at her dressing cabinet. She took the shell pins from her heavy hair. It fell like a dark cloud over her white shoulders. She began to brush vigorously with long swift strokes.

Barton took a dress, cream silk flowered in rose, out of the big oaken press, and laid it carefully on the bed, the embroidered petticoat beside it. She carried the woollen frock Gabrielle had been wearing to the window. Gabrielle watched her scratch a spot on the full skirt with her fingernail, then sniff at it with her long sharp nose.

"Tar," she said. "As I live, a great spot of tar on your second-best wool dress. Wherever did you find tar, to ruin a good woollen?"

Gabrielle peeped out of a cloud of black hair. Her eyes were merry and her strong white teeth gleaming. Barton did not wait for an answer. "You've been down on the docks again, mingling with the scum of the universe and goodness knows what barbarians."

"I didn't speak to a soul," Gabrielle said quickly, to prevent a scolding.

"No matter. The sight of the ungodly is a taint. This time I shall surely tell the Master. I shall be silent no longer. What will he think of a great, grown girl like you, striding along the wharves of Bristol, stepping over tarred ropes and hawsers and rubbing shoulders with Lascars and Portuguese sailors and those pagan, bedevilled Spaniards? 'Tis a man you should have been." She stood with her hands folded across her meagre bosom, her righteous anger flowing from her eyes and her narrowed lips. "How ye can be the daughter of that delicate lady lying in there on the bed, I cannot fathom."

Gabrielle drew her hair into a smooth knot and twisted a long curl into place. "I wonder myself sometimes," she replied soberly.

Barton continued to look at her severely. After a silence she spoke again: "It is said in the kitchen that the Master is going out to the American Plantations."

Gabrielle looked over her shoulder. "What did you say?" she asked, surprised at the abrupt change in conversation.

Barton repeated. "So Cook says. And David, the new gar

dener, was telling the same tonight at tea, that the Master is thinking of going out to the Plantations."

"I don't know whether it is true or not, Barton. My father has not told me whether he has come to any decision."

Barton stared out the window. Her lean face was expressionless. "I have no objection to the Plantations myself. As for setting foot on a ship, I was born Clydeside and many a ship my father helped to build. The smell of tar is in me nostrils."

Gabrielle jumped to her feet and threw her arms about the gaunt frame. "You are a fraud, Barton. A moment ago you were scolding me for getting tar on my skirts, and for walking along the quay to see the ships. Now you tell me you are a Clydeside lass."

"That I was and so I will say again. There's a mighty difference between the daughter of a poor shipwright and the daughter of a fine Huguenot gentleman. A long difference, and you will please keep away from the docks on Kingroad or I'll surely speak to the Master."

"But you were talking about America," Gabrielle said quickly.

"So I was. I have nae objections to the Plantations at all, nor to the long voyage across the Western Ocean. So please tell your father, when the time is proper." She poured the hot water into the copper basin and laid a cloth and a cut of fine Castile soap on the washstand. "Now scrub your neck briskly, and don't forget your ears. I can't abide a dirty skin, even if it's on a duchess covered with fine brocade and drenched with sandal oil." Barton walked towards the door, pausing long enough to say, "You'll never be as bonny as your cousin, Miss Molly, but you can be clean and pleasant." Having finished her tasks and dissertation, she walked quickly from the room. She shut the door firmly behind her, in time to cut off Gabrielle's indignant:

"I won't be treated as if I were a child and told every day to wash my ears."

They sat long at dinner that night, Robert Fountaine and the two young girls. The meal was simple—a fine Dover sole, cooked in oil, a jugged hare with root vegetables. For the young women there was a trifle, smothered in cream. For the Master, Cheddar cheese with his Madeira.

Robert Fountaine sipped his wine and smiled at the bright faces of the two girls engaged in an animated argument over the merits of King Charles spaniels versus toy Chinese, lately the fad among fashionable ladies. He thought in all the city of Bristol there could not be found two more attractive young women, so young, so alive, so opposite in looks and temperament—Gabrielle his daughter, and Molly his ward. Gabrielle's hair was black as a rook's wing and her large dark eyes had the dreamer's imprint. She had more poise than Molly, he thought, although Molly was a year older and spent much of her time in a worldly household. Molly's hair was pale yellow. Her cloudy greenish eyes changed colour with the passing clouds of her mood, sometimes amber, sometimes, when the velvet pupils enlarged, as dark as Gabrielle's. Gabrielle's features were clear-cut and regular, while Molly's nose turned upwards, giving her a quick, inquiring look, and her lips were fuller and her mouth smaller.

Robert's thoughts turned to the woman upstairs, lying so quietly she seemed scarcely to breathe as he bent over her to touch her thin hand with his lips, before he came downstairs to supper. His eyes sought Gabrielle. It was a responsibility to be father and mother to a young girl. The two boys did not trouble him. He had them well placed in Mr. Hay's school at Bedford. When they came home last holiday, he was well pleased with their progress. René was very tall for fifteen. Etienne promised to be stocky in build. Yet they had presented a problem—whether or not to take them to America, if he decided to make the move.

Gabrielle recalled him. "What are you dreaming about, Father? Is it about the new serge, or about the Plantations?"

Robert set the wine glass on the table and settled back, his dark eyes on his daughter's eager, questioning face.

"I will set your mind at ease, Gabrielle, my child. I am seriously inclined to go to the Carolinas. Wait. Wait. It is not a settled thing," he exclaimed, as Gabrielle jumped from her chair and ran to his side.

"I know," she said, seating herself on the arm of the Jacobean chair. Her voice had a gay lilt to it. "I know. You must consider very, very carefully." She began checking on her fingers. "We must consider Mother's comfort; second, cost; third, the servants' welfare; fourth, your sons' and daughter's education."

"A man must improve the conditions for family living, my child, and the welfare of his dependents."

"Yes, I know. I know. But if you will only make up your mind, Father, all we have to do is to go down Kingroad and get aboard a ship."

Robert laughed. "Not as easy as that, my dear one. There is the matter of a land grant, a suitable ship, what household goods to transport—"

"Why not everything, Father? When Mamma is well she will want the things she loves about her. There is not a piece of furniture in this house we can leave behind."

"The boys," Fountaine interrupted. "That I have decided. The boys will remain at the school in Bedford until we are firmly established. As for the servants, I must consult them first."

"Barton wants to go. She told me so before supper."

"Splendid. I cannot imagine a house of mine without Barton."

A slight frown came on Gabrielle's broad white forehead. "I'm not certain I want Barton."

"My child!" Fountaine's voice was shocked.

Gabrielle's words rushed from her red lips. "If you take her, will you please give her strict orders to treat me as a young woman, not as a child? I won't have her telling me when to wash my neck and ears."

"So Barton is still the nurse, and my child is a grown woman," Fountaine said amusedly.

"Yes, Father, I am." She turned to Molly, who had not entered into the conversation. "You are lucky not to have a woman who treats you as a child. . . . Why Molly! Whatever is the matter?"

Molly was sitting quietly, her hands clasped in her lap, great tears falling down her cheek. "I can't bear to hear you talking of going away to the Plantations, and leaving me all alone." She put her bright head on the table, heavy sobs shaking her body. "How can you talk about going away, Uncle Robert, and leaving me behind? Then I will have nobody. Nobody!"

Gabrielle's tender heart was touched. Molly weeping! She ran to put her arms about the girl. "There, don't cry, sweet Molly. You have your cousin. You know you will have pleasant and gay times at the Hall and in London at your Aunt Lepel's great house."

"I don't like my aunt. I can never, never please her." She sobbed harder. "Mary Lepel hates me. She told me so. She won't let me come into the drawing-room when she has her company. She hates me."

Fountaine listened thoughtfully. His ward's words did not shock him as they did Gabrielle. Surrounded as she had always been with love and consideration, she did not recognize the jealousy or impatience of a woman obliged by her husband to accept a beautiful girl into her own household. For all of Robert's quiet living, he had seen something of the world in his younger days in Paris. That was while he was a law student, before his father professed Protestantism and they were banned from the gay court of Louis. He recognized Molly's troubles. The jealousy of her aunt and her cousin was not pleasant. Should he take her with him, if he decided to go? Molly's voluble, impulsive nature presented more problems than he faced in the less complicated Gabrielle. Could he undertake it? He did not want to commit himself now. He hesitated to say the words: "Come with us to America."

"It is early to become emotional, my dear," he said instead. "We haven't gone. Even if I decide on the Carolinas, it will be months before we can be ready to sail."

Gabrielle said, "Oh, Father! I thought we were going at once, right away, for dear Mamma's sake." She ran a hand over his greying hair. "I thought perhaps we would go out on the *Delicia*, with Captain Woodes Rogers and the Bahama Adventurers, when they sail in April."

Fountaine smiled. "Wouldn't it be wiser to wait for an invitation to sail on the *Delicia?*"

"I saw her again today, when I was walking along Kingroad. A beautiful stout ship, newly painted, with golden carvings on her deck. They told me that she was Captain Roger's ship."

Molly cried, "Oh, now I *have* caught you, Miss Gaby. You do go to the ships. You love an officer, a beautiful officer on a ship of war."

"Molly, please!" Gabrielle's tone was pleading. "I only walked that way to take the pattern drawings to Madam Ertz." She looked fearfully at her father, but he had not heard. He sat staring at the floor, his straight black brows drawn together, making two deep furrows between his eyes.

Gabrielle sighed in relief. He had not heard Molly's reckless accusation. Instead he rose to his feet and started to pace the floor, back and forth, back and forth. Presently he left the room. A moment later they heard the door of his workroom close.

The two girls went into the salon, where Barton was lighting the candles. After she had left the room, Gabrielle said, "I think you are very unkind, Molly. You know I don't even know a ship's officer."

Molly threw her arms about Gabrielle. "Now don't be cross, sweet coz. I didn't think of Uncle Robert when I spoke, truly I didn't! You are such a prim little person, I love to tease you." She got up, her long silk skirts floating behind her as she moved gracefully around the room. "You are as naïve as a child, Gabrielle, or a country woman, you——"

"And you are a worldly woman of fashion. You tell me that half a dozen times in one day," Gabrielle laughed. She could not long be angry with Molly.

"So I am. Worldly. At least I keep my eyes and ears open and behave as a woman of fashion should behave."

"Woman of fashion! You know that our church does not approve of worldly vanities, you know that, Molly." This time it was Molly who laughed her husky thrilling laugh.

"I'm not a true Huguenot, remember. Only half. Half of me is French and half of me is English, as English as an oak tree. That is from my mother. I propose to marry an Englishman, not one of our reform French, my dear, so I may as well attend the Established Church."

"Oh, Molly! How can you say such a thing? It would hurt Father so much."

"There are many Huguenots who are of the Established Church. It's Protestant, too, isn't it? Can I help it if good Uncle Robert chose to be a Presbyterian?"

The argument was closed by Barton coming back into the solon. She looked quite flustered for Barton. "The Honourable Councilman," she said breathlessly. "The Honourable Councilman Tuker and his son. They wish to speak with the Master."

"Goodness!" Molly began to pat her hair into place, her white hands fluttering nervously. "A Councilman and his son—whatever will you do—where is Uncle—oh——"

Gabrielle said quietly. "Show the gentleman in here Barton, then inform my father. I think you will find him in the weaving room." She rose from her chair and stood beside the table, waiting to greet her father's guests. Molly looked at Gabrielle's calm face. She settled herself in a chair, her skirts spread decorously, showing only the tips of her satin slippers, a studied position that looked as natural as the art of Sir Peter Lely or Godfrey Kneller.

The Councilman was a short, stocky man, with a red-veined, choleric face. He wore a white wig, and his dark cloth coat was of elegant weave. Gabrielle knew he belonged to the Weavers' Guild. In his youth Tuker had been a good craftsman and was not above himself now, for he often mentioned in his public utterances that he came from humble folk, although he now was known as an importer and manufacturer of fine woollens, and he traded outside the British Isles as well as at home. But his civic duties kept him occupied, and his son, the young man who followed him into the room, took charge of the business of Tuker and Son. Both men paused at the door of the salon. There was a startled look on the face of the older man, and quickened interest in the eyes of the younger, at the sight of the two young girls.

Gabrielle stepped forward, making a small curtsy. "Sir, this house is honoured," she said. "Will you step in and have a chair? My father will be informed of your presence."

Councilman Tuker smiled blandly at the formality in Gabrielle's greeting.

"I am Gabrielle Fountaine," she continued, "and this is my cousin, Miss Lepel."

"My son," the Councilman said carelessly. His small black eyes darted about the room, a puzzled expression on his face, almost as if he asked, "How does it come that humble folk live so well?" But he did not speak. Instead he sat down on the blue satin sofa while his son took a chair near Molly.

The Councilman leaned forward and picked up a panel of Gabrielle's flowered gown. "Very pretty," he said, fingering the material. "Very elegant quality."

A flush rose on Gabrielle's cheeks at the man's impertinence.

"The pattern is excellent. Did your father import it?"

" 'Tis my own weaving," Gabrielle said distantly.

"So?" said the man. "So? And the design as well?"

Gabrielle bowed slightly. The horrid, ignorant fellow! But her face did not betray her thought.

At that moment the door opened and Barton stood in the doorway. "The Master says will you step this way, sirs?"

The younger man hesitated. He was well content to stay where he was, but a sharp word from his father brought him to heel. He bowed very low, first to Molly, then to Gabrielle, to show that he was not lacking in the niceties. "Your servant, Mistress," he said, sweeping the floor with his beaver. He followed his father from the room.

Molly jumped to her feet and sped to the door, opening it

34

a crack. "They are going to the weaving room," she said in a horrified tone. "Whatever can Uncle be thinking of to receive the Councilman in the weaving room?"

Gabrielle answered, "I don't think Councilman Tuker is here in any official capacity, Molly. Doubtless it is something to do with weaving, or the Guild." She tried to speak lightly, but she was secretly troubled.

"He was almost handsome," Molly said, speaking of the son. "Although he fancied himself a little too much." Molly laughed gaily. "Did you ever see such a bow?" She put her hand across her breast and bent her body forward. "Your servant, Mistress," she said, dropping her voice an octave. Gabrielle laughed with her. Molly was so engaging. But her heart was troubled for her father. Ireland had been like this. Men calling, asking questions about weaving; then more men with inquiry about the Guild! Was it to be the same thing over again, here in England?

No, that couldn't be. England had been refuge for the Huguenots ever since King Charles the Second's proclamation. Queen Anne, too, gave them haven, and Queen's Bounty. Now with the new King, the Huguenots had consideration. She was magnifying the visit into something sinister, when doubtless it had a simple explanation.

In the weaving room, the Councilman and his son were asking questions, one after another. Intimate questions concerning a man's business, his income from importations, and the list of his exports.

Fountaine's face was pale, his dark sombre eyes fathomless and unreadable. He answered some questions quietly, evading others. All the time his mind was leaping ahead of his words. These were not important questions. Tuker was leading up to something. Fountaine was glad he had laid the new double-weave material in the chest after Mr. Wainwairing had left. That was it. The Councilman had heard of the new process. Fountain felt the bright little shoe-button eyes boring in. He is coming to it, he thought. If I refuse to let him see the material or keep secret the process, what happens then? How did he get wind of the new work so soon? In a moment Robert realized the truth—the slovenly, sullen weaver he had discharged last week. It was clear to him now.

The Councilman cleared his throat. "And now, Mr. Fountaine," he began, his voice taking on his official tone. At the moment the son took out his watch from his pocket.

"I am sorry," he said, breaking in, "so sorry to interrupt, but it is nine o'clock. At what time was your appointment with Captain Woodes Rogers and Mr. Colston?"

"Bless me!" The Councilman started up from his chair. "Bless me! It is time now, at this moment. We must make haste, Oliver." He turned to the silent Fountaine. "We will discuss these very interesting matters of weaves at some near time, Mr. Fountaine."

Clapping his hat on his head and taking up his gold-knobbed stick, he walked quickly out of the door, followed by his son. Fountaine went after them, bearing a lighted candle to show the way.

At the salon door young Oliver paused. "I should be very happy if you would permit me to call upon the charming young ladies of your household, Mr. Fountaine."

Fountaine hesitated, not appreciably. He knew he must give no offence to these men, powerful in the Guild. "We shall be honoured," he said.

The Councilman's servant waited at the door with a lanthorn. A gust of wind blew out the candle. Fountaine fumbled for the latch, to close the door. Young Oliver's words carried back. "I spoke in time to keep you from making a fool of yourself," he said, scorn in his voice. "Do you want all Bristol to know your plan? Leave it to me, and you will be clear, quite clear of any suspicion. We have seen the weaving room; now all we——" The words were cut off by distance.

A chill wind seemed to touch Fountaine. He shuddered. It was beginning again, the old persecution. He stood in the dark hallway, thinking, thinking. From the salon, the gay, lilting voice of Molly rose over the accompaniment of Gabrielle's harp, singing some lines from "The Constant Lover":

> "Out upon it, I have loved
> Three whole days together!
> And am like to love thee more,
> If it prove fair weather."

Robert walked slowly to his room. Once inside, he sat down near the window. The moon was rising. He saw the crowded hulls of ships, sides almost touching. Tall masts carrying riding lights rose above the low walls of the quay.

Masts and sails and the Western Ocean. He knew now what his next step would be. He lighted a candle and drew

36

his knee desk from the table. Taking up a quill, he began a letter. He wrote for a time, then folded the letter into envelope shape and sealed it. Across the front he wrote:

"The Right Hon. Lord John Carteret, Palatine of the Lords Proprietors.
"Albemarle Street.   London."

The address sanded, he took up his hat and cloak and went down the stairs. Calling to a serving boy to bring a lanthorn, Fountaine walked down Meg's Lane in the direction of the Fox and Grapes Inn, where the stages changed horses. If he hurried, with good fortune he would be in time to send the letter by the midnight coach for London.

After he had deposited the packet in the pouch, he walked home with a light step. The die was cast. Now he could make his plans with a clear head—not next autumn, or sometime in the future, but now. The men he wanted to accompany him had all been approached. As soon as he could arrange passage, he would take his family and his people to the American Plantations. The first step had been taken.

"Pray God that I have chosen the right road!" he said aloud.

He went to his room, and there for half an hour he read his Bible, to clear his mind and strengthen his faith.

Before he slept, he went to his wife's room, walking softly in list slippers. The night candle burned on a small candle table, throwing a ray of light under the heavy curtains of the bed. She was sleeping quietly. Her pale gold hair flowing over the pillow half concealed her pallid features under the delicate lace nightcap. Her arms was thrown outside the silken cover. The fine lace of the wristband of her night wrapper half covered her fragile hand. The candle ray caught the thin gold band of her wedding ring.

Robert fell on his knees beside the bed and pressed his face against the soft down of the cover. "God, in Thy divine mercy, make her mine again, as once she was, or give me strength to bear the burden."

Chapter 4

THE LORDS PROPRIETORS HOLD
A MEETING

It was a rare day for February. A light wind from the river carried in it a hint of spring. Two mouse-coloured sparrows fought over a length of string, half buried in the slimy grey mud of the cobbled street, while a crowd of idle boys and men stood on the cobbles and laid wagers on the outcome.

Old Timothy Whitechurch, Secretary to the Lords Proprietors of the Carolinas, paused for a moment in the shadow of the Holbein Gate, with a quickening pulse, to watch this first indication of spring. Nest-building was as eternal as the rising of the moon, he thought. March would bluster but April was close following. It wanted but a little time until country lanes would be pink with the bloom of hawthorn, and the old courtyard where he lived, at the edge of Whitehall, crowned with plane trees in full leaf. He was weary of grey winter and dreamed of green spring. When a man presses seventy, the blood runs thin, and the passing of winter is welcome.

A gust of wind whipped his long blue kersey cloak about his thin shanks. He moved to the protection of the pedestrian arch of the gate as a fine coach whirled through the broad archway. It came swiftly, with clanking of harness chains and shouts of coachman and outriders, who cursed roundly at the rabble that stood with gaping mouths and avid eyes, peering through the coach windows to see the gentry ride by.

Timothy stepped back, flattening his spare frame against the stones of the gate. But he was not quick enough to escape the shower of mud flung from the cobbles by the flapping mudguards of the coach. The slime of the street found lodgment on his kersey cloak, dribbled downward to his long pearl-grey silk stockings and his well-varnished buckled shoes.

Not a profane man by habit, Timothy was ready to let fly a strong oath when he recognized the occupant of the coach, Lord John Carteret, Palatine of the Lords Proprietors and, as such, his employer. Timothy's Adam's apple trembled in his long thin throat. What a catastrophe had the "damme" escaped from his lips, instead of being swallowed and reposing now in the pit of his stomach! As the coach careened around the corner, he saw that Lord Carteret was accompanied by his aristocratic mother, Lady Granville. Her proud head rose above a mink-skin cloak. Her clear, straight profile, set against the rich plum colour of my Lord's cloak, was like her son's as two peas of the same pod. Broad forehead, curved haughty lips My Lord's brown wig hung heavy to his shoulders. Her hair, more auburn, swept downward in long curls. The Countess held her muff against her cheek with one hand, a furred bulwark between her proud head and the stares of rude London people. On the seat opposite, two little King Charles spaniels sat on their haunches, their long silken ears fluttering, their bright, round eyes staring haughtily out through the glass windows with the same disdainful condescension as their mistress showed.

" 'Tis my Lord Carteret, home from abroad," a man called out. "He goes to the King's levee to tell his Majesty what the Irish have to say about war and trade."

Whitechurch quickened his pace towards the park. He had a good two hours ahead of him before the time set for Lords Proprietors' meeting. Time aplenty to arrange the books and see that the reports were in order. He had not known until now that Lord Carteret was home from his mission to Ireland. When he was on hand, there would be penetrating questions asked, for his Lordship was not indifferent to the business of governing the Carolinas, nor was he indifferent to making money on the investment. Besides, today was not just another meeting. Today the Lords of Trade and Plantations would be present with the Lords Proprietors. A meeting of some moment; a discussion of importance and consequence to both august bodies. Now that the Spanish wars were over and the nation at peace, his Majesty's ministers were thinking of the development of trade with the West Indies and the Carolina Plantations, for Britain, a maritime nation, must now turn her ships to pursuits of peace. The life-blood of the nation was an ever-developing trade with her colonies, with South America and the South Seas, with India and China. Trade was the wealth of the Empire.

Timothy turned into St. James's Palace through a side entrance that took him directly to the great panelled room where the Lords would hold their meeting. Two lesser clerks waited for him. His desk was spread with papers and the book of Minutes. The secretary gave his cloak and silver-trimmed beaver to one, and to the second he gave the privilege of brushing his pearl-grey stockings, to get rid of the mud splashed from the Palatine's carriage. He pulled his knee-length vest of dun-colour taffeta into place, straightened his periwig, then walked to the high-backed chair the younger clerk held for him in front of the heavy oaken desk, at right angles to the great board table, and sat down. He glanced through the papers to see that they were in order, opened the long Minutes book to the proper page. He chose a fresh-cut quill with deliberation, and wrote a line across the page:

"Lords Proprietors of the Carolinas. Meeting at St. James's Palace—
    "19th of February, 1718.
    "Present:"

As he held the pen poised over the paper, the great bell of St. Paul's boomed out the hour. Three full round pulls of the bell-ringer's rope. In one hour's time eight of the first nobles and gentlemen of England, or their proxies, would enter the room, to be joined one-half hour later by the Lords of Trade and Plantations.

"An historic meething today, me lads," he said solemnly to the two young clerks. "Something for you to remember when you are old men. Old as I am now."

"Yes, sir," the clerks said in unison, looking solemnly each to the other. "Yes, sir. Are we to stay in the room, sir?"

Whitechurch bit the end of his quill, considering the matter. "I may need you to get papers from the ante-room, but it would not be becoming for you to be here with the great Lords and Gentlemen. You may wait in the withdrawing room."

"With the door open?" asked the younger, a rosy-faced blond boy with bright, eager eyes. "You said it would be historic. You know, sir, I am going to the Carolinas as soon as I get my articles."

Timothy nodded. He remembered so well—it was in 1694—that Governor Smith wrote from the Carolinas urging the Proprietors to send one of their own number as governor of the Province. All the Proprietors pitched upon Shaftesbury as being the one qualified for the work, but he desired to be excused on account of his particular affairs in England. It was then the Quaker, Mr. Archdale, was chosen, a good and just man who led the dissenting people out of the confusion into which they had been plunged by feeble and unjust government. Timothy recalled himself from his abstraction.

"I know, Bates; a very good plan," he said. "I'd have been in the Carolinas at this moment, myself, if Lord Shaftesbury had lived a few years longer." The boys drew long faces. They had heard old Timothy tell the story many times, how my Lord Shaftesbury, the great minister, had promised to take Whitechurch to the Carolinas when he went across the sea to visit the Plantations with his friend Locke. "But he never went to the Colonies; instead he went to his just reward." Timothy shook his head sorrowfully.

" 'Tis well to make your adventure to the New World," he said, nodding approvingly. "I tell you what we will do. Put the seven-leaf screen back of my table and place your table behind it. Then you can hear without being seen, and you will be in a position to get my signal for papers or books, without delay."

"Thank you, sir. Thank you." The two voices came as one.

Timothy allowed his spare, bony frame to lean against the tall chair back. He was well pleased with this solution. Now he could gaze at the portraits of the first Lords Proprietors, which adorned the panelled room, beginning with the blue-cloaked figure of the Duke of Albemarle, first Palatine, which Sir Peter Lely had painted so vigorously. It hung over the great fireplace. Set in panels were the other Peers of the Realm to whom Charles the Second had given the Great Charter, The True and Absolute Lords Proprietors of the Carolinas.

Whitechurch's eyes rested on one painting after another. They were men, the eight Peers of the Realm, worthy of the land they had by charter. That was fifty years ago, and the great Lords were gone. Albemarle dead. Clarendon, the Chancellor, banished by his niece, good Queen Anne, his name besmirched by lesser folk. The narrow proud face of Shaftesbury, the greatest of them all. It was he who drew up the constitution, with the help and advice of Locke. The Grand Model that gave men more freedom and liberty than common men had ever enjoyed before in all the history of the world.

Timothy sighed again as he opened his snuff-box. He wished the present Lords were made of the same bone and sinew as those before his eyes. The second and third generations were thinner in blood and brain than the giants. Fifty years, he thought. Fifty years, and he had never seen the great Sound that bore Albemarle's name, or the river called Clarendon. His feet had never touched the gracious soil of Roanoke Island where Sir Richard Grenville had planted his cousin Raleigh's ill-fated colony. His canoe had never gone upstream on the Roanoke to the whirling rapids, or the far reaches of the Chowan; nor had he sailed over the dangerous shoals of Cape Fear, or stood on the deck of a ship as it found safe harbour at Charles Town built near the Ashley and the Cooper.

All he had done for fifty years was to lean over ledgers and books, writing items that concerned the Plantations and planters who had made their adventure to the new land of the Carolinas. Land grants and quitrents and taxes, items of trade and naval stores, set in thin columns in great calf-bound ledgers.

Bates tiptoed up to him, interrupting his dream. "The planter gentleman from Carolina, Mr. Roger Mainwairing, is waiting in the antechamber, and Justice Christopher Gale," the clerk said in a whisper.

"Take them into the small cabinet," Timothy said briskly. "Say you will notify them when their Lordships arrive. See that there is wine on the side table, and remember in the future that a justice takes precedence over a planter."

"Yes, Mr. Whitechurch."

The other clerk, Wilde, came in, his eyes wide with excitement. "The Lords are coming down the hall from the audience with the King. They are dressed in their fine court clothes, and Captain Woodes Rogers is with my Lord Carteret. Crikety, the Captain is taller than anyone and he's got a great scar on his jaw. Crikety, look at the scar on his jaw," he added. "He's a proper hero, he is. He looks a man who'd sailed around the world and fought the Spanish and the French and all the King's enemies."

Timothy silenced his exuberant clerk with a lifted finger and sent him scurrying behind the screen. He rose quietly and stood waiting behind his desk, modest in demeanour, as befitted a servant of the Lords Proprietors of the Carolinas, but his old eyes were fixed on the heavy panelled door of the board room. He too was eager to see Captain Woodes Rogers, the bold navigator who had circumnavigated the globe, and now the lessee and new Governor of the Bahama Islands in the West Indies.

The door was opened by a lackey in red livery. Whitechurch heard a strong, clear voice: "Trade, Lord Carteret, is the very life-blood of England. If we are to be a great sea power and a great nation, as we were in the days of Elizabeth, we must look to our trade with the Indies and the South Seas—yes, and with our American Plantations." With these words, Rogers set the stage.

Old Timothy's faded blue eyes swept the board room. Men of circumstance and wealth, every one of them. If only they cared, as he cared, for that far-off country. They came in from the audience, carelessly throwing cloaks and plumed beavers on chairs and high tables near the door. They unbuckled dress swords, which clattered against benches or the polished side tables. Gay brocaded coats, and brocaded vests laced in silver and gold. Some of the older men wore full-bottomed periwigs; some wore their own hair, cut shoulder length, or even shorter, hanging in heavy curls.

They stood in small groups near the blazing logs of the great fireplace, or sat in careless attitudes in the padded seats of the deep window embrasures.

Lackeys passed noiselessly among them, serving hot possets, for the day was cold.

No one noticed Timothy Whitechurch after the first careless greeting, with the exception of Lord Carteret, who put an affectionate hand on the old man's bent shoulder and inquired after his rheumatism.

"Better, your Lordship. Much better, now that the winter is passing."

Lord Carteret smiled absently, his quick active mind already on something else. Timothy looked at him, eyes filled with admiration. He cared little that people said Carteret was drunken and arrogant. He had found him kind and understanding, the only one of the Lords that gave a tinker's curse about the Carolinas, other than making money from their shares.

"Have you heard from Mr. Mainwairing, Whitechurch? Has he sent in the report on the Albermarle Plantations?"

"Mr. Mainwairing and Justice Gale are in the small cabinet, my Lord."

"The French Huguenot, Fountaine, who wrote us about taking settlers to the Cape Fear—is he here?"

"Not yet, my Lord, but a messenger came earlier to say he would be here by five." A faint semblance of a smile came to Timothy's lips. "The Bristol coach was waylaid by a highwayman, near the Heath, and Mr. Fountaine was obliged to appear before a magistrate to identify one of the robbers."

Carteret smiled, then his dark face clouded gravely. "Too many highwaymen on our roads, Timothy. I'm afraid the enforcement of law is lax these days."

Timothy did not reply, knowing no answer was expected. Carteret examined the outline of the meeting.

"The Lords of Trade will join us around five. We will get through this business as quickly as possible: first Mr. Gale, then the Huguenot."

"Then Mr. Mainwairing's report?" Timothy asked eagerly. He liked Mainwairing. He wanted to hear what he had to say of progress in the Carolinas.

"Not until the Lords of Trade arrive. I want them to hear what he has to say. Let him appear last, after Captain Woodes Rogers. He had promised us a few minutes."

Carteret turned away and joined Sir Francis Shipworth, who had just come in the door. Timothy heard the newcomer say, "His Majesty detained me. He says he is eager to have a complete report of the American Plantations."

Carteret took a glass from a lackey. "Do you think his Majesty is really interested, or has Walpole been prodding?"

Sir Francis shrugged his heavy shoulders. "I don't know really. To tell you the truth, Carteret, I had a wretched time trying to talk to him without an interpreter. German is not my language and his Majesty will not speak a word of English."

Carteret's face showed nothing. Shipworth broke off as Mr. Danson approached them.

Timothy went back to his table, sat down and, taking up his quill, continued his writing in the journal. "Present: Lord John Carteret, Palatine; Mr. Ashley; Mr. Bertie, for the Duke of Beaufort; Sir John Colleton; Sir Francis Shipworth, for Lord Craven; Mr. Danson." To this he added a few lines, anticipating regular business which was to follow.

It was agreed that Mr. Gale should have a new commission for Chief Justice of the Carolinas; he was to produce his credentials to qualify himself, and take oath, in two weeks' time.

He was interrupted by the sound of the gavel on the ancient oak table. Lord Carteret as Palatine had taken his place at the head of it. The others got up from chairs and the benches below the mullioned windows and made their way towards the long table.

"Will you sit beside me, Captain Rogers?" Carteret asked. "The others in their usual places." He turned to Ashley. "You have proxy for the Earl of Bath?"

"Yes, and for Madam Blake." He spoke carelessly, then turned back to Sir John Colleton and took up the conversation where he had left off. The Palatine glanced at him a moment, a look of annoyance on his face. Then he turned to the business at hand.

"My Lords, Gentlemen: I declare the meeting open."

Timothy leaned back. He could sit quietly and listen, watch the little group of Lords and Gentlemen take up the business of governing a land so far away. A feeling of revolt entered into his thought. Strange, for old Timothy knew his position too well to criticize his betters. But the thought persisted. Not one man present had ever viewed with his own eyes the deep shadows of the vast forest, or the broad river roadways, the hidden harbours and the lush river bottom lands, not one. Yet they held the destiny of the Carolinas in their aristocratic hands.

Chapter 5

THE LORDS OF TRADE AND
PLANTATIONS ATTEND

The great hero of the sea, Captain Woodes Rogers, was speaking. The Lords Proprietors had been augmented by men from the Lords of Trade: the Earl of Westmorland, Sir Francis Cook, Mr. Chetwynd, Mr. Bladen, Mr. Docminique and Mr. Secretary Craggs. The Captain stood erect; his strong, tall frame shut out the light of the narrow leaded window behind him. His long oval face was bronzed by wind and he had a network of fine wrinkles radiating from the corners of sharp blue eyes, seaman's eyes, used to looking long distances towards far horizons. He brought something of the strength of the sea with him, in the bold, free glance of his eyes, and the confident way his words fell from his lips. Here was a man who had fought many a good fight with the elements. The wind and the storms were his companions and he was not terrified of their strength. His sober dark coat was a uniform on his broad shoulders. He stood with legs apart as he would on the deck of a ship.

Timothy did not give him close attention. He had heard the Captain more than once, even before the Merchants of Bristol had sent him forth to circumnavigate the globe in the interest of their trade. Now he had leased the Bahama Islands from the Lords Proprietors and proposed to set up a colony. His voice was strong and clear. "In April I will sail my ship to New Providence and seat my colony—" he paused a second, a slight smile at the corner of his lips— "then, so that we may come into an era of great prosperity, I have only to sit under a banyan tree and govern; nothing at all to do but clear the sea of a thousand pirate ships."

A spontaneous laugh went up. "You call that nothing, Captain?" asked the Earl of Westmorland, a heavy man, unsmiling, with the cares of his position a stone's weight on him. "You call pirates nothing, when Vane and Blackbeard, Rackham and Stede Bonnet still roam the Caribbean?"

Young Ashley inquired negligently, "What about the women, Mary Read and Anne Bonney? Do you propose to hang them higher than Haman?"

The navigator brushed the questions aside. "The King has given amnesty to every pirate who comes into Nassau and surrenders himself and his ship." His bold glance swept the table. "And I propose to be there to hand out the King's Pardon. If Anne Bonney or Mary Read want pardon, they will get it, provided they swear allegiance to the Crown."

Carteret, who had been a silent observer, said quietly, "And the pirate who doesn't surrender to you, Captain?"

Captain Rogers' face hardened. "I shall deal with him suitably," he said. No man present doubted his ability to deal suitably and effectively.

"God help the poor pirates!" Ashley whispered to Danson. Danson tittered, then put his hand to his mouth quickly to hide the smile from the Palatine's eagle glance.

Mr. Secretary Craggs, of the Lords of Trade and Plantations, had a question for Captain Rogers. "Are your old friends the Merchants of Bristol behind you in the new project of the Bahamas colonization?"

"Some of them, as individuals, but not the organization as a whole."

"Why is that?" Craggs asked.

"I did not invite them all. Mr. Colston made the arrangements for financing the expedition. His grandson goes with us as an observer. He will take a report back to Mr. Colston. If more financing is necessary, more ships and supplies, it will be handled by him."

"A very good arrangement, indeed," Craggs condescended. "There is not a merchant in all England of more weight than Mr. Colston."

The Captain did not answer. Timothy thought he did not hold a high opinion of Mr. Secretary Craggs. Most full-bodied men did not. A man who played on the King's weakness, fetched young maids to his Majesty, deserved an ancient and obscene name which Timothy would not foul his thoughts, much less his lips. He didn't like Craggs for other things. . . . What was it Craggs was saying?

"Mr. Colston might have employed his funds to better advantage by investing in the South Sea Company."

"So say I," muttered Ashley.

"A swindle!" Rogers burst out. "A rotten swindle!"

Craggs sat up. "You forget that my father is a director in

47

the company, and the Bank of England is guaranteeing
to——"

"A swindle," Woodes Rogers interrupted, "I still say. I
can't see why men don't realize that they cannot make
money in trade with the South until the land is developed.
What on God's earth have they to trade?"

Craggs bristled. "Gold and copra, and the King has put
money——"

Woodes Rogers' face was red, but he held himself in
check. "Mr. Secretary, I've sailed the whole length of South
America, down the east coast, and I've sailed up the west,
putting into every town of consequence. I've taken my ships
up the California coast and crossed the ocean to the Philippines; from there to the island of Guam. There is little there
to trade for yet. In the Indies, yes—but that trade goes
around Africa to England, not by way of South America. I
tell you, you will wake up one morning and find you have
indeed put your money in a bubble."

Mr. Ashley's eyes smouldered but he did not enter into the
discussion. Mr. Secretary Craggs had not the finesse to with-
draw gracefully; he blundered on, "I thought you were all for
trade, Captain Rogers. Trade with the South Seas and South
America."

"So I am," snapped the Captain, "but I want honest trade
for commodities, finished products for raw materials. I don't
want trade based on joint stock issued by wolves who do
business in the City."

Carteret listened to the irate Rogers, a cynical smile on his
lips.

"I'm glad to hear you say that, Captain. Some members of
this group are about to propose that we sell out our shares in
Carolina, and invest the money in the South Sea Company."

Ashley's and Danson's eyes met. They had not meant this
to come out before the Lords until some future meeting,
when their plans were better prepared.

Carteret thumbed through a mass of papers on the table
until he found one he was looking for. He lifted it up.

"If I may interrupt for a moment, Captain Rogers, I had
intended this matter to rest, but since it is in the open we may
as well get it over with. Mr. Ashley has written this letter to
my mother, the Countess of Granville, begging her to use her
influence to have her shares in the Carolinas sold and the
money put in South Sea joint stock. In this he has the
concurrence of Mr. Danson. In fact he has gone so far as to

have the documents of transfer made out with a note where she was to sign. Only the stroke of a pen, and Carolina would be thrown to what Captain Rogers called the 'Wolves of the City.'

"I ask you to bear with me, Gentlemen, since this letter concerns you all:

" 'The day your Ladyship went to Beachwood, I was in Kensington to wait on you, intending to inform you of a proposal in respect to Carolina. It is of such advantage to the Proprietors that my single share may amount to thirty thousand pounds.

" 'Term of agreement, your Ladyship will find enclosed, drawn in form and ready to be signed by Lady Granville, for her son Lord Carteret. . . .' "

Carteret raised his eyes from the paper. "It will be remembered that I was, at the time, in Ireland. I will not accuse Mr. Ashley of taking advantage of my absence, but certainly he timed his proposal." Ashley did not glance up. He sat looking at a spot on the table, as if fascinated.

" '. . . and by Mr. Bertie, guardian for the Duke of Beaufort . . .' "

Mr. Bertie spoke with heat. "I swear I never signed any such paper."

Lord Carteret raised his hand for silence and continued:

" '. . . by Mr. Danson and myself. I have no reason to question your Ladyship's interest in this matter for your son and his family.

" 'I entreat your Ladyship to treat it as a secret, since we have the prospect of something so considerable.

" 'Give me leave now, Madam, to make your Ladyship a request for our brother Proprietor, Mr. Danson. He has a mind to concede a thousand pounds in next subscription into "South Seas." He desires your Ladyship to request the favor of 1000 pounds subscription for me. I will willingly lend him my name. He hopes your Ladyship will answer soon.' "

Carteret dropped the letter on the table and wiped his fingers with a fine cambric handkerchief, as if the touch contaminated him.

"The gentlemen must have been dealing with Sir George

Montgomery and been taken in by his extraordinary scheme for leasing the Carolinas.

"Fortunately my mother turned the letter over to me. I will give the answer now, Mr. Ashley and Mr. Danson. Never, so long as I draw breath, will a Granville's share of the great Empire of Carolina be sold for stock in the South Sea Company or any other share of stock. If any man present wishes to sell his share, I am prepared to buy—nay, I demand the shares be brought to me for my refusal.

"It is a disgrace to us, as Lords Proprietors of the Carolinas, to consider such an eventuality. King Charles the Second, of saintly memory, gave the land to our fathers. We as their sons will hold the land as they gave it to us endeavouring always to develop it into a great colony for the glory of his Majesty's realm. Not an inch of ground shall be exchanged for a worthless share in a worthless company." His closed fist hit the table. "To that I give oath, so help me God."

Ashley was angered by Carteret's words. He sat looking down at the table while Danson bit nervously at his fingernail. Neither spoke, although out of common decency Carteret gave them a moment to reply. He turned to Captain Rogers. His voice was quiet, his manner contained.

"I am sorry for the interruptions, Captain, but it seemed the time to declare myself on the subject on which you, an expert in trade, have spoken so vigorously. Thank you, Captain Rogers. I want you to call on me, either as Palatine, or personally, for any help I may give you in developing your new colony in the Bahamas."

There was a moment of silence during which Captain Rogers sat down. The Palatine said:

"My Lords and Gentlemen, we are ready to hear the report which his Majesty requested on the condition of the Carolinas." He spoke as if nothing had happened. "Instead of reading the lengthy report prepared by our Deputies in the Plantations, I have asked Mr. Roger Mainwairing, a planter of Albermarle County, in North Carolina, to give us a summary, and to answer such questions as we think necessary to clear any obscure points." He lifted his eyes from the voluminous report he held in his hand and glanced in Timothy's direction. "Mr. Whitechurch, will you be so good as to ask Mr. Mainwairing and Mr. Gale to step in?"

Timothy rose and laid a paper before the Palatine. "Your

pardon, my Lord. This note has just arrived, my Lord. The gentleman is waiting."

The Palatine glanced at the paper. "Monsieur Robert Fountaine, the Huguenot gentleman to whom we have given a grant of 8500 acres on the Cape Fear River in North Carolina, has just arrived from Bristol. I asked him to appear before this board today. With your permission, I think it would facilitate matters if he came in first, before Mr. Mainwairing. His business will take but a few moments."

"Let us see him, by all means," Sir Francis Shipworth said. "I have a curiosity to see a man who has the courage to venture into the wilderness and seat a new colony."

Lord Carteret said, "You will see a very fine gentleman, one who has suffered almost beyond belief for his religion. A saintly man, yet, being French, he finds it possible to combine thrift and business acumen with saintliness." A slow smile lighted his dark face. "That would not be possible in a Briton. A saint, yes; a thrifty man, yes; but not the combination."

"Let us see this saint," Sir John Colleton said, adjusting the ruffles in his sleeves. "I've often wondered about saintliness. Does it set heavy on a man's brow? Does he wear it as a halo?"

The Palatine frowned at the hint of raillery in Sir John's voice. "Ask Monsieur Fountaine to honour us," he said to Timothy, and the form his words took erased the smile from Sir John's face. He settled back in his chair, pouting his full lips, like a child when punished.

Timothy went to the door and held it open. The Huguenot came in with a quick, firm step, paused a moment until his eyes met those of the Palatine. "Ah, my Lord. It is with pleasure that I come before you and this honourable body." He bowed slightly to the table and stood waiting, a slim, wiry man of medium height. His oval face, with arched brows, had the pallor of an indoor man, but not unhealthy. His smile was kindly but his quiet eyes had the stamp of sorrow and tragedy within their depths. His suit was of a modest grey, but excellent in texture, a woollen that had the sheen of satin. The buckles on his shoes were silver and his stock and ruffles of the finest Brussels. But it was the beaver, carried in his hand, that attracted the attention of the young men present—of such fine texture that it was like the fur of a kitten or a young rabbit. He wore no sword.

Lord Carteret waited until he was seated, then spoke directly to him.

"I am happy to tell you that the Lords Proprietors have granted you 8500 acres of land, facing the River Cape Fear on the north, and straddling Old Town Creek. I am assured that it is excellent land, and it lies exactly on the spot of our early settlement of Charles Town, of Sir John Yeamans' colony."

"Near Charles Town?" exclaimed Mr. Danson. "I thought the grant was to be in Northern Carolina."

"I am afraid the gentleman hasn't studied the maps of Carolina possessions, or perhaps he is ignorant of the history of our colonization." The look that accompanied the words was contemptuous. "I recommend that Mr. Danson apply to Mr. Whitechurch for information concerning early settlements of Charles Town on the Cape Fear, the Barbados Adventure, in 1663, proposed by 'several gentlemen and persons of good quality,' which came into being under the leadership of Sir John Yeamans, and the Vassel attempt."

Mr. Ashley inquired, "I thought the Lords Proprietors were on record as opposed to any colonizing other than the already established settlements in Albemarle County and the present Charles Town, on the river named for my illustrious kinsman."

"If you attended our meetings with more zeal, Mr. Ashley, you would know that we have voted to cancel that fifty-year-old prohibition." Lord Carteret took up a parchment roll from the table and handed it to the Huguenot. "Here is your grant, Mr. Fountaine, signed by me as Palatine of the chartered owners of the Carolinas, the Lords Proprietors. We wish you every success with your Carolina adventure."

Fountaine rose and took the roll from Carteret's hand. His face bore a look of solemnity as he said, "With the Grace of God and His divine help, my associates and I will endeavour to seat this grant in a way to bring honour to the honourable Lords Proprietors, and to the nation."

"Hear! Hear!" said the gentlemen present.

Lord Carteret sat down. "Now, Mr. Fountaine, I am sure these gentlemen want to know a little of your plan. Tell them the number of men you are taking, your ideas of planting and trade."

The Huguenot looked about the table, his dark sombre eyes missing not one of the Lords and Gentlemen. He saw no particular interest in any face save Mr. Chetwynd's and

Captain Woodes Rogers', who smiled encouragingly. What he read in the other faces was indifference, incredulity and a little condescension. Why should they waste their time with the plans for seating a small parcel of land in the wilderness of the American Plantations? A great colonization scheme, such as Captain Rogers had laid out, was something different. Rogers spoke in large terms—of great tonnage of ships and consequent pounds sterling. A man of wide vision and accomplishment. Success was his bedfellow; success was his before he put his foot on his ship; but this little man, without a name of consequence! Why was Carteret backing him for success?

All this Fountaine could guess ran through the minds of the gentlemen seated at the long table. The combined thought of incredulity and condescension beat against the Huguenot with the force of a great wave. He faltered a moment; then, raising his troubled eyes, he encountered those of the old Secretary. Whitechurch was leaning forward, his thin bony face alert, his eyes eager and friendly, his smile encouraging.

Fountaine, heartened by the look and the smile, raised his head and began to speak rapidly. Twenty men he was taking with him—artisans of various sorts, many of them with more than one trade. Farmers and husbandmen, a furrier and four weavers. When he said that, Captain Woodes Rogers spoke involuntarily.

"Weavers?"

The Huguenot smiled. "Yes, Captain. That explains my plan. I shall set up weaving as an industry. We will raise our own flax and cotton and our own sheep. I am taking with us the looms and the machinery. I am taking also cattle, horses and sheep."

"But what will you do with your weaving?" Sir Francis Shipworth asked, becoming suddenly interested. "Aren't you taking a large number of weavers for a settlement of twenty people?"

A slight smile passed across Fountaine's face. "It will be five, to be exact. I am myself a master weaver."

Ashley turned to the Palatine. "I thought you told us last meeting that this—this gentleman was a lay reader in the Huguenot Temple in Bristol."

Fountaine answered, "So I am, Mr. Ashley. I am also a barrister, an advocate, in France, or I was before the Revocation of the Edict of Nantes. I fled France to your great

53

England, which has ever opened it gates to the oppressed. But a poor refugee must think of his family when he flees to a strange country, so I apprenticed and learned the trade of weaving."

"By gad, a man of energy!" Sir Francis said admiringly. "I believe you will succeed. By gad, I wish you success, sir!"

Carteret smiled but said nothing. Captain Woodes Rogers did not disguise his interest.

"I see you have an idea that coincides with my own. You propose not only to colonize and plant but to develop an industry as well. Trade will follow. Is it not so? Trade with the Bahamas perhaps?"

"Yes, Captain Rogers, I hope for trade to the Bahamas and Jamaica as well as coastal trade to other colonies— Virginia, Southern Carolina and New York."

"And run afoul the navigation laws," Sir John Colleton said sourly. "It's a pretty scheme but it won't work, unless you hope to make money by stock-selling in your venture."

Fountaine drew himself up. "There are no shares to sell. It is not a bubble. The project is financed within the group."

Rogers spoke again. "I must talk to you later, Mr. Fountaine. I'm sailing with the Bahama settlers in April. Perhaps you will go with us. We have room, as we are taking several ships."

Fountaine bowed, well pleased with Captain Rogers' interest. The representatives of the Lord of Trade and Plantations began to show interest, now that Captain Rogers had expressed himself favourably.

Carteret, leaning back against the tall oak chair, said, "It will be a thousand pities if you don't succeed, with such high plans, and I'm sure you will. I can see, sir, that some of these gentlemen are looking with envious eyes at the cloth of your coat. I imagine that they will be asking if it is from your own looms, once this meeting is over."

Danson flushed darkly at the Palatine's words. He had scarcely taken his eyes from the Huguenot's garments while the talk was in progress. He was annoyed that Carteret had caught him.

Ashley laughed. "By gad! That I will and I shall ask him where he got that superb beaver, also. Never have I seen a finer laced hat."

"Gentlemen!" said the Palatine sharply. "Come to order, please! I shall now ask Mr. Whitechurch to request Mr. Roger Mainwairing and Mr. Christopher Gale to join us here. Take a chair, Mr. Fountaine. You will be interested in what Mr. Mainwairing has to say about affairs in the Plantations."

Old Timothy's eyes wandered over this scene. On the arrival of two representative men of their Carolina Plantations, the Lords sat back in their chairs, at ease. Someone called for pipes and the meeting took on a more informal aspect.

Christopher Gale, Timothy had heard often during his sojourn in London as Chief Justice of Northern Carolina and responsible agent for the affairs of the province. He had appeared before the board from time to time, laying before them the cause of the colony for better laws and government. His slim, energetic body, his thin face and deep-sunken dark eyes were familiar in London. Gale's sharp, caustic tongue had warded off many a defeat in argument before this august body. He did not hesitate to criticize government, governors; even the Lords Proprietors themselves were not exempt.

Today he did not speak. He accepted his renewed commission as Chief Justice with a few words, and gave way to his friend from the Albermarle, Roger Mainwairing, planter.

The Palatine spoke. "I have asked Mr. Mainwairing to come down from the Midlands, where he is staying, to give us an opportunity to learn first-hand of some matters under dispute in our providence of North Carolina. For the information of the honourable Lords of Trade and Plantations, Mr. Mainwairing is one of our prominent planters in what is called the Albermarle, the country adjacent to the great Sound.

"At the request of his Majesty we have recently had our eight Deputies of the district prepare a report. Most of us have read that report. Mr. Mainwairing's presence in England at this time is propitious, for he knows, as well as anyone in the Carolinas, the conditions there. I know him to be a man without prejudice. I am sure he will speak openly and frankly, and we will question in the same manner.

"We are all here for one purpose today: to judge the best means we are to employ, to open and develop trade with our plantations in the New World and the West Indies. My Lords and Gentlemen, Mr. Roger Mainwairing."

Carteret sat down and adjusted his long body comfortably, his thin dark face quiet and composed.

Timothy had looked quickly about the circle. The Lords of

Trade and Plantations showed more interest and anticipation than the Lords Proprietors. That worried Timothy. He had long been an admirer of Mr. Roger Mainwairing. Over the years he had corresponded with the planter, always satisfactorily. He glanced behind the screen. His two young clerks had moved a leaf of the high screen so that they had an uninterrupted view of the speaker. Timothy was pleased at their obvious interest in the affairs of the Province. His eyes rested long on Bates. He sighed a little: if he were only young, without ties to hold him, as Bates was, he would embark on the great venture and go out to the Carolinas when Captain Woodes Rogers and Mr. Roger Mainwairing sailed in April. Age had its compensations, but its drawbacks were many. His glance went back to the table as Lord Carteret was saying, "My Lords and Gentlemen, Mr. Roger Mainwairing."

The planter of Albemarle pushed back his chair and got to his feet. He stood for a moment in silence, his eyes following the long table, including every man present in his glance. He was tall, well over six feet, with broad shoulders and narrow waist and hips. His blond hair was his own, and his blue eyes clear and cool. He had the habit of direct look, appraising swiftly. His hawk nose was as high-bridged as my Lord Carteret's and the long line of his jaw was firm. He had the easy confidence of a man who has met life and danger boldly, with a certain quiet exhilaration, and the deeply indented corners of his firm lips were not without laughter.

"He has an arrogant look," whispered Ashley behind his slim hand to his neighbour Danson, "too bold for a provincial planter."

Danson nodded. He had the same thought. "I swear his coat is as well cut as Sir John's and the Mechlin at his wrists as good as Chetwynd's. One does not expect such elegance in a planter."

"It savours of insolence," Ashley added, then leaned back as the Palatine's sharp glance met his.

"My Lords and Gentlemen." Mainwairing's voice was full and strong, matching his hard sinewy body and his firm features. "I have laid before Lord Carteret the report sent to me by the Lords Proprietors' Deputies in Northern Carolina. You, my Lord, have asked me questions concerning the political conditions of the Carolina Plantations, the prospect of trade and the progress of the settlers in seating the country. I must warn you I am no politician, nor am I a

56

dealer in words to mystify and evade. I am accustomed to plain speaking." A slight smile crossed his lips, passing immediately. "There may be words which will not please some of the gentlemen present, if they expect praise for their procedure in administering government in North Carolina."

There was a stir at the table and inquiring glances exchanged. A smile lurked in Carteret's dark eyes. Mr. Chetwynd smoothed one hand over the other slowly, as if he anticipated and relished plain speaking. He leaned forward a little and said:

"The committee, the Lords of Trade and Plantations, is here to learn the truth about conditions in the Carolinas, relative to increasing trade. We expect, also, open discussion of any subject that is detrimental to the free flow of trade. We have had reports from the governors of Antigua, the Bermuda and Jamaica Plantations. We anticipate that Captain Woodes Rogers will change New Providence, the pirates' fortress, into a fortress of free and lawful trade with all plantations and the mother country. With the honourable Palatine's permission, I will say for my committee, 'Speak out, Mr. Mainwairing.' "

"Hear! Hear!" said several gentlemen in chorus.

Lord Carteret voiced his agreement. "We want frankness, not evasions, Mr. Mainwairing. We have had many contradictory reports from our governors and our deputies, and from Governor Spottswood, of Virginia, and his boundary commission." He paused. "We have heard only one side of the disagreement between the Governor of Virginia and Mr. Byrd."

Mr. Ashley tapped the table with a long forefinger. He was unsmiling; his assumed air of indifference had vanished.

"Gentlemen, I protest it is not necessary to bring up the everlasting disagreement between the Burgesses of Virginia and the North Carolinians over the boundary line. Since Mr. Mainwairing is not a member of that commission, his opinion would be hearsay only. Let us keep to the questions with which he is familiar—planting and trade. Let us leave affairs of government to men who govern."

Roger turned. The eyes of the two men met and clashed— Ashley's haughty, disdainful, Roger's cool and dispassionate.

"I shall speak also of government, gentlemen. Since I live under your provincial government, I have the privilege of criticizing that government openly, with the intent to better certain obvious mistakes."

"People who throw out one governor after another make rebellion against constituted authority a habit," Ashley said sharply.

The eyes of the two men met again. Roger said quietly, "I had not intended mentioning the subject of inadequate governors, but since you paved the way, Mr. Ashley, and it could readily be classed under restraint of trade, I will speak out.

"We Carolinians have absorbed the habit of free speech from our British forebears, a privilege won at Runnymede. We have repudiated adventures, and greedy men who sought to mulct the province for their own selfish ends, though they carried the title of Governor. Witness the regime of John Archdale, your father-in-law, Mr. Danson. He gave us good government: a quiet term during which many colonists came to seat the rich bottom lands. Mr. Hyde, of happy memory, had the support of the best of our people, in spite of the rebellion of your brother-in-law, Thomas Cary. If Edward Hyde had lived, we would be by now in excellent case, what with the Indians subdued and the planters given a fair opportunity to get ahead with the business of colonization and prosperity."

Timothy put up his hand to hide the satisfied smile that came to his thin old lips. This was as it should be. The New World striking out at the decadent injustices of the Old— Ashley, hot to sell out his share of the Carolina empire, and Danson too, the weak son-in-law of the strong Quaker, Archdale. Timothy looked covertly at the Palatine. Carteret was leaning back in his chair, watching the by-play with a certain pleasurable satisfaction.

"I suppose you agree with your radical friends Edward Moseley and Maurice Moore, ready to write complaints of your new governor, Charles Eden, with every post, accusing him of all sorts of misconduct," Ashley said, a note of sarcasm dominating his voice.

The planter's face was without expression. "I have not been in the Albermarle for some months," Mainwairing said noncommittally. Without showing any rancour towards Ashley for the covert goading, he went on. "Under the Grand Model, the Fundamental Constitution sponsored by Mr. Locke and your ancestor, Mr. Ashley, the distinguished Earl of Shaftesbury, we of North Carolina were granted more privileges and liberties than any government heretofore. We enjoy that freedom and will defend it. We have so far discarded only one section of the Constitution."

"What is that, may I ask?" inquired Mr. Docminique.

"The section which deals with the power of the Lords Proprietors to establish a caste system, or to grant patents of nobility and confer titles."

There was silence. No one made comment.

Lord Carteret said, "Will you pass on to the next obstacle to trade beyond that of ineffectual government and administration, Mr. Mainwairing?"

"Have you a remedy to offer, Mr. Mainwairing?" Sir John Colleton questioned. "Do your people still contend that they are neglected?"

Roger replied, "It has been a very long time since a Lord Proprietor visited our hospitable shores; not since the day of our good Quaker governor Archdale many years ago." Mainwairing did not wait for an answer to his comment. "I·usurp Mr. Gale's prerogative and mention bad laws: navigation, duties, adjustment of quitrents. Particularly I ask you to give consideration to the unjust Virginia Tobacco Act, which sets a prohibitive tax on all North Carolina tobacco sent out through Virginia ports, showing that a Crown Colony has privileges that proprietary government does not enjoy."

"Why not use your own ports instead of those of Virginia?" Danson asked, overlooking the inference of bad government.

"Because of geographical reasons, Mr. Danson, we have no proper ports. The long sand banks of our coast make passage of larger ships dangerous, if not impossible." Mainwairing turned slightly and looked directly at the Palatine.

"I would suggest, my Lord, the opening of the Clarendon— I mean the Cape Fear—River to seating. North Carolina would then have a harbour for our ships comparable with any along the coast." He paused a moment. "For fifty years your Lordships have prohibited settlement of that fine, fertile land along a great navigable river. I am happy today to learn that you are at last encouraging settlement at Old Town, and that Mr. Fountaine will make the attempt to reopen the river to trade."

Ashley said, "I thought the Cape Fear was the haunt of pirates—of Blackbeard and Vane and Rackham."

"And Stede Bonnet," Sir John added.

Mr. Secretary Craggs spoke: "Pirates' River they call it, do they not? If Captain Woodes Rogers succeeds in driving the pirates out of New Providence, will they not continue to forgather in the Cape Fear and the Carolina Banks?"

"I think we planters will take care of that, although you have given us no help," Roger said drily. "Captain Rhett, of Charleston, has already made some progress."

Mr. Ashley said, "If I remember, those troublesome Moores from South Carolina were petitioning for land on the Cape Fear."

Roger said sharply, "We have one of that ilk, the 'radical' Maurice Moore, in the Albemarle. May I remind you that we think highly of the Moore family in Carolina, Mr. Ashley?"

Mr. Chetwynd interrupted. "Always returning to the subject of trade: Have you seen this River Clarendon, Mr. Mainwairing?"

"They call it the Cape Fear now, Mr. Chetwynd. Yes, I have crossed it more than once, following the Great Road to Southern Carolina."

"Do you believe that the Cape Fear can be seated without loss to the Albemarle or Charles Town? They are both thin settlements and can ill afford to lose population."

"I had hoped the honourable gentlemen would advertise for new colonists and not draw from the North or the South."

"That answers my question. I know that the harbour is good, once the shoals off the entrance are passed. Is the land fertile, Mr. Mainwairing?"

"After the first few miles of sandy soil it is good land with fine timber, oaks of great size, tulip poplar, turpentine pines and a dozen hardwoods. It has a bank on the west side and many coves and tributary streams. That is why it has become 'Pirates' River,' a safe place where they can sail into fresh water to unfoul their ships."

Ashley could not give up his attempt at breaking through Mainwairing's poise. "Are you thinking of changing your residence and moving to the Cape Fear, Mr. Mainwairing?"

Roger was unruffled. A slight smile played on his lips, but his eyes were cold and watchful. "If we continue to have unjust government, I dare say I will."

"Mr. Mainwairing seems to enjoy moving about. If I remember, he moved from England to the West Indies—St. Kitts, was it not?—under government compulsion." Ashley raised his arched brows suggestively.

Roger's eyes had steel in them. "I also moved from Sedgemoor Field direct to the Tower."

"Ah, yes, I do remember. You followed Monmouth. A

sad, sad fortune. You had a price on your head and became a bondman."

"With many of my betters," Roger retorted.

"It seems that I have heard, more recently, that you cast your fortune with Monmouth's dazzling sister, my Lady Mary Tudor."

Roger looked squarely at his interrogator. "I understand the greensward at Hampstead Heath is quite suitable for sword-play," he said, his voice as suggestive, as smooth, as Ashley's.

"Gentlemen!" the Palatine interrupted. "Mr. Ashley, if you will kindly refrain, we will get on with the business at hand."

Old Timothy drew a deep breath. For a moment he had thought something untoward would happen, something unbecoming the dignity of a meeting of the Lords Proprietors of the Carolinas. He would have loathed that, before the honourable Secretary of the Lords of Trade and Plantations, Mr. Secretary Craggs. He glanced sidewise, out of the tail of his eye. The Secretary's clerk was writing busily. He hoped he would not set down all that had been said. The Palatine had the same thought. He said, "We will strike out all extraneous matter from the records, gentlemen." The clerk's scratching ceased suddenly. Timothy drew a deep breath. As he turned, he encountered Mr. Mainwairing's clear blue eyes. There was a smile of understanding in their depths. Thought Timothy, The New World is better than the Old. Men have other things to think about than quarrels with their neighbours over nothing, but they are not averse to a fight. He took satisfaction in that and in the look of discomfiture on Mr. Ashley's face. That pleased him. He didn't like Mr. Ashley. Mr. Ashley was constantly talking of selling his share in the Carolinas. To old Timothy Whitechurch that was sacrilege.

He wanted Roger Mainwairing to win. To Timothy he was more than a planter in the Carolinas; he was the land itself, strong in body, strong in character, with the vital strength of the vast forests and deep rivers and a young world; an unwavering man who had followed his adventure and gained strength and character in so doing. Now in the middle years he had the vigour of youth. He put to shame the youthful debauchees at the table.

Timothy sighed for his dream. Always he had been put off—by his old mother, by his crippled nephew. Lord Shaftesbury had promised to take him there. "Wait, Timothy.

Wait until I go out to see the New World. We need you here." So it was until age had overtaken him, and his great patron was dead and gone, and a lesser man sat in his room; so it was with all the great Lords Proprietors; all gone, and weaker men in their stead, who did not think of the land, only of the gold it would bring. All save my Lord Carteret. He loved the land as the old Lords had loved it.

Timothy closed his books and put them away in a box with a great brass-bound lock. The Lords and Gentlemen stood talking in groups, buckling on swords, lifting plumed beavers from benches and tables, throwing bright cloaks over satin-coated shoulders or arranging wigs before mirrors. Within easy earshot, Lord Carteret was talking with Captain Rogers. Rogers was saying:

"If you will join me at supper, my Lord, I shall be most honoured. With your permission, I will invite Mr. Mainwairing and Mr. Fountaine. We will join Mr. Addison at the Tennis Club. I am sure it will be a memorable evening."

Lord Carteret smiled. "I shall be honoured to sup with the Secretary of State and the first sea captain of our Empire." He turned his head to include Timothy Whitechurch in the conversation. "Old Timothy and I have burned midnight candles looking at maps, talking of the time when we would take ship and sail away to our New World adventure."

Timothy's eyes glazed over. "It is too late for me, my Lord. I'm too old. But you are young. You will hold the land until it is a great golden empire in your hands."

"God grant that that day will come, Timothy! But in the meantime, we have three emissaries to make the way clear for us." He threw his arm carelessly about Timothy's bony shoulder. "I've a feeling, Timothy, that I've done a good thing this day. I've brought together three men—you, Captain Rogers, the sea captain; Robert Fountaine, the colonizer; and Roger Mainwairing, the planter. It is strong in my mind that you three will play a great part in the destiny of the New World."

Chapter 6

MERCHANTS OF BRISTOL

The farewell dinner for Captain Woodes Rogers and the Bahama Adventures brought all the great Merchants of Bristol to the Guildhall.

Edward Colston, aged but active in mind and body, presided. With a lionlike head set on a short heavy neck, he had an air of power that overshadowed Lord Hervey. The young Lord was attending the banquet as the representative of his father, the Earl of Bristol, who lay abed with the gout. At the high table sat the captains and lieutenants of the *Delicia*, H.M.S. *Rose* and H.M.S. *Milford*, interspersed with the Councilmen. At lower tables sat masters of ships and their mates, with lesser merchants to act as hosts. Everything was done in good order. It might have been the Guildhall in London, and the Lord Mayor himself presiding, Robert Fountaine thought, as he watched, from a lower table, the prominent men file in to take their places. Fountaine was there by invitation of young Edward Colston, due to the fact that Robert and his family were to sail on the lead ship, *Delicia*, of Woodes Rogers' Bahama Adventurers.

He recognized Sir John Hawkins and John Romsey at the high table; near them old John Duckenfield, who had representation in the Carolinas. Beside Duckenfield was Thomas Goldney, the leading Quaker of Bristol. Present were the eighteen worthy Merchants of Bristol, who had financed Woodes Rogers' earlier venture in trade, when, in 1708, he took the *Duke* and the *Dutchess* for a privateering journey around the world, with the great William Dampier as navigator. They sailed around South America to the South Seas. That cruise made the Bristol merchants rich men, and they were more than willing to follow wherever Woodes Rogers led them.

Robert Fountaine, soberly dressed, stood out boldly among the brocades and silks of the merchant princes, as did Thomas Goldney in his Quaker garb. Once he caught the baleful eye of Councilman Tuker fixed upon him. Robert turned away, the old torment sweeping over him. The Councilman would hurt him by some underhand means—get his trade from him, wean away his workmen. He had made the mistake, since establishing himself in Bristol, of being too successful. His cloth was too good, his purchase of foreign goods too clever. He couldn't help knowing which way fashion would run. He was too much the Frenchman not to have the gift of good taste. All this was a mistake. Too late he recognized it. That day he had drawn money from the bank and bought Boston and Jamaica exchange notes, to be ready. Ready for what? He did not know. It seemed unreasonable that the hatred of one man could drive another from the country, but it was truth that he had encountered once before. Bewildered he was, that he created such deep hatred in any man, when he wanted only peace and a reasonable amount of security for his family.

The man seated next to him was looking at him curiously. Robert became aware that he had been spoken to and had not answered. "I beg your pardon," he said. "I am abstracted. It is a habit I have, a bad one."

The man laughed. His ruddy, round face with a long scar crinkled in good humour. "I've been that way myself more than once. That was after I escaped from prison, where the Barbary pirates sent me. May they rot in hell!"

Robert scrutinized his companion more closely. The bloodthirsty words were spoken with mildness, almost as a child would speak, but there was no weakness in the man's face. It was the countenance of one who had faced danger and hard living.

"Bragg is the name. Zeb Bragg. Lately master of the Royal Africa Company's ship *Lobita;* now sailing master of Captain Woodes Rogers' *Delicia.*"

He grasped Fountaine's hand with such vigor that Robert almost cried out. He mentioned his name.

"Huguenot?" Bragg said, looking at Robert with his sharp, shrewd eyes. "Many's the Huguenot gentleman I've picked up off Lorient and St. Malo and sailed across the Channel. A fair company of them at one time or another."

Robert said, "You took risks for your kindness, Captain."

The Captain shrugged his bulky shoulders. "I was young then, and seeking adventure . . . I couldn't abide persecution," he said, as an afterthought. He looked at the Huguenot thoughtfully. "It sets its mark on a man, persecution, a wound that leaves a scar on the soul."

Robert had not expected such sensitive feeling in the bluff fellow.

Bragg looked towards the door. "Ah, there he comes—my Captain." Robert saw again the tall, dark man with thin, brown face. The side towards them showed an injury to the jaw that changed the lean contour. His brown periwig fell in curls below his shoulders. The eyes were large and dark and had the piercing quality that sweeps wide spaces at a glance. Heavy brows and a strong nose gave him a hawklike look.

He was dressed now in the height of rich fashion. His powder-blue coat was of brocaded satin. His white waistcoat, covered with gold and silver braiding, came almost to his knees. His cravat, of heavy Tuscan lace, cascaded to his chest, and ruffles of the same lace fell over his long brown hands. His breeches were plain blue satin and his long white stockings, of silk, were held in place with paste buckles. Paste buckles were on his red-heeled shoes. He stood easily, his hand on the hilt of his dress sword.

Bragg said, "A fine man. If you've seen him aboard ship, as I've seen him, you would know that he is a man who will always do what he sets out to do."

"You've sailed with him?" Robert asked, watching Captain Rogers take his place between Edward Colston and Lord Hervey.

"That I have—with him and Dampier, when the *Duke* and the *Dutchess* sailed around the world. We were a-seeking a new passage by way of the Philippines and the Solomon Islands; and crossed the Dampier Straits. 'Twas on the journey we picked up a castaway on Juan Fernandez. Alexander Selkirk was his name. It fair makes me laugh still, to think how he could chase the island goats. Says Captain Rogers, 'I believe I have a desire to eat mutton with caper sauce for my supper. Mate, send a man ashore with a blunderbuss to get me a young 'un.'

"Selkirk would all but scream in his anxiety. 'My Captain— if you please! I will bring you a fine young kid, but don't let my goats be disturbed by gunfire,' says he. And so he'd go ashore and run down a couple of swift-footed animals, wring the necks with his two hands, without a quiver, but he couldn't abide the thought of having one shot. The noise would startle his fleet-footed friends. Did ye ever hear of such, sir?" Bragg paused to lift his glass to his lips.

A blow of the gavel under the stout hand of old Edward Colston brought the room to attention. The usual speeches followed. The eighteen men who had financed the privateer cruise of the *Duke* and the *Dutchess* each rose to bow acknowledgement. A toast was proposed by Lord Hervey, "To the Captain of the *Delicia,* and all who sail in her!"

Then Captain Rogers rose to speak. The clatter of dishes stopped. Even the rustle of the silk skirts of the wives, who were seated behind the screens, quieted. The Captain spoke briefly. A graceful word of thanks to the gentlemen Merchants of Bristol, gratitude to Edward Colston for his vision in building trade with the colonies in America and the West Indies.

"Gentlemen, you did me the honour to approve of my proposals for the long voyage in 1708. Your generosity fitted out two ships, the *Duke* and the *Dutchess,* in which you gave me principal command. You had the courage to adventure your estate on an undertaking which, to men less discerning, seemed impracticable.

"We had success. Make no doubt, this will be to your lasting honour that such a voyage was undertaken from Bristol at your expense.

"Now the wisdom of the nation has agreed to establish trade with the South Seas—which, with the blessing of God, may bring great riches to Great Britain and her colonies.

"I am no speaker, gentlemen, with fine words. I choose rather the language of the sea, which is genuine and natural for a mariner. My men and my ships are my first concern, for a ship is a commonwealth, and must be so treated.

"If I concern myself with the welfare of my men, I get returns, as you get returns when you concern yourselves with the welfare of your nation.

"I have no other words than to say that, in taking the government of the Bahamas, I will devote myself to ridding the seas of pirates, who interfere with trade with the mother country. Those who accept the King's Pardon, I will treat as citizens of New Providence. Those who resist, I will chase from the seas.

"Trade is the wealth of nations, and I, with the help of God, will do my endeavour to make my country great, on land and on the seas—as great as it was in the days of Elizabeth, God rest her soul!"

He leaned forward and took up his wineglass. Lifting it high, he said: "To his Majesty King George!"

The company rose, "The King! The King!"

Robert Fountaine slipped out through a side door and was

on the street before the crowd had made its way from the hall. A dozen link boys stood at the curb looking for patrons. He hailed one and walked off quickly in his wake. His mind was alert and active, impressed by Woodes Rogers' words and the man himself. He was more determined now to go to America with the Bahama Adventurers. He hurried after the link through dark streets onto Kingroad, where ships lay, side to side, in the dark water.

The immense wealth of the West Indies was the bait to draw adventurers and merchants and men who followed the sea to Caribbean islands and the southern Plantations of the mainland of America.

Trade with the South Seas caught the fancy of merchants and gentlemen, and the coast cities of England outfitted ships and sent them voyaging into the Western Ocean and around the stormy tip of South America to the Pacific. Woodes Rogers had come back once with the wealth of the Orient in his hold. He could do it again. Cottons and silks, gold embroideries, musk, cinnamon and cloves, by the thousands of pounds. Benjamin by the hundred pounds, beeswax, and gum elemi, chinaware, and nuts and great jars of ginger; petticoats of taffeta, sooseys and silk stockings. Forty pounds of raw silk from China, a fortune in itself! Thrown silk and sewing from China and rich silk from Bengal, and golden fringe and flowered taffetas, embroidered in gold and silver and set with jewels. Is it any wonder the Bristol merchants fell across one anothers feet to sign the register of those who paid for shares in the Venture?

The West Indies trade was established and flourishing. Save for the pirates, it would have brought wealth of Elizabethan times to England. The West Indies had pearls, emeralds and amethysts and virgin silver; pieces of eight, and virgin gold, as well as doubloons. Then there was cochineal and Granta Silvestre, wild scarlet from the islands and Campeche; indigo from Antigua and the new plantations at Charles Town; logwood and braziletto. From Nicaragua came lignum vitae and other hardwoods that polished high as silver.

Think of sugar and ginger and cacao; think of cotton and redwood and tobacco in roll; tobacco in snuff, to please the Scandinavians as well as the British. Raw hides and tanned. Ambergris, grey and black. Balsam of Peru, Jesuit bark and jalap. Sarsaparilla and sassafras; fruits to tickle an epicure's palate. All these commodities in the hold of a merchant ship—holds of a fleet of merchant ships, plying across the

Western Ocean, to return home with turpentine and tar and fur skins from the Carolinas, and naval stores to keep the Grand Fleet moving. Here was wealth for merchants, for gentlemen adventurers, aye, wealth for a city like Bristol—wealth for a kingdom.

A stop on the way, to careen a ship, would add wealth, for it would give time to trade. Ironware from Biscay, steel and white wax; wine of St. Lucar; oil from Seville; figs and raisins from Arcos, put in barrels. Black silk from Granada, coloured silk and flowered, such as the Spanish ladies wear. Toledo silk and Toledo blades. Hard soap from Alicante and almonds from Valencia; wool and wheat and barley from the high mesas of Spain. Two-pile velvet from Italy, and Genoa paper; mohair stuffs from Smyrna; Genoa golden thread and rice from Milan.

These words fell from the lips of the Merchants of Bristol as beads of a rosary. The smell of spices seemed to fill the great hall as men talked of the Spice Islands, the Sugar Islands and the treasures of the Indies.

Robert's mind caught up the long vista; his imagination carried him far beyond his widest horizon, into a new world of trade. His step was firm and ringing along the flags. Even with the land grant from the Proprietors in his pocket, he had not been wholehearted in the Venture. It took the Merchants of Bristol and Woodes Rogers to open the door so that he could see the long vista. The load of uncertainty dropped away from him. Unequivocally, his heart and soul were in the undertaking. It was not only his and his family's benefit that pushed him forward. There were larger issues—the issue of a man's freedom of worship, and freedom to trade as he willed.

He tossed a coin to the link boy. The lad ran off. The link was only half burned; he could find another patron and make double money.

Fountaine heard voices in the salon. Gabrielle and Molly must have waited up to hear of the banquet at the Guildhall. He had much to tell them. At the door he paused; his eyes swept the room. At the far corner Barton sat, nodding over her knitting. Gabrielle was near the tea table on which were piled empty cups, Molly on the stool before the fire. Seated on chairs on either side of her were two young gentlemen—young Edward Colston, the merchant prince's grandson, and Councilman Tuker's son. The young men were glaring at

68

each other like two young turkey cocks. No one heard Robert open the door, so intent were they on something that had been said. Molly waved a lace handkerchief to and fro, idly, as if to ward off the odour of brimstone.

Colston said, "I repeat, the green beyond St. Michael's is a fair spot in the morning." There was a slight sneer in his fine clear-cut features, and his voice had a ring of contempt.

Tuker was silent, his face sullen. After a time he said, "I'll not let you force me to challenge you. Not that I fear you, Mr. Colston, but it is on account of the Councilman, my father. He does not hold with duels."

"So," said Colston. "So!" The contempt was open now.

"Nor would I fight with swords," Tuker continued. "Fists are made for weapons."

"Fists?" Colston's eyebrows raised. He flicked his cravat into place and stroked his sleeve ruffles. "Fists! My word! I would not have believed it, sir. Your fine clothes fooled me for a moment. Fists!"

His words flicked Oliver Tuker on the raw. "Ye needn't be high and mighty, your granda' no more than a merchant, same as mine."

"Indeed?" Colston smiled. He was getting the fellow!

Gabrielle said, "Mr. Colston, Mr. Tuker, some more tea— or perhaps you would prefer a bottle of Madeira. My father has some excellent Madeira that came in only yesterday."

Colston rose. "Thank you, Miss Fountaine, I must be leaving. I only ran in for a moment, from the banquet. I must be getting on. Captain Rogers is our guest, and they will soon be leaving the Guildhall." He bowed to Molly. "Do not forget, Miss Lepel, Mistress Martha Blount asked me to tea with you the next time I visit London."

"I shall look forward to the meeting, Mr. Colston," Molly said in her grandest manner. "Good evening, Mr. Colston."

Robert moved off to his workroom. He had no desire to linger for explanations, or interrupt what seemed to be an embarrassing situation for at least one of the number.

In a short time he had the small loom going. The rhythm of weaving the threads in and out quieted him, as it always did. Tangled thoughts straightened themselves as tangled threads unravelled. Life held new promise.

Deep in the night Gabrielle woke. A muffled noise far below took her from an untroubled sleep and set her wide awake. She sat up quickly. A thud like a heavy object falling took her out of bed to the window. The moon was on the quarter, the garden in shadow. She thought she saw a light flash for a moment across the half window of the weaving room. Without waiting to put on her sandals, she caught up a shawl and ran down the stairs. The dark halls did not bother her, or the long passage from the house to the weaving room. She moved swiftly, her heart beating violently. Had something happened to her father? Had the sound she heard been the falling of an inert body? She pulled the door to her cautiously. A tallow candle had been placed on the long stretcher table, held erect in its own grease.

Half a dozen burly figures moved about the shadows in their errands of destruction. She heard the sound of shears ripping through cloth. The new material! They were destroying the new-cut woollen! A man stumbled over some object. A voice out of the darkness came sharply:

"Not so much noise, fool."

" 'Twas the peddle of the loom. I barked my shin."

"Come on. Get through the business . . . What's that?"

The voice at the door answered, "The watch. Be quiet until he passes."

Gabrielle heard the footstep of the watch as he passed by, his halberd tapping the cobbles. In a moment he would be at the gate. She moved into the room to the open window.

"Watch!" she called sharply. "Watch! Help! Thieves!"

"God's death, what is this?" A man ran by her so close that she smelled the foul odour of his clothes. Others were scrambling out windows. The shadow at the door was there no longer. The moonlight played on the floor. She saw a man on his hands and knees, creeping out of the door.

"Watch!" she cried again. "Watch, by the door! Thieves running through the garden!"

The watchman pounded through the gate. She saw the moonlight flash on the point of his pike.

"Ha! I've got one," he called. "Make a light, Mistress."

Gabrielle turned to the table; the candle had been blown out. She took a taper from the basket near the hearth. Blowing on the coals, she ignited the taper and lit the candles.

"Hum. A pretty fellow you be, entering a good man's house." The watch addressed the culprit. "I know the man, a low ne'er-do-weel from the wharves. I'll take him off. Much harm done, Mistress?"

Gabrielle lifted the candle. "See for yourself, watch." The

room was a shambles. Lengths of good cloth, bales of silk, ribboned and slashed; the threads of the loom cut; the spindles wrecked.

"See for yourself," she said dully, thinking of her father, thinking of another time, in Ireland, when the looms were wrecked and the cloth cut, just as they were tonight.

The watch's weathered red face looked shocked. "A villain's mean trick, Mistress. 'Twill send this fellow to gaol for a year and a day."

" 'Twas another that gave the orders, watchman. I heard him speak, but I didn't see him. He ran away, leaving this poor wretch behind."

"That's what I say, Gov'nor," the captive put in. " 'E ran off, like that." He snapped his dirty fingers together. "And Oi tyke the bag an 'e never so much as paid me the shilling 'e promised."

David, the gardener, came running up the path. "I've chased two of them up the lane, but I lost them at the docks. Fleet enough they were. What have you got, officer?"

"A thief, that's all. The young leddy was a smart one—she called 'Watch, watch, a thief' and I came quick as God let my two legs carry me."

David turned slowly. "I didn't see you, Mistress," he said. Under his gaze Gabrielle was conscious of her disarray—her nightdress showing under her loosely hung shawl, her bare feet.

"Perhaps the officer needs help, Moray," she said.

David looked about the devastated room. "God's death! They didn't leave much. I wonder——" His eyes searched hers. "The first man was familiar, but I can't place him."

Gabrielle said nothing. She too thought she recognized the voice of the man by the door—the Councilman's son. But that could not be. Surely no man could come to the house as a visitor, and a few hours later destroy as the marauders had done in the weaving room.

She remembered the look on Tuker's face when Edward Colston had turned his back on him, and Molly's air of contempt. He had cut a poor figure, but he had brought it all on himself, trying to annoy Colston by veiled allusions to gay women and parties held at country houses. Edward restrained himself until a woman was mentioned by name, then he turned on Tuker. Gabrielle was frightened. She thought Tuker would challenge to fight. Surely such contempt could not pass unnoticed. But Tuker had backed down. Even that could not explain what lay before her eyes.

Something in Moray's eyes revealed her own condition of mind.

"I will call my father, officer," she said, and went quickly from the room. She met her father in the hall. He was dressed and carried a bed candle in his hand. He listened to her words without comment. He opened the door. Gabrielle saw the look of despair on his face as his eyes took in the havoc that had been created. Months of work of his men and his own hand lay on the floor, wantonly destroyed.

Gabrielle caught his hand and held it against her cheek.

"There is not a man in the world to whom I have done harm," he muttered. "Not one man in all Bristol——"

He went into the devastated room.

She shut the door quietly. There was nothing she could do or say to lighten his despair.

Molly waited at the head of the stairs; Barton and Celestine were behind her, their faces white with anxiety, their eyes glowing with startled surprise in the light of the candles they held.

"What has happened?" Molly caught Gabrielle's arm. "Why do you look like that? What has happened?"

"Thieves came in. They destroyed my father's looms and all the new cloth——"

"Oh, Gabrielle!" "Oh, Mademoiselle!" "Not the new cloth!" Celestine's and Molly's words ran together.

Only Barton was silent, her face grim and determined. "It is Ireland all over again," she said finally. "The puir good mon."

Gabrielle said, "The watch has one of the men. Perhaps he will talk and then we will know who ordered the others to wreck my father's looms and destroy the patterns and the woollens."

Molly's eyes were round. "Did you go down there? Alone?"

Gabrielle said, "I heard a noise. I was afraid that something might have happened to my father."

"But alone! I could never have gone. I would have been terrified to go alone."

"Miss Gabrielle! Your feet! They are bare!" Barton's shocked voice interrupted. "Get into your bed. I will bring a hot salt bag. Dear God knows what will happen to you. Miss

Molly, get you back to bed. Must I spank you both this night?"

Molly ran down the hall to her room. Gabrielle made no protest. She moved quietly into the dark bedroom and let her body sink into the comfort of soft feathers. Her heart bled for her father. She knew she could not help him now. All she could do was to be ready if he needed her.

In the morning the watchman called. Robert Fountaine was not inclined to prosecute the man taken the night before.

"He is not the principal," he told the watchman, who looked at him with growing suspicion in his sharp eyes.

"'E's guilty of malevolent and wilful destruction, and he is so charged by me. I have already given 'im purpose to talk, sir. 'E says 'e'll talk fast enough if 'is principal don't come an' lay bail on the table."

"We will see when the time comes for that," Fountaine said. "I am a Huguenot refugee in this country and I do not know what my status will be in the courts."

The watchman's eyes brightened. "I can tell ye somewhat. I know that in the time of Queen Anne, of sainted memory, the French gentlemen refugees petitioned her Majesty about the Queen's Bounty, under which they lived. The officers in charge cut down the poor fellers' pensions from twelvemonth to ten, and put the over in their own pockets. But the Queen made it right, I'm a-telling ye. She saw that her Bounty was rightly distributed and the French gentlemen and their ladies had their full twelvemonth pension. She was a fine lady and a good Queen and it was good times in her reign for poor folk of England."

Robert listened. It hurt him that French gentlemen should be so reduced as to claim Queen's charity. But that was the way of nobles. They would not demean themselves by working. Rather they would accept a Queen's Bounty.

The watchman picked up his pike and his lanthorn and walked to the door.

"Please to thank the young Mistress for sending the ale for the missus and fruit for my child. She's a rare thoughtful one, she is, with her bright 'Good evening, Bramston, how is the little girl today?' A man remembers the like of her, sir."

Robert stood at the door, watching the man as he made his way down Meg's Lane. It was like Gabrielle to know that the watchman had a sick child. He had never given the watch a thought. He was just a raucous voice calling the hour.

He had turned away when the gardener, David Moray,

73

came around the corner. He took off his cap and stood bareheaded, waiting for Fountaine to speak.

"Thank you for clearing the weaving room, Moray. I could scarce make myself face the destruction, but when I opened the door this morning I found the litter cleared away. Best of all, the loom was mended and in working order."

"Huggins did that, sir. He has a fair light hand with tools. He saw your Worship set great store by that loom."

"You must have worked the night through to finish it," Fountaine said. "I will not forget your service."

" 'Tis naught. I've stayed up many a night until the sun rose, roistering and having my amusements. This wreckage has a bad odour to me, Mister. 'Tis not the work of thieves."

Fountaine's eyes became blank. "Some lengths of cloth were missing. Enough to make it thievery."

"But, Master—there is more behind it."

Fountaine raised his hand. "Say no more, Moray, let it stand thus. I do not care to make charges which can only lead to a judicial rebuff, perhaps a reprimand."

"But you have appeal through the Court of Oyer and Terminer," the man said. "Surely you will not let the rascals divest you of your invention."

"I cannot win a case against the instigators of this devastation," Fountaine said sadly, "so we will drop it, Moray. I thank you for your interest. You are a good man." He went to his desk and took out a paper stamped with a red wax seal. He turned it over once or twice before he handed it to the bondman.

"Your bond is abrogated, Moray. You go to the New World a free man, not one with a debt hanging over him, or a prison record. I never believed that tale of debtors' prison."

He smiled a little at the incredulous expression on the man's face.

"Sir, sir——" Moray's self-contained manner deserted him.

"I've been fugitive myself, Moray, and a political refugee. The insurrection of '15 led many a good man through prison doors and to the block. You are lucky to have had only prison."

"You knew I was a follower of the Pretender? You let me stay at your home?"

"Why not, Moray? I have no prejudice, political or religious. I have been persecuted by a few Papists and by some
74

Protestants, for that matter, but I do not take all the Romans or all the Established Church men to be evil because a few have been overzealous in their religious fervour. No more do I hate all the Bristol merchants because some of them have sworn to work my ruin."

He walked nervously about the room. Moray watched him with sympathetic eyes. Presently Fountaine halted in front of his ex-bondman.

"Your passage is on the *Bahama Venture,* mine on the *Delicia,* so I will not see you before we reach New Providence. I am putting you in charge of my servants, my cattle and all the household goods. When we are loaded you will go aboard and take over. I have already given the necessary orders."

Moray hesitated, then spoke: "Is it wise, Mr. Fountaine? The servants may resent taking orders from one they knew as a bondman."

A smile twitched the corners of Fountaine's lips. "You underrate my people, Moray. The servants do not need to be told who is a gentleman and who is not. Amos Treloar will assist you. You will find him shrewd and capable and the others trust him. Lean on him if necessary." Fountaine shuffled through a pile of papers. "My London agent has arranged all the papers, and expense money is laid out. If you have personal matters that need your attention, you may have a few days to yourself." He took a cash box from his desk and counted out some paper. "Here is your wage, and you earned it, my lad."

Moray accepted the bills and held one up to examine it. He smiled as he put it in his wallet.

"Thank you, Mr. Fountaine, 'Tis the first money I ever earned of my own endeavour, and I've a mind to have it framed and tack it up in Stationers' Hall. Thank you for a few days' leave. I'll be back by Monday without fail. You may trust me. I will watch your interests for the voyage."

Robert smiled. "And since you want to be a planter, I suggest that you consult Mr. Mainwairing. He will be glad to advise you about taking up land. You'll earn what you make in the Provinces, my lad, and don't forget that working on the land bears fruit, twofold."

Moray walked slowly down the path to the little garden house where he had his quarters. The room was not unattractive. Gay chintzes curtained the casement windows which opened into the garden, away from the house. A channel coal fire burned on the hearth. An old work chair covered with faded red leather was placed near the fire. Books on gardening and on soil were spread open on the long table within reach of the chair. A couch covered with a dark counterpane was along one wall, a high chest on the other.

Moray glanced about. He had comfort in the little room. More peace than in the rambling old manor house in Scotland where he was born and grew up. He reached to the shelf above the window and took down an iron key. With this he unlocked the long oak chest by the fireplace. Out of the chest he took a dark brown coat of excellent cut and weave, a snuff-coloured waistcoat with golden buttons. The breeches were made of soft-tanned doeskin, as fine as any skins in Mr. Fountaine's stock.

The water in the kettle on the hob steamed noisily. Moray turned it into a pewter basin and laid a rough crash towel on the base by the washstand. He got out his razor and lathered his face. He would rid himself of his Stuart beard. Then he stripped himself of his dusty, earth-stained clothes. Standing on the rug by the warm fire, he flexed his muscles, stretching his arms and legs as animals do, to feel his strength. A smart rub with lather, a still smarter rub with the rough towel set his blood tingling. He was young and a new life was opening to him. He broke into song in a round, lusty voice:

"Gather ye rose-buds while ye may,
Old Time is still a flying:
And this same flower that smiles today
Tomorrow will be dying.

"Then be not coy, but use your time;
And while ye may, go marry;
For having lost but once your prime,
You may forever tarry."

As he sang, he dressed himself, turning about to get a full view in the cracked shaving mirror above the basin stand. Satisfied, he went back to the chest and took out a full-bottomed wig that matched his own reddish-brown hair precisely. Boots and a light sword, and his dressing was complete—all save a wide beaver hat of russet brown with a long dun-coloured feather.

He threw a dark cloth cloak over his shoulders and started for the door, stopping long enough to kick his worn garden clothes half across the room, under the couch.

"Avast to you, and a triple damn!" he cried aloud. "I'm through with you, my hearties. You stink of the stable and barnyard. Bah!" He held his fingers to his nose.

He opened the wooden door and all but banged it against Gabrielle Fountaine. She gave him a quick glance in which there was no recognition. "I am looking for the gardener," she said, when she had recovered from her astonishment at the sudden appearance of such a brave gentleman in the gardener's cottage.

"Gardener?" he replied in the fashionable, affected voice. "I am not sure but I believe the fellow went down the lane. Some matter of—ah—fertilizer, if one may mention such a thing in the presence of so charming a young woman. On the other hand he may be snoozing inside."

He made a sweeping bow and walked jauntily down the path to the gate.

Gabrielle watched him go, a puzzled frown on her smooth forehead. There was something familiar about the man. She tapped at the closed door, but there was no answer. The second knock was peremptory. "Moray!" she called out. "Moray!" After waiting a moment, she tugged at the latch. The door swung open. The gardener's clothes lay on the floor in a heap, the washing basin and soap near the fire. A hot flush mounted her face. Suddenly she knew. She had not recognized the bondman in his fine raiment.

The impudence of the fellow! The impudence!

Chapter 7

LUSTY WIND FOR CAROLINA

The quay was alive with people. Half a dozen ships were sailing down the Channel, from Kingroad, with the turn of the tide.

The Bristol merchants were out in force to pay their respects to Captain Woodes Rogers, and to scan his vessel. The *Delicia* looked fine and brave in her new suit of sail and gaily painted poop. The ship lay in midstream, waiting to catch the first breath of breeze at the turn. Men sweated and swore, trundling cargo to the end of the docks, ready for loading barges.

Woodes Rogers' Bahama Adventurers consisted of men of every class and condition—tailors, haymakers, peddlers, fiddlers and tinkers. Yeomen, he had; farmers and husbandmen and drovers, a goodly number of men, young and adventurous. Some brought their buxom wives and towhead children. Some started with wealth, in cattle or sheep. Others had no more than clung to their backs. They looked with anxious eyes towards the west, for the fortune the fifty acres of virgin land would bring them. There were white-faced men who slunk into the crowds, casting anxious eyes over their shoulders. They gave off the dank odour of dungeon and cell, and their furtive eyes blinked and grew veiled in the light of the sun.

The Huguenot, Fountaine, and his men had loaded the day previous. Their household goods, their cattle went aboard the smaller ship, the *Bahama Venture*. Fountaine's servants and settlers came in an orderly manner, with their goods well packed, labelled for Carolina, via New Providence. At Nassau they would transship to a Jamaica packet, sailing north along the coast. A three months' journey lay ahead.

The crowd was dense, pushing and shoving good-humouredly. Porters carrying bundles and boxes shouted for gangway through the crowd, to get their patrons and their luggage aboard the lighters.

Fountaine had arranged with the master, Captain Bragg,

78

about the complicated matter of getting his wife aboard on her litter.

" 'Tis easy as nothing," the bluff Captain told him. "We will bring her aboard when we ship the Captain's company of foot. A hundred of them there are, and they will make a guard for her, and no one will even see the litter, with no discomfort for Madam Fountaine."

With Fountaine and Celestine came the doctor, to hold Madam's wrist. Celestine showed nothing of her feeling as she walked sturdily beside her mistress to the dock landing. She looked to neither the right nor left at the line of soldiers. She wore a sober black cloak, and her head was decently covered by her frilled Norman headdress. But she told Barton later that she felt much as a queen must feel when she reviewed her palace guard, which showed that Celestine was not lacking in imagination.

Barton came in a hackney with the young ladies. Molly had begged to come. She would go back to London on the coach, with Captain Woodes Rogers' wife.

"I declare! I feel my courage oozing," Molly said, looking at the crowded street. "I don't see how we can alight from the coach and make our way through that odious mob. Where is Uncle Robert?"

Gabrielle craned her neck to look over the crowd. But she saw nothing of her father or any of their servants.

Barton said, "Have no fear, young ladies, I will make a way through. 'Tis nothing. Many a time I've seen the like at a ship's sailing, or at a ship's launching." She punched the coachman's back with her stick. "Coachman, drive to the curbstone."

"I can't, miss. A great coach blocks the way—the coach of Councilman Tuker."

Molly reached for the door knob. "I see Edward Colston. I do believe he is waiting for us." She pulled the door open, but Barton detained her.

"Wait, Miss Molly. I will 'light first. If there is any jostling by that crowd, I will use my staff." She gathered up her case and bundles and stepped down.

"Make way," she said truculently. "Give us a path to the dockway."

A man laughed. "I'm pressed so hard from my rear that I couldn't move if I tried, my good woman. Best you wait for police to clear your way."

Barton was a tall woman. She looked over the crowd and

attracted Colston's attention. He spoke to his men. Four stout porters in the Colston livery made their way through the crowd, joking good-humouredly with the men and women who stood on the curb.

"Barton will walk before you and I will follow," he said, after he had made his duties. "My fellows will separate the crowd and together we will manage to get to the ships." They moved along slowly to the complimentary remarks of the good-natured crowd.

" 'Tis a shame to allow such beauty to leave England," one old woman cried as Molly passed. "God's truth! What have we come to that we send our best to the colonies?"

Molly blushed and slipped her vizard so that it covered the upper part of her face, but her red, petulant lips and her delicately cleft chin still brought forth complimentary comments.

"Pay no heed," Edward Colston said to Molly. But he tossed the woman a coin. "Our people always have an eye for real beauty." She gave him a quick, appraising glance from under her long lashes, showing that she recognized the compliment. He was not bad to look at. Medium height, he looked shorter because of the width of his shoulders. He wore his clothes well, but not foppishly. The cloth of his coat was excellent. The lace at his neck and sleeves, good. Upper middle class; rich merchant class, at its best, she thought. It might not be a bad match. With plenty of money and a little influence, a title might be had. Her cousin Mary Lepel could manage it, if she was so inclined. She, as lady-in-waiting to the Princess, had opportunities. 'Twas said that the Duchess of Kendal was not averse to bribes, but they must be in jewels, not money. Heigho, her thoughts were running wild again, but she turned and flashed a dazzling smile over her shoulder at Colston, who was close behind her. He moved forward. In the press their shoulders touched. Edward leaned down, his cheek close to the fragrance of her pale gold hair.

"May I have the honour to drive you to London in my coach, Miss Lepel?"

Molly's lips smiled. "I should love to come with you, but my uncle has already made arrangement for me to ride to London with Madam Rogers."

Colston's spirits, dampened for a moment by Molly's refusal, rose. "I will invite Madam Rogers also. I am sure she will be willing. I have heard that her father, Admiral Sir William Whitstone, is to furnish his coach for the journey."

Colston laughed. When he laughed, his dark blue eyes crinkled at the corners and his strong, white teeth showed behind his minute moustache. He is almost handsome, Molly thought. "We will save Admiral Sir William Whitstone's fine horses by keeping them in their stalls."

Gabrielle was pushed close to them for a moment in the crowd. "Father said you were thinking of coming out to the Plantations, Mr. Colston."

Edward answered, "Yes, I am. My grandfather wants me to go to New Providence."

"Are you going to Carolina?" Molly asked. She had taken off her vizard now, and was looking at him with questioning eyes.

Edward's spirits soared higher. She *was* interested in him, in his comings and goings.

"I do not know yet. Perhaps I shall go no farther than New Providence and Jamaica, where my grandfather has interests in sugar plantations."

Molly sighed. "I should like to go to a sugar plantation." Gabrielle glanced at her. "Don't look like that, Gabrielle. It's quite different from your primitive Carolina. I've been told that the great plantations of Jamaica have splendid houses and each planter has hundreds of black servants. People of the nobility live in Jamaica, and the other Caribbean islands."

Edward looked at her quizzically. "So you'd like to queen it in the islands, Miss Molly?"

Molly flushed. "Yes, I would, I'm frank enough to say. I'm tired of being a governess and living in someone else's house. I——" She paused suddenly, her eyes fixed on a tall figure standing near the open door of the stone warehouse.

Gabrielle followed her glance. " 'Tis Michael. Michael Cary," Molly whispered to Gabrielle. "I must talk to him, but I don't want Edward to know. Engage him in conversation as we pass the door."

"Molly, don't do anything rash," Gabrielle pleaded. "You told me he is married."

Molly's mouth was stubborn, her little chin thrust forward. "I will speak to him. Do not turn to look for me. I will follow you to the ship. If you love me, keep Colston engaged."

They were, by now, opposite the warehouse door. Molly edged close to the outskirts of the crowd. If Edward turned, he would think the press of people intervened. Gabrielle saw the expression on the man's face as Molly caught his eyes. A handsome, reckless face, with a sort of bold strength. She saw him catch Molly's hands and swing her out of the crowd into the dark cavern of the warehouse.

A moment later she and Barton were separated from Colston. She tried to reach him, but the press bore her onward. Perhaps it was not bad. It would cover Molly's disappearance. Since she, too, had been separated from the others, Molly's absence would not be conspicuous. She hoped she would not do anything rash.

After a time they reached the stone steps where the barges and lighters landed. To Gabrielle's surprise, Molly was there before her. The girl's eyes were unnaturally bright, her cheeks delicately tinted, her half-parted lips soft and red. The little pulse at the base of her throat was throbbing.

"Gabrielle. Gabrielle. I shall see him in London tomorrow, at Miss Blount's. He loves me. I swear he does." She looked anxiously into Gabrielle's eyes. "Would you know I had been kissed?" she whispered.

"You look very wonderfully happy," Gabrielle said grudgingly.

Molly pulled a long face as Edward came up. "A poor protector you are, Mr. Colston, getting yourself lost just when the press was heaviest."

Colston looked from one to the other, bewildered at Molly's attack. "Why, I thought it was you who were lost. I tried to follow you, but you got out of sight. Once I thought I saw your back disappearing into the warehouse. But I must have been mistaken."

"Indeed you were, Mr. Colston. Gabrielle and I have been waiting here ever so long."

Gabrielle and Barton exchanged glances. The serving woman had missed nothing of the little incident. She shut her lips firmly. Curious how both of them were protecting Molly in her indiscretions.

Madam Woodes Rogers sat in the Captain's commodious cabin, pouring tea from a handsome silver tea service. The merchant princes were there, and their wives. Sir John Hawkins, the ex-Mayor of Bristol, was talking with the present, Mr. Lydgale. Councilman Tuker, puffing with importance, tried to edge in a word whenever conversation lapsed. He kept well away from Robert Fountaine, but cast envious glances as the latter spoke long with Mr. Colston.

Madam Rogers, a frail, delicate woman, spoke little, and then of her two children, a boy and a girl, who waited for her in London.

She said to Molly, "Mr. Colston has arranged for his grandson to drive us to London in his coach. Very thoughtful of him, don't you think?"

"Indeed yes," said Molly absently. "Very thoughtful."

She has lost interest in Edward Colston, Gabrielle thought; a pity, for he is so fine, and the other—she thought of the handsome, reckless face. The other was just the man to sweep Molly's emotions out of control.

"Oh, Molly, promise me not to see Michael Cary," she said when the two were alone. "Promise me."

"I won't promise," Molly said firmly. "But I won't get into trouble. If I did, Aunt Lepel would cast me out." She kissed Gabrielle's cheek. "You are to have no worries, my sweet Gaby. I know my way about. I can take care of myself."

"I believe Edward loves you," Gabrielle whispered.

"He is so heavy," was Molly's reply. "Heavy and triple dull," she added, her eyes glowing. Gabrielle said no more. Her father was moving across the deck. A seaman beat a gong, shouting "All ashore!" Men were swarming up the rigging. The master stood on the high poop, shouting out his orders in a heavy voice that bore down the wind.

Canvas flapped and shrieked. The heavy anchor chain grumbled as four men worked on a capstan winch. The great standard had been raised.

Molly threw her arms about Gabrielle, tears streaming down her cheeks.

"Write me. Write every day of the voyage," she said. "Oh, Gaby, how can I ever let you go? I'll never see you again!"

Gabrielle fought back tears. "Nonsense. Of course you will see me. You will come out to the plantation yourself, before the year is out." Tears streamed down her cheeks.

Molly bade a wordless good-by to Robert Fountaine. Edward Colston took her arm and drew her to the gangway. The confusion and noise of a ship's sailing rose above farewells shouted from the shore.

"A lusty wind and a fair sail," the shout came, as the sailors hauled at the tops'l mainsheet.

Shouted Bragg: "Move, boys, move! It's out into the Channel to catch the tide."

Masts creaked with the new load; master and mates shouted orders—"Weigh, boys"; the winch creaked. "Bring ship to proper station," shouted Bragg in his great voice. "Hand the tops'ls." There was scrambling as seamen raced barefoot across the clean scrubbed deck to their stations.

The master's great voice formed a background to the sound of departure. The shoreward passengers stood on deck waving bright scarves and handkerchiefs. Madam Woodes Rogers, Molly Lepel and Edward Colston were in the last shore boat to leave the *Delicia*.

"Put out the fo's'l—trail up the mizzen." The canvas billowed, the tide was turning, the ship began to move, slowly, guarded on either side by barges, until she should be free of the hulls of the near-by ships.

Bells chimed and pennants dipped as the *Delicia* advanced from Kingroad down the Bristol Channel.

Molly and Madam Woodes Rogers faced the ship, waving damp handkerchiefs. Gabrielle stood at her father's side, her hand in his, watching the widening stretch of water between the ship and shore. The colour of the crowd on the quay was lost to her as she watched Molly and Madam Rogers land, followed by Edward. With increasing disquiet, she saw the tall figure of Michael Cary step beside Molly, linger behind the others. She could not see the expression in Molly's face, but she saw her reach out her hand to meet the hand of the handsome Cary. A note passed? She did not see such an exchange but she could well imagine.

Her father's voice engaged her attention. "The die is cast, my dear. God knows what awaits us on the other side." His voice had a note of weariness, of intense sadness.

"Only happiness, my father. Health for my mother and a fair portion of wealth for the good people who go with us."

"Your confidence is contagious, my dear. Now I must go below to see that your mother rests comfortably. Then I will speak with Mr. Mainwairing in his cabin."

"Mr. Mainwairing? Is he aboard?" Pleasure shown in Gabrielle's face.

"Yes, at the last moment arrangements were made and he transferred from his Majesty's ship *Rose* to this ship."

"I am glad," she answered. "He will be a good companion for us all." She started to follow her father but he waved her back. "Stay on deck to watch the passage down the Channel and see the sunset, my child. It will be something to remember, this last day in England." He disappeared down the companionway.

Gabrielle stood alone, watching the movement on the quay.

Presently someone stood beside her, not speaking. Gabrielle turned and looked up into the brown eyes of David Moray. "I have come to speak with the Master," he said, his wide hat in his hand, his red-brown hair blowing about his shoulders. "I have been to the cabin on the poop deck and to the Captain's cabin, but I have not found him."

"He is with Mr. Mainwairing, Moray. You will doubtless find him in his cabin."

David Moray still lingered, looking down at her, until she grew impatient under his scrutiny.

"You must hasten, else the ship will be under way."

"No haste," the man said carelessly. "The ashore gong is only for visitors who do not know the way of ships."

"And you do, I presume?" She let a sarcastic note creep into her voice.

"Yes, Mistress. I've been across the Western Ocean to the Indies once or twice." He spoke carelessly, as if crossing the great ocean was no more than crossing the Channel to France. Gabrielle noticed his dress. He no longer wore clothes such as bondmen or servants wore. His clothes were not unlike Edward's, and his topcoat had three capes and a dark velvet collar.

"You are sad at leaving England?" he asked, moving closer to her to make way for some passerby. He did not move back, but inclined a little so that his arm touched hers. "You are sad to leave old England, yet you look forward to the new." Gabrielle nodded. He had read her thoughts.

He bent his head slightly, his voice lowered. "There is no one you leave behind? Any friend to draw you back again?" He asked the question lightly. She answered, not remembering he had no right to speak so familiarly with her.

"Yes, there is Molly."

There was laughter in the man's voice, and in his eyes. "I'm not speaking of young women. I mean a man who would hold your thoughts, draw you back."

"You are impertinent, Moray," she said indignantly.

"You have answered me," he said, a certain exultation in his voice. "You have answered me. There is no man who distracts your thoughts. Let me change that."

He put his arms about her with cool deliberation, lifting her chin with his fingers, until she looked deep into his red-brown eyes. What she saw disturbed her, raced her pulse.

"Your eyes are as clear and as cool as a Highland lake." He bent over her.

"I want your lips," he said, "your sweet red lips." His voice burned into her consciousness. She made no effort to move. She felt the growing strength of his arms about her body, drawing her to him.

"Your sweet red lips," he murmured. Then he kissed her, deep kisses. She felt shaken. Her pulses pounded against her ears. She drew back in the circle of his arms, struggling. In all the movement and hurrying about them, it was as if they were alone on the ship's deck.

He let her go. She could not read the look in his eyes. Where was her just and righteous anger? She felt none, only a strange bewilderment.

He drew her to him. "I must kiss you again, my sweet, my sweet." His lips were strong against hers. Then he left her. Striding across the deck of the *Delicia*, his tall figure moved with quick easy grace.

She wanted to call after him, to speak her indignation, but he was gone. She leaned against the narrow rail of the ship, trembling and afraid.

David Moray stood on the quay, packed in with the crowd as close as Norway sardines. The *Delicia* was moving slowly, catching the light breeze that came with the turn of the tide. His eyes were fixed on the red-coated figure by the rail of the ship. He could make out that Gabrielle had turned to look towards the shore. Were her eyes fixed on him or on the neat, strong-shouldered figure of Edward Colston? Anger rose in him, a swift burning anger against the merchant prince's grandson. But in a moment he was sane again. He could not understand how he had allowed himself to take the girl in his arms and lay his lips on hers. Soft lips they were, trembling and warm. He burned now to think of the pressure of her body against his, as she lay for that brief moment in his arms. There was something vital, alive in the touch of her lips. She did not hate him; her lips, her body loved him. He hummed the little song:

> "Gather ye rose-buds while ye may,
> Old Time is still a flying;
> And this same flower that smiles today
> Tomorrow will be dying."

"You are gay, sir," a voice addressed him. "You sing a pretty ditty." David turned as well as he could in the press. A man as tall as he, well turned out, with merry eyes and a restless look, was hemmed close against his side.

"Gay enough," David said, "leaving the old for the new."

A look of interest showed in the stranger's face. "So you go to the New World?"

"In the *Bahama Venture,* tomorrow morning."

"Ah, to New Providence."

David gave the man a closer scrutiny. "You know that part of the world?" he asked.

"As well as the lines in the palm of my hand," the stranger replied. "You have a treat ahead of you, sir." A sudden push and a fat red-faced farmer was thrust between the two by a sudden convolution of the crowd.

David saw Madam Woodes Rogers and Molly Lepel on the stone platform that led to the street. The tall, brown-eyed man moved close to the landing. Molly Lepel came tripping up the steps, lifting her skirts daintily to avoid contact with the wet stones. When she reached the top, she looked up and encountered the gaze of the tall stranger David had talked with only a moment before. A rosy blush crept from her throat to her cheeks as the man edged closer. David saw him manoeuvre Molly away from her party. They stood talking, screened from the others by piles of bales and boxes.

Moray whistled softly. Interested now, he examined the fellow closer. He was handsome, well turned out, and had an air of command about him. A seafaring man, perhaps, or one of the gentlemen lieutenants the government was now sending out on merchant ships, to act as diplomatic contacts with consuls and legations ashore. But how did it happen that he spoke to Mistress Molly so surreptitiously? Why did he not address her openly?

Squeezed and pushed by the slow-moving crowd, David Moray edged his way towards the cobbled street. He could do with a drink of ale to wet his parched throat and wash away the dust of the mob.

He made his way up to the Rose. He knew it for an inn where Jacobites forgathered. He did not want to get involved in any more Jacobite plots. The experience he had in '15 was enough to last him for some time, but his feet seemed to take him along the familiar path.

He entered the low, dark-panelled room and sat down at an oak table, well seasoned and nicked over the years by many knives.

He had no sooner thrown off his cape and tossed it, along with his beaver, on a bench, than the tall stranger came in, ducking his head to enter the low door. He stood for an instant, searching the room with his brilliant eyes. He saw David and swaggered across to the table.

"With your permission," he said, and tossed his beaver on the bench beside David's cape. Standing, he unbuckled his sword, surveying the room as he did so, looking into each gloomy corner as if searching for some hidden foe.

He called a pot-boy and ordered a pot of ale. "So you are off for New Providence tomorrow?" he said by way of opening a conversation. "I need not ask if you go as a pirate or settler, since your sober dress and good demeanour show your gentlemanly status."

David laughed, thinking of his work in Robert Fountaine's garden. "You honour me, sir," he said, a little mockery in his voice.

The stranger gave him closer attention. "Ah, a Scot," he said with satisfaction.

"From the Firth of Moray," David said, without giving his name.

"My name is Michael Cary. Sometime captain in his Majesty's Royal Navy, at present without ship."

David was forced to say his name.

"Ah, Moray, a good Highland name. You are going out with Woodes Rogers to the Bahamas."

"Yes," David said.

"You must drink with me to that, sir. Boy, a bottle of your best whisky. 'Tis a man's drink for a man's venture, we must have."

The barman himself brought the bottle and set it on the table with conscious pride. "The best, the very best," he said, and picked up the gold Cary tossed on the tray. Other customers had come in and the opposite tables were filling. The barman glanced at David and raised his brows. David nodded. The man left and came back with two glasses, crystal, fine-etched with a four-petalled rose with one bud.

Cary took up the bottle and filled the glasses. He did not seem to notice the etching on the glasses. He raised his glass and met David Moray's eyes squarely; his voice dropped. "To your safe journey 'over the water'!"

David raised his own glass slowly. Should he, or should he not, answer the challenge? The man was watching him covertly, waiting. "Over the water," David said suddenly. "Safe journey over the water."

Cary smiled. He leaned forward. "I want to know nothing of your plots and counterplots, but I have my suspicions; when a gentleman, undoubtedly an officer, seeks the New World—" Cary shrugged his shoulders—"it is either a woman or——"

"Or '15 and Argyll." By these two words David indicated the story of his adherence to the lost cause of the Stuarts and the ill-fated Argyll.

"So I suspected. The Stuarts have always commanded loyalty and given nothing in return." He spoke with bitterness. Cary poured another drink apiece. "I advise you to have done with lost causes. Start anew in the Bahamas."

"Carolina is my objective, not the Bahamas. Have you visited the mainland?"

Cary did not move or change expression. David had the impression that he was waiting for the next words. Being a Scot, he withheld the words. After a moment Cary said, "I am not welcome there. My uncle led the rebellion against the government of Carolina. His name was Thomas Cary."

David nodded. He knew of Thomas Cary, the Quaker Governor. "Against Governor Edward Hyde?" he asked.

Cary nodded. "Yes, against Hyde, and Hyde and his people won."

"Have you been back?" David asked.

"Not yet, but I will go, one day before long. There is no real reason not to go. There is no Hue and Cry against the Cary family, now." He poured a drink and tossed it off. His face was growing flushed. The last drink was taking effect when Cary's tongue loosened. David wondered about Molly Lepel and her connection with this man.

"I'm waiting. Waiting until I can take my wife back." David thought he might be speaking of Molly.

"Oh, you are going to marry?"

"Not going to marry. I am married. But my wife's mother, gad blast her soul, stands between us."

David raised his brows. "How is that? A husband has his rights."

"Not when the mother is who she is." He gulped down the drink, looking at the aroused interest in David's face. He closed his mouth to a thin line. "But I'll win one day."

David poured the drinks this time. His mind was on the soft lips of a girl. "Here's to winning!" he said.

"Here's to the others, the substitutes for the one you dream of!"

David downed his drink. He had no interest in substitutes. He wanted Gabrielle Fountaine.

Michael Cary got to his feet. "A pleasant voyage, Moray. Perhaps we will next meet in the Carolinas." He buckled on his sword. "I'm booked on the London coach at eight, so I'll be on my way." He stopped long enough to pour another glass of whisky. He lifted it, his hand a trifle unsteady, "To a beautiful substitute! May she be willing!"

He watched Cary as he swaggered across the room and out of the door. He pushed his glass aside with a feeling of distaste.

The ship was moving easily down Channel. The Captain came up and stood beside the sailing master and the pilot. There was no wind to speak of, and the ship moved slowly. Some of the sailors were asleep in the fo'c'sle, others drank their daily can of flip and swung their hammocks for the night.

Gabrielle leaned on the rail. She heard one poor fellow lamenting his decision to sail to America. A Devon man, he boasted he belonged to seafaring folk since the days of Queen Bess. But he had turned to the land and was tithing man of his parish. His grievance was that his wife might have to pay forty shillings to make up the deficit.

"I will send forward the money from Cork," said Captain Rogers, who also had heard the complaints. "I like not complaining men on my ships," he told Gabrielle, as he turned from watching the men on the deck below. "A ship is a commonwealth, and I try to govern it so. A happy ship is a safe ship, Miss Gabrielle, and it carries its fortune under its flag." He waved to the ensign. The sunset gun sounded from the shore at the same moment that two seamen hauled down the great flag at the taffrail.

The sun was low; a light mist from the shore spread a thin haze across the breast of the Channel. Sailors went aloft with riding lights. The night settled down, slowly. A vast spread of April darkness lay over the land, pierced by little flames of light. At the mouth of the Channel the light showed strongly, a warning to seamen. Two sailors were braiding rope ends by the light of a great lanthorn. One of them sang in the full, sweet tenor voice of a Welshman:

> "Give me a spirit on life's rough sea,
> 　Loves to have his sails filled with a lusty wind,
> Even till sail-yards tremble, his masts crack
> 　And his rapt ship run on her side so low,
> That she drinks water and her keel ploughs air.

Others joined in the chorus.

> " 'Till the ship drinks water
> 　And her keel ploughs air,
> Oh heigho, and a lusty wind."

Gabrielle, stirred by the loneliness of the fog-blanketed shore, shivered and drew her crimson cloak about her. The thought came over her that she would feel loneliness a thousand times, and then a thousand, before they reached the Canaries, and again after that, westward, across another expanse of ocean, to the alien shores of America. As she crossed the deck and mounted the poop companion-way to where their cabins were, the voices of the sailors came from below, dim and rhythmic. She must become attuned to the loneliness of the vast Western Ocean, and, after that, to the loneliness of a primitive land.

The *Delicia* picked up her convoy which was southward bound acruising, H.M.S. *Rose,* and H.M.S. *Milford.* For company they had the *Scipio, Peterborough Frigate, Prince Eugen, Bristol Gallery,* and the *Bahama Venture.* At night a wind rose and the Captain signalled the fleet to anchor between the Holms and Minehead. For two hours they lay waiting, then he ordered a gun fired, and all came to sail, in a fine gale, southeast to south-southeast. They ran by Minehead at six in the morning.

They had a message that a French man-of-war, carrying forty-six guns, was cruising between England and Ireland. The master ordered the hammocks up so that the decks could be instantly cleared. He wanted no surprise attack. The fleet lay astern. No Frenchman was in sight, which pleased Captain Woodes Rogers.

"We could have put up but an indifferent fight, for want of being better manned," he told Roger Mainwairing. "In open sea we have a chance, for the *Delicia* can outsail most."

The *Arundel,* a King's ship, came up and ordered the Captain to strike his pennant. He immediately obeyed the order, as he was obliged by his instructions to pay all respects to his Majesty's ships and fortifications.

The morning brought dirty weather. Gabrielle stayed in the cabin, helping Barton unpack. Her dresses hung on pegs on the wall, well covered with Holland linen.

Gabrielle felt sleepy and languid. From time to time Barton gave her a suspicious look. Presently she left the cabin and returned after a short absence. She was followed by a cabin boy, who carried a tray on which were a cup of hot broth and a few toasted biscuits.

Barton said, "Drink this. You need something hot in your stomach. Then get out of your clothes and into a warm wrapper. I've turned down your bed and the boy is heating a hot salt sack to put at your feet."

Gabrielle protested feebly.

"Do as I say, miss. I'm not going to have you seasick on my hands." Barton bustled about, getting off Gabrielle's clothes, tucked her in, wrapped warmly in a blanket, a salt bag at her feet and one at the pit of her stomach.

Gabrielle attempted a few indifferent protests which Barton ignored.

"You'll be all right when you have a good rest and get your sea legs. It's a nervous girl you are, shedding all those tears, leaving your friends and England. But the sea air will set you right in a day or two."

"I wanted to go to my mother," Gabrielle said. Her eyelids were heavy and her voice thin.

"Madam is quiet. You know Celestine will not allow you to do for Madam."

Gabrielle did not answer. Her eyes closed. She was fast asleep. Barton stood looking down, her habitually grim expression softened. "Poor bairn. Poor little bairn," she said softly. She pulled the blanket closer. She put on her bonnet and cape and went on deck. The salt tang of the sea was in her nostrils. It made her lift her head high as she walked the deck with firm sure tread and easy balance. Barton was at home on the deck of a ship. At home and happy. The land years fell away from her like a cast-off garment. She was a girl again, sailing down the Clyde at her father's side. The sea was in her blood. She heard the sailor's song. It was all natural and part of her life. She hummed a little, under her breath, as she moved easily among the coils of rope and anchor chains and bales of provisions not yet stowed, her green cloth cape swinging with the breeze.

> "Oh heigho, and a lusty wind,
> 'Till the ship drinks water
> And her keel ploughs air.
> Heigho, and a lusty wind."

Chapter 8

THE PRIZE

Six weeks later they came upon blue water and flying fish. When Gabrielle rose from her bed in the morning, the purple tips of mountains rose from the horizon. The Canaries lay dead ahead. Aside from the grumbling among the crew about close quarters and bad food, and the threatening mutiny of the crew when the ship sprung a bad leak before they put in to Cork harbour, the only untoward incident that had marked the uneventful journey was the meeting the Spaniard off Teneriff.

By four in the afternoon Pico Teneriff was in sight, distant about eight leagues. The Captain stood on the forward deck, his glass following the horizon.

"A sail under our lee bow," he called out, "between the Grand Canary and Forteventura." They set sail to chase, having letters of marque to make such capture legal and not piratical. About seven o'clock they came up with her. It was still light and a glorious sunset aftermath glowed in the west, reflected in the bank of cumulus clouds that rose beyond the dark peaks of the island and spread across the horizon.

The consorts stood off under full sail. The Delicia was nearest. She fired a shot across the bow and made the bark heave to.

There was excitement on the deck of the *Delicia*. Seamen rushed about, stripped to the waist. The women were ordered to their cabins, but Gabrielle slipped up to the high waist of the poop deck where she could watch the action.

It was a Spanish bark, owned in Orotava on Teneriff. She was bound for Forteventura, a near-by island, with fifty passengers. Gabrielle watched them leave their ship and come aboard the *Delicia*, escorted by Mr. John Finch, the London oil wholesaler, now a lieutenant on the *Delicia*.

The prisoners shouted and laughed out in their happiness when they found themselves aboard an English ship. They feared they had been captured by the Turks, since a piratical Turkish ship was about in these waters.

Four friars, in long black robes and with tonsured heads, stood to one side, sliding the beads of their rosaries. Captain Woodes Rogers came down from his position, to pay his respects to the gentlemen of Holy Church.

One proved to be the Padre Guardian of the Island of Forteventura. He had a thin pleasant face, with honest blue eyes.

Captain Woodes Rogers requested Roger Mainwairing to escort the Padres to his cabin, and had his servant serve wine and biscuits while a suitable meal was being prepared for them.

Some men were prisoners, with leg irons. The Captain ordered the chains removed. He had his men give them straw mats so that they could sleep on the deck. This was no hardship, since the weather was balmy and the breeze soft and pleasant.

The London merchant reported the Spaniard a small, unimportant prize. Butts of wine, hogsheads of brandy, olives and fresh food—a cargo of small moment, it proved. The men were disappointed.

Master Bragg suggested, "Let us take the ship into Teneriff, Captain. Then we can have her hull ransomed by the owners. It will add ducats to our prize, and the bouquet of good Madeira will make the *Delicia* as sweet smelling a ship as her name."

The company supercargo, Thomas Vinsend, pressed the Captain for permission to go ashore. The Captain was reluctant.

"I don't trust these people, Vinsend. We've not been at peace long enough for them to have forgotten the habits of war. If you go with the officer, who will treat for the ransom of the prize, it isn't wise for you to leave the small boat or get out of the protection of the *Delicia's* guns."

The Captain watched the boat making swift headway towards the shore.

"I don't feel easy about Vinsend," he said to Roger Mainwairing. "He has poor judgment and ill luck. He is always into some pocket but it's never his fault. I don't like men of ill luck on my ships, but in spite of my protests, the merchants employed him."

"He has a great amount of energy," Roger said, remembering how the supercargo had busied himself about the dock on the day of sailing.

"And curiosity to the point of snooping." The Captain's scarred jaw clamped down. "I lay you four to one, Mainwairing, he'll go ashore in spite of my orders."

"Done," said Roger, who liked to bet. The Captain walked away. Roger went up to the poop deck where he found Robert Fountaine and Gabrielle. She was lying in a long chair under a bright strip of canvas that had been rigged up as a shelter from the vertical sun.

"It is a day to laze and dream," he said, looking down on Gabrielle. She smiled back, raising the book she was reading.

"I'm almost halfway through Mr. Lawson's book," she said. "I feel that I know Carolina in all its beauty."

Roger sat down on a canvas stool. "He makes a case for Carolina, doesn't he? I think no one has written so vividly of our country."

"How did he die?" Robert Fountaine put down the small Bible he was reading and drew his chair a little closer. "I seem to remember someone telling me that he was killed by the Indians."

Roger glanced at the young girl.

Fountaine persisted. "Did Lawson go among the redskins to teach them the word of God?"

Roger hesitated. "No, he did not try to proselytize. That is the work of the Church. Nor did he trade, although he always carried some small gifts. He was surveying the outlying country beyond the Tuscarora villages, well up the New River tributaries. Some trouble arose, and he was killed, although Baron de Graffenried, who was with him, escaped and returned to the colony to tell of Lawson's death."

Fountaine looked off across the deep blue water. He passed over the surveyor's death without comment. Roger was glad.

Fountaine said, "It would be a great work to bring these pagan peoples to God. A great work for the Lord."

Roger glanced up quickly. He saw an almost fanatical look in the Huguenot's deep-set eyes.

"Better to colonize and plant and make a place for men to live their lives in plenty and in peace," he said grimly. "Let the missionaries and the traders look to the Indians. There's work enough on the land for the rest of us."

The look faded from Fountaine's eyes. "Yes, you are right. That is today's concept. Food for a man's body, but let his spirit starve."

Gabrielle's troubled look warned Roger. He pushed his stool around so that he could see the shore. The little red-roofed, whitewashed houses struggled up the steep hills, clinging to the mountain sides as white mountain goats cling to the rocks. Half a dozen ships lay at anchor in the crescent of the harbour. He saw a shore boat put out from the wharf.

"I think the *Delicia's* boat is coming," he said. Fountaine looked up, then away, indifferent to the coming and going of a ship's boat. The man's head is in the clouds, Roger thought. I don't believe he knows we've taken a prize; certainly not that the Captain has demanded ransom.

He got up. Making some excuse, he left and sought Woodes Rogers.

The Captain was seated in his cabin. At the table with him were the friars. They were making a toast to King Charles the Third, as the Archduke Charles of Austria was popularly called.

"Come in and join us," the Captain said hospitably, brushing the long tails of his brocade coat aside to make room on the bench for Roger.

"Come, have a glass of golden Canary," he urged, signalling his servant. "Fetch out another bottle," he said.

Roger did not sit down. "The shore boat is on its way, Captain," he said.

Captain Woodes Rogers pushed the oaken bench back against the wall and got to his feet. He clapped his beaver firmly over his long brown periwig and went to the door.

"With your permission, I will leave you, gentlemen. Another bottle is on the way, good sirs. You will, I hope, help yourselves, and drink such toasts as you deem suitable. Mr. Mainwairing, I will follow you."

On deck they waited for the long boat. A cabin boy came up with the Captain's spyglass, which he put to his eye.

"I fear me I have won the wager, Mr. Mainwairing. I get no view of our supercargo, Mr. Vinsend."

John Finch came aboard and brought a letter to the Captain. Before he broke the official seal, Captain Rogers said, "Where is Mr. Vinsend?"

The Lieutenant was troubled. "You will see by the letter, sir, they are holding Mr. Vinsend for ransom."

A flash of a smile crossed the Captain's dark face, " 'Twas as I thought." He broke the seal, scanned the letter. "Ah," he said, "from British merchants—what does this mean?"

"CAPTAIN WOODES ROGERS"
"GENTLEMAN:

Your lieutenant coming ashore and having given an account to our Governor of your having taken a boat belonging to this place, bound for Forteventura, we must inform you that his Majesty is graciously pleased to allow a trade between his subjects and the people of these Islands, whereof we suppose you are not ignorant.

"His Catholic Majesty of Spain has given orders that none of his men-of-war will molest any trader vessel. For the last year we have had orders not to molest any Spanish barks.

"With due regard for the interest of his Majesty's subjects, we expect the return of this boat. You will make restoration of said bark, otherwise Mr. Vinsend will not be permitted to go off, and there will be extravagant reprisals on our estates and persons."

"We are your very humble servants,
  J. POULDON, Vice Consul
  J. CROSSE, Merchant
  BERNARD WALSH, Merchant
  G. FITZ-GERALD, Merchant."

"Dammit to hell!" The Captain's face was red with anger. "I was prepared to have the islands raise Cain and Abel. But not a lot of whiney, white-livered English merchants! His Majesty's orders, indeed! I never heard of any orders to let any Spanish trader go. I'll deal with Messrs. Merchants and Sir Vice Consul." The Captain stode off to his cabin. Roger heard him shouting for his boy to bring ink and a quill.

Roger Mainwairing was in his cabin, some time later, when Woodes Rogers' cabin boy knocked at the door.

"The Captain's compliments, and will Mr. Ma'n'ring step to his cabin?"

Roger slipped on his coat, which he had removed, for the room was hot, and went forward. He found the Captain seated at a table on which were papers, an ink-horn and a sanding box. Three broken quills lay on the floor. The Captain was coatless and wigless; perspiration dripped from his forehead.

Opposite him sat Zeb Bragg, sweat streaming down his cheeks. Roger smiled. It was evident the men had been struggling over the wording of the document in Woodes Rogers' hand.

"God's truth!" swore the Captain. "I'd as leave grapple a ship as write this. A seafaring man hasn't use for words—it's action he wants—but since I must account to the owners of this vessel, and since I now carry the title of Governor

General of the Bahama Islands, I must needs be diplomatic."

Zeb Bragg uttered a sound, somewhere between a grunt and an expletive. "I'd ha' shelled the town on the instant," he complained.

"Diplomacy is our word now," the Captain countered. "Gone are the days of free sailing, and free sacking a town, my good Zeb."

Zeb took up his cap and put it on his close-cropped head. "'Tis your show, Captain. I'm blest if I can stomach the diplomatic approach. 'Stand by to fire' is what I'd say." He stalked out of the cabin, his square, strong figure stamped with disapproval.

Woodes Rogers laughed. "Zeb is a sailorman, and as such, I want no better companion, but what I want now is advice from another man who can think of something beside guns to settle a difference. Listen:

ON BOARD H.M.S. DELICIA

"GENTLEMEN:

I have yours, and observe its contents, but having no instructions given us by our Commission, relating to Spanish vessels trading among these islands, we cannot justify the parting with this bark on your single opinion.

It is Mr. Vinsend's misfortune that he went ashore against my instructions. If he is detained, I cannot help it.

To convince me, you must send a copy of his Majesty's Orders or Proclamation regarding this case.

Immediately ransom the bark; else we will set the prisoners down at next island and sink bark, after we have stowed cargo in hold of *Delicia*.

I would advise you to see that this is done at once, by suitable agents. It is fortunate that I do not say, I will shell the town and raze it."

"Gentlemen,
Your Humble Servant
WOODES ROGERS"

The Captain turned his eyes towards Roger. "What do you think of it, Mainwairing?" he questioned.

"It sounds final," Roger answered. "It leaves no alternative but to pay ransom, or——"

The Captain nodded, well content with the answer. "That is what I mean it to be," he said. "I would hesitate to shell the town, but these gentlemen need not know that."

Roger laughed. "They won't, from that letter."

Woodes Rogers called a boy. Handing him the letter, he gave instructions for the Lieutenant to carry it back to the merchants. Not satisfied, he got up hastily and followed the boy. Roger heard him shouting to Bragg to get the guns in place, ready to sweep the shore.

"In case they're looking through their spyglass, I'll give them something to digest," he said with a laugh. "Now I'll go and return to the friars their goods and their relics, for I do not doubt that the ransom will be here by sundown."

Roger went back to his cabin. It occurred to him that if he wrote a letter to Rhoda, it could be sent back by one of his Majesty's ships stopping at Grand Canary. He sat down and drew the paper to him. He wrote a full letter to his wife—a few instructions about household goods she would have sent out, a description of the ship and the people on her.

Of Robert Fountaine he said:

"He is a godly man, but I doubt his ability to become a planter. I may have made a wrong estimate of his ability. I hope I have. His daughter—yes, I believe she will be happy in our world; a fine young girl, she is assuming responsibility too great for a young woman. The wife I have not seen. She remains always in her cabin, guarded by a faithful French woman. Fountaine says little about her. In answer to my inquiries about her health, he says: 'Better, I think, a little better than yesterday, yet far from well.'

"I have an idea it is consumption of the lungs. If it be that, I do not know whether the change will benefit. I suggested they move her to the afterdeck, where Captain Bragg has rigged up an awning to keep off the sun, but Mr. Fountaine says she must remain very quiet. I believe her daughter only goes in for a few moments each day.

"By the way, do make inquiry from Martha of Teresa Blount, about a young girl who is a frequent visitor at Mapledurham. Molly Lepel is her name, a connection, I believe of Mary Lepel, the Queen's maid of honour. I thought her a very interesting young woman. It may be that she will be ready to come to Carolina when you come in the spring. She has been acting governess in her aunt's family, and she may be the very person you want for our young ones at Queen's Gift. I fancy she will be lonely without Gabrielle Fountaine, and her life in the Lepel household is very trying. This I had from Gabrielle, not from Miss Molly herself.

"Now, my dear, I must finish this letter so that it may go ashore by Captain Woodes Rogers' boat, when he sends the ship's pouch. Kisses for the children, and my love and affection for my very dear wife.

ROGER

Off the Grand Canaries,
12th May, 1718.

He sealed the letter and left it with the Captain to be sent ashore.

"By sundown we will have the ransom," Woodes Rogers said confidently. "Want to lay a wager?"

Mainwairing shook his head. "No, I haven't settled with you for my last. Anyway, I think you'll win this one."

"Let us hope so. I shouldn't like to raze that pleasant little town."

Roger glanced up quickly. There was a look of determination on the Captain's face as he looked towards the red-roofed houses scrambling up the mountain. This was a new side to the usually good-natured Woodes Rogers. A hard, determined man, to whom blood-letting was a necessity, when occasion justified.

"No. I won't like to lay the little village to waste."

Late afternoon, half a dozen boats and a barge put out from shore. Roger Mainwairing was taking a stroll about the deck before supper, when he saw the little fleet approach. As it came nearer he saw the boats contained wines, grapes, fruit, hogs and other food necessities.

The second boat had quite a variety—limes, oranges and other tropical fruits. A flatboat, manned by a Negro dressed in ragged white linen, was loaded high with bananas, musk and watermelons. On top of the fruit and melons were half a dozen long wicker chairs, birdcages of wicker with birds of variegated hue huddled inside. There were rolls of hand-woven mats, all products of the island. On a small barge stood three good black cattle, and in a small boat, a dozen wicker coops of fowl—chickens and guinea and a few Muscovy ducks. The ransom had arrived.

Captain Woodes Rogers received the British merchant, Mr. Crosse, and the Spanish owner, in due state in his cabin. The paper signed, he sent for the friars and presented each of them with some bottles of Holland gin and a cheese. They went away happy, speaking well of their treatment by the Englishman.

The Spanish owner, a swarthy low type of coastal cross-breed, was inquisitive as to where the convoy was sailing.

"To the West Indies?" he asked. A look of cunning in his eyes made Captain Woodes Rogers wary.

"West Indies, no. We sail for the Cape of Good Hope, and from there to the South Seas."

The Spaniard showed his disappointment.

The English merchant, Crosse, lingered for a moment for a private word with Woodes Rogers. " 'Tis rumoured that a pirate ship, *Queen Anne's Revenge,* is lying off the islands now. That rascal Rackham, with two women pirates, Anne Bonney and Mary Read, are aboard her. A diabolical crew, Captain, so be on your guard."

The little man moved uneasily, looking out through the door. "They watered on one of the out islands three days ago, on their way up from Madagascar. They are searching for an East Indiaman, due about this time with a cargo of spices and precious stones. I feel I am duty bound to warn you."

"Thank you, Mr. Crosse."

"Yes, yes, Captain. Another thing: I was all but forced to write you the letter. Mr. Vinsend is on the way. I convinced them it would be dangerous to hold one of your men."

Woodes Rogers nodded. "You are right, Mr. Crosse. It would have been very dangerous. Thank you for the warning. I shall be on the lookout for strange ships. I've long wanted to overtake that rascal Rackham."

The man scurried through the door after the Spaniard.

That night they raised sail, and by morning had overhauled their consort, which had watered on another island. Early morning they were in sight of Palma and Gomera. A stiff gale caught them, one that worked to their advantage. They sailed westward when out of sight of the island.

For several days the crew "licked their chops," as Zeb Bragg put it. The Captain had posted a notice to let them know that the ransom money would be divided according to the percentage arranged before sailing. Not so much of a prize, but enough to whet the appetite and keep up good will to "a Captain who looks after his men."

Gabrielle Fountaine lay in her long wicker chair. She had purchased it from a brown boy with flashing teeth, who rowed out to the ship to barter with the passengers, and to dive in the clear aquamarine water for pennies which the sailors threw overboard.

The day was warm and she was glad of the shelter of canvas to protect her from the glare of the sun. Behind a screen of canvas Celestine sat beside the cot where Madam Fountaine lay sleeping.

Gabrielle could see her mother when the soft breeze stirred the curtain. She lay so still and white that she scarcely seemed to breathe. There was no colour in her cheeks. Celestine had made long plaits of her pale golden hair, and thrown a light cover of rose-coloured taffeta over the cot. Once in a while her father would come from his cabin, the length of the deck away, to look at his sleeping wife.

"It should benefit her," he said to Gabrielle, "the sun, this mild, soft air. It should bring colour to her cheeks."

"She will be better soon," Gabrielle said. "Celestine thinks so too. She says she rests more quietly now. That is the first step. Sleep and rest are the restorers." She took his thin hand and laid it against her cheek.

"Sleep?" he repeated absently. "Sleep? So it has been for month after month. She only opens her eyes to stare at me, then closes them again. Sometimes I wonder——" He shut his lips firmly.

Gabrielle knew the deep anxiety that lay behind his words. "We must be patient, Father. God, in His goodness, will help us."

"Yes, my dear, you have more faith than I." He leaned over to touch her forehead with his lips. "You show me the way again. I must turn to God. He will help me." He walked quickly away towards his cabin. Gabrielle did not need to see with her eyes; she could follow with her thought. He would close the door and take down his Bible, and read until dark closed the square porthole.

The ship was sailing along under a good steady wind. Gabrielle watched the sails catch the wind and billow out. On the lower afterdeck, sailors were sprawled, some sleeping, some at cards or dice. One fellow, apart from the others, his back against a roll of rope, was reading a book, laughing aloud. Someone outside the range of her vision was playing a Jew's harp, a gay, rollicking tune. Another squatted cross-legged in front of a parrot's cage, repeating over and over, "Damme, shut up, damme, shut your mouth, damme."

At the far end of the deck the cook prepared a meal for the fo'c'sle. His small iron stove was set in a large box of iron. The smoke rose thin and grey against the high curved deck. A light veil surrounded the gilded figurehead of a Greek woman, carved in feeble imitation of the Winged Victory of Samothrace.

103

A quiet ship, sailing on a great ocean. Gabrielle's eyes closed slowly and she slept.

"Sail to starboard." The hoarse shout of the lookout entered Gabrielle's dreams. "Sail to starboard." The ship came to life. Bare feet pattered across decks to stations. Any strange ship was danger in these waters. Long days ago they had lost their convoy, for the *Delicia* was swift and Zeb Bragg a good sailor, who took advantage of every turn of the wind.

"Sail, northwest," came the shout.

Gabrielle sat up. She glanced towards the canvas curtain, but the space was empty. Celestine must have moved her mother to the cabin. The confusion on deck became more apparent. She heard Captain Bragg shout:

"A frigate of seventy guns, by the Eternal."

"Spaniard or French?" called Woodes Rogers, as he came out of his cabin.

"Can't make her yet, sir. She's moving fast, under full sail."

"Let us fall to windward," Rogers said, taking the glass from the sailing master. "That gives us good latitude and a proper station. If she is one of his Majesty's ships, well and good. If she prove an enemy——" He left the sentence unfinished and picked up the glass again.

The foresail and mainsail were up, the breeze stiffening.

Bragg shouted orders through his cupped hands. "Trail up the mizzen, lay the ship ahull." His voice set the men into action, climbing shrouds, hauling and unfurling. "Sixty guns, if one," he shouted to Woodes Rogers. "She's no ship of his Majesty's Navy; she's a Spaniard, from her build. Do we give fight?"

Woodes Rogers glanced at the gun deck. Thirty guns was *Delicia's* complement.

"A brave, lusty ship," the master shouted.

"So much the better," Gabrielle heard Woodes Rogers answer. "So much the better. I can see from here that the ship has a deep load. Like enough she's foul."

Bragg leaned over the rail and shouted to the men: "Set sprits'ls, sprit tops'ls and flying jib. Man the topgal'nts. Haste, men, haste, have you iron for feet?"

"We'll pace her in three glasses," he said to the master. "Order the men aft, to remain quiet there. The ship steers better. She's too much by the head as she is."

"Yon's a foul ship, all right," the master said. "See how

104

slow she is to come about . . . Get to windward and keep her there!" he called to the steersman.

Roger Mainwairing came up to Gabrielle.

"The noise wakened me from sleep," she said. "A ship?"

"She's a fast-sailing ship," he said under his breath.

"What are we doing? Are we trying to overtake her? What does it mean?" Gabrielle asked.

"We're signalling to find out what ship she is," he answered, keeping his face expressionless.

"Captain Bragg said she was a Spanish frigate." She followed Roger to the rail where he was watching the action on the deck below them. Gunners were clearing the decks. Hammocks were unslung. Seamen knocked down bulkheads about the swivel guns.

Bragg ordered, "Get a good store of cartridges, ready filled. Fill the garlands with shot, between guns and 'round the masts and hatches."

"She's hoisted a Spanish flag," Roger said. "But that means nothing. She may have good intent . . . or evil."

"Are we going to have a fight? We seem to be drawing nearer."

Roger did not turn his head. His eyes were fixed on the stranger.

"I don't know," he said, scarcely heeding her. "One never knows the nationality of a ship in these waters."

"But the men are at the guns," she protested. "See, they are bringing out arms—blunderbusses, muskets——"

"Cutlashes and poleaxes and pikes come next," he said, without turning.

"How do you know that, Mr. Mainwairing?"

"I've been in a seafight or two. That ship is handled by someone who knows his work."

Captain Woodes Rogers came within speaking distance.

"If there's any trouble, take Miss Gabrielle below," he said, and strode off.

"I want to stay on deck," she said to Roger.

"You had better go below. The deck is no place for a woman when there's fighting going on." He went back to the rail.

"Ah, so I thought!" he said after a time. "She's raised the black flag!" His voice mingled with that of the lookout:

"The Jolly Roger, sir! She's raised the Jolly Roger!"

A pirate ship! Gabrielle clung to the rail. The frigate had

swung about. In place of the Spanish flag, a great black flag, splashed with white, caught the wind.

The boatswain's shrill whistle sounded below. The call to quarters.

Captain Woodes Rogers' voice came out strong and full, carrying with it a certain gaiety: "She's a larger ship and she carries more guns, but we will match her. Every one of our men will outfight two of the pirates. We will win, for we carry the colours of St. George."

A shout came from the deck: "St. George and England!"

Gabrielle watched the Captain. The pleasant, gracious manner that she knew was gone. Instead, a man of action stood on the deck facing his men. His voice was harsh and confident. Here was the Woodes Rogers his seamen knew, a captain who knew how to manoeuvre his ship and how to put life and fight into his men.

He raised his hand for silence. The deck became quiet. There was only the sound of the wind whipping the sails as they sped towards the frigate and danger.

"Up the trumpets!" he ordered. "Hail our prize!"

The ship's musicians responded with a will. Trumpets sounded. What if the pirate was a greater ship and carried more guns? They had a captain who would lead them to victory.

Gabrielle's heart beat fast. Her blood leaped in response to the wild huzzas of the seamen, as she watched the great ship draw near.

The wind caught the black flag. Gabrielle saw the white skull and crossbones, the symbol of the Fraternity of Pirates.

Chapter 9

QUEEN ANNE'S REVENGE

Terror gripped Gabrielle. Without speaking to Roger Mainwaring, she turned away, running down the narrow upper deck to the cabins.

Roger did not notice her departure. His only interest was in the onrushing ship. She was too beautiful to be an evil ship of rapine and death. Her graceful gilt figurehead reached out to meet the sparkling water. The gold of her heavily carved prow caught the light of the sun and seemed to break into a hundred little pinpoints of flame. But the sinister dark spots at the ports gave a different aspect. He estimated more than fifty guns, with the nest of cannon aft. He turned to speak a reassuring word to Gabrielle, but she had vanished.

Roger's long strides covered the deck swiftly. He, too, must be ready for action. The seamen he passed were stripped to the waist, their breeches turned up well above their bare feet and ankles. Their long hair was bound in kerchiefs of coloured cotton, and they carried sidearms and knives thrust through their sashes.

He closed the cabin door and removed his coat. It did not take him long to change to leather breeches and sleeveless waistcoat and pull on his high jackboots.

He had no wig to discard, for he wore his own blond hair, shoulder length. He braided it into a club and set it in a black sheath, a new style but convenient for a fight where long locks got in one's eyes. If there was a head wound long hair matted and clouded the vision—an accident that he did not want to happen if he used sword or cutlash.

He buckled on his sword over his waistcoat and thrust two duelling pistols into his belt, having first looked well to the priming. If there was to be a fight his sword was at the disposal of the Captain.

When he had finished dressing he went down the passageway and knocked at Robert Fountaine's cabin.

"Come in, come in," Fountaine called. He opened the door

and went in. It was a small cabin without a portlight. Fountaine was seated at the table, his Bible open in front of him.

Mainwairing said, "We have sighted a frigate of fifty guns which carried the Spanish flag. The Captain was suspicious of her and we are going after her."

"We are not at war with Spain," Fountaine interrupted. "Surely we will have no trouble from a Spanish ship."

Roger said, "I was going to add that the flag of Spain has been hauled down and the pirate flag hoisted in its place."

Robert Fountaine was not disturbed. "We have the convoy to protect us. There is no need to be alarmed."

Roger looked at him a moment before he spoke. "Haven't you noticed we lost sight of our convoy four days ago?"

Fountaine looked bewildered. "I have not noticed. I have been thinking of other things. But surely Captain Woodes Rogers will not seek a fight with a ship that is larger than the *Delicia*."

Roger grinned. "I think he will. Our Captain doesn't like pirates. I'm going on deck. It may be that I can help if we board her."

Robert let his hands drop to his knees. "I'm no use in an emergency like this, Mr. Mainwairing. No use whatever."

Roger Mainwairing agreed mentally. Aloud he said, "Perhaps it would be best for you and your womenfolk if you were to stand guard at your wife's cabin."

Robert got to his feet. He was eager to go, now that Mainwairing had made the suggestion. "Yes, yes, of course I will go to my wife. She will be frightened if there is any shooting." He lifted the Bible from the table and went out of the room. "I wish I might be more useful."

Roger watched him walk away. Fountaine's unawareness of impending danger troubled him. How would he govern a colony in the Carolina wilderness unless he recognized an emergency?

He heard the shrill pipe of the boatswain's whistle followed by the patter of bare feet running across the deck.

Woodes Rogers' voice sounded above the noise of canvas, as the sails caught the heightened wind. Roger climbed to the upper deck and took his stand on the leeward side. The wind had risen sharply; that was good.

The ship was running into head seas. The seamen had stripped the ship of all unessentials. There was no cordage left loose to rattle and shriek. The small articles were roped so that there were no loose things to fetch away.

The crew were at their posts, grim-faced and expectant, as they watched the pirate ship. There were some seasoned men among them who welcomed a good fight, and green young ones looking to their betters for guidance and assuming the grave determined air of men who have no thought of giving way.

Bragg shouted orders: "Two more men up the main topmast. Look for the shape of any ships on the horizon. There may be a sister ship. Keep a sharp lookout for our convoy."

Mainwairing thought: Up until now we have been proud to outsail his Majesty's ships. When trouble approaches, we are willing to hover and wait for the convoy, as a covey of partridges seeks the hen. He felt his blood rising at the prospect of a fight. He laughed aloud and laid his hand on his sword hilt. As though I were a young blade, he said to himself, itching for the fray; but a swordsman is always a swordsman, even when his arm lacks power to follow the thrust. There was no lack of power in Roger Mainwairing's sword arm. He was as tough and hard as seasoned oak—muscle and bone and sinew, as becomes a man who rides hard and walks with strong stride over the ploughed fields of his own land.

Hard riders, hard drinkers and keyed to laughter in a fight, was the way of the Carolina planters, and Roger was no different from his fellows, save that his sword was swifter and his arm was longer because of his height. Pressing middle age, he could outfence anyone in the Province.

The pirate ship was approaching swiftly. It had the advantage of a west wind. All her sails were set. She rode the waves easily, well balanced and trim.

"I believe she's got sixty guns at least. Bragg says she resembles the Spanish frigate *Reina Isabella,* which he saw in Havana last year."

Roger turned at the sound of Woodes Rogers' voice; a look of surprise crossed his face. The Captain had dressed himself in the fine clothes he had worn at the banquet given in his honour by the Merchants of Bristol. He smiled crookedly at Roger's questioning look, a glint of mockery in his eyes.

"You see before you, not a simple sea captain, but his Excellency, the new Governor of the Bahamas, also titled Admiral and Captain General. If we should be forced to strike our colours it must be done in good style."

Mainwairing grinned. "I have no fear that you will strike

colours, Captain. You are too skilled a navigator to be outsailed by any Spanish-built ship even if you are outgunned."

"A greater captain than I was forced to surrender in these waters. It wasn't many leagues from here that Richard Grenville engaged forty ships of Spain, and met his heroic death."

Mainwairing said, "I had forgotten that it was here that the *Revenge* made her last fight."

Woodes Rogers did not answer for the moment. He lengthened the telescope, wiped the lens with his sleeve ruffle and sighted again on the pirate ship.

"She's coming about, Bragg," he called to the master. "She's a foul ship. Observe the way she handles. She's not been careened and rummaged for a long spell."

Bragg took the glass, his feet wide apart, his stocky figure set to the rise and fall of the ship.

"We do well to study the Elizabethans." Woodes Rogers took up where he left off. "We can learn from them. They had the demoniac determination, the self-dedication to victory or death, that we have lost. The Spaniards used to say that Grenville's soul was possessed of devils and that accounted for his victories. But Grenville himself said that it was the 'valiant, resolute seamen' who won sea battles, not the heroism of captains."

Woodes Rogers walked back and forth, his hands clasped under the tails of his long coat. Mainwairing started to leave but the Captain detained him.

"Don't go now. It will be some time before we are within shooting distance."

He wants to occupy his mind while he is waiting, thought Roger. No doubt he has his plan of battle complete in his mind.

"To go back to Grenville. The Spaniards held him in great respect as a man to honour and admire. It is from them that we have his dying words." Woodes Rogers stopped in front of the planter, repeating Grenville's last words with reverence: "'Here die I, Richard Grenville, with a joyful and quiet mind; for I have ended my life as a true soldier would, who hath fought for his country.'"

The planter said nothing. He seemed to see the deck of a ship—and men dying.

After a pause the Captain said, "'Sail into the enemy's formation boldly, and give him a broadside port and starboard. He daren't return the fire for fear of raking his own ships.' That was Grenville's battle plan. He was a bold navigator. Bold strategy is always good strategy."

Roger said, "Grenville explored the Albemarle Sound, when he brought Raleigh's settlers to Roanoke Island, and came as far as my plantation. He tells of mooring his pinnace and going ashore to eat his dinner. He carried his gold table service and his musicians went with him to play soft music while he dined."

The Captain laughed aloud. "Trust the Elizabethans never to change their way of living, no matter in what country they found themselves."

The Governor moved to the rail. He had observed some change in the position of the frigate. He called to the sailing master, "Point directly to her bow. We'll be on her before the sand has run half a glass. Give your men their orders."

"Aye, aye, sir," Bragg answered. He shouted to the master gunner on the deck below: "Down with gun bulkheads."

"Down with gun bulkheads." The master gunner took up the cry; the crew passed it the length of the *Delicia*.

"Is all well between decks?" Woodes Rogers called to the master. "See that the guns are all clear and nothing loose on deck."

Roger Mainwairing looked over the rail. The men had stowed the hammocks. They were taking down the deck cabin partitions so there would be no hurts from splinters. Cartridges, ready filled, were stacked neatly against the side of the one remaining cabin. The shot was disposed of in garlands between the guns and piled high around masts and hatches. Rammers, sponges, ladles, pruning irons were being carried out of the hold and passed from one seaman to another. The *Delicia* was prepared to give fight.

Fountaine came up beside Roger. His face was pale and very grave, but Roger saw no indication of fear in his eyes. Gabrielle followed her father. She had put on a dress of some dark cotton stuff, ankle length, and a white kerchief covered her shoulders and bosom. Her heavy dark hair was braided and wound close to her small head. She, like the ship, was trim and snug, ready for action.

Gabrielle spoke, raising her voice against the confusion of sound below. "Have we a chance against such a great ship, Mr. Mainwairing?"

He nodded towards Woodes Rogers who was standing where he could be seen and heard on both decks. "I think the

Captain's about to address his crew. I expect your question will be answered."

Woodes Rogers' voice rang out confidently: "My men, I expect the impossible of you. But we have done the impossible before. We shall match the pirate in courage, if not in men, for our colours are St. George's."

A lusty cheer broke from the barefoot seamen.

"Well said, Cap'n!" an old gunner shouted. "Remember how we took the *Manila* galleon?"

"Hist!" a sailor cried. "Don't you see the Cap'n has more to say?"

"Gentlemen," Woodes Rogers went on, "we are maintained by his Majesty George First, and our country, to keep the sea free of his Majesty's enemies; to put down piracy and robbery. Therefore I desire, for your country's honour, in his Majesty's name, that every man behave himself like an Englishman, courageous to do the word of command, and to do his best endeavour to clear the sea of all obstacles to trade."

He held up his hand. Gabrielle thought of a bishop, blessing his people. His voice swelled out, encompassing his listeners.

"Repeat these words after me."

The sailors' voices came reverently from the gun deck and from high in the mast stations, as they joined the Captain in prayer. "We commit ourselves, and our cause, into God's hands. For King and Country, and may God grant us victory!"

Bragg called out the ship's musicians: "Up noise of trumpets and hail our prize!" A stirring call that set the blood atingle.

The answering sound of trumpets came over the water as the pirate took the challenge that the *Delicia* had thrown down.

"Hold fast. Do not fire until alongside, within musket shot," Woodes Rogers' voice warned the gunners. "Hold fire until I give the signal."

The boatswain stood near the mainmast, his head bound in a scarlet cloth, his bright sash stuck with pistols, repeating orders in a steady sing-song.

"Load the guns with cross-bar and langrel. We'll split the enemy's rigging first of all. Bring up the musketoons and the pistols. Has every man got his cutlash?"

"Aye, sir, and our poleaxes and pikestaffs."

112

"Good men! Have your falchions handy. Gunners, turn your swivels till they point direct."

Bragg's voice interrupted: "Have the chambers of the stockfowlers full of good powder, and load them with bags of small shot. Save them to clear the deck when the enemy boards."

"Aye, sir, aye. Clear the decks we will."

The chase shortened sail. The Captain strode up and down, his eyes measuring the distance between the *Delicia* and the frigate. Waiting the signal to open fire seemed interminable. The silence was like the quiet center of a hurricane. At any moment the storm would break in all fury.

Suddenly Woodes Rogers dropped his outstretched arm. His voice rang out, "Give him a broadside."

At the sound of the *Delicia's* guns, the frigate was alive with pirates, crowding the deck, running like monkeys up the shrouds.

Fountaine took Gabrielle's arm, hurrying her along the deck aft to the cabin. "Bend low. Run, run. Get inside the cabin and bolt the door. Go, my child, stay close to your mother while I am away."

Mainwairing noticed then that Fountaine had a sword in his hand and a pistol thrust in the front of his tightly buttoned coat.

"I am a man of peace," he said, encountering the planter's inquiring glance, "but a man of peace must fight if need be."

"We'll be needed right enough," Mainwairing said grimly. "The frigate is as alive with pirates as a dog with vermin. Look out!" He pulled the Huguenot to a protected spot behind a cabin as a pistol shot splintered the wood behind them. "No need to rush into exposed positions. We can serve the Captain best by keeping alive."

Woodes Rogers' confident voice reached them from the after deck. "Another broadside! Trim! Run in close under their guns."

The helmsman manoeuvred swiftly, putting the ship in close.

"Good, my hearts! They can't touch us with cannon now." A cheer went up from the crew, stopped on their lips by a great burst of heavy cannon from the pirate.

They lay close enough to read the name *Reina Isabella* under the gilded oak figurehead. The pirates had crossed out the Spanish name and painted *Queen Anne's Revenge* upon the hull, but the gold letters shone through the new paint.

The first broadside from the *Queen Anne's Revenge* shot high over the decks. The *Delicia*, being smaller, was lower in the water, out of range of large fixed cannon.

"She'll rake us through and through with her small pieces," Bragg cried.

"No fear. Our turn next. Edge closer," Woodes Rogers ordered the helmsman. "Edge towards him. Port your helm! Port your helm!" The Captain's voice cut across the noise: "Damn it, I say port your helm! Hold fast, gunner. Starboard a little. Right your helm and close in. Well done! Broadside gunner, now is your time!"

The pirates fired at close range. The shots from their mortars hit the target and the *Delicia's* deck was strewn with wounded men.

Gabrielle stood alone, flattened against the door of her cabin, her eyes closed to shut out the dreadful scene of carnage. The cries of the wounded beat in her ears and her heart. She ran to the rail so that she could see where the wounded lay. She might be able to help in some way.

She saw a lad dragging a bag of small ball across the deck. A shot caught him as he ran. He spun around and fell, his leg blown away. Gabrielle's grip tightened on the rail; the sea and the deck spun crazily.

She could not see men die before her eyes like this. There must be something she could do to ease the wounded men. She flung open the door of her cabin. Barton was inside, methodically tearing linen petticoats into strips.

"I've a boy heating water on a brazier." She spoke quietly as she piled the linen into Gabrielle's arms. "Come, my child, 'tis better to have your hands busy doing for the hurt men."

She followed Barton to the lower deck where some of the wounded had been dragged in the shelter of a deck house. The cabin boy, carrying a pail of hot water, made his way to them, crouching low to keep out of the range of fire.

Barton sponged the dirt and powder from wounded arms and legs and bodies while Gabrielle bound their wounds and tried to speak words of encouragement.

The boom of cannon was continuous. Each volley of musketry was followed by curses and cries of fighting men, screams of the injured, and Woodes Rogers' shouts of encouragement.

"Cheerily, my men. That last broadside did the execution." A crash followed the Captain's words.

"His foremast is done! His foremast is down!" the boatswain took up the cry. "His foremast is down."

Gabrielle glanced up. Zeb Bragg's arms were going like flails.

"Port hard! Port hard!" The Captain's and the master's voices overlapped.

"Bear up and give him our starboard broadside! Load with double head, round and case!"

Gabrielle saw the pirate ship looming above. The boatswain repeated an order: "Lashers and grappling hooks ready."

Two grievously wounded men were dragged across the deck at her feet. As she washed the wound in a man's chest she heard the Captain's encouraging voice. "Well steered, helmsman. Edge closer."

"Load with case shot. Bring the guns to bear among his men."

Roger Mainwairing and her father were running to the starboard side where a pirate had flung a blazing rope dipped in pitch. They beat out the flame with strips of wet canvas.

Smoke from cannon fire obscured the guns and hid the wounded piled on deck. The ship shivered with every broadside as though the concussion would tear it apart. The bare torsos of men glistened with sweat and powder grime; their bright turbanned heads rose out of the drifting smoke as they rushed the side of the enemy ship. The smell of sulphur was overpowering and mingled with the sweet sickening smell of fresh flowing blood.

Gabrielle swayed dizzily. Blackness came before her eyes. She felt Barton's bony hand clutch her shoulder; her harsh voice rang in her ears.

"Don't go into vapours, girl, there's work to be done."

Gabrielle braced herself to go to the next man lying on the deck. It was an old seaman with a weathered face, lips twitching with pain.

"God! God! Help me, for the love of God!" But there was no help for a man raked with langrel. Langrel designed to tear canvas into strips did the same for human flesh. He looked at her, his eyes glazed.

" 'Tis a long hard life I've lived, young mistress," he whispered. "I'm not afraid to face my Maker." For a moment he gained strength. "May the devils rot in hell," he cursed. "God," he whispered, "God."

"God is with you," Gabrielle said softly.

Barton pushed her aside. "This is my work," she said. She closed the man's staring eyes, murmuring, "God receive his soul." Then she turned from the dead to the living.

A powder-marked gunner tossed the gun swab to his mate and ran to Woodes Rogers.

" 'Tis the devil himself, sir!" he cried, gesticulating violently towards the frigate. "Calico Jack. Calico Jack Rackham."

Woodes Rogers saw a tall spare man wearing a printed calico shirt and drawers, standing on the deck of the frigate shouting orders—an evil face but not without strength.

The gunner caught up two hand grenades from a pile and started across the deck. The Captain stopped him.

"What are you doing?" he demanded.

"Goin' to blow up that devil, Cap'n. God damn his rotten soul. He won't send any more good men to the bottom."

"Put those down. I'll deal with Rackham," Rogers said sharply. "I want him taken alive. Let the swaggering braggart know what it means to surrender."

The gunner put the grenades back on the pile and ran back to his gun.

The Captain watched the narrowing strip of water between the *Delicia* and the frigate. The crew waited, cutlashes in hand, for his order.

"Cut his quarterdeck. Now throw the grappling hooks. Steady, boys. Guns starboard, fire! . . . Well done, my hearts. Stand by to board."

"Up, boys, and board! Board!" The stentorious voice rang the length of the decks.

The boarding crew swarmed up the nets and ropes, grappled with the pirates who rushed to meet them. The fight raged over the sides, men fell into the sea, others hung from the ropes. Men cut and slashed, cursing and screaming.

Pirates jumped to the *Delicia's* deck, to be met by cutlash and pistol fire. The enemy had the advantage in numbers, seasoned men who fought savagely. They pushed the *Delicia's* seamen back. Was the fight going to be over before it began?

A bugle sounded, sharply staccato. The Governor's company of foot, which had been waiting below, rushed to the deck, driving the pirates back, crowding them to the rail. While the crew hacked and thrust and killed, the company of sharpshooters picked off pirates in the frigate's rigging and the crow's-nest.

The enemy's helmsman fell and the released wheel spun round, rocking the ship violently. In the confusion that followed, the *Delicia's* men swarmed the nets. When a pirate appeared at the rail, a well-placed shot from a soldier's musket caught him before he could mount and jump. The fight was turning.

Rackham cursed and swore and beat the bare backs of the men near him with the flat of his cutlash, driving them towards the rail.

"Swine! Cattle! Cowardly bastards!" he roared. "Haven't you the guts to fight?" He pierced the buttocks of a seaman with his weapon and kicked the wretch when he ran screaming across the deck.

Mainwairing made the deck of the pirate ship with half a hundred of Rogers' foot soldiers. Trained marksmen, they fought methodically. The deck of the ship was the same as the land to them. Row by row they fell to one knee, fired and dropped back to reload while a second row took up the fire. The orderly precision of their gunfire confused the pirates. Their own helter-skelter, every-man-for-himself method met an organized rebuff.

"Captain Rackham! Captain Rackham!" a pirate shouted. "There's no stopping them."

"Let us beg for quarter."

The pirate captain sped to the quarterdeck.

"God's death to you for cowards! Turn the small cannon on them. Load and make ready."

In the confusion of battle, bloodletting and killing, Anne Bonney came on deck.

Roger Mainwairing, who had just fired his pistol at a snarling devil with one eye, halted in the act of reloading his weapon. It had been six years since the leet girl, Anne Bonney, had disappeared from the Albemarle, on a pirate ship bound for the Caribbean.

He recognized her without difficulty. Anne did not look his way. She was intent on the battle that raged on the deck below.

She was dressed for fighting, in men's clothes, high boots pulled up over white linen breeches that displayed her shapely thighs. She carried as many pistols and knives in her girdle as the most villainous of Rackham's crew. A thin white cambric blouse with a cascade of fine lace at throat and wrist costumed her becomingly. The blouse, open at the neck, showed her white throat. She wore a chain of linked emeralds, set in Venetian gold, with a large square-cut stone as a pendant. The emerald lay in the hollow, accenting the swelling whiteness of her breast.

She had a cat-'o-nine-tails in her hand. Without speaking, she laid it on the back of the wretch who had first cried for quarter. He covered his face with his arms but she drove him backwards.

"Mercy, mercy! I will man my guns," cried the terrified man. The whip curled around his bare torso. "Mercy, Mistress, mercy!"

"No mercy for cowards," she shouted, her voice, high with anger, rising against the heavy staccato of musket fire.

The pirate's agonized cry went unheeded. Anne's whip drove him back until he hung against the rail. An instant later his wretched body plummeted through the air into the sea.

"I'll teach you to cry 'Quarter' on this ship!" she shrieked. "Die, you cowardly nothing. Die!" Her face was hard. Her pale blue eyes glittered as she watched the bleeding body strike the water. "Shoot the coward," she called to a pirate. The man aimed his musket towards the water.

"Back to your stations!" Anne Bonney snapped, raising her whip. "Back to your stations!" She drove the open-mouthed men before her to the gun deck of the frigate.

No one seemed to notice Roger, crouched by a fallen mast, half hidden by a tangle of ripped and tattered canvas.

The woman waited a moment at the rail, looking down into the water. Satisfied, she turned and mounted the steep companionway that led to her cabin.

Roger watched her go. If he could only consider Anne as a pirate with as evil a reputation as any who sailed the Caribbean, he might have shot her with the pistol he carried in his hand. Instead he remembered her as a young outcast, hounded from place to place by ignorant people, because her foster mother was reckoned a witch. Pictures of her flashed through his mind—a lonely girl hiding in the forest and the swamp, a great Irish staghound her only companion. He thought of the stormy night when he found her huddled beside the body of her mother, still hanging from the gibbet. The bitterness of her early life looked out of her cruel ice-blue eyes, and her loose, indulgent living with pirate captains had left its mark on her wide, sensuous mouth.

The noise of battle came louder to his ears. A bullet grazed his arm and ripped the cambric sleeve to the shoulder. He had no time to think of the wound. He saw a pirate in the shelter of the wheelhouse aim his pistol at Woodes Rogers as he stood on the deck of the *Delicia*.

Mainwairing leaped forward. The two grappled and rolled on the deck. The shot went wild. Roger's pistol slid along the boards. The fetid odour of dirty flesh was nauseating. The pirate fought viciously, clutching, gouging, his pock-marked face close, his greasy black hair falling against Mainwairing's cheeks.

Exerting his strength, Roger tore himself free of the man's embrace. He sprang to his feet, dragging his sword from its sheath. He had him then. The pirate lunged forward, but Roger drove his sword at the man's throat. The blood spurted from the ripped jugular and made a pool on the deck where he fell.

Wiping his sword on the dead man's shirt, Mainwairing looked about him. The fighting was fierce and bloody. He saw the evil-faced Rackham, naked sword in hand, a look of bestial rage on his face, run across the deck and disappear through a door.

Making his way closer, Mainwairing took shelter at one side of a deckhouse. He would wait until Rackham came out. He would like an opportunity to cross swords with the villain.

The fight was all below now. The big guns were quiet. Only the rattle of small ordnance and pistol fire broke the noise of men's curses and death screams.

Suddenly the door of the cabin was flung open. Rackham strode out followed by Anne. They were quarrelling violently. Roger slipped further back in the shadow of some crates which were lashed to the deckhouse. Rackham's face was black.

"Christ Almighty, woman, I'm captain of this ship. I'll do what I please!"

"Coward!" The contempt in the woman's voice cut like a falchion.

"They've damaged our rudder; they've cut down our mast. I tell you I'm going to surrender. I'd rather be prisoner than have my ship blown up under me."

"Coward!" she repeated. She walked close to him and slapped his cheek with the back of her hand.

Surprise held him motionless; then his rage and hatred blazed from his blood-shot eyes. He made a step towards her but checked his stride as two men armed with pistols took their places behind Anne.

119

"Listen to me!" Rackham said without glancing at Anne's guard. "I'll surrender my ship but I won't hang. Do you think Jack Rackham is a fool?" He dropped his voice too low for Mainwairing to hear what he said.

After a moment Anne's face cleared. She nodded once or twice. Mainwairing wondered what the pirate had said to his woman. Some evil design—some trick to outwit Woodes Rogers? He wanted to warn the Captain but the way was blocked. He edged his way cautiously around the deckhouse. On the opposite side was a companionway leading to the gun deck. If he could reach the steps . . . He was halted by a shout from above.

"Four sail, nor'-nor'east," the lookout's voice repeated. "Four sail, nor'-nor'east."

Rackham spun around and looked towards the horizon. "Christ! The convoy!" He rushed into the cabin. The woman stood motionless, her hand over her eyes, looking across the water. A moment later Rackham came out carrying a white cloth. He thrust his sword through the linen and waved it about, shouting: "Quarter! Quarter! Quarter!"

Anne Bonney turned her back on Rackham. She walked into her cabin and closed the door.

"Quarter! Rackham sues for quarter!" The cry echoed and re-echoed along the decks.

Mainwairing clattered down the companionway and ran across the frigate's deck to the rail. A few moments more and he had let himself down the nets and back on the *Delicia*.

The drums rolled; a trumpet blew a blast of victory, while Zeb Bragg, dirty and dishevelled, stood on a coil of hawser, shouting:

"An extra tot of rum, my lads, and praise to the lot of you. A pint of Jamaica for every man and boy."

His words were drowned by the wild cheering of the *Delicia's* crew.

Chapter 10

BAHAMA LANDFALL

His Excellency the Governor General of the Bahama Islands sat in a carved chair behind an oak table, carelessly spinning a globe of the world with the tip of his long fingers. Battle stains had been removed. He had changed to a wide-skirted coat of plum colour, trimmed with gilt buttons and loops of gold braid. The coat was unbuttoned to show a tucked shirt of finest white linen, and his cravat and sleeve ruffles were of Venice lace. Over the back of the chair, a cloak of dark red had been carelessly thrown, and he wore his orders and decorations.

Master Bragg and the other officers were in the wardroom when Mainwairing entered, in response to Woodes Roger's summons. He, also, had removed the signs of battle and was dressed in a dark blue coat with sand-coloured breeches buckled over his long silk stockings. He wore red-heeled shoes and his dress rapier.

"Sit down, Mainwairing," the Governor said. "I've sent my Lieutenant, Mr. Finch, to the frigate with my terms. He is to tell Rackham that quarter will be granted, provided they lay down arms, haul down all sails and furl them. They are to loose the lashings, while we steer off and hoist our boats. If they offer to fire or make sail, no quarter will be granted except death."

"Fair terms," Roger observed. "You have a boarding party in the frigate?"

"Yes. I've been aboard myself and left a crew." He got up and took a turn around the room. "When I had the hatches opened, what a sight met my eyes! Twenty Spanish prisoners together in the hold. Richly dressed ladies, white and still, huddled together, rigid with horror. Christian gentlemen, bound hand and foot, looked at me with flaming eyes, furious that fate had thrown them to the mercy of the fiends. Their gratitude when my men released them was pitiful. They fell to their knees, tears streaming from their eyes."

He ceased speaking, his face grave. The silence continued a few moments, then Zeb Bragg said:

"Did you get a squint at the booty, Cap'n?"

The younger officers looked up, their eyes eager, but they did not speak.

Woodes Rogers allowed a slight smile to cross his lips. "Booty enough. Rich goods. Cordovan leather, fur-lined cloaks, velvet, and gold cloth in bolts, olives, oil and wines— yes, a rich haul." He rubbed his fine long hands together, anticipating the division of these riches. " 'Twill please the Bristol merchants and our boys will have a goodly share. It will make them happy. A happy ship is a good ship, Mr. Mainwairing."

Footsteps rang on the deck. Roger got up and took a seat near the wall. The room was in shadow. A cabin boy was lighting the lanthorns already. Through the door he saw the sun setting on the western horizon, crimson and aflame with the afterglow.

The room was quiet. Woodes Rogers settled his ruffles. Every man looked towards the door to see the pirate Rackham, in his hour of defeat.

The heavy footfalls ceased outside the door; only one advanced, curiously light. Roger saw the flutter of a skirt; a moment later Anne Bonney stood in the doorway, framed by the crimson light of the afterglow.

There was an involuntary sound, like an indrawn breath, as the men moved in their chairs.

Anne Bonney walked into the room alone. She had discarded the fighting clothes of a male pirate. She had clothed herself in a soft floating garment simply ruffled in delicate lace at the neckline and square-cut bodice. Her pale golden hair, bound with a riband, hung to her waist. The eyes that were lifted to the Governor were soft and a little frightened, as appealing as a child's.

No one spoke. They could not look away from Anne Bonney or conceal their astonishment. She sank to her knees before the Governor and held up her long pale hands in supplication. Her low husky voice trembled.

"Your Excellency, I implore his Majesty's pardon for my ship and my men."

The governor was first to recover. "Rise, Madam," he said, his voice level. "It does not pleasure me to see a woman kneeling."

She rose with easy grace and stood erect. Her eyes did not

move from the Governor, nor did she glance about the room. The two might have been alone. Woodes Rogers tapped the table with his fingers. After a moment he said: "I prefer to deal with the captain of the frigate *Reina Isabella.*"

"I'm the captain of the frigate *Queen Anne's Revenge.*"

"I am speaking of Rackham."

"Captain Rackham is confined to his cabin." After a moment she continued, "He is wounded, your Excellency. One of your men shot at him while he carried the white flag."

Her clear-cut profile was turned to Mainwairing, so he could not see the expression of her face. He thought he detected subtle mockery in her words and her husky voice.

"I am the captain," she repeated. "I ask for the King's Pardon. I am within my rights according to his Majesty's proclamation, that any pirate, seeking to live a new and clean life, would be pardoned, provided he took the oath of allegiance and turned his ship to the Crown."

Zeb Bragg uttered an oath. Woodes Rogers checked him with a glance.

So that was Rackham's plan, to turn the prize ship to the Crown, not to the men who won the fight. Captain Richards of the *Milford,* as Commodore of the convoy, would turn the prize money to the crown.

Woodes Rogers' face was expressionless. He rose to his feet.

"The matter of pardon will come before me when I land at Nassau. You may return to the frigate."

"In irons, your Excellency?" Her voice was openly mocking now. She knew she had won.

The Governor ignored her words. "Mr. Finch, see that Madam Rackham has suitable escort."

The woman curtsied to the floor, the soft skirts spread about her.

"Mistress Anne Bonney, if you please, sir."

The Governor left, bowing slightly as he passed. Anne, looking neither to right nor left, went out of the room. At the door, her woman met her, carrying a black and white spaniel. Anne took the dog and tucked it under her arm. She walked across the deck to the boatswain's chair, her head thrown back, her expression arrogant.

Mainwairing glanced at the officers. Consternation was mirrored in the face of every man present. Instead of a rich prize to divide between the Merchants of Bristol and the

Delicia's officers and men, the frigate would become the property of the Crown.

A signal gun sounded, a clang of ship's bells. With an oath Bragg left the room, the others after him. Close by they saw the *Milford* and the *Rose*. Others of the convoy were spread out along the horizon.

A moment later the boatswain's whistle sounded. Side-boys rushed to the ship's rail and stood stiffly at attention.

Mainwairing turned his head as Captain Woodes Rogers strode past him on his way to meet the Commodore of the convoy, Captain Richards, of his Majesty's ship-of-war *Milford.*

The days were warmer now. A steady wind filled the sails and drove the ship westward. The confusion of battle was far away; the thought of England grew dim in Gabrielle's mind as she reclined day after day in the low chair on the after deck.

The young crescent moon changed to the quarter, the half; now it was at the full. Gabrielle had no wish to think beyond the day. The New World was as far away as the Old.

Then one day the Captain pointed out low-lying clouds along the western horizon. The following day two seagulls hovered over the ship and flew westward. Land was not far away.

She lay in her chair watching the constellations brighten in the heavens. The stars seemed close enough to reach with her slim hands. The deck was quiet. The men were in the Captain's room to make their final plans for disembarking at Nassau and the transfer of Fountaine's people, their goods and cattle from the *Bahama Venture* to a smaller ship, bound from Jamaica to the Carolinas.

The moon was rising, blood red. It sent a fiery path of light on the dark water. Gabrielle fancied she could pick out the *Bahama Venture* from the other ships of the convoy, their sails plainly visible.

Moonlight and the soft warmth of the tropic night set her dreaming. Moonlight befuddled one's wits. She did not want to think of David Moray, but his image rose before her. Her heart beat swifter when she remembered. Was it because no other man had pressed his lips against hers? It was not his kiss that she remembered so vividly. It was the strength of his muscular body as he held her in his arms. Even now she was ashamed of her sudden surrender to the hot pressure of his

124

lips. She closed her eyes, but she saw only his face bending over her, his brown eyes dark with emotion.

She rose swiftly. She did not want to lose herself in a dream so fantastic. Where was her pride when her thoughts clung to a man she did not know, a servant, whom her father had bought at auction in the market place? She would blot remembrance. She must re-establish in her thoughts the old footing of mistress and bondman.

She went to her cabin and began to dress for supper. She was seated on the edge of her cot when a knock sounded on her door and Celestine came quickly into the room.

Gabrielle knew from her face that something was amiss.

Celestine tried to speak but no word issued from her lips.

Gabrielle grasped her arm. "What is it, Celestine? Quick. Tell me. Don't stand there. What is wrong?"

"It is Madame. She is awake. She called me by name, but she thinks she is a young 'demoiselle. She thinks we are in France at the chateau. Oh, Ma'm'selle, please come. I am afraid."

Madam was sitting in bed, propped up with pillows. She wore a thin cambric night rail, over it a short jacket made of rows of lace and tucked cambric. Her hair was piled up in curls and bound with a broad satin riband, to match her cornflower-blue eyes. She looked at Gabrielle without expression, watching her walk across the floor as a cat watches, waiting to scent friend or enemy. She spoke to Celestine, calling her by name. "Celestine, who is this you bring to my boudoir? Have I not told you I do not feel equal to seeing strangers?" Her voice was thin and querulous. "Take her away. . . ."

"But, Madame, this is Gabrielle—"

"Gabrielle? Gabrielle? I do not remember any of our servants named Gabrielle. I do not like Gabrielle for a name." She began to cry quietly. "I do not like Gabrielle," she whimpered.

The shock struck Gabrielle full force. Her mother did not know her. She thought she was a servant in the old chateau of her childhood. She stood still, without the wit to move or speak.

Madam Fountaine clung to Celestine, burying her face in the good woman's ample bosom. "Send her away. I do not like her. I will not have her near me."

Celestine smoothed the sick woman's hair with one hand; with the other she motioned Gabrielle to leave the cabin. The girl went quietly, propelled by Celestine's gesture rather than by her own volition. She had no sensation of sadness or anger, nothing but intense bewilderment. She had waited, day after day, month after month, to hear her mother's voice, to see the light of warm affection and love in her eyes.

The querulous voice flooded her consciousness. "I do not like her. ... I do not like her. ... I will not have her near me."

Gabrielle went blindly down the narrow passage to her cabin and threw herself down on the bed; after a time tears came.

Barton found her asleep, her face wet with tears. "Puir bairn," she murmured, "puir bairn." She had talked with Celestine. She knew why Gabrielle sobbed even in her uneasy sleep.

Barton went to the door of the cabin, her mind troubled. For a long time she stood looking down the passageway, unable to make up her mind to speak to Gabrielle's father. Finally her face cleared. She would go to him; she would tell him that he had a duty to Gabrielle. It was well enough to sit the whole day reading the Holy Word, but a man had earthly duties as well as spiritual. He was leaving his daughter too much alone. It was not good for a young girl to take deep sorrow to her heart, without sympathy and help.

She walked firmly, her mind made up, and once decided, Barton did not know compromise. "Speak freely, and let the chips fall," she often remarked to Celestine. She struck the cabin door briskly with her closed hand.

"Who is it?" Robert Fountaine asked.

"Barton, sir. I would like to speak with you, if you please."

"Come in, Barton, come in."

Barton said, "I am sorry to disturb you when you are reading Holy Writ, but I'm sore troubled about Miss Gabrielle."

"What? Is my daughter ill?" He half rose from his chair.

"No, sir. It is not illness of the body, it is a wound in the heart. Her face is wet with tears, and the sobs rack her though she is sleeping, the puir lambie."

"What is wrong, Barton? Tell me what is wrong with my child."

" 'Tis not that I like to tell you, Master, but Gabrielle went to see Madam ..." She hesitated a moment, but words rolled across her mind. "To make the telling easy, Madam did not

126

know her. She thought she was a new servant at the chateau. She cried out that she did not like her and asked Celestine to take her away!"

Robert turned pale. His hands, clasping the hard edge of the table, whitened at the knuckles as he strove to control himself. He muttered, "Poor little Gabrielle, my poor child!" He looked straight at the serving woman without seeing her. "My poor child!"

"That's what I've said a hundred times, Master, the puir bairn. She'll be old before her time, bearing such burdens without anyone to help, and her so young and tender."

"But she has me, her father."

Barton looked at him steadily, her goose-grey eyes hard and unyielding. "Has she? Do you help her? Mr. Fountaine, I must speak, though it cost me my place. You do not know your daughter, nor try. You are a good man, but you are wrappit in your own world among the Saints, and think little of what goes on below, with your bairns. Before Madam fell ill in Ireland, you thought only of her, never the childer. It is not fair to put so much upon Miss Gabrielle. It is pitiful to see herself, no more than a child, try to help you in your sorrows. But do you help her? I ask you to examine yourself. Do you help her?"

With this Barton turned and marched out of the cabin, trembling inwardly at her brash speech, yet glorying in standing behind her young lady. "I've said my say, now I've done with it. If the Master shows his anger, I will ride back on the next ship. It is time someone put his foot on the earth," she said to herself. "Yes, time enough for him to think of Miss Gabrielle."

Gabrielle was surprised at her father's attention that night at supper. A number of times she found him looking at her questioningly, as if he were trying to read her thoughts. The talk at Captain Woodes Rogers' table was gay. They spoke of the Out Island where Christopher Columbus first landed in the new world. A case for the Spaniards, Captain Rogers said with a laugh, but Roger Mainwairing stood stoutly for Sebastian Cabot. "He discovered the mainland of America years before any other nation set foot on the mainland. Spain didn't send a man until 1527, when Narvaez came. It was 1539 before DeSoto came up to Florida from Havana and made his long journey, searching for mines."

The Governor turned to Robert Fountaine. "I like to

127

engage in an argument with Mainwairing. He is always so positive!"

Roger grinned a little sheepishly. "I've been reading reports of the Council of Trade and Plantations in regard to Carolina discovery," he said, "I don't usually know my history dates so readily."

Gabrielle said, "I thought Sir Walter Raleigh discovered Carolina."

Woodes Rogers answered her. "Sir Walter didn't have to leave his fireside chair to discover or colonize Carolina. He sent his cousin, Sir Richard Grenville, instead. Grenville assumed the danger, and Raleigh the glory." The Governor's expression showed his bitterness. Perhaps he was thinking of the analogy of his own adventurous life. Certainly he had taken the danger.

A seaman came from the bridge. "The master's compliments, sir. Land ahead, south by sou'west, sir."

The Governor rose, laid his napkin on the table, and with a word of excuse left the dining hall. Robert Fountaine and Mainwairing pushed back their chairs, followed by Gabrielle.

"Captain Bragg said we would be in sight by sunset. Is it New Providence Island?" she asked Mainwairing.

"No, not yet. One of the Out Islands—Eleuthera, mayhap Guanahani where Columbus landed."

They found the moon well up, the sea calm. The island was a long stretch of dark cloud along the horizon.

"Is that land?" Gabrielle asked her father. "It looks like a cloud to me."

Roger Mainwairing, who stood by her side, laughed. "You wanted waving palm trees or a mountain, like Teneriff Pico?"

"I don't know what I expected, Mr. Mainwairing. Perhaps I expected land to be solid and substantial. Yonder is something that floats on the breast of the ocean, ethereal, without substance."

"By morning the islands will be solid enough, Miss Gabrielle. A day or so more and we will be at the end of our long journey."

Gabrielle did not answer. After the others had gone below, she pulled her chair beside her cabin door to watch the moon swing higher and the stars take their places in the great vault above. The voice of a seaman rose, calling the depth of the water.

The master was taking reckoning by Polaris. "Watch that

you be not ahead of your reckoning," he called to the helmsman. "It is safer to look for land before we come at it, than to run ashore before we expect it."

"Aye, aye, sir," the answer came.

The silhouette of the pirate ship, running close, was deepened by the rise of the moon. Beyond, the sails of the convoy closed in, a little covey of birds with widespread wings, running in the bright moon.

A soft breeze, a land breeze, blew across her face, stirring her hair as she sat looking at the stars. The horror of the day was lost in the beauty of the night. She thought how little, in all these days and nights, she had looked backwards, remembering what she had left behind.

A voice came to her, a strong, vibrant man's voice, saying, "Is there no one to draw you back to England?" David Moray's face rose to her mind. His hazel eyes looked deep into her own. His lips came close. She closed her eyes. For a moment she let herself go back to the brief moments when she lay in his arms, her lips warm and pulsating under his.

All the ship was quiet. Sleep had come to the weary seamen. The luminous beauty of the stars reached down to her, soothing her with their tranquillity. Fish were jumping in the water, turned to silver by the moon. The moon rose higher, making a path to the island, which seemed now to rise out of the water and take form—one of the long low outpost islands that guarded the New World.

Chapter 11

GARDEN IN NASSAU

The first person Gabrielle saw when she stepped ashore at Nassau was David Moray. He was standing on the beach watching the horses and livestock being unloaded from a long barge. His Majesty's ships *Rose* and *Milford* lay in the roadstead, outside the entrance of the harbour. The smaller ships of the convoy, the *Delicia* and the *Bahama Venture*, rode at anchor near them.

Inside the harbour, between New Providence and Hog Island, half a hundred small vessels, sloops and flyboats and pinks of the pirate fleet were anchored. The large vessels, frigates and barquentines, belonging to the well-known freebooters and pirates, were sheltered in small inlets and bays on the opposite shore of the island.

The Governor remained on the *Delicia*. He wanted to stay on board his ship until the plans of the ceremony when he would officially be made governor were completed. That was to be in three days' time. On the same day he would read the King's Pardon for pirates. No one knew just what would happen. Some said there were a thousand pirates now on the island. That might be an exaggeration. On the other hand, from the number of people gathered on the beach to watch the ships unload, a thousand might not be too great a number.

Gabrielle and her father came ashore to the house of a merchant friend of Robert's, Mr. John Graves, now Collector of the Customs. Gabrielle was to stay as their guest for a few days, while the unloading was going on. After a week the *Delicia* was to proceed to the Carolinas, with Fountaine's settlers and trade goods for Charles Town. Madam remained on board the *Delicia*, with Barton and Celestine to look after her. These were the ship's doctor's orders, and Fountaine fell in with the idea eagerly.

Madam Fountaine had gained in strength, day by day, as she lay on the deck in the long wicker chair Gabrielle had purchased at Grand Canary. But she gave little or no heed to anything that happened about her. Nor did she call anyone by name, or seem to recognize anyone, save Celestine.

Gabrielle followed her father when he went to speak to Amos Treloar and Moray. She stood a little apart as they talked, watching the movement about her. Black men in tattered white garments, wearing broad-brimmed hats of braided coconut fibre, carried great bundles of goods from the barges to the fine coral sand of the beach.

Black women, dressed in variegated calicoes, stood by, some lending a hand. They were straight-backed women accustomed to carrying burdens on their heads; they had thin legs under their bright garments, and flat splayed feet. They laughed and made rough jokes with the men, and rolled their languid brown eyes at the sailors. Some wore scarlet hibiscus flowers in their kinky hair, others white flowers, heavy-scented and waxen. Children clung to their mothers' legs or straddled their backs, their thin legs over the protruding stomachs of the women. Young girls with wreaths of flowers around their heads, and gaudily striped and flowered calicoes bound tightly about their brown bodies walked back and forth, edging closer and closer to the sailors as they unloaded the barges. They laughed and chattered, showing gleaming white teeth and waved feather fans languidly, aping the wives of the white merchants and government officials.

The seamen, shut up for months in the hold of the ships, looked at the brown women with lascivious eyes, thinking of nightfall and lonely coral beaches, and the rustling palm trees.

Back of all—the press of town people and the Negroes—were the pirates, heavy-browed and sinister, with the cruel faces of men who had killed over and over with unlicensed wantonness. Heavily armed, they hovered like evil birds of prey, waiting.

Gabrielle, while her father gave directions to his men, had time to see all this, to look with curious eyes on the ships in the harbour and the squalid huts near the beach. Farther up the hill the houses were larger, for people of means. All the houses were within the stockade and sentries watched from towers and blockhouses. One house on the high ground was far more pretentious than all the others. It must be the Palace Woodes Rogers had spoken of, the Government House, where he would live with his officers and his civil staff. A wooden house, rambling and not ill-conceived, thought Gabrielle. Tropical vines and bushes grew lavishly in the

131

gardens, and the walls of coral shell were whitewashed or coloured a delicate pink or blue, as the walls in Madeira and the Canaries.

She moved up to the higher ground, to the shelter of a great tree with a heavy crown of shining green leaves and long seed pods. She took off her white leghorn hat to let the soft breeze blow through her hair. Her embroidered muslin skirt swayed as she walked, and the sash of taffeta matched the cherries on her wide hat.

The sea sparkled in a thousand facets of light and the water and sky were deep blue, a deeper blue than she had ever seen. She sat on a wall and took her fill of beauty. She saw David Moray leave her father and Amos Treloar and walk away. She knew he was coming to her, not by a direct path, but deviously, passing the loads and boats as if to give directions to the blacks.

His face was tanned and he wore no coat over his ruffled cambric shirt. His light breeches were tight-fitting and his high boots wrinkled about the ankles, over which brass spurs were strapped. He went up to a horse that had been slung off the boat, and patted its lathered neck as if to quiet it, then swung himself over the horse's back, without saddle, and trotted down the white coral beach. The people watched him, a man and horse moving as one. Riding easily, he turned and trotted up the hill to where Gabrielle sat on the wall. She watched him slide from the horse's back and walk towards her.

She made no sign, but her heart was beating swiftly. She met his eyes firmly. She forced indifference into the appraising look she gave him. She might have been judging the horse and the man as one, so little expression showed in her face. Once she thought to upbraid him for his impertinence on the ship. But how could one speak angrily of kisses given three months past? Better to ignore the past.

"Do you like the mare?" Moray asked, patting the arched neck of the hunter. "It is one that Mr. Mainwairing is taking to Carolina."

"She is beautiful," Gabrielle said, relieved that he had been so natural. "Is she easy-riding?"

"Very. Would you like to try her?"

Gabrielle looked down at her ruffled skirt. "Thank you, not now. One day when I am more suitably dressed." She hated the words, once they were out; they sounded so stiff.

132

"Mr. Mainwairing would be pleased to have the mare exercised."

Gabrielle said nothing. David went on, "There are beautiful paths about the island for riding."

"Thank you. I shall ask Mr. Mainwairing to accompany me one morning." A dark flush spread over the man's face. Without speaking, he caught up the reins and swung himself on the back of the mare and trotted down the beach. He needs restraining, Gabrielle said to herself, but she was not pleased with the part she was playing.

One cannot be friendly with a groom, she thought. Even a handsome groom. For it was evident now that he had stepped out of the shoes of the gardener into the boots of a groom—Mr. Mainwairing's groom. She followed her father up the hill to the low spreading house where the Collector lived behind a pink-walled garden.

It was past midnight and Fountaine and Bragg excused themselves and left Woodes Rogers' cabin. Roger Mainwairing remained at the Governor's insistence.

They had been, for the past hour, diminishing a huge bowl of rum punch which the Governor had brewed with his own capable hands. The room was heavy with the smoke of their pipes and half a dozen tallow candles, although the two square ports and the doors were wide open. The long stretcher table was littered with maps and sailing charts.

Reminiscence lay heavy on the navigator. He spoke again of the rescue of Alexander Selkirk, who had been marooned on Juan Fernandez Island for four years; of his visit to Guam and the Philippine Islands and on to the Solomons. "Those islands were a disappointment to my seamen," the Captain said. "They were ceaselessly searching for gold. They would not listen when I told them that trade would bring in as much gold as ever they could dig from the ground. They wanted the shiny yellow metal."

"Like the Spaniards, in Florida, always going west in their search for free gold. If they had planted and seated the land, they would have had riches," Mainwairing commented.

Woodes Rogers nodded. The flickering light of the candles cast shadows that elongated his face and accentuated the livid scar where his jawbone had been shot away. That accident had happened when his ships, the *Duke* and the *Dutchess*, fought with the Manila galleon off the shores of the island of California.

"They were outside themselves with joy when we captured

133

that treasure ship of gold from Manila," he said absently, rubbing his jaw with a long forefinger. "The prizes kept them satisfied for a time, but they wanted to see gold, hold it in their hands, and let the pearls of India drip through their gross fingers. Bah! Men without imagination disgust me." He dipped the silver ladle into the punch bowl and filled two glasses.

"I have a task on my hands now," he said, "a task I cut out for myself: this trick of governing the Bahamas, and ridding the seas of pirates. Sometimes I think it would have been wiser to press the Bristol merchants to take Madagascar—" He tilted his glass.

"Then you would have had a pirate crew on your hands," Roger said. "I believe you will have success here, sir, for you will have support from the mainland. Captain Rhett of Charles Town has sworn on his honour to capture Stede Bonnet. Governor Spottsswood of Virginia wants Blackbeard."

"What about your North Carolina Governor Eden?" the Governor questioned. " 'Tis rumoured that he consorts with Edward Teach—Blackbeard, as you call him."

Roger did not want to enter that controversial subject. "I really know nothing of Eden," he said. "I've been in England most of the time he's been in office." The Governor did not seem to hear his words. His thoughts were on some problem of his own.

"Do you think you will get the support you want from home?" Mainwairing asked the question after a long silence, in which the Governor sat with his body slumped in the chair, his head supported by one long slim hand. He was not drunk. The planter knew it would take more than a bowl of punch to put that hardened seaman under the table. He had taken off his wig and coat, and sat shirt-sleeved.

After a pause Woodes Rogers looked up. The expression of hopelessness in his eyes stirred Roger Mainwairing to pity. "I don't know. I don't know," he said slowly, tamping a long clay pipe. "If I go back to the early history of our colonizations, I would say no support will be forthcoming. You know your own experience in Carolina. Did they send ships to help out your Roanoke Colony?"

"Sir Walter Raleigh sent ships a year too late."

"Well, that's what I'm afraid of. I've been promised three hundred extra troops, and as many settlers. They're supposed to be sent in three months' time, but I am not too sanguine."

"Does this trouble your Excellency?"

"Not too much yet. 'Tis the damn pirates and the King's Pardon for Rackham that keep me awake of nights." He got up and walked about the cabin. Stopping in front of Roger Mainwairing, he said, "I've been told that there are a thousand pirates on the island and in the surrounding waters. I've got three hundred settlers—men, women and children—and a hundred soldiers. The inhabitants of the islands are a poor lot; they have consorted so long with the pirates, they will be on their side. They trade with pirates. They make money off pirates. What can I expect of them? Nothing."

"Nothing?" Roger said. "Nothing at first. Later perhaps, when they see you are here to protect them." He knew what the Governor was thinking. He would have to prove to the pirates and to the island people that he had the strength and power to hold his high position.

Woodes Rogers continued his walk—up and down, up and down, without pause.

"It is ridiculous," he said. "Tomorrow my men and I march up to the fort when my commission as Governor and Captain General of the Bahamas will be read aloud." He paused. His voice was bitter when he said, "We haven't enough powder to waste on a proper salute in honour of the new governor."

Roger said, "Why not let the pirates fire the salute? No doubt they have powder, shot and shell."

"That's the trouble. They have all kinds of ordnance, while I have nothing—nothing save a few outmoded cannon and mortars." He threw himself into his chair and poured a glass of punch. "After this ceremony is over, I will read the King's Pardon for pirates. What happens then, Mainwairing? Do these tough, reckless devils walk up and throw their arms and ordnance at my feet, because I read a proclamation saying that I am Governor of this island? No, they do not. The whole idea is ridiculous!"

"But the ships-of-war, the *Rose* and *Milford*? Surely it will have a salutary effect to have them at anchor outside, with their guns pointed inshore. Let the ships fire the salute."

The Governor let fly a string of oaths. "By the blood, I'll have Whitney's hide before I'm done with him! The *Rose* and the *Milford* will be gone by morning," he said more quietly. "I've just had a session with Whitney. He refuses to stay to back me up."

"I'll be damned if that isn't a scurvy trick!" Roger Main-

135

wairing's words came without thought. "Surely you can persuade Captain Whitney——"

Woodes Rogers drew himself up, his shoulders back; his features took on a new sternness. "I'll not sue for help from Whitney or any of his sort. I am the Governor of the Bahamas. I'll conduct myself as a governor tomorrow and every day hereafter."

Roger got up. He felt a little wobbly on his legs, but he managed to stand erect. He laid his hand on his sword hilt.

"I salute your Excellency. Command me in any way you desire. My sword is at your service, sir."

"Thank you, Mainwairing, thank you. Sit down. I'm not through. I want to show you this list. Here are the names of the pirates that sail off the Spanish Main, the Caribbean and the Carolina coasts. Vane is the leader; Rackham, his lieutenant. Well, we still hold Rackham and that devil woman, Anne Bonney. At least they are bound to accept pardon. Then there's Stede Bonnet. And Blackbeard, the deepest-dyed rascal of them all. I'm told Captain Hornigold and Captain Burges and Captain Peers are off the eastern shore of the island; Leslie and Nichols and Henry Jennings are sailing in from Eleuthera and Harbour Island. Why are they gathering here? To accept pardon?" He hit the table with his clenched fist, so hard that the candles bounced and one fell over to the floor. Roger picked it up and put it in its place. "Of course not. I can't conceive any reason why they should." He had control of himself now. "They are coming in to see how I conduct myself, and how I'll handle the situation."

"How many people are here altogether? Inhabitants, I mean?"

"We have three hundred settlers' houses in Nassau," the Governor said. "Mr. Thompson has seventy families on Harbour Island and Mr. Holmes about the same on Eleuthera. They have a company of militia on each island—the only drilled men besides the company I brought over. But, as I said before, the merchants want the pirate trade. Pirates are their market for buying and selling." He sank back in his chair, his elbow resting on the table, his hand before his face, lost in his sombre thoughts.

Roger got up and went out on deck. The Governor did not seem aware of his good night. The soft warm air cooled his brain. Overhead millions of stars shone in the dark dome of the sky. Little lights along the shore line of the harbour marked the pirate sloops and schooners, while the great frigates were anchored outside.

A quiet, dreamy night of soft perfumed winds and beauty. Underneath the darkness was the stench and rottenness of the pirate stronghold. They would pit their strength against the law and order that Woodes Rogers stood for. No doubt they knew his weakness and the weakness of his little garrison as well, or better, than he. A fort with walls crumbled from repeated attacks by the Spanish; a pitifully small garrison, without proper ordnance.

Roger made his way to his cabin. For once he felt disheartened. He understood too well the problems of governing a colony—the indifference of the Proprietory Government and the Crown, the savage cruelty of ravaging pirates, who held full command of the seas between islands and mainland. Woodes Rogers was a strong, resourceful man, but was one man of strength enough to carry the burden of government of a lawless people? It was a task that required a man of fearless disposition, and Woodes Rogers would not shrink from his responsibility.

In the smoky cabin, Woodes Rogers pulled the candles close and took up his quill.

"To the Honourable Richard Steele.
To be left at Bartram's Coffee House,
in Church Street,
opposite Hungerford Market
in the Strand, London, via Carolina.
"SIR:

"I hope this writing does not fall into the hands of pirates, who teem these waters as full as a school of 'Passing Jack'; a fish, which enters the Caribbean, sometime in midsummer, on its way from the African Coast.

"I have been given a problem to solve: all I have to do is to clear the sea of pirates, so that British Trade may be free-moving, in all seas.

"Every capture of a pirate aggravates the merchants, whose market they are, and to apparent inclination of the commanders of our Men of War; who, learning that the greater number of pirates make their suitable advantage in Trade; for merchants are, of necessity, forced to send their goods in King's bottoms, when they, from every port, hear of the ravages committed by pirates.

"There has been no governor in these American parts who has not justly complained of this grand negligence.

"I am in hopes the Board of Admiralty will be more strict

137

with their orders; Spaniards and pirates both threaten the Islands. If the Spaniards defer their coming until I get my forts rebuilt and cannon in place, it will be God's Mercy.

"Captain Whitney, of His Majesty's Ship, *Rose*, Man-of-War, being one of the three that saw me to this place, leaves me in the utmost danger. He pretends knowledge of you, but he has behaved so ill, that I design to forget him as much as possible.

"If he is acquainted and sees you in London, I desire you know his character is not what it appears to be at home.

"I hope this finds your hands in perfect health and that you have thrown away your great cane and can dance a minuet; and will honour me with the continuance of your friendship, for I am, good Sir

> "Your most sincere and humble servant
> WOODES ROGERS

"My humble service to Mr. Addison.

"I humbly propose that two guardships of twenty-four or thirty guns can be stationed here. One ship and a sloop always in the harbour, as guard."

He closed the pages and set his seal upon the flap. He felt easier in his mind, now that he had set some of his thoughts on paper.

It took him some time to undress, for his fingers fumbled with buttons and ties. At last he was free of his fine garments. He threw himself upon his bed and lay uncovered so that the light land breeze might cool his body. He hoped for an untroubled sleep. He wanted to be strong for the morrow. He did not know what danger might be ahead.

The sun was up when Gabrielle woke. She lay for a moment in the bed, her eyes on the voluminous mosquito net held in place by a hook in the ceiling. The long window that gave on the balcony was wide open. The early sun shone in on the polished floor boards. Mr. Graves had a fine, well-built house, as befitted a rich merchant.

Gabrielle pulled the netting aside, slid off the side of the high bed and stepped to the floor. Without waiting to dress, she threw a dimity wrapper, sprinkled in pink rosebuds, about her and stepped out on the balcony.

The garden was a mass of bloom. The sun was already drinking up the dew that lay heavy on tropic shrubs and vines. The wall that surrounded the garden was built of crushed coral, shell and cement, painted a soft faded pink. Golden shower and jasmine hung over it, mixed with honeysuckle and stephanotis. The garden bloomed with frangipani and red hibiscus. Trees with cerise and blue blossoms made a bright background for a hedge of Spanish bayonet and flaming flowers. Great chalice flowers grew rank and unashamed climbing up to the second balcony. A pair of flamingos, with clipped wings, added their coral beauty to the scene. Gabrielle drew a deep breath. Could such fragrance and such beauty be of this world?

The harbour was alive with small ships and sloops, and beyond it the larger ships lay at anchor in a deep blue ocean. White coral sand edged the water and the sky overhead held great puffs of white clouds.

Little houses of wattle and daub, whitewashed, glistened in the reflected light from sea and sky, smothered in bright flowers that took on new beauty in the daylight.

Gabrielle noticed that the *Delicia* had come over the bar and lay at anchor within the harbour. The quay was alive with white-clothed people, black and white. Under a great silk-cotton tree a crowd of black people stood watching the activity on the shore with sullen faces and curious, roving eyes.

Through the drooping limbs of a casuarina tree, she saw people walking up the hill towards the frame house that had been prepared for the Governor. It was an old house, owned by a merchant who had grown weary of island life and gone back to England. It was well placed, with a view of the harbour from its double balconies. It, too, had a walled garden, where vines grew in exotic luxuriousness, a contrast with the sterile land beyond, covered with tamarisk and Spanish guava, that ended in mangrove thickets at the water's edge.

A slave, carrying her morning tea, brought Gabrielle back into the room. The bronze body of the young girl glistened beneath the bright red calico with which she was wrapped. Hansu was her name, and she smiled at Gabrielle, a wide smile, showing her brilliant white teeth.

"*Moni*," she said. "*Moni*."

"Good morning, Hansu. I slept late. Is everyone gone?"

"Master goes to the custom-house. Madam rides away to the market. She say, Will Missy please to dress and be ready when sun strike there?" She pointed to a spot in the garden near a clump of great-leafed plantains. "Mis' says, Please to wear something cool and pretty, to go to the Governor's house. She wants Missy to look pretty-pretty."

139

Gabrielle laughed. "You will have to work hard then, Hansu."

The girl took the robe and helped Gabrielle lift her night robe over her head.

"Bath laid." The Negro girl waved to an open door. She stood aside until Gabrielle had gone into the little porch room off the bedroom. Then she closed the door and pulled the jalousies so that no stroller in the garden could glance in and look upon the white body of the Huguenot girl as she bathed in the little floor pool.

The bathing room was open to the sky. A vine of orange jasmine, mingled with honeysuckle, made a trellis. Gabrielle could see the garden through the slanting louvers, and the white puffs of clouds overhead. The Negro girl crouched on the rim of the pool, a white sponge in one hand, a slice of soap in the other, ready to lather Gabrielle's back and legs, and her flat stomach and rounded breasts.

A moment of shyness overcame Gabrielle. To expose her body. naked to the sky and the sunlight and the clouds, was something new to her. The soft wind seemed to slide across her body, caressing as it passed. This was not strange to the brown girl. A bath under the sky was a daily event, for the slaves bathed naked at nightfall, in little out-of-the-way coves along the beach. Men and women, boys and girls. It was a good time, with songs and laughter and couples stealing away into the darkness. White people also bathed in the sea, but they wore heavy clothes, and they kicked and panted under the confining heaviness of skirts and breeches.

Dark people knew better. They knew the pleasure of water sliding softly along their bodies, and the heavy, strong pull of the breakers against their strength.

These thoughts came to the serving woman as she moved the sponge gently over the white skin of Gabrielle's body.

Wrapping the dripping girl in a Turkey square, Hansu took a handful of fragrant leaves from a great bowl—frangipani, ginger, jasmine—and rubbed the petals over Gabrielle's arms and shoulders and throat.

"It makes smell nice, so men like." Hansu smiled at Gabrielle; her deep eyes held knowledge that Gabrielle could not comprehend. "All way, men like good sweet smell of body. No?"

Gabrielle turned away. The colour came to her face. Her thought turned to David Moray. Hansu laughed.

140

"Dere is somebody, no? Somebody who like meet Missy in garden?"

"No," Gabrielle said coldly. "There is no one."

"Too bad." Hansu shook her small head sadly. "Much too bad." Then she brightened. "Maybe Missy find nice man today. Soldier man, no?"

"No?" Gabrielle repeated. "No."

Hansu slipped a thin white garment over Gabrielle's body. "If Missy want, I will see Guinea woman. Get Missy some perfume pomade. Missy rub pomade on man she like when he pass by. Oof! and he turn and follow her at once, all hot with love."

"Hansu! Do not talk that way. I don't believe in charms."

" 'Tis the truth, I swear. I know. It was like that with my man, Puti. He love another, but I go to woman and give her one shilling for pomade. Then I go walk where all lovers walk, in moonlight. I am all dress' fine in new red calico, wrapped tight, and I have a red flower over my ear. I see those two laughing and talking together, and holding arms, lak' they love much. I walk by. I make my hips go so." She moved across the room, swaying her lithe body seductively. "I say, 'Good evening, Puti, good evening,' and they don' answer. They do not see me. They look in each other's eyes."

The girl sighed as she began to brush Gabrielle's long black hair. "But I do not despair. I have yet my pomade. I walk past them slowly. They are now sitting on wall. He have he arms about that woman. I am annoy', Missy, very annoy'. I take out my little box of pomade. I rub it one finger dis han'. I stop behind them and I put my han' on the back he throat, and I draw it along, like dat. Then I walk away, so." She rubbed her hand over the back of her neck and walked slowly across the room, looking over her shoulder.

"Puti, he put he han' against he throat. He jump up. That woman she hand on he arm, but he push her off. Push so hard she fall down. He run after me. I run too, fast. But not too fast, so he catch me at the far end of the quay, where is all nice shadow."

She gave a low laugh, remembering. "After that we go bathe in the moonlight, and walk once more in the shadow. So it goes. Puti is my man now. I gave the Old One another shilling. 'Twas worth."

Gabrielle listened, wondering a little. Many people had told her of strong charms the Negro witches made. Could the girl be speaking the truth? But she said nothing, only smiled back at the girl in the mirror and shook her head.

Hansu shrugged her shoulders, pouting up her lips. Ah well. White folk had strange ways. Their blood ran cold in their veins. They had no warmth or laughter. She was glad she had not been born white.

Dressed in a white ruffled frock, with coral ribands at her waist and in her hair, Gabrielle walked in the garden, waiting for Madam Graves to come down. The little carriage with two small ponies stood at the street door. The crowd at the harbour wharf was a throng now, a motley throng made up of native Caribs, Ivory Coast and Guinea slaves. Inhabitants of the Island of New Providence—fishermen, farmers, carpenters and farriers, and kindred tradesmen—leaned against the walls. White officials, merchants and upper-class folk sat on balconies or in their little carts. Some men rode, mounted on small Spanish ponies.

Madam Graves came out, a comfortable body of a woman with a good-humoured expression on her round face. She wore a dress of black Spanish lace and her large bosom pushed up over her stays. She had a small hat with feathers set atop her piled-up hair, already greying. Ribands streamed from her waist, her throat and her wrists. She waddled down the path towards the iron door set in the wall, beckoning Gabrielle to follow.

"You look very pretty and simple," she said, giving Gabrielle a searching glance. "Put your hat on, dearie. The sun plays tricks with strangers."

Gabrielle obediently put on her large flower-laden leghorn.

"There. That is better," Madam said. Two slaves came out of the house to help her mount the carriage step; another held her bright red parasol. Gabrielle got in and sat opposite Madam Graves. Hansu and Madam's woman squeezed in with the coachman, who was dressed for the occasion in a dark wool livery with buff trimmings. The day was hot. Sweat oozed above the fellow's collar and at his wristbands, ran in streams from under his stiff hat. Gabrielle thought how much better he had looked the day before, when he came to fetch her from the ship, a pair of ragged white trousers his only garment, and a broad hat of woven coconut fibre on his round head.

"It's a first time we have had a real elegant governor, and I don't want he should think we are too provincial out here."

142

She smiled a complacent, satisfied smile and reclined, elegantly, against the carriage cushions.

"There are only two carriages such as mine on the island," she explained to Gabrielle as the ponies toiled up the hill towards Government House. "Mr. Robert Beauchamp owns the other. He has lent his to the Governor for the ceremonies. He could well do it, as his lady is in Jamaica making a visit."

Gabrielle did not have to answer her hostess. Madam did not expect it. A steady stream of words issued from her lips—some, pearls of wisdom, Gabrielle thought, others toads and snakes, bits of venomous gossip about officials and their wives.

"The Governor will have to put some women in their places," she said, her voice rising angrily. "They overstep themselves and think they run the island, while decent folk await their pleasure."

"What women?" Gabrielle asked.

"That pirate, Anne Bonney, for one, and her body-companion Mary Read. Two bloodthirsty creatures as ever walked this earth."

"Captain Woodes Rogers captured Anne Bonney," Gabrielle said. "He brought their ship into port."

"So I heard from my husband. I hope you never turned eyes to the vile creature." Madam peered under the drooping brim of Gabrielle's hat.

"I saw her but once. She is very beautiful."

Madam made a sound of disdain. "She's evil. Evil, as poisonous as a fer-de-lance, and as venomous as an adder. She poisons everything that she touches. Young island boys run off to join the Brotherhood of Pirates because of her dulcet voice. She ruins lives of men, too! Even pirates fight and kill for a word or a smile from Anne Bonney."

The sound of shouting and high words rose from below. Gabrielle looked down towards the harbour. Boats were moving and a long procession was coming down the twisting street from the south side of the village—men wearing broad hats, who swaggered as they walked. They were armed, for she saw the gleam on musket and sword sheath as they moved.

Hansu squirmed in the seat, turning her head. "Madam, Madam," she said, her voice high, "Madam, the pirates are marching down the street. See, they come in quantities, all with arms."

"Merciful Mary!" Madam breathed heavily, trying to turn, but she found it too difficult. "Look, Gabrielle. Tell me, do they seem to be making a disturbance? My husband is fearful lest they attack. He told me not to speak of it, but all the government officials and all the responsible merchants are afraid something will happen today."

Gabrielle did not listen to the long explanation. She saw a shiny great bay hunter coming up the hill. As the rider came near, she saw it was David Moray. He was dressed in the clothes he had worn that day in the garden at Meg's Lane, the time she had not recognized him. Blood rushed to her cheeks. She looked down at her clasped hands to recover her composure. But she was not quick enough to hide the blush from the brightly curious eyes of Hansu.

Moray stopped beside the carriage. Sweeping his hat from his chestnut locks, he made a deep bow to Madam Graves. "His Excellency's compliments to Madam Graves. Will she be so good as to wait their party at Government House, and see that the guests are made comfortable? He begs to apologize for not sending the message earlier, but he has only now ascertained from his good friend, John Graves, that Madam is in Nassau."

"Will you please give his Excellency my deep thanks and say to him that his guests will be made comfortable and the hospitality of the islands extended to them? Thank you, Captain." She bowed regally, already the lady pro tem of Government House. Gabrielle smiled at the look of satisfaction on Madam's face.

David rode around to Gabrielle's side of the carriage. "Your father has asked me to stay near you, Miss Fountaine."

Gabrielle tossed her head. "I do not need a guard." She could not keep the tremor out of her voice.

"Do not be angry," he said, mistaking her meaning. "I would not have you think that I relish being a guard to two women." He reined his horse and dropped back out of the dust the wheels made.

Hansu was squirming and wriggling in her seat, endeavouring to see Gabrielle's face.

"He is handsome, ver', ver' handsome. I shall get the pomade for Missy tonight," she whispered later, as she helped Gabrielle straighten her frills in the little hall powder room. "I do not blame Missy for being in a flutter, so that the blood rushes to the cheek."

144

"You are not to speak of these things," Gabrielle said haughtily. She marched from the room, her head high. Hansu watched her move away down the long hall, a knowing little smile on her full lips.

David Moray galloped down the hill, faster than was good for his horse. He was angry clear through. Why was it that a chit of a girl could so unnerve him? He sought her out, time after time, always knowing he would leave her in anger. She had the power to annoy and anger him, with her remote air of superiority. Yet she was not a snob. Too often he had seen her talking with the common people on the ship. No Lady Bountiful airs about her. A friendly, common touch she had—with all save David Moray. She had been in his thoughts on the long journey from England. Could it be that he was in love with the girl?

He came to the beach where the *Delicia* was unloading. He saw something that put all thoughts of a perverse willful girl out of his mind.

A sloop of twenty-two guns, carrying the French flag, had crossed the bar and was sailing into the harbour. Flames shot up from her decks and sides. He could see the black figures of men running on deck and jumping overboard into the warm water of the harbour. A steersman and a few sailors remained aboard the doomed ship. Why didn't they leave? He realized what was happening. They were endeavouring to run her up to the *Delicia* and let her drift against Woodes Rogers' ship. Some dastardly pirate trick, was his first thought.

He cupped his hands, shouting: "Fire! Fire-ship!" His voice rang out over the water, but the watch aboard the *Delicia* had discovered the ship. A warning cry went up. A moment later the deck was alive with hurrying men. The helmsman and two men at the sails of the fire-ship jumped, leaving it empty of men. Captain Bragg's voice came to him: "Stand by to man the boats."

Good old Bragg! He was going to send a crew aboard to combat the flames or run the ship aground below the *Delicia*.

Moray jumped from his horse and gave the reins to a black boy to hold, while he ran down to the water's edge. He saw the Governor come out of his cabin dressed in light blue brocade coat and white breeches, ready to go up the hill to Government House.

He stood beside Bragg, watching the *Delicia's* boats close

in on the burning ship. The crowd from the wharves had run down the beach until the press about Moray was dense.

" 'Tis Vane's work," a man near him said. "Vane will be up to his dirty pirate tricks."

The man with him looked fearfully over his shoulder. "Hist, man, hist. They are swarming over the town. Hundreds upon hundreds. Have a care they don't hear you, else they'll be firing your warehouse."

The men moved on and David heard no more. It was as he thought. Vane, the leader of all the pirates in the Caribbean, would not give up without a test of strength. He looked over the crowd. On the outskirts he saw a dozen men dressed in true pirate garb, with high boots over coloured breeches, with knives and pistols stuck in their gay sashes.

Brutal faces, under wide black hats or coloured kerchiefs; some wore golden earrings, and one had a rosary of gold and ivory beads about his neck, with the crucifix lying on his bare stomach. A rascally lot of thieves and cutthroats they were. How would Woodes Rogers handle the lot of them? Certainly he had not the strength to combat them by arms.

The *Queen Anne's Revenge* lay off the entrance. The *Rose* and the *Milford* were not in sight. David wondered what had become of the ships-of-war that they were not standing by when they were most needed. He wondered about the pirate Rackham and his woman, Anne Bonney. Where had Woodes Rogers sent them? Did he intend to drag them, in chains, captive to his chariot wheels, as the conquerors did in the days of ancient Rome?

A detail of militiamen ran down the beach, led by a stout corporal.

"Stand back! Stand back!" the corporal shouted. " 'Ware of fire!"

David saw that the *Delicia's* men had taken control of the ship and they would beach her a short distance below. Woodes Rogers put out from the *Delicia* in a small boat. He stood in his fine raiment, directing the crew of the fire-ship. "Port hard!" he shouted, his great voice covering the water. "Beach her! Beach her!"

There was a murmur of approval from the crowd as they hastily backed away from the water's edge. A good man was the new Governor; a man who kept his head.

The French ship swung shoreward, now under control. Woodes Rogers' men were running about the decks with buckets of water, fighting the fire. The crowd shouted encouragement. It was a brave fight, they saw, but a losing fight. A dull explosion sounded; boards and deck planking rose into the air.

"Set the helm for shore and abandon ship!" Woodes Rogers shouted. "Abandon ship!"

The crowd saw the helmsman swing the vessel directly towards the beach. He lashed the wheel, then ran across the deck, the flames licking his clothes as he dived overboard. He was followed by the boarding crew. With singed hair and smoke-begrimed faces, the men swam towards the beach, or were picked up by the small boats from the *Delicia*. The crowd on the beach was in a panic; pressing and pulling and shouting, they ran from the water to safety inland.

Woodes Rogers' boat was last to pull away. He continued to stand, shouting directions to his men. He was still standing when the French ship blew up, scattering masts and sails and timber into the air, hurling bits of iron and wood along the beach among the fleeing people. Many were knocked over by the impact, others hit by flying debris.

From the water Woods Rogers' confident voice exhorted the people to be calm; the danger was past.

The French ship was deep in the sand, lying on her side. She was still burning, but the flames were dying down. She would burn to the water's edge and no more. The ammunition, set to explode when she neared the *Delicia*, had gone off too soon to do any damage, except the few cuts and bruises among the curious crowd that had lined the beach.

The *Delicia's* boat rowed by, close to the shore. The Governor was seated; oblivious of the crowded beach, he took a fine cambric handkerchief from the wired tail of his brocade coat and mopped the soot from his face. David saw a trickle of blood on his forehead where a flying splinter had put a gash.

All about, he heard satisfied expressions of approval. The new Governor was a man for an emergency. He turned to look at the spot where the pirates were. They had disappeared, lost in the fringes of the crowd. Woodes Rogers had met the pirates' first challenge.

Chapter 12

KING'S PARDON

Woodes Rogers, wigless and coatless, was washing the blood from the cut in his forehead made by flying splinters when the fire-ship blew up. On the other side of the cabin, near the door, his manservant was sewing up a rent in the sleeve of his blue brocade coat. The servant's face was perturbed, and he squinted with one eye, as he needled the thread.

" 'Tis bad luck, very bad luck, to tear a coat on the first wearing," he said dourly. " 'Twould be better to wear the puce coat, sir, and leave this tailoring to a proper tailor, if there be such a thing in this benighted spot."

The Governor smiled into the mirror. He was accustomed to the man's talk of omens and portents.

"Just mend the rent, and I'll make out with it, Briggs. It's God's kindness that I didn't have the coat torn off my back, so make haste. We must go up the hill within the next glass. It will never do to keep the people waiting for a sight of their new governor."

"A poor lot they are, sir," the man growled. "What kind of people are they, who leave their dead from the last contagion unburied outside the palisades? I tell you, sir, the stench of rotting carcasses is horrid in the nostrils; the air is putrid."

Woodes Rogers frowned. "I've appointed a health officer and I gave orders to have the corpses buried in quicklime. I do not want the fresh European blood of my people to draw in the infection."

He took his wig from the wooden stand and placed it on his shaven head. It was a full-bottomed wig of brown curls that came well below his shoulders. The colour became him well, and made his face less thin and long. A handsome man, for all the scar on his jaw. He slipped on the mended coat and smoothed his lace cravat into place. He turned slowly as the servant pulled at the wide coattails, smoothing out each small wrinkle. His jewel-hilted sword in place, the Governor took a pinch of snuff from a gold box, and went out on deck.

There was still half an hour before time for him to start up the hill, to the fort where the public ceremonies were to take place.

Most of his officers had gone; only a skeleton crew remained on the *Delicia*. They lounged near the guns which were pointed shoreward.

Woodes Rogers turned the spyglass on the hill. The winding road was lined with people from the beach to the crest. Between the town and Hog Island hundreds of small craft lay at anchor. The pirates were still coming. If he carried a secret worry, the Governor did not show it. His hundred foot soldiers were on the beach, waiting to march up the hill when he gave the signal. His secretary had gone up to the fort half an hour before, carrying the proclamation and his commission. He would see that the red carpet was unrolled and the great chair in place.

The notables of the town had waited on him earlier and breakfasted on deck. He had then announced his Councilors: Mr. Beauchamp, Mr. Fairfax; Messers. Hooper, Walker, Taylor, Thompson, Holmes, Blanchard. Spencer, Watkins and Captain Wingate Gale. William Fairfax he had made Judge of the Admiralty; John Graves, Collector of the Customs; and for Chief Justice he sent up the name of Christopher Gale, who would represent them in London for the present. He considered Gale an honest and genteel character who would serve him well.

Woodes Rogers' selection met with hearty approval of the merchants. He had nothing to fear from them. He had to fear the pirates and the lesser merchants who traded with them, and he had also to fear the apathy of the government at home.

He turned his glass towards the crumbling fortifications. The breaches in the walls and stockade had not been repaired since the last invasion by the Spaniards. This was an indication of the apathy and indolence of the inhabitants of the island. How could he raise the living standards of the colony, if they did not want to rise beyond the place where they had food for the day and a place to lay their heads at night?

The sound of angry voices and scuffling on the deck drew his attention. Two sailors were struggling with a native fisherman, urging him forward at the point of their bayonets. The older sailor touched his cap. "Sir. We found him rowing around the ship, so we fetched him aboard. He says he's been turtling off the islands. But now he says he's been at Green

Turtle Cay, near Abacoa. That's where Vane lies up. I thought you'd want to see the fellow, sir."

The Governor nodded approval. "Very good work," he said to the sailor.

The fisherman, a sullen heavy-browed fellow of jaundice colour, was reluctant to speak. Plainly nervous, he shuffled his feet and turned his bright stocking cap in his hand. He wore only one garment—a ragged, once-white shirt, the tails of which came halfway to his kness. His upper lip protruded from the roll of snuff that lay on his gum above his broken teeth.

The Governor was stern. His questions came sharply. Yes, Vane had an anchorage at Turtle Cay, the fisherman acknowledged, but he had left some time the previous week.

"To sail to Nassau?"

The fisherman shook his head. He didn't know. The Governor raised his brows and the sailors came forward until their bayonets were close to the fisherman's buttocks. The man paled under his yellow skin. He glanced over his shoulder, then said, "So it is said, Master."

"What else is said among the fishermen?"

Grudgingly the man answered. " 'Tis said Vane comes to offer terms to the new Governor."

"What terms?"

"That was not known among the men; only it was said that Vane would demand freedom to trade as he saw fit. That is all I know, sir. I swear by the Virgin Mary, I am an honest fisherman, sir."

Woodes Rogers' long jaw clamped down. "Take him away. Keep him where you can watch him, but no irons. I am not satisfied whether he is an honest fisherman or a pirate sent to spy out the lay of the land; but don't be too harsh." The grinning sailors followed close on the heels of the fisherman, their bayonets showing him the way to the forecastle.

So Vane would set the terms. By God, he'd see to that. The insolence of the fellow! The Governor paced the deck, anger boiling within him. What if they outnumbered him ten to one, in men and in ammunition? One thing was certain: Woodes Rogers, not Vane the pirate, was Governor of the Bahamas.

In this mood he went ashore. He found the carriage waiting to take him to the hilltop, but he would have none of it. Instead, he beckoned to Roger Mainwairing, who was at the landing talking with a group of merchants.

"I'd like one of your horses, if you'll be so kind, Mr. Mainwairing."

"Certainly. My man is beside the warehouse with the horses. I'll have one here in a few moments."

The Governor stood apart, but his sharp, penetrating glance swept over the crowd. An ominous quiet prevailed. Black-browed, bronzed men off the pirate ships pressed against the lower-class townspeople, making a wall along the roadway to the old fort.

David Moray galloped along the beach, leading a fine hunter. He dismounted and brought up the horse to the Governor. Making a cradle of his hands, David gave the Governor a leg up for swift mounting. Settling his sword in place, and his plumed hat more firmly on his head, Woodes Rogers set out with his mounted escort.

The trumpeters came first, then the Colours, followed by the Governor's Independent Company of Foot, in a column of fours, brave in their new uniforms and brightly burnished brass buckles.

The Governor looked neither to right nor left, but, with eyes front, he guided his cavorting horse with steady hand. After him marched the island militia in sombre, worn uniforms. The procession moved up to the entrance to the old fort, now defended by one gun and sadly breached walls.

Here he paused long enough to have Mr. Secretary Beauchamp read the Governor's commission, and he was sworn in before the Council. This brief ceremony over, the party moved on up the hill to the house that had been the residence when Ellis Lightwood was governor. Here most of the prominent townspeople awaited their new Governor.

The crowd looked on, silent, sullen. Among the townspeople, the gaily dressed pirates stood out menacingly. At the crest of the hill the company of foot made an aisle through which the Governor rode.

There was a stirring in the crowd, and the sound of a trumpet. A moment later, the boom of a cannon rent the still air. The people looked to the harbour. A great frigate lay off the entrance; a small puff of smoke floated upward against the clear blue of the sky, followed a moment later by a second shot.

"Vane's frigate!" went from mouth to mouth. "Vane's frigate!"

There was no change in the Governor's face as he rode onward. No sign that there was anything unusual in the

151

Governor's salute being fired from pirate cannon. He had almost passed through the lines of his men when he saw the ranks of pirates. For an instant the hand on the bridle rein hesitated; then he touched the shining satin flanks of his mount with his spurs.

The pirate crews were drawn up on either side of the road, taking over the lines where his soldiers left off— hundreds of them, dressed in gay raiment, velvet coats and satins, and fine cambric shirts, as if they had raided the chests of many a French trading ship and Spanish galleon. Broad plumed hats, or striped satin turbans. Some wore jackboots, heavy and spurred; others had on gentlemen's fine Morocco shoes, with silver buckles and red heels. Arms they had aplenty. Dress swords and cutlashes and broadswords. Duelling pistols and long-barrelled, evil-looking pistols, thrust through sashes, along with daggers and curved knives of the Barbary pirates.

Bristling with knives and matchlocks and pistols, the pirate crews stood along the roadway, making a guard of honour for the new Governor. They bowed low, with exaggerated courtesy, as he passed, watching him with bold, glittering eyes, in which malign challenge lurked.

Behind the front row was a second—pirates dressed in fine female toggery, displaying a king's ransom in jewels and silks and satins. They ogled and waved their gay feather fans, and walked mincingly, showing heavy jackboots and spurs under their trailing robes.

At the steps of the house a group of pirate captains waited, Hornigold, Stede Bonnet and John Angus among them. Vane was absent, firing a salute—a challenge—to the arrival of a governor, from his pirate frigate.

Woodes Rogers ground his teeth in rage at the irony of it. But the fact remained that he did not have powder to waste to fire a salute from the *Delicia*, or from the fort. His stern expression did not change. He dismounted, threw the reins to a groom and strode up the steps. There was no air of defiance about him. Nothing to show pleasure or displeasure. If the pirate captains had planned all this to annoy or intimidate Woodes Rogers, the plan fell flat.

The Governor's head was high, his fine tall figure erect, but his hawk eye did not miss the challenge of the pirates or the terror of the groups of townspeople pressed back against the doorway and walls of the house, the width of the broad gallery between them and the pirate captains. He saw Robert

Fountaine and his pretty daughter, and Roger Mainwairing near the door, directly back of where he would stand.

Mounting the red-carpeted steps, he took a place just in front of the open door, and faced the crowd. The people who had lined the roadways moved forward; together with the pirate crews, they made a great throng in the open ground in front of the steps.

The soldiers marched forward to take their places on either side of the steps, but the Governor motioned them to one side. Let it not be said among pirates that the Governor of the Bahamas was afraid to stand alone, in close proximity to them, or any men or body of men.

For a moment his eyes swept the crowd boldly. He was princely in his bearing and his disregard of danger.

Mr. Secretary Beauchamp came forward, a parchment in his hand. Again he read the commission from the Lords Proprietors which made Woodes Rogers Governor of all the Bahamas, as he had read it at the fort before the common people of Nassau. There was a little scattered cheering, but it was quickly stilled.

The townspeople were in dread of the pirates and what they might do. So easily they could turn on them and ravage and kill. Their ships lay in the harbour, deck guns mounted. They dominated the crowded beach and hillside.

The Governor turned his back on the pirate captains while his clerk took the ivory-coloured parchment with illuminated letters from a Morocco case. Then facing the outlawed men, he began to read the King's Pardon:

"By the Grace of God, I, George the First, of England, Ireland and Scotland, and the British Territory in all Oceans and Seas, do hereby grant free and full pardon . . ."

The words came from the Governor's lips in full, sonorous tones that all the crowd could hear. He spoke slowly, giving every word of the document its utmost value. Full pardon to those who took oath and forswore their evil ways. Full pardon and free land to farm and cultivate. Useful Citizens was the term used—Useful Citizens, with all crimes forgiven and forgotten. King's Pardon, a gift from a benign and generous King to his erring children.

There was a snickering at this sentence, quickly suppressed by the warning looks from the group of captains. The reading went on, uninterrupted to the end.

When Woodes Rogers finished the proclamation, he rolled it and handed it to his secretary. Then, for the first time, he turned his full bold eyes on the group of pirate captains. For a moment there was no word. Then Stede Bonnet stepped forward—"Gentleman Stede." He moved close towards the Governor, drawing a letter from his sash. He bowed solemnly. "With your Excellency's permission, I beg leave to present a document from our leader, Captain Charles Vane, whose frigate lies off the entrance, and whose gun has just furnished your Excellency a proper salute."

Woodes Rogers ignored the suggestion of sarcasm in the last sentence. He took the paper and read it with great deliberation. His face was expressionless as he handed it back to Bonnet. "You may say to Vane, the pirate, that I will not make terms with him, or any man, who is an outlaw to his Majesty's government. If he wishes to speak with me, he will first come forward and accept pardon, so graciously offered by King George. That applies to all pirates and lawbreakers. From now on there is but one Governor of New Providence and the Bahamas, and that Governor is Woodes Rogers."

He turned on his heel and walked into the house followed by his staff.

The pirate captains were left standing at the steps, taken aback by their reception. They had thought to intimidate the Governor by the show of strength and armed force, but they had not succeeded. Bonnet looked at Hornigold and shrugged his shoulders. There was a gleam of reluctant admiration in his eyes as the three pirate captains moved off and made their way down the hill; the lesser pirates fell in behind them, a goodly number of villains, marching towards the town.

The merchants and the officials watched the departure of the pirates uneasily. They did not know what to expect. Perhaps the pirates were honest, and did intend to accept the pardon; perhaps they were only play-acting and would fall upon the town with fury in the night.

The Governor crossed the hall to the great room and seated himself in the elbow chair. The honourable gentlemen of the Council made a semicircle. Flanked on either side by standards of the colours and battle flags he had captured from French and Spanish ships, the Governor met the people of the island. Mr. Watkins, the Provost Marshal, and Captain George Hooper, the Naval Officer, acted as his aides, and all went forward decently. in good order.

Madam Graves held a small court at the entrance of the

dining room, introducing her guests—the Fountaines and Roger Mainwairing. Young officers hovered about Gabrielle, bringing her cool punch made of limes and island fruit and rum.

No one spoke of the uncertainty of the pirates' action, or that danger hung over them like a dark cloud from the Caribbean. It pleased the representative people to ignore the pirates, taking their cue from the Governor's words. If he defied the known strength of the murderous Vane, he must have sufficient arms and guns to carry himself through a possible attack.

They were pleased with Woodes Rogers. He carried himself as a Governor should. There would be no shilly-shallying. It was no weak Governor that the Lords Proprietors had sent out to New Providence, but a man of power. So they fell in with his programme.

The musicians, hidden behind vines on the gallery, played softly. The men and women in their grandest clothes moved in and out of the long dining-room, feasting on the good food that covered side tables and hunt boards. The young people, drawn by the music, crowded into the great room which had been cleared for dancing, while the older men gravitated to the punch bowls in the dining-room and the broad gallery.

Woodes Rogers led off the dancing, taking the first minuet with Madam Graves. After it was over, with Roger Mainwairing he joined a group of men in the little office at the end of the gallery. Here eight or ten of the merchants and Councilmen joined him. A slave brought in a silver bowl filled to the brim with punch.

Woodes Rogers himself ladled the punch into each cup, and a toast was drunk to the Governor, followed by one to the island and the islanders.

Said John Graves: "Your Excellency, do you think there will be any pirates who will accept the King's amnesty?"

Woodes Rogers knew these men were curious about his plans, and what he intended to do if the pirates chose to take his words as a challenge and make a fight to maintain their hold on New Providence as their bailiwick. He glanced out through the window. Most of the crowd had departed, but little knots of people still lingered about the entrance to the grounds, and crowds were thick along the beaches. Save for the double sentry at the gates, there was no effort to make a display of military power. The soldiers moved about the grounds, or ate their dinner at the tables set up in the side garden, and there was ale for the commonality served at the gates. It was all easy and informal. There was a suggestion of careless indifference to the pirates and what they did, and confidence on the part of the new Governor that the law would be maintained. All this was as Woodes Rogers had planned.

"Some of the pirates will be pardoned," he said lightly. "Others will refuse to receive the benefits of the King's great generosity." His voice changed. The expression of his face was stern and unyielding. "Those who are so foolish as to refuse his Majesty's grace will suffer for their folly."

The Councilmen looked one to another. Robert Beauchamp, tall, dignified, with cold grey eyes under his white wig, said, "We have heard from Governor Nicholson of South Carolina that Captain Rhett is outfitting a ship to hunt Stede Bonnet down. And we had a letter this morning from our Virginia agent that Governor Spottswood would send a guard ship out to hunt Blackbeard."

"I thought Teach—Blackbeard, as they call him—had the patronage of the Governor of North Carolina."

"So he has," answered the Provost Marshal, "but the more responsible citizens have appealed to Spottswood to come to their aid."

Woodes Rogers turned to Roger Mainwairing. "Mr. Mainwairing, have you had any news of this effort on the part of the Governor of Virginia?"

"No, your Excellency. I have not had any news from the Province since I left London."

"What do you think of Eden, Mr. Mainwairing?" Beauchamp asked. "Is he to be trusted to help clear the Carolina Banks of pirate nests?"

"I am afraid I can't answer that, Mr. Beauchamp. I've been in England for a considerable period, and out of touch with provincial affairs," Roger said noncommittally.

The Provost Marshal was outspoken. "I believe Governor Eden and his Deputy, Knight, are hand in glove with that villain, Blackbeard. Why, the fellow has a house in Bath Town, and lives there openly with his thirteenth or fourteenth wife."

"Governor Eden has a house in Bath Town also and he's building a road there from his house on the Chowan River, at Edenton—a wide road, straight as a string, which he is pleased to call the Governor's Road. What do you say to

156

that, Mainwairing?" Beauchamp pressed for an expression of opinion.

"Mr. Eden is ambitious," Roger said cautiously. "Ambitious for the Province and for himself."

A laugh went up. The Provost Marshal clapped his hand on Roger's shoulder. "You are cautious, Mainwairing. You don't intend to commit yourself."

"I don't like to express an opinion of something about which I have no firsthand knowledge." Roger spoke good-humouredly.

"Well, I have firsthand knowledge," William Watkins said. "I have just come back from Charles Town. I met Edward Moseley and Maurice Moore from the Albemarle. They did not hold fire when they talked about Eden. They breathed brimstone."

Someone laughed. "Like the brimstone matches Blackbeard lights in his beard, to frighten captives?"

"God damn him!" one of the men said. "He captured a bark I was bringing from Jamaica. He took all the sugar and sold it to his profit; then he had the impudence to come to my warehouse and tell me that he picked up the bark abandoned, and he wanted to collect salvage."

Roger Mainwairing went out into the garden through the long window. The room was hot and filled with smoke and the fumes of punch. Music came faintly from the great room, and the gay, bright sound of women's voices, and the movement of dancing feet. It was near sundown. He strolled to the garden wall and watched the sun flatten to a lanthorn, then drop below the rim of the Western Ocean.

He turned towards the town. From King Street into George Square, where the King's flag waved, it was crowded with black figures, and in Fort Street people were moving from the beach to Prince Street.

There was a restless movement in the crowd, and from the distance a sound like a muffled roar came to his ears. He didn't like it. He didn't like the ominous silence of the pirates. Vane was no man to take the Governor's words without some reprisal. Woodes Rogers seemed not to be fretting over what the pirates would do; but Mainwairing understood the man well enough to know that under his calm, casual exterior the Governor had some plan to meet eventualities.

He leaned against the wall, watching the streets leading to

157

the old fort. They were changing the guard. He heard the sound of the sunset gun as the colours were lowered from the flagpole. The air was soft, laden with heavy perfume of jasmine and ginger flower and frangipani. There was a rustling along the path, made by a woman's silk skirts. Roger turned to face Anne Bonney.

The pirate woman was elegantly dressed in priceless India silk. Her long pale gold hair was held by a band of velvet set with pearls. Pearls were about her neck and on her fingers, and the blue of her gown matched the ice blue of her eyes.

"I saw you on the ship, Duke Roger, but you did not speak."

Roger felt the blood rise to his tanned cheeks. "You did not come to talk with me, but to see the Governor," he said brusquely. "I would have left the cabin, but there was no way."

"So you hid behind the curtain to hear what the pirate woman said?"

"That is not true. I have no interest in Anne Bonney's affairs."

"There was a time when you felt kindly towards a lonely girl." The voice was dulcet, with flowing, husky undertones. It was no longer the sweet, thin voice of girlhood. It held challenge and dark suggestion of passion. "I remember a night when you helped a frightened girl cut down a woman they had hanged for witchcraft. I remember other times, when your people left food in a cabin in the swamp."

"Your wolfhound still lives," Roger said, passing over the words she spoke of days that were gone. "He is my companion at Queen's Gift."

"If you had taken me, that night I came to you, I might never have gone from one pirate to another, and ended up with Rackham."

There was silence for a moment. Then Roger said:

"What are you seeking, Anne Bonney?"

The woman moved away and sat down on a stone bench that backed against the wall. A shower of gold flowers fell about her, pale yellow as her lovely hair. Even when he looked closely he could discover nothing in her face or clear-cut features to show the dissolute life she had led. Only in her eyes, pale blue, cold and cruel. They had looked on death, and evil and they had lost the wide-eyed innocence that Roger remembered in the leet girl.

"Why do you go from one man to another?" he asked suddenly, his voice harsh.

She glanced at him insolently through half-closed lids. "Why should I answer you, Duke Roger?" She used the old name he had been called in his younger days. "But I mind not telling you. The first time I went with a Portuguese sailor, because he would take me away from a country I loathed. I thought because he was a pirate, he was strong and brave; but he was a weakling and I left him. Each time I have hoped to find strength in a man, but——" She shrugged her shoulders. "Even Rackham has a weak, cowardly streak. He's always talking of his bravery and high courage. But now, at this moment, he is sueing for King's Pardon, down yonder at the fort." She got up and moved swiftly to the wall. "Down there: Rackham and Hornigold and Burges and many of their men, more than a hundred of them, all accepting King's alms."

Roger was astonished at her words. He had not dared to hope that so many of the pirates would come to Woodes Rogers and accept the terms of the amnesty.

"It is well," he said. "It is better to live, pardoned, than die from a yard-arm or hang on a gibbet in George's Square."

"I would rather hang than surrender," she said fiercely. Her eyes blazed; her face was set in cruel lines.

"But you must surrender with Rackham."

"No. No. I'll never surrender. I'd rather put my dagger through my heart."

It occurred to Roger now to wonder how it was that she was free. In the surprise of seeing her, he had not remembered she was left a prisoner on the frigate.

"How did you get free?" he asked.

Her eyes lighted; a soft, sensuous smile curved her full red lips. "Stede Bonnet set me free. Stede Bonnet and his men." She repeated the name as if she liked the flavour of it on her lips. "Stede will not take pardon."

"What will Vane do?" Roger asked the question not expecting an answer. The woman moved close to him, so close the fragrance of the heavy perfume of amber filled his nostrils.

"Have a care tonight, Duke Roger. Vane will not stomach the words that Woodes Rogers spoke today. Have a care. 'Twas Vane who sent the fire-ship against the *Delicia*. He will stop at nothing."

The music came louder, as if doors and windows were thrown open. They heard the clear laughter of women, and a man's voice saying, "The garden is the place to be at sunset."

Anne Bonney turned quickly. She laid her slim hand for a moment on Roger Mainwairing's arm. He felt the blood rise in him. Her lips were near his cheek as she whispered, "Set a guard on your ship tonight, Mr. Roger Mainwairing." She turned and walked swiftly down the path, and was lost in the shadows of the shrubbery.

Roger went back to the Governor's little office. It was empty. The odour of pipe smoke lingered, and a litter of empty glasses filled the table. He went down the gallery to the great room. The crowd had thinned. The Governor's guests were moving across the garden to the road down the hill.

He saw Gabrielle Fountaine standing near an open window. She was talking with someone in the garden. As he came closer, he recognized David Moray's voice.

"It is your father's wish, not mine, Mistress Fountaine. It is he who asked me to escort you to Madam Graves's house. Believe me, I have no wish to intrude myself."

"Very well. I am ready," Gabrielle answered. Then she saw Roger Mainwairing. "Oh, Mr. Mainwairing, you come at an opportune time. Will you walk down the hill with me?"

"I shall be honoured, Miss Gabrielle."

"Do not let me detain you," Gabrielle said over her shoulder.

Mainwairing moved to the window. "Have you seen the Governor?" he asked Moray.

"He went down to the fort, sir. I understand some of the pirates have surrendered." He spoke evenly, but his face was a thundercloud.

Mainwairing wondered why the girl's words should anger Moray so, but the thought gave way to something of more immediate importance. "Take my horse and ride to the fort." He leaned down so that his words could not be heard by Gabrielle or any passerby. "See the Governor immediately. Say you have a message from me, to be delivered in private. Tell him I suggest that he put a guard on the *Delicia* at once. Tell him I will be down in half an hour and will explain in full. Wait, Moray. I will ride down myself. It will simplify matters." He turned to Gabrielle. "My child, I am afraid I'll have to forego the pleasure of the little walk with you. Moray will see that you reach Madam Graves's safely."

He bowed and went swiftly down the walk to the rack where his horses were tied.

160

Moray looked at Gabrielle. A little smile touched the corners of his firm lips. He bowed deeply, his broad hat sweeping the ground. "Mistress Fountaine, will you give me the honour?"

Gabrielle did not glance at him or take notice of his proffered arm. She marched off, her head erect. Moray fell in behind her. The little smile still quirked the corner of his mouth. He knew the path was rough and the shadows deepening. The girl would turn to him for help before they had gone far. The perfume from the garden flowers was all around them, and the breeze from the sea was soft against their faces. As the wall cast a shadow on the path, Gabrielle stumbled and put out her hand to steady herself against the stone. Instead, she touched the strong, firm arm of the bondman.

"Thank you, Moray," she said coldly. "I will take your arm. I find the shadows are misleading."

"Shadows are like to be misleading, ma'am." There was hidden laughter in his deep voice. He said no more, but fell in step beside her.

Her hand was on his arm. He moved closer, pressing her fingers between his strong arm and his side. They walked in silence. The first bright star was rising over the shadowy sea. A few riding lights were visible on the ships that lay at anchor. Voices were far off, rising softly as the people below them walked down the path. She could feel the steady beating of David's heart against her hand. Anger fell away from her. It was a quiet world, soft in beauty and serene peace in which anger had no place.

The scene Roger walked in on was one he never forgot. The barrack rooms of the old fort had been cleared. A long table made of planks was set up at one end. Provost Marshal William Watkins, Judge of the Admiralty William Fairfax, and the Naval Officer, Captain Hooper, sat side by side. At the end was the Governor. The table was littered with papers and lists.

A hundred or more men crowded the room, guarded by a few soldiers. Roger thought he had never seen a more villainous lot in all his days. Rackham had a pardon and was leaving the room when Roger entered.

Hornigold, beetle-browed and obese, Burges, thin-lipped and pock-marked had already passed the questioners, and held the King's Pardon in their hands. The wretches who were in line were of every race and colour—the dregs of

London and Glasgow, sullen Spaniards and captured French; Caribs and Negroes, Barbary Moors and men of Madagascar.

A clerk was droning out the crimes of each man as he passed—rapine and murder, plundering towns, sinking ships, sack of villages and towns, evil practices and perversion forced on prisoners. Hacking ears, slitting noses, forcing prisoners to walk the plank were some of the crimes listed. Once in a while a pirate would add an item to his villainies, speaking gloatingly of some heinous crime he had committed that was not on the list.

Roger sent a soldier to the Governor, asking to speak with him privately on a matter of immediate importance. Woodes Rogers got up and walked to a small room at one side. Mainwairing joined him there. The Governor listened with close attention to the warning Roger had received from Anne Bonney.

"Whether it's the truth, or a bit of malicious gossip to annoy us, we must not overlook the fact that neither Vane nor Bonnet has come in. I mistrust the lot of them, but am obliged to give them pardon if they ask for it and take the oath of allegiance."

He stood for a moment, smoothing with his fingers the scar tissue along his jaw, a habit he had when in deep thought. After a time he went on: "I cannot leave at the present. Will you take the message to Captain Bragg to put an extra watch aboard the *Delicia* and have guns loaded and ready? I will send a platoon of soldiers to the beach. I cannot send more without arousing suspicion. As soon as possible I'll come aboard."

He turned and went back to the barrack room. Roger passed the pirate Rackham as he crossed the square. He was swaggering, accompanied by half a dozen of his fellows. They were headed for a grog shop near the beach. Rackham was shouting to every group he met that he was a free man under King's Pardon and fit to drink with the best merchants of Nassau. People moved out of his way as he went down the road, taking refuge in shop doorways and alleyways. Giving the man a wide berth was safer than drinking with him. He understood why the townspeople had little faith in the regeneration of the Brotherhood. Rackham was joined by a band of the pirates dressed as women. They had already visited the grog shop and carried bottles in their hands, and most of them had stripped off one or more of their feminine garments—a bodice, leaving a hairy chest above a trailing silk skirt; or a skirt, leaving short-cut trousers and boots, and a woman's bodice or underbody. A lewd mob of the scum of the earth. It was a mistake to allow them to hide behind a pardon. They should have been strung to the yardarm or raked with grape, according to Roger Mainwairing.

He found Captain Bragg walking the high deck in the darkness. He followed Roger into the cabin and called a boy to light the candles. His face was grave and troubled. His men had brought in fragments of gossip, which the shrewd seaman fashioned into a pattern. He had already set an extra watch and made preparations to repulse attack.

"Take a look at the shadow across the channel, Mainwairing," he said. Roger went to the door. A great dark hulk loomed up against the water, the tall masts pointing to the stars. "Vane's frigate," Bragg said succinctly.

"Is she making ready to sail?" Roger asked.

"Shouldn't wonder. Don't expect she'll sail without doing some devil's work first. Trouble is, we can't do aught but wait and see what she's up to."

"The *Bahama Venture* is lying on that side."

"Yes. And half a dozen fishing boats. More than that, a ship from England is lying outside the entrance, and that damned Whitney has taken the *Rose* and the *Milford* off to Jamaica, to join Admiral Vernon's fleet. Scut and be damned to the fellow!"

"Go get some rest, Captain. I'll stand watch for you."

"Couldn't close an eye," protested Bragg.

"Well, lie down anyway. It's a long time until daylight."

The Captain's protest was weaker. Finally he stretched himself on a berth. A moment later he was snoring loudly.

Roger went on the high deck. The planets were glowing like great lanthorns in the sky. Venus shone brightly, and red Mars glowed with baleful intensity. He looked at the shadow of the frigate. After a time it would be moonshine and he could watch Vane's ship more closely. Below him he heard the swish of bare feet on the deck as the watch moved slowly back and forth. Landward, lights glowed from bonfires on the beach and a few lights, no larger than fireflies, gleamed in serried rows up the hill, where people walked, carrying lanthorns, or a post light marked the entrance to some hidden garden.

He wished he knew what move Vane would make. A school of fish hurtled their silver crescent bodies against the dark water. "Passing Jack," which had crossed from Africa, swam up the warm water of the channel. A quiet night— ominously quiet, Roger thought; the scent of danger lay in the soft warm air.

Gabrielle and David Moray walked slowly down the hill. They were at the wooden gate, set into the wall which surrounded the Graves's garden. They had walked down the path without words, Moray watching the rough places in the roadway and holding back branches and vines that hung over the wall.

The heady perfume of tropical flowers was all about them. The moon was rising, a shimmering silver light lay over the island and the sea. It was a night for lovers, not for two antagonistic people. Gabrielle withdrew her hand from Moray's arm; she was on familiar ground now and needed no support.

Suddenly two men detached themselves from the shadows, between Gabrielle and the gate.

" 'Tis a maid. I swear by St. Hubert 'tis a fine, fair maid." The man's voice was drunken, and as he lurched closer, the fumes of wine polluted the still night air.

"Hold the lanthorn, and let us look upon the maid's face." The second man spoke with a slight French accent.

"Higher. I can see only a slim, elegant figure, but often the face belies the figure."

Gabrielle felt Moray's unspoken anger. He slipped his sword from its sheath. His extended arm pushed her gently backward until he stood between her and the drunken men.

"Put down the light," he said quietly.

"Ah, the lady has a cavalier. Do I see the flash of naked blade, or does moonlight befuddle me?" The taller man with the accent stepped forward, his hand on his sword.

" 'Tis not the moon that befuddles you, Monsieur Bonnet." David's voice was quiet.

Stede Bonnet! Gabrielle shrank back into the shadows. She remembered his eyes on her that afternoon, when the pirate captains held speech with the Governor. Loathsome eyes that roamed over her slowly, as if they were stripping her of her garments.

"Raise the light, you fool." The servant swung the lanthorn high; the yellow rays detached Gabrielle's white face and great dark eyes from the surrounding blackness.

"Ah, the Huguenot!" Bonnet swept the ground with his

plumed hat. "My duty to you, Mademoiselle Fountaine. I am Stede Bonnet, at your service." He gave the French pronunciation to his name. "We are fellow countrymen, and should be friends. Is it not so? Do not be frightened, because, as a pirate, I have a rough name. 'Tis only a name. I do assure you I am a gentleman who would never harm a fair lady."

The servant came closer, swinging the lanthorn so that the light fell full upon Gabrielle. She showed no fright; her white face, her enormous dark eyes held only contempt.

"Lower that lanthorn!" David Moray said. The man pressed closer.

There was a flash and a clatter of metal, as Moray's sword struck the lanthorn to the ground and grazed the man's arm. He let out a yell.

Bonnet drew his sword. "Ah! So the gentleman wants satisfaction. Well, he shall have it. A duel by moonlight is an oddity, but Stede Bonnet will always oblige when it comes to sword-play."

"I don't duel with pirates," Moray said contemptuously. "I fight, but I don't give satisfaction under rules set for gentlemen. On guard, rat!"

Bonnet lost the gay banter in his voice. "Young fool! You don't know Stede Bonnet's reputation with a sword."

"On guard!" was Moray's answer. "Slip through the gate as I drive him backward," he said to Gabrielle. But she did not move. She flattened herself against the wall, her light dress showing plainly against the blackness.

The swords crossed. Moonlight flashed from hilt to point like lightning flashing in a thunder-rocked sky.

Slowly, guardedly, David Moray fought. Stede Bonnet was not boasting. He was master of the blade. He fought, not brilliantly but consistently, watching for an opening in Moray's guard. The two stood in a bright patch of moonlight, the trees casting dappled shadows about them.

"Shall I use my dagger?" the servant cried.

"Stand back, fellow! I want no help from you," Bonnet's voice commanded. "Stand back!"

Little by little David forced Bonnet backward, until he was beyond the garden door.

"Now!" he called to Gabrielle. "Go inside!" She did not move. "Do as I bid," he said angrily. Gabrielle tried the latch, but the door was locked. "Ring for the porter," he called.

"No. Do not ring," Stede Bonnet cried. "We will settle this by the sword. We fight for the lady."

"May God damn you!" David said.

"Ah. My opponent grows wrath!"

David said nothing; he needed a steady hand and a quick eye.

Warily they circled, each seeking an opening. Gabrielle watched them, fascinated by the flashing sword blades. She was so engrossed that she did not notice the servant drawing near, in the shadows, until his rough hand was on her arm.

She opened her mouth to scream, then closed it. If she cried out, David might turn and Bonnet run him through. She fought against the strength of the evil-smelling creature. Pressing back against the door, she found her hand against the bell. A violent peal rang out, the high cracked peal of a rusty old bell. Twice she pulled before the pirate could stop her.

There was the sound of running feet. Voices cried out. Heavy, lusty voices caught up the cry. "Coming! Coming," the porter shouted.

The man turned and Gabrielle wrenched her arm free from his hand. She saw that Moray was aware of what was happening, but he went on fighting. He was driving Bonnet farther back, away from the wall. Bonnet was breathing hard. An older man, and half drunk, he was wearing down under the weight of Moray's attack. A sudden feint and a quick thrust, and Bonnet's sword made a flashing arc in the air.

Oaths flooded the night air, oaths from Bonnet and a warning cry from his servant: "Quick, Master, the guard."

Bonnet snatched his quivering sword from the ground and turned towards the town. "I'm not through with you, my fine guardsman," he shouted at Moray.

His servant was tugging at his arm. "Quick, Master, quick. See the signal flares on the ship! Quick!"

The two disappeared into the darkness as the hurrying porters reached the gate and flung it open.

Gabrielle entered the garden.

"Is there trouble, Mistress?" the porter cried, breathless from running.

Gabrielle's voice was almost gay when she answered, "There was trouble, Porter, but it has passed. This gentleman took care of it." She turned to speak to Moray; with a bow and a mumbled word, he too disappeared in the darkness.

"Don't go! Don't follow Bonnet! David!" she cried alarmed.

There was no answer. The quiet garden was filled with her terror.

She waited for the porter to fasten the lock on the gate.

"There will be trouble this night, Mistress," the porter said as he held the door for Gabrielle to enter the house. "The town is filled with the scum, drinking and carousing. Two of the devils tried to carry Hansu off, but we beat them back with staves."

Gabrielle hurried through the silent hall. There was no one in the drawing-room. A few candles sputtered and gave off a feeble light. She went upstairs. The Graves family had not returned. Hansu was not in sight and no one answered her when she called for the slave. She undressed herself and got into bed.

The boom of cannon wakened Gabrielle from a restless sleep. She sat up in bed. Her room was illuminated from a great fire on the beach. Footsteps, racing down the hall, stopped at her door. Hansu beat on the panel with her fists, crying, "Wake, Mistress! Wake! The pirates are sacking the town."

Gabrielle jumped from her bed. Throwing a wrapper about her, she ran to unlock the door. The terrified slave girl fell into the room, gasping for breath. "Madam says dress swiftly. It may be that we must go to the fort for protection. Hurry, Missy, hurry."

Gabrielle hurried, finding her fingers all thumbs and very clumsy. She wished Barton were there to help her, but Barton was on the *Delicia*. An overpowering terror struck her. They were all on the *Delicia*: her mother and father and Celestine. Half clothed, she ran to the window. Through the slanting jalousies she saw black figures against the scarlet flames and the outlines of ships at anchor. "Hansu, Hansu! Is the *Delicia* burning?"

"No, Mistress. The warehouse at the foot of Fort Street. The guns! The pirates are shooting."

A splash of fire rosetted out of the blackness. A bursting shell fell on the beach, clear of the ship. The moon was up now and made a faint glow on the water. She could see that the *Delicia* was firing on a ship on the opposite side of the channel, a great ship, with sail spread to catch the land breeze. A smaller ship was afire. It lit up the water and the beach and the running dark figures.

"Come! Come!" Hansu tugged at Gabrielle's arm. "The carriage is waiting to take us to the fort. All hell is loose tonight. Come, Mistress; you do not know your danger."

Buttoning her overdress as she ran, Gabrielle followed the terrified slave girl down the hall to the gallery.

Madam Graves was already seated in the carriage. The moonlight showed her white, frightened face, framed in dark flowing hair. "Come! Come!" she screamed. "We must get to the fort."

Gabrielle piled into the carriage. The horses started before Hansu was seated. She pitched forward onto Madam's ample lap.

"Get off me, girl!" Madam shouted angrily.

The slave crouched at Gabrielle's feet, her body a bent bow. She was shaking with terror. "The pirates!" she kept whispering. "The pirates! They will kill the men and ravage the women."

"Merciful God!" whispered Madam, her lips moving in prayer. Then she was aware of the frightened slave, kneeling in the bottom of the carriage. She shoved Hansu with her slippered foot. "Quit snivelling, girl. Sit in the seat. No pirate is going to get you. Do you not remember we have a fearless Governor and an Independent Company of Foot?"

Her words brought solace to the girl, and to herself. She sat up stiffly and gathered a Spanish shawl about her to cover her bare neck and arms. She had forgotten her bodice.

Gabrielle sat with her fingers intertwined in her lap. "Dear God!" she kept saying over and over. "Dear God, save my loved ones! Save them! Save them!"

Mr. Graves met them at the gates of the fort, which swung open to receive the carriage. Gabrielle could have laughed, had she not been too terrified—women in every stage of dishabille; children crying, clinging to their mothers' skirts; soldiers and militiamen running back and forth; slaves carrying bags of sand, building up the breached walls; officers shouting orders in high, ringing tones. The sky was brilliant with flames, and the town as light as day.

Near Gabrielle a man was wringing his hands, crying, "My warehouse. My beautiful warehouse, burned to the ground."

Over and above the shouting and confusion came the booming of cannon. After a time the interval between the booms grew longer, and finally they died into silence. Women and children lay on the ground. Many had fallen asleep.

Hansu got a rug from somewhere and spread it for Madam and Gabrielle. "It is not well to sit on the ground. Chigoe is a terrible plague. It will bite and lay a sack of eggs by your toes. Then you will lose a foot, maybe."

Hansu spoke cheerfully. Her first fright had faded when the guns had stopped. She leaned against the wall and talked to a young Negro coquettishly. She broke a flower from a vine and set it in her hair above her ear. Gabrielle wondered if she had her little shell box of pomade to rub on the slave's neck. Or perhaps this was Puti, her man.

At dawn Gabrielle got up and walked to the gallery of the old building. From there she could see over the wall to the beach. The *Delicia* lay in the stream, but the *Felicia* was burned to the water-line. Outside the harbour, Vane's frigate, under full sail, was fading from sight.

Roger Mainwairing, his face grimed with powder, his clothes scorched, was coming across the parade ground. She ran to him. He would tell her of her mother and father.

"Your people are uninjured," he said, seeing the anxiety in her white face and questioning eyes. "We got off remarkably well, considering Vane's frigate had the better of us in guns and men. But he got away, damn his villainous hide!" He caught himself. "I'm sorry, Gabrielle, but if ever a man deserved to be caught and strung to the yardarm, it's that rascal Vane. Instead, he gets past our fire, over the bar and out to sea."

"And all the pirates?"

"Thirty or more, including Stede Bonnet. The rest of them remained ashore—those who took the oath. Woodes Rogers rounded them up and put them underground for the night, otherwise they would have made off."

"You don't believe they intend to keep their oath?" Gabrielle asked.

"No, I don't. I think they will all slip away with their spoils and rendezvous on the Carolina Banks." He said nothing of Anne Bonney. There was no doubt in his mind that she sailed in Vane's ship. She and the gentlemanly Stede Bonnet.

Gabrielle turned to him. "Take me to the ship, please, Mr. Mainwairing. I want to see for myself that my mother is uninjured."

Leaving a message for Madam Graves, who was still asleep, they walked down to the beach. As they were about to step into a boat to be rowed out to the *Delicia*, a small boy, in one ragged white garment, thrust a folded piece of paper into Roger's hand. With a word of apology to Gabrielle, he read the note as they were being rowed to the ship.

"HONOURED DUKE ROGER:

"I have left Rackham since he proclaims himself, by oath, to be an honest man. Mayhap he is honest. Mayhap, by so doing, he gets away from Vane and Bonnet, who hate him.

"I walked with Stede Bonnet on the beach tonight. It was he who planned for Vane to take his frigate and get out to sea, after they fired the town and ships in the harbour. 'Tis their way of telling Woodes Rogers that they are his enemies.

"They will burn his guard ship and leave him without protection.

"Bonnet planned it all. He is a man of superb courage.

"Anne Bonney does not forget kindness done to her in the past. Therefore she spared your life this night."

"QUEEN ANNE,
of the Caribbean."

"The brazen baggage," Roger said. He tore the paper into small bits and cast them overboard. Gabrielle looked at him with inquiring eyes, but he made no explanation.

Vane and Bonnet had got away and were headed for the Carolinas, where Blackbeard, the most odious pirate of them all, had his rendezvous in Pamticoe Sound, in the little town of Bath.

Roger didn't like it. He wished Woodes Rogers had moved more swiftly, with a sterner hand. Appeasement was not the way to treat murderers and men filled with blood lust. Death was the only answer. Death, with their vile heads on pikes, so that people could know.

BOOK TWO

Chapter 13

THE RIVER

The journey from New Providence to the Cape Fear was a matter of weeks. Becalmed for days, followed by contrary winds, they made slow progress up the Florida coast, keeping well out to avoid Spanish ships of war.

Between Charles Town, on the Ashley, and the shoals that marked the tortuous entrance to Cape Fear River, they ran into the fringe of a hurricane, which blew them back almost to the Charles Town harbour.

Then one morning at sunrise, Master Bragg manoeuvred the *Delicia* over Frying Pan Shoals into the channel.

The faint light of soft dawn lined the eastern horizon when Gabrielle awoke on that long-dreamed-of morning as the *Delicia* entered the river and found safe harbour behind the shoals and the protecting Banks. She got up quietly from the little cot behind the screen in her mother's cabin, where she had slept since the ship sailed from Nassau. She dressed hurriedly in the dark, moving softly so that she would not disturb her mother. Even though she did not waken, she would be restless and talk in her sleep of her old home in France. Celestine, sleeping on the floor on a pallet at the side of Madam Fountaine's berth, snored intermittently, her mouth half open in her full moon-face.

Gabrielle closed the cabin door and made her way up the companionway to the deck. She was eager to have her first glimpse of the river and the land at sunrise. She wanted to see the sun bring the river banks out of the deep shadows and flood the river with daylight. There was a portent in seeing a new land at sunrise.

Early as it was, there were others before her—dark shadows at the rail, facing shoreward, trying to pierce the gloom, waiting for the massed shadows to dissolve under the first light of the new day. A crimson glow through the dark sky marked the horizon. In a moment the sun would rise and she would see what her inner eye had long envisaged: the new world of the Carolinas. The sound of myriad song birds came

173

from the near-by shore. But there was no vibrant cock's crow to mark a civilized world, only the song of the forest and wild places.

The muffled sound of voices and the creaking of the anchor chain sounded far away. She peered down the deck, only to find her vision blunted by a grey mist. She realized then that a low-flying fog shrouded the river and the shore. She felt a vague unrest, the weight of disappointment. She had always had the vision of a sun-drenched shore line, pointing the way to the forest. Fog belonged to the old world of sorrow. She must have spoken aloud in her disappointment, for a figure detached itself from the shadows and stepped to her side. From the height and carriage she recognized Roger Mainwairing.

"The sun will soon dispel the mists," he said. "At this season of the year the mouth of the river is often obscured by fog. Ships are obliged to anchor, as we have, in the lee of the islands and wait for a clearing before they sail upriver."

As they stood side by side at the rail, waiting for the fog to drift seaward, Gabrielle thought how many times during their long voyage from England, and the wearisome wait at Nassau, Roger Mainwairing had spoken his quiet words of comfort and reassurance. It was his confident bearing and vigorous action that helped give them victory over the pirate ship, captained by the notorious Rackham and the unspeakably wicked Anne Bonney. It was also he who helped Captain Woodes Rogers through those first trying days, when the Bahama settlers and the seamen from his little fleet had threatened mutiny. It was Mainwairing who had suggested that Captain Zeb Bragg take the *Delicia* and bring her father's people to the Cape Fear. There had been muttering among them at the delay in the Bahamas, when they heard that the Jamaica packet, which was to carry them to the Carolinas, had been scuttled by Vane and his men. Mainwairing kept half of them from leaving the ship at Charles Town to join Huguenots already settled on the banks of the Ashley and the Cooper. Working quietly, he had accomplished these things without their being aware. Certainly her father had given no indication that he had any knowledge of the help the Albemarle planter had been to them. Robert Fountaine's mind was fixed on the ultimate; the present had little of his attention. His trust was in God's wisdom and the right. He believed that all things would adjust themselves, if one had faith. It was Roger Mainwairing who, out of his wide experience, had smoothed the difficulties and kept Robert Fountaine's group together.

They were almost at the end of the journey. Sixteen miles upriver to Old Town Creek, which had been the site of Sir John Yeamans' ill-fated colony fifty years before. Here they would go ashore and make their settlement within the old stockade that had protected Sir John's small party of Carolina adventurers. There was an advantage to this. Fields had been cleared and ploughed, although since grown over. Some of the log houses would be left standing.

"It is easy to repair log houses already built," her father had told her, when she questioned. "A little chinking, perhaps some flooring and roof patching, and we'll have a place to lay our heads until we build proper houses."

It had all sounded so encouraging, especially when he told her that Tomothy Whitechurch had sent word to Mr. Pollock in the Albemarle to send men to the Old Town settlement, in order to repair the old cabins for Fountaine's settlers. A good woodsman or two and half a dozen men handy with axe and saw and hammer would set things right in no time. Such cheering words from Whitechurch had lifted the worry from Robert Fountaine's mind, and from Gabrielle's as well.

Now doubts beset her again. Suppose the ship bearing the letter of instruction to Mr. Pollock were held by pirates. Suppose she had been lost in a hurricane. . . .

Roger Mainwairing said, "Look to the east." Gabrielle raised her eyes. Broad rays of gold pierced the grey of the fog, rolling it into little wisps, shattering the gloom with shimmering vibrations of light. The wind from upriver tossed the soft fragments, pushing them along as a wind scatters unreality gave Gabrielle the impression of being caught up and suspended between earth and sky, with no object of weight or darkness as a guide-post. Even the river was invisible, the hull of the ship floating in a moving cloud of mist. Half frightened, she moved until her shoulder touched the solid figure of Mainwairing. He was real. Real and strong and steadfast. She took comfort from his nearness.

"It is an inferno, turned grey," he said. "We are floating in the nether world between earth and sky."

"You feel that too?" she asked quickly.

"Yes. I was thinking of Dante's Inferno. We want only the tortured wails of the earthbound spirits to lend it support."

"Please!" Gabrielle spoke quickly. "Please do not give voice to the thought. I cannot help feeling something sinister, some portent of evil. It makes me fear for this venture of ours."

Mainwairing laid his strong firm hand over hers. "No fears. You are almost at home, my child. You have had rare courage all the long journey. Do not lose faith now you have reached the goal."

Gabrielle was silent, her mind not at ease, clouded with fear of the unknown. The raucous cry of a whistling crane broke the stillness. It, too, had a portent of evil.

"No fears," he repeated. "See, the mist has vanished. You can see the shore line rising, and the long spires of the pines piercing the fog."

The fog had departed. A high bank along the shore was visible through drifting fragments. Marshland skirted the water's edge. The tall marsh grass was a sea of green. A million iridescent jewels sparkled on every waving blade of grass and cane where the heavy dew of early morning caught the sunlight.

Beyond the marsh, half a mile inland, the high banks of the river rose to twenty or thirty feet. There the deep forest stood, quiet and imperishable, light green upon darker green, in heavy, unbroken masses. Over the tall trees the thin streamers of mist floated, marking the lazy breeze. The forest was at once beautiful and inhospitable. Gabrielle wondered what dangers lurked there in its ancient fastness. Would it be her friend or her implacable enemy?

The lush green of the marshland gave off a strange yellow light from the slanting sun—the light of a sky under a hurricane. The marsh crept inland, long green fingers clutching at the land, making patterned inroads into the bank and into the lowland. She could see piles of earth where the banks had given way to the greedy marsh. Only the stately marching cypress held out against the oozing strength of the swampland.

"It is so beautiful, and so lonely," she whispered, turning to the man beside her. He was looking at the land, exaltation in his face and in his eyes.

"It is never lonely," he said quietly. "There is solitude, but not loneliness, under the trees. Men need solitude. The forest is strong and men must have strength to fight it. But strength comes as one needs, my dear. Always remember that.

"Do not fear the forest and it will not hurt you," he went on, his voice quiet. "It will give you strength and courage. It holds everything you need for your living—your habitation, the food for your existence. It solaces you with its beauty, it soothes you with its many voices." He gave a short laugh as if half ashamed of his words. "You will think me a young poet under the influence of spring, instead of a middle-aged planter with a deal of work ahead of him. But I love the deep forest, Miss Gabrielle. More than once it has given me the strength to live out my life."

With a slight bow he moved away. His strong lean face was expressionless but his words set her wondering what was the secret of his strength, and what caused the underlying sadness that showed for a moment and was gone.

I wish I had known him when he was a young man, she thought. And then she forgot Roger Mainwairing in her interest in the passing shore.

The ship was moving slowly now, under a light sail. The opposite shore became visible, a low line with strips of sand beach but no high banks. She was glad that Old Town settlement was on the west side, where the forest was heavy and the banks high. Somehow there was protection in high banks—protection from the pirates, who sought refuge in the river. Folk in the Bahamas said the Cape Fear was called the Pirates' River. She was disturbed until Captain Rogers assured her that the pirate ships hid behind the Banks, along Topsail Inlet, or Hawlover. They seldom went up the river farther than the first creek, where they filled their water tanks.

Two of the women, Mary Treloar and Eunice Caslett, walked by. Gabrielle had heard their names from Barton. "It is beautiful country," Gabrielle said to them, after the morning greeting. "See the long streamers of moss hanging from the oak trees. 'Tis like a tissue veil."

Mary Treloar said glumly, "More like an old man's beard. I never could abide dirty grey beards on old men."

The younger woman looked startled, started to say something, but the older woman had her by the arm, pulling her away. Gabrielle watched them cross the deck to join a group seated on corded sea chests. She was disturbed by the woman's ill temper. The morning was so beautiful. There did not seem room for ill temper in the world. She had noticed Mary Treloar before—always with some scare story or ill-humoured remark. Her eyes were black, set slightly aslant and too close together in her swarthy face. She was the wife of Amos Treloar, shipwright, one of her father's trusted men. They were Devon folk, and Amos had built many a ship to sail out of Plymouth harbour. He was a quiet man who had little to say. Aside from his gift for hymn singing, he scarcely ever opened his mouth. But his bright little eyes missed nothing. Gabrielle rather liked him. He reminded her of a squirrel, with hanging jowls and sharp quick eyes. She had watched him on the journey from New Providence, sitting on a coil of rope, listening to the seamen's tales, laughing at their bawdy jokes but not joining in the lewd talk.

Gabrielle looked around the deck at the little group of settlers. For the first time she saw them as individuals. She had had little conversation with any of her father's settlers. She had been too busy during her mother's long illness, and in the evening she sat at the Captain's table, with her father and Mr. Mainwairing, listening to the talk of planting and seating the new colony. Most of the people were of the lower class of workers, selected by her father for their skill in trades. Yeomen and husbandmen were on the second ship, which carried cattle, sheep and horses. Some of the people looked pleasant and cheery, others were sullen, scarce lifting their eyes from the deck when she said good morning. Two men from the debtors' prison never came on deck at all, but stayed in the forecastle with the crew, drinking rum and lying half drunk in their berths. Her father had voiced his distrust of these men one night at dinner, but Captain Bragg had laughed and said that you must have a few tough men to use as whipping-boys, to keep the stocks from falling apart. Gabrielle was horrified at this bald statement from the outspoken Captain, and her father quickly changed the subject to something more agreeable. Now that her mind was turned to the details of their new life, she hoped there would be some pleasant people. Barton had long since told her that there was scarce a woman among them that one could sit down with to have a cup of tea.

Gabrielle had spoken to her father about Barton's comment. He was as near angry as she had ever seen him. "These people are all equal in the sight of God, the Heavenly Father. That is one reason why we came. The Carolina constitutional charter gives equal rights and religious tolerance to all." An almost fanatical light burned in his deep-set eyes. "Let me never hear you speak of anyone as inferior again, nor use the term of lower class or upper class. This is a New World in which the integrity of every man denotes his station. Please remember this, Gabrielle."

"Yes, Father, I will remember."

The ship rounded a point. Cypress trees with heavy buttressed trunks pushed their grotesque, snaky knees out of the black swamp water. Water hyacinths, with full purple bloom, choked the streams that flowed into the river. White cranes circled overhead, disturbed in their nesting places by the flap of sails or the sound of voices carried over the water to the swamp. Loneliness, immense and undisturbed. An ancient loneliness that had carried through the centuries.

A log came suddenly to life, raising a long head and great gaping jaws to snap at a mullet that broke the quiet water. Gabrielle put her hand to her mouth to keep from crying out.

"Don't scare at a 'gator." Captain Bragg had come up quietly without her knowledge. "You'll see plenty of the beasties before you've been here a sennight, Miss Gabrielle. Big ones, too, but not so big or so fierce as those down in the Spanish country."

"I thought it was a log," Gabrielle said. "I didn't think of alligators."

The Captain took a pinch of snuff. He sneezed three times into a big red handkerchief. "Well, do you like what you see, Miss Gabrielle, or shall I stop on my way down from Edenton and take you back to the Bahamas?"

Gabrielle smiled. "No, Captain Bragg, you will not have me for a passenger on the return voyage."

"I'm athinkin' there'll be some of yon company that will be applyin' for passage back on the *Delicia*." He motioned his thumb over his shoulder towards the after deck where a little group of settlers stood talking near the piled anchor chain.

"Why do you say that?" said Gabrielle, startled at the sailing master's words.

"Oh, I hear things. Folk think because I'm on the bridge, I don't know what's going on below. That's where I fool them. A captain must have long ears, and have ways of knowing things as go on, on his ship. That is, if he's a good captain," he said without undue modesty.

After a moment she said, "Some of the women complain of the swampland. They didn't know about the swamps, they say. But there is high land also. See up there, under those great oaks with the Spanish moss hanging long from the boughs."

The Captain squinted in the direction Gabrielle pointed, with a morose eye. "Yes, that bank's tolerable high. But there's rutting stags there, and mean brown bears and foxes big enough to attack a man. Timber wolves, too. The sneaking kind that follow a man lost in the wood until he runs clean out of food and lies down to die quietly by starvation. Then those great grey beasts close in on him." He shook his head. "And the snakes! Nothing worse than those pizon swamp snakes——"

"Ever kill a moccasin, Captain?" Roger Mainwairing's voice broke in on the master's gloomy recital.

"No, can't say I have, Mr. Mainwairing, but I've seen aplenty in the water. Poplar leaf, too. Now that's a mighty mean snake; can't tell it from a bunch of brown leaves."

"We've snakes on my plantation in the Albemarle, though I don't think I've killed half a dozen in my life." Roger smiled at Gabrielle. "I'm minded of my Negro Primus. Someone asked him if he had seen any poisonous snakes when he came through the swamp. 'Warn't lookin' fo' none,' Primus answered."

Gabrielle laughed. "I'll remember Primus when I get ashore. I won't be looking for snakes." She turned to the ship's master, "When will we reach Old Town Creek, Captain Bragg?"

The old man squinted at the slack canvas. "Next full moon, if this calm abides much longer," he complained. "With a breath of wind we should anchor off Old Town this afternoon, late."

Robert Fountaine joined the group. His dark eyes were alive with anticipation. "You have not said half enough about the beauty of this Carolina of yours, Mainwairing," he said, waving his thin hand shoreward. "I had no idea the wilderness could be so beautiful. And that timber!"

"Wilderness," grunted the Captain. "Wilderness, an untracked wilderness. It will take a smart two-legged animal to hack his way through that tangle of vine and brier. Why, I've made my way through the Guinea Coast jungles in Africa; 'tweren't as deep as that—and those *blanked* redskins——"

Fountaine watched Bragg stalk away, his heavy shoulders sagging. "The Captain has had great sorrow in his life. Is it not so?"

Roger looked at the Huguenot, surprised at his keen perception. "Yes," he said. "Yes. How did you surmise?"

"Some sorrow that had its foundation in the wilderness. I can see it in his eyes and the words he speaks. A great sorrow that has left great bitterness."

"Yes," Roger repeated. He did not speak of Miss Mittie,

180

the one gentle thing in Bragg's rough, tempestuous life, killed by the Indians in the massacre at Bath Town six years before.

Barton appeared, carrying a little tray with a pot of tea and some hard biscuits. "You must eat something, Miss Gabrielle. You've been on deck since before sunrise, with never a hot wash to comfort your poor little stommick."

Gabrielle shook her head, protesting she did not feel hungry.

"Flutters come to the stommick when one is excited. Take your tea, miss, like a good child." Barton balanced the tray between the rail and her arm and poured a cup. "Drink it all and save yourself. You'll have need of strength before this day is over."

"Drink the tea, Gabrielle," her father said. "I am going below to see my people. I had thought to have a small vesper service on deck tonight at sundown. A thanks to God for giving us safe journey to the New World."

Barton watched him walk away, her face grim. "The guid mon," she said, dropping into Scots. "The puir guid mon," she muttered. "He's fair too guid for such as they."

"What do you mean, Barton?" Gabrielle asked.

Barton shut her lips in a thin line and her features might have been cut from Cotswold stone.

"What are you saying, Barton?"

"Naething, Miss Gabrielle, naething. It's no good anticipating trouble. Time enough as it comes o'er the bridge." She took the tray and walked off.

Gabrielle followed the serving woman with her eyes. It was no use to question Barton when she made up her mind to be silent. She would follow her to the cabin to see if she could be wheedled into plainer speaking. At the foot of the stairs Gabrielle met Celestine. The woman's eyes were round with excitement, and her hands, which held a water ewer, shook.

"Madame is awake! She has asked for her chocolate. She said, 'Celestine, I am hungry. Bring me my chocolate.' She said me by name—Celestine. Oh, Miss Gabrielle, it is weeks since my poor lady has said me by name." Tears ran down her fat cheeks.

Gabrielle's heart beat to suffocation. "God is good," she whispered. "It is an omen. On this, our first day in the new land. A good omen." She wiped the tears from the woman's face with her handkerchief. "I am so glad she said 'Celestine'

181

first of all. You have been so faithful and so kind all the long dreary weeks. The good God will reward you."

"He has already done that. My lady has said my name."

"May I go in?" Gabrielle asked eagerly. "Perhaps she would know me."

"*Non, non,* not yet. I must speak to the Master first, and fetch the chocolate. When she has had the hot drink, she will feel stronger. My dear lady is weak, so very weak. When she raises her little hand you can see through its thinness."

Gabrielle sighed. "Yes, you are right, Celestine, we must not press too closely. I thank God. He has given her back to us this day, this first fair day in our new life."

"Sit beside the door, if you please, Miss Gabrielle. I will hurry." Celestine hastened away towards the galley, where she had long since become a familiar visitor and had the good will of Captain Zeb's black cook.

When Gabrielle came on deck, a few hours later, she saw Mary Treloar and Eunice Caslett sitting under the deck shelter. Both women were knitting heavy grey wool stockings, while several small children played at quoits near by. They glanced up as Gabrielle approached, then looked down at their knitting, their faces expressionless.

The *Delicia* was well upriver, moving easily under light canvas. The river was swifter and the water roiled and muddy, carrying small limbs of trees and brush. Tangles of water plants, still abloom, broken from the banks or lily beds farther inland, floated seaward. The cypress growth at the water's edge was heavy. Great trees waded deep in the water and made an outer bulwark for the marshland. Wild marsh birds rose from the reeds and floated across the low swamp with a lazy sweep of their heavy wings.

Mary Treloar's voice drew Gabrielle's attention. The woman had laid her knitting on her bony knees and turned her deep-set hard black eyes towards Gabrielle. Her voice was harsh and carried accusation in it, as if she held Gabrielle responsible for her woes. " 'Tis God's forsaken country," she said bitterly. "Since early morning I've sat me here on this deck, and never once have I seen human being, no habitation, nor a friendly column of smoke that marked a cottage where humble folk dwelt. Where is this village of Charles Town, where we are bound?"

Taken unprepared, Gabrielle forgot, for a moment, the old Charles Town settlement which was their objective.

"Why, we are far north of Charles Town, Mary. Don't you

182

remember, it is in South Carolina, on the Ashley River and the Cooper?"

Mary brushed the answer aside. " 'Tis not the spindlin' Huguenot colony that I speak of, 'tis the old Charles Town, where my man said we were landing this day. Where is it, I say?" She glanced upward. "Look at the sun; past midday and we be'n't come on the outskirts of a town yet."

Eunice took up the stocking, counting the rows with her long needle. "I did not know it would be like this either; so wild and lonely. I don't like it." Her voice was the flat voice of the deaf. She reached out her hand and drew her small daughter close to her. "I did not know it was wild like this. I thought it would be like the Midlands with a bit of land to farm. Not this swampland." Fear and uncertainty clouded her mild blue eyes.

Gabrielle said, "I think it's beautiful and peaceful. Did you ever see such great oaks?"

The women did not hear her. They had turned again to look at the shores. They did not heed the children who were clapping their small hands with delight as a great blue heron rose from the bank and dropped on a fish breaking water.

"He got the fish in his claws," Eunice's girl cried out. "Mother, Mother, see, he is carrying the fish away in his claws."

"The marsh is horrible: full of rottenness and poisonous creatures." Eunice's face worked painfully. "So lonely, so lonely," she whispered.

"Come, Mrs. Caslett. Look at the children. Do not kill their happiness with your fears."

The woman did not meet Gabrielle's eyes. "I shall die of loneliness. I want to go back. I'll tell Tom I cannot abide the marshes." She rose suddenly and walked away. The long grey stocking coiled on the deck where she had dropped it.

Mary Treloar picked up the knitting and put it into her bag. She had a determined expression on her grim countenance. She moved off without a word to Gabrielle, who stood looking after her. Somehow she had failed her father. She had spoken no words to quiet Eunice's fears. The attitude of the women had had its effect on her. Why could she not have comforted them, given them her own feeling of the beauty and quiet splendour of the land? But she had been speechless under their accusing looks.

She wondered, with sudden trepidation, how far this out-spoken discontent went. Mary Treloar was a strong vigorous woman who spoke her mind. How far did her influence reach? A group of men had their heads together. They were too intent to notice Gabrielle. Broken bits of conversation reached her.

"I've counted hardwoods. Did you ever see so many trees? Oak, poplar, hickory, walnut. I'm thinking I'll have heartwood floors in my new house." Gabrielle recognized Amos Treloar, the Devon man.

" 'Tis well enough to say, Amos, but cutting hardwood is a rare heavy task."

"Mr. Fountaine's brought a little sawmill. Did you not see it in the *Bahama Venture*, with the farm implements? A millstone he has, and the machinery for a fine gristmill. We sha'n't go hungry."

"Too late to plant corn this season," a grizzled old man said. "We'll have to wait a year."

John Caslett broke in: "We're carrying a sight of corn and wheat in hogsheads. Our leader bought food in Charles Town. Where were you lads when the trading was going on at the market-place? Off in some grog shop, swillin' down bad ale. I be tellin' you."

"Ah, John, have done with your preachin'. Just because you be teetotal don't be hard on us lads as want a drap now and then."

A man said, "Why don't you set yourself up as a cabinetmaker, Treloar? I saw the chest you made as we came across. You're better than a joiner or shipwright; you're a rare artist, you are."

A second voice joined in: "Why, yes. Why not, Amos? You can sell your furniture to Captain Woodes Rogers' colony and to Charles Town. Trade, that's what we want. That's the life of the country."

Amos Treloar's eyes were on the river. He said firmly, "I shall build flat-bottomed boats of stout oak. That's what I'll build. Leave the frills to someone who likes that kind of work. See the fish leaping from the water? Mullet. September mullet, a good fish."

"Yes, we must have boats, Amos Treloar, and you're the man to build them. Fish is good eating."

Another voice cut in: "I can scarce wait to turn my spade in the virgin soil—rich soil, never turned by plough."

Gabrielle took comfort. The doubts and fears, the worries were blotted out by the confident words of the men. They were looking ahead, planning for their future, each man

184

thinking in terms of his trade. The great wilderness was nothing to them now. Its hardships had no terrors. They were exhilarated by its richness, its wild fertile abundance.

These men would attack the forest with axe and adze, with saw and plane, and subdue it to their need. They would turn the deep furrow in virgin soil and lay the fruitful land open to the rains and warm sun.

The great panorama of virgin riches, so fertile, so tender, so undiminished by the ruthless havoc of man's necessity for his material wants! Here was a vast country waiting. No more tiny farms, overcrowded cities. Here was the promise of plenty, where a man might look forward, not backward.

Follow the rivers and their rich, lush bottomlands; conquer the wildnerness and the unknown. What splendour life held for men of stout hearts and strong bodies, who had in them the unquenchable fire of conquest, and the courage to fight and conquer!

At vespers Fountaine called his little band of thirty souls to service on deck. The *Delicia* lay becalmed in the middle of the Cape Fear River, off the mouth of a creek whose black water soon disappeared into a tunnel of green trees and greener swamp grasses.

He read, without comment, the story of Moses leading his people out of the wilderness. The settlers sat quietly on deck, their eyes turned shoreward. No words were spoken. They were silent with the strange inner excitement that comes to people at the end of a long journey to an unknown destination.

The thoughts that crowded Robert Fountaine's head did not find utterance on his lips. How could he tell these people what driving force prompted him to face the unknown. Let the Bible speak for him. Let it give voice. Let them all find comfort and guidance from Holy Scripture, as he did, day after day.

Chapter 14

PROMISED LAND

It was late afternoon when the *Delicia* anchored at Old Town Creek. Long shafts of sunlight slanted through the trees on the high bank. In the woods, back from the shore, the shadows lay heavy. The tide was high and the ship made her way slowly, tacking across the shallow bay under a foresail.

Along the rails of the ship the passengers crowded, waiting for a sight of their new home. What picture each one of them had in mind was impossible to tell, but expectancy was high. The background of forest, the winding creek with the high land on one side, were no different than they had been gazing upon in their slow journey upriver for the past twelve hours.

Robert Fountaine watched his people, looked from their expectant faces to the land for the first sight of the stockade and the log houses which marked the site of Sir John Yeamans' settlement. He could see nothing but the bank, overgrown with bushes and a heavy tangle of vines; some with orange lustre-like flowers; others morning glories, white as snow and larger than any he had ever seen. Two deer stood knee deep in the water of the creek, looking up with startled eyes. They stood motionless for a moment, then crashed into the bushes, leaping a great log of cypress that had fallen into the stream from the bank above.

There was no docking place. A few rotting piles on the north bank marked the place where a road ended and a dock had been. The roadway was overgrown and tangled into an almost impenetrable barrier of vines and brambles. A wilderness of trees grew along the bank without an opening, and there was only a small stretch of beach showing at high tide.

"This can't be the place," Farmer Caslett said, his harsh voice breaking the silence and reverberating against the bank. " 'Twas set to farms, so Mr. Fountaine said: fields that had been planted and had felt the plough. 'Tis a wilderness, this, a domned wilderness, I'm athinkin'."

His words let loose a torrent of disappointment and despair for the people at the ship's rail, the heavy voices of men pierced by the shrill voices of women.

"He said there'd be houses ready! And a stockade to protect us from the red Indians."

"God's mercy! What is this we've come to? I knew all the time we weren't canny to trust a Huguenot, a refugee Frenchman."

"I shall stay on the ship!" a woman cried hysterically. Gabrielle recognized Eunice Caslett's voice. "I shall go back. The Bahamas are better than this."

Fountaine's face was white, but he stepped forward, his eyes boring into those of the yeomen.

Gabrielle watched him, her heart heavy with anxiety. She, too, was cast down by the desolation, the heavy threat of the forest, the gloom of the mouldering swampland. It was cruel to bring them here, cruel and tragic.

Fountaine raised his hand. "Listen, men," he said without raising his voice. "Wait until you have seen the plateau above the bank, where the farms lie. As for the houses, Mr. Whitechurch, the Secretary of the Lords Proprietors, wrote explicit instructions to Deputy Thomas Pollock, of Edenton, to send men down to put the places in repair for us. The letter went off two ships preceding the *Delicia*. They sailed the shorter way, via Boston. Let us not despair until we have investigated, and if we do not find things to our liking . . ." He paused a moment.

John Caslett broke in: "Let's make them to our liking. Many among you have raised a rooftree and laid a sill before this day; aye, and thatched a hut. So I say, like our leader, let's not despair."

Farmer Neely stepped forward, his face dark. "Well enough to speak fine words, Johnny, but doing is another thing. I say, let's go ashore and see for ourselves what may be on the top of the bank."

"Aye. That is well," said half a dozen men. "Let's see for ourselves."

Gabrielle looked about anxiously. Her father, having said what he had to say, turned away. She watched him, her heart beating swiftly. She had known of men mutinying on ships. Captain Rogers had told them of more than one occasion when he had "taken a strong hand" to quell an uprising. Her father would not take strong measures. He would say his say and have done.

She heard footsteps. She looked over her shoulder. Captain Bragg and Roger Mainwairing were strolling down the deck, talking quietly. Somehow she knew they had overheard the talk and were coming to her father's assistance.

The Captain stood at the rail, a little apart from the group of angry men, sweeping the shore with his spyglass. "I won't put up the creek until daybreak, when the tide's running in. It's better so. It's better for the ship and for the men. 'Tis possible that there might be redskins in the woods at this time of year."

"Redskins?" Farmer Neely stepped up. "Did you say redskins? Dommit all, man, they told us the redskins were peaceable-like."

"So they are," the Captain said, the glass still at his eye. "So they are. But they come down the river this time of year to go fishing on the Banks—crabbing and clamming. They are peaceable enough. But the point is: Are the white men peaceable? That's what they don't know, and if they are camping at Old Town, 'tis better they are approached peaceable-like first, before a crowd of men, women and children swarm ashore on their camping ground."

" 'Tis a right idea you have, Captain," one of the elder of the Shore brothers said. "We must step softly, and not rush into the unknown."

"Besides," the Captain continued, "I won't let 'ary one of you ashore until daylight comes; so ye may go back to your places and settles yourselves comfortable."

There was some discussion, but the Captain did not listen. He turned to Robert Fountaine. "With your permission, Mr. Fountaine, I planned to have a supper tonight, something special." He grinned his toothless smile. "The Captain's dinner, as it were, to bid ye all farewell on your last night aboard the *Delicia*." He looked expectantly at Fountaine.

"You are very thoughtful," Robert Fountaine said, "very thoughtful. I am sure all of us will be pleased to attend the Captain's dinner."

Captain Zeb walked across the deck, turned and said as an afterthought, "Ladies, better pin on your ribands and get out your finery, for I'm going to give you a surprise dinner. Something you've never eaten before, something which belongs to Carolina—and remember, it is the full of the moon tonight."

A woman laughed. "I shall get out my green taffeta, Captain."

They rustled away towards their quarters, talking and laughing, followed by questing children. "A party, Mother? A really party?" The men followed more soberly, perhaps not quite satisfied.

Captain Zeb wiped his bald head with a great red silk handkerchief. "Whew! That took some talking! More talking, Mr. Mainwairing, than I've done since I talked myself out of trouble with the Barbary pirates."

Roger laughed. "I was right behind you, ready to take up where you left off. But I need not have worried. Your dinner turned the trick."

Gabrielle looked at her father; he was standing at the rail, facing the shore, his lips moving in prayer. She realized that he had not been aware of the design behind Captain Bragg's words, nor Mr. Mainwairing's. He was taking his trouble to his God, as he always had done.

She looked into Roger Mainwairing's kind, understanding eyes. "I can never thank you enough," she said, watching the Captain climb the narrow steps to the high bridge. "He came at the right time, said the right words. Oh, Mr. Mainwairing, sometimes I wonder." She drew her breath inward, so that she would not say the words that were on her tongue. Her loyalty to her father forbade saying the thing that was in both their minds. How would he be able to lead disgruntled, disappointed men? Had he the stamina to lead them to a successful colonization in this dark wilderness?

Roger took her hand. "My child, I've seen men—devout, quiet men, like your father—inspire the greatest loyalty. I think it will be like that with him. His very gentleness is his strength."

Tears came to Gabrielle's eyes. "I am ashamed that I faltered a moment," she said, her voice very low. "Ashamed. I should have remembered. Christ was a gentle man, gentle and quiet."

"He turned the other cheek to His enemies." Roger spoke soberly.

He was interrupted by the appearance of the mate and two seamen, armed with a fowling-piece and fishing tackle. They lowered a longboat over the side and rowed up the creek. They were soon out of sight.

"I think they have gone after the Captain's supper," Roger said, a twinkle showing in his blue eyes. "Let's wish them good fortune, so that we may have a good dinner."

As Gabrielle turned to go to her cabin, she saw the small

189

schooner that carried the remainder of their company, the farm animals and horses. She smiled a little, watching the flapping sails catch an offshore breeze; David Moray was aboard the *Bahama Venture*. Her heart beat faster when she thought of him.

They and the young yeomen and their wives would bring youth and enthusiasm. They would not hold back for danger or hardship. Suddenly her fears left her. The symbol of her mother's return to consciousness came to her mind. It was a good omen. Surely all would go well now.

She had not seen her mother, nor had her father. After her breakfast Madam Fountaine had fallen into a natural sleep. How long it had been! Ever since the Irish mob stormed the weaving room and the rock crashed through the window. She could never forget her terror when she saw her dear mother, white and still, on the floor, the blood flowing from the ugly cut on her temple. Ever since that time, those periods of unconsciousness had come, like an ever-flowing wave, now light, now heavy. The doctor had given them assurances of her ultimate recovery. But her memory had not returned. She seemed unaware of the passing of time; days seemed only a night's repose to her, and sometimes an hour seemed an eternity, when she woke, querulous and fretful, scarcely recognizing her husband or Gabrielle or good, faithful Celestine.

Ah, well. In new surroundings, it would be different; of that Gabrielle felt sure. The sun was down, and a gentle breeze came up that wafted away the heat of the afternoon, a soft, languorous breeze that touched her cheek gently. The tide turned outward, towards the sea, evenly, and from the land she heard the song of birds, as clear and high and melodious as their own nightingale. She took off her frock, slipped a dressing robe over her shoulders and lay down on the cot to rest, falling instantly into a deep and dreamless sleep.

Barton wakened her. It was near to six o'clock, she announced, and great preparations were going on for the dinner, which would be served on deck within the hour. Gabrielle turned and stretched her white arms above her head. Her dark hair, unpinned, hung in two long plaits over her shoulder. Barton said, "There's a hot drink of tea on the table and Mr. Colston sent you flowers for your hair." She held up a long vine of small pointed green leaves with snowwhite glories. Gabrielle read the paper Barton had given her:

"A wreath for your hair. I went ashore to gather the first Carolina blooms for you. I attempted to compose a sonnet to my lady's tresses, but I got lost in the mazes of time and rhyme and gave up. I have made friends with your Captain Zeb, so that he will seat me near you at his dinner. Heavenly Day, how long it has been since I have seen you, my sweet friend! Can you imagine my exasperation to have the sails of your ship constantly within vision, and not see you? Until the supper hour—

"EDWARD

"I have a packet of letters from Molly Lepel and some others which arrived in Nassau the day after the *Delicia* sailed."

Gabrielle smiled as she slipped the spray of flowers into the water ewer on the washing stand. She laughed at Edward's nonsense, but in her heart she was pleased.

"Mr. Colston is a fair, gentleman and has as many years to his credit as yourself, Miss Gabrielle." Barton spoke primly. "I'd be thinking of that, my Mistress, and think a little of his grandfather, the richest merchant in all of Bristol."

The laughter left Gabrielle's eyes at the maid's words. "No matter what his grandfather's position may be, he is in Bristol. In Carolina a man must stand on his own feet, not in his grandfather's shoes."

Barton rattled the wash basin to show her complete disapproval of such utterance, but she said no more. She could convey more disapproval by her silence than by her words, a fact of which she was fully aware. She went about laying out Gabrielle's underpetticoats and chemise, and a pair of bright crimson sandals to go with the ruffled white dimity frock.

"The deck is dirty," Gabrielle suggested, "and the rope and chains are tarred."

" 'Tis an occasion," Barton said shortly, "and I know ways of removing tar." Gabrielle laughed. It was only a few short months ago Barton had scolded her for walking along the Bristol waterways, because she got tar on her skirt.

"You are a romantic old dear," she said, giving Barton a squeeze which disarranged her prim, fluted mob-cap.

"Have done with child's play," the maid said, but Gabrielle knew she was not displeased.

The moon had risen. It laid a full, rippling path on the breast of the river from the far shore, breaking into sparkling fragments against the sides of the ships. The stars were luminous and close, a great blue canopy spread with light.

Gabrielle thought she could reach them with her hands. Above the trees, the evening star glowed.

"What luck! Venus in the ascendency tonight." A gay voice interrupted her meditation. Gabrielle turned to find Edward Colston coming towards her from the shadows of the charthouse. He wore a brocaded coat and flowered waistcoat and his breeches were heavy silk, as if he were on the way to the pump room at Bath.

Behind him was Roger Mainwairing. He, too, was well coated, more sombre, but as richly dressed. Both men wore small swords. Edward's hair was tied back in the new fashion that had just made its appearance in London.

Gabrielle thought that Barton was right. Edward Colston surely was a fair, fine gentleman, for all his grandfather was in trade. But so was her own father, for that matter. Why should she feel superior to a man in trade, when she was the daughter of a weaver? Such thoughts must be banished. This is a New World, without class or distinction among peoples.

"You look too serious, much too serious for a gala fête."

Gabrielle touched the wreath of white glory that bound her smooth black braids. "Thank you. It is lovely."

"You have honoured me by wearing my flowers," he said hand to sword hilt, bowing deeply.

"Stars in your hair," Roger Mainwairing said, joining them. "How appropriate for you!"

"Edward Colston found them on the shore. Was he not thoughtful?"

Roger glanced at the youth. He looked a little sulky to have had the tête-à-tête interrupted, but he was too good-humoured a person to be annoyed long.

"By gad! What splendid odours arise from the galley! Methinks the Captain is outdoing himself."

The ship's gong sounded. Gabrielle looked around for her father. She saw him walking along the deck with the ship's master.

"May I offer my arm?" Edward Colston said.

Gabrielle smiled and laid her hand lightly on his crooked arm. She held out her other hand towards Roger. "I think I am a fortunate girl, to have two escorts to my first supper in Carolina."

The sailors had made tables of planks and sawbucks across the after deck; on these long tables they had spread the supper.

The grinning black cook came from the galley. He was

closely followed by two half-grown boys carrying a great iron pot, swung on a pole. From it came most entrancing odours. The cook and two messboys managed to set a tripod, from which the iron pot was swung.

Captain Bragg came up with Robert Fountaine. When they had taken their places, the others found seats. The Captain nodded to his cook. "Bring on the Brunswick stew," he ordered. "And tell Hector to pass the fish."

"Fish?" someone called.

"Fresh fish," Bragg said proudly. "My men caught them upcreek, five pounders."

"Five pounders? Did you say a five-pound game fish?" The men looked at one another, pleasure showing in their faces.

"And rabbit and squirrel for the Brunswick stew," the ship's master added. "That's my surprise—Brunswick stew, as good a dish as a woodsman ever tasted. Mr. Fountaine, if you will say grace, these good people may start eating."

Robert Fountaine bowed his head.

> "For this food, Lord, we thank Thee.
> May we eat with Thy blessing."

The people ate fresh food with zest. But one or two men and more than one woman sat silent and did not join the gaiety induced by the food and the Captain's good Madeira.

Gabrielle noticed Mary and Eunice. They ate sparingly and had no laughter on their lips. She saw Roger Mainwairing shrewdly observing a group of men who sat apart at the end of the table. Whatever was going on, Roger Mainwairing was aware of the implication. Discontent on an expedition she was sure he would not tolerate. From what knowledge she had gained of the planter's character on the way over, she knew he would punish insubordination swiftly and with severity commensurate with the offence.

She thought of his conduct at Nassau, when the pirates had threatened to unseat Governor Rogers. She remembered his stern, set features as he rode with Woodes Rogers from the ship wharf up the hill to Government House, between the rows of pirates bristling with sidearms. He was without fear, but with that instinctive caution that belongs to brave men, who count recklessness a sign of stupidity.

Try as she would, Gabrielle could not see her father meeting the responsibilities that would attend this Carolina adventure in the way a Woodes Rogers or a Roger Mainwairing would meet them, with firmness bordering on brutality, if the occasion demanded.

The thought brought back that old feeling of fear at the pit of her stomach. Her father had no physical fear, but he was too saintly to combat ruthless, brutal people. Perhaps his saintliness would hold rebellious colonists in check, but she wondered.

Her thoughts were broken by Bragg's rough voice calling for silence. The Captain was standing at his place at the head of the long table.

"It is the privilege of the master of a vessel to make a speech on the last night of a successful voyage. I am more at home shouting on the quarter deck than saying fine words. I have asked Mr. Roger Mainwairing to speak instead. You all know him well from the voyage. During the pirates' attack ye saw him in action. But ye have no knowledge of Mr. Mainwairing as a planter, and as a planter, he is a most successful one, I may say. He will hold talk with you now. Mr. Mainwairing."

Roger Mainwairing rose to his feet and took a place behind the tablebench, against the background of the dark wooded shore line. The moonlight was on his face. Shadows thrown by the ship's lanthorns, swung from the rigging, fell upon the men and women at the tables. They were quiet and expectant, leaning forward, their eyes fixed on the man they had come to respect during the long voyage from Bristol.

"Looks like a stone figure," Edward said in Gabrielle's ear. "Strong, and all that."

Gabrielle put her finger to her lips. "Hush."

Edward leaned back, fingering the ruffles at his wrist and neckband, as if indifferent to the company and the planter, as indeed he was. His eyes turned to Gabrielle's face. He could look at her now, unabashed by any reprimand she might speak. She was watching Roger Mainwairing, listening to what he said with undivided interest.

Edward moved slightly, piqued that he could not attract her attention. After a moment, Mainwairing's quiet spoken words held him, reluctant as he was to admit to himself the planter's command over the company.

"You are tonight in the position I was in one evening, years ago, when I sailed up the Albemarle Sound and anchored off the tiny village that is now known as Edenton, then Queen Anne's Town.

"The soft breeze off the water was pleasant; the shadows

194

of the shore, pierced by fireflies' lamps, drew me. Instead of waiting, I went ashore. The dusk covered all defects of the village. It was a spot of romance. Soft voices of women, sitting in the galleries, behind vines of jasmine and honeysuckle; the heavy voices of men answering; men on fine horses riding down the street, followed by Negro grooms carrying lanthorns; the post lights at the cross streets, and the village green. The moon rising, almost at the full, fell on cypress trees standing deep in the dark water."

He paused a moment, turning his head slightly towards the shore, where the cypress swamp reached out from the land and waded into the river.

"I resolved that this place was the one I had been searching for. It has been my home for years now, and never once have I regretted my decision of that July night.

"The country was a wilderness. Only a few staunch spirits had fought the wilderness and built permanently—old James Blount and Pollock, Lillington and Edward Moseley; the Quakers, at Hertford, a few miles eastward; the Harveys and Durants and the Skinners, and all their kin and connections.

"I mention these names because you will meet them again and again, as you develop the Cape Fear. Your problem in establishing your homes, planting, developing trade, will be the same that the Albemarle planters and the planters on the Ashley and Cooper have already met. You will have their experience to guide you, if you wish to draw on it."

He turned then towards the Huguenot, Fountaine.

"Mr. Fontaine has only to ask and we will be glad to help, in giving advice about planting, in augmenting his stock of seeds, or enlarging his herds and flocks."

He stood silent for a moment, looking down as if lost in some recollection of past hardships, then took up his story where he had left off.

"We have treaties now with King Blont of the Tuscarora Indians. If you are wise in your treatment of the coastal tribes, you need have no repetition of Indian war. If you are tolerant in your religion, you need have no repetition of religious wars.

"You will have the privilege of living under the greatest freedom ever given to man, our Fundamental Constitution, devised by Locke and the Earl of Shaftesbury. But—" here he paused, his searching eyes following the company down the long table—"soon you will be raising your own rooftrees. Nothing can quite equal that, save perhaps—" he waited a moment; his voice took on a sterner tone—"the moment when your first-born is laid in your arms.

"Half a dozen planters from the Albemarle and Charles Town settlers have already taken up grants along the river. The Moores, Lillingtons, Swans, Moseley and I have grants farther up the river. We hope to develop a trade in naval stores, tar, pitch and turpentine, cedar poles, resin. I believe in the future of this river. Plant the land. Let the forest furnish you with masts and planks for building ships. Let it feed you and protect you.

"It will not be easy, this fight for new land. You must give labour or the land will not yield its fruitfulness. I speak as a planter, not as a trader. Trade comes after planting. Hard work, loneliness, frugal living, until the harvest.

"But there is this thing to remember: Carolina is not a land for the weak. It wants men of strength and fortitude and high endeavour. It wants no timid souls, afraid of the forest and river and marsh.

"We want men and women of strength and substance, who will build and not destroy. Only by these can we conquer and build this generous, fertile land into a great empire.

"Tomorrow you will put foot on shore. Whether you walk into a reconstructed village, or the ruins of an old one, you will have made a great stride forward. One day you will say to yourself, 'That day was the turning of my good fortune.'

"I am reminded, as I look at your faces, eager with anticipation, of something Captain Woodes Rogers said to us one night when we were crossing the Western Ocean: 'Necessity has more than once sent simple private men on a noble undertaking.' I have often thought of his words. Surely the colonization of this New World is a noble undertaking. Its success rests on the united endeavour of simple private men."

He sat down. There was a long silence. Gabrielle's heart seemed to beat in her throat, choking her. Tears came to her eyes. Even Edward was still, his bold eyes on Mainwairing. No one stirred or spoke. Men and women rose, quietly filed past Roger Mainwairing. Some of them shook his hand, thanking him with their words or their eyes.

Gabrielle looked up and saw David Moray among the unmarried men seated at the end of the long table. His eyes met hers and lingered for a moment.

Edward Colston grasped Roger's hand. "For the first time I feel my good fortune in coming to Carolina, one of a band of valiant men who have built and will sustain her."

Gabrielle waited until all were gone. "Thank you. Thank you," she said, her voice scarcely above a whisper. "Thank you for my father and for his people."

Roger looked down into her wide, dark eyes. He saw that she knew the reason behind his words. "It was the least I could do for a splendid gentleman. I could not endure to see discontent rise, without making my endeavour to crush it at the beginning."

She repeated, "One day you will know how much I thank you."

That night, before moon fall, two ships slipped over the shoals at high tide and took harbour behind the banks of Topsail Inlet, not many miles downriver from where the *Delicia* lay. Flags flew from the masts, black flags with white skulls and crossbones.

Men dressed in weathered velvets and woollens, stained by salt spray and wind, climbed down ropes and into small boats and rowed to the sandy beach of Barren Head. There they made fires and roasted a pig, and broke open a keg of Jamaica rum with an axe.

All night they drank possets and took turns in digging deep into the sand, under the palm trees of the island.

A tall, wiry man, well favored, of good bearing, stood on a high sand dune, watching them, his hand on his belt, where cutlash and pistol were close to his fingers' ends. Stede Bonnet, the Huguenot pirate, watched his men bury treasure from sacked Cartagena and the Spanish Main and the Caribbean islands. He trusted no one, not even his partner in crime, Rackham, and least of all did he trust Anne Bonney, Rackham's pirate wife, or her familiar, Mary Read.

The pirates sat on the beach, eating well-done pig garnished with roasted sweet potatoes, and drank their rum neat, without diluting it with sweet water or a dash of fresh Cuban lime. Evil company kept Stede Bonnet, for a gentleman of France. Evil company. Did coffers filled with gold compensate for the life he had lost? For family, friends and high position? No one knew. None could read in his face the thoughts that tortured him each time he took life. Gold and jewels exacted their price in manhood and honour, and Bonnet knew this. He had known it since the day he saw the tall daughter of the Huguenot Fountaine walk up the hill to Government House and the party of the new Governor, Captain Woodes Rogers.

Something in the calm serenity of her clear features, the straightforward look of her large eyes made the evil thoughts that had so long been a part of him fall away and leave him as he once was, with laughter and good feeling for everyone in his gay heart.

The men on Barren Head completed digging. Their feast consumed, Bonnet's harsh voice ordered them back to their ships. They went reluctantly, some staggering, others dragging the drunken by heels or shoulders.

Anne Bonney came over to the dune where Bonnet stood alone. She laid her white hands on his arm. The men's clothes she wore revealed her sweet feminine charm. Her deeds of violence had not brutalized her as they had Mary Read. She grew with the months more lovely; her pale blond beauty took on a more delicate charm.

She pressed close to him in the shadows. Rackham and Mary Read, hidden from them in the dunes, were on their way to board the vessel.

"Stede. Stede," she whispered. "If there is a child, it will be yours, not Rackham's."

"You lie," Bonnet retorted. "You lie! It will be no more mine than Vane's or Rackham's or half a dozen other men's."

The girl drew back as if hit by a lash. "You hurt with your insults. Only you have that power, because I am mad for you."

"It will not be my child," he repeated, but his tone was not so grim, nor his denial so firm.

"I swear to you, Stede. It was the night on the beach at Nassau. The night you refused to take the King's Pardon, from Woodes Rogers' hand. Don't you remember? You took me in your arms, and told me my body was warm and soft for loving and forgetting."

The man did not reply. The woman pressed against his side, swung around in front of him, her arms about his waist, drawing him to her. Her mouth was close. His lips came to hers with a firmness that hurt her. She moaned softly, glad to be hurt by the pressure of his lips, by the strength of his firm body against her yielding.

"I do not love you," he said, wanting to hurt her.

"You find solace in me," she rejoiced. "Only in me. Not in the women you take captive and force to submission. Oh, Stede, it's not submission you want. You want what I can give—passion to meet your passion—fire to meet your need,"

His lips went down on hers, smothering her words.

After a long time she said, "I sleep with Rackham no more. Never since that night at Nassau." He said nothing, but his arm was hard about her. "Do you remember the waves pounding against the shore?"

"Rackham is a coward." Bonnet spoke with contempt.

"I found out too late." The girl's bitterness was in her voice. "Courage I must have in a man. Courage and no cringing fear." She sighed. "When one has mated with the eagle, one cannot endure the crow," she said after a silence.

"You're a bold woman, Anne, bold as a man." His praise came grudgingly. Why should the clear, clean features of a young girl come between him and this strong, desirable woman in his arms? He would blot out thought of her, lose her in the arms of this fierce, burning woman.

"Bold as a man, but soft as a woman." Anne laughed, a deep-throated laugh. "It is the woman who is near you now, waiting, Stede, waiting."

"You are a very devil!" His voice was gay and warm. He drew her to the shadow of the palm trees, pressed hard against her yielding body. "A very devil."

"The eagle and the devil," she whispered. "A noble battle, my Stede."

Gabrielle, unable to rest, stood at the door of her deck cabin, looking eastward. The bright moon made the river a shimmering roadway of silver, moving seaward. Suddenly her eyes were arrested by a column of smoke drifting skyward, pink tinted with the glow. Fire a long way downriver, it seemed to her, almost at the entrance to the sea. The red smoke disturbed her. Did it mean danger to them? Indians? A pirate ship taking refuge within the shelter of the Banks?

She stood for a long time, looking eastward. Perhaps it was not evil, but a favourable portent, sent to guide them. "A column of smoke by day, a pillar of fire by night."

Chapter 15

WHAT WENT YE OUT INTO THE WILDERNESS TO SEE?

Morning brought fog. A heavy miasmic mist rose from the swamp. On the *Delicia* men stood on the decks gazing shoreward, waiting anxiously for sunup, so that the ship's small boats could take them up the creek to the hidden landing place. Five men had been chosen to go ashore with Robert Fountaine—Amos Treloar, John Caslett, the husbandman Neely and the two Shores, steady men, all of them, men who would not be readily discouraged.

By now they were resigned to one thing. The carpenters and joiners had not come down from Edenton, as Fountaine had been promised. They were prepared to see, not newly made log houses, or old ones comfortably repaired, but ruins of an older settlement.

The sun came up, a crimson ball above grey mists. The boats were lowered. Captain Bragg and Roger Mainwairing were to go in one. Three seamen came along to fill the water casks from the creek. Fountaine, David Moray and two yeomen were in the second boat. Gabrielle joined the women who stood at the rail, watching their men row away from the ship towards Old Town Creek. The entrance to the creek was concealed by the water reeds and cane of the swamp.

The women were silent. There was no sound but the *swish* of water against the sides of the boats, the dip of oars and the rattle of oarlocks.

Gabrielle thought, We are people at a play at Drury Lane, waiting for the curtain to rise. We are not real. This lush greenness I see is not real. It is painted on a backdrop of canvas. We are waiting for the actors, not knowing whether it will be tragedy or comedy that will be played before our eyes.

Soon the boats were out of sight, lost in a tunnel of green. She drew a canvas chair to the rail and sat down. She would read Molly's letters now. There had been no time last night. It was a thick packet. Molly was an enthusiastic correspondent, and her letters, like her conversation, were full of gossip and personalities.

> "In care of Mrs. M. Lepel,
> next door to my Lord Carteret's
> in Albemarle Street.

"MY LITTLE GABY:

"Did you see the tears running down my cheeks when you stood on the deck of the *Delicia* looking so statuesque, in your brave crimson cloak?

"I wept, 'deed I did; my eyes were streaming and I thought not at all of my appearance. My heart was ice. You, my darling, and my darling Uncle Robert carried away from me, out on the stormy sea to some unknown world.

"I watched Captain Woodes Rogers (What a handsome man, my dear! I envied you, sitting at his table day after day) on the bridge, giving orders in that fine clear voice of authority, so strong, so different from the thin, lisping voices of our fine gentlemen. I watched the strip of water widen between the dock and the ship, and I wept aloud. That is, until I heard a voice say, 'May I offer my shoulder, and my handkerchief?'

"My dear, I swear by Venus, guardian of lovers, that I did not raise my eyes, but before I knew it, my cheek was against a man's shoulders and I was wiping my eyes with a fine cambric handkerchief that smelt of amber.

"When I realized what I had done, I pulled back. 'Unhand me sir,' I said to save my dignity.

"'As my lady wishes,' and I was standing without support. I ventured, then, to look upward through my lashes (I swear this is a telling trick of the eyes, Gaby. Try it some time, on that very nice Edward Colston, from Bristol, whose grandfather owns all the *Venture* ships.)

"What I saw made me sorry I had not looked earlier, and stayed against that strong shoulder longer.

"A divine man with such an air, and dressed in the very latest mode. Such eyes, and a gallant moustache, and his hair set to the latest fashion. He was smiling, and I had the very good fortune to blush naturally, without holding my breath.

"'You are overcome,' he said solicitously.

"'Indeed, yes. My guardian and my dearest confidant have sailed away to the New World.'

"'Ah,' he said. 'With the Bahama settlers?'

"'No, they go to Carolina, to take up their grant of land on the Cape Fear River.'

"'Ah, the Pirates' River.'

"'Why do you say that?' I said, alarmed.

"'Because the lower Cape Fear and the Banks, along the Carolina coast, harbour a host of pirates! Blackbeard, Vane,

Rackham, Stede Bonnet and half a hundred others, including the two women pirates, Mary Read and Anne Bonney.'

"'You are well informed about pirates,' I said, hoping my voice sounded cutting.

"The gentleman laughed. (By this time we were walking towards my chair, where my aunt's woman was waiting for me.) 'Indeed yes. I come from the Indies, and I sail the Carolina coast. I am captain of one of his Majesty's privateers, at your service.' He put his hand on his sword hilt and made a fine bow, raising his eyebrows, waiting for me to say my name. But I didn't tell him, not then. I slipped on my vizard, for we were at the docks and many mean-looking ruffians were about us.

"'When may I see you again?' he asked.

"'Never,' I said, frightened at his boldness. 'Never.'

"'Never is a long time, and London is small. You go perhaps to the masquerade, after Nicholi's performance at the theatre?'

"As a matter of truth, I was going with Teresa and Martha Blount, who are in town now, at their house, near my Lord Salisbury's, in King Street by St. James's Square.

"'Indeed no. I do not attend the theatre.'

"'Then you go to Ranleigh's, or down to Twickenham on the river, or to St. Paul's of a Sunday.'

"'I attend St. Michael's in the Fields,' I said before I thought.

"'Ah! How pleasant! My name saint. I am sure St. Michael will bring us together one day. Perhaps tomorrow, since it's Sunday.'

"'Tomorrow I am going to Mapledurham.'

"'Ah!' he said smiling. He said nothing more, but put me into my chair.

"My aunt's woman looked on with stern disapproval, until my fine captain walked around to her window. I saw him slip a coin into her hand. I thought he would follow my chair, but he did not. He stood quite still until we were out of sight.

"'A very fine gentleman,' the woman said. 'I presume he is a friend of your guardian's?'

"I swear I had not the slightest intention of telling even a white lie; I was gravely astonished to hear the words from my lips: 'Captain Cary is a friend of Gabrielle Fountaine's,' and the lie didn't burn my tongue in the least.

"'Ah, inded.' My aunt's women settled back in the chair. She was disappointed. No romance in that. These women are terrible harpies. They make a small fortune in accepting fees from the young gallants who pursue fashionable women. Sometimes they arrange assignations, or even kidnappings, when some bold young lordling seeks a new mistress. All this is embroidered to make a fine tale. You know it is Michael, whom you saw at the dock.

"But I forgot my great news: I am to go to Mapledurham for a fortnight with Miss Martha Blount. You know I adore her, and there is always such refined, intellectual society at their home. Not dull, oh no. All the great wits gather about Miss Martha and Miss Teresa. First, Mr. Pope, who is their daily visitor, Mr. Addison, Mr. Steele and that very young and attractive Mr. Fielding. They say he starves in a garret in order to write a great novel. He won't take money from his father, with whom he quarrels about writing books.

"He is a cousin of Lady Mary Wortley Montagu, and for a wonder she is friendly towards him, and doesn't turn her biting wit on him as she does on others.

"Lord Hervey is mad about her (nobody seems to' remember her husband, Mr. Montagu). This worries my Aunt Lepel, for she is determined to get him for my cousin Mary. I can't see why. Hervey is unhandsome and he has fits, and diets on the most peculiar things, to keep from having them—fits, I mean. But he has position. He is wealthy, and it will be a step up the ladder. If I were seeking position, I'd turn my eyes towards Lord John Carteret, who lives next door to my aunt, in Albemarle Street. He is patrician, and his wife, the plump Carteret, can't live forever, they say.

"Heigho! All this amuses me, but not you, my serious Gabrielle. You are burning to be a builder in a new world. I am content to live in the glamour of the old, even as a poverty-stricken cousin, who fetches and carries for a temperamental aunt and a jealous cousin.

"The reason that I like Mapledurham is, I am myself there, Molly Lepel. Miss Teresa and Miss Martha like me. We play on the harpsichord and we read French novels. Miss Teresa was born in Paris, so she cannot inherit this wonderful little gem of an Elizabethan house, Mapledurham. But she will have heaps of pounds sterling, instead.

"Now I must close this for tonight. I wonder if I shall ever see Michael Cary again? Something tells me I will.

"You naughty girl, why did you not tell me that you were taking your handsome gardener with you? I do not trust the man. Twice I saw him standing under your window in the middle of the night. He is either in love with you or he is planning to murder you.

"No more nonsense tonight, for I must sleep to be in good health for my trip down into Oxfordshire to Mapledurham tomorrow.

"Oh yes, one of the guests will be Lord Bolingbroke. You know he is the great friend of Mr. Pope. I like him. He is a man of power.

"Kisses—from your worldly friend

MOLLY"

"April 23, 1718
"P. S. I liked Mr. Roger Mainwairing's wife Rhoda. She has

203

asked me to visit her in the Midlands. Perhaps I will later, for then I can get away from my dear aunt and cousin, but right now I do feel inclined to leave London, I might, by chance, meet the handsome Michael.

"P. S.

"MAPLEDURHAM

"Sunday, three days later.

"I had not sealed your letter, which was good fortune. Now I can make an exciting addition. On Friday, who should come out by coach but my adventurous Captain, Michael Cary! It seems he is sometimes a guest here. So he got himself an invitation. He is handsomer and more fascinating than I dreamed; and so mysterious! I don't know what it is, but he conceals something. I feel that he is not wholly frank. He pays attention to all the women present, including the brazen Duchess D—— that Harry Fielding is so mad about. However, it is good fun. I am glad to meet him here, instead of at Aunt Lepel's, where I am constantly belittled as a poor relation. Heigho! You have the easier life, my sweet friend. You have nothing to keep you from planting your garden and making a bare house into a home, while I have to use my wits. I am determined to make a good match. But how can that be managed, when I have no dot worth the mentioning? Perhaps Cary, coming from the Plantations, will not be interested in the size of a maiden's dot, as are the young gallants of London. By the way, the country squires still wear the Monmouth cock, and when they go a-wooing they put on a red coat!"

Gabrielle slipped the letter into her writing case. Out of all the long letter one fact only made an impression on her mind. The sentence about their gardener, David Moray. Molly could not have been speaking the truth about seeing him standing beneath her window in Meg's Lane. Molly was flighty, with little regard for truth.

"Why do you look so troubled on such a fine midsummer morning? Has the spritely Molly written a tale of woe?"

Gabrielle looked up. Edward Colston drew a canvas stool across the deck to her side. He looked in fine spirits, with untroubled brow and clear eyes, although she knew some of the men had drunk deep last night after the women and her father had retired. She had heard the Captain's voice, and Roger Mainwairing's. She was sure it was late when he left the *Delicia,* for she heard the boat being lowered, and Colston calling good night in a gay, cheerful voice.

"On the contrary, she is extraordinarily cheerful." Gabrielle smiled.

"Ah, a new love affair. That girl is bound to have a dozen gallants at a time, she is so gay."

"Men like gaiety in women?" Gabrielle spoke before she thought that the question might be taken as disapproval of Molly Lepel.

"Indeed yes! It pleasures them, when they are seeking a good time."

"And that is all the time," Gabrielle retorted.

"Please. Please. Don't *you* fall into the fashionable habit of sarcasm. The delight you give us poor men is your frankness, your natural wit; not the fashionable London ladies' aping of Lady Mary Montagu and her circle."

Gabrielle laughed. Edward's dismay was so plainly written on his mobile features. He was a nice person, she thought. "Very well. I shall be natural. Really it would be hard to be otherwise. I haven't the brain for posing. It takes so much energy to act a part, and such a good memory."

Edward Colston dropped his superficial manner. "You asked me if men liked gaiety in women. I said yes, but that is not all the truth. A man could easily tire of a woman who was all gaiety. There are times when one wants to go deeper than the surface. I, too, will be frank. I was so much interested in your Molly Lepel. I saw her half a dozen times and my head and heart were in a whirl; I went so far as to talk with my grandfather about her."

Gabrielle's face showed her interest, but she said nothing.

"He told me to ask myself if I could stand gaiety and frivolity at breakfast and lunch, at tea and at dinner. Put that way, I knew I could not. So I did not see Molly again."

"You're unfair, Edward. You made no attempt to find out if there is another side to Molly. I assure you there is. She is impulsive. She makes an effort to be gay when she is in company; but I do assure you that she has her bad moments, when her heart is heavy."

Colston fingered the seals dangling from his watch. "I am glad to hear you say that, Gabrielle. . . . I may call you Gabrielle, may I not? . . . Perhaps I have been hasty. But it is too late now. Before I sailed from Bristol, I was for a month in London. I was told in London that Molly was seeing a good deal of Michael Cary."

"Michael Cary?" She tried to speak as if she had never heard the name.

"A privateer captain from the West Indies, I think he claims to be. Privateer implies so much these days. It may mean a captain in the King's service, set on legitimate business for our government; or it may mean something a little less than a pirate——"

"And Michael Cary?" she asked.

"I don't know whether he is a privateer or a pirate. But I do know that he is reckless and swaggering. You know—the kind all women adore."

"And who adores all women?"

Edward's glance was one of approval. "You *are* quick," he said, and let the subject rest.

The conversation gave Gabrielle some small worry. Edward Colston was the type of man Molly should marry. There was honesty and a fine, straightforward look in his blue eyes. A man to trust, she would say. But how could she speak for unpredictable Molly? Molly's London connections with the fine world would look down on a merchant, even the grandson of a merchant prince.

After a silence Colston said: "I suppose Mainwairing told you that the Edenton workmen who were supposed to be here to repair the houses have not come?"

Gabrielle turned her eyes from the shore. "No, he did not tell me, but I was afraid my father had not allowed enough time for the letter to arrive at Edenton and the men to get here. What will happen now?" she asked, dropping her voice so that the women seated across from them would not hear.

Colston hesitated. "I don't know. I only hope that Mainwairing's talk last night will influence the settlers so that they will not make any hasty decision if things go wrong in the beginning. Mr. Mainwairing has great influence. The men admire him because he has struggled and overcome the obstacles that were in his way. They will listen to a man whom they respect."

"It was good of him to address them last night. He has been a strong support to my father from the first."

Colston nodded. "Yes, I've noticed. To be frank, I've wondered if your father realizes that there are times when a leader must be harsh, to maintain discipline."

"The Saviour was a mild man."

Colston had no answer for her words.

A moment later they heard one of the women call out, "The boats are returning. Look, they are coming out of the mouth of the creek. My husband is holding up a fish."

206

Gabrielle's eyes met Colston's. He smiled encouragingly. "No fear now, Gabrielle. This is the time to show staunch faith."

Mary Treloar cupped her hands so that her voice carried over the water. "Have the carpenters been?"

No one answered. Instead Caslett cupped his hand behind his ear to indicate that he did not understand her words.

Colston walked away. Gabrielle stood up and moved close to the rail. David Moray was rowing. He had taken off his jacket and rolled the sleeves of his white shirt above the elbow. Her father sat in the stern, his eyes fixed on the water. Her heart sank. She wondered what the next move would be. The woman Caslett was looking at her, resentment in her eyes.

The boats hit against the side of the *Delicia*. The men clambered up the ladder; each one carried a gift in his hand; some had nuts, one a handful of berries in a basket fashioned of grape leaves, held together by thorns. Amos Treloar had a bit of polished cypress wood which had been roughly carved into the semblance of a doll, a reminder of some child whose name they would never know. He gave the crude toy to Akim's little girl. The child laughed and clapped her hands and begged her mother's kerchief to wrap around her treasure.

Eunice Caslett let the white lilies John gave her drop to the deck. "The stems are slimy!" she said. "You haven't told us about the carpenters. Are the cottages ready?" she cried, her voice rising.

"Now Eunice . . ." John began.

She interrupted him. "No. Of course, they've not been. Always promises. Promises." She caught his arm. "Speak out plain, man! Are there carpenters or not? Has anyone been there to fix our houses?"

"No, Eunice. From the look of it no one has set foot on the place for many a year."

Eunice Caslett said, "Let us women go ashore and see for ourselves. It is our right. What do you say, Mistress Fountaine?"

Gabrielle, caught by surprise by Eunice's question, hesitated. The woman's husband spoke soothingly. "You shall go . . . tomorrow or the next day; no hurry. This ship won't sail for Edenton until she's rummaged and made clean. We've a sight of clearing and wrecking to do before we begin to build on the old foundations."

"I never saw such lush growth," Michael Neely the farrier interrupted. "It is a jungle of berry vines and bushes. I saw a grapevine with a trunk as big as my two wrists."

"I never expect to see such fertile soil." John Caslett looked at his wife. "You can have a posy bed as big as my Lord of Bristol's glass house; the soil will grow anything."

"Soil! Soil! That's all you and Josh Benning think of. What about the fine cottages we were promised? Didn't *he* tell us in Nassau that they'd be ready when we came? Didn't *he*?"

"Hush, Eunice! Hold your hush!"

Josh Benning spoke up. "Hist, woman, don't bedevil John. Land is what we've been promised and I'll have a hundred acres. Think of that, woman, a hundred acres!" He put his hand on his wife's arm. "I'll be a land baron, Martha. I'm going to build you a fine house. There're plenty of hewn logs left from the old."

His plump little wife looked at him. "With a great room, Joshua—I want a great room."

"You shall have one, my dear. I'll build you a room twice as big as the cottage in Devon."

"Truly, Joshua, truly?"

Gabrielle moved silently away. She had the feeling that the men had planned it this way. Their disappointment was as great as the women's, but they were resolved to keep a bold face before their wives.

Robert Fountaine sat at the long table in his cabin. Before him were his papers, scattered helter-skelter. Gabrielle found him there, his brow lined with the bother of separating his lists of names, equipment and stores. Gabrielle set to work without words to bring order out of chaos. After a time the frown left Fountaine's brow and he lay back in the chair, looking with satisfaction as he watched his daughter set the papers into neat orderly piles.

"Read me the list of men," he said after a moment. "I want to check those I think will stay and those who will back out."

Gabrielle looked up, surprised. Her father had known all along the discontent and unrest that beset his little colony. She picked up the papers and began to read:

Amos Treloar	Carpenter & Boatwright
John Caslett	Yeoman
Joshua Benning	Yeoman

Jean LaPierre	Weaver
Michael Neely	Husbandman & Farrier
Shore Brothers	Metalworker & Brickmason
James Hawksworth	The Smith
Marius Akim	Yeoman

He interrupted before she could continue the list.

"I've checked fifteen of whom I am sure. Of the others I cannot say." His voice sounded tired.

"Didn't they express themselves?" Gabrielle asked.

"Some of them did." A faint smile came to his lips. "Violently. I must confess, Gabrielle. The place where the old settlement stood was a scene of desolation. Houses tumbled down, overgrown with brambles and vines. Only by hard work could the men find the outline of the stockade. The fields—what had been fields—were grown with young vines and oaks, some six feet high."

"I heard Joshua Benning say that the heavy growth showed the soil was fertile."

"Yes, he did. That was David's influence. It was David who called their attention to the heavy growth. Then Mainwairing came up and added encouraging words. The soil was more sandy than the rich dark loam I had thought of."

"Perhaps it is as fertile as the dark soil," Gabrielle ventured.

"So Mainwairing explained. He said it was excellent for potatoes, melons, small vegetables, as well as cotton, tobacco, corn, and the marshland, for rice. Gabrielle, Mainwairing's presence, his encouragement saved me from complete failure. I venture to say every man of them would have turned back when he saw the desolation and ruins of the old settlement." He put his elbow on the table, his long thin fingers covering his forehead. He lifted his head, smiling a little. "Then Josh Benning caught a seven-pound fish. A seven-pound fish! On such small things the fate of empires may hang."

"That made them all happy?" she asked.

"That and the fine buck one of the Captain's seamen brought down. Someone discovered a hickory tree with plenty of nuts, another a walnut tree. After that they scattered, each returning, well pleased, with some discovery of his own. The situation righted itself. I walked in the forest alone, Gabrielle, asking God's help. I am sure my prayers are not lost."

To divert him, Gabrielle said, "I can see from here that the oak trees with hanging moss are tremendous."

"Yes, yes, we shall have our house in that grove of oaks. There is a foundation of a two-story log dwelling with part of the walls standing. It must have been Sir John Yeamans' residence. The south wing shall be for your mother and Celestine, detached a little from the confusion of the main house and the weaving shed. The stockade must be rebuilt. The walls of a little chapel are standing, four square with the compass, Gabrielle. The roof has fallen in, but the oak timbers are stout and well mortised. Is not that a symbol?"

"Indeed yes, dear Father. I can almost see you now, in your long robe, mounting the lectern, turning over the leaves of your old Bible."

Fountaine's eyes were dreamy. "I know my text—Matthew 11:7: 'What went ye into the wilderness to see? A reed shaken by the wind?' "

Gabrielle put her hands over his. "Dear, dear father. You have led us out of the wilderness of evil men and evil thought into a New World."

Robert did not hear her. His mind turned to his ailing wife. "Now I must go to your mother," he said, pushing back his chair.

"Celestine told me she spoke yesterday and called her by name."

Robert's brow clouded. "Yes, for a short time she knew Celestine; then all was dark again. But it is a good sign, a good sign. Soon she will know us all and we will have her again with us to make our days bright and happy once more."

"Yes, Father," Gabrielle said, tears falling down her cheeks. "Yes, Father, we will have her again, you and I, by the time the boys come, perhaps."

"When the boys come? Yes, yes, of course, when the boys come." He was silent a moment. "Let us hope and pray, Gabrielle. God will reward our prayers if we speak to Him humbly, from full and contrite hearts."

"Yes, Father."

Gabrielle came on David Moray as she walked to her cabin. He was standing near the companionway, watching the women who were gathered in a close group on the after deck. She paused when she saw him. She wanted to say something to show her gratitude for the help he had given to

210

her father. He bowed and moved aside as she came near, but did not speak.

She paused, embarrassed that she could not find the right words. Something in his attitude made it hard for her to speak; he was aloof, as though she took liberties in speaking to him, instead of the other way around.

"My father told me you were a great help to him this morning, when the men were so disappointed and discouraged. I want to thank you . . ." She paused, unable to continue.

"It was nothing," he answered unsmiling.

"My father thinks differently and so do I." She hurried on, the color mounting her cheeks. "You turned the men to think of the good soil instead of allowing them to brood on their disappointment. Indeed, I am grateful, I . . ." She broke off. Was he not going to help her at all? In some mysterious way he managed to show his strong disapproval without uttering a word. She was bewildered first, then a little angry.

"You could do as much yourself, if you cared to take the trouble." He indicated the group of women by a nod of his head. "But no, you would rather laze in your chair on deck and listen to the adulation Colston pours into your willing ears, instead of preparing those poor women to meet disappointment you know they must suffer when all their fine hopes are dashed. You must play the fine lady and hold yourself above common folk." He turned and strode away, his heels making a fine tattoo on the deck.

Gabrielle's face blazed. He was unfair. She didn't hold herself above anyone. She was trembling with anger. He had no reason to say a thing like that. Then a thought came to her: Was he angry because she had sat on deck talking to Edward Colston? A little smile touched her lips as she watched him go. She had made a discovery about David Moray and the discovery was not displeasing to her.

Chapter 16

WHERE PAST YEARS ARE

Roger Mainwairing leaned against a timber in Fountaine's new house and mopped his forehead of the perspiration that ran in rivulets from his brow to his throat. All about him were the sound of the axe ringing through the forest, the regular whine of the saw and the whistling and shouts of the men, working at accustomed tasks.

Two weeks had seen a change in the ruins of Old Town. A new hamlet was springing out of the old. Bragg complained that his seamen were slipping away from caulking the bottom of his ship to drive pine stakes for the stockade. There seemed to be an unspoken purpose among the settlers and the men of the ships to get the stockade built, snug and tight, with a blockhouse at one corner near the river, before the *Delicia* set sail for the Albemarle.

Men from the *Bahama Venture* had come ashore, bringing horses and cattle. Each morning they staked the livestock out in the old fields, where they grazed to satisfaction, even to surfeit, on succulent green grass.

By common consent, after one view of the location, most of the women had remained on shipboard. But their men had to set up tents and make a camp, so that they could use the long hours of daylight. By October they must be well housed, for although the climate was mild there might be snow, even ice on the river when deep winter came.

The men welcomed work after their long holiday from labour, and under the guidance of those who knew woodcraft as well as housebuilding, the work of rebuilding the log houses moved forward swiftly.

Gabrielle came across the open clearing, her full skirts tucked up in her belt to ankle length, showing her sturdy buckled shoes. She wore a wide straw hat, wreathed in field flowers, which sheltered her face from the hot sun. She had a cluster of water lilies in her hand, held together by a grapevine. She was smiling. She, too, was encouraged by the work she saw.

Roger Mainwairing and Edward Colston were seated on the stump of a pine tree when Gabrielle came into sight.

"A fine strong girl," Roger said as he watched her walking towards them. "She will need to be strong, to bear her share of the burdens of this settlement."

Edward opened his snuffbox and pinched a bit of powder before he answered. "Her shoulders are broad. She will bear burdens easily."

Roger said, "Even so, 'tis too much responsibility for a young girl."

"She has her father." Edward paused, sneezing into his large silk handkerchief.

"He is a dreamer." Roger spoke impatiently. "He doesn't know half that is going on—between his sick wife and his dreams."

Edward leaned forwards, his homely intelligent face alive with interest. "What are his dreams?" he asked of the older man. "He never talks to me about anything of moment."

"Fountaine dreams of equality for all men, all races. Impossible in practice. Men are not born equal nor can they attain equality. He talks of men being free. Well, freedom is a word of indefinite meaning. What is freedom to you might be slavery for me. What men need is opportunity. That is the value of a new country. Opportunity. Then let each man show his ability to attain equality with his betters and work his own way to freedom."

Colston turned over a small turtle with the toe of his boot and watched it wriggle its small feet in the air before he righted it again. "I don't know whether you're right or wrong, Mr. Mainwairing. My grandfather maintains that there are very few men worthy of freedom. Most of them wouldn't know what to do with freedom except to abuse it."

"Your grandfather is a wise man, Colston, but we are getting off the subject of Miss Gabrielle. She needs someone stronger than she is to lean on, someone like you, Edward, who appreciates her."

Colston laughed. "If you mean a husband, I'm afraid I'm not the strong one for her. I admire Gabrielle. I admire all her fine qualities. I suspect she thinks I am still an ardent admirer of her friend Molly Lepel, and that I want to marry her." His face darkened. There was bitterness in his tone. "Molly's aunt will see that she marries one of the gentry. She looks down on men who are in trade. It has never really bothered me because we are middle-class folk. The gentry may look down on me and the nobility hold their heads with more arrogance, but when they want something that requires money, it is to us traders that they must come. My grandfather has done a thousand times more good for the people of Bristol than his Lordship, the Earl of Bristol. He has built almshouses, homes for wretched girls and fatherless boys. Since the time of Elizabeth it has been the Merchants of Bristol who have made England great. The great John Cabot and a hundred lesser navigators have carried the Bristol flag to every known portion of the globe; aye, to unknown seas, to carry English goods and build up our trade."

"Why not be a planter-trader and cut the Gordian knot?" Roger said.

"I'll be damned if I will," Colston said sharply. "I can never follow in my grandfather's footsteps, for I haven't his ability, but I surely hold myself above the profligate frequenters of Will's Coffee House or the Tory clubs, where after the play, green and blue ribbons and stars distinguish the great from the commoners. These are the people Miss Molly Lepel admires. No doubt she will marry one of them and be well satisfied."

Roger did not answer. Gabrielle was near them now. He rose from the pine stump and offered her the seat, dusting it off with his handkerchief.

Gabrielle sat down. She pushed her wide hat from her forehead until it slipped to the back of her neck, held in place by the blue riband ties. Perspiration beaded her white brow. A little dew showed above her firm red mouth.

"It is very hot," she said. "Perhaps I walked too far in the heat of midday."

"I'll get you a drink of water," Edward offered. He came back quickly with a gourd of water from the spring. "It's delightfully cool," he said as he stood watching her drink. "How fortunate to find such a clear good spring bubbling up within the stockade."

Roger smiled. "All colonists benefit from those who have gone before them, even if the settlement was a rank failure, as were the two that preceded this one."

Gabrielle turned her troubled eyes towards him. "Do you think this settlement will succeed?"

"Without doubt," Roger said firmly. "The time is ripe for colonization now. You do not stand alone. You have two strong neighbours, one north of you, one south. It is good to remember that. Two hundred miles north to the Albemarle and two hundred miles south to Charles Town. Soon the lower Cape Fear will be . . ."

"As successful as your Albemarle?" she interrupted with a smile.

"Stronger, I think, because you have the river and safe harbour."

"I pray you are right, Mr. Mainwairing. It would kill my father if the colony did not succeed."

"It will succeed," Roger repeated. "Have no fear. I believe in its future so firmly that I have made up my mind to join Maurice Moore when he lays out his town just below here, on the river."

Colston showed his interest at the name of Moore. "I called on James Moore in Charles Town. I had a letter to him from my grandfather. I found him very interesting. I heard on all sides that he is a man of importance in that settlement."

Roger smiled. "He's a thorn in the flesh to the government."

"Is this Maurice Moore a connection?" Colston asked.

"James Moore is the father of my friend. Maurice has lived near me for some years now—since 1710, in fact, when he came from Charles Town in command of a company of men sent to rescue the Bath settlers at the time of the Tuscarora massacre."

He paused and called their attention to David Moray who was jumping a bay hunter over a hedge of flowered shrubs. "Isn't the bay a beauty?" he said. He did not want any discussions of Indian massacres before Gabrielle.

"Moray has an excellent seat. He rides as though he had the advantage of military training," Colston commented, watching the bay skim over a high hurdle. "The fellow knows horses."

Mainwairing started to make a comment but refrained. It was evident that Edward didn't know Moray's story.

Gabrielle had eyes for the man and not for the horse. She had never seen anyone who seemed more at ease on a hunter. How could she have been so blind, not to have recognized at Meg's Lane that he was no ordinary bondman? Perhaps it was the reddish beard he wore. The gardener's smock disguised his soldierly carriage. She felt chagrin when she remembered the time she had not recognized him in gentlemen's clothes.

"Suppose we walk to the landing. I see our boat has put

out from the ship. My groom is bringing the pack ashore for a little run and exercise."

"I saw the foxhounds on the ship," Colston said. "You have made a good selection, Mainwairing. I suppose you hunt in your part of Carolina?"

"Indeed yes. My wife wouldn't live there if she couldn't hunt."

Colston said to Gabrielle, "Coming?"

"No, Edward. I think I'll stay here. I like to watch the men raising their rooftrees, and hear the sound of the axes. Listen: the men are singing as they hoist the ridgepoles."

> "Sing the song of a hammer,
>   Sing the song of the nails,
> Sing the song of strong men
>   Lifting heavy rails.
>
> "A rooftree is a home
>   Wherever you may be,
> Home for wanderers on the land
>   And a safe haven from the sea."

Mainwairing and Colston moved away. Gabrielle sat quietly watching the workmen. It gave her a good feeling to see everything going so well. Aside from a few grumblers and malingerers, most of the settlers worked with a will.

David rode up and reined his hunter close to the log where she was seated. Gabrielle hoped the admiration she felt for the picture did not show in her face, for a picture they made, man and horse in perfect accord.

"The mare is beautiful," she murmured. David leaned forward, his long, strong fingers caressing the satin neck.

"Madam Mainwairing is a fine horsewoman and she keeps fine horses—only the best blood for her hunting stable,"

"Yes," Gabrielle said. "You will enjoy being Mr. Mainwairing's groom." She spoke indifferently, "Horses must be more exciting than gardening."

David's face reddened. "You know how to stab," he said bitterly.

Gabrielle had regretted it as soon as the words left her lips. "I'm sorry, Moray," she said impulsively. "I can't imagine why I spoke those miserable words. What I mean to say is that you love horses and Mr. Mainwairing will be the best of masters."

The look of anger faded from his eyes, "Mainwairing is

216

not my master," he said quietly. "You don't seem to understand that I've come to Carolina for quite another purpose." He paused. He had said enough. Let her think what she pleased. He slipped from the back of the horse to the ground and stood straight and tall beside her. He did not look the same man who had been trundling a barrow about the garden paths at Meg's Lane.

"You are so different, Moray," she exclaimed, realizing the change in him. "Vastly different."

"Yes? No doubt 'tis this balmy Carolina air."

"Your speech is different, too. It was broad Scots. Now it is that of a . . ." She paused, not wanting to hurt again.

"More like that of a gentleman." He finished the sentence for her.

She had the grace to be confused. "Without dialect," she said lamely. "David, I do not know what ails me. I say things to you I do not mean. Not the things I am thinking."

He took a step towards her. "What are you thinking now?" he said, bending close. "Tell me, what are you thinking about me?" His face changed. He had seen someone approaching. He said a little too loudly, "Thank you, Miss Fountaine. The mare is a beauty. Her name is Dierdre, after the lovely Irish queen."

Mainwairing joined them. "Oh there you are, David. Did you bring the other hunters ashore?"

"Yes. They are out on pasture." He pointed to the cleared grasslands, where half a dozen horses were racing about, kicking up their heels in their delight to be on land again.

The men walked away. She heard broken sentences drifting back on the wind— ". . . plenty of foxes . . . a good run . . . exercise . . ."

After a time Mainwairing came back. "Your father told me to tell you that he was going out to the ship by the next boat."

Gabrielle rose slowly. "Then I must go back," she said reluctantly. "I know he will want me to work on cargo lists again."

"Dull work but necessary," Roger said absently. He was watching the horses. Moray remounted the mare and rode off.

They went down the little path through heavy vine-covered bushes, to the water level. Here the great cypress grew heavy and close, at the edge of the marsh. A bridge of poles, side by side, had been laid across the fringe of the marsh. The

217

black marsh mud oozed up between the small poles and made walking difficult.

"Keep close to the middle of the path," Roger said, leading the way. "The walking is easier." He carried a long stick in his hand; it did not occur to Gabrielle to ask why. He would not have told her that the men had killed three flat-headed water snakes on the causeway that morning. Poisonous moccasins, the Albemarle men called them.

Gabrielle lifed her skirts above her ankles. Her stout buckled shoes sank into the mire with each step. But they made the landing, where the seamen, with long sweeps upright, sat in the shoreboat waiting to take them back to the ship.

"Are you going aboard?" Gabrielle asked Roger.

"No. Not now. I've sent for my fowling-piece. Colston and I are going out on a turkey-shoot. If we are fortunate, we will have wild turkey for dinner tomorrow, or perhaps we may even have the luck to fall in with a young deer; so wish me good fortune."

"Good fortune, brave hunter," she said with a smile.

Men were fishing in the creek. One had a strike as they passed. With an exclamation the fisherman rose to his feet, his rod bent almost double. The oarsman rowed frantically trying to keep pace with the flashing silver fish as it churned the black water of the creek under the overhanging bushes.

At the mouth of the creek the workmen had set up a shelter of boughs on the narrow sandy beach. A smith was at the forge. The ring of hammer on anvil sounded across the water. Two men worked with a cross saw cutting a great cypress log, while others with frows split shakes for the roofs of the new houses. No temporary thatch for them, but good cypress shakes. Other men were squaring logs for joists and fitting mortises. They were laughing and shouting to one another. Surely when men worked with laughter and snatches of rollicking song on their lips, all was well.

She found her father on deck, sitting apart. He was holding his well-worn pocket Bible, the one he had brought from France when he made his escape after the Revocation. His face was very white and his fingers that held the leather-bound book were trembling. Alarmed at the expression on his face, she hurried to him.

He raised his eyes as he turned a page. She read anguish in them, deep undisguised anguish.

"Father," she cried, "Father, what is it? What is wrong?"

"Sit down, my daughter. Draw a stool near me." She drew a little canvas-covered stool to his side and waited for him to speak.

"I have something to say to you, my child. Something I wish with all my soul could remain unsaid."

The feeling of tragedy deepened with his words. She caught his arm with both of her hands. "My mother, is she ... is she dead?" She scarcely breathed the words.

"No, she is not dead," he said slowly. "Her body remains alive. She even seems stronger than she has been. Gabrielle, you must bear what I have to tell you with courage. Your mother has returned to complete consciousness, but she is not herself."

He closed the Bible, his thin forefinger holding the place where he had been reading. "Her mind has turned back. She is a girl again, a young girl no older than you. She lives her life as it was before we were married; when she was still the Countess of Marsanac."

He bowed his head, but Gabrielle saw the burning tears that fell on his thin white cheeks. "Celestine she knew, but not me, her husband."

After a silence, he read aloud:

"Deliver my soul from the sword; My darling from the power of the dog."

Gabrielle got up slowly to go to her cabin. Her father did not seem aware of her departure. Barton waited for her, her kind, homely face working. She held out her arms: "My lamb. My wee, wee lamb!" she whispered. Wordlessly Gabrielle went to her and found comfort in her arms.

Chapter 17

GREEN SWAMP

Towards the end of September the day came when Captain Bragg announced at breakfast that the *Delicia's* repairs were almost completed. In two days' time they would be ready to sail for Albemarle Sound. A heavy feeling came over Gabrielle Fountaine, as if a great weight had settled down upon her. As long as the ship remained, Roger Mainwairing and Edward Colston assumed responsibility for the welfare of the little colony. Now they were going away. She looked at the shipmaster. He was eating his cakes and treacle with relish. His weatherbeaten face was calm and undisturbed. He did not realize the weight of worry his casual announcement had laid upon her. How was she to carry the burden without Roger Mainwairing's wise counsel, Edward Colston's encouragement? For Gabrielle had now acknowledged to herself that her father would not, could not, carry the task of governing these people. He had the iron necessary to meet the hard conditions, but not the iron necessary to hold his people with firm hand and will. They loved him but they did not respect his judgement. She pushed her plate aside, her breakfast untouched.

"We are hunting this morning. Will you ride with us, Miss Gabrielle?" She turned at the sound of Roger Mainwairing's voice, shaking her head in the negative.

"It has been so long since I have ridden, Mr. Mainwairing. I am afraid I should hold you back."

Roger laughed. "Indeed you won't. We've no manners in our hunting, my dear. Each of us goes his own way. Ride as far as you like and drop out when you like. Our Albemarle workmen are joining us, following the hounds on foot. They have worked so faithfully they have earned a holiday."

Robert Fountaine looked lovingly at his daughter. "Why don't you ride, my child? It will do you good. You look a little pale this morning." He turned to Mainwairing. "Gabrielle has been acting as my secretary. I am afriad I have kept her confined too closely."

220

"But you need me, Father," Gabrielle began.

Her father interrupted. "No, not this morning. I am going ashore to see about the work on the little chapel, and the unloading of our household furniture."

Gabrielle said quickly, "I must be with you then. The arrangement of the furniture——"

"Yes, yes I know, that is woman's work, and you shall not be deprived. It will take us half a day to unload and uncrate, a whole day perhaps. So run and change and don't delay Mr. Mainwairing."

Gabrielle hurried away to change to her habit. For some reason care slipped away from her. For the first time since her father had told her two weeks before that her mother's mind was clouded, she felt free to enjoy herself.

"You must humour her," Robert had told his daughter. "Do nothing, say nothing to cross her in any way. She is happy as she is. We must not go before her with unhappy faces, or show our distress or sorrow, for fear she may notice. Perhaps this is a temporary phase. Perhaps someday she will return to us."

Gabrielle wiped away her tears. She could not show less fortitude than her father was showing, or do anything to destroy his courage and faith. Since that day they had both been actors upon a stage, each one playing the part as best he could. Gabrielle was young, and youth is resilient. Robert grew whiter and thinner, and his dark eyes were set deeper under his heavy brows. But he said nothing. The secret of his wife was locked in his heart and in the hearts of his faithful servants. They guarded that secret well. No one on the ship suspected the truth. Madam Fountaine was ill of a lung complaint, most of the people thought. It was well to leave it thus, for she was safeguarded.

Barton hovered about, waiting to assist, but Gabrielle's swift, impatient fingers buttoned the dark blue bodice and hooked up the long riding skirt. Barton helped her struggle with the high boots and handed her the beaver with its drooping crimson plume. Gabrielle tied it into place over her slick black knot, which was held secure by a net.

"You look almost yourself, Miss Gabrielle," Barton said, as her young mistress slipped on her fringed gauntlets. "Have a care. Don't let the horse fall on you and break a leg."

"You have the gloomiest thoughts, Barton." Gabrielle laughed. "I won't fall off. I'll slide off—in the swamp most likely, and spoil this nice habit Molly gave me."

"Have a care," Barton repeated, as Gabrielle ran out of the door and sped down the deck.

The morning was cool. The sun, rising above a low-hanging bank of fog, was a great red globe on the eastern horizon. As their boat neared the shore and entered the cheek, they disturbed two white cranes that stood knee-deep in the water, intent on their morning fishing. They rose with a rush of great wings and sailed lazily upcreek. Cardinals flitted from bush to bush along the path that led from the little strip of sandy beach to the high ground above, where the houses were being built, while starry glories hung from the dark green vines that twined over bushes and trees. Birds sang; flowers bloomed in the dark aisles of the wood; tall grass glittered with dew. The land was flooded with the soft beauty of early morning.

Edward was dressed in a fashionable riding suit of bottle green with tan leather trimmings, and his boots were soft tanned leather, as was his broad silver-buckled belt. A short hunting dirk in a leather case hung from his belt, and he carried a crop with a loaded silver handle.

He was mounted on a tough brown hunter that looked a veteran of many hunts. He waved a gauntleted hand to Gabrielle while his horse drank at the newly made trough that had been set up at the spring near the centre of the compound.

Men were working at all the log houses within the stockade. The houses were in every stage of construction, from two with only the framework up, to their own house with the roof shingled and sideboards in place. Built of cypress, it looked large and commodious, with a two-story central building and wings of one story on either end. It was set in a grove of large oak trees, from which streamers of Spanish moss hung, swaying with every passing breeze.

Her father had built on the foundation of a former dwelling; from its size, doubtless it had been the residence of Sir John Yeamans of the earlier colony.

The central log house was found to be sound enough to use. By re-roofing and fitting clapboards of cypress over the logs, it had not taken the Albemarle workers long to finish. Now they were working on the inside panelling and setting the bricks in the fireplace. The fifteen other dwellings were well advanced, and the high stockade of pine stakes, twenty feet high, was finished. A little world of its own, Gabrielle thought, as she walked across the cleared centre of the compound, where the horses were tied to a long hitching rack.

Mainwairing said, "We are riding across the fields, outside the west gate. There's a fox den down to the right, near where the creek runs through that little pine thicket. If he crosses water, ride along the path to the wooden bridge. There's open country beyond and no brush under the pines. Keep away from swampland and you will be quite safe."

He made a cradle of his clasped hands. Gabrielle put her booted foot in his palms and sprang lightly to her seat. David Moray was on the other side of the hunter, sliding the girth through a ring to keep it from flapping.

He touched his cap. "A fine huntin' mornin', miss," he said. Gabrielle nodded acknowledgement. "I hope ye enjoy yer hunt, miss."

It angered her that he should speak in dialect, for she knew he used it only when it suited his mood. Just now it pleased him to act the boor. But he didn't look the north-country boor. His thick chestnut hair was brushed smooth and hung waving to his shoulders. He was shaven close. His hands were clear, not grimy as they were when he had acted as their gardener. She noted that his leather clothes fitted well, his coat laid smooth across his broad shoulders, and his Glengarry bonnet on the side of his head gave a swaggering air to the fellow.

"Thank you, Moray," she said, as he handed her the crop.

"Ride close after Miss Fountaine, David," Gabrielle heard Roger say. "I hold you accountable for her safety."

"Right," David answered. "I'll guard her well."

Gabrielle felt the hot blood rush to her cheek. She remembered vividly how resentful he was when he had been asked to guard her the night in Nassau when Woodes Rogers was made Govenor. There was not time to protest to Roger Mainwairing. The hounds were giving voice; they were away, noses following a first fox scent across the uneven field. Colston and Mainwairing rode through the gate first, followed by the men on foot, who made for a cross-path along the creek. Her horse took its head, following the pack. She heard the heavy hoofbeats behind her, and the voices of the men on foot, raised in unison with the hounds. The hot excitement of the chase settled down upon her when she saw the red streak of a vixen's body flash along a fallen log and the defiant waving tail disappeared among the young pine trees.

Dierdre took the bit and ran. Gabrielle was not the horse-woman to check her in her flight.

"Draw up slowly. Talk to her." David Moray's voice came from a distance. " 'Ware of the trees," he shouted. "I can't overtake you."

The mare sped on, running wild. Far away to the west she heard the baying hounds, hard on the chase. After the first turn Gabrielle felt no fear. As long as she stayed on the horse's back she was all right. She ducked low as they went under half-grown pine trees. A limb bent back and lashed across her face, tearing her plumed beaver from her head; over her shoulder she saw the brave scarlet plume lie like a wounded thing on the ground.

She tried to steady the horse by talking. She realized that the strength she could exercise on the reins was nothing now. The horse was following the chase across a pine barren. She had a glimpse of the pack and two horsemen. She would come up to them when she crossed the creek. She remembered Mainwairing's admonition about the bridge, but there was no bridge here. The horse plunged, over her depth; she began to swim. Gabrielle's skirt billowed up like a haycock. It grew heavy and waterlogged, but she dared not let go the pommel to hold it away from the water. On the other side, the horse plunged into a maze of trees, where animal trails crisscrossed, going towards water. How long she rode she could not tell. A maze of trees separated her now from the pack, the baying of hounds and the shouts of men far away. She came to a small black lake, set deep in a cypress grove. A dark, weird spot—the sunlight came slanting down in narrow shafts of pale yellow; green lily pads grew thick, while blossoms lay heavy on the black mirror of the lake. All was silent. No bird call, no gay twittering in the heavy crowns of the trees. Even the breeze had died. The air was heavy, fetid, with decayed vegetation of the centuries.

The mare was puffing heavily; foam, flecked with blood, came from her lips and nostrils, but she held her head hard against the bit, pulling savagely.

"Steady, girl, steady." Gabrielle tried to soothe the animal with her voice. A small path followed the contour of the lake. They crossed a low swale, waist-high in tall, waving, swordlike leaves and plumes of wild oats. The path ended at another lake, larger than the first, deeper in lily pads. The green vegetation around her was heavy and dense; the trees rose tall, their crowns shutting out the sky; the earth was soft under the mare's hoofs. They came to a cross-path. The fox, tail low, flashed by. The scent of the frightened animal cut through the air. The mare trembled, as a dog trembles, at the heavy vixen odour, sickening in its intensity.

She sank deep in the slime. Gabrielle grew alarmed. "Keep away from the swamps," Roger Mainwairing had told her. Well, she was in the swamp, the deep heart of the swamp; behind her was the black glossy water of the lake, on three sides the heavy, dank swamp.

Looking down to see what the footing was, Gabrielle saw a water snake, heavy, with a short stumpy tail, lift its vicious head from the water. The mare trembled violently, and with a great effort pulled her hoofs free, to firmer ground. She stopped under a great tulip tree, panting for breath.

Gabrielle could do nothing. She dared not dismount for fear of snakes and quivering ground. She looked over her shoulder. Where was Moray, who was to protect her? She had left him far behind. She could not even hear the pack. She was lost.

She sat quietly, trying to think what to do next. The mare had run her course. She stood quietly, with tired head drooping. Two paths crossed, a little to the left, almost overgrown with brush, yet she could see that something—animals or man—used the path to the edge of the lake. The ground under the tree was firm, but how far did that firmness extend? Not behind her, for there the quivering ground began. The mare must have crossed the upper edge of the area. She must go on, trusting that there was another way out. She knew there was a narrow road that followed the river, to the west. Perhaps if she took a path, she would come to Far Reach, but which path?

She remembered reading of a traveller in Scotland, lost in the Highlands, who gave his horse its head, and the horse brought him home. This queenly mare under her might choose the path that would take them to Far Reach.

Gabrielle lifted the reins. The tired horse responded. She set off, taking the eastward path without hesitation. She tried not to be alarmed when they went deeper and deeper into the strange oppressive green of the swamp. She could not see the path for the heavy growth of swamp reeds and cane. But it was a path, and firm, though on either side the swamp water lay, dark and dismal, with black cypress pushing their grotesque knees out of the water.

After a time they came to a small grove of tulip trees.

Low osier bushes, covered with grapevines, made a little cover. The ground under the trees was firm, and there was a fallen log that she could use for mounting. She resolved to get off the mare and rest. Her back was tired; her arms ached; her great braid of hair had tumbled down her back.

She unhooked her skirt from the pommel, kicked her foot free from the slipper and slid to the ground, holding the reins so that the horse could not run. She sat down, her back to the trunk of the tree. The mare began at once to nibble grass.

Her eyes closed. She was tired, more weary than she realized. Whether she fell asleep or not she did not know. She wakened at the barking of dogs; they were nosing their way down the path that crossed the one she had been following. They nosed about the earth, moving in circles which led always nearer to the tree under which Gabrielle sat. "You've lost the fox," she said, pushing one of the bitches away from her. "Don't come looking here. Reynard outwitted you."

She got to her feet; if the dogs came, Mainwairing or Edward would be close behind. But there were only three dogs; they were separated from the pack. They, too, were lost.

Just then one of them put its paws against the tree, looking upward into the leafy branches. It lifted its head and bayed deeply. The others joined, all looking skyward.

Gabrielle lifted her eyes. At first she saw nothing in the heavy green shadows. Then she saw a bare black foot, hanging below a limb out of reach of the dogs. Her heart almost stopped beating as a black face looked down at her with wild rolling eyes—a Negro man, obviously frightened by the dogs. She knew what that meant: a runaway black. She had heard of runaway Negroes when she was on the ship and while in Nassau.

They had beaten paths like their old jungle tracks, through forests; they hid in swamps and along the banks.

"Come down!" she cried. She tried to steady her voice. She must show no fear now. "Come down, I say."

"Mistress—the dogs. They'll tear my flesh, Mistress."

Gabrielle caught the lead dog by the collar, then secured a firm grip on the second. The third answered her command and lay down on the grass, his red tongue lolling out of the side of his mouth.

A moment later the black man was on the ground—an old man with greying hair, bent of back. As he turned she saw

226

the mark of the lash, not yet healed. The sight sickened her. He looked at her sullenly and did not speak.

He was tall and incredibly thin. It seemed as if the black skin of his cheek lay against the bony structure of his face, without flesh between to build the contour of a face. His forehead was scarified, three vertical lines above his brows, three on the chin and two on each cheekbone. Caste marks, such as Captain Bragg had described when he had talked to them of the distinctive differences in the various African tribes.

She might have been frightened, but she saw how frightened the African was. He clasped his hands together, showing where ropes and chains had cut into his wrists. He kept repeating a few words, over and over, *"Bu Mwatu-anga. Inzho Twa-Bebe"* (Since you tied us so, we have repented). *"A-mu-tu-tole a Bwina, mu-ka-tu-yayile Ngona"* (Let you carry us to our burrow, that you may kill us there).

"Speak so I can understand," she said. "Where are you going? Speak English. Do not be afraid," she added kindly. "I will not hurt you or give you up. Tell me where you are going." From his expression, she knew he understood her. "Speak English," she repeated. "I want to help you. Where are you going?"

"Hiding, Mistress. Hiding from the old men who run after me."

He lifted his head. Far-off voices sounded, carried by the wind. Soon there would be more dogs and men. They would send this poor wretched fellow to a cruel master. She couldn't bear it. Every instinct in her rebelled. Had her own father not been fugitive, hiding as this man was hiding?

"Have you a place to hide?"

The man looked at her steadily for a moment, moving about her. She thought of the way a dog sniffs at a stranger. Satisfied, the black said, "Yes, Mistress. A place of hiding, near. Safe place. I myself know."

Gabrielle listened. The voices were more distinct, the hounds quite clear. A thought came to her. She acted at once. "Get on my horse," she said quickly. "Ride down that path. When you get to your hiding place, turn the mare loose. I hope she'll find her way back."

The Negro looked at her a moment, not comprehending. Then he saw freedom ahead of him. His face cleared; all suspicion fled from his heavy eyes. He fell at her feet and kissed the hem of her sodden habit.

"Go quickly," Gabrielle cried. "Quickly! They will be here in a moment."

"I go to Green Swamp, Mistress. There is safety for fleeing men. Tomorrow the horse——"

"Go! Don't wait!" Gabrielle looked fearfully over her shoulder. She heard a new sound—the crash of breaking boughs down the path she had just ridden.

The man leaped to the saddle. The hounds made a great effort to follow, but Gabrielle managed to quiet them. She sat down on the log again and began to bind up her hair.

She thought, This will not do. How could she account for the loss of her horse if she had not been thrown? She stretched out on the ground. She hoped she was in a position that looked as if she had been thrown. Her soiled habit, her dishevelled hair would help the illusion. The dogs lay quiet. They were winded, glad of a resting place on the soft earth.

She heard her name called—Moray, stumbling along the edge of the quivering ground. For a moment she had a struggle to keep from crying out, to warn him of danger. His horse might not be so fortunate as hers had been, but she saw, through half-closed eyes, that he was on firm ground. She shut her eyes quickly—too quickly to observe his expression when he discovered her.

"Christ! She's dead!" she heard him cry out. Then he was off his horse and at her side. He lifted her up. Her head fell back, the long braids of hair falling over his shoulder. For a moment he held her against him. Then he laid her down gently. He walked swiftly to the edge of the lake and filled his hat with water. Gabrielle did not relish being deluged with black swamp water. She opened her eyes slowly.

"My horse. My horse," she whispered, as if dazed by the fall.

"You've had a spill," Moray said, anxiety in his face and in his voice. "Move your arms and limbs, please."

Gabrielle moved languidly.

"Nothing broken," he said shortly. He stood up and looked around. Gabrielle was suddenly filled with consternation. Had the Negro's bare feet left a mark in the earth? The falling leaves made a thick carpet. She hoped the mare's hoofs had trampled out all other tracks.

"I'd follow the mare, if I did not fear to leave you alone," Moray said. His voice sounded gruff.

Gabrielle sat up. "I'm quite all right. Won't the horse find its way back?"

"I don't know. This is a strange country." He stood silent, considering. While he waited to make a decision, Mainwairing and Colston rode into sight.

Moray rode to meet them. The three crowded the narrow path, the dogs milling about the horses' feet.

Moray said, "Miss Gabrielle has had a fall from her horse. No bones broken. Fortunately the ground is soft here."

Gabrielle felt guilty, but when she thought of the wretched black, she was firm in her determination.

The men hurried over to her. Both showed concern in their faces. On her feet, she had no sense of hurt, but only a slight dizziness, she assured them.

The river road was only a few hundred yards down the path. If she felt able to mount Moray's horse, she would be in the clear in no time. She mounted; Mainwairing and Edward Colston went ahead; David Moray walked by her side, to steady her if her dizziness returned. Gabrielle thought, I would make a liar of myself if I really set about it. I don't seem to mind. Evidently my conscience is not troubled by these matters. The man would get away to Green Swamp. He would be safe.

"It is well I came up when I did," Moray said. "I saw the tracks of bare feet under the tree where you were lying. We are not far from the river and only a few miles from the Banks, where the pirates hold rendezvous."

"I saw no pirates." Gabrielle was pleased that she could speak convincingly. Could she have done as much if he had mentioned runaway slaves?

"Please don't ride out alone in this country without protection. Pirates are a real danger, and so are Indians, Miss Fountaine, and next time don't let your horse get out of hand."

"Do you suppose I wanted the horse to run? I made no pretensions, but it seems to me if I were so competent a rider as you are, I'd have made some effort to overtake a runaway horse."

She looked at him steadily, scorn in her voice. A dull flush came over his face. He opened his lips to speak, then closed them firmly.

If she didn't know that to run after a wild horse only maddened it the more, he would not inform her. Why should he defend himself, or tell her that his mount was too slow? Even if he had charged after her, he could never have overtaken the swift-going mare.

They went in silence towards the River Road. Gabrielle's anger subsided after a time; her thoughts turned to the other runaway. She hoped he would get safely to Green Swamp. "Green Swamp!" Suddenly she realized the extent of the Negro's trust in her. He had told her the name of their hiding place. Green Swamp was the sanctuary of hunted men.

Chapter 18

SCOT FROM UPRIVER

The last day the *Delicia* lay in the river was a busy one for men of the new colony. The unloading was completed. Boxes and bales and barrels were carried by small boats to the beach. There, under hastily improvised bush tents, each householder stored his possessions, to await the completion of the houses, or for help from his neighbour in transporting his goods to high land.

Fortunately the fine weather held. The heat had given way to a cool east wind, a blessed relief after the heavy, humid days of early September.

There were chores for everyone—men, women and children. The children drove the swine and sheep up to the common pasture. The cattle and work horses were already at grass, kept in bounds by hastily constructed fences of split rails, set zigzag about the small plantation of half-grown pines.

One of the men, more ingenious, or lazier, than the others, had rigged a pulley and tackle secured to a great pine tree, and was dragging his goods up the bank instead of uncrating the furniture and carrying it up by hand. This effort proved so successful that an ox was hitched to the pulley, and no manpower was needed except for direction.

The Devon man, Amos Treloar, was the instigator of this labour-saving.

"Trust a Devon man." Roger Mainwairing laughed as he stood near by, watching the first load over the brink.

" 'Tis so, sir," Amos replied, a twinkle in his bright blue eyes. " 'Tis always so. We are fair clever to save ourselves from labour."

"It is good," Roger said, nodding approval. "Now if you rig a high line to carry your goods right to your doorstep, it would be even better."

"I'd thought of that, Mr. Ma'n'ring, but I'd no' see my way clear to get the lines goin'. So I give up. Let well en' be, I say to my missis, let well en' be. Didn't I, Mary?" He turned to the woman seated on the ground, busily engaged in polishing her pewter vessels with white beach sand.

"He's slick enough when it comes to saving hisself," she said grimly, but there was pride in her face, too, as she watched the net holding her fine oaken dresser swing over the bank. "At savin' hisself, he's a master hand."

Roger made his way across the open space to the Fountaines' house. On the way he was intercepted by an old hunter and Indian trader he had not seen for some years, MacAlpin, a sturdy, square-shouldered Scot with sandy hair and a beaked nose. His green-grey eyes were set in a network of fine lines, under low-hanging brows. He was a strong man, of hard, long sinew, and his dress was made of the buckskin that only the Indians knew how to tan. His musket, in the crook of his arm, the hunting knife at his belt, the moccasins on his feet, told of the woodsman.

A snuff stick protruded from his thin lips. He chewed as he surveyed the activities of the settlers with a quizzical look in his eyes. A suggestion of skepticism hovered about his lips. "Third time's the charm, Mr. Ma'n'ring?" he said by way of greeting.

Roger knew he spoke of the two unsuccessful attempts to settle along the Cape Fear. "Let us hope so," Roger said, eyeing his companion. He knew MacAlpin for a shrewd, far-seeing woodsman, a man familiar with the country. He had been his guide more than once in journeys Roger had made up the Roanoke as far as the rapids, then into Virginia through the long valley.

"I'm glad you came, MacAlpin. I want you to know Mr. Fountaine, who has charge of this colony."

"Fountaine? Any kin to Fountaine in Virginny?"

Roger didn't know. "This man is a Huguenot."

"Oh, one of those. Well, I can't be bothered with them that's thinkin' all the while of religion and disputin' which church is best, when God Almighty shows us something to worship, every day of our lives, right here in His own church. The forest, I mean. Ain't it better'n any church man built?"

Roger headed off an argument by agreeing.

"There's Parson Urmston, of Edenton," MacAlpin went on. "We have arguments, but I can't convince him. He thinks the Friends will go to some particular hell and sizzle there. He says the Established Church is the only one whose folk will go to heaven."

232

He spat out the snuff stick and took a leaf of bright tobacco from his pouch. "I met one of those Jacobites in Charles Town. He says the Roman Church is the only enlightened one. Then my folk in Scotland, they were Knox followers, and so——"

Mainwairing broke in. He had no intention of allowing MacAlpin to continue along this line. "Where have you come from this time, Sandy?"

The woodsman waved his hand westward. "Far Reach, up to Tuscarora Town. Been tradin' with King Blont."

"How are his people? Friendly?"

"Yep. Smoked a peace pipe. Taken to ploughing fields. Through with war, he says."

"I hope so. Come with me, MacAlpin. I'd like to take you to Mr. Fountaine. He was talking yesterday about wanting a guide who knows this country to teach his men to hunt and fish and train them in woodcraft."

"I'm their man, if he's got the shillin's to pay. I've been thinkin' I'd like me a rest for a spell through the winter. Next spring I've got plans——"

The two men walked over to the small building back of Fountaine's house. The weaving room. Roger knew he would find Robert Fountaine there, supervising the placing of his loom.

The front of the house was cluttered with furniture. Four of Bragg's men were breaking open the crates and taking off the wrappings. Barton, her mob-cap pulled down over her head so that not a lock of hair showed, in a Holland linen apron, stood near, supervising, her sharp tongue ready to scorch the hide off a man who pulled a nail wrong or scratched the satin mahogany and walnut. The subdued seamen were working with a will, the sooner to get out from under her rule.

Roger thought there was something almost tragic in the sight of the delicate, spindly French sofa and the blue satin-covered chairs sitting out under the oak trees. He recognized the furniture from the little salon in Meg's Lane. Well, that was the woman of it. They must carry their own civilization with them wherever they went. The amenities meant so much. Perhaps it went deeper. Perhaps the elegance of fine furniture and plate would create a new elegance in living in a New World. He knew he was happier in the background Rhoda had created at Queen's Gift than in bachelor Queen's Gift.

"Looks mighty elegant to me. Mighty elegant and mighty frail, for a he-man to set on." The woodsman's bright eyes twinkled. "That lady there, she be mouty proud of those little chairs. Is she Madam Fountaine?"

"She is Mis' Fountaine's woman."

MacAlpin whistled. "Great day in the mornin'!" he said under his breath. "We have gentry among us, just like James River, Virginny."

Robert Fountaine was seated on the long wooden bench threading his loom when Roger knocked at the door. He looked up. When he saw Roger his face brightened.

"It seems home to me, now that I have my loom," he said after the first greeting.

"May we come in, Mr. Fountaine?" Roger asked. "I have Sandy MacAlpin with me, a man who knows more about Carolina than anyone but the Surveyor General, Edward Moseley." He turned to Sandy. The woodsman stood with mouth sagging, looking from the loom to Fountaine. Mainwairing could read his thoughts, for his face was as open as the page of a book. How could one who got pleasure from weaving at a loom control men, or lead a band of settlers, or establish a new settlement in the wilderness? Roger had his own doubts, but he kept them well within himself.

"Mr. Fountaine is a famous weaver from Bristol. His woollens are known all over England," he said to MacAlpin.

Sandy's face cleared. A manufacturer of woollens. That was a different thing. He was enough of a trader to know the value of a good length of fine woollen cloth.

"Step inside, gentlemen." Fountaine's voice was cordial. He swept a bolt of cloth off a rush chair for Roger, and pointed to a bench.

"Have a seat, Mr. MacAlpin. You arrive opportunely. I have been talking with Mr. Mainwairing about the necessity of having a guide and practical woodsman attached to our little colony."

"I ben't a guide, sir. It's an Indian trader I am." The expression on Sandy's face was forbidding. Roger knew he would be hard to handle in this mood. He said nothing. Let Fountaine make the bid.

"We know nothing of the woods," the Huguenot said frankly. "We have among us carpenters and smiths, boatbuilders, husbandmen and yeomen, men who understand tilling the soil. But we have no hunters, though every man has a fowling-piece or a musket and is a proficient marksman. I

234

would gladly pay well to have you instruct our men. You'll find them eager learners."

"Thank you kindly, sir, but I be on my way down the Great Road to Charles Town for a supply of trade articles. I trade with Indians, sir. I'm nothing of a teacher."

A shadow came over Fountaine's face; his shoulders sagged a little and the light went out of his face. "I am sorry for that. Perhaps someone else will come who will undertake the work."

"The season is late. Traders have gone up the Virginia rivers."

Roger opened his lips to speak, but at the moment Gabrielle Fountaine opened the door opposite the loom and came into the room. Her arms were piled high with lengths of silks and woollens, a mass of bright colour as varied as a rainbow. She was wearing a flowered cotton frock, turned back over an embroidered ruffled petticoat. A bright gauze scarf, twisted about her head, hid the mass of dark hair, but its brilliance gave colour to her clear skin.

She dumped the armful of cloth on the top of a cedar chest, holding out both hands to Roger. "Isn't it nice that cook says we are to have supper for you here tonight! Think what it means to us, to have our dear friends with us at our first meal."

"Think what it means to your friends to be with you, Miss Gabrielle." Roger was smiling down at the girl. "I shall look forward to tonight with greatest anticipation, but pardon me. Here stands my old friend, Mr. Sandy MacAlpin, waiting to be named to you. Sandy, this is Miss Fountaine. I swear she has been bedevilling me to find someone to teach her to shoot, and tell her the names of the birds and the flowers and the trees of Carolina. Miss Gabrielle, no one knows these things better than friend Sandy. 'Tis a pity he must go to Charles Town, instead of tarrying here for a month or two."

Sandy glanced at the lovely young girl, then looked away, a bright pink flooding his face, setting every freckle into bold relief. He made one or two attempts to speak, and finally managed, in spite of obvious embarrassment, to say, "Haven't yet said when I were going down the Great Road. Mout be tomorrow, mout be a month from now. I——"

Gabrielle took his hard, gnarled hand. She smiled up at him; an engaging smile it was. "Oh, Mr. MacAlpin, you will teach me to shoot before you go, won't you?"

Sandy glanced quickly at Roger from under his shaggy

brows. Roger looked away to hide a smile. "Mout be, miss—providin'."

He would not say 'providin' what,' but Roger was quite satisfied.

"You must dine with us," Robert Fountaine said cordially. "We cannot promise much, the first evening we are in the house, but there will be an omelet of fine herbs, and a sweet."

MacAlpin hesitated, looking down at his travel-stained clothes. "Just as you are," Robert continued, with quick perception of the man's reluctance. "The young people will dress, but we older ones will not change."

Gabrielle went over and touched her father's hand lightly. "I must leave you. Barton and I are determined to set the furniture in place in the salon—great room the workmen call it—so I must fly. We will have supper at nine, when it is dark, so we can light the candles."

She went out the door. Roger saw her run across the path that led from the weaving room to the house. "Come, Sandy. I want to talk with you about my land up the river at Rocky Point." He turned to Fountaine. "Sandy carried chain for Mr. Moseley when he surveyed my grant, twelve or fifteen miles up the Cape Fear on the North East Fork. I haven't seen it myself, but Moseley tells me it is fine, fertile land."

"As good as can be," Sandy said with enthusiasm. "Rich bottom land. Perhaps you will be persuaded to leave the Albemarle for the Cape Fear, Mr. Mainwairing; I don't believe you have worn out your enthusiasm for virgin soil."

"No, by gad, I haven't. There's something that gets into a man's blood and drives him to seek new land in the wilderness."

"Amen to that," said Sandy. "Good day, Mr. Fountaine."

Fountaine was already at the loom. "We will see you at supper. Until then——"

Roger and Sandy MacAlpin walked to the high bank that overlooked the river. Roger sat down, his back against the rough bark of a great oak. It was shady and cool, and the long streamers of moss swayed gently in the passing breeze. Below them, the *Delicia* lay in the river, and farther down, the shallop's sails were drying in the sun. Several small boats were on the water, shuttling back and forth between the ship and shore. On the narrow beach, men worked.

"I am minded of another time when settlers came, filled with joy to gain a new free land." MacAlpin's words broke in on Roger's abstraction. "That was Sir John Yeamans' colony. They came in great ships, larger and higher than yon, and they came ashore with flags flying and the trumpets' blast and the roar of their field pieces, and Sir John stood beneath the flag, and a priest of God blessed the land, and blessed the new adventure. But it did not stand. No more than stood the earlier one of the Bermuda Adventurers. 'Tis a cursed land and no one will have dwelling on the shores of this river."

"Why do you say such things, MacAlpin? Colonies fail because the people who come are not men of strength. They have no iron to fight. They want gold lying on the ground, with no muscle expended to dig. It has been so always. Many a man, yes many a hundred, have gone back from the Albemarle, from Virginia and from the northern colonies. Look at Roanoke Island. Three times it failed. Do not say such words within hearing of these new men, to dampen their hopes."

Sandy nodded his head. "I've looked about. I've seen some gude men and some thin timber that will break like a reed. Mr. Fountaine's a breakable man, I say."

Roger said, "No. He's a man tempered to adversity. He's been a refugee from France. He's withstood persecution and hardship, and has risen above them."

"A Frenchman. I know them. They dwell on Goose Creek, and along the Ashley. Ravenels, Trenegasts, Manigauls, Laurents, Légares and a dozen more."

"Good men?"

"Aye. If you understand their talk, I suppose." The woodsman acknowledged grudgingly.

"And those others, they who reached the great river of the Mississippi, who travelled through the Spanish country—were they not Frenchmen? La Salle, Crèvecoeur?"

"Aye, but this man. He looks weak. How can he govern? How can he resist the forest and the wilderness and the Indians? He has built a stockade. So did Sir John's men, but it could not shut out the loneliness. When that came, where was the colony?"

Roger did not answer. Instead he said, "His daughter, Miss Gabrielle . . ."

The woodsman rose to the cast. "She is bonny, verra bonny. I think she might hold a fort from hostile foe."

"You will stay, Sandy? I'll leave with an easier mind, if you're here to guide them through the first winter."

"What of Mr. Moore, Mr. Roger Moore, who has sent for me to come to Charles Town?"

"Roger Moore? What does he want of you?"

The woodsman shook his head. "I don't know. Of a truth, I don't know. But Moore's son has a grant on this river, from the mouth northward. I don't recollect how far his grant runs. What land does Fountaine hold?"

"I do not remember the exact acreage. It lies along the river front from Old Town Creek."

"That would run t'ward the Forks. Moore won't like that. He wants the river-front land, I've been told. Does Mr. Fountaine hold by settling or by grant?"

"Both. Every settler one hundred acres; wife and servants fifty each. A separate grant of land for Fountaine—a larger acreage."

"By grant of the Proprietors?" Sandy asked shrewdly.

"Yes. Signed by the Palatine, my Lord Carteret."

Sandy squatted down on his heels. He took out his knife and began to fashion a face on a hickory nut. "Mr. Moore is a quick-tempered man, with a lordly way. Do you know him, Mr. Mainwairing?"

"No, but his brother Maurice is a friend of mine. He lives not far from me."

"The Colonel? I've guided him more than once. I walked with him the time he came with his troop of nigh a hundred men to help the garrison at Bath."

Roger nodded. He didn't add that he himself was at that garrison when the Tuscaroras came down the Pamticoe.

"I'm thinking that the Moores and their friends mean to settle this river. Old man is at outs with the government. He's fighting with the Governor and the Council. Some say Moore fought a duel with the Governor. I don't know, but they are talking revolt in the South. They don't like the Lord's Proprietors' ways."

Roger thought a moment. He remembered Maurice Moore's talk of laying out a town on the banks of the Lower Cape Fear. Perhaps the plan had gone forward while he was in England. So much the better; there would be activity on the river, and people. The chances for success of Fountaine's colony would be greater if others came. Of this he did not speak. He said, "I must go back to the ship. I'll speak to one of the men to assign you a bunk in the loghouse where the bachelors sleep."

"You take for granted." Sandy bristled a little.

"Yes. I take for granted you will stay, MacAlpin. Whatever Fountaine pays you, I'll double. It will be worth your while. When spring comes, you can go to Charles Town. Mr. Moore has waited this long. He can wait a few months longer."

"Aye, that he can. I have no love for young Roger Moore. He's too arrogant. If 'twas Maurice who sent for me, no one could hold me back."

"Not even——" Mainwairing laughed knowingly.

"Not even a fair, bonny maid, with kind ways of talking." MacAlpin spoke earnestly. "Don't think I raise my eyes to that fine lady. 'Tis protecting she needs, not from men but from this wilderness. If I can discover this country to her in its badness and in its goodness, I can make her strong to defend herself."

Roger shook the woodsman's gnarled hand. "You're a good man, Sandy MacAlpin. I have no fear for these people under your guidance. They will learn the way of the wilderness, if they are men of strength. If not, let them go back to England."

MacAlpin rose to his feet, his eyes turned towards the west gate. "There's a Core Indian down there, riding a mighty fine bay mare. I wonder where he got the animal."

Roger turned his head. "I don't know where the Indian found the mare, but she's mine. She threw Miss Fountaine this morning, and ran off somewhere by the lakes, four or five miles below here."

"Um-m." The woodsman's eyes travelled over the horse. "Looks as if she's been well curried."

"So she has." Roger slanted across the compound. "Come on. I want to question that Indian. Do you know him?"

"Yes. His name is Kullu. He's a grandson of Atta Kulla Kulla, the most steady friend of the English."

"Is this young one a good friend?"

MacAlpin pursed up his lips. "Can't say. I've had no truck with the Cores for some time. Good enough, I suppose."

Roger nodded. They had come within a few feet of the horse, When they came up, the Indian slipped to the ground and extended the reins to Roger.

"Your horse?" he asked in the Tuscarora tongue.

"Where did you find her?"

The Indian nodded his head in the direction they had hunted that morning.

"You've given her a good brushing," Roger commented,

239

running his hands over the horse's legs. He turned to MacAlpin. "Shall I give him money? I don't know the customs of these Banks Indians."

"No. Tobacco would please him more. Let me take care of it. You just take your mare and move away. I'll talk to the fellow."

Roger watched the trader and the Indian for a moment. The Indian answered questions rather sullenly. He pointed towards the forest once or twice, shaking his head.

MacAlpin wasn't satisfied with the story the Indian had told him, but he went to his pack, which he had left near the little chapel, opened it and handed the Indian a pipe, a pouch and two twists of dark tobacco. The Indian took the gift and went off.

Roger noticed that the men near by had stopped their work. They watched the Indian with curiosity and some uneasiness. This nearly naked red man was the first Indian they had seen. They did not understand his presence.

David Moray came up from behind. He took the reins from Roger's hand. "She looks none the worse for her run," he remarked, his eyes going over the mare. "Someone has given her a good vigorous currying since I saw her last. The Indian?"

"I wonder," Roger answered.

"Has Miss Fountaine recovered from her fall?" Moray questioned.

"Why don't you ask for yourself, David?"

Moray grinned. " 'Twouldn't be seemly for Mr. Roger Mainwairing's groom to inquire about the health of Miss Gabrielle Fountaine. That would be presumptuous."

Roger said, "Why do you keep up this disguise? Surely you are safe enough, here in Carolina."

"It pleases the young lady to treat me as a bondman. Why should I spoil her innocent pleasures?"

"You're a good hater, David. Surely it's not the girl's fault, or her father's, that you got yourself into the mess so that you were auctioned off, sold for your participation in the Stuarts' cause."

David interrupted. "Pardon me, Mr. Mainwairing not auctioned off—taken from debtors' prison."

"Oh, that's the story? Well, it's your affair, David, but it seems to me——"

David said, "I'll take the mare out to the ship, Mr. Mainwairing. All the other horses are already aboard."

From the change in Moray's voice and attitude Roger discerned that someone was approaching. He turned his head. MacAlpin had come up. He stood to one side, looking steadily at Moray, a puzzled look on his brown face, as though he were trying to remember something.

"Moray is in charge of my horses," Roger said by way of introduction.

"Moray?" the trader said. "I've known many a Moray in the old country. From the Firth of Moray country?"

" 'Tis a large clan," David replied noncommittally.

MacAlpin watched the groom striding along the path that led to the bank. "Walks like a soldier. An officer, I'd be thinkin'. Did you say he was your groom, Mr. Mainwairing?"

"No, I didn't. I said he was in charge of my horses for the trip over. Before that, I believe he was Mr. Fountaine's gardener."

"I'd ha' sworn he was gentry. But many a man nae cares to tell fra whence he came. That's the good of a new country. We don't inquire too closely."

"What information did you get from the Indian?" Roger wanted to switch the subject.

"He says he found the mare down by the second lake, just as you see her now. Swears he didn't rub her down. I believe him. Never knew an Indian to exert himself thataway."

Roger asked a question: "What are you thinking, Sandy?"

"I'm a thinkin' that it mout hae been a pirate, or a runaway slave, that got her first. Did ye note one rein was broken off, as if she'd pulled herself loose?"

Roger dismissed the idea of pirates; his mind caught at the other alternative. "Runaway slave? Is there a station near here?"

"Green Swamp is where they hide. Sometimes a hundred there at a time, going and coming."

Roger turned this over in his mind. "So there's a sanctuary for runaway slaves at Green Swamp," he said thoughtfully.

Chapter 19

THE HEARTHSTONE

The room was ready, the furniture in place. The long narrow table of oak, with matching benches, was set with pewter and the second-best china. Barton had been firm about this; the best china was for Madam, no one else. It was bone white with delicate gold bands. The second-best pleased Gabrielle, for it was gay, with pink roses and dark blue borders, and went well with the pewter goblets and dishes. A Holland linen cloth lay over the table and, in the centre, Gabrielle had arranged a low centrepiece of green leaves and cloudlike blossoms of Queen Anne's lace, that grew wild along the old fields.

The room was pleasant and comfortable; the cypress lining set over the old logs of Sir John Yeamans' dwelling was too new to have taken on any lustre, but the wood was beautiful in grain, and the fireplace was large, so large it carried six-foot logs. It was made of old ballast stones, and had needed only to be mended in places to be ready for use. The crane swung from the side and a trivet sat on the hearth. The evening was cool enough that flint had been touched to the resinous wood, which Sandy had brought from the forest. Lightwood, he told Gabrielle, as he laid thin slivers under the great logs. It came from the turpentine pines that grew strongly along the rim of the banks, back as far as Far Reach, and beyond.

'Twas turpentine that would make the colony rich and prosperous, Sandy told her; naval stores were in demand at Jamaica and Bermuda as well as England. Tar and turpentine and pitch—he could readily show the men how to tap and box the trees and fire the wood for tar and pitch. Then there would be charcoal for cooking.

"There are many ways to make money from the land," Gabrielle said, watching the fire blaze brightly.

"It is a good land." Sandy wiped the pitch from his hands with a handful of Spanish moss. "Good if a body treats it good." He looked at Gabrielle earnestly for a moment. "I
242

want that your father makes success here. Twice people have come and gone away. They say they starved here. Hell's fire, how can anyone starve on the land that will grow anything? They were lazy, shiftless folk; that's what they were. I've heard them talk. I know."

"You've been here a long time, Mr. MacAlpin."

"Sandy's what I'm called, miss, from the coast to the rapids."

"Sandy." Gabrielle smiled as she said his name.

"Aye, Ma'am. Fifty years, if my count is right. A man loses track of time in the wilderness, but I've a notched tree up Far Reach. My calendar, I call it. I go by the moon."

"You must have come in with Sir John," Gabrielle exclaimed.

Sandy nodded. He stood, back to the fire, his thin, sinewy frame silhouetted by the flames. "I'm nigh on seventy years, miss. I came up with Sir John from the south. I was with him in Bermuda too. A big man he was; it broke his health, those snivelling weak-livered people belly-achin' and cryin' to go home to their comforts. Great day in the mornin', miss, nae one of them but had his record—debtors' prison, Bridewell an' the like—yet they wanted their comforts."

Gabrielle looked at him more closely. Not a grey hair showed in his thick sandy mane. He looked like a lion, she thought, unafraid of the forest, or the forest people.

"Are you the only one who stayed?" she asked, as she put the candles into the pewter sticks and placed them at intervals down the table.

Sandy shook his head. "No, Ma'am. There's a few like myself, trading up the river, and a family or two living up Far Reach."

"How do they live?" Gabrielle asked.

"Mostly huntin' and trappin' and a little plantin'. They'll be glad that a settlement's come. Makes them feel safer from pirates."

"Pirates?" Gabrielle set a candle on the table and turned to see if Sandy were serious. There was no twinkling laughter in his pale eyes.

"Pirates' River—that's what we call her. Didn't no one tell you about pirates hidin' in Topsail Inlet? Or about Blackbeard and Vane and Rackham?"

"No," Gabrielle said. "Those men were in Nassau. I saw them there when they came to Captain Woodes Rogers to receive King's Pardon."

"King's Pardon!" Sandy threw back his head and laughed aloud.

"But they signed the papers."

"Put their hand to signin' King's Pardon?" Sandy chuckled, his body shaking with mirth. "More'n likely they'll put their hands to King's Treasury."

Gabrielle was silent. Barton had come quietly into the room carrying a tray of dishes. She balanced it on the edge of the table, and turned her eyes on MacAlpin. "It's a puir fellow who'd make up tales to frighten a young girl," she said scornfully.

"Hist, woman! 'Tis no makin' of mine. This river is Pirates' River. Stede Bonnet called it that and he's the king of all the waters around here. Best tell your father that. Tell him to pay tribute when the pirates ask, if he wants to plant in peace."

"Pay tribute to pirates! How horrible!" Gabrielle's foot came down on the hearthstone smartly. "No, never!"

Sandy said, "Better do it. 'Twill save lives and property."

Barton looked at him, her hands on her hips. "'Tis the first time I ever heard of a Scot willing to pay tribute," she said scornfully. "'Tis a Highlander you must be. No lowland Scot would utter such words."

"Woman," Sandy retorted, "have done! No one can accuse me of giving a shilling tribute to any mon."

"Ha! But you tell us to give our money to loathsome pirates."

"So I did. I said it would save lives and property. Those fellows would as lief burn off this compound as eat. Rather, I think."

Gabrielle interrupted. "Please say nothing to my father yet, Mr. MacAlpin. He has so many worries."

"Better to know danger and be ready for it," the Scot said sagely.

"I know. But we can be prepared as we are prepared for Indians, or wild animals. A heavy stockade, with a blockhouse and sentries posted at all times. That's all we can do against any danger that threatens us."

Sandy nodded, admiration strong in his shrewd eyes. "Yes, miss. That is all we can do."

Barton moved about the table, placing dishes. She emptied the tray and turned to Sandy. "We ain't fearful folk, MacAlpin. Ye and the like of ye can't afright us by your tales."

"Don't want to 'fright you." Sandy was somewhat subdued under Barton's eagle glance. "Jest want to warn, that's all."

Barton didn't trouble to answer. With the tray under her arm, she marched off with firm, decisive tread.

Sandy whistled. "A prickly pear, that one," he commented.

Gabrielle, amused by the little exchange between the two, smiled. "She has a stout heart, my Barton."

Sandy left the room for a bundle of lightwood to lay on the hearth. Left alone, Gabrielle looked about to see that all was in order. She was satisfied with the result. The oaken furniture suited the great room. Chairs, benches and presses, the Welsh dresser and the long hunting board from her father's weaving room seemed to fit in as if they had been built for it. Covers and curtains of crimson cloth, of their own weaving, gave life and colour. The French furniture from the little salon at Meg's Lane would go into the wing they had set apart for her mother: a bedroom and a sitting-room. She sighed a little, and her fine eyes grew thoughtful. They would bring her mother ashore tonight, late, when the moon was up and the people were in their houses or their tents. It was Celestine's idea to give Madame a sleeping potion. Then she would not know of the change. It would be easy: a litter swung from the ship's side to the periauger, a few trusted men to carry her as she slept. Yes, that would be best. In the morning she would wake surrounded by her own things, sleeping in her own bed. Her father approved of Celestine's suggestion. Gabrielle saw by the expression of relief that crossed his thin face how deeply he had dreaded the move. If she could be brought secretly . . .

Satisfied with what she saw in the room, Gabrielle walked out under the great oak trees that grew in a circle near the edge of the bank. The sun was low, almost at the top of the forest trees that cut the western horizon.

The river below was quiet, dark with shadows. The marsh-grass, bent by the gentle wind, resembled the green waves of the sea. In the centre of this sea of green, a flight of egrets rose and flew along the slow-moving river. The evening was quiet. The men who lately sawed and hammered and sang lusty, rowdy songs as they worked had left the forge and the work bench and gone to their new homes. Tonight they would eat at their own hearths for the first time.

Gabrielle's throat tightened as she thought of this. She turned from the river to look towards the compound. Little grey columns of smoke were rising here and there from the new, half-completed houses. Small cooking fires burned beyond the field where some men camped in the open. The sharp bark of a dog and the lowing of cattle sounded far away, across the great clearing. She stood for a long time, seeing, yet not seeing, these evidences of a new colony, her active mind trying to penetrate the grey obscurity of the future. What lay ahead of them? Success or failure—which?

She felt a tugging at her brown woollen skirts. Her mother's two little King Charles spaniels cavorted at her feet, demanding attention. How they had escaped from the south wing she could not imagine. She lifted them and, with one tucked under either arm, went back to the house. The sun was down. Plumes of crimson flared in the western sky. Crimson was reflected on the great bank of cumulus clouds that hung along the coast, driving seawards. Violent colours lay across the sky, and shadows over the untracked forest. What mystery it held in its depths! Mystery and death. She shuddered involuntarily and accelerated her pace. She had time only to bathe hurriedly and step into her white flowered taffeta before it was time for the guests to arrive. Those dear guests, who would be gone on the morrow.

The dinner was over. Cook had done herself proud. Carolina food, Gabrielle told the guests—the wild turkey Sandy had shot, the sea bass Captain Bragg's men had landed in the creek, the entree of rabbit, delectably cooked with dried pease, and a pudding made of raisins and currants.

The serving boys had cleared away when Roger Mainwairing's man came in, bearing a hamper of wine.

Gabrielle rose. "I'll sit in the other end of the room while you have your port," she said, making a slight curtsy, first to her father, then to her guests.

Roger would have none of it, nor would Edward Colston. "No, you must stay." Roger got up from the bench to place her in her chair at the foot of the table.

"I have brought the wine for a purpose," Roger said. With his own hands he filled the glasses his servant placed on the table. "A rare purpose, to which I have been looking forward."

Instead of sitting at his place at the table, he moved across to the fireplace. Standing with his back to the fire, he raised his glass high.

"To the Hearthstone! God bless all who dwell within this house, and the guests who gather under this roof." He touched the glass to his lips, and spilled the wine on the hearthstone. "I pour libations to the household gods," he said, smiling at Gabrielle.

The toast to the hearth was drunk to the last drop. Tears were in Gabrielle's eyes, and Robert Fountaine's were misty.

"To Carolina!" he said. "May its waters bear our ships; may its forests house and give us warmth; may its earth sustain us with plenty! To Carolina!"

"Hear! Hear!" shouted Roger and Edward.

Only Sandy MacAlpin sat silent, his thoughts far away. He caught himself, and lifted his glass to Gabrielle. "To a gracious lady! May she love Carolina and find comfort in her bounty!"

Gabrielle smiled, touched by the old man's words.

"I am minded," Sandy said after a pause, "of another evening at this hearthstone. I seem to see that gay company now, laughter and singing. And another night, six years later, Sir John walking across the floor, back and again, his chin sunk on his breast, his hands clenched together. He did not like failure, Sir John Yeamans, but his people would not stay; they were too weak. His voice rose. He spoke solemnly, as if he were taking an oath. 'We do not want weak men. Carolina is a jealous mistress; she asks for strength.' "

Roger Mainwairing broke the silence that followed MacAlpin's words. "If Sir John Yeamans had settled Old Town with men who, of their own choice, made the venture, it would have been different. He took what they sent—political prisoners, who had the choice of America or the block; men from debtors' prison or worse." He turned to Robert Fountaine, who sat silent at the head of his table. "If Sir John's colony had been settled by free men, as your colony is, Mr. Fountaine, the colony would be here to this day. Only free men can build a free country."

No one spoke. The truth of Mainwairing's words had made too deep an impression on everyone at the table. After a time Colston said, "By God's hand, I think we do well to send free men to the New World. I shall write to my grandfather this night."

Barton entered the room then. She had in her hand a flat woven basket of some native handcraft. It was lined with grape leaves, deep green touched with silver; on the leafy cover lay a great mass of tawny grapes. She placed the basket on the table in front of Gabrielle. "They were left for

247

the young mistress," she said. "A red Indian brought them to the kitchen door."

Sandy leaned forward. "Scuppernongs. I did not know they were ripe. They're early this year."

"Scuppernong grapes," Roger said, smiling. "The purple James and the amber Scuppernongs are prized. They grow in the forests along the streams."

Gabrielle selected one from the vine. Roger passed the basket down the table. As she lifted the amber globe to her lips, Gabrielle saw David Moray pass the open window. A slow colour burned her cheeks. She did not need to be told who it was that had sent the fruits of the forest to grace the first feast at the hearthstone.

The *Delicia* crossed the bar at sunrise and turned northeastward, to follow the Banks to the entrance to Albemarle Sound.

Roger Mainwairing was on deck as the ship sped on a good southeast breeze. As they passed Barren Head and Topsail Inlet, he saw the masts of three ships rising over the sandy banks. He spoke to the Captain, who put his glass on the shore line.

"No flags visible," Bragg said shortly. "I'll bet my chance in Mohammed's paradise that pirates air nestin' there, hatchin' out trouble for some poor merchantman. Lucky for us, we are ridin' high with no cargo. Not that they are likely to attack Captain Rogers' guardship."

Roger said, "I heard in Charles Town that Captain Rhett was out to run Stede Bonnet down. Rhett boasted that he'd have Bonnet's head on a pike at Charles Town wharves before the year is out."

"Only three months to run," Bragg said. "Bonnet's a shrewd sailor. For the life of me, Mr. Mainwairing, I never could understand Bonnet. A French gentleman born, they say down south; and him consorting with Rackham and Vane, and Blackbeard. Greatest scoundrels as ever drew suck from mothers' milk."

"I've never heard Bonnet's story," Roger said; "only that he never murders his captives."

"So they say, but I don't believe it. He's after the women captives quick enough—takes them, dresses them up in pearls and gold chains and keeps them prisoner in his cabin to serve his pleasure. Like old Borgia, he wants a virgin every night."

"Boastful," said Roger, still watching the coast. "Ah! There! A black flag at the masthead."

Bragg grabbed the glass from his hand. He looked long, then shouted his orders. "There's a pirate ship about to take after us."

Colston joined them. He was fresh from the barber; his cinnamon-brown coat had fine lace ruffles, and his breeches of doeskin were strapped with small silver buckles below the knee. "Pirates, you say? Where?"

Roger pointed to the square black flag, plainly visible.

"Ah! So it is the Jolly Roger. I say, Captain Bragg, do you think they'll try to follow?"

"I'd like them to try," Bragg said, his mouth grim. "We'd blow the spume in her eyes and rake her with our deck guns; but she won't try, whoever the captain is, when he makes out the *Delicia*. There's scarce a ship in the Caribbean that's got the canvas to overhaul her; but if there's one of them two captains there, Rackham or Vane, they'll haggle like traders of Javvy to take a prize. I'd like to see their faces when we fetch them a blast of our deck cannon."

Roger Mainwairing looked grave. "I don't care to lose my merchandise, so lets' not test the guns, Bragg. It's canvas you want, not a fight, this time."

Bragg nodded. "You're right," he said, visibly reluctant. "I know you're right; but I'm fair spoilin' for a good fight."

A ship came out of the inlet, a high-waisted galleon, canvas spread. She hung for a time at the entrance, as if unable to make up her mind in which direction to set sail.

"A Spaniard! By the Eternal!" Bragg said.

"More likely some pirate has taken a Spanish frigate prize," Colston exclaimed. "See, she's veering south. She doesn't want to give chase."

"I'm well suited," Roger said, handing the glass to the Captain. "I've had enough of storms and sea fights. I'll be glad for safe harbour in the Albemarle."

Roger saw David Moray at the rail, watching the Spaniard. He left the Captain and Colston talking breakfast, and went to join David.

"Have you made up your mind, David? Do you come with me to the Albemarle, or do you go on to Virginia?"

"The die is cast. Last night I flipped a coin; Carolina turned."

"Well enough. No need, now, to have more words of

bondman. You can come before the Council and apply for a grant of land, and become a freeholder."

"I'm not sure that I can pay the price, Mr. Mainwairing."

"It is little. Whatever it is, I'll advance it to you."

"I don't want help." Moray spoke shortly.

"Against your first crop," Mainwairing went on, without heeding the interruption. "I know a parcel, vacant for want of proper seating; not more than a dozen miles from Queen's Gift on Harvey's Neck."

"Is it water-front land?"

"Yes, and a smal house on it. In fact it is now in my name. You can go on as tenant, if you like, or as owner."

"Thank you. You are kind." David Moray said slowly. I don't want to be stiff-necked——"

"As if a Scot could be otherwise!"

Moray laughed then, a great rolling laugh that had youth and strength behind it.

"That's better. I've wondered at your glumness. You used to be glum when you were a child and I visited your father on Moray Firth."

Moray looked up surprised. "So you've known all the while!" he exclaimed.

"Yes, since the night I saw you pass at Meg's Lane. You look the image of your father."

"God rest his soul!" David said. "But it seems centuries since you could have been at our house on the Firth. I can't think much farther back than '15, and the Jacobite uprising. And the Jacobite uprising? Best forgotten. A new world, a new life. Is it not so?"

"As you will," Roger said, grasping his hand. "The past is dead; let it lie. But tell me why you stay in Carolina rather than the more settled Virginia."

"Virginia is a Crown Colony, and an escaped Jacobite might not be welcome."

"That's not the answer. Nor do I believe that you flipped a coin to settle your mind."

"If you must know, I like the country. The grapes are superb."

"Ah," said Roger. "I understand."

David burned a dusky red, "A check on my tongue," he said angrily. "I talk too much."

Roger smiled. He knew who had sent the great basket of Scuppernongs to the lovely Gabrielle. "Not that I blame you," he said, apropos of nothing.

250

On the deck of the Spanish frigate two people, a man and a woman, leaned against the rail, following the spread sails of the *Delicia*.

"You could have overtaken her, Stede," the woman said, disappointment on her mobile face.

"I did not wish to, my dear; Stede Bonnet wastes no shot on cargoless ships."

"I'd like to sink every ship sailing to the Albemarle and every ship sailing from that river," the woman said vehemently.

Bonnet's eyes were admiring Anne Bonney. "You're a vixen. You hate well and strongly, my queen, but why the Albemarle? Why not the James River?"

"Because I hate the Albemarle and everyone who lives on its shores. I wish death and torture for them all."

"You're venomous, my dear Anne." He looked at her fondly; he liked her thus, cold and cruel and vindictive. "You must have some reason——?"

"Reason enough!" she said shortly. Twisting her lithe body around, she threw her arms about his neck and pressed his face against hers with her clasped hands. "Promise me you will raze the town on Queen Anne's Creek—fire, pillage and rapine. They're rich, those planters. They've gold. Promise your Anne. Promise." She laid her mouth against his, holding him to her. "Promise, my Stede. Promise."

"I promise. This ship, which I bought of Rackham at your request, shall justify her name, *Queen Anne's Revenge*. We'll sail up the Sound—" he stopped, his face darkening—"if Rhett doesn't track me down first."

She held him close, laid her hand across his mouth to smother his words. "Don't, dear heart. Don't speak. It is evil to speak of such disaster."

He looked gloomily across the water. "They say in Charles Town that Rhett is getting ready an expedition. Gold, much gold, is offered for my head."

She glanced at him. Her pale blue eyes seemed almost black in her emotion. "Come," she whispered, "come to our cabin. Why should we think of evil when we are together? We must make up for the days and months we have lost, Stede."

Her passion lifted his blood until it showed throbbing in the veins of his temples. They moved swiftly across the deck, through the open door of the cabin. The evil-browed men

251

who were on deck looked at each other and laughed knowingly.

One dark-visaged fellow began a pirate ditty:

> "With pitch and tar, her hands were hard
>   Though once like velvet soft.
> She weighed the anchor, heaved the lead
>   And boldly went aloft."

"Best not let Captain hear you, sonny," Graves, his companion, offered. "He'd cut the ears from your head, easy as that." He slashed through the air with a knife.

The other laughed loudly. His grimy hand pressed back the long oily locks that hung to his shoulders. The ear was gone, shaved close to the head, only the gaping orifice visible.

" 'Tis been done already," he said. "A better man than him got there first."

"Drop your hair," the other said. "I can't stomach the sight."

The earless one laughed louder. "Proper pirate you be, Juan," he taunted. "Earless man be nothing to a noseless man. You'd be a pretty pirate in a fight."

"Have done," said the second. "I came piratin' for gold, not to scallop men's faces."

Chapter 20

THE CLOSED DOOR

Gabrielle missed her friends—Roger Mainwairing most of all, then Edward Colston. She had come to feel close to him, a strong, sisterly affection. Then there was David Moray. . . . She found herself thinking of him often, wondering why he had not come near her before he left.

But why should he? She had not been kind to him. She had been superior, putting him always in the servant's place. She did not do that to actual servants—Barton, or the serving boy. . . . Still, a fine strong man who languishes in jail for debt was not worthy of her compassion. She resolutely turned her thoughts away from the former gardener to her present complexities.

The new life was so different from the old well-ordered existence at Meg's Lane that Gabrielle had to use all the fortitude her strengthening character held to meet the change with equanimity.

Celestine was difficult. She did not meet change as readily as Barton. She wanted this and that for her mistress— impossible things, such as special herbs and spices, a length of satin to cover a chair or make a pillow, a bolt of fine Flemish lace for Madame's night robes.

Gabrielle grew weary of saying, "It is impossible, Celestine. We have not the things with us. Make a list. When the ship comes in again, I'll send a letter to the Bristol shop, or to Jamaica. Do not be impatient."

"But Madame has nevaire, nevaire wear a night robe that is not edged with Valenciennes or Flemish lace. It is horrible to contemplate." Her black eyes filled with tears of anger.

"Perhaps we could rip something off one of my dresses," Gabrielle suggested.

Celestine held up her hand in horror. "Madame wear something belonging to another person! No. No. Better a night robe trimmed only by fine tucking, than to borrow."

Gabrielle had a thought. "Why not a trimming made of a strip of scalloped linen—handkerchief linen?" Barton could flute it. She was sure there was a fluting iron. Celestine was satisfied. It would mean work, hard work for her, but the good God knew Celestine had nevaire, nevaire spared herself or her eyes where Madame was concerned.

"I know that, Celestine." Gabrielle put her arm over the woman's fat shoulders. "What would we have done without you? To think you are the only one, the only one my mother recognizes. See how she loved you and depends on you."

"It is true," Celestine said, quite mollified now. "I will make the fine little ruffles, hand-scalloped, and Barton will fetch me the iron for fluting. It will be work, but Celestine does not abandon herself to idleness."

The woman went off through the door that led from the great room to the wing given over to Madam—a door that was never opened save when Robert Fountaine or his daughter went through, or Celestine came out.

Gabrielle's eyes were fixed on the door long after the compact figure and sleek glossy head of the maid had passed through. It was a door brought from England, panelled with double crosses—the Crusaders' door, or as the poorer folk called it, a witch door. Safeguarded by the crosses, the door was protection against all evil spirits.

Gabrielle thought of the old superstitious belief. She hoped that a blessing and a protection lay in the Crusaders' cross. It seemed to her that a light emanated from the door, bringing the cross into prominent relief. A sign? Or only a passing shaft of sunlight, filtered through the swaying moss that drooped from the limbs of the great oak beside the outer door?

It was Monday. Gabrielle Fountaine smiled as she stepped outside and walked across the garden. As yet there was nothing to show but rank carpet grass, grown thickly, in what was once the Governor's garden. But it would be different in the spring. She had had plans drawn, and in walking about she had found outlines of old beds, framed with ballast stones that had been taken from ships which sailed up the river long years past.

The thought of the sacrifices that had been made to found the colony, the evidences of its tragic ending, saddened her. Yet as she looked about her, almost every house held something of the old—a door reset, square-hewn cypress sills laid anew; logs carried from a ruined cabin, to form the walls of a new dwelling. The new building on the old. That was as it

254

should be—moving forward from the old, yet holding the foundations intact.

She made a little wager with herself as she walked along the path. Next year would see a garden as gay and lovely as any in Old Town.

Monday, without doubt, and clothes-lines filled with gay washings. A rivalry existed in every small cottage and log house. A good housekeeper sets clothes to soak Sunday night, to be ready for early washing. To be first to hang out the week's wash—that was an accomplishment worthy of the best Old Country tradition.

For the New World carried over the habits of the Old, she thought as she made her way towards the stockade where she was to meet Sandy MacAlpin. People would live here, as they had lived at home. Women wanted to be surrounded by familiar things—the Welsh dresser, the wedding chest, the china tea-set which belonged to mother or grandmother, the shining pewter. So it was with lesser folk, so with greater. To carry over the Old World to the New was the part women played in the scheme of things. She laughed a little, walking through the forest path. She was getting to be a philosopher these days.

Just beyond the east gate of the stockade she came on Sandy. He was sitting on his haunches, whittling some small wooden object from a cypress knee, which he had polished until it looked like old ivory. With him was the Indian Kullu, standing against the trunk of a great tulip-poplar tree. The Indian was talking, making what sounded to Gabrielle like a series of guttural sounds, almost grunts. Near him, against a log, Sandy's long musket and powder horn were visible.

When he saw Gabrielle, Sandy got to his feet, pulled off his dented bonnet, and spoke his good day.

"I've a range all ready, Mistress—a good open place in the woods near the creek, where I've set up a target. Only a step this way."

Gabrielle followed Sandy. The Indian moved in behind her, following without sound. His presence made her look nervously over her shoulder from time to time. The bronze oiled body moved silently, as sinuously as a forest animal.

When they came to the spot Sandy had selected, she saw he had set up a crude bull's-eye target on a tree.

"We start on this," he said. He pulled a rag through the barrel of the fowling-piece, squinted through the bore to see that it was well cleaned. He put in the charge and handed the

255

piece to Gabrielle. She had shot before, in Ireland, when they had gone out on the estate of my Lord Carteret for pheasants. But she did not tell this to Sandy. She was not sure but that she had forgotten all the gamekeeper had taught her.

"Lay the piece on my shoulder," Sandy said, "and close one eye. Take a squint along the barrel to the marker out there. Take your time, Mistress. No good shooting comes from a quick aim. Your flint? Yes, now you are ready."

Gabrielle laid the musket on his shoulder, sighted carefully until the bull's eye lay well within her vision.

"By the great Jehovah!" Sandy shouted. "You've hit the outer ring of the target."

Gabrielle was disappointed. "I should have hit the centre!" she exclaimed. "Let me reload."

"'Sdeath! You've shot before," Sandy chided. "You did not tell me. Where was that—in England, in Scotland?"

"Neither. 'Twas in Ireland, when we went shooting pheasants one autumn. The gamekeeper instructed me."

"And you did not tell me. You would make a fool of old Sandy."

"No. No. It was so long ago I might have forgotten." She shot twice after that, each time close to the large central ring.

"Well enough," Sandy observed. Sandy was pleased. He turned away. "Where is Kullu?" he exclaimed. The Indian had disappeared.

They prepared to go back to the stockade. Sandy had shouldered his fowling-piece when an arrow sped through the air, straight to the heart of the bull's-eye.

"Ah!" Sandy said. "That's shooting."

Kullu came out of the forest. He stood close to them, bending the string to a feathered arrow. "Mistress she try," he said.

Gabrielle looked at the yew bow. "I don't believe I can bend it," she said dubiously.

"Try," Sandy said. "No success without trying."

She shot. The arrow went wild. The Indian took another from the quiver and stood before her. "Watch," he said. "Watch feet so, arm so, eyes to look forward. Pull slow."

Gabrielle hit the tree that held the target, but above the marker.

"Too fast. Two three days try, then Mistress know how shoot like Cherokee."

Gabrielle smiled. "I don't think I can learn so quickly, Kullu, but I'll try."

"Good," said the Indian. He picked up his quiver, slung the bow over his shoulder and plunged through the bushes to the river. Sandy and Gabrielle went back to the stockade.

"I'll try to teach all the women to shoot. If they can't learn to shoot, they can learn to load. It is well for women to know how to take care of themselves in a new country."

A shiver passed over Gabrielle's body. A shadow of things to come fell over her path as a great bird flew before them.

" 'Sdeath! A hen turkey, a twenty-pounder!" Sandy shouted. He began to make ready his piece, but the great wings were less strong. The bird flew heavily, close to the ground. After a moment it dropped in the path. When they came close, they saw an arrow embedded under its wing.

Sandy shouldered the slain bird. "Here's your supper. A present from Kullu."

Gabrielle looked over her shoulder.

"No use looking. He's gone. Just left a visiting card—a farewell card, you might say."

"But I want to thank him," Gabrielle exclaimed, taking a step in the direction of the creek.

"No need," Sandy was laconic. "He's gone—halfway to Far Reach by now, Mistress."

Gabrielle stopped at Amos Treloar's log house. There she left Sandy, who went on to Fountaine's kitchen with the turkey. She found Mary hanging out a line of clothes, her red skirts turned back over a short black petticoat, her mouth full of wooden pins.

Gabrielle sat down on a bench near the wooden tubs and waited until the goodwife had finished.

When Mary saw Gabrielle she was horrified and ran to bring a rush chair. " 'Tis a shame for a fine leddy like Mistress Gabrielle Fountaine to sit on a washing bench. You'll be spoiling yer pretty skirt, you will."

Gabrielle pointed to her hem stuck with beggar lice, the sticky burs of a plant that grew by the stream.

"I've been practising shooting at a mark. I walked along the creek and see what happened."

Mary held her hands aloft. "Dearie me! That I'd live to see the day when a fine leddy do the like! Shootin' is man's work, miss, and not for dainty hands."

"I want to know how to shoot," Gabrielle said. She saw it was not the time to broach to Mary Treloar the subject of learning to shoot. She must be allowed to get used to the idea that it could, conceivably, be woman's work.

"The kettle's aboil, and a dish of tea will be good." Mary bustled into the kitchen, a lean-to of the log house.

"Thank you. It's what I need."

A few minutes later Mary came out. "I'd be asking ye within," she apologized, "but we're in a fix inside. No time to settle ourselves yet. But yesterday I baked a saffron cake and a wee pastie for Amos. I'd be proud if you'd try 'un."

Gabrielle drank her tea and ate the little meat pastie with relish, and broke a piece of saffron cake. "It's delicious," she said. "I'll have to ask you to give Barton your rule for pasties."

Mary reddened with delight. "I'd be proud to show her the real Welsh way, though maybe she would want the Cornish. Myself, I hold the Welsh to be finer."

"Whichever rule this cake is made by," Gabrielle assured her.

Gabrielle rose and carried the dishes inside. The room was large and most of the simple cottage furniture in place. "What beautiful old furniture!" she said, admiring the Welsh dresser, already laden with its display of pewter and Dutch china.

" 'Tis my own mother's," Mary said. "I'm sorry that the room is not so tidy as it belongs to be, but I'll have it righted by the week's end."

"It's nice. So comfortable."

"Yes'm, that's what Amos says last night when we ate our first supper in our own house."

Gabrielle went outdoors. Mary followed her. "I'm ready to say I made something of a fool of myself, there on the ship, Miss Gabrielle. 'Twas the long journey, and I was fearful. But now that we have the house, fine and big, and I'm getting down to me work again, I feel different. It's idleness makes us women restive." She added in a burst of candor, "Idleness gives women into Satan's hands, Mistress."

Gabrielle walked down the narrow road that led to her house. She must take time to go to the homes of all the settlers. It would be well to know how they felt and what progress they were making. She hoped they were all like Mary, more content when they took up their routine duties of making a home. She saw plainly that the success of the venture rested on the women, not on the men. No matter how content a man might be, a discontented woman could pull everything awry. She sighed. At the moment the task ahead of her loomed large.

The first week in October her father held service on Sunday morning. The chapel roof was still not finished. The men had set up a bush tent roofed with brush; under this they placed the panelled pulpit her father had brought over. It was a gift from one of the older Huguenot temples in London, and it carried the good wishes of the London congregation. The benches were made from newly cut cypress logs, the sap still running.

Robert Fountaine read the service, dressed in the black robe and white linen falling-band of the lay reader. He appeared fragile, with a spiritual fervor not of this world. It tore Gabrielle's heart to see the sorrow in his eyes, and the deep lines from nose to chin. She knew it was the condition of her mother that caused the change in him. She wished he would talk freely with her about her mother. It would lessen the sorrow if they could only share it together. But he drew more and more within himself and she had not the courage to press her way into his secret thoughts. So they went on, each one ignoring the tragedy that lurked behind the closed door.

In a clear voice her father spoke out of his heart. His inherent goodness reached the people. More than one woman reached for her handkerchief and touched her eyes.

"He is truly a man of God," Gabrielle heard Eunice whisper to her man. "He is so saintly God will take him to Himself one day."

A wave of fear swept over her at the woman's words. Her hand went to her throbbing throat. What if Eunice were right? What if God should take him? What would she do? What would all the little colony do without him, now that the winter was coming? Her heart went out to him in tender affection. If she could only take his burdens! She was young, her shoulders were broad.

Gabrielle waited near the chancel for her father to leave the people who had gathered about him and walk home with her. The settlers were standing about, dressed in Sunday clothes, each talking to his neighbour with animation, just as though they had not seen one another and worked side by side every day. It always seemed to Gabrielle that they took on a new dressed-up personality when they donned Sunday raiment. Women wore bonnets and India shawls, for the day had the bright tang of autumn. Children moved quietly instead of rushing headlong about the fields and down the paths. A man and a woman, in black, left the group to walk to the rear of the chapel to a little mound marked by a crude cross: "The La Pierres' little boy Jean." Ill all through the long sea trip, the child lingered only a few weeks after the landing in the new country. The small mound, now covered with green moss, was tragic in its loneliness. The boy's parents had accepted what they had known was inevitable, had borne up, the mother better than the father. There was a deep-seated hurt in a father losing his first son that sprang from something fundamental in a man's nature. The instinct of survival, the carrying on of a man's name—"bone of my bone, flesh of my flesh"—a blind unreasoning emotion has come down through the centuries.

A loud cry from the sentry broke the silence with a sonorous cry: "A ship! A ship sailin' up the river! A ship!"

"Man the guns," ordered Amos Treloar, breaking away and running to the stockade gate. "It may be pirates. Every man to his place. Look sharp now!"

"It flies our flag," called Caslett's boy, who had climbed a young sapling the better to see over the low bushes.

Men ran across the compound to the river bank. Half a dozen mounted the ladders that led to the outlook. The women waited anxiously, gathering the small children near to them as mother partridges flutter their children into hiding with their wings.

"A British ship!" a man called out exultantly. "A British ship!"

A few moments later this cry was repeated by a second sentry. "They're dropping anchor in midstream. They've launched a flyboat to come ashore."

From their high places on the stockade the sentries reported the movement of the seamen.

Gabrielle followed her father to the gate. Three men from the settlement ran down the path to the landing. A young mate jumped out of the flyboat before it landed—a ship's officer, by his cap. Behind him came a cabin boy carrying a canvas sack.

A lookout called, "I can make out the name, sir. 'Tis the *Bristol Venture*, from Bristol."

"By gad, the lad's carrying a post packet. We'll have letters today."

There was a rush down the path to the landing place. Robert Fountaine sat down on the circular bench which the carpenters had built about a great oak. Festoons of waving moss, moved gently by a light breeze, floated above his head.

He leaned his thin hands on his ivory-headed cane, waiting for the approach of the young officer. Gabrielle sat down at his side. She watched the path eagerly. The *Bristol Venture* might bring letters from home, from Molly or some of her Bristol friends.

"I hope the gardening and farm tools have come," her father remarked, as they watched the men coming along the path. "I left the order before I left Bristol to send with the next Jamaica convoy. There has been time, if the ships went through safely. The men are making ready for the spring planting next month. After the first spell of autumn rain, before the heavy rains set in, they will plough."

Before she could make any comment on her father's words, the young officer stood before them. Back of him was a cabin boy with the post bag.

"I'm Mitchell, mate of the *Bristol Venture*. Captain Graves, the master, sends his compliments to Mr. Fountaine and asks if he will do him the honour to have supper with him aboard his ship."

Fountaine, rising, took the outstretched hand of the young officer. "My daughter, Miss Gabrielle Fountaine."

The rosy-faced, blue-eyed young man bowed politely and turned to a young gentleman, dressed in a cinnamon-coloured suit, who had come up. "Mr. Fountaine, may I present Mr. Thomas Chapman, a planter of Jamaica and brother-in-law of Mr. Roger Mainwairing?"

Robert grasped Chapman's hand cordially and introduced him to Gabrielle. The low, courtly bow, the glance of admiration from the young planter caused a flush to glow on her ivory skin.

Her father said, "A connection of Mr. Mainwairing is very welcome to the home of Robert Fountaine. Your sister, Mrs. Mainwairing, is known to me. I spent a week-end at her home in the Midlands before I left England. I trust Madam Mainwairing is quite recovered."

"Yes indeed, Mr. Fountaine; she recovered her health in record time. In fact, I doubt not that she will be hunting with the Quorn by November."

"The child?"

"A strong girl. Strong and healthy." A slight cloud crossed his hazel eyes. "I wish I could say as much for the boy. He's a bright lad, but not so strong as we could wish."

Fountaine turned to Mitchell. "Will you walk to my house?

I should like to offer some refreshment—a glass of Madeira and a biscuit."

The ship's officer bowed. "I should be delighted. We have a bag of letters and parcels for your people. Shall I allow one of my men to distribute them?"

Robert Fountaine glanced at the settlers standing in respectful little groups some distance away while he and the officer had been talking.

"Yes. Yes, indeed. I know my people are anxiously awaiting their letters from home." He beckoned to Amos Treloar, who came across the intervening space swiftly. "Amos, the ship has brought letters for us. Will you see that they are distributed? Sit here on the bench and let the people come forward." He beckoned to the groups. "Come, my good friends. Mr. Mitchell has brought the post. Come under the tree, and Amos Treloar will distribute them. I trust they bring good news to all of you."

The groups dissolved, as men, women and children came forward, eager to see what the post would hold.

"Letters from home!" one woman cried as her name was called. Tears streamed down her cheeks. "From home!" She held out her hand to receive the packet. Clutching it against her bosom, she ran towards her cottage, unwilling anyone should see her break the seal.

There was something for everyone except Hawksworth the smith. The settlers all knew his good wife had died not a month before they had set sail from Bristol, and his daughter Ellen had run away to London with a fine young gentleman who had had no thought of marriage behind his ardent wooing. Hawksworth walked away, smoking his pipe.

MacAlpin saw him go. Walking quickly, he overtook the smith. "Come along with me, Jamie. I'm going down to the ponds. The Indian says the ducks are lightin'. Bring your fowling-piece. Mayhap we'll blow up a few birds for supper."

The smith's face cleared. "I'll overtake you as soon as I put on my heavy shoon and gather up my shootin' gun. 'Tis a fine fair day for a walk."

"Five miles there and five back," MacAlpin commented. He watched the smith hurry away. "Puir mon," he said aloud. " 'Tis lonely he is this day, with all his friends reading their letters and talking of home." A grin overspread his weathered countenance. "Better to cut all ties. 'Tis been many a year since Sandy MacAlpin had a bit of scrawled paper from Lothian. Ah weel. Better so." He rolled a ball of snuff and laid it along his jaw under his lip. "Better to make a clean cut," he repeated.

In a short time the smith came up, carrying his fowling-piece over his shoulder. They walked along the path single file. At the junction of Far Reach they found Kullu waiting. He dropped in behind them and the three walked silently into the deep forest.

"We have some Virginia gentlemen on board the *Bristol Venture*," Tom Chapman said, as he walked across the clearing at Gabrielle's side. "Mr. William Byrd . . ."

Gabrielle said, "I've heard of Mr. Byrd, in England. He's a very fine, worldly gentleman."

Tom Chapman laughed a hearty, infectious laugh, so natural that it warmed Gabrielle's heart towards the young planter. "Mr. Byrd would like that. He wants nothing so much as to be considered one of the fine young blades who attend the Prince's Court."

"Mr. Byrd is on his way to Virginia?"

"No, Miss Gabrielle. The *Bristol Venture* put into the James River before sailing south to Jamaica. Mr. Byrd joined us there, as well as the Williamsburg gentlemen, Mr. Bray and Mr. Harrison. . . . But to go back to Mr. Byrd. Already, in these days we have been on the ship, he has told me a dozen times how well befriended he is by my Lord Peterborough, and my Lord Bolingbroke, Lord Hervey and Carteret. How often has he talked of Will Urwin's Coffee House, where the wits forgather! He knows them all by familiar names: Tom Addison, Alex Pope. He does not call the gloomy dean Jonathan, but he speaks of Vanessa and Stella constantly. Well acquainted with these ladies he must be. As for Lady Pomfret and Lady Mary Montagu, he sees them daily."

Gabrielle thought of her cousin Molly and her chatter; she had heard the same names from her lips. She felt remote from everything that touched high life and great people.

She said, "I'm glad to talk with you. You're a planter. Before the year's out, I'll be a planter too. I'd like advice about this soil. Mr. Mainwairing suggests potato seed from Ireland. Potatoes do well in sandy soil, and melons."

Chapman kicked at the overturned earth beside the path with the square toe of his buckled shoe. Leaning over, he gathered up a handful of soil. It was light, and ran like sand between his fingers. "I'd take Roger's advice," he said. "He knows this country better than I. Jamaica is tropical. We grow tropical fruits, vegetables, not suited to this soil. But your wealth lies in your forests." He turned his eyes to the pine woods. "Naval stores, tar, pitch and turpentine; mast poles. Here you have wealth at your doorstep." He turned to Gabrielle again. "But you said you were going to be a planter. Why did you say that? Do you mean you'll have flower-beds and a fine kitchen garden?"

"No. I'll have flowers, of course, but I shall plant corn and tobacco, rice for the swamps, they say, and perhaps I shall try indigo."

Chapman's face lightened. "Indigo? I can help you there. I'll send you some young plants this spring. I don't know if they'll prosper. They want warmth, but you can use a protected spot. 'Tis worth trying, for there's money to be made in indigo."

Gabrielle nodded. "So I was told in Charles Town."

Tom Chapman looked at the girl with deepening interest. "I say, is your father as enthusiastic over planting as you are?"

Gabrielle shook her head. "No. He thinks only of trade and manufacture. My father is a master weaver. He'll raise sheep for wool, cotton——" She laughed as a rabbit skipped across the path in front of them.

"There you have material for his hats," Tom said, "rabbit or beaver for fur felts. So he plans to make woollens and hats. Where will he sell his product?"

"My father has already plenty of orders in England and the Bahamas. Then, when the New England traders see his fine products, ships will come from the North." Her eyes smiled as she watched his changing expression.

"By the Lord Harry! I believe you have a plan that will make your fortune."

"I hope, for the sake of all these good craftsmen my father has brought over, that it will be a success. But we must make haste. My father will want me to see that you're well served with wine and some of Barton's seed-cakes."

Tom Chapman lengthened his stride to match Gabrielle's, though he had rather linger. Talking with her held a peculiar interest. Never had he seen a girl so lovely, who had such rare good sense.

They entered the house close after her father and the ship's officer. The sound of a harp came to them, and a light, clear voice singing a gay little roundelay in French. The men, hearing the voice, looked towards the door of her mother's rooms, which was ajar. At a glance from her father, Gabrielle moved across the room. Before she reached the door, Celestine's broad, ample body was revealed in the opening. She stood for a moment surveying the room with her sharp black eyes. Then she caught the door knob in her pudgy hand and drew it shut. The scraping of the bolt sounded across the silent room.

The eyes of both strangers were turned towards the door.

Robert broke the silence. "Gabrielle, will you ask Barton to fetch the wine? Our guests must want refreshment after their journey."

With a start Thomas Chapman's eyes turned from the closed door to his host. "Thank you, Mr. Fountaine. I'm sure we'll be delighted to drink a toast to the new colony, and the new Palatine."

"Palatine? I do not understand." Robert's face showed perplexity.

Tom Chapman took the glass from the tray Barton held before him. Lifting it, he said, "My Lord Carteret's appointment is in the post you will shortly receive. He has nominated you a Palatine, to sit on the North Carolina Council, with the same prerogatives granted to the Baron de Graffenried, chief of the New Berne Colony."

"Oh, Father! How nice!" Gabrielle said quickly, to cover her father's hesitation.

"Yes. Of course, Palatine," Robert said. "I had forgotten. A colony must have an official head. It cannot function without authority." His voice was an indication of his sadness.

"Of course you must have discipline," the officer said, swallowing his wine, "strong discipline, to hold people in order."

Robert's bewildered eyes met those of his daughter. She knew what was going through his mind. He had never considered himself a leader. He was a father to his people. He had no thought of discipline or of invoking order. The people were adult. They would behave themselves.

"We have a good set of slave laws for the blacks in Jamaica," Tom Chapman said matter-of-factly. "One has to deal strongly with the raw natives until they are broken to the plough."

Robert, realizing what Chapman had in mind, said stoutly,

"I'll have no slaves in this colony, neither white bondmen nor Negro slaves. This is a colony of free men."

Tom Chapman stared, bewildered at Fountaine's words. "No black slaves or bondmen? Who in the world will do the labour?"

"Every man has his share in the work, and every woman also," Robert said.

"Ah, one of those Utopian colonies, like Sir Tom Moore's."

Mitchell spoke. "Well, I'll lay a wager it won't work. A ship and a village, they're alike; they each have to have a head. What makes a good ship is a good captain that the men respect. Aye, and fear, too. This all sounds pretty, but it won't work, sir."

"We shall see." Robert smiled. He was tranquil again. "Now, Mr. Mitchell, if I may see the cargo lists of my merchandise."

Tom Chapman kissed Gabrielle's hand in farewell. They would be sailing in the morning before she was awake, he told her. "Do not forget me, Miss Gabrielle. As for that matter, I won't let you. When my sister Rhoda is at Queen's Gift, I come up twice a year, at least. I'll stop at the Cape Fear, going and coming."

Gabrielle smiled. "Please do," she said.

"I'll tell Rhoda to have you come to visit at Queen's Gift, when I'm there," he added, pleased with the idea. "Your father will be in Edenton often, now that he's a Palatine. His duties will require it. You'll like that, won't you?"

Gabrielle hesitated. "I'm not sure," she said. "Is it wise for a planter to leave his work at any time of year?"

"Certainly. One always has an overlooker to take care of details. Come, confess you would like to tread a Sir Roger, or hunt with the best pack in America."

"Perhaps," Gabrielle said. "Perhaps."

"You'll like the Albemarle people—the Moseleys, the Pollocks, the Moores and Blounts and Lillingtons. They all gather at Roger's house. He and my sister Rhoda love people to come to them. You'll like Rhoda and she'll love you."

"I hope she will like me," Gabrielle said, caught by his enthusiasm. "Mr. Mainwaring spoke of her so often, and my cousin Molly Lepel wrote me that she visited Madam Mainwaring in the Midlands."

"Molly Lepel?" Tom's voice changed. "Do you know Molly Lepel?"

266

"She's almost a sister. My father's her guardian. Do you know her, Mr. Chapman?"

"No," he said slowly. "No, I've never met her. But a man I know speaks of her often enough—Captain Michael Cary, whose ship comes to Jamaica and to Carolina at least once every year."

He said no more. To her anxious heart there was something ominous in his sudden change of manner.

He raised her fingers to his lips a second time, and followed her father and the ship's officer.

Her father came to her room when he returned from the ship.

"Did you have a pleasant time, dear Father?"

"Yes, very pleasant," Robert replied, but he spoke absently. After a few moments he said, "Mr. William Byrd, of Westover, is a gentleman of parts. Worldly, but shrewd, when he talks of business."

Gabrielle waited, but said nothing. Her father walked about the room, picking up a book, laying it down again without looking at it. "But he is intolerant. Intolerant of the North Carolinians, whom he despises. 'Ignorant, lowly, rough people,' he calls them."

"But Father!" Gabrielle exclaimed.

Robert raised his hand. "I know you are thinking of Roger Mainwaring. Byrd had nothing to say against him, but much to say against some of the Council—Anthony Lovyck, Edward Moseley and Maurice Moore. He can see no good in them. He even quotes the King in speaking of 'those troublesome Moores.' But he also had much to say against the Virginia governor, Colonel Alexander Spottswood. He doesn't like the Governor. In fact they've quarrelled, bitterly."

"But why should he say these things about the people of Edenton?"

"I don't know, Gabrielle, but I think it's some matter of the boundary between Virginia and North Carolina. Whatever it is, it distresses me. I confess, when I heard him talk, my heart sank. Intolerant words. It is the same intolerance we found in France, in Ireland, in England. I'd hoped we would not find it here in the new country."

He turned and walked slowly from the room, his head bent, his hands clasped behind his back.

Poor Father! Gabrielle thought. He cannot face life that is unpleasant. It hurts him so deeply. But the life he dreams of

267

can't be. It is impossible for people to live together without jealousy and hatred and intolerance.

She sat down to read Molly's letter. Enclosed was one from her brother René. In spite of the airy, casual words, she could see that Molly was worried. And from Tom Chapman's manner it was evident that her flirtation was far from secret, and it was also evident that Tom was not one of Michael Cary's admirers.

London, 16 June, 1718

"MY DARLING GABY:

You have been gone three months. To your Molly it seems three years. I wrote you at Nassau, and I have had one letter from you from that place. I read it aloud at a gathering at my Aunt Lepel's. Lord Hervey was there, and our neighbour Lord John Carteret and his wife and half a dozen others. They screamed with laughter at your description of the Nassau pirates, armed to the teeth, making a guard of honour for Captain Woodes Rogers as he went up the hill to the fort. They screamed even louder when I came to the part where the doughty captain did not have sufficient power to fire a salute in honour of his own arrival as governor of the Bahamas. Everyone laughed by my Lord John, and he said, 'Dash me, that's courage!' Then the others held their laughter, because my Lord Carteret is showing signs of being in power politically, and no one wants to offend him. The King turns to him frequently for advice. So you see how it is, and so Captain Woodes Rogers is now a hero, and the wits and scribes are talking about his extraordinary command of the pirates, and how he will soon drive them from the seas, and trade will progress.

"I might say all London, perhaps all England, talks trade, or rather about the new South Sea Company, which is a company to trade with South America and the South Seas. If you haven't heard of it, you will before many months. I don't understand it, but one hears nothing but buying shares. It is said that Lady Mary Montagu has scandalized her name by borrowing many, many pounds from a Frenchman who is desperately in love with her. Tongues wag. Mr. Pope wrote to Miss Martha Blount, when I was at Mapledurham, advising her to buy, saying he had invested heavily. It's so wild and fantastic that people lose their heads over the idea of such enormous returns as they are promised. Mr. Craggs, Secretary of the Lords of Trade and Plantations, is in the middle of the plan, working both ways. He's a loathsome creature. They say he acts as agent for the Prince and the King, bringing them young maidens (country type preferred) for their amusement.

"I've had a wretched time, of late, at my aunt's, all because

268

of a little escapade of mine that went awry. Of course you know it's about Michael. I see him frequently. He always seems to know where I will be at a given time. (I suspect he fees my aunt's woman.) He implored me to go out to East India Warehouse, where the great musicians gather to have recreation by playing trios and quartettes. It is dusky and eerie gloom in the great cavernous building, so lovers go there, the ladies with their vizards on, to hear the music. They sit in spooky corners, behind great bales of goods and crates of spices, and sip China tea.

"Michael importuned me for a long time before I consented to go. (You know young girls have no liberties. That's the reason I long to be a young married woman.) I dressed darkly and inconspicuously and borrowed a vizard Mary had brought from Venice, made of black satin and a fluting of lace. Really it's remarkable how becoming a vizard is if a patch or two is well placed on the chin or brow.

"The music was not too loud, the room dusky, the tea fragrant. Michael held my hand and talked sweet promises which I vow he will never keep. All went well until I got into my chair to go home. It was dusk and I was really frightened, because I had stayed too long and my aunt would be angry. If she was very angry, I vowed I would tell her I saw Lord Hervey and Lady Mary sipping tea in a corner. That would divert her anger.

"Michael had put me into a chair and called a link boy, when six or seven half-drunken gentlemen—Mohawks, they call themselves—came rolling down the street, peering into chairs, shouting to women as they came out of the warehouse.

"Michael muttered an oath, a strong one, and pulled out his sword. 'Move on quickly,' he shouted to the chair-men. But they were slow in moving and the fellows were upon us.

" 'Who's this?' they shouted, spotting my chair. 'Let the lady raise her masque.'

" 'Get the devil out of here!' Michael said. He was magnificent, Gaby; he didn't raise his voice, but he had his sword in his hand.

" 'Ah, the lady has a defender. Let's take the defender first.'

" 'Not so,' said one, more sober than the others. (Mind you, these Mohawks are all fine gentlemen, dressed in the very height of court costuming.)

" 'Let the lady remove her vizard and we will allow her to pass. If she won't do that, let her give her name.'

" 'God's death!' said Mr. Cary, and he lunged at the leader with his sword, piercing his arm. The fellow let out a cry and clutched his sword arm.

" 'Have the villain!' he shouted, mad with rage. The others jumped forward, swords flashing. Michael wounded two, but he

269

had a long scratch on his hand, and the blood drained on the white ruffle at his wrist.

"'Her name!' shouted the leader. 'Tear off the vizard.' Then I saw one of the men sneaking about to come up behind Michael.

"'Michael,' I called, 'defend your back.' But he was too late. The fellow had him by the arms.

"I cried to the leader, 'Let him go. I tell you, call off your men.' The fellow made a sweeping bow with his hat before my chair.

"'If Madam will tell her name, and——'

"'Come hither,' I cried, distraught. 'Come hither. I will tell you. I am Mary Lepel——'

"Just as I said it, my Lord Hervey and the masked woman I took to be Lady Mary Montagu came out of the building. Lord Hervey grew whiter than usual. He shouted to his lackeys, who had been lounging about the door, never coming to Michael's aid. 'At them, fellows! Lay on with your staves!' The good fellows did, and the Mohawks fled.

Michael thanked Lord Hervey, saying, 'Six to one is not healthy for the one.'

"Lord H. did not answer. He made a deep bow to me, whilst I huddled back in the chair. Then he turned to Michael and said, 'I was wrongly informed. I had understood that Miss Lepel was too ill to go out today.'

"He walked away before I could explain. Of course he thought I was my cousin, and although he was out with Lady Mary, he didn't like the idea that Mary Lepel should be out with a handsome cavalier like Michael.

"So I am in bad odour at home. I had to confess my misdeeds. Aunt Lepel said nothing about my going to the East India warehouse. She was furious because I spoke my own name in Lord Hervey's hearing. Heigho! I don't know what will happen now. Anyway, I can always come out to Carolina, when Madam Mainwairing goes to join her husband this winter.

"Would you like that? Can you imagine your Molly living in the wilderness? I might even fall in love with a pirate. They say some of them are handsome and have untold riches in jewels and pearls.

"Ah, Gabrielle, I've written so lightly, but my heart is not light.

"Your
"MOLLY"

Gabrielle put the letter away in the drawer of the press. Somehow she could not picture Molly living as she was living in the New World. Molly would not be able to adjust herself to the changed conditions.

Gabrielle was sure now that she could meet anything that

might arise. She had accepted the weight of her responsibility in the success of this venture. She realized that every individual must carry part of the load if it was to be a success.

Gabrielle broke the seal of René's letter.

"MY DEAR SISTER:

"Etienne is at prayers but I am in bed with a sniffle and have been excused. I will take my spare time to write you since Etienne has written to Father and sent the report cards of our headmaster.

"I wish I knew what to write that would be of interest to you. School is very dull. We want to go to America. Dear Sister, plead with Father to allow us to go out this summer holiday. We are not learning anything useful here at school. What good will Latin conjugation do in America?

"I hope Mother improves. Greet Celestine and tell Barton to make some seed-cakes for us. They starve us at the school.

"Your loving brother
"RENÉ

"*Postscriptum* 1. The boys tell stories every day about highwaymen. Each one tries to top the other. Please write me a good tale about pirates so I can top them all.

"*Postscriptum* 2. Your letter from Teneriff was read in the classroom by our master Mr. Oglethorpe. He gave us a lesson in geography and showed us the maps of Captain Woodes Rogers' earlier voyage in the *Duke* and the *Dutchess* and the location of Teneriff.

"*Postscriptum* 3. I am the tallest boy in the form."

Gabrielle smiled as she folded the letter and tucked it into her portfolio. Dear René. She wished he were with them, and Etienne. She must write to them and tell the story of Woodes Rogers and the pirate ship. She was sure it would top all the Jack Sheppard stories of René's schoolmates.

Chapter 21

PLANTER'S RETURN

The *Delicia* lay off Queen's Gift, Roger Mainwairing's plantation on Albemarle Sound. Pontoons, as they called the long loading barges, were secured alongside the ship for the removal of horses and cattle Roger had brought from England; Highland cattle, shaggy and sturdy, low to the ground; Shropshire ewes and rams. There was a great shouting of the seamen on the ship as the animals were swung to barges, and answering shouts from the shore where Roger's overlookers, field and household slaves waited to welcome him home after a year in England. A small group of men on horseback showed that some of his intimates were there to greet him, as well as the members of his own household.

Roger stepped into his own canoe, pulled by three slaves, guided by his personal servant, Metephele, a great African warrior from a fighting tribe.

"Master, all is well when the Master returns," the black man said, smiling his welcome.

"All is well," Roger replied. "Wait," he said, as the men touched their paddles to the water. "I have two guests."

Edward Colston appeared on deck, followed by David Moray. They got into the canoe and Metephele shoved off. He stood in the prow, a long sweep in his hands, steering the canoe. As the boat swung round a cluster of cypress trees that jutted far out into the water, the manor house came into view, a broad-galleried house with long, low wings on either side. A garden, laid out in geometrical form, swept from the house to the water's edge. Roses bloomed in the garden, and a great crescent of crepe myrtle was crowned with masses of dark pink blossoms. Great trees made a background for the house.

Colston drew a deep breath. "I never dreamt it could be so beautiful here. So beautiful and so civilized."

Roger smiled. "Wait till you see Pollock's plantation Balgray and the Blounts' Mulberry Hill. They have great holdings, much larger grants than mine. They came early and have the cream of the river lands. Pollock has fifty thousand acres at least."

"He's one of the Lords Proprietors' Deputies, is he not?"

"Yes, and a good one; a thoroughgoing old Tory, for all the world like Addison's fox-hunting Squire; but he's the salt of the earth."

David Moray had not entered the conversation. He was looking at the heavy forest, the deep swamp, which framed two sides of the little cove that held the wharf and landing.

"A man can be master of himself here," he said as they walked up towards the house.

"Yes," Roger answered. "A man can build a little kingdom of his own. That's what I hope will happen on the Cape Fear."

Colston fell back to join the conversation. "I'm afraid for them," he said soberly. "When I left, I looked back. Fountaine and his daughter stood close together. It came to my mind that the man grows frailer each day."

"And his daughter stronger," Roger interrupted.

"Yes, perhaps, but the chances of success are small. With a couple of men of strong character they might manage."

"That's why I persuaded MacAlpin to stand by through the winter. He's worth a dozen ordinary men."

Moray looked at Roger attentively. "So it was you?"

"Yes. I couldn't rest in my bed if I went away and left those babes in the wilderness."

David started to speak, then thought better of it. Roger looked at him once or twice, but nothing more was said about the new colony on the Cape Fear.

They had come to the long, wide steps that led to the first gallery. Half a dozen men had dismounted from their horses and were seated on the broad gallery. Slaves were hurrying back and forth, setting decanters of whisky and glasses on the long table, where food was spread. Black faces beamed a welcome to a loved master. One by one the house slaves came. Standing in front of Roger, they crossed their arms over their breasts and made an obeisance.

"*Moni*, Master, *moni*."

"*Moni*," Roger replied in their tongue.

He turned then to greet his neighbours, mentioning their names to Edward Colston and David Moray.

Edward Moseley, the Surveyor General of the Colony, who lived at Moseley Hall, the plantation adjoining Queen's Gift; Frederick Jones, the Chief Justice, whose plantation

273

was beyond Moseley's, on Queen Anne's Creek; Lillington, from Pequimans; Anthony Lovyck, the Secretary to the Deputies, whose seat was at Sandy Point; Blount, of Mulberry Hill, next plantation west; and Colonel Maurice Moore, the soldier turned planter.

A sturdy group of individuals, thought Colston, appraising them shrewdly; landed gentry, much like the people in England, except they seemed more vigorous, more individualistic.

The talk took a political turn, after proper inquiry had been made about Rhoda and the new baby, and several healths drunk.

In fact toasts had been drunk to a number of reasons—to the safe return of the planter; to Mr. Edward Colston, on his first journey to the New World; to Edward Colston the elder, well known to these gentlemen; to David Moray and his prospective venture as a planter.

Colston was glad to see food being placed on the table. He had not the hard head of these Albemarle men. Already his was spinning, for he had not had his morning tea, and his stomach was empty. He looked at the Scot. He showed no outward effect of the liquor he had drunk.

Roger took the head of the table, with Colston and Moray beside him. The men who had not finished their whisky drained their glasses and found places. As soon as they were seated, they dropped their heads, as Roger said grace: "O Lord, for these benefits of food and for our freedom, we thank Thee."

The amens were lusty and rousing. Every man went at the food with relish. The long hunt board by the south wall held ham and bacon, cornmeal grits and cold Guinea hen, dishes of honey and conserve; dishes of peaches and small russet pears. An oblong silver fruit bowl, filled with amber Scuppernong and wild purple fox grapes, and their trailing vines, graced the centre of the table. Negro table boys, dressed in white robes, feet bare, passed hot bread made from cornmeal, and scones. Tea and coffee were served.

Roger motioned to Metephele, who was watching to see that each boy did the work assigned to him. "Take my keys, go to the wine cellar and bring a dozen bottles of Vale de Pines, from Spain, which I sent over last spring. Have the boy set proper glasses at each man's place."

"The Spanish wine?" Metephele asked.

"Yes. This is a homecoming."

"Yes, Master." The slave moved, noiseless, across the gallery.

Colston said, "I've heard that planters in the West Indies live like kings, but I didn't know, until now, that Carolina boasted such bounty."

Moseley, a tall, extremely thin man, with burning dark eyes, said, "Better than kings, I think, Mr. Colston. We haven't the uneasy heads that go with a crown."

"The Governor's head is uneasy enough," Maurice Moore commented, helping himself to a slice of ham.

"Why is that?" Roger asked. "You must inform me on our politics. I'm sadly behind."

Moseley and Lillington looked at each other. "Ask Justice Jones," Lillington said, a smile lurking in the corner of his full lips.

Jones was not eager to speak; to be conciliatory was natural to him. "I hear a few rumours," he said by way of explanation, "and I take it that all these stories about Governor Eden are rumours."

Moseley spoke out unequivocally:"If you mean no one has seen him dividing the spoils with Blackbeard, you speak truly of rumours, but——"

"Nothing has been proved, or is likely to be." Lillington supported Jones.

Anthony Lovyck's handsome face darkened; fire flashed from his black eyes. "They are all afraid to speak aloud. Well, I'm not, Roger. Our handsome, gallant Charles Eden, Captain General, Admiral, and Governor of their Lordships' Province of North Carolina, is accused of having truck with the notorious pirate, Edward Teach. A more malicious set of lies has never been spoken about a great man."

There was complete silence at the table. Then a chorus of voices spoke at the same time: "Not accused, surely; rumoured, suspected, but not accused."

Moore's voice was cool. "You accuse us of defaming Mr. Eden, Lovyck?"

"Certainly not. I'm saying aloud what the rest of you are whispering. As for me, Charles Eden is my superior, I hope my friend. I'd be the last person to believe him capable of so dastardly an act against law and justice as to barter with pirates. But you know our people, Mainwairing; they must be fighting someone. The Indians kept them occupied for a time. Now they've turned against the freebooters."

Roger Mainwairing saw the black looks Moore and Moseley cast at Lovyck. He spoke conservatively. "Mr. Colston, Mr. Moray and I were in Nassau when the pirates walked up the hill to accept King's Pardon from Captain Woodes Rogers. It was an inspiring sight—hundreds of heavily armed men laying down their arms in exchange for a bit of paper."

Lovyck leaned forward. "That pardon proclamation is the cause of these rumours about Governor Eden, Mainwairing. Blackbeard came to the Governor, at his home at Bath, and accepted King's Pardon at his hands. Now these good people raise their voices in criticism of the Governor for dealing with a pirate, when he is only following his Majesty's orders."

"What about the French sugar ship Blackbeard seized after he had called on the Governor and taken King's Pardon?"

"Tobias Knight is implicated," Moseley said to Roger. "A pretty mess it is when the Governor of the province and one of its chief Deputies hold commerce with Blackbeard and Rackham and Stede Bonnet."

"Don't forget that woman devil, Anne Bonney, the daughter of that old witch we hanged on the gallows a few years ago."

Faces were flushed, angry voices raised. Roger must act to save his welcoming-home breakfast from disruption. "Gentlemen, gentlemen, I've heard enough of pirates for a lifetime in Nassau. We were all but wrecked on the shoals off Cape Fear entrance by a freebooter who was hiding in Topsail Inlet, and that caused more talk and speculation. I can't stomach any more pirate talk before breakfast. I propose that we eat hearty and drink hearty. This fine Spanish wine was a present to me from Mr. Colston's grandfather, the greatest merchant in England, Mr. Edward Colston of Bristol."

Everyone drank to Mr. Colston with extra heartiness. The merchant prince was known to every planter in the Carolinas. They were happy to do honour to his grandson.

"We hope you are long with us, Mr. Colston," Edward Moseley said, setting his glass on the table.

"Unfortunately I'm sailing tomorrow on the *Delicia*, or whenever Captain Bragg takes her up the James River."

"That's too bad. We'd like to show you our upriver plantations before you leave."

"Is old Zeb master of the guardship?" Maurice Moore asked. "I must go out to call on him."

"He'll be coming ashore before the day is over." Roger stood up. "Suppose we adjourn to the paddock. I want you to have a look at my wife's new hunters, and see the Highland cattle."

Chairs scraped, men rose and began to talk of plantation matters. The tension was broken. They took up wide beavers and riding crops and went down the steps to the hitching rail at the side of the house, where the stable boys had tied their horses.

Maurice Moore walked with Roger. "I must have a talk with you about this new Cape Fear colony. Do you think it will interfere with our plans?"

"No. On the contrary, if it succeeds, it will assist us."

"But Huguenots—won't they be clannish?"

"It's not a Huguenot colony in the true sense. The leader, Robert Fountaine, is French. The others are artisans and yeoman from Devon and Cornwall and around Bristol. Another Frenchman, La Pierre, brother of Jean, comes by the next ship. He's a Church of England pastor. He'll minister to the spiritual needs of the colony. All will go well with them, if industry is the essence of success."

"I do hope there will not be another failure at Old Town," Maurice Moore said dubiously. "Three failures would scare away colonists. That's Carteret's fear. We should watch them closely and try to prevent failure. I don't want my plans for the Cape Fear predoomed."

"Don't worry. I've put MacAlpin there for the winter."

Maurice Moore's face cleared. "Good! Good! MacAlpin's just the man. By the way, I want you to see the plans of the townsite on the lower Cape Fear. Moseley drew them up for me."

Roger said, "Bring them over the first of the week. Since my visit to Old Town I'm as interested as you about the value of a deep-water harbour for the Province."

Moore's eyes shone. "Moseley is also a convert. So that makes two besides the 'troublesome Moores.'"

"Is there anything to this talk of Moseley's about the Governor?"

Moore was evasive. "No smoke without fire," he said shortly.

They had come to the paddock, a good thickly tufted pasture enclosed in a whitewashed fence. Jumps and brush hazards had been set up. Small Negro boys sat astride the six new hunters. The men dismounted and climbed on the fence rail to watch the tryouts.

David Moray sat on the fence, apart from the Albemarle

277

planters, facing a long vista that was broken by the Sound. The *Delicia*, trim and shapely, cut his view of the Tyrrel shore. Along the narrow beach, up the path to the warehouses, a long line of Negroes walked, balancing bundles and bales of merchandise on their heads. Heavier loads were swung in rope hammocks stretched on long poles. These were carried by four men; the poles rested on well-padded black shoulders. The Negroes moved at a loping trot, a jungle trot, which covered the ground swiftly. The fine blue sky, the tawny water of the Sound, the dense green of the swamps and forests that enclosed the plantation on three sides made a deep impression on the erstwhile bondman. He thought: It's a man's world, this America, a world where energy and strength hold sway, a Utopia, set in a lush, fertile wilderness.

After a time Roger came over and climbed up on the fence beside him. "I wish you could see your way clear to stay on at Queen's Gift until my wife returns in the spring, Moray."

David opened his mouth to protest, but Roger intercepted the words. "Wait till I've finished. I'd like someone to train my men to get these hunters in shape. My men are good, but they do not know the fine points of conditioning a horse for hunting."

"I'd hoped to get some land ready for spring planting," Moray said.

Roger elaborated. "I'll send some of my men to Yaupim Creek to plough, and others to get the house in order, so you'll lose no time."

Put that way, Moray hesitated. He was under an obligation to Mainwairing that could not be ignored by a man of honour.

"Damn it all, Moray, I want someone in the house. It's lonesome with Rhoda away."

Moray perceived that Roger spoke the truth. It was a companion he wanted in his big manor house.

"I've company enough," Roger went on. "Every day someone drops in. Overnight visitors once or twice a week. It isn't that. But I've come home with big plans chasing themselves around in my head, plans for building up trade with the Indies, and I want someone to listen to me. A man thinks better if he can speak his plans aloud."

Moray looked up, interested. "I heard Captain Woodes Rogers say something of the future of trade between the
278

West Indies and the Carolinas, a natural trade that would profit both."

Roger nodded. He beckoned to a young Negro standing a short distance away. "Go to the house and tell Metephele to have rum and whisky on the table."

"Yes, Master."

Roger slid down from the fence. He stood for a moment, beating off the heads of a bunch of wild oats with the leather of his crop. "Don't make up your mind now, Moray. Think it over. Three months with me on the plantation will give you a good idea of the way we run things here." He smiled a little. "Farming in Scotland is different from planting in the Albemarle. Different land, different methods." He smiled wryly. "I've made my mistakes, and still do——"

"I can give my answer now, Mainwairing. I'll be delighted to stay with you until Madam Mainwairing comes back."

"Good!" Roger said in his pleasant, level voice. "Good! Another thing: Moseley told me he was going to the Cape Fear early this spring. He's planning to survey his grant. I think I'll have a new survey made of my holding upriver from Town Creek. I may want you to go with me."

A pleased look crossed David Moray's face, gone instantly. "Spring's a long way off. Let's think of the present."

Roger watched the tall Scot move away towards the stables, a slight smile on his firm mouth. Let him have something to dream about, he thought. A man is only half a man who has not a dream to force into reality. He walked across the paddock with his long swinging stride and joined his guests.

"The sun is at the yardarm, gentlemen, and Metephele is waiting to serve you."

"I'm ready enough," said Moseley, his thin face brightening. "Dust creates a deal of thirst." He laughed as he pointed to a little cloud of dust that followed the trotting horses. "A deal of thirst. Besides, I lay a wager you have brought home something from the islands worth testing."

"Right. I laid in a supply—enough for two years, I hope—when we touched Grand Canary. At Nassau a ship came in from Jamaica; I bought rum, hogshead, which I must bottle. You have a choice, gentlemen—Canary wine or one of Metephele's lime and rum punches."

At Roger's words the men moved more rapidly. A comfortable chair on the gallery, a long glass of Metephele's mixture, drew them.

Colston went to his room. Roger had asked him to stay at Queen's Gift while the *Delicia* went to Edenton wharves for a cargo of pork in barrels, destined for Governor Spottsswood at Williamsburg. His head was splitting. The last glass of rum punch had put him at the border line and he had left the hard-drinking planters while he could still retreat in good order. He threw himself on the bed. His last thought, before he drifted off into deep slumber, was of his grandfather. He must write a letter, explaining these men who lived in the New World. They were different. He had not yet satisfied himself where the difference lay. They were strong and vigorous from out-of-door living. But that was not all. The difference lay deeper. They seemed more purposeful. They made great plans for the future. They had more independent thought. What the Hanoverian King and his ministers thought seemed to matter little to them. They were law-abiding, but it was their own laws that held their adherence and their loyalty. "Our sovereign rights," he had heard Mr. Edward Moseley say. "We will uphold our sovereign rights." He had not been part of the group to whom Moseley made the declaration, but he overheard the words, spoken truculently. Moseley's face had an almost sardonic look when he spoke, and his tone was sharp. Something to do with his Excellency, Governor Eden, something about a pirate named Blackbeard. . . . He must write a letter. . . . Colston's thoughts were confused. He dropped off into deep slumber.

A short time later, Metephele, the great Angoni warrior who was Roger's *capita* and principal house slave, came into the room quietly, saw Colston's flushed face and noisy breathing. He shook his head. Deftly he slipped off the sleeping man's jackboots, then, rolling him over, he removed the stiff skirted coat and embroidered waistcoat, unwound the fine Mechlin lace stock, and opened the silk shirt at the neckband. The Bristol merchant slept on, all unknowing. After placing a blanket over Colston's stockinged feet, Metephele hung up the garments and left the room. Outside the door he stood for a time, his black face immobile, unreadable. Could he have been thinking of the old days when, night after night, he had put his master to bed in like case? But that was long ago, in Roger's bachelor days, before Madam came. A slow smile lighted the strong dark face of the slave as he turned away and went down the hall, his bare feet making little sound on the puncheon floor.

The gallery was deserted. Only glasses on the table and gallery railings and the drained punch bowl gave evidence of the meeting of Albemarle planters to welcome home one of their own.

In the library Roger Mainwairing and his neighbour Edward Moseley sat with their long clay pipes, smoking this year's bright leaf.

Moseley's dark, intense eyes were resting on Roger as he talked, as if to drive home his words. "Your homecoming finds us in evil case, Roger. His Excellency grows more arbitrary each day. He is usurping powers of the Council and of the Assembly. He's mad to retrieve his fortunes."

"I hear he's courting Madam Galland."

"Yes, that's true. He aims to draw to his side all of her connections—not an inconsiderable number, I must confess, and important. He's built himself a fine house on the Chowan River, above Pollock, and a straight road from there to Bath Town, which he calls the Governor's Road."

"What about the Government House Hyde started in Queen Anne's Town?"

"Edenton, my dear Roger, Edenton, we are to call it from now on."

"I say! He *is* high-handed, to give the capital town his own name."

"Eden will never suffer from overmodesty, although he works, clumsily, through Anthony Lovyck."

"Lovyck?" Roger questioned, raising his heavy brows.

Moseley laid his thin fingers together. "They are like that. You find his Excellency, you find Lovyck hard by. I was surprised that Lovyck was here to greet you this morning. He's usually not out of voice range of Eden when he's in residence."

"Perhaps he stopped en route from Sandy Point. The river road to the village passes my gates."

Moseley pulled at his lip, a habit he had when thinking. "No. The explanation is too simple. These two familiars like devious ways best. I fancy it's to woo you that he came. The opening gun of a campaign to get you firmly on the side of his master, the Governor."

"Lovyck knows that I take no part in politics, even if Eden doesn't."

Moseley laughed. "You'd be surprised how many people are showing interest in government affairs who never did before."

"How's the division? Where does Pollock stand?"

"With the Governor, to be sure. The Maules and Gallands

connections, and most of the planters along the Salmon and the Keshai and the Chowan make up the Tory contingent. On the other side we have the lower classes and radicals."

Roger raised his brows.

Moseley's face darkened. "That damned radical rascal Moseley; that radical Maurice Moore, Lillington, Swan, et al., et al.," he quoted, his voice deeply sarcastic.

Roger laughed. "So you're now the 'damned radical rascal.'"

"Yes. These are the mildest expressions the Governor uses when he is surrounded by his familiars. In public he presumes to be polite and exceedingly dignified."

"I see. And what brings on all this?"

Moseley tapped the bowl of his pipe. He emptied the dottle into the fireplace and put the pipe in the rack before he said, "It has to do with piracy and kindred crimes. Roger. It's too long a story to go into now. In a few days Maurice and I will talk to you. I think we can give you a good account of what has taken place in your absence. But I must be off."

At the door Moseley said, "I've talked too much about *our* disturbances. I haven't even asked what London is like under a Hanoverian King."

"Like you, I'll say it's rather a longish story. Part of it will come out tomorrow when I make my report to the Deputies."

"I'll be there. I want to know how our betters are behaving." His tone was caustic.

Roger raised his eyebrows. "Will you attend the Council?"

"Yes. It's an open meeting of the Council and townsmen, to hear your report, and the one Gale has sent over."

As he swung onto his horse, he added, "It's nice having a neighbour again. I've missed the evening glass of brandy and our talks. It's been damnably lonesome."

Roger stood for a moment on the steps to watch the line of slaves carrying merchandise from the *Delicia* to his warehouse, and a second line carrying bales of tobacco to the ship. It made him damned mad that he had to pay a tax to Virginia for his tobacco. Technically, he was loading for the James River port. The customs would regrade it there and, like as not, throw out a third. They did that to North Carolina products. Damn the law, anyway! It was never a just law, from the time it was made.

He forgot his brief annoyance as his eye turned to the east

field, where his men were ploughing. He pulled his chair close to the end of the gallery and stretched his long legs, in heavy riding boots, on the rail. His thoughts cleared as he contemplated the scene—the new turned earth, the pasture where the cattle grazed. It was good. It was good to be home again. Winter work ahead of him, and then the spring, with green fields and pasture and growing crops. He would clear two more fields this winter, plant more cotton, double his tobacco. He would enlarge the turpentine output on his Tyrrel land—produce to trade in the Indies. A fine new market opened with the coming of Woodes Rogers and his Bahama Adventurers.

He leaned his head against the back of his chair. He wanted to fill his eyes with the prospect before him. His eyes and his soul wanted reviving, by the green of the forest, the smooth amber waters of the Sound.

A great Irish wolfhound came out of the house and laid his long head on his knee, looking up with great liquid eyes. Roger's hand sought the dog's head, stroking it absently.

How long he sat looking across the Sound to the cool green turpentine woods, he had no idea. He was interrupted by the noise of footsteps. He looked up. David Moray came striding across the broad gallery. He walked with a long swift stride, his broad shoulders well back—a military carriage, Roger thought. For the first time since he had seen the man at the Huguenot's house in Meg's Lane, he wondered about his experience. But he had said nothing of this. Let him give his confidence when he was ready.

"Sit down, Moray," he said, indicating a chair.

But Moray preferred to stand, leaning against a pillar. "It's amazing how those Negroes understand horses," he said. "I've never seen anything quite like it."

"They have patience, and a light hand," Roger answered, "the two things necessary to gentle a horse. Help yourself to a drink."

"Where's Colston?" Moray asked as he poured a glass of whisky from a decanter. "Gone on a tour of the plantation, or did he go back on the *Delicia?*"

Roger's eyes crinkled at the corners and his lips twitched with the shadow of a smile. "My man Metephele told me that Colston was 'resting.' Between us, I don't think he can stand up to the drinks we serve here in the Plantations."

Moray grinned. "I noticed your planter friends can take care of themselves."

Roger gave an answering smile. "That's right. We take care of ourselves. Sit down, Moray. I want a word with you."

David sat down, his glass in his hand. His shrewd, intelligent eyes were guarded.

"It's about your position here," Roger went on. "I see no reason for you to mention anything about your life in Bristol. You came here as a planter, seeking to establish yourself in a new world. Not that being a bondman would stand in your way here, any more than it has stood in my way, but until you get your affairs straightened out I think it the part of wisdom to forget it. There may be some zealous patriots who would find it their duty to report your presence here to his Majesty's government, and someone in authority might seek to gain favour with that government by sending you back to England to stand trial. His Majesty's government doesn't look with favour on Jacobites, you know."

Moray was silent, turning Mainwairing's words over in his mind. "I expect you are right, Mr. Mainwairing," he said after a time. "I am one David Moray, lately come from Scotland to seek my fortune in the New World."

"Good. Very good. I don't want to lose a prospective planter to a law made to entrap political malefactors." He smiled again. "I'm not forgetting my own youth and my adherence to a lost cause. So, from now on, you're my guest and my friend, and I hope you'll be content here at Queen's Gift until you establish your own home." He waved his hand toward the Sound. "I've been thinking of a piece of land between Mulberry Hill, Blount's plantation, and Greenfield. Bluff Point, it's called. It belongs to one of the Porters. I think it's available." He hesitated, then said, "I could buy it and let you take your time to pay off."

Moray gave him a look of gratitude. "You're very kind, very kind, Mr. Mainwairing. But that won't be necessary. I took occasion to get notes of exchange on Jamaica and on Boston before I sailed. It's never been a question of money, for all the tale of Mr. Fountaine having bought me from debtors' prison. I preferred that tale to the truth. There are too many others involved in the Jacobite plot who might have been traced through me. I did not want to take the chance, so I did not deny the other story."

"Quite right. Your decision does you honour. As for the land, we'll ride over, tomorrow or the next day, and you can have a look at it. I'd first thought of a plantation on Yaupim

284

Creek, near Greenfield and Drummond's Point, but I think Bluff Point would suit you better."

"You've mentioned Greenfield. Who owns Greenfield?"

A shadow crossed Roger Mainwairing's face. His eyes were expressionless. "Greenfield has an absentee landlord. It is run, at present, by two overlookers—Scots, by the way. A woman owns it." He paused as if he were reluctant to pursue the subject. Thinking better of it, he said, "Madam Michael Cary is the owner. She's in England."

"Michael Cary!" Moray said impulsively. "Captain Michael Cary?"

Roger turned from contemplating his boot tips at David's words. "I believe he calls himself captain." Mainwairing's tone was level. "Captain, sailing under letter of marque."

David said, "I wonder if it could be the same." He described the man he had seen and drunk with at the Rose Inn near the Bristol docks.

Roger nodded. "That's the fellow, all right."

"You don't seem to hold with Captain Michael Cary. He appeared a man of parts." David raised a questioning eyebrow.

"Appearances are not the heart of a man," Mainwairing said. "I'd not trust Cary very far."

"Ah!" David whistled through his teeth, thinking of Molly Lepel. Mainwairing was about to say something more, but Metephele came up with a question that required his master's consideration. With a word of excuse Mainwairing got on his horse and rode off towards the tobacco barns.

David finished his drink and went upstairs. It would be too bad if the handsome Cary were playing with Molly Lepel. David liked her. She was frivolous and flirtatious, but there was no more harm in her than in some gay child, unless her dormant emotions were stirred. He hoped the fellow wasn't a blackguard. He was married. But perhaps Molly knew that. If so, she was playing with fire. He thought of the times she had run into the garden to talk with him over some trumped-up excuse. Just a female on the prowl, had been his first thought. Later he had changed his mind. A lively temperament, a young girl, without home or kin. He shook his head. He hoped nothing would happen to spoil her, to make her unfit for the man who really loved her. Too bad she had not come out to the Carolinas with Robert Fountaine. She needed a restraining hand, or the influence of Gabrielle, to steady her. "Gabrielle." He almost said the name aloud, but checked himself in time. He had no time to think of Gabrielle Fountaine, or let his thoughts wander. There was work ahead of him if he was to become a planter and set up a "new empire in the New World," as the advertisement said.

He ran up the stairs to his room in the east end. As he passed a door, he saw Colston, sleeping peacefully.

Edward wakened from his heavy sleep. He looked about the room blankly, not able to remember where he was. When he sat up, the thumping in his head reminded him of the breakfast and the toasts that had been drunk. One thing was certain: he would never take drink for drink with the rugged Albemarle planters; why, he believed they could put the gay London men of fashion under the table without an effort.

He looked at his watch—nine o'clock. Night or morning? He got up and pulled the chintz curtains. The sun was shining on the broad expanse of the Sound. Slaves were ploughing in the fields; half a dozen white men and as many slaves were at the paddock watching Moray put a great bay hunter over a brush barrier. It was morning. He had slept the clock around.

Edward looked about him. He was a merchant and, without conscious thought, he at once set a value on the contents of the room.

The furniture was Queen Anne, of good make. There were a mahogany highboy and tables and a great canopied bed, with slender high carved posts. Flowered chintz decorated the bed and hung at the windows, and the broad floor boards were polished and covered with small hooked rugs, decorated with floral patterns. The sun streamed in the east windows, and the fire in the bricked hearth burned cheerily behind a gleaming brass fender.

Edward walked out to the upper gallery and faced the broad waters of Albemarle Sound. The opposite shores were heavy with forests. Spires of green pine and cypress rose to the blue sky. The Sound was dotted with sails of fishing boats, and on the *Delicia* the seamen were drying canvas. Queen's Gift was on the north shore of the Sound. Well-cleared land, with forests between the fields, and a great cypress pocosin ran along the curved shore to a point beyond the little bay. In the fields Roger's people were working, stacking cornstalks; some slaves were ploughing, getting ready to plant winter grain. Negro children ran about, playing with dogs and chasing small shoats. From the end of the gallery he saw Roger and his overlooker galloping down the long, magnolia-lined drive towards the tobacco barns and smokehouses.

"It's a little empire," he said. "And Mainwairing is its ruler—'Duke Roger,' Captain Bragg called him." He had told Colston it was because Mainwairing had "ridden with the Duke." That designated the men who followed the Duke of Monmouth when he led his rebellion. To have "ridden with the Duke" sent many a man to his death on the gallows, like Argyll, or into exile, like Andrew Fletcher of Saltoun.

Roger Mainwairing had escaped the gibbet and been sold as a bondman to a West Indian planter. Colston had heard bits of this tale from Captain Bragg and from Mainwairing himself. An adventurous man was the planter. He had lived life firmly and with zest. Colston thought of the counting-house desk where he had spent many a weary hour, and he was suddenly dissatisfied, sorry for himself.

"Dammit! I've missed a lot in life." He spoke the words aloud to the accompaniment of his jingling watch fobs. "I've missed a lot in life, sitting at a desk, my nose in a ledger."

An eagle planed across the sky and hung for a moment suspended in the blue, then dropped to a bare, lightning-stripped tree in the pocosin and settled on a branch above a great bundle of twigs set in a fork of the treetop. An eagle's nest! He was in a world where eagles nested! A lordly world, primitive and young.

Refreshed, he opened the door into the wide hall. His boy was crouching there. He rose quickly.

"Master want hot water for shaving?"

"Yes. Bring me hot water."

"Master Mainwairing says horse is ready saddled to ride to Moseley Hall for morning tea."

The idea pleased Colston. A clean shave, clean clothes; a ride in the clear, crisp air to a near-by plantation for a dish of tea, or a hot rum punch. He smiled as he began to divest himself of coat and brocaded waistcoat. He smiled while the black boy shaved, and then began to hum a little tune. A good world, this Carolina. Pleasant. He understood why Roger Mainwairing's face always lighted up when he spoke of Queen's Gift. Why, he grew younger-looking and happier the nearer he got to his home.

"Master is happy?" The soft Negro voice penetrated Edward's consciousness. "Master is happy and he sings."

"Yes, Master is happy," Edward said, breaking into a laugh. "It must be the Carolina air."

"At Queen's Gift people are happy," the boy said, wielding the razor swiftly and deftly. "Master happy, his people happy. That is good."

Colston and Roger found Mosely working on a map that was stretched out on a long table in one end of his book room. He greeted Roger warmly, holding his hand with both of his. A tall man, with deep, burning eyes, a strong aquiline nose and firm, wide mouth; a thin face in which the cheekbones were too prominent and lines too deep for a man of his years, the late forties.

He clasped Edward Colston's hand warmly. "I did not properly express a welcome to you yesterday, Mr. Colston. A real pleasure, sir; a real pleasure to have you in the province. I've known your grandfather since I was a young lad at school in Yorkshire. A grand man, Edward Colston, one of the great men of our times."

A feeling of warmth came over Edward. He recognized the genuineness of Moseley's words. His reserve melted.

"When is Rhoda coming home?" Moseley asked Roger, as the men seated themselves.

"She'll come in the spring. She did not want to take the long voyage until the baby's a little older."

"I miss Rhoda. I declare I believe I've missed her more than I have you, Duke."

"That's what I hear on all sides," Roger answered, smiling. He turned to Colston. "Rhoda pampers these men. She sees that they get the things they like to eat and drink, and she makes them comfortable."

"Don't forget that she listens to our vexations," Moseley interrupted. "You know Rhoda is a genius for listening to a man's troubles."

"That's true. She's a good listener and that's always flattering to a man."

Moseley leaned against the mantel board, smoking. "It is lonely without a woman about. They give life to a house." He turned to Edward. "Are you married, sir, or a bachelor?"

"A bachelor, Mr. Moseley. But I'm beginning to think I've been wasting a deal of time."

Roger looked up at his words. "You aren't, by chance, thinking of taking up land on the Cape Fear?"

Edward's face flushed. "Well, no, not seriously, but there's something about this country that makes me think it would be a good thing to have a home and establish myself."

Roger laughed. "What did I tell you? The country will get you, sooner or later, as it did me."

Moseley listened, a half smile on his lips. "The Cape Fear. That's a good place for seating. A good spot, with a wide river roadway." To Roger he said, "While you were gone, I made a preliminary survey on the Cape Fear. I've applied for land on the northeast branch of the river, near Rocky Point."

"Have you?" Roger's pleasure was evident.

"Yes, Maurice Moore and I. Maurice has been talking about it ever since he came up from Southern Carolina at the time of the Tuscarora War in '12. He has a plan to lay out a town near the mouth of the river. Wait, I'll show you on the map I've been making."

He walked across the room to a cabinet and took out a roll of maps. After a moment he found the one he was searching for and spread it on the table, weighted down with books. He pointed with a long thin finger at a spot not far from the mouth of the river on the west bank.

"Here's where Moore proposes to lay out the town of Brunswick. Here, next to it, is a grant his brother Roger has taken up, and north of it James, another brother, has his holdings."

"That brings him up to Old Town," Roger exclaimed, looking more closely. "Yes, here is Old Town Creek. Fountaine's holdings go from there, on the north side of the creek, and follow up the river for several miles."

"What's that you say?" Moseley asked, suddenly becoming interested. "Who has several miles of water front near Old Town?"

"Mr. Robert Fountaine, a Huguenot, has brought out twenty settlers. They're already building their dwellings at Old Town Creek, Yeamans' old settlement."

"How do they hold the land—did they buy it or is it a grant?"

"A grant, I believe."

Moseley pursed up his lips. "The Moores won't like that. They have applied for all the land along that side of the river from the mouth to the forks."

"That's a good deal of territory," Roger said, tamping his pipe. "I suppose our law limiting the amount of water front a man can own does not apply on the Cape Fear."

"No. Just on Albemarle Sound, and the Chowan. That's one reason Maurice wants to go to the Cape Fear. He can carry out his scheme of colonization. I think this Fountaine settlement will annoy him."

Edward Colston shook his head when a slave brought in a decanter and glasses. "I have to admit that I can't keep pace. I'm just a soft-headed merchant from Bristol," he said ruefully.

Moseley smiled. "Don't be discouraged at your first experience in the Carolinas. A hard head is acquired over a long period. It is not come by readily, Mr. Colston. We spend so much time out of doors that we eat heartily, and drink ditto."

"As a guest, I'm a failure," Colston said. "I'm humiliated."

Mainwaring drained his glass and got to his feet. "We'd better be getting on. Going to the village, Moseley?"

"Indeed yes. Do you think I'd miss hearing what you have to say about your meeting with the Lords Proprietors?"

The three men went out of the library, down the hall to the front stoop, where the horses were waiting. Mounting, they trotted down the cedar-lined drive to the River Road.

Colston looked back at the house. While Moseley Hall was well located on the point, with a sweeping view of water and forest, it had not the dignity of Queen's Gift. Mainwaring was thinking of the untimely death of Moseley's wife Anne. The absence of a women was evident. Even in her long illness Anne had held the reins and guided her household with a skilful hand. Now that she was gone, the house slaves had grown slack. Moseley didn't see the disorder; his mind was on other things. Solitary by nature, Moseley had set himself apart from the majority of the planters.

Roger Mainwairing was not only his close neighbour, but the only one to whom he gave his confidence.

They had passed Vaile's and Justice Jones's plantations and come to Queen Anne Creek. Moseley pulled his horse to a walk.

"You'll find changes, Roger. Alarming changes. We are almost in armed camps here in Edenton—those who are for the Governor, and those who are against his high-handed dealings with the pirates. I thought of talking with you about this situation last night, but I decided against it. It's something you must think out for yourself. I don't like schism in a small community. It savours too much of the Old World. But there must be someone who cries 'Halt?' to these lawless people. We are living over a volcano, Roger, one that may throw off steam and hot lava at any moment." Moseley's thin-lined face was grave and his deep-set eyes troubled.

The planking of the bridge rattled under the sharp impact of the horses' hoofs. A few moments later they rode through the East Gate into King Street. Before them lay the Village Green. Crowds of men and women were moving towards Cupola House. There Governor Eden waited with their Lordships' Deputies who formed his Council.

When the workmen returned from the Cape Fear, ten days before, they had brought the word that Roger Mainwairing would return on the *Delicia* in time for the fortnightly meeting of the Council. Today the Council meeting would be augmented by planters from the Sound and the great rivers, the Roanoke and the Chowan, and their tributary creeks, by merchants of the village, lawyers and doctors and representatives of the common people. They would ride for many miles, eager to hear Roger Mainwairing's report of his talks with the Lords Proprietors, and of the meeting with the Lords of Trade and Plantations at King James's Palace.

Every man in the province, rich or poor, of high condition or of lowly birth, knew that their future and the future of the country itself lay in the aristocratic hands of eight Lords Proprietors of the Carolinas.

Chapter 22

EDENTON

Government House, which many of the villagers called "Madam Hyde's Folly," had been finished half a year. His Excellency Governor Eden used it for an office and a residence when he came to the village from his country residence, Eden House, on the Chowan River. The house was not large, but it was well proportioned and stoutly built. It was well placed in a large plot of ground, west of the green, and fronted on the cypress-lined bay.

Madam Catha Hyde, the wife of the former Governor, had brought the original plans of the house from London. She was disappointed when the Council and her own husband cut her ambitious plans by half. The cupola was not nearly so large or towering as she had dreamed suitable for the residence of a Governor of Carolina who was own cousin to Queen Anne. She envisioned something not quite so large as St. Paul's dome, but of a size. Poor, ambitious lady; she never saw the completion of her dreams. Before the house was finished, her husband died of yellow fever—so the doctor pronounced it—but Baron de Graffenried, who was at the deathbed, declared he died of eating too many green peaches.

The province lost a good governor when Edward Hyde passed away in 1712. He was a just man and sincere in his devotion to duty and to the welfare of all the people of the province; his death was a loss to poor folk and wealthy alike.

Madam Hyde's grief was assuaged when the government sent a ship-of-war to take her back to England. She never saw her "miniature capitol" building in its finished state. Charles Eden took up where Madam Catha left off, and, as a bachelor governor, made himself very comfortable at Cupola House when he chose to honour the village with his presence.

Charles Eden was a man of parts. Tall, imposing, he carried himself with dignity. He liked pomp and demanded a certain amount of subservience in those close to him. This defect in his character did not please the planters of the

Albemarle, where each man was a monarch on his own land. In the beginning, the larger grants of land, those that went to the Palatines, were called baronies, and carried certain privileges. The next grade called their homes manor houses. Some of these planters dealt with slaves and bondmen with a high hand, aping the manners of the Court. But for the most part, they were cognizant of the rights of the people, and there was a friendliness and good will among all the classes.

Governor Eden did not like this. He wanted well-drawn lines between classes—those who belonged by birth to the noble families; the country families; the middle and lower classes; the white bondmen and women; and last the Negro slaves. In this way his administration would take on the likeness to a small European state, rather than to a Crown Colony such as Virginia, where all the people had certain liberties. But he was wise enough to move slowly, through his Council and his staff, rather than show his hand. Charles Eden was ambitious and poor. He meant to be successful and rich before he returned to England. He took infinite pains to draw the well-to-do and powerful to his side. He made friends with Thomas Pollock, the wealthiest planter in the country, who was a conservative and a believer in the old forms. Anthony Lovyck, who had been secretary to the late Governor, he attached to his staff at the beginning. He saw in the young, handsome Anthony a man secretly selfish and ambitious, and one who would serve him well. Besides, he was married to a daughter of John Blount, of Mulberry Hill, a wealthy planter, and connected in England with the famous Blount family. Martha and Teresa Blount were his relatives, those beautiful belles who were made famous by their friendship with Alexander Pope. Then there was Sir Thomas Blount, the financier, who was now heart and soul in the new South Sea Company; and Mary, who was the wife of Norfolk and close friend of the Prince and Princess. These connections would be good for the Governor's designs, later, when he would appear before the Lords Proprietors to ask for all the honours guaranteed in the original Charter to governors and Palatines.

Some of these thoughts passed through Roger Mainwaring's mind, as he sat in a back-row chair in the Governor's room in Cupola House.

Charles Eden sat near the fireplace in a large elbow chair covered with red brocade. The Council were in semicircles, before the Governor's chair. Chief Justice Jones and Clerk of the Court William Badham were near him. Anthony Lovyck sat at a small desk, at his side, his quills and paper ready.

Roger noticed that the Deputies were better dressed than in the old days. His Excellency was somewhat of a stickler for form and fashion, and this had its effect on the other men. He took his snuff elegantly from a gold box bearing a miniature of Queen Anne, of sainted memory. His cambric handkerchief was edged with lace. His coat was puce brocade, his breeches were of the finest serge, and his Flanders lace cravat and ruffles in the latest fashion. He wore Morocco shoes with high red heels, and diamond-clasped garters held his silk hose in place.

The curls of the Governor's periwig, which came halfway down his back, were of a russet colour. He boasted that he went to the same wigmaker that served my Lord Carteret, and he had the same bootmaker. It was rumoured that his wigs cost forty guineas. His watch was made by Richards, with a gold and carnelian seal and a pair of drops dangling. He wore a mourning ring, left to him by some high-born woman of fashion, whom he spoke of to his familiars as the Duchess of K——; he wore also a signet with the effigy of Charles the Second, cut into a gold-flecked bloodstone.

His Excellency was a first-rate swordsman. A pupil of a famous fencing master, Charles Eden had more than once fought duels at Lincoln's Inn Fields. He spoke French and Italian, having studied the latter with Peter Bisson at St. Amant's Coffee Shop, by Charing Cross.

Roger felt the Governor's cool grey-green eyes on him while Anthony Lovyck was reading the minutes of the previous Council meeting, a speculative, appraising look without warmth.

Roger leaned back, relaxed, waiting for his time to speak. Edward Colston was next to him, his fine clear eyes missing nothing that went on, from the significant grouping of the Council according to their standing with the Governor, to the gathering throngs of village folk, who could be seen on the green through the many-paned windows. The room was crowded, and the only empty seats were near the Governor. Edward Moseley came in late and stood near the door, leaning against the panelled wall. The Governor saw him enter. A slight scowl creased his forehead, quickly smoothed.

He interrupted Lovyck. "Will the Surveyor General, Mr. Moseley, please take a seat? There is one vacant."

He nodded to a chair near him. Moseley hesitated the fraction of a second. Bowing, he moved through the close-packed chairs to the seat near the Governor, where he sat with arms folded, his dark, sombre eyes on the floor.

Lovyck's voice took up the reading: "A letter from Governor Spottswood, of Virginia Colony, asks that a committee be appointed to make a *new* survey of the boundary line in the spring. He has again appointed Mr. William Byrd to serve on the commission."

Thomas Pollock, the red-faced country squire from Balgray plantation on the Chowan, said, "I thought Mr. Byrd had gone to England, sir."

"No, he went to Jamaica. He will be back by June, when the survey will be made," Lovyck answered.

The Governor said, "I quite agree with Governor Spottswood. This stupid controversy over the dividing line should come to an end. It is farcical that it has been drawn out all these years. No wonder the other colonies call the strip between the two colonies 'Rogues' Harbour'. It is just that. As it stands, the section belongs neither to Virginia nor North Carolina, and consequently no laws are enforced. It is an abiding place for criminals and refugees and I want that condition wiped clean. Mr. Moseley, as Surveyor General, will head the commission, naturally. I am appointing Mr. Little and Mr. Anthony Lovyck as members. I hope this time we will be able to arrive at a satisfactory solution, as his Majesty has indicated that he will not brook further delay."

Pollock was the first to speak. "I'm minded that we could ha' settled the affair in Governor Hyde's time, your Excellency, had it not been for the stubbornness displayed by one William Byrd. He nae wants to give up his idea that all the Albemarle, down to the south shore of the Sound, should become part of Virginia."

Chairs scraped the floor as members of the Council moved, and voices were raised in unison.

"By God, he won't get our consent to that move." It was Moseley who spoke. "I beg your Excellency's pardon, but it makes my gorge rise when I hear anyone talk about making Albemarle Sound the dividing line; nor do I hold with the others who want the southern tip of the Great Dismal as a marker. The line should cut the Great Dismal, east to west, through the centre."

The Governor said, "Yes, that is what I think. I see no

reason to give way to the persistence of the Virginia committee."

Moseley said, "If I may offer a suggestion to your Excellency, put in the letter, 'This time, the North Carolina commission will furnish their own surveying instruments, so that we will have a check.'"

The Governor nodded. "You hear, Mr. Lovyck? Please incorporate Mr. Moseley's suggestion in your letter of acceptance to Governor Spottswood."

Mainwairing noticed glances exchanged. James Blount leaned over to Roger and said, with his hand over his lips, "His Excellency's wooing Moseley. Wonder what's behind it?"

Mainwairing didn't answer. He thought it within the range of possibility that the Governor hoped to soften Moseley's feeling towards him, so that Moseley would not pursue his investigation of Knight's complicity and Eden's with the pirate Teach. The Governor was wasting his time. Moseley wasn't so easily deviated from anything he had once undertaken. By nature he was a pathfinder, willing to sacrifice himself to anything he considered for the good of the people or the province. Eden had skill, shrewdness and diplomatic experience. Moseley had tenacity and integrity. It would be a bitter fight. His thoughts were interrupted by Lovyck, speaking his name.

"Mr. Roger Mainwairing will now give us his report of his recent interviews with the Lords Proprietors."

Edward Colston gave the closest attention to Roger Mainwairing. He presented his facts from the point of view of the colonist. It opened Colston's eyes, and gave him a different perspective. He saw that the colonists had a case against the Lords Proprietors, who were indifferent to their welfare.

"Only one of the Proprietors can be counted on to recognize our needs," Mainwairing said when he finished describing the meeting he had attended in St. James's Palace. "Lord John Carteret. When you realize that of the eight Proprietors, two are minors, and two extremely anxious to sell their shares, you can understand why we are in sad case."

"Do you think our protest will have any influence?" Foster Tomes, Quaker Deputy from Pasquotank, asked.

Mainwairing hesitated. "Christopher Gale and Micajah Perry, our provincial agent, are both satisfied that we will fare better, now that Lord Carteret is back from Ireland. He is interested in developing the province through enlarged trade; but both Danson and Ashley want to make swift money through shares in the new South Sea Bubble. They want either to deal with Sir George Montgomery, who desires to lease the province as a lifetime governor, or sell outright to the Crown."

Roger glanced about the room, smiling a little. "That would please those among us who contend that we would prosper, as Virginia has prospered, if we were under the Crown, instead of under a proprietory government."

John Blount said, "My relation, Sir Thomas Blount, writes me that there is a great opportunity for wealth through the South Sea Company. He, with Mr. Secretary Craggs, has had a great deal to do with its organization. Blount is a sound man when it comes to finances."

Roger knew from the way he spoke that his neighbour John Blount had laid out money in the company.

The discussion became informal. Questions were asked about the company and whether it was hard to get shares. Roger's answer was short.

"I don't know. I'm not interested in making money through speculation."

Pollock interrupted the talk. "Let's return to our immediate interests," he said. "That is, our trade. What about navigation laws? Will there be any change in the old ruling, Mainwairing?"

"Not that I know of. But I was told privately that there would be no interference if we wanted to deal with the West Indies. I think we can disregard the ruling that all the trade must be with the mother country. We'll continue to trade with New England, as we have been doing, laws or no laws. I told the Lords that any interference with coastal trade would meet with stubborn resistence on our part."

There were nods of approval at his words. "You're right, Mainwairing. We'll hold out for our trade."

Moseley's voice dominated. "I hope I've made it clear that we would also disregard the Navigation Act of 1696—a most obnoxious act, detrimental to our welfare and growth. Why shouldn't we trade with other nations besides England? We do well to trade with Portugal and her islands, and with Spain and Italy, now that the wars are over and the Peace of Utrecht is signed."

No one answered. The Governor was looking out the window and a frown deepened on his face as Moseley continued: "In Massachusetts, they are in violent conflict over the seizure of Boston ships accused of violating acts of trade. When the Governor made threats, his windows were smashed by a mob, so the cases were dropped." His words almost constituted a defiance.

Roger Mainwairing glanced about the room. His eyes rested on the Governor's fine profile. "We've had a reputation in North Carolina for harbourage of pirates. It was suggested to me in London that clearing our coasts was the business of the Province, not of the Lords Proprietors."

At once, Chevin from the eastern end of the country and Maule from upriver were on their feet. Before either could speak, the Governor tapped the table smartly. "Mr. Mainwairing, we have heard you with great interest. I personally want to thank you for your faithful report of the meeting of the Lords Proprietors and the Lords of Trade and Plantations. I am sure our Province had been well and faithfully represented by you and our Chief Justice, Mr. Christopher Gale."

He glanced at the clock. "We appear to have used up our time. Other matters can rest until the regular meeting of the Deputies, two weeks hence. If you and Mr. Colston will be so good as to remain, I'd like further conversation with you."

The men left the room in groups of twos and threes. Roger saw from their expressions that some of them were not too pleased to be so summarily dismissed by his Excellency. Roger thought Eden had moved with adroitness out of what might have been deep water. The Governor wanted no discussion in open meeting about sweeping the sea of pirates.

Moseley, Tomes and Nathaniel Chevin remained outside at the stoop, where they were joined by Colonel Maurice Moore, who had ridden up too late to attend the meeting.

Roger watched them as they moved across the Green towards the coffee house. He would have preferred to join them. He wanted to know what they thought of his report. He had deliberately brought up the subject of piracy, hoping that open discussion of that major problem would follow. But Eden had been too quick for them.

The Governor waved Colston and Roger Mainwairing to comfortable armchairs and seated himself near the fire, drawing a rabbit-lined cape over his shoulders. "I feel the cold. I shiver up and down my spine," he complained, after he had rung the bell rope to summon a slave.

"A touch of fever," Roger suggested. "'Tis common to have chills and ague at the first weather change."

"A villainous climate," the Governor went on. "These swamps let off poisoned air that hangs like a blanketing miasma along the shore. It's deadly. I've built a house on a bank above the river. I hope I'll escape the fever there." He turned his cold greenish-grey eyes on Roger. "Eden House is completed now. I want you to see what I've done in the way of a comfortable place to live. Perhaps you can bring Mr. Colston up on Saturday this week and stay until Monday."

Colston answered, "You're very kind, your Excellency, but I am leaving in the morning on Captain Bragg's boat, so I'll be unable to accept."

"So soon? Why, you've just arrived. I'd hoped to have the pleasure of entertaining you under my roof. I've had the honour of knowing your grandfather for some years. He's been always kind and hospitable to me when I've had occasion to visit Bristol."

"I'm so sorry," Colston said. "Perhaps if the *Delicia* stops on the voyage back from York, I shall be able to do myself the honour."

"Consider Eden House your headquarters. This little residence is not supplied with enough rooms for more than my official family, but it's necessary to have a place to lay one's head in the official village of the Province."

A light knock at the door interrupted him. The Governor called, "Come."

A slave entered carrying a silver salver, with decanters and large-bellied glasses.

"I'm fortunate. A friend sent me a dozen bottles of French brandy." He turned to Edward. "Good liquors are a rarity in this province."

Roger wondered whether the "friend" was Blackbeard.

The slave, dressed in dark maroon-coloured coat and breeches, the Governor's livery, passed the decanter. Edward and Roger helped themselves. The Governor lifted his glass. "Allow me to drink to your return to your home, Mr. Mainwairing, and to Mr. Colston's early return to the Albemarle."

"Your health, sir!" Edward said, rising.

"Your very good health!" Roger echoed.

"Thank you, gentlemen." The Governor set his glass down on a small tripod table which the slaves had placed beside his chair. His fingers turned the stem absently as he spoke to

Edward of his grandfather, and of Bristol. Roger thought the Governor showed good grasp of the affairs of trade and commerce.

He looked about him. A pleasant room, well panelled and furnished. A wine-red Turkey carpet on the floor gave warmth to the sage-green walls. Through the two south windows, the bay and the Sound were visible. The windows that flanked the fireplace faced the Green. The rail in front of the East Gate Inn was close-packed with restless horses. Slave boys stood near by in groups, waiting for their masters to come out.

Across the upper Green was William Badham's house, set well back in a little grove of trees and the remains of a well-planted garden. Gardening was Mary Badham's life, and she was earnest in her endeavour to introduce new flowers and shrubs into the winding paths and beds.

He noticed Pollock's coach in the driveway, and a dozen saddle horses tied at the rack. He could easily imagine who the guests were: Pollock, the Lovycks, Duckenfield, Willie Maule and his wife Penelope Galland; perhaps the Jacocks from the Chowan River plantations. The division in the community was widening, for he had seen Moseley, Swan, Henry Clayton and Lillington go into the coffee house. He didn't like this lining up on opposite sides— the Governor's friends and the Governor's enemies. It made for dissension in the community, when what they needed was unity of purpose, so that the country could prosper. If the leaders disagreed so openly, the common folk lacking leadership would be confused, and that would open the way to disorder.

They finished their drinks and Roger rose, followed by Edward, to make their adieux. The Governor did not rise. He was shivering again.

Roger said, "If it's a chill, bed and blankets and a hot posset will help. I'm sure Dr. Allen would tell you to take Peru-bark tea."

The Governor's face darkened. "I don't like Allen. He's a know-nothing. But what can one do?"

Roger said, "We have always found him competent and faithful."

The Governor did not reply. He pulled the cape closer about him. "Will you be kind enough to pull the bell for my man? And if you see Lovyck, ask him to stop by. I want to see him before he leaves for Sandy Point. I am sorry to have this wretched thing come up, Colston. I wanted to talk with

300

you . . . but my head . . ." He leaned back in the barrel chair and closed his eyes. The men left quickly. At the door they met the Governor's man.

Lovyck had already left, a slave told them. Perhaps he could be found at the inn, or at Mr. William Badham's house on the Green.

Colston's keen bright eyes were alive with interest. He made pertinent comments on the ships in the bay, the shops along Broad Street, and the fishing boats. They passed many groups of men standing at street corners, men from different ranks—well-dressed planters, yeoman and herders with cotton smocks under their sheepskin coats, woodsmen in their leather garments, and a sprinkling of Negro slaves. All of them touched their caps as Roger went by. Some stopped him to bid him welcome home.

The taproom was heavy with smoke and the acrid odour of lightwood from a newly lit fire. Roger saw a group of men seated at a table on the far side. Moseley rose from his chair and beckoned to the two men.

Colston said, "I fancy this group will have little to say in favour of the Governor."

Roger gave him a quick glance. "So you noticed?"

"Who could avoid seeing there's a distinct rift?"

Roger nodded. "I do not know the extent. I have talked to no one about the affairs of the Province since my return."

"The tension was evident at the meeting. I fancy I could tell where each man stood when you made your comment that ridding the Carolina coast of pirates was the business of the provincial government, not of the Lords Proprietors."

"I hoped it would have that effect," Roger said calmly.

Colston whistled. "Ah! So you wanted to make trouble."

"Not make trouble. Bring matters to the open. It came in naturally at the moment."

"And Governor Eden circumvented you."

Roger laughed but made no answer. They were nearing the table. Colston dropped his voice. "Have you chosen sides, Mr. Mainwairing?"

Roger hesitated to answer Colston's candid question. Finally he said, "No. There seems something on both sides. Until I know more of the details I shall steer clear of controversy. I'm inclined to a middle course."

Colston looked at him. His eyes were shrewd and knowledgeable. "I think the time has gone by for a middle course, Mainwairing."

Moseley pulled a chair for Edward next to him. Mainwairing sat down opposite. He mentioned the names of the other men to Colston.

There were Justice Thomas Relfe, from the eastern end of Albemarle County; Samuel Swan and Alexander Lillington, his neighbours; Thomas Garrett, also from near the Eastern Banks; and Colonel Maurice Moore.

"We've ordered dinner in a private room," Moseley told them. "I took the liberty of reserving places for you."

Roger hesitated the fraction of a second.

"Don't say you've other plans, Roger," Maurice Moore said. "We want to ask a dozen questions that did not come out at the meeting this morning."

"The Governor handled it his way," Thomas Relfe remarked, acidly. He was a fine-looking man of substance, with a broad open brow and clear-cut features.

Jacock and William de la Mare, Garrett and Relfe had all served as justices in the provincial courts, Moseley told Edward Colston. "At present we have no resident Chief Justice."

"So Gale remains in England?"

"Yes. He serves us better there than here."

"Does he favour the Governor?"

Colston's shrewd question gave Moseley pause, but only for a moment. Then he said, "Gale's first and only desire is to serve the Province."

Colston said no more. His question was answered.

A servant came to announce dinner, a round-faced man wearing a long leather apron over his striped breeches and brown woven shirt. He carried the cellar keys at his belt, and he waited until the company was seated before he took their wine orders.

Four Negro slaves brought the food—a fresh ham, baked in a ring of apples, surrounded by sweet potatoes; cornbread; a great dish of sweet butter; and a boat of rich onion gravy. Hearty food for hearty men, who spent most of their days out of doors. The talk was easy, with polite questioning of Colston, who had no hesitation in telling them he was so impressed with the country that he hoped to return again, after he had reported to Bristol the findings of his journey.

This statement by the visitor called for a toast. Edward only touched his glass. He had not forgotten his unhappy experience at the first breakfast at Queen's Gift.

Thomas Relfe said, "I wanted to ask about the health of

our good friend and correspondent, old Timothy White-church."

Roger smiled. "Timothy is in excellent health—a little more withered, a little drier than the last time I saw him, but he stills talks of the time when he will come to Carolina."

Relfe picked up his knife and fork. "A fine old man, one we can always count on to watch our interests. Too bad he can never see the country with his own eyes."

"Too bad, indeed," Roger rejoined. "I must write to him."

Relfe raised an inquiring brow. "Does old Timothy also keep you informed?"

"On political matters? No. We correspond about crops and turpentine woods and, sometimes, the herring run."

"Ah, yes, I see," one justice commented. "Old Timothy takes his pioneering vicariously, through Roger Mainwairing, planter."

During the meal the talk ran mostly to questions about affairs of the mother country as related to the Province. More than once the South Sea Company was mentioned. "A man has little chance in the Provinces to better his condition except by hard work on the land," Lillington observed. "It would do me good to lay down a certain amount of money and let it pyramid to twenty times its value without any effort on my part."

Justice Relfe smiled crookedly. "I've never known money to linger long that comes so readily."

Swan, a quiet-spoken man, leaned forward to get an uninterrupted view down the table. "One of my friends has written me that the Bank of England is trading its stock for shares. Did you hear anything about that, Roger?"

"That was the rumour. I never took the trouble to verify it. I'm not concerned with making money by speculation." Roger's tone was a trifle contemptuous.

"Why should you?" Lillington asked. "You own some of the best land in the whole county. But what about some of the rest of us, whose land is not so fertile, and whose income is unstable? Why shouldn't we take a gamble?"

Roger shrugged his shoulders. "Every man has a right to do as he pleases," he said, "unless he has a responsibility to other people. Take the case of Anthony Ashley and Danson. They're trying to persuade the Lords Proprietors to sell out the Carolinas and invest the money in South Sea shares, which to this moment have nothing but paper profits."

There was a moment of shocked surprise. Then Moseley

said, "They'd never do that! Why it's unthinkable! Sell this great productive land and our immense forests for pieces of paper!"

Roger said, "It's the truth. I heard Ashley bring it up in the meeting at St. James's Palace."

Moseley's fist came down on the table. "By God! How often have I told you we're ruled by a bunch of nitwits? To think such people have power of life or death over us is galling to me. If we had red blood in our veins we'd rebel."

Maurice Moore, who had been out of the room, entered in time to hear Moseley's words. He closed the door and stood at the end of the table, his arms folded over his broad chest, a man of soldierly bearing, with jutting jaw and firm wide mouth, but his deep-set eyes and broad forehead bespoke the dreamer. He waited for Moseley to finish his impassioned words before he spoke. "Perhaps that will not be so far off as you imagine. The southern end of the Province has leaders who do not propose to accept the neglect of the Proprietors much longer. There's a little group in Charles Town, headed by my father, who have already sent a memorial to their Lordships reciting our wrongs. It's a strongly worded document, and if no notice is taken of it—" his fingers touched his sword hilt—"suitable action will be taken."

He smiled as he spoke, but a vibrant quality in his voice showed his audience that action, rather than reform, would be the consequence of the memorial. An impressive silence followed. Moore sat down. His voice lowered. "I need not warn you, gentlemen, that this is a confidential matter."

Lillington addressed Edward. "Mr. Colston, you probably know more of this South Sea business than we do. Isn't it true that Mr. Secretary Craggs and Sir Thomas Blount are heading the lists and are responsible for the organization? Doesn't that indicate it's sound?"

Colston glanced quickly around the table. "You must understand, gentlemen, that I speak without authority. That is, I do not speak for my grandfather. I'll be frank to say that before I came to Carolina I might not have considered the sale of this Province for other investment was reprehensible, but now, from the small part I've seen, I consider such an act little less than treasonable. I might add—again my own opinion—that I do not like either of the Messrs. Craggs, father or son. They are bootlickers. They serve his Majesty with servility and without dignity. As for Sir Thomas Blount, I believe the Craggs have pulled the wool over his eyes.

They've made him think that all England needs in order to restore her trade to the glorious days of Elizabeth and her adventurous sea captains is to send a few ships to South America and the Solomons and the South Sea Islands. Why, we do not yet know what wealth these islands contain! Only a few sailors have visited these places. We do know about gold in the Philippines, and something of the wealth of India. But trade with the other islands and South America is pure venture. This last is not only my opinion but that of Captain Woodes Rogers. Mr. Mainwairing can tell you more about that than I."

The cautious Swan questioned Roger Mainwairing. "Is Captain Woodes Rogers an authority on trade?"

Roger said, "No living man is better qualified to speak. He and Dampier made the round-the-world journey together. As you know, Dampier is dead, and like to be forgotten, except for the straits in the Solomons that bear his name. Woodes Rogers is a firm believer that the wealth of England lies in the development of her colonies in America, and in the further development of trade with her rich Indian possessions. The Western Ocean once cleared of pirates, both the colonies and the mother country will enter into a fabulous era of prosperity."

"Which brings us back to the very thing I've been talking about," Maurice Moore exclaimed. "And it's in direct line with the thought of the liberal leaders in South Carolina. For some time I've held that we in the Albemarle are too engrossed with our individual problems to take the long view. We're far behind Virginia and South Carolina. It's high time we took some action."

He got up and strode to the door, threw it open quickly. Satisfied no one was within hearing, he continued: "We may as well admit that we have a Governor who closes his eyes to practical operations. Some of us suspect that he benefits from illicit freebooting. We know he's built a tunnel from Eden House to the Chowan River. We know he's built a fast road directly from his house to Bath Town on Pamticoe Sound. We know he spends as much time at his summer house on Pamticoe as he does at Eden House or his residence in Edenton. We know that Tobias Knight is his alter ego. We know that Tobias Knight has more than once defended the pirate Teach, or, as I prefer to call him, Blackbeard. We know that Blackbeard has a house close to Knight's dwelling at Bath Town, where he lives with his thirteenth wife. These are indisputable facts. What we don't know, and what we must find out, is whether his Excellency and his satellite Knight have benefited by the cargo of sugar which Blackbeard took from a French ship he captured off the Bermudas this midsummer. I've had a letter from Christopher Gale. If we get factual evidence on this transaction, or any other, he may be able to put the case before the Lords Proprietors."

There was a moment of shocked silence, following this bold statement and its implications.

Edward Colston felt Moseley's eyes boring into his, but he said nothing.

Alexander Lillington pulled his chair forward, so that he had a better view of Maurice Moore. He seemed to have forgotten the presence of the stranger. "Do you think there are such records? Where would they be kept?"

"To the first question, I don't know. To the second, I've ascertained that the Customs Records are now in the hands of Lovyck, at his Sandy Point plantation. Perhaps other records also may be in the same place."

Edward Moseley interrupted. "You've given us something to think over, Maurice. For me, I don't like the idea that we North Carolinians are lagging behind any of the colonies. But whatever course we decide on, it should be taken after due consideration, and not in anger or impetuous rashness."

Moore answered in a level voice. "There speaks the lawyer. I'm a soldier and accustomed to speedy action. A bold attack, a surprise attack, wins battles."

Thomas Luten, who had had nothing to say up to this point, put in, "I agree with Moore. We lose by delay." He turned to address Edward Colston. "Perhaps it's not hospitable for us to ask a pledge of secrecy from a guest, Mr. Colston. But I do ask the pledge of you, to forget what you've heard today."

"For shame. Nonsense, Luten." Several men spoke at once.

Colston smiled. "You're quite right, Mr. Luten. I'll be glad to give my word. I have already forgotten."

Roger Mainwairing pushed back his chair and got to his feet. "I think we'll be going. I promised Madam Badham to bring Mr. Colston to her house for a toddy."

Luten and several others rose at the same time. Luten put his hand on Roger's arm. Always outspoken and direct, he said, "We haven't had a chance to find out where you stand,

Mainwairing. I think it's appropriate to ask the same pledge from you."

"My gentleman's word," Roger said. "You know I've never taken much part in politics. I must know more of the circumstances before I make any decision. Be assured that what you've said will go no further. Good afternoon, gentlemen."

Colonel Moore and Moseley walked out together. As Roger was taking his coat from the rack, he heard Moore say, "I just met Lovyck. He told me that the Governor had asked him to stay in town with him for a few days."

There was a significant pause, and Moseley said, "Good. Very good indeed."

Chapter 23

HIGH CRIMES AND MISDEMEANOURS

The sound of laughter greeted Roger and Edward Colston when the Negro house slave opened the door of the Badhams' house—women's laughter and the deeper voices of men. The door of the drawing-room was open but the room was empty.

"Madam says please bring all de guests as come direct to de dining-room, sir. Dey's eatin' and drinkin' back dere."

He took their cloaks, folded them carefully and put them on a long chest near the door. "It's mighty fine to see you home again, Mr. Ma'n'ring. We missed you droppin' in. Yes, sar. We missed you ridin' 'round dis place."

"Thank you, Israel. I'm glad to be home again."

Colston stepped in front of a mirror to straighten his cravat and flip the ruffles of his sleeves into place. "And do I hear female voices?" he asked, meeting Roger's eye in the mirror. "I've been going to ask you if this was an Eveless world."

"By Jupiter, that's true. You haven't laid eyes on a woman since you came here. We'll have to attend to that right now."

Almost in answer to his words, the door at the end of the passage was thrown open. "I told you it was Mr. Mainwairing," a woman exclaimed. "I'd know his voice anywhere."

A moment later the hall was filled with the flutter of varicoloured skirts and the clatter of high heels on the bare floor. A group of young women hurried down the hall towards Roger. Hands were outstretched in greeting. There were low graceful curtsies to the floor, the rustle of silk and satin, flashing smiles of greeting, as the young girls surrounded their friend. Sweet clear voices rose in chorus.

"Did you bring the packet of dresses from my cousin Martha?"

"Victoria said she was sending a Spanish shawl. Did you bring it.?"

"Tell us about Madam Mainwairing and the new daughter. Is she as pretty a baby as Hesketh was?"

308

"We expect you to tell us everything about the new London fashions, and all the latest gossip."

Roger laughed and put his hands over his ears, looking down at the girls who hung on his arm and plied him with questions, all talking at once.

Edward thought he had never seen so many charming creatures, so natural, so unaffected. Roger turned his eyes towards Edward, who was standing back of him. "Just a minute, young ladies, I have a guest."

The pretty babble ceased. Brown eyes and blue turned towards him. There was an instant change in their demeanour. Six young ladies of fashion bowed slightly, with easy dignity, as Roger mentioned his name.

"May I present Mr. Edward Colston, of Bristol. Edward, these young ladies are our friends and neighbours. I'll go round the circle from left to right: Mistress Maria Blount, of the bright blue eyes and the coal-black hair. Maria lives at Mulberry Hill, not far from Queen's Gift. This is Madam William Maule—is she not young to be a wife? Cullen Pollock, with red hair and a fiery disposition to match, lives at Balgray, upriver."

"Oh, Mr. Mainwairing, how can you?" the girl cried. "You've no idea how I've changed." She curtsied to Edward, spreading her green skirts wide. "Do not believe him." She looked at Colston, her green eyes dancing. "He loves to tease."

Roger put his hand on her shoulder and kept her at his side, while he finished. "Then we have Alicia and Prudy Jones, our very near neighbours. And here's little Mary Badham, grown four inches at least."

A tall, slender, dark girl came out of the dining-room. She went straight to Roger and kissed his cheek. "How nice to have you back again," she said.

Roger held her hand and looked into her eyes. "My dear, I'm happy to see you." He turned to Edward. "This is Madam Anthony Lovyck; until a few years ago she was Sarah Blount. She and Maria are sisters. You saw her husband today at Cupola House."

Edward bent over Madam Lovyck's hand. A lovely creature, but her eyes were too brilliant and the little spots of colour on her cheekbones were too brightly red for perfect health.

Madam Badham and William hurried up, and the young girls went into the drawing-room.

"You must have some refreshment," Mary Badham said after the first greeting.

"We have dined," Roger said.

"But you'll have a glass of Mary's Scuppernong wine. Five years old, Roger." William addressed Edward Colston: "Mary, my wife, and Duke Roger have a feud of long standing over their Scuppernong. But step into the dining-room, sir."

A dozen older men and women were at a long table. House slaves passed back and forth with plates of ham and cold joints. Badham indicated a seat beside a dark handsome woman with a regally held head. "Madam Pollock, may I present Mr. Colston? He's Roger's guest and comes to us from Bristol."

Madam Pollock inclined her head graciously. Her large dark eyes surveyed him with interest. "You're Mr. Edward Colston's son?" she asked.

"His grandson, Madam Pollock."

"I'm acquainted with Edward Colston. I admire him extravagantly. A great man, a very great man."

Edward was a little embarrassed by the fulsome praise. "Thank you, Madam. I agree with you," he said, as he slipped into the vacant place.

His host introduced him to the woman at his left, Madam Galland. The opposite in colouring to Madam Pollock, she was blonde, with a pretty face and candid blue eyes. A little inclined to plumpness. She had beautiful arms and hands. Madam Hester Pollock immediately engaged Edward's attention by asking him numerous questions of his voyage, of his stay in the Bahamas and of Captain Woodes Rogers. Even before he finished answering the last question, she had whispered a word to the house slave to summon her stepdaughter to her side.

"You must meet Mr. Pollock's daughter, a most charming girl, so full of vivacity and life. She has become as close to me as if she were a child of my own." She laughed a little self-consciously. "That is, if I were old enough to have a child of her age."

Edward felt a stir at his side and a sound that might be a sniff of derision. He saw, from the expression of Madam Galland's face, that she and Madam Pollock were not too friendly. Madam Galland leaned forward a little and said, "My dear, I've not asked you recently how the little affair of Martha and the Reverend Bray is progressing." She included

310

Edward in a warm smile, and without waiting for his neighbour to answer, she explained: "Martha and the charming
young clergyman are so sweet together. I do hope that the
course of true love runs smooth for them."

Madam Hester's black eyes flashed fire, but no shadow
disturbed the serenity of her smooth brow. "My dear," she
said, "it's not serious. They're only friends." She, too, included Edward in her word of explanation. "Such a worthy
young clergyman. The Squire and I ask him frequently to
stay at Balgray. He's so forlorn. You know there are very
few people for a cultured man to associate with, in this little
wilderness settlement of ours."

Madam Galland passed the explanation without comment,
but her silence spoke her disbelief. She beckoned to a young
girl who was sitting in a doorway. "Penelope, my child, come
here. Take Mr. Colston into the drawing-room, where the
young people are going to dance."

Edward rose and followed the girl, inwardly chuckling. He
had not reached twenty-eight without having had designing
mothers lay little traps.

Others had noted the by-play. Edward overheard two
women as he passed into the drawing-room:

"Madam Galland gives herself airs, since the Governor has
been riding to Mount Galland to court her."

"I expect his Excellency finds Eden House lonely," the
second answered. "A bedfellow is always comforting these
cold winter nights. If he's really serious and marries her,
Queen Hester will be dethroned."

"Sssh. She'll hear you."

Edward's smile deepened. Even in this fine New World,
ambitions and jealousies played a part in the daily life of the
people. So the Governor was thinking of marrying. That was
interesting. He looked down at the girl by his side. Her
cheeks were scarlet and there were tears in her round blue
eyes. He felt suddenly sorry for her.

"Let's go into the little room across the hall and sit down.
I'd like to talk to you about this lovely country of yours."

The girl flashed him a grateful smile, and attempted to
steady her trembling lips. "It is lovely," she said. "If only the
people were as lovely as the country."

"It was as good as a Gay comedy," Edward said, as he
recited the incident to Roger while they rode back to Queen's

311

Gift an hour later. "But I felt sorry for the girl. She is a sensitive little thing."

"Several people told me that Eden is very attentive to the Widow Galland. It would not be too bad a match, for her husband left her many acres and a well-feathered nest. She has a talent for home-making," he added as an afterthought.

Edward said, "I take it Madam Pollock will not like that."

Roger laughed. "Madam Hester has had full sway in our little social world for a long time. She was vastly uneasy when I brought my wife out. But she soon saw that Rhoda had no ambitions in that direction."

"And what about the Squire? Does he have ambitions?"

"Not along that line. All he wants is land and to take up more timber holdings than anyone in the county. And he has realized his ambitions."

Roger's horse shied when a white-tailed deer ran through the underbrush and leapt across the road in front of them. Roger gave him his head and Edward pounded after him. There was no more conversation.

At supper that night Captain Bragg announced that he would not be sailing for two or three days more. Squire Pollock had a cargo for Williamsburg, and if he went that far upriver, he might as well go into Bennett's Creek to fill his casks with sweet water and give his crew a chance to do some fishing. He had allowed them to come ashore and go into the village for the night.

"I find it pays to let my men see a little life when they're in port. If they get too much of the bad liquor that's served along the water front, they return to ship better satisfied with the pannikin of good grog I give them every night. Sailormen have to run the devil out of them every so often."

"Not only sailormen," David Moray said with a laugh. "It's the same with soldiers. You've got to give your men some leeway. That's the reason Albemarle was a great general. 'Tent your men warm, fill their stomachs, and once in a while let them have their fling,' was what he said to explain the extraordinary loyalty of his men—and that was something for a Cromwellian General."

Colston selected a grape and skinned it with a silver fruit knife. "So you *were* an officer," he said, without looking at Moray. "I thought so, from the way you carry yourself."

"I don't seem to have fooled anyone," Moray said. "I thought I was being very clever."

"What does it matter?" the Captain observed sagely. "You

312

got away without being arrested by the King's men for treason."

"I came near joining the Duke of Argyll myself," Edward said reminiscently. "I was hot to right the wrongs, and put the Stuarts back on the throne, but my grandfather managed to dissuade me. He said there wasn't a chance for the Pretender."

"No one attempted to dissuade me," David said ruefully. "I was the head of my clan. We had always ridden out with the Stuarts, so I went along in the old way. It was just luck, on my part, that I wasn't arrested when they caught Derwentwater."

Bragg's eyes shifted to Mainwairing, who was looking down at the table, his fingers turning the stem of his wineglass, his face without expression.

Mellowed by the wine, David was loquacious. "A fine man at heart, Derwentwater. Most people thought him eccentric, but I never saw it. Even his estranged wife, Lady Mary Tudor, begged the King on her knees to give him pardon. For the life of me, I don't see how any man who was a man could have refused that beautiful woman."

There was a sound of glass shattering. The stem of the wineglass that Roger had been holding snapped in a dozen pieces. He sprang to his feet as the red wine spilled over the white cloth and spattered against his waistcoat. Metephele came forward quickly to sop up the wine.

"Don't bother," Roger said. His voice was curiously harsh. "Let's go into the library. I'm sure there's a fire there."

The men rose and crossed the hall into the book-lined room. Rain was beating against the window, and the wind rattled the shutters. The fire burned brightly, and the brass of the andiron and fender gleamed in the light. Metephele followed them with a tray of decanters and glasses for brandy. The three guests sat down in the comfortable leather chairs, but Roger stood in front of the fireplace, his hands extended to the warmth of the flames.

Bragg watched his host while David and Colston talked. He alone knew what lay behind the shattered wineglass. He alone knew the story of the brief and tempestuous love of Roger Mainwairing and Lady Mary Tudor, the natural daughter of the Stuart King.

Their host's silence became noticeable. The Captain knocked the dottle out of his clay pipe and got stiffly to his feet. "My old aches come on the joints when the rains begin. Think I'll be going back to the ship, for we'll be sailing upriver by daybreak. Do you want to go with me, Mr. Colston? Or had you rather stay here in comfort, whilst I'm loading Pollock's stuff?"

Edward hesitated. "I'd like to see Balgray plantation. Madam Hester gave me a cordial invitation. What do you think, Mainwairing?"

The sound of his name brought Roger out of his reverie. "Sorry to disappoint Madam Hester, but I can't let you go. Half the village and all our neighbours will be here tomorrow. The girls exacted a promise from me, to have my boxes opened so that they could get their presents. At least that's what they used for an excuse. Actually, I think they want to see the two strange young men who're visiting Queen's Gift. Madam Hester and the Squire are coming too, so there's no point to going upriver this time."

Edward's face brightened, and David Moray looked interested.

"That will be pleasant, Mainwairing," said Edward. He turned to Moray. "An extraordinary group of young people, Moray. I'm sure you'll enjoy it."

Roger pulled the bell cord. "Metephele will have a boy light you down to the boat, Zeb. I'll walk to the door with you."

He put his hand on the Captain's shoulder, and they walked down the hall together. A slave was waiting on the gallery. The two men stood in the door, discussing the cargo of tobacco which Roger was sending in the *Delicia* for reshipment abroad. Roger still had his hand on the old man's shoulder. Giving it a slight pressure, he said, "Good night, and thank you, old friend."

Bragg had no words, but they both understood. He buttoned his pea-jacket tightly around his neck and pulled his hat well down before he went out into the rain. Roger watched the stocky figure, with head bent against the force of the wind and the driving rain, until he disappeared into the grey shadows. "Good night, old friend," he repeated, "good night."

In the morning the wind had died down. By afternoon the rain was only a light mist. Towards dusk four horsemen met on the River Road, at the little creek that turned into Sandy Point Plantation. Edward Moseley arrived first, followed shortly by Thomas Luten, who had ridden by a short cut through the pocosin. Maurice Moore and Henry Clayton came together. They had spent the night with Samuel Harvey at the plantation at Harvey's Neck. Their greeting was quiet and serious. The lively banter that usually marked the meeting of the lighthearted Albemarle folk was absent. They were on serious business which might involve breaking the law by forcing their way into a man's house and abstracting government property.

This was an extreme step for Edward Moseley, who had, from the first, when he was acting Chief Justice under the short-lived Cary government, stood for law and the settlement of disputes under law. Since the earliest settlements every planter had been his own law, settling disputes by duelling pistols or swords, or even fists, before they took recourse to public law. The crowded dockets of the General Court and the Court of Oyer and Terminer were now proof that the people were falling into the habit of using the established means of justice. In this they had followed Moseley's lead. Now he was setting out deliberately to break the law. What made it more culpable was that as the Surveyor General of the Province he held high office under his Majesty's government.

The four men rode down the lane that led to the plantation house. Anthony Lovyck had purchased Sandy Point from the Porters a few years before, when he received the appointment of Secretary to the Deputies' Council and married Sarah Blount, of Mulberry Hill, the next plantation to the west. Lovyck was the Governor's man, as he had been the preceding Governor's. He was gaining prestige and fortune rapidly by currying the favour of those in power. In spite of all this, Moseley liked Anthony. He was especially fond of Sarah, but he held the welfare of the Province above personal preferences.

He was sure that the Governor was implicated, with Tobias Knight of Bath Town, in unlawful trade, through the pirate Blackbeard. Knight's position with his Majesty's Customs made this possible, for Knight could cover illegalities. In order to prove this, Moseley knew he must get a look at the books that held the records and manifests of ships trading into Edenton and Bath Town. The books were public property and should be open to inspection by any citizen, but Eden had arbitrarily ordered them removed from the Clerk's office and secreted. Only the week before, Maurice Moore had ascertained they were in the custody of Anthony Lovyck. Moseley was determined to see them. So was Moore. Clayton and Luten had fallen in with the idea.

When the house was in sight, Moseley drew rein. "Since we're going to be Jack Sheppards and engage in banditry, we may as well use proper procedure. Luten, you stay here and give the signal if anyone approaches by the road. Clayton, you keep an eye on the main house."

"Do you know where the books are likely to be kept?" Moore interrupted.

"The strong-box is in the plantation office. We'll go there first, Maurice."

They rode off towards the small building, connected with the house by a grape arbour, now denuded of leaves.

"The responsibility of this venture is mine," Moseley said as they rode along. "I'll do the housebreaking, if it's necessary. That's the reason I put Henry and Tom on watch. If we get caught, they'll be only accessories to the crime. And you're to stay outside."

"We're in this thing together," Maurice said gruffly. "I don't think we'll run into any difficulty. You made sure that Lovyck's staying in town with the Governor, didn't you?"

They encountered no one. They could hear the sound of voices in the distance, near the slave quarters. They dismounted and tied their horses at the grape arbour.

The door to the office was unlocked. The strong-box was under the steep stairway that led to the attic. The plantation books were scattered about, on the desk and table, and the Council journal lay open on a small table. The last item was dated two weeks previous, and it concerned a grant of land in Tyrrel County, to the Widow Hassel, described as lying up and against Edward Moseley's White Marsh tract. The men looked at each other. Edward smiled quizzically. All the Albemarle knew that he was rumoured to be courting Madam Hassel's daughter Ann.

"I'll have to find something to break open the strong-box," Moore said. There was nothing in sight. "I saw a sledge at the end of the arbour. I'll get it." Moore strode out of the room and returned in a moment with the hammer in his hand. It took but a moment to break the flimsy lock. Moseley flung the door open. The books were there, wrapped in a packet labelled: "Tobias Knight. Bath Town." A second packet, "Cargo Inventory. Property of Charles Eden."

"Here you are," said Moore. "What are you going to do with them?"

"I'm going to put them in my saddlebags," said Moseley, tucking them under his arm.

316

"Why not look at them here?" asked Moore. "Wouldn't that rate as a lesser crime?"

Moseley laughed shortly. "We're in so deep now, one more indictment will make little difference. I must have time to compare these items, to be sure that I've got a case against Eden. Come on, let's get out of here."

Moseley mounted his horse.

"Wait, Maurice. I've thought of something. I'll go back and leave a note to say I've taken the records. That saves us from being out-and-out thieves."

"Put my name to it," Moore said. "We share and share alike in this."

"Well, 'tis accomplished. If the Governor gets us into court, you may have to build your city of Brunswick on the Cape Fear earlier than you planned!"

The books were safely stowed in Moseley's saddlebags, and the men mounted their horses and signalled Clayton. Before he could join them, an old Negro, crippled with rheumatic fever, hobbled out of the house.

"Evening, Masters," he said. "Master Lovyck, 'e's gone to Edenton, two days ago excusin' one. He be mighty sorry if you don' come into the house and have a glass of sumpin."

"Thank you, Eph," Moseley said calmly. "We haven't time today. Tell your master that we got what we came for."

"Yas, sir."

Clayton came up and the three rode down the lane, where they were joined by Tom Luten. When they came to the River Road, Mosley said, "Best all separate and go to your homes. I believe that's the proper procedure of thieves. I'll communicate with you." After discussing it a few minutes, they agreed.

Moore lingered after the others had ridden away. "I think I'll go along with you," he said, putting his horse beside Moseley's. "You might come on some trouble and need a lusty sword by your side."

Moseley made no comment and they rode on in silence, as far as the entrance gates of Mulberry Hill.

"Ah! Here comes trouble," Moore said. Looking up the driveway, Moseley saw Anthony Lovyck, with Sarah riding postillion, her arm around her husband's waist. She smiled and waved to them. They were obliged to pull up. Moore, as always, taking the bold course, said, "We've just come from Sandy Point. Eph offered us hospitality, but we didn't have time to linger."

"I'm so sorry. You should have stayed to have supper with us. The men have been killing this week, and we have some excellent spiced sausage."

"That would have been nice," Moore said. "But we have to get to the village before nightfall."

Anthony was looking at the two men, a shadow of suspicion in his eyes. He said, "Why not come back, if you have business with me?"

Moseley allowed a thin smile to cross his lips. "Thank you, not tonight, Lovyck. Some other time will do just as well. Good night, Sarah. Better get on. This mist is bad on the throat." He spoke to his horse and the two men trotted on towards Moseley Hall.

"Well! That was a near call!" Moore exclaimed. "We haven't much time ahead of us now. What's our next move?"

Moseley did not answer at once. He was thinking. There were ten or twelve hours of work ahead of them, trying to dig out incriminating evidence from the books. It would not take Anthony very long to find out what had happened, and ride back to the village to report to the Governor. Eden would swear out a warrant and send a constable after them. Moseley Hall would be the first place they would look for the books. They would lose too much time going to Moore's place in Pequimans.

"I think it would be wise to stop at Queen's Gift. Roger will give us a quiet room where we can take our time on the books."

Moore objected. "Mainwairing hasn't declared himself and he has two strangers with him. Do you think it well to go there?"

"Can you think of a better plan?"

Moore had nothing to offer.

Sorry weather was no damper to the young people. They came from the village and the neighbouring plantations by carriage and on horseback.

The Pollock family arrived in their fine coach, which Madam Hester had bought in Williamsburg from one of the Harrisons. She had had it smartened up, and a small crest of the Pollocks' outlined in gold put on the door. Old Tom had been blasphemous over this, but Hester had paid no heed, and since there was no coach painter in the village to obliterate it without ruining the looks of the door, that little symbol of the superiority of the Pollocks remained. The village only

318

laughed. Hester's vagaries caused on annoyance or envy, only amusement.

The horseback riders brought changes of attire in their saddlebags. The carriage people had boxes. House slaves showed them to the guest rooms, where they would change. The gay voices and laughter which filled the rooms gave Roger a momentary wave of nostalgia. It was always like this when Rhoda was at home. He missed her. Half of his morning had been wasted in consultation with cook and housekeeper—questions about food and drink; the keys to the linen closet had to be found and the fruit storage closet opened. Primus wanted to know what grade hams to get from the smokehouse and cook wanted to know how many chickens to roast. Roger had no idea how many people would come. He did not even know how many he had invited. All this confusion annoyed him. He realized suddenly how smoothly the household ran under Rhoda's deft guidance. By four o'clock, thirty or more had arrived. A fire was burning in the fireplace in every room and the candle loft had been robbed of wax myrtle tapers.

Roger had had the boxes and packages he had brought from London sent up to the nursery. Almost every woman in the village had commissioned Rhoda to buy clothes. Then there were gifts sent by relatives and friends, from London and the provinces—bandboxes and boxes and even wicker cases, bearing the tags of various London manteau and slipper-makers. Voices rose to a babel of sound and floated down the stairs as the women unwrapped parcels and boxes. The menfolk gave their sodden capes and hats to the houseboys. The older men shook out their wigs and made their way quickly to the morning room, where Metephele was serving steaming punch from a silver bowl. Here they took solace in numerous cups of hot toddy and talked about tobacco crops and affairs of the Colony.

Seeking to remove himself from the temptation of taking too many toddies, Edward wandered into the hall and looked into the drawing-room. It was empty. He heard the soft-voiced Negro houseboys moving about. He looked in. The table was set. Piles of plates and silver were on the long hunt board. Metephele stood near the door that opened to a pantry; this in turn let to the passageway and the kitchen wing. The giant Angoni was dressed in a long robe of white linen; about his waist he wore a girdle of gay striped cloth. A hunting knife with a handle of ivory was thrust through the sash. On his head he had a cap of red felt with a long black tassel that reached to his shoulder. A short bolero of red cloth, embroidered in gold and silver thread, completed his costume. Barbaric and splendid he looked, with his straight clear features and bronze skin.

The houseboys, too, wore long white garments with red sashes, their bare feet thrust into red leather slippers. The slaves' costumes and the lavishly set table were like some story out of the tales of Damascus or Zanzibar, some fabulous Eastern world.

The words that greeted him, as he stepped back into the hall, completed the illusion. "Please, Mr. Colston, do you know how to wrap a turband?"

He looked up. Two girls stood at the head of the stairs, their wide flowing skirts sweeping across the polished treads. Each carried a length of tissue trailing from her hands.

Maria Blount came first. It was she who had asked the question. Behind her was the auburn-haired Cullen Pollock. Maria had a sheet of paper in her hand.

"My cousin, Miss Teresa, sent me a length of tissue and directions for wrapping a turband. It's exactly like the one Lady Mary Montagu imported from Turkey." She held up the gold tissue for his observation.

Edward shook his head smilingly. "I've seen many a turband stuck with feathers and artificial flowers, but strike me! I've never tried tying one of the things." He hailed David Moray, who had come into the hall. "Here's Mr. Moray. He's somewhat of a ladies' man; perhaps he has had experience."

"Egad, no!" David exclaimed.

Maria pouted. "I think you're too unkind. We have all these silk lengths, and the directions my cousin sent, but we simply can't make them out."

The Vaile girls and Prudence Jones clattered down the steps. They also trailed lengths of silk in their hands; their long curls were awry, their cheeks red.

"We've tried every way. They look dreadfully funny."

"They do look funny," Edward assured them, "particularly when they have great diamond pins and towering plumes."

Maria went into the drawing-room and pulled a chair in front of a long mirror. "I'm going to sit right here until someone shows me how it's done." She tilted her head to one side and began to wind the gold scarf over her dark hair. The tissue was slipping. It caught in her hair and disarranged it. Her cheeks grew red with vexation.

320

"Wait, Maria," Cullen Pollock exclaimed. "I've an idea. I'll read the directions and Mr. Colston can follow." She thrust the scarf into Edward's hands.

Moray laughed at the expression on Edward's face.

"And you, Mr. Moray, will you please arrange mine?" She dragged a chair and sat beside Maria, spreading her green skirts and smoothing her auburn hair.

"Oh, I say, Mistress Pollock. My hands are too heavy to handle such delicate fabric," Moray protested.

"I heard Roger say you had a light hand on the bridle." Her greenish eyes twinkled.

"Come, gentlemen. A race."

Other young people came into the drawing-room—the Blount brothers, Johnny and Thomas; the two Vailes. Tom Benbury and young Allen, the doctor's son, stood against the wall, while the girls clustered around to watch and give advice.

Tom Benbury took out his watch, his fob dangling. "Why not time them? Who'll lay a bet on Mr. David Moray? Who on Mr. Edward Colston?"

The laughter rose as the two men struggled with the scarves.

"This is monstrous!" groaned Colston. "My fingers are all thumbs."

"The silk eludes me. I swear it is magicked," Moray exclaimed. He tried to wind the girl's long red tresses into folds of the silk, but the silk slipped from his grasp.

Drawn by the laughter, older men and women looked in, and stayed to join in the hilarity.

Roger Mainwairing came to the door of the drawing-room and stood watching the young people, a smile on his lips. He beckoned Metephele to come to him.

"I give up," Colston said, as for the fourth time he unwrapped the scarf from about Maria's head. She tried to smooth her hair to a semblance of order.

"I think you're awkward, Mr. Colston."

"I am. I'm frightfully awkward," he admitted. Perspiration was standing on his forehead.

"I, too, admit defeat," Moray said. "The silk will be in a string if I keep on."

Roger motioned to the slave. "You show them how to roll a turband, Metephele."

"The Master wants it should be in the manner of Zanzibar, or of India?"

The eyes of all the young people were turned towards the slave.

"India! Zanzibar! I choose Zanzibar, because it is such a beautiful word," Maria Blount exclaimed.

Metephele slipped the ivory-handled knife from his girdle and handed it to Primus. He unwound the long striped silk scarf from his waist. When he finished, the sash was in a tight roll. He spoke to a small boy, Nick, who mended the fires. The boy stood in front of him, facing the mirror. Metephele laid the tightly wrapped silk against the lad's head above the ear. Nick held a skinny finger against it, to hold the silk secure. Metephele unwound the tightly wrapped sash swiftly, giving it a square turn over each ear, so that the lower edge remained taut and conformed to the shape of the head. Round and round the silk flew, until it rose towering over the boy's forehead. He made a skilful turn at the back and drew the remaining silk through the folds in such a way as to make the whole edifice secure, and the fringed end hung down over the shoulder.

"Oh! I could never do that," lamented Mistress Pollock, and immediately began to wind her scarf into a roll. Every girl followed her example, striving to learn the trick of turband rolling.

"This is the way of Zanzibar," Metephele said. "It is warry simple, not complicate' as the turband of India." He said a word, in his native tongue, to the wood boy. The picanin' tore himself reluctantly away from the mirror and followed the *capita* from the room.

Slaves went about lighting the candles in the wall sconces, on the tables and mantel.

Roger stepped to the gallery that faced the Sound. He met Captain Bragg face to face as he opened the door. "Why, Zeb! I thought you'd gone upriver."

"No," said Zeb crossly. "The wind died. I won't get off before early morning. Thought I'd come up and ask myself to supper. I didn't know you were having a ball." He shook the water from his short coat, for it was raining steadily.

"Only the neighbours. Come in, come in. Everyone will want to see you, Zeb."

Roger had his hand on the doorknob when he heard horses sloshing in the heavy mud at the side of the house. "Someone is arriving," he said. He lifted a hurricane lanthorn from the rack. "You go on in. There's a bowl of toddy in the morning room. Help yourself. I'll be in in a moment."

He walked the length of the gallery to the farther end. The light from his lanthorn illuminated the face of Edward Moseley, who was dismounting. He swung the lanthorn. The tall stalwart figure of Maurice Moore came into the circle of light. The sound of music came from the house. The two men stopped and looked at each other, then at Roger.

"This is unfortunate. We wanted to see you alone." Roger noticed that Moseley had his saddlebags over his arm. The faces of both the men were grave. Roger sensed something out of the ordinary was afoot.

"Come in. We can go to the library. No one is in there."

Moore shook his head. "We don't want anyone to see us at present. I mean no one. It's imperative that we have a few hours without interruption while we do some work. Moseley thought if we came here——" He left the sentence in the air.

Roger thought for a moment. "Go around to the plantation office. I'll get the key and join you there."

The two men moved off in the shadows, following a little brick path that led through the garden to the small building which Roger used for the estate work. He hurried through the hall, up the stairs to his bedroom. Here he got the keys from the drawer of the highboy, and went back to the lower floor. Metephele stopped him at the foot of the stairs.

"Hannah she say, food ready this long time. Very bad for gentleman to drink long time with nae food in stummick."

Roger laughed. He went into the drawing-room and started the guests to the dining-room where the food was waiting. The young folk left off their dancing and went to the long table where the food was waiting. The men about the punch bowl were harder to move. But some of them, urged by their wives, put down their glasses. Roger looked into the dining-room and saw that everyone was occupied. Then he slipped out the side door and hurried to the office. Moore and Moseley were standing under the little porch, out of the rain. Roger opened the door and put the lanthorn on a table. Striking a flint, he set fire to cobs under the logs, in the little brick fireplace. The flames blazed up cheerily. The two men took off their damp riding capes and shook the raindrops from their wide beavers. Moseley unstrapped his leather saddlebags and removed the books. Without a word being spoken, Roger knew what had happened. They had been to Sandy Point and abstracted the Customs books that had been placed in Lovyck's care.

Moore's piercing hazel eyes bored into Roger's. "We're

going to check the books. Then we plan to return them."

Roger said nothing. He was waiting for Moseley. It came to him that he was, without any intent on his part, involved in an act that might have far-reaching effect on the Province. For good or evil he did not know. It passed through his mind that Moseley intended it to be this way. He wanted Roger on their side, not on Eden's.

Moseley opened the books and sat down in front of the table before he spoke. "We met Lovyck as we passed the gates of Mulberry Hill. It won't take him very long to discover his loss. In fact I left a written message, saying I had exercised my rights as a citizen to see the public records. Since he had seen fit to sequester them, I had no recourse but to take the books by force."

Roger lifted his heavy brows. "Will that action lessen the crime?"

Moseley smiled grimly. "I doubt it, but it was a salve to my own conscience. You see, Roger, we need time to go over these records. I'm sure Lovyck will go to Eden immediately. The Governor will at once send the law after us. At all costs he must keep us from making a thorough search. The fact that he had the books hidden shows something. Either they've been in league with the pirates or there's some other nefarious work going on. In either case we, the people of the Province, should know the truth. That's our legal and moral right under a free government, such as our Charter gives us."

It was like Moseley to appeal to Roger in this way. He wasted no time in explaining the personal squabbles and factional differences. He placed the whole affair on high moral grounds. Sacred rights were at stake, liberties being violated. Edward Moseley had given most of his mature life to a struggle over the rights of all the people as guaranteed by the Magna Charta and the Great Charter of the Carolinas.

"You'll be safe here, unless . . ." Roger paused.

Moseley nodded in affirmation. "Unless the constable, not finding us at Moseley Hall or at Benbury's, will come here. I know that. We must take the chance. I only want time to complete this search. Then I'll go into Edenton and call on the Honourable Charles Eden. It will not be necessary for him to send a man with a paper in order to take me to gaol."

"I'll get word to you, if Lovyck or anyone from Edenton

324

arrives. I'll send Metephele with some food. You know he's to be trusted."

Roger pulled the heavy curtains across the window so that no glimmer of light would show, and left the room. Already the two men were deep in the work of going over the great books, item by item. A full night's work lay ahead of them, he thought as he closed the door behind him.

Roger regained the hall without meeting anyone. The sound of laughter and gay voices fell on his ears, a shock that brought him back from the heavy sense of apprehension which had surrounded him in the little office room. He squared his shoulders. He was smiling when he joined Squire Pollock. His face did not show at all a fear that two of his close friends were near danger, that they might lose the liberty for which they had fought so earnestly and valiantly. He talked about things of no consequence, listened to Tom Pollock and John Blount argue about the strange actions of Parson Urmston, who had recently come back from a visit to England.

"I can't see why the Society for Propagation of the Gospel returned him to this Province. He doesn't like us and he doesn't like the country. He writes violent letters to the Lords telling the most outrageous things about our morals and our conduct." John Blount spoke with emphasis. "I'm going to write the Bishop and ask him to recommend that the Society send out someone else."

"Poor old Urmston," Pollock said as he lighted a church-warden pipe a slave handed him. "I think his judgement is crippled, just as his leg is crippled. He has vinegar and gall as a drink instead of honey and spice. Poor mon."

Roger heard shouting outside, the sound of several voices and the neighing of horses. With a word of excuse he went swiftly out of the room. He had recognized Lovyck's voice. He did not want to see Lovyck until he had warned Moseley. He knew that he'd find Bragg in the room where the punch bowl was. Bragg set down his cup and came into the hall when Roger signalled him.

"Bragg, I want you to do something for me without asking any questions," Roger said, walking towards the hall door, away from the room where the dancers were.

"Afoul of the law, Roger?" Bragg queried, his old eyes lighting up in anticipation.

"I hope not. But we must act promptly. Go to my office. Tell Moore and Moseley that people are here to ask questions. Then I want you to take them on board the *Delicia* and set sail as quickly as possible. Upriver for a day or two is all they need to complete what they're doing."

Bragg snatched his heavy jacket which hung on a peg by the door. He refused a lanthorn. It would be a give-away. "I've the eyes of a cat, Roger. I can see in the dark. Lucky I left my boy in the boathouse to wait for me."

"Take the path through the lower garden. It isn't visible from the house, in case they start a search."

"Five minutes and I'll get them to the water's edge. It's too dark for them to see the boat anyway and I'll have the boy pole, so as not to make too much noise."

"Good! Now I'll go in. You'll be back in a couple of days?"

Captain Zeb didn't answer. Walking swiftly, he went down the familiar path that led to the lower garden and the plantation office. The driving rain erased the bulky figure and made it part of the deep shadows.

Roger went into the hall and closed the door. When Anthony Lovyck and his party came into the lower hall, he was mingling with the dancers in the drawing-room. He walked forward to greet the newcomers. Lovyck did not take his extended hand. His cloak streamed with water; water dripped from the brim of his hat. His dark face was clouded and his lips drawn to a thin line. Behind him on the stoop stood the village constable and two other men whose faces were in shadow.

"I'd like to speak to Colonel Moseley," Lovyck said. "I have a matter to take up with him."

"Moseley is not here," Roger answered, hoping he spoke the truth.

"Then Colonel Moore will do." Lovyck's tone was sharp. He was worried and it showed in his face and in the quick nervous movement of his hands. The Governor had doubtless lifted Lovyck's hide with his scalding tongue. He could be venomous to foe or friend when he dropped into a fit of rage.

"Moore isn't here either. Sorry. Come in, Anthony, and have a glass of toddy and some supper. You too, constable. Send your men around to the back and they'll be fed."

The constable's face wreathed in smiles. From where he stood he saw the dining table and the outlay of food. "A hot drink would be welcome, Mr. Mainwairing. Don't care if I do. Thank you, sir." He spoke to his men, who went down the steps.

Lovyck did not appear to hear the conversation. He allowed Primus to take his dripping cloak and hat, and walked into the drawing-room. Standing in the door, he glanced around the room, his dark eyes taking in the people with a swift glance. He did not reply to greetings, but went to the morning room. Here were the men he knew would be on his side. He put one hand on the side of the door but he did not enter.

He fixed his gloomy eyes on Thomas Pollock, who sat in a fireside chair, a silver cup filled with a hot drink in his hand.

"The Custom Books have been stolen from Sandy Point," he said without raising his voice.

Every eye was turned to the newcomer.

The Squire's hand trembled, and the liquor dribbled from his cup upon his flowered vest.

"Moseley, Edward Moseley did it. Have any of you gentlemen seen him tonight?"

"No," came in unison. "No."

"Or Maurice Moore?"

"Is he in on it too? How do you know it was Moseley?" Roger asked. He felt the necessity of saying something to show that he was interested.

"He had the impudence to tell me so." Lovyck drew the paper from his pocket and read Moseley's words. Roger glanced swiftly about the room. The older men's faces expressed astonished disapproval.

Pollock's face was red. He was so angry he sputtered. "That rascal, that radical rascal. I'm not surprised at anything he'd do against his Excellency. But Moore! That's something I can hardly credit."

"Moore was with him. I saw him myself."

The constable came to the door. His round blue eyes shifted from one to the other. "My man says that the Governor has sent a platoon of militia to scour the country. He wants you shall have Moseley in his hands by morning. Those were his words, Mr. Lovyck."

Lovyck glanced at Roger. His eyes were hard. "I'd like your word that neither of these men is in your house or on your plantation."

Roger was standing near the window. As Lovyck spoke he saw the riding light on the *Delicia* raised and lowered twice—

the old signal they had used on the voyage to hail their convoy. That meant the men were safe aboard Bragg's ship.

"I give my man's word," he said quietly.

Lovyck took up a glass of punch and drained it. His dark olive skin was pale, his eyes burning. His hand shook as he ladled out a second glass. He set the glass down carefully and moved towards the hall. At the door he turned, his hand on his sword.

"I swear I'll have the men who committed this outrage at the point of my sword." His voice shook with rage. "At the point of my sword," he repeated.

He went down the hall quickly, followed by the constable. The men left in the room looked one to the other with apprehensive eyes.

"Maurice Moore is a master with the sword," Squire Pollock said glumly. "A master——"

Lovyck had no more than got to the front hall when a loud knocking was heard, a voice rang out:

"Open the door, for his Majesty's Governor. Open."

Metephele and Primus moved swiftly, their white robes fluttering over their lean brown legs. Roger took his place at the stair, ready to welcome the new guest. The dancing stopped; the men in the morning room hastened to the entrance. Every door that led to the hall had its complement of astonished folk.

Metephele flung the door wide. Charles Eden strode in. He stopped just inside. His long cape dripped water to the polished floor. The plumes of his beaver hung as draggled as a cock's tail. His face was black with rage, and his hand clenched his riding whip with enough force to whiten the knuckles.

"Where's Lovyck?" he demanded, without word or greeting to his host.

Lovyck stepped forward. If his face had been white before it was livid now.

"Where are the books?" The Governor's voice was sharp. "Where is that villain Moseley?"

"They eluded me, your Excellency. I've searched everywhere, but I cannot find them."

"Nonsense, utter nonsense. I thought you said you knew where they would hide."

"So I thought. but I was mistaken."

The Governor passed him without another word. Stopping in front of Roger, he said, "You have him hidden in your plantation. Produce Moseley—and that other rascal Moore—or it will be worse for you, Mainwairing."

Roger faced the excited man calmly. "You have made the mistake this time, your Excellency."

The Governor whirled about, scanning the faces of all the guests. His voice rose excitedly. "You're all against me. All against Government. You're hiding two criminals from the law. I'll have the law on all of you, all——"

Old Tom Pollock pushed aside the men who stood between him and the door. He bowed to Eden. "You're making a grave mistake, your Excellency. We have all been here for the past four hours. Neither Moseley nor Maurice Moore has been here."

"Mainwairing may have concealed them. Isn't that possible?" The Governor faced Pollock.

Roger stepped forward. Pollock raised his hand to deter him. "Your Excellency, Mr. Mainwairing has been here at all times, exercising his talent as a gracious host. Any one of us, all of us, will give our sworn word to that. Do not be discouraged, the books will be found. As soon as it is daylight a search will be instigated."

The Governor's rage dropped from him. Instead, his face showed utter discouragement. He laid his hand on Roger's arm. "Forgive me, Mr. Mainwairing, for my high words. The provocation has been great, a series of provocations; rather, one piled above the other. . . . I've just had advice from Williamsburg that the Virginia Assembly has offered a reward of one hundred pounds for the arrest of Teach, fifteen pounds for the arrest of each of his officers and ten for every member of his crew."

The Governor paused and glanced about the room, to see the effect of his words on the company.

Thomas Pollock was the first to speak. "By what right does the Virginia Assembly deal with matters that concern North Carolina?"

"That's not all," Eden said, when old Tom had finished. "They say, in Virginia, that many North Carolinians have written to the Governor of Virginia for aid in ridding the country of pirates. They realize they must look elsewhere for help than to North Carolina's Governor."

The Governor leaned forward, grasping the back of a chair with one hand, as if his rage made him unsteady. "This calumny, because I have followed his Majesty's order and given pardon to Teach, when he came to my place at Bath to sue for amnesty!"

The righteous look on Eden's face did not fool anyone. He was making a case for himself, in attacking the Virginia Assembly.

"That is not all the infamy," he continued. "Governor Spottswood himself has gone down to Hampton Roads and engaged and equipped two sloops at his own expense: the *Lyme*, with Captain Brand, and the *Pearl*, under Lieutenant Maynard. They have instructions to repair to the Carolina Banks and bring Teach and his crew to Virginia, dead or alive."

Tom Pollock spoke again. He was edgy over Virginia's taking action. He didn't hold with Spottswood on other matters. "In God's name, by what right does a Virginia ship invade North Carolina waters?"

Eden gave him an approving look and waited for others to speak. They were all aware that the Governor was creating a diversion. He had brought this up to extricate himself from an unpleasant situation which he had created by his loss of self-control. In the back of the room a man said to his companion, "Tobias Knight had better be padlocking his barns."

Someone snickered. It was rumoured that Knight had lent his barns and dependency houses to Teach more than once, when the pirate had a cargo he wanted stored.

The Governor cast an angry look towards the two men, but he could not tell the speaker. He let the implication pass.

Edward Colston and David Moray stood near the door of the drawing-room, where they could both see and hear Eden. Grouped about the hall, the young women stood silent, not understanding. Their flowing silk gowns and the gold tissue turbands they had bound on their heads made the scene as unreal as a stage setting, and as fantastic.

"The villains are in the right, and the heroes in the wrong," Colston whispered to David. He was thinking of Moseley and Moore breaking into a house to steal records in order to right a wrong. He had no doubt in his mind that Eden and Knight were in league with the pirates. Eden's anger rose from fear, not from righteous wrath.

"I'll appreciate it if you come with me, Colonel Pollock. I want you to see the letter I write to Spottswood. As a member of my Council, I need you."

"Certainly, your Excellency, I'll come at once." Pollock

signalled his wife, who went quickly up the stairs to get her outer garments.

Roger said, "Metephele, call Mr. Pollock's carriage." To the Governor he said, "Sir, will you honour me by having a glass of brandy while you wait?"

The Governor turned his cold protruding eyes on Roger, "It is not the habit of the Governor of North Carolina to wait for anyone, not even a Councilman."

He stalked to the door, his head thrown back, his shoulders stiff and straight.

"Exit majestically," said Edward behind his hand.

David laughed. "I was thinking the same thing. But the bedraggled, beaten and sodden cloak is more reminiscent of the Woeful Knight."

The door was closed behind the Governor and the Pollock family. A torrent of excited voices rose, men and women asking one another could it be true that Tobias Knight was actually in partnership with the murderous Blackbeard? They spoke aloud of Knight, but the unspoken question in every mind was Charles Eden, Governor of North Carolina—was he an accessory after the fact, as deep in the dark villainy as Knight himself?

Two days later, the Council met at the home of Chief Justice Jones, the plantation which adjoined Moseley Hall. Present were the Honourable Charles Eden, Esqr., Governor and Captain General; Pollock, Ffrancis Ffoster, Frederick Jomes, Esqrs., Lords Proprietors' Deputies.

After a heated and acrimonious debate, in which swords and a duel were mentioned, an order was passed and written into the minutes, Ffrancis Ffoster alone, among those present, protesting, although several members of the Council voiced their opinion by remaining away.

The Deputy Secretary, ANTHONY Lovyck, was ordered to write the following into the minutes:

"Mr. Edward Moseley and Mr. Maurice Moore, on 27th December last, having been committed to the custody of the Provost Marshall for illegally possessing themselves from the Secretary's office, the Journals of the Council, and several other papers, relating to the Government, lodged at Sandy Point, the dwelling of Anthony Lovyck, Esqr., Deputy Secretary; and the Honourable Charles Eden, the Governor, having called the Board upon same, and laid before them his reasons for so doing:

"It is ordered that said Edward Moseley do stand committed for charge of high crimes and misdemeanours, for which he is now in custody until next General Court . . . unless said Moseley and Moore give sufficient bail to Richard Sanderson, Esqr., in the sum of Two Thousand Pounds, and in the meantime to be of their good behaviour, and that the Attorney General be ordered to prosecute them for their offenses.

"Ordered that the Secretary prepare a proclamation for the better preserving the King's peace and for the observing the penal Laws, and that it be published as soon as possible."

Chapter 24

RENDEZVOUS ON OCRACOCK

For all of Anne Bonney's admiration, Stede Bonnet had no seamanship and she knew it. She thought, But he is brave, courageous, bolder than if he were an accomplished seaman. She was opposed to his alliance with Blackbeard. She was afraid that horrible rascal would outwit Stede, if the two entered cruise together.

Anne herself refused to go on cruise with him. She said she was weary and proposed to remain at the Rendezvous until Stede returned. She wanted rest and time to repair her wardrobe. Since falling in love with Gentleman Stede, she had cast off men's attire and had her woman fashion garments from the wealth of material found in captured ships.

She gave great heed to her appearance and spent some hours each day brushing her long silky blonde hair with a tortoise-backed brush. Her fine fair skin came in for attention. She smeared it with papaya fruit, brought from Jamaica. This she let dry, and washed it off carefully with cool water brought from a spring.

She set up a camp at Ocracock Island in the Carolina Banks, a half mile away from the main camp, where Vane held rendezvous whenever he came in from a raid. The great tent was divided with curtains made out of India prints from an East Indiaman Rackham had taken between Madagascar and Cape of Good Hope.

She lazed under the awning and held court for the pirate captains on moonlight nights. Here they ate at table like civilized folk and drank good wine from glasses, not from mugs and tin cups. Half a dozen captains were in harbour now, Charles Vane among them. Vane was a cold-blooded man, stony and cruel, who had never given Anne Bonney a passing look.

She was too clever to use the wiles of a woman, but guile was a different story. With him she was cool, remote, speaking only of matters that had to do with fights, disposal of cargo and the like, waiting her time to bind him to her. For

333

Anne had determined to become the most powerful pirate in the Caribbean. She had her father's shrewd, unscrupulous brain, as well as her mother's seductive body. Get Vane to her side, she would, whether or no.

Rackham was off on a cruise, near Honduras. Mary Read was with him. Acting as Vane's chief lieutenant, he had only courtesy command, since he had lost the ship to Woodes Rogers. Anne announced, publicly before pirate company, that she was no longer married to Rackham. She went down to the palm grove one evening, and stood before the cooking fire. Clapping her hands to gain the attention of the pirates, who were lounging on the beach, she made her announcement.

"What will Rackham say to that, Mistress Anne?"

"What matter?" Anne replied, tossing her head.

"Making bid for a new husband?" a man in the shadows shouted. Anne did not even look in the direction of the speaker.

"Hold your tongue. Let the lady speak as she wills." It was Vane who gave that command. He had come upon them without their notice. He stood at the edge of the ring, watching the men. His cold eyes swept the circle. Not one but did his bidding. He knew this and it gave him no exhilaration. Nothing elated him but the clash of arms and the boom of cannon and a ship under full rig, moving towards the grapple.

"Have a care, ye clumsies, you muck minds. What the lady says is her own business and nothing of yours. Get you to your watches."

The men got up and moved away. Only the captains remained, and of them two or three wandered off.

Vane indicated a canvas stool. "Have a seat, Madam."

"Thank you, Captain." She sat down and arranged her skirts about her, covering her red-slippered feet. She wore a dark dress, and her hair was in long braids on either side of her neck, falling to her slender waist. She drew the Spanish shawl, embroidered in gay flowers, closer to her shoulders. "I've wanted to speak with you, Captain."

"Yes?"

"Yes. Ever since the night I heard you say you were thinking of setting up a law for pirates at this rendezvous. I have thought of it often since. I've come to a conclusion."

"Indeed?" There was a faint sarcasm in his tone and his face showed no interest.

Anne appeared not to notice. "Perhaps you did not know, sir, but my father was a solicitor, both in Ireland and in this country. I know something of legal procedure."

"Indeed?" Vane repeated, but instead of faint sarcasm there was now faint interest.

She opened a velvet reticule she carried on her girdle and took out a paper.

"I've made out a list of benefits for injuries received when crews are under fire. I believe it to be fair and just to the captain and to the crew." Without waiting for Vane to give permission, she began to read:

	"Pieces of Eight
"Loss of right arm	600
"Loss of left arm	500
"Loss of right leg	500
"Loss of left leg	400
"Loss of eye	400
"Loss of finger	100"

When she finished reading, Anne folded the paper and returned it to her bag.

Vane sat for a long time without speaking. Anne sat quietly too. A man pushed the trunk of a tree farther into the fire. Anne's body, touched by the firelight, was immovable. After a long time Vane said, "You have a man's way of putting things, clean and straight with no extra words."

Anne said nothing. She was pleased at his words. Let it go at that for the present. She rose to go. Vane held out a protesting hand. "Have patience. I've a paper to read, also." He went inside his tent. Anne saw him moving about, heard him speak to his servant, who held a lanthorn for Vane to open a great iron-bound chest.

In a few minutes the Captain came back. He moved close to the fire, holding a piece of paper close to his eyes.

"'Tis an outline of pirate law I have made up," he said abruptly.

"1. Every man obey civil command. Captain full share and half of all prizes.
    "Master Carpenter, Boatswain, and Gunner 1¼ share.
"2. Man who offers to run away, or keeps secret from company, he shall be marooned, with a bottle of powder, one bottle of water, one small arm and shot.

"3. Pirate who strikes another, Moses' Law, of forty stripes lacking one.

"4. Stealing, to the amount of a Piece of Eight; marooned or shot.

"5. Man who snaps his arms or smokes tobacco in hold of ship, without cap to his pipe, or carries lighted candle without a lanthorn, shall suffer same punishment.

"6. Man who does not keep his arms clean or neglects his business shall be cut off from share. He shall suffer such punishment as captain or company see fit.

"7. If a man shall loose a joint, in England, he shall receive 400 Pieces of Eight, if a limb 500.

"8. If at any time he meet a prudent woman and meddle with her, without her consent, he shall suffer punishment by death. "All company shall swear to those rules and laws on Bible. If company has no Bible, swear on hatchet."

Anne listened to the relentless words that came so readily from Vane's thin bloodless lips. A shiver went over her. A passionate woman, she could do evil on impulse, but she could not premeditate punishment. She had never heard of harsher terms, under any earlier pirate law.

Vane was waiting for her to speak. She struggled to steady her voice. "You are just, Captain, and you protect women."

"There's no scoundrel so low as the one who commits rape on a helpless female. That man I'll kill in my own way. It's known on my ship. My company does not attack women. There are enough willing girls in every port to satisfy their man's need. If a case of attack is called to my notice, I kill. Yea, I torture the man first, a heavy long torture so that he may repent his heinous crime of violating a woman's body."

Anne felt a chill creep up her spine. Vane was fanatic. She drew the Spanish shawl across her breasts. "You're quite right," she said, her rich voice smooth as honey. "A woman deserves honour from men."

"If she be a pure woman," Vane said evenly.

Anne got to her feet. "Thank you, Captain," she said, sweeping a curtsy. "Thank you for allowing me to learn about your new rules."

"I'll include your insurance list, I believe it to be a fair adjustment in money for a wounded man to receive. Thank you, Madam Rackham."

The last two words made Anne shudder. Vane had disregarded her attempt to rid herself of Rackham. He stood beside his lieutenant, and he let her know it.

336

She walked slowly across the beach towards her camp. Vane's servant, carrying a lanthorn, walked behind. Her thoughts were on Vane. He was hard and cruel and dealt swift punishment to offenders. By these means he held control of his men. Hard and cruel, swift to punish. Fair in his treatment in regard to prizes and privileges. Was that the secret of Vane's undisputed captaincy of the Caribbean?

Blackbeard she abhorred, with his filthy body and filthy talk. He was a show-off, trying to scare grown men as he would scare children, putting sulphur matches in his great matted beard that teemed with vermin. His horrid glassy black eyes, his open lascivious mouth. He was no captain. He gained by striking fear, by tricks . . . a trick captain . . . but no honesty in his bravery. She was sure he would be a cowering knave, whining and slobbering. Bah! It sickened her to think of him.

She stripped off her garments and sent her woman to bring fresh water and a sponge. She would wash herself clean and fresh. Even thinking of Blackbeard brought repulsion.

She was long in getting to sleep that night. A thought had found lodgment in her mind that disturbed her. Would Stede Bonnet display swift courage in time of stress? He could think up ways to manoeuvre and gain his position. But was he really brave? Did he have real power to command, behind his gentlemanly ways?

Anne Bonney waited impatiently for the end of the week. Stede Bonnet had told her he would be at Ocracock by that time. He would anchor at Teach's Hole, behind the island, by the Sabbath day at the latest. "I have a rendezvous with Teach himself on that day," he had told her before he sailed for St. Thomas. "We have a plan, Teach and I. We're going to combine our forces and rule the Caribbean."

"I don't trust Blackbeard. He's a low scoundrel, keeping faith with no one but Blackbeard—if indeed he keeps faith with himself," she added contemptuously. "He owned to me that he took oath before Governor Eden last January, laughing up his sleeve the while."

Bonnet grinned, showing his strong white teeth. "I took an oath before Eden, too, at his fine house at Bath—but I made mental reservation. You're a child, Anne."

Anne had not liked that. "If I give oath, I give oath. Blackbeard never will keep word with any man," she insisted. "Have a care, Stede. Don't trust that villain."

Anne thought of the conversation as she sat before her tent at the Ocracock Rendezvous. Stede was more gullible than she. At heart, he was a gentleman. He loved the adventure and the wild life, but he was no match for Blackbeard, and the two together were no match for Vane. Her thoughts turned back to Vane, calculating, cruel in the extreme. He out-thought them all. Stede she loved for his body and his gay, reckless nature. Vane she admired. She could not win him as she won other men.

Vane had taken $6,000 in specie from Samuel Wragg, a member of the Provincial Council, as ransom for himself and two merchants of Charles Town, when he overtook and captured the ship in which they were returning from London.

Vane had been bold. He threatened to batter down the defenses of Charles Town, if it didn't give ransom. Anne knew Vane would have made good his threat.

Now Stede had larger plans. He had hinted at them without giving details. He would raze towns and cities along the Carolina coasts, as Morgan had razed towns and cities in the Golden Isles and on the Spanish Main years before. Blackbeard also was ambitious to carry the fame of Bold Henry Morgan, but he had not Morgan's brain. Man of many names—Drummond by birth, Blackbeard, Thatch or Teach by choice—he had brute courage and ferocity, but not the ability to plan. That was why he wanted Stede. Anne saw through his cunning. Stede Bonnet would be the brains; Blackbeard would execute the plans.

These thoughts disturbed her. She got up and walked down to the beach, in front of her tent; a small cove shut off from Vane's camp by a series of dunes. Her woman followed her. Anne sent her back. She did not trust this low-browed, sullen creature, a Carib from one of the Spanish Islands. Stede had given her the slave: "She can use a knife as well as a man. She'll protect you." Anne laughed at the time. Anne Bonney need protection! Yet her heart was touched. For the first time in many years, a man was thinking of her as men thought of other women. "Protect and guard and love—" that was Stede's attitude towards her. She made no effort to command him as she had commanded the others. She took pleasure in playing the part he had assigned to her. Yet her mind was filled with a new idea.

Matched with Vane, she might win her great desire—to rule the Caribbean. Anne still loved Bonnet passionately, but she began to set his limitations. The humour "to go apirating" had overtaken the Bermuda merchant, and he had sailed to join the Brotherhood ... but Stede was not the equal of Blackbeard in cunning or cupidity or stark brutality. He was squeamish at the sight of blood.

She strolled up and down the beach, her mind filled with uneasy thoughts. Like many another woman, she let her emotions cloud her cool judgement. Power was what she wanted, power in herself, or in her mate. She didn't care, just so long as she had a part in ruling the Caribbean. She stopped suddenly. Shielding her eyes with her hand, she looked seaward. Two vessels were in sight, tacking to make the inlet.

She recognized the *Revenge*, which Blackbeard had wanted to take as his own. The other was the *Royal James*, carrying a long homeward-bound streamer, for all the world like a homecoming ship of H.M. Royal Navy.

She laughed with delight at this conceit of Stede's. Such little things gave flavour to his personality and added zest. He was flying the long homecoming pennant because he was coming home to her. She walked swiftly to the tent and called the Carib woman to aid her in dressing. She wanted to be as alluring as he dreamed her. After all, perhaps it was an experience, to be loved by a man full of quaint and beguiling conceits. Let the dream of power rest for the moment. There was time ahead.

Anne was hard to please. Twice she rapped the Carib over the knuckles as she brushed her long silken hair. Dress after dress came from the great oaken chest, only to be discarded. Velvet and silks she put aside, for a simple white muslin with a pelisse of blue taffeta, from some English woman's wardrobe captured off Jamaica. A blue riband bound her hair. She looked at herself in the polished mirror, well pleased.

Captain Charles Vane was a man of simple tastes. When she sat, that afternoon, in council with Vane and Teach and Stede Bonnet, she would play a role—a young woman without guile. So doing, she might learn more of their plans than she now knew. She would take her place at the council table on equal terms with any pirate captain. Aye, share and share alike with Vane and Teach and Bonnet. No longer would she accept half of Rackham's share, or half of Bonnet's. She would stand on her own. Then, one day, she would build a great house—perhaps on Jamaica, or New Providence. She would have slaves and live a great lady, in a great house.

In her mind she saw the slaves moving about its halls and

339

rooms. But it was not one of the great houses of Jamaica that she envisaged. It was Queen's Gift, Roger Mainwairing's home on Albemarle Sound.

She remembered a lonely girlhood, when all man's hands were against her, all save the owner of Queen's Gift.

Her woman's gutteral voice broke her dreams. "Master's ship at anchor in Teach's Hole."

Anne gave one look at her mirror. What she saw satisfied her. She ran her slim hand over her hair to smooth it into place. When she rose to walk across the sand to Vane's camp, she was ready to give battle. By nightfall she would be a fourth member of the company.

Stede met her halfway. He was walking quickly down the beach. His face and his dark eyes showed his impatience to be with her. He caught her to him in a hurried violence that marked his rising passion.

"Anne! Anne!" he whispered, his lips against her. "Come, let's go to your tent." He caught her arm, half dragging her with him. "Swiftly, Anne, come swiftly. Can't you feel my impatience to be with you?"

Anne unclasped his fingers from her arm. "And leave Vane and Teach to plan behind your back?" She tried to keep the scorn from her voice. "Let them plot and scheme and divide, while we sport in each other's arms? No, my Stede, no. We'll sit at the council."

Bonnet stood with dropped arms looking at her. Anger, bewilderment gave way to admiration. "By God's breath, you are a woman!" he said. "Come, we'll go to Vane's tent. Already that snake Teach has taken one ship from me. He says I have no seamanship."

"Well," said Anne noncommittally, "have you?"

"I'm a captain, not a navigator," Bonnet said, sullen in a moment. He caught her and pressed against her firm strong body. His lips went hard against her mouth. "I'll kill anyone who looks at you in desire." He released her as suddenly as he had taken her.

Anne's red lips caught against her white teeth; a stealthy, feline look came into her light blue eyes. "You *are* a lover, Stede," she whispered. Her voice was husky. "Tonight, when we have showed Vane that we will not be belittled . . ."

"Aye. And that scoundrel Blackbeard. He stinks with treachery and foul thoughts."

Anne smiled, but she said nothing. It suited her plan to have Stede enraged with Blackbeard. Stede was French.

Laughter came easily with him, and his rage was quickly spent. Well. Now it would be different. She would see that rage, once lighted, would smoulder until she was ready to have it burst into flame. Blackbeard they would outwit. When she thought of Vane, a shiver went over her, as if an animal had crossed her grave.

She shook off the feeling with an effort. Stede lifted the fly of Vane's tent. Anne Bonney entered first, her face calm, her eyes serene and untroubled.

Blackbeard and Vane were seated at a small table, a map spread out before them. Blackbeard was tracing a line along the coast with the point of a black-tipped fingernail. He stopped speaking when the woman entered, a scowl on his face.

Vane looked up. Slowly he got to his feet and pushed a bench to the table. "Sit here, Madam Rackham," he said with rigid politeness. "Bonnet, good day to you."

Blackbeard started to roll the map. Vane lifted his hand. "No. I want Bonnet to see."

Blackbeard's scowl deepened. "Bonnet knows enough. It's the woman . . ."

"Madam Rackham has the privilege of entering this consultation. She sits in the room of her husband, my lieutenant."

Bonnet started to speak, but a glance at Vane's cold eyes deterred him. Blackbeard's eyes were pin-points of black anger, but he, too, knew the lash of Vane's tongue and wanted none of it. Besides, Vane had four hundred men or more at the Rendezvous, while Blackbeard had but ninety on the *Revenge*. He spread the paper again.

"Tell them the conversation you've had with me, Teach. Begin with the report from the man you sent into Williamsburg from the York River."

With a baleful glance at Anne from under his bushy brows, Teach told them how he had sent men ashore. They had gone into Williamsburg and mingled with the people on market day dressed as yeoman. At a tavern they had heard talk that Governor Spottswood was sickened by piracy. He was determined to clear the James and York Rivers to the Capes. He had gunboats and guardships. He proposed to send his ships, not only along the Capes, but as far south as the North Carolina Banks. "Since Eden will not prosecute pirates," Spottswood would unite with South Carolina men of his will. They would both enter North Carolina waters, one

341

from the north, one from the south. Between them they would blast out all pirate rendezvous along the Banks.

Vane sat silent at the recital, which was mixed with blasphemy and vile oaths until he set a check. Bonnet had heard the story before. He made no comment, waiting respectfully for Vane to speak.

Anne watched Vane's face. It was impossible to see behind his granite mask. His eyes were granite and held no reflecting light or depth. After a time he turned to Bonnet. "What say you? Do we clear ourselves out of the Banks and Sounds of North Carolina and hold rendezvous in the Virgins or Honduras, or do we fight along the Carolina coast, as we always have?"

Bonnet answered, "The Virginia Governor has well-equipped ships, well-manned, well-gunned. Perhaps the part of wisdom would be to drop down to the southern islands, to rendezvous and lay across the plate routes."

Blackbeard growled, "New Providence, Green Turtle Cay gives one a good base for northern trade or for Jamaica."

Vane said nothing for a few moments, then he spoke to Anne. "Madam, what do you say? Shall we turn south?"

A small smile appeared at the corners of Anne Bonney's red lips. "Run, Gentlemen? Turn sail at some old wives' yarn of ships of war and guardships, and Governor Spottswood's threats, or the Charles Town merchants' glib speeches? No, gentlemen. No! I lay my vote to stay as we are; fight when need be; sail away when necessary; but do not turn tail!"

No one spoke, waiting for the captain to express himself. After a time he said, "Why do you say that, Madam?"

"Why? Because every year brings more trade to the Carolinas and the coast. Every year the planters grow richer and buy more goods abroad. There's a new settlement on the Cape Fear River. They make cloth and beaver hats, which they're already sending to Charles Town and Woodes Rogers' city of Nassau. Let's glean the benefits of the trade. Let's take their prominent men for ransom, as you, Captain Vane, took Wragg, of Charles Town. Why should we run from a few empty threats of Virginia's Governor, or Charles Town merchants? We have refuge in North Carolina waters. We're protected by her honourable Governor and his equally honourable Secretary, Mr. Knight."

Vane let his cold eyes rest for a moment on Anne's face. He saw her, not as a desirable woman, as the others did, but as a strong, bold woman, with courage and a clear mind.

342

"Madam, I salute you," he said, bowing in Anne's direction. A slight flush came to her face, her lips parted, showing her white teeth.

Bonnet glanced from one to the other uneasily. Teach glowered. He wanted no women to have voice in the Brotherhood, yet he dared not dispute Vane.

A slave came to the tent and waited for permission to speak. Vane looked up and nodded. "The dinner is set," the Negro said, and limped away.

Vane got up. "Let's eat. After that we can talk further." As they walked across to the bush tent, where the meal was spread, Vane fell in step with Anne Bonney. "I like your decision and your clear judgement. I shall continue to allow you voice in council, in Rackham's place."

Anne said, "I've divorced myself from Rackham. I would sit in no man's place. In your council I want it to be Anne Bonney's voice that speaks. That or not at all."

Vane's cold eyes met hers, as unyielding, as cold as his own. They held for a moment, then his gaze moved away. "You have a bold tongue, Madam."

"Not bold, Captain Vane. Frank. I speak my mind to you forthrightly, without withholding my desires. I want full voice."

"You have no ship," he said. "Without a ship and men to sail her, how can you expect to hold enough power to have a voice?"

"Give me a ship and I'll get the men to sail her."

"You speak confidently."

"I am confident," she said quietly. Vane did not reply.

Anne had not intended to bring things to a head. She had planned to wait and give more thought, to study the character of Vane, probe his weaknesses, but by the living God, he had no weak side! Well, her tongue had spoken for her. Let it go as it was. She had an Arab's thought, derived from the years she had sailed with Arabs in the India Sea off Madagascar: "Whatever will be, will be, for that is Allah's will." She had spoken out. Wait now for the development. She did not even glance at Vane, but moved ahead into the tent and took her place at the table.

Vane called for Madeira, and sent the slave back the second time before he got what he wanted. He was patient with the blundering Negro. No blasphemy, no cursing, no venting his rage and passion on trifles like the others, yet she sensed that he would kill as readily as he spoke if the

343

occasion came. She wondered what was going on behind the stony exterior. Nothing showed in her face, either. It was open and childlike, her red lips quick with laughter, as she turned to Stede Bonnet.

She felt Vane watching her, but she gave no heed. Blackbeard soon showed the effects of numerous cups of heady wine, which he downed one after the other. He attempted to eat, belched noisily. Vane motioned to two slaves to lead the drunken pirate away, but not before he had vomited down the front of his waistcoat.

Anne turned her shoulder. She could look on carnage and blood, but vulgarity disgusted her.

That night Stede had her in his arms. He took her roughly, without wooing. He spoke no words of love and endearment.

Anne knew from Stede's glances towards Vane earlier in the evening that he was wondering why the Captain should give her privileges no woman had had before. The speculation had not come to the point of suspicion. She would not allow that.

She got up and walked out of the tent into the moonlight. The light muslin wrapper that she wore was near transparency, but not quite. Bonnet followed her and they stood watching the moon reflection break upon the sea, ride in on the crest of a great wave and break into fragments, turning the spume into particles of light.

She threw one cool arm across his shoulder. "You've not forgotten your promise to me?" Her voice was low.

"What promise?"

"The promise you made that night at Nassau—that you'd raze the towns along the Carolina coast, go into every river and creek and sound, despoil their plantations and collect tribute."

Bonnet said, "You are a bloodthirsty wench, or you carry a great hate."

"I remember, and remembering I want vengeance."

"Why should I be the instrument of your vengeance?" He spoke without rancour.

Anne's temper rose suddenly. She held it in check. No use to antagonize Stede yet, not while she still felt emotion for him. She removed her arm and walked a few steps towards the beach. Across the water came the sound of harsh voices, singing ribald songs. Half a dozen small fires burned along the beach—fish being roasted or crabs boiled. She could tell

344

that an extra allowance of grog had been issued because of a capture, or because of a fight on the morrow.

"Go back to your tent," Bonnet said. "Some of those dirty snakes may walk this way and see you."

Anne did not answer. She continued walking on the beach. Stede stood still. He watched her lift her skirt and step into the little pool of water left by the last wave.

"Come back," he called. A great wave rolled in and enveloped her. She flung herself to meet it, lifting her arms ecstatically, turning to drift in on its cool green bosom. She rose dripping, her garment clinging to her lithe body.

A dark shadow lurched from behind the dunes, calling to her. Blackbeard, a bottle clutched in his hand, came reeling toward her. "Come to my ship. Come to my ship," he called drunkenly.

Stede Bonnet ran down the beach, drawing as he came. "Get away from here, Teach. Get away or I'll skewer you on my blade."

"Ha, ha! The watchdog, a little dog yapping on a chain. Ha, ha!" The drunken laughter roared out, striking the dunes, drifting back.

Stede sprang forward. His sword flashed in the moonlight.

"God damn you!" cried Teach. "You've pricked my right wrist, my pistol wrist!"

"Next time I'll do more. Get you gone. Don't let me hear of you coming this way again."

Blackbeard had dropped the bottle. He stood swaying, his wrist clutched in his left hand. "Meant no harm." His voice was oily. "No harm. My madam asks Mistress Anne to visit her aboard my vessel."

"Tell Madam Teach Madam will not visit on your vessel, now or ever. Get out!"

"Nice words for a partner to speak to a partner!" There was an underlying threat in Blackbeard's tone. Anne wondered if he were as drunk as he appeared to be. After a moment he turned and lurched off.

Stede Bonnet thrust his sword deep in the sand, to clear the point of Blackbeard's blood.

"You have made an enemy," Anne said.

"Pah! What do I care? I've a hundred enemies. Besides he'll have forgotten by morning. His wits are befuddled. I won't have the beast coming around you."

"I have my pistols," Anne said. "Good night, Stede." She walked into the tent and dropped the flap.

Bonnet stood for a moment, then walked away through the dunes, in the direction of Vane's camp.

That night late, before moon fall, Blackbeard and his men went out on Stede Bonnet's swift-sailing *Revenge*, and sailed north, knowing that Bonnet could not overtake him in the smaller, slower *Royal James*. Blackbeard had thrown down the gauntlet.

Chapter 25

TRADE

Carolina was not too young to have factions rampant. In the north it was the Governor's party against the Popular party led by Edward Moseley and Maurice Moore. In the south, there had been even more unrest between the Governors and the people; the question of unjust taxes was before the people every hour of the day and night. The strong man in the southern end was Colonel James Moore, father of Maurice of Albemarle, and of Roger, who remained in Southern Carolina. He had trusted men to stand by him: John Ashe, who was once the provincial agent, Howe and Colonel William Rhett. The last was a courageous, bold man of high temper, who used cane or sword with equal facility. In the "Five Day Riots" he had caned a justice of the peace, and taken sides with people of "lower classes."

Governors came and went with surprising rapidity. The Lords Proprietors appointed each new man with the hope that he would secure peace within the Colony. Indian uprisings in the south had been settled, the Spanish quieted. But internal friction held the growth of the Colony in check.

Woodes Rogers endeavoured to co-operate with South Carolina to sweep the waters of pirates. The merchants who benefited from illegal trade were almost as dilatory as Eden in the north.

At a meeting in Charles Town words ran high and tempers broke. Rhett pounded the table with his clenched fist until the glasses jingled. He swore he'd take Stede Bonnet if it were the last thing he did in his life.

Johnston, the former Governor, was almost as violent as Rhett in his denunciation of the pirate crew that lurked off the entrance to the harbour, making shipping dangerous at all times, and holding down a free flow of trade. Blackistone, one of the Carolina agents in London, complained to the Lords Proprietors that the Ashley and Cooper Rivers were fortified more for beauty than for strength, and the pirates took full advantage.

The six bastions were enclosed by a line. The Cooper River had the Blake and Granville Bastions, a half-moon, and Craven Bastion. At South Creek were the Palisades and Ashley Bastions. On the North Line, facing the Ashley River, were the Colleton Bastion, a drawbridge-covered half-moon, in the line, and another drawbridge in the half-moon of the Carteret Bastion. A fort was erected on a point of land at the mouth of the Ashley River, which commands the Channel.

Mr. Landgrave Smith's house on the key, with a drawbridge and a wharf in front of it, was the target of pirates. Colonel Rhett lived on the key also, and Mr. Bone and Mr. Logan and ten or twelve more families had lodgement there. No wonder those men, exposed to depredations of Spanish and pirates, wanted the waters cleared. Many of them, being merchants, wanted to build up wealth through the sale of their goods.

Then there were the planters up the Ashley River, John Bird in particular, who concurred with Rhett in saying the waters must be made free for shipping. They influenced other planters near Charles Town—Ferguson, Underwood, Gilbertson and Garett. Colonel Rhett rode up and down the highways trying to organize the planters. Exterminating the pirates would be for the benefit of every planter in the Carolinas—yes, and the Bahamas and Jamaica. He called on the Cooper River planters, Matthews, Green and Starkey. He found most of them favourable. Izard, on Turkey Creek, and William Corbin, who had a congregation of Church of England men on Goose Creek, were more than favourable. Next he rode to Colonel Moore and the Quarry Plantation, these two on Back River not far from the barony of Mr. Thomas Colleton.

A tiresome task, but the sturdy, dark-visaged Rhett was insatiable in his determination to get the principal people roused to the height of his own temper. Planters were lazy by the very method of their living—slaves to do the labour in the fields, bondmen and women, and white overlookers. They'd agree to a thing, then grow lax. This Rhett would not permit.

He checked off the list of men he had seen one morning, and found he had only a few of the Ashley River planters left to see: Colonel Gibbs, Dr. Trevillian, Mr. Pendarvis. He met with them. He conferred with Arthur Middleton in Charles Town. That finished the task. The merchants, both Huguenot and English, he was confident would support the idea.

348

The spadework done, he called a meeting at the parish house of St. Philips and the greater part of the substantial people of Charles Town attended. Rhett was a stickler for detail. He had made exhaustive search in the public library for figures and facts about shipping, and when he got to his feet, his words flowed as freely as he wanted trade to flow from Charles Town harbour. He spoke directly to the point, of the necessity of a well-developed trade. He gave examples.

Fifty thousand barrels of rice employed ten thousand tons of shipping, and would bring to Great Britain eighty thousand pounds sterling per annum. Silkworms, resin, tar and pitch needed more. Seven or eight hundred ships were necessary to healthy navigation.

There was cattle in quantities. In the early days, if a man had four or five cattle, it was good. Now some men had a thousand black cows, and it was not uncommon for a planter to have two hundred. Hogs were in abundance, well fed on acorns and nuts and the gleanings of the field. For these commodities they had an excellent market in the Sugar Islands.

Rhett picked up a paper and studied it for a moment. "It may seem odd to you planters for me to harp on figures of the products you raise and ship. In order to let you see the great volume we're shipping I recommend a study of the imports and exports in the trade report sent recently to the Council of Trade and Plantations. Even as far back as 1700 Sir Joshua Childs's book on trade affairs said that the Plantations employed two-thirds of England's shipping. How much this could be increased if we were encouraged to ship direct to other countries instead of having to transship from England!"

Rhett looked at the faces of men squeezed into the parish room. He was flattered by their close attention. Perhaps never before had they listened to a recital of their growing trade, or envisioned the development of the colony.

There was some movement in the back of the room, as if a man would question. Rhett held up his hand. "Wait! I've one or two more items I want you to hear. Then we'll be ready for questions and free discussion."

He glanced at the paper in his hand. "We have a trade with Madeira, small but steady." A laugh went up, but Rhett did not change expression. "Wine from Madeira and the Western Islands, for which they receive from us provisions, staves and heads for barrels. From Guinea, we get Negro

349

slaves, but the ships that bring them, being sent from England, return to England. All this is settled by bills of credit on Boston, New York or Jamaica; as you know our Carolina money is not acceptable except for local trade. It runs one hundred and fifty pounds sterling to the one hundred pounds sterling. Spanish gold is used. French pistoles still circulate for trade, although the Act For Regulating Coin in the colonies at six shillings three pence a pennyweight has been passed. We use also Dutch dollars and Peruvian pieces of eight in trading.

"All these figures I've given you have been put together to show the extent and scope of our present trade and how golden would be the prospect of the future, except for one thing . . ."

Rhett paused. Half a hundred voices finished in accord: "Pirates."

Rhett smiled grimly. "Yes, pirates!"

Izard got to his feet. "Why not sweep the dastardly Brotherhood from the seas? Why not petition the Lords of Trade and Plantations to send the Jamaica Fleet?"

Rhett countered: "We have already done that. They're having even more trouble in Jamaica, and they need their ships of war. We must do this ourselves. Are we not men enough?"

"Yes! Yes!" was the general answer. "No," a few replied.

Rhett did not pause on the interruption. "I choose to be the man to capture Stede Bonnet. I owe him for a ship of mine he scuttled off the bar."

There was instant response—volunteers in men and money.

Colonel Thomas Broughton, speaker of the House of Assembly, asked for the floor. "I wish, for a moment, to digress from the subject of pirates to the subject of trade. You'll see, by the figures Colonel Rhett has given us, that for a village of three thousand souls we're advancing, but not advancing enough.

"I suggest that you all study the list of the commodities we import. You will see many things on the list that could be as readily manufactured here as in England. Take hats, for instance. I've been talking this very morning to my friend Légare. He tells me that a new settlement has been made on the Cape Fear. They plan, through their leader Mr. Fountaine, to set up weaving and hat manufacture. A good thing, I think. If we study the lists of importations, we'll find other articles can be made here as well as in England or France or Spain."

"Hear! Hear!" came in hearty answer.

"In other words, when Colonel Rhett clears the seas, nothing need stand in our way to make a great self-sustaining colony."

Job Howe, once Speaker of the Assembly, had a word to add. "Colonel Rhett paints a bright picture of our future. His is a hard task, since he has to break down the great obstacle which stands in our way. He will not be alone in this. Robert Johnston, once our honoured governor, could not be with us today, but he has commissioned me to say that he will outfit ships to take after the pirate Richard Worley. Worley's ships, the *New York Revenge* and the *Eagle*, have been playing havoc with our coastwise shipping, as you know."

Loud shouts of approval followed Howe's announcement. Howe clasped his lean hands on the back of the chair in front of him. "We are talking of expanding trade. It is well. In this lean time of peace, between wars, we must make the adventure of trade. We're in good position now, with Captain Woodes Rogers, of the Bahamas, and the Jamaica Fleet at work for the same purpose—the destruction of pirates and the extermination of their leaders in the western world. We must not lag in our endeavours. I am assured by a letter from Virginia that Governor Spottswood is fast sweeping the pirates from the waters of Virginia."

Someone called out: "What about North Carolina? Is Eden doing anything to clear the Banks?"

A great laugh went up. Eden was a byword along the coast for his lax methods of dealing with Blackbeard.

Howe's serious expression did not change. "When the time comes, the people of North Carolina will act. I've never known them to hold with indignities for long, without doing something about it. Have you, gentlemen?"

"No! No!" came the unanimous answer.

Rhett saw that the meeting was moving in the direction of political discussion. That he wished to avoid. He pounded the gavel sharply. "I believe we have unanimity. With God's help, we'll have success in our undertaking. Gentlemen, the meeting is dismissed."

A few days later Rhett began preparing his vessels, the *Henry* and the *Sea Nymph* for the task he had set for himself. He had Captain John Masters for the *Henry*, and

Captain Frayrer Hall for the *Sea Nymph*. He was ready in a few weeks. The final preparations were being made at Sullivan Island, across the harbour, for his voyage to the Cape Fear. There he would wait for Stede Bonnet, who was rumoured to be preying on coast-wise shipping along the Banks.

Sail was up when a small sloop from Antigua limped into the harbour, reporting that she had been all but captured by the infamous Charles Vane.

Vane was patrolling the entrance to the harbour with two vessels. Already he had captured a Barbados ship, and a brigantine from the Guinea Coast with a cargo of a hundred Negroes. Vane had sent the Negroes to some rendezvous along the coast.

Instead of sailing after Bonnet, Rhett now made haste to set sail after this new menace to Charles Town.

He searched creeks and inlets and several leagues of coast, but Vane was too wily. He had escaped again, whether north or south no one knew.

After a week's delay, during which time he discovered the hidden Negroes on Edisto Island, Rhett sailed north in his quest to rid the seas of Stede Bonnet, gentleman pirate.

The settlement at Old Town Creek moved forward at a snail's pace. In spite of careful preparations, many necessary tools and implements had been overlooked, or not even thought of. Household necessities had been forgotten. Women were without pots and pans, iron pudding moulds, and great kettles of brass and copper. This caused worry and discontent until May Treloar, at Gabrielle's instigation, called a meeting one afternoon to discuss the housewives' problems.

Most of the settlers had a roof over their heads and many of the log houses were completed, inside and out. Not the cottages they had dreamed about on the voyage over, but the rooms were large and the logs well chinked and all had floors. Most of the log houses had more than one room, and lean-to-kitchens. Several had followed MacAlpin's suggestion and built dog-run houses, the open space between the two large rooms to be used for eating, when warm weather came. Every habitation had a fowl run near by, well fenced by driving sapling stakes deep into the ground, close-joining to keep out the varmints such as weasels, foxes and the like that preyed on fowls.

These cabins and cottages were built close to the stockade

so that, in case of emergency, the women could reach safety with little delay. For the most part they were erected along the high ground, above the river, so that each cottage had a view of the water. A few large oaks and tulip trees provided shade.

The fields were communal. The old fields of Sir John Yeamans' colony had been grubbed out and ploughed. New fields were added, the men cutting and hacking into the heavy forest growth to make space for them. The forest gave way slowly, fighting every inch of ground, showing its wrath against man, making every day difficult, defending its deep, ancient darkness. The swamps sucked into the firm land, the daily river tide inundating and breaking the heavy ground, undermining the high banks. Great cypress trees tottered and crashed into the river, floated down the amber stream to become a menace to ships.

Men waded knee-deep in the swamp to fell cypress trees, for cypress made strong uprights and cross beams, and wide floor boards.

The light soil sifted and moved, blowing dust into the bright new houses, discouraging the women. There were, as yet, no grass plots or heavy turf to anchor the soil; where the old gardens had been was only a tangle of rank growing weeds and brambles. This had to be burned off before any progress could be made. The men were concerned first with houses, then with fields. They knew that they must plant and have good crops the next season, for their provisions would not hold out. The women concerned themselves with kitchen gardens, vegetables and herbs for seasoning.

Working, they had high spirits, but when the rains came, would they remain content? Gabrielle did not worry about the men. Autumn brought the ducks and geese from the north, and the marshland was alive with migrating birds, pigeons in such numbers that even the small children clubbed them to earth. The autumn brought deer-shooting in the deep woods, and down by the little lakes south of Old Town Creek. Deer hides were salable, after they were tanned. MacAlpin showed the men how Indians tanned the hides and made tunics.

Fish were plentiful. September mullets, in schools, swam up the creeks and inlets and were readily netted. Larger fish, sea bass, fought and gave zest to fishing. The women and children went into the adjacent forest for hickory nuts and walnuts, and each house had its store put away for the winter.

Black cattle roamed in the woods, and came home for milking. The swine were penned near the swamp. They were held by the community, as were the fields. There was milk aplenty for every household. That meant butter and cheese for the thrifty housewife.

With all this plenty and promise of plenty, there remained some discontented women. Gabrielle wanted especially to convince Eunice Caslett that she must be contented with things as they were, and the promise of better to come. Eunice's gloomy and unsmiling face, her constant complaints since the moment she sailed from Bristol, were having a bad effect on some of the other women.

Mary Treloar, on the contrary, had dropped the outspoken criticism which she had voiced on shipboard. On the completion of her snug, comfortable log house, with its "great room" and wide fireplace, Mary seemed to take on a new character. She sang as she worked. She washed on a Monday, cleaned on a Friday, and baked of a Saturday, with in-between days for sewing curtains, making shag rugs, carding wool and spinning.

Some of the women followed Mary's lead, but others, weaker or lazier, followed Eunice, muttering complaints, worrying their menfolk. It was these women Gabrielle wanted to meet. She did not wish to talk to them as individuals, but in a group.

She went with her trouble to Mary Treloar, and Mary came through with the answer. "I'll have a tea party, miss. 'Tis high time we lay off work for a little entertainment. A meat tea it will be, Miss Gabrielle."

"With some of your fine pasties, Mary?"

"And saffron cake." The woman smiled, flattered at Gabrielle's suggestion. "And when we have filled their stomachs with hot tea and good food, they'll be more like to listen to a word of advice."

"You'll invite all the women, Mary?"

"Yes, Ma'am, and their little ones. That will make them able to come with a free heart and not be aworritin' about the young ones running off to the swamp and getting bit by water snakes. Don't trouble your heart none, Miss Gabrielle, they'll all come."

And so they did. When Mary opened the door in answer to Gabrielle's knock, every woman in the settlement was seated in Mary's great room, with their children slicked and clean, the girls in starched pinafores and the little boys in clean blue smocks and gaiters. The women were in their best, as they sat in the rush chairs and wooden benches which Mary had placed with definite precision about the walls. They sat in solemn silence, their faces blank, their hands folded on their laps.

A moment of sheer fright held Gabrielle motionless at the door. The critical eyes of sixteen women scrutinized her face, moving slowly down to take in the detail of her costume. She was glad that Barton had insisted she wear her light blue pelisse, with the dark blue quilted petticoat.

"Wear something elegant, Miss Gabrielle," Barton had told her. "If you dress too simply, they'll think you're looking down at them and don't consider them good enough for your fine clothes. I know countryfolk."

Barton was right. Gabrielle knew it when she encountered these wary, observing eyes.

"Good afternoon, ladies," she said, smiling. "Good afternoon, children." She swept a curtsy as if she were at Court.

The women rose and half curtsied; the children bobbed; no one spoke.

This is going to be awful, thought Gabrielle. She was of a mind to turn and flee, but Mary Treloar was at no loss. She singled out several women as her assistants. "Eunice, you and Deborah and Millie come out to the kitchen. I'll need a bit of help. Miss Gabrielle, will you be so good as to sit at the table? I'll be honoured if you'll pour tea for us."

Gabrielle sat down at the end of the table, which was placed in the centre of the room, a blue and white cloth covering it, and a bowl of bright bittersweet berries for decoration.

A big log blazed in the fireplace and gave off a cheerful crackling, and the odour of pitch, from a knot of pine, permeated the room.

A little girl, the daughter of Marius Akim, a yeoman from the Midlands, stole from her bench at her mother's side to stand close. Gabrielle smiled at the dark-eyed, solemn-faced child. There was no answering smile but the little girl drew near enough to touch her skirt.

How strange it seemed! These silent, critical women were strangers, yet she saw them day after day, spoke to them as she rode by their cottages and gave them good day. She realized that company behaviour was something apart.

In a few minutes Mary came in carrying a steaming kettle, which she hung on the crane to keep boiling. Eunice brought in the brown earthenware teapot on a little pewter tray and set it before Gabrielle. Mary put on the table a large dish piled high with pastry cut in triangles, stuffed with meat and potatoes. The flaky crust was rich golden brown and hot from the oven.

A young girl of fifteen or sixteen, Daphne, daughter of Lockwood, who had put up a toll house on the Great Road to Charles Town, carried in a great saffron cake, with currant filling and a hole in the middle. A pretty, shy girl with round brown eyes and black hair and high color, she moved like a faun in the forest.

Gabrielle smiled at her, and she smiled back, timourously, a swift flush mounting her smooth cheek. Gabrielle had seen her once before at a distance. She knew the girl was staying with the Akim family, who had built their house near the bridge on Old Town Creek.

Mary turned to the child, who had not left Gabrielle's side. "Say a little prayer of thanks, Gwennie, my love. The nice one I taught you last week."

Gwennie moved to the table. She closed her eyes and clasped her plump little hands together. Lifting her face heavenward, she said in a sweet childish treble that touched the hearts of her listeners:

> "Here, a little child I stand
> Heaving up my either hand.
> Cold as paddocks though they be,
> Here I lift them up to Thee
> For a benison to fall
> On our meat and on us all."

The moment food appeared, the silence was shattered. The women began to talk and laugh and show their appreciation of Mary's superior cooking by asking for her rule for pasties and cake. The little girl touched Gabrielle's quilted petticoat and said, "Pretty. Pretty." Gabrielle patted her hand and said, "You're pretty yourself, little Gwennie," and the mother smiled.

The tea things cleared away, Mary took over. She stood near the fireplace back of the tea table, a comfortable round figure in a neat grey woollen frock with a decent white frilled apron to cover it.

356

"The thought comes to me," she said, glancing about the room to take in all the listeners, "that we women need to meet together, now and then, to have a dish of tea and a bite, and to gossip a little. Me mother always said, 'A good gossip and a good cry does often a woman satisfy,' and 'tis the truth as I know it. Now our menfolk are smarter than we. What did they do first, when they come to land at Old Town?"

"Built a church, a house ... and a club!" some of the women answered.

"That's it. A club. A man must have his club, where he can go and set a spell, smoke his pipe and drink his ale and talk to his neighbour.

"Women, they stay at home and dry the dishes and set the risin' bread for next day's bakin' or knit a round or two on a sock, and sit and rock and think about their troubles."

There was a movement among the women, an "Oh" and an "Ah."

Wise Mary gave them no time to break in. "'Twas in my mind that we women might have a club of sorts. No house like our menfolk have, but meeting each week at a different house. A guild or an auxiliary to do some work for the church, mayhap, or help each other sewing or cutting out clothes for the children, or make curtains for the new house. At any rate there's a lot of us here, a village of twenty families. 'Tis right we should help one another."

Eunice Caslett said, "What if we didn't want to be helped?"

Mary did not lose her composure. She smiled at Eunice. "Well, one can't do much for a body who don't want anything done. I mind there were folk like that in our village, at home in Devon, and I expect folk are no different in America than they were at home. But some of us will be glad of help; I for one. I never could turn a proper heel in Amos' socks, and Deborah here can turn a heel without looking."

"I'll trade heels for pasties," said Deborah, catching the drift.

"I'll make curtains for a saffron cake."

Half of the women entered into the plan. Eunice and three or four sat silent.

Mary appealed to Gabrielle. "Mistress Fountaine has something to say to you that may be a help to all of us." She smiled at her. "Please stand here, Mistress, so all can see you."

Gabrielle stood up at the end of the table. She hoped she'd say the right thing. It meant so much to get the women interested and enthusiastic over the progress of the settlement. Her father's sorrowful face, his tragic eyes rose before her. It must be a success, for his sake.

"I know, from what Barton has told me, that many of you are having the same trouble we're having. In spite of making out long lists of household articles we would need, we find we've forgotten many useful things that help make the work easier. It occured to me we might do what the men have done. They've made a list of their field and farming implements and posted it at Peter Wynne's blacksmith shop, so if a man needs an anvil, a sledge-hammer, brick, iron, a hand mill, frames or stones, he knows where it is and who owns it. Then he can go to the owner and make arrangements for a loan or a rental. The hand mill, for instance, is a rental; so is a fish seine, or cooper's tools. Other things are lent or traded.

"Why can't we women do the same? Yesterday we wanted to make soap, but we hadn't a kettle big enough, so we came to Mary Treloar and she lent us her big iron washing kettle."

She glanced around the room. There was a little response, but not enough. "I thought we might list the things we needed most and did not have, and we might send to Charles Town or Edenton or Williamsburg, and buy them."

"Where's the money coming from, Mistress? There ben't a store of gold for buying and bringing in luxuries. We be poor common folk, not rich folk like some I know," Eunice Caslett snapped.

Gabrielle kept her composure, though she felt her blood rising. "I haven't spoken of money, Mrs. Caslett. I had thought some of the things would be bought from a general fund my father has set aside. For instance, we need more great kettles, and large pans and baking pans. When we have a social evening for the church, we need quantity pans and kettles, cups and saucers and plates. We should have demijohns and glass bottles, for wine, and big copper preserving and pickling kettles. My father has brought extra wool wheels, that anyone may have for the asking, also carding machines and linen wheels. We need big iron hooks to swing our preserving and washing kettles, bell metal, spice mortar and pestle and grinding stones to make coarse cornmeal, grindstones for house knives—and many things I have not thought of yet."

358

Mary Treloar said, "Candle moulds—mine only makes three at a time."

Someone said, "Knives for tanning. Mr. MacAlpin is teaching us to tan the deer hides but we haven't the proper knives yet."

A little dark woman said, "I wish I had brought more buttons to cover, and more needles and flax thread."

"Why not have a supply on hand? Keep it in someone's house," another suggested.

"A very good idea," Gabrielle said heartily. "If Mary will give me a quill and a scrap of paper, I'll make a list to send to Charles Town by the next ship."

"When a ship comes, I'll sail out on her," Eunice said loudly. "I and my husband and some others," she added mysteriously. "Mout be a lot of others to go with us."

Gabrielle wrote busily on the paper Mary brought.

"Stone jugs and crocks," one woman said. "The cows are giving such a bounty of milk. I could set it in the spring house if I had crocks."

"I'd make some Devon cream, if I had flat saucepans," another broke in.

"I need pudding moulds. I forgot to bring my iron moulds."

"I need a common weighing scale if I am to preserve the walnuts."

Everyone had a suggestion, everyone except Eunice and her little group of three. They took their children and left, with no more than a slight nod at departure.

"Poor Eunice!" some woman said.

"Poor husband! say I." Another woman spoke vigorously, "That poor man is fair crazy about having a farm, but Eunice, she's a city girl from Bristol, and she wants nothing but to sit on her back doorstep gossiping with a lot of sluts as lazy as she be herself."

"Hist!" another said, glancing at Gabrielle. "Hist!"

Gabrielle did not appear to listen. She was busy with her lists. After a time she rose. "If everyone here will bring to Mary a list of the household things she has, and is willing to lend, Mary will combine them and put them up in her kitchen. When that is done, anyone will know where to go for a preserving kettle or a flax wheel or a churn, just as the men know where to get a fluke plow or a bar plow, a runner millstone or a warping bar box."

One woman rose when Gabrielle did and dropped a curtsy

when she departed. The atmosphere was friendly now, and Gabrielle was well content.

Mary followed her to the door. "It is as you wish it, Mistress Gabrielle?"

"I think so, Mary. But I was frightened at first!" She laughed as she thought of the first half hour.

"They're always so. 'Tis the custom. One does not speak much until food comes."

"Oh!" said Gabrielle. "I did not know."

"You haven't been much with common folk, Mistress. We have our way, same as great folk." Mary bobbed and said her adieus.

Gabrielle thought of her last remark as she walked along the narrow corduroy path to the stockade. It was all so complicated. The gulf that divided people was deep and wide. She wondered if it would be possible to bridge that gulf in this new world of theirs.

As Gabrielle walked through the forest, she heard children laughing and singing. She stopped. Two little boys were standing close to the trunk of a great tupelo tree, watching a bright green lizard crawl up the rough bark. They were crying, "Lizard, Lizard, show your blanket," and the lizard obliged by puffing out its bellowslike throat, which turned a bright pink from the effort. The children were happy. They had quickly adapted themselves to their new surroundings. If only! . . . She sighed a little as she made her way homeward.

She came into the stockade. There was no sentry at the open gate. She noticed men running towards the river bank. Others were mounting to the lookouts at the corners of the stockade.

"A sail! A sail!" someone was shouting.

She quickened her steps. Without stopping at the house, she hurried to the bank. It had been six weeks since a ship had put into the river—only the small fishing boats from the north; none of any consequence. She saw the ship. It was under full canvas, taking advantage of the off-sea wind that blew upriver at sunset. A goodly ship. Could it be the *Delicia*? She was due now, after her journey northward to the Albemarle Sound and the James River.

Barton came out of the house and ran after her. When they got to the bank, they saw men on the decks, waving their hands.

" 'Tis the *Delicia*," Barton said. "I know the cut of her. I'll run back and see about supper. No doubt your father will be

wanting the Captain and half a dozen others for the meal."
She started off, then came back. "Better you come with me,
and put on a fresh frock and brush your hair and make
yourself tidy, Miss Gabrielle."

Gabrielle looked at Barton, smiling. "Who do you think
will be aboard the *Delicia*, Barton?"

Barton had no answering smile. "The good God knows,"
she said non-committally. "But is well to look one's best."

"I know. You think Mr. Edward Colston will be on her."

Barton did not reply. She picked up her wide woollen skirt
and ran towards the house. Gabrielle followed, not running
but walking swiftly. She felt the pulse quicken ever so little.
It would be nice to see Edward again ... very nice indeed.
Her stride lengthened. After all there was little enough time
before a shore boat put out. She would not want Edward to
think she had gone stale since coming to the settlement, and
relaxed in her grooming. No indeed. She must look as well as
though she were in her own drawing-room in Meg's Lane in
the city of Bristol. She began to run.

Edward Colston appeared to be pleased to see her. He
kept the dinner table lively with gossip, and he and Zeb
Bragg together recited the story of the theft of the records
from Sandy Point.

"Mr. Moseley was hard pressed to raise the bail, but he
managed somehow. He was quite angry when he appeared in
court. He said that it was very strange that the Governor
could not find men to arrest the villain Teach, but could
readily spare officers to search out and arrest honest citizens."

"The Governor went into a rage at Moseley's charge,"
Bragg interjected. "He said that Moseley's words were treasonable, an accusation against his Majesty's government."

Robert Fountaine listened without taking part in the conversation. Gabrielle understood his feeling. He did not want
to think that there were quarrels and jealousies in the New
World.

After dinner Captain Bragg handed Gabrielle a ship's
manifest. "I've fetched the box down from Virginia, Miss
Gabrielle, I swear I had a time getting it from Robinson. He
wanted me to give him a paper showing I was your assign,
but I convinced him, over a bottle of Irish whisky I had
stowed away in my locker, that it was a favour he would be
doing to a fine young leddy, to let the box come down with

361

me, instead of waitin' for some little coastin' boat from New England to come up in the Cape Fear."

"Thank you so much, Captain. You're so thoughtful. I don't know what it can be, or who sent it."

The Captain indicated the paper Gabrielle still held in her hand.

"Read it. Read it. Perhaps it will be informative. Sometimes they be, you know. Read it aloud."

Gabrielle read:

"Shipped, by the Grace of God, in good order and well conditioned, by James Hamburg & Company, agents for Mistress M. Lepel, in and on the good ship called the *Balderson,* whereof the master, under God, for this present voyage and now riding at anchor in the River Thames and, by God's Grace, bound for Virginia,

"ONE BOX OF MERCHANDIZE

"being marked and numbered and to be delivered in like good order and well conditioned, at the aforesaid port of Virginia, (the danger of the seas only excepted), unto Mistress Gabrielle Fountaine, in care of Robert Fountaine, Esquire, at the village of Old Town, on Old Town Creek, on the Cape Fear River, (formerly called the Clarendon River) in North Carolina, or her assigns.

"The freight for the aforesaid goods being payed with coinage at average accustomed for said goods, Instructions whereof, the Master or Purser of the said ship has affirmed to,

"Bills of lading of the Tenor and Date, the one bill accompanies, the other, to hand,

"and so God send the Good ship to her desired Port in Safety. Amen.

"Dated London, 7th August, 1718.

"Inside and contents unknown to Robert Robinson, Capt."

Gabrielle looked from the Captain to her father. "I still don't know what's in it."

"Neither did Captain Robinson," laughed Edward. "I venture a surmise that Miss Molly has sent you some fine new clothes from your mantuamaker in London."

Gabrielle shook her head. "I didn't have any order for clothes." Her face brightened. "Perhaps it's books, and the new *Spectators.*"

Zeb Bragg pulled himself out of his chair. "I have to get back to my ship," he said. "I'll send it up. Then you can satisfy your curiosity, Mistress Gabrielle. I'm like Mr. Colston: I'll lay a wager it's new clothes."

Gabrielle looked at them and laughed. "If Molly could see the way we're living, she wouldn't be sending me any fine London gowns. With rains beginning, I think that doeskin breeches, such as Sandy MacAlpin wears, and a pair of jackboots will be my winter costume."

Robert Fountaine looked at her gravely. "That might not be a bad idea, my child. Under your long cape, of course."

Colour came to Gabrielle's cheek. "Father, I was only teasing. I couldn't think of wearing breeches. It would be too . . . too . . ." She paused, embarrassed to have said so much in front of Edward.

"You do wear breeks under your riding skirt," Captain Zeb observed.

Gabrielle said nothing, and the Captain made his adieus. "I'll send the box up," he said as he left the room.

"Thank you, Captain," Gabrielle said. "I'm curious to know what Molly has sent me."

"So I thought. For all your quiet ways, you're just like any girl when it comes to a surprise."

Gabrielle laughed. "Indeed I am. I like presents." She stood for a moment in the entry, watching the Captain go down the path, following his man who lighted the way with a ship's lanthorn.

"I'm glad to hear you say that."

Gabrielle turned quickly. Edward was standing behind her, in the entry. She had not realized he had followed her from the room.

He put his hand in his coattail pocket and drew out a slim black shagreen box, and gave it to her, bowing as he did so. "A tribute to a fair lady," he said, smiling at her bewilderment. "If I'd had the time, I'd have made a sonnet to my lady's white throat, but I declare, words would not rally to my aid."

Gabrielle walked back into the drawing-room. Her father had left it. They were alone save for Barton, who drowsed in a chair at the far end, her knitting in her lap. Gabrielle sank down on the little settee before the fire. Edward sat opposite her, watching her open the box and peep in. A look of surprise crossed her face when she saw the neck chain that lay curled inside, so well shown on the white velvet lining of the shagreen box.

"Oh Edward, how lovely it is!" She lifted the chain from

its bed and let the golden links fall through her long, slender fingers. She raised questioning eyes. "For me?" she said.

"Who else?" he replied, happy that he had pleased her.

She shook her head. "But it's too costly a gift for me to accept."

"I asked your father before I gave it to you. It's a small thing, Gabrielle, only a little memento. It's one of Monsieur Légare's pieces that were on display at Williamsburg. Let me."

Gabrielle bent her head, and he clasped the shiny chain about her white throat. She rose and looked at her image in the gilt-framed glass above a small table. The chain circled her throat and fell between the curves of her breasts. She smiled and held out both her hands, a graceful spontaneous gesture.

"Thank you, Edward. Thank you so much."

He lifted her hands and brushed them with his lips, one and then the other.

"Now I must leave you for a few minutes, Gabrielle. Your father asked me to come to his office in the weaving room. Don't run away, for I'm coming back. Perhaps we may have a game of bezique." He left the room, walking rapidly.

Gabrielle settled herself into her chair, her rose-coloured skirts pulled in primly to cover all but the tips of her buckled shoes. Edward was sweet, she thought. He was nicer than she remembered. She had been so interested in what he had told them of his visit to Virginia. His talk made the northern colony seem quite close. Williamsburg must be a very lively little city where the people lived well and fashionably. Colonel Alexander Spottswood must be a very fine gentleman. The Virginia planters prospered. Trade was excellent, excepting for the pirates that infested the Carolina Banks and preyed on the Virginia shipping off the Capes. Spottswood was of a mind to send a ship-of-war after the pirates, since Governor Eden wouldn't take steps to go into the Carolina waters to catch them.

Zeb Bragg had agreed with Edward. "We can't call ourselves civilized people, and let that dastardly pirate band have their way with our shipping," he told Fountaine.

Robert was bewildered by all this talk of pirates and ships-of-war.

"I thought they took King's Grace from Governor Woodes Rogers," he said.

Both men laughed. "They're all out again. A few at a time they've slipped away from New Providence and gone pirating," Zeb told him. "We had a scare coming over the shoals yesterday. Thought we were being pursued by a frigate that had the earmarks of a pirate, but it sailed north, past Barren Head."

Robert shook his head. "I don't like this news," he said slowly. "We have no protection here, only a six-pound cannon mounted, and two small mortars."

This conversation came to Gabrielle as she waited for Edward to come back from her father's office. She pulled the card table before the settee and got the picture-back cards from the mahogany box, which held chessmen and checkers.

It was almost an hour before Edward came back to the room. Gabrielle noticed that the gay expectant look that had been on his face when he left the room was gone. Instead he was serious, almost distant.

"Please sit down. I have laid out a hand, but perhaps you'd rather deal a new one."

"Let's play this." Edward took up the cards. They played a round, without words. As he was marking the score, Edward said, "I wish you'd told me about Paul Balarand."

Gabrielle's surprise was genuine. Edward looked puzzled. He started to say something, then thought better of it. He played the cards indifferently. Gabrielle glanced at him once or twice but said nothing. Long ago she had learned the value of silence.

After a time he said, "I felt all kinds of a fool."

Gabrielle laid her cards, face down, on the table. "Edward, what are you talking about?"

"About Paul Balarand. Don't you think you should have told me about him?"

"I still don't understand. I haven't seen Paul Balarand since I was a little girl. His father and my father were friends when they were boys in France. What has that to do with us?"

Edward took her hand in his. "Because you are going to marry him."

Gabrielle drew back. "Edward, have you had too much of Father's port?"

"No, my dear, I wish I had. I may as well tell you, now that I've blurted out this much. Gabrielle, I asked your father for your hand in marriage. He told me he had betrothed you to Paul Balarand."

Gabrielle withdrew her hand from Edward's. She sat for a moment, her hands clasped in her lap, too stunned to speak.

Edward watched the changing expression in her clear, candid eyes.

"I did not know," she said in a low voice. "My father has not spoken to me of any betrothal to Paul Balarand."

Edward said, "I'm sorry, Gabrielle. I wronged you in my thought. I thought you saw I was growing fonder of you every day I was here. These weeks I've been away, I've come to know that my feeling for you is much deeper than friendship. I've missed you. I found myself thinking of you constantly."

"I did not guess, Edward. I thought it was Molly. I . . ." She stopped, not knowing what to say. A dark flush mounted to Edward's cheeks.

"Molly bewitches a man, but . . ." He would be a cad to say more.

"My father has never mentioned marriage to me at any time, Edward. He thinks I'm a little girl still."

"So, you are, an adorable girl."

"I'm a woman. Ever since I've been here, I've felt old, old and settled." She smiled faintly. "I've never disobeyed my father in my life, Edward, but . . ."

He got up and sat down beside her, catching her hands in his. "Gabrielle, I won't attempt to persuade you against your father's wishes. I want you to know that I am always at your service. Always. You have only to call me."

He kissed her hand lingeringly. The little act of courtesy became a lover's plea. Tears filled the eyes. She started to speak, but a knock at the door made her turn her head. Barton woke. She got to her feet and crossed the room to open the door.

Gabrielle felt her pulse quicken. She hoped that the telltale colour did not show in her cheeks. David Moray stood in the hall, with him a stranger, a lean tall man of commanding presence. Edward dropped Gabrielle's hand and straightened himself quickly. From the look in David's eyes Gabrielle knew he had seen and misinterpreted Colston's action as he had once before, the day on the ship.

David said, "Miss Gabrielle, Colonel Moseley has just ridden down from Albemarle. He wishes to speak to Mr. Fountaine."

Gabrielle rose, curtsied and extended her hand. Edward crossed to the fireplace.

"Colonel Moseley, we are indeed honoured to receive you. My father is in his study. I will send for him at once."

Moseley held her hand a moment. "Pray don't send. Let me go to him."He recognized Edward. "Ah, we meet once more, Colston! I thought the *Delicia* was well on her way to Charles Town by now." The two men shook hands cordially.

"We ran into a stiff wind off Hatteras Cape and were obliged to take shelter behind the Banks until the storm blew itself out. You came overland, Colonel?"

"Yes. Two days' hard riding and a night's rest at Bath. I introduced Mr. Moray to our new road, the Governor's Road. I want to convince him that the Albemarle and the lower Cape Fear are not too far apart to be neighbours."

"A pity to interrupt a little game *à deux*," Colonel Moseley said, seating himself beside Gabrielle. He seemed to have forgotten he had expressed a desire to be taken to Fountaine's study. "The privilege of age." He looked from one young man to the other. "Two of you, of an age to fight for a boon from so sweet a lady, but I, with my grey hairs, pre-empt the desired place by her side." He smiled.

Gabrielle smiled back at him. "This is the way I wish it," she said, catching his banter and returning it. "Barton, will you have some brandy brought for these gentlemen? Please sit down, Edward." She hesitated a moment. "Please sit down, Mr Moray."

Edward took the chair on the far side of the little card table. David moved over near the fire, his elbow on the mantelboard. He stood easily, not in the least perturbed by her rudeness. He was quite poised and a little amused; the old smile lurked at the corner of his lips. She saw his eyes fall on the golden chain at her throat. His quick glance sought Edward who was staring moodily at the floor.

He knows. He has seen the chain before, she thought. She turned away and spoke to Moseley. "I hope you're going to be with us for some time, Colonel Moseley. Captain Bragg told my father that you were coming to survey the land grants along the Lower Cape Fear."

"Yes. That's why I'm here. That and another reason." He addressed Edward Colston. "Eden has allowed me to go free on one thousand pounds bail. I suppose I should be honoured to have the highest bond ever placed on a citizen in the province, but I'm not. It was deuced hard to raise the amount. I've mortgaged all my plantations." He smiled ruefully.

"Will the case ever come to trial?" Edward asked.

"I think so," Moseley replied. "Charles Eden is a stout

enemy, of vindicative nature, one who does not forgive anything he thinks is an affront to his dignity."

Gabrielle asked, "What did you say, Colonel Moseley, to arouse the Governor's anger?"

Moseley fingered his watchfob, a smile on his lips as though he thought of something that gave him pleasure. "I am afraid I lost my temper, Miss Fountaine. It annoyed me to see Mr. Eden sitting in his elbow chair assuming the air of outraged innocence, when I knew he was as guilty as Blackbeard. So I spoke my mind when he said I was guilty of high crimes bordering on treason to the Crown."

Edward said, "I think you should tell Miss Gabrielle what you answered."

Moseley's face became grave. "I said to his Excellency, 'If the law be for the King alone, I am guilty. But if the law be for the common people I am not guilty.' No, Eden will not forgive me. He will use all his influence to see that I am punished."

"What about Mr. Maurice Moore?" Colston asked.

"Moore did not anger the Governor by defying him, so he will have a lighter sentence when the case comes up in the General Court next session."

Robert Fountaine entered the room followed by Barton carrying a tray with decanters and glasses. He greeted David warmly and extended his hand to Moseley who had risen to his feet. Gabrielle left before the men seated themselves. David opened the door for her, bowing easily. She smiled a little timidly. It was difficult to adjust herself to his new status in the household. She started up the stairs to go to her own room. Her father's voice came through the open door.

"Bragg tells me that you have decided to come back to us, David. I am glad. It is a comfort to me to have you close by . . . you and Sandy MacAlpin."

"Thank you, sir," David replied. "I found when I got to Edenton that the land which Mr. Mainwairing thought was open had been taken up."

"The best open land is on the Cape Fear River," Moseley said. "According to my survey, the parcel just beyond here is still open for seating. I advised Moray to apply for the patent, which he did."

Gabrielle was deeply moved by what she heard. The heaviness that hung over her vanished. She felt lighthearted. She told herself it was because David was strong and resourceful, and would be helpful to the men who still remained.

She opened the door of her room. Barton had unpacked the box which had been sent up from the ship. Molly's clothes lay on the bed, overdresses and ruffled petticoats, modesties and underbodies, delicate pale colours which Molly affected to compliment her lovely hair.

She took up a primrose taffeta petticoat. A faint fragrance of lavender rose as she shook out the garment. The perfume recalled the garden in Meg's Lane and Molly seated at the harpsichord. She put the petticoat on the bed. Her lips began to tremble. She realized how much she missed her friends, how starved she was for companionship. As she crossed the room to the dressing table she saw Molly's letter on the desk. It must have come by a Virginia convoy, brought down on the *Delicia*. She broke the seal.

"DARLING:

"Do not be amazed to have a letter following so close after my last, but a friend of mine is bound for Virginia and will carry it with him.

"Your Molly is vastly disturbed and in the depths. Aunt Lepel and my cousin Mary are not speaking to me although I still remain in the house. It is all on account of the affair of the warehouse and Lord Hervey.

"Miss Teresa is angry with me too, because she came on Michael making love to me in the summerhouse at Mapledurham. She gave me a great lecture. She said Michael was married to the granddaughter of a king and he could bring me only trouble and heartache. . . . I'd better marry Edward Colston if I had the chance.

"I cried and protested I would never see Michael again. But what good are promises where one loves as I love? I want no one but Michael.

"I have made up my mind to leave England and come to you in America. Yesterday I wrote Madam Mainwairing asking her if I could go out when she goes to Carolina. If she will not take me, I'll go on another ship. Whose? I don't know, perhaps Michael Cary's.

"I decided to send some clothes to you as I may have to steal away from my aunt's house with only one little boy, like a heroine in a play by Mrs. Centlivre I saw in Temple Garden. I sign myself

"Your perplexed and bewildered
"MOLLY

"I saw the boys on their holiday. They are such dears. They are as eager to go to Carolina as I.

"The new fashions are monstrous. Ladies show their necks

to their waists, without benefit of modesties or tuckers. Lords and ladies vie with each other in silks and satins and cloth-of-gold. The gallants even powder their periwigs in perfumed powder from Araby, and 'tis the fashion to smell of all the spices of India and the Golden Isles."

Gabrielle smiled at the last postscriptum. She wondered whether Molly were really serious when she wrote of coming to Carolina. No matter how dire her situation, Molly could always find some diversion, a bit of gossip, a malicious little tale or the always absorbing subject of fashions.

Then she forgot Molly and thought of her own problems. One thing she determined to do—to talk with her father about Paul Balarand. It was unfair for him to betroth her to one she scarcely knew. That was the custom of France, or the nobility where great estates were involved. Simple folk had more freedom in England. She dreaded to go to him. He was so kind and gentle, yet when he had made a decision it was difficult for him to change.

She opened the door of her room and went into the hall. From the head of the stair she heard men's voices—her father's, David's, then the sonorous voice of Colonel Moseley and Edward's lighter tone.

She turned back, for the moment relieved that she could put off until another time the disagreeable subject of Paul Balarand.

Chapter 26

A TALL SHIP

Trouble was brewing along the Carolina Banks, at Teach's Hole, behind Ocracock. Half a dozen pirate vessels lay at anchor for a meeting of captains to consider Vane's plan to divide the waters off Carolina and in the Caribbean. A determined effort was to be made to keep the New England pirates in northern waters. Of late, too many had come surging south, to terrorize shipping in the Chesapeake and off the Virginia Capes. Low and Moody must be reasoned with or driven back. Since Woodes Rogers had come to govern the Bahamas, Nassau was no longer a safe place for rendezvous, and Green Turtle Cay less desirable. St. Thomas was fine harbour, but too far south for the Virginia and Carolina trade. Mono Passage caught the ships sailing south, but they were not so many as in the days of great Spanish trade. New rules must be made and adhered to if there was to be booty for all.

Anne Bonney lingered on at Ocracock. No one told her, but she scented something of moment was in the air, and she wanted to be there when plans were made and have a voice in council. Some time since, she had made up her mind to have a ship of her own. How to get it was troubling her day and night. Vane had no idea of giving her a prize someone else had fought for and won. She must gain a prize of her own. But how was she to do that without a crew or money to pay? Foolishly, she had let Rackham have the chest of money they had captured off Jamaica the year before. A ship she must have, and soon. She sat before her tent, watching the waves breaking on the beach, her chin clasped in her long slim fingers, trying to devise a way.

Tomorrow or the day following, Stede would come. He had been north, trying to overtake Teach, after the latter had taken the *Revenge*, and left him only the *Royal James* to make depredations along the coast. Arriving at Bath, he had found Teach had already sailed for the Albemarle or Currituck Sound. Stede did not know these waters and had no trustworthy pilot. He cursed and swore revenge, but he had not the fortitude to run down the bold Blackbeard.

When Bonnet came in that night, he was in a vile mood. A few months before, in the first bloom of their passionate love, Anne would have endeavoured to woo him into good humour. Now she let him sit and gloom, without asking what troubled him. She didn't care. Only one thought was in her mind—to get her ship.

"How many captains are in?" Stede asked after a long silence.

"I don't know," Anne answered indifferently. "Some came in today; yesterday the New Englanders came, Moody and Low. I heard them say that Worley would anchor in a few hours. He's been taking more prizes than any of the lot."

"God blast him!" Stede muttered. "He's been lying off Charles Town, *my* territory, while I was north on a worthless voyage."

"Better let Blackbeard have the *Revenge* and call it quits." She was unsympathetic.

Stede laughed harshly. "He says he's paying me in my own pieces of eight. He's wroth because I turned soft and rescued those men he had marooned at St. Thomas."

"I hear you're calling yourself Captain Thomas nowadays." Anne was brushing her long silken hair. She did not look at Stede as she spoke. She felt his eyes on her.

"Well, what of it?" he growled.

"I wondered. I should think the name Stede Bonnet was one to conjure with in these waters."

"Yes. 'Tis so. The British Fleet is after me for that Jamaica affair. I may as well be Thomas for a time. That's the reason I called my ship *Royal James*. She stinks under the name *Adventure*. I've got papers now. I can sail under King's license. I can be a privateer captain, if I so wish."

Anne let a long look of contempt rest on Stede, as he lay in the sand at her feet. "So! Playing it both ways?"

"Why not? I suffer no pangs of conscience. If I ship as a privateer and the exigencies of battle put me under the black flag, well and good, or the other way round."

Anne laid the shell-backed brush on the table and began plaiting her long fair hair into two braids. "What has come over you, Stede?" she asked as she bound the braids about her small, proud head. "There was a time when you stood where you stood, without cavil, and your name brought terror to the snively people of Charles Town and Nassau and the Southern Islands. Now you go from King's man to pirate and back again." She looked at him strangely. "Are you losing courage? Has that beast Blackbeard frightened you by his threats?"

Bonnet sprang to his feet. "Christ A'mighty! I've a notion to put a whip about those pretty white shoulders."

She laughed scornfully. "You wouldn't dare. I'm the one to use the *kiboka*, the rhinoceros whip I brought from Africa."

He looked at her a moment, then the hot rage died in his eyes and passion took its place. "I adore you, Anne Bonney. You're a leopard, ferocious and untamed, with your claws unsheathed." He drew her to him roughly, his mouth against her throat. "I thought I'd tamed you, my girl, but sometimes I'm not sure."

Anne suffered his embrace but no passion rose in her eyes to meet his. After a moment she disengaged herself impatiently. "We must remember that we go to a council in half an hour. We must know what we want, and be prepared to trade and bargain with shrewd, sly bargainers."

"I want nothing," he said, sullen that she had left his arms. "I have my ship and my crew and my woman."

"Ah, I come last!" she answered, but without rancour.

"That's as it should be; a man and his ship, and all else come after."

Anne's woman came to the tent carrying a yellow silk dress, pale as her hair. Anne stood up, her white arms above her head, as the dress was slipped over her shoulders. She turned slowly. The Carib woman wound two sashes, one powder blue, one rose, about her trim waist. Anne held a mirror to scrutinize her face. A bright circle, where the blood had come to her neck from Bonnet's kiss, annoyed her. She spoke sharply to the woman. "Cut two bands, like my sash. I must cover this hideous spot."

Stede looked at her. "Once you would have been proud of the mark of a kiss from Stede Bonnet."

Anne did not lift her eyes from the mirror. "I do not wish to make a spectacle of myself before the captains."

Bonnet caught her arm. "Who is it? If I find you've turned to another man, by the breath of God, I'll kill him."

"Save your anger, my Stede. There is no one."

"You no longer love me," he said, waiting for her denial.

"There's a time for lovemaking and a time for the business in hand. And the business in hand is to see that no one outsmarts us in this trading for position—Vane, or Blackbeard, or his henchman Worley, or any of the New Englanders."

"What do you want, my lady? Haven't I given you everything, silks and velvets and fine jewels?"

Anne was preoccupied, tying the double ribands about the slim column of her throat, so that the bow hid the red mark. "I want a ship," she said, as she patted the bow into place. "A tall ship, a proud ship."

"Christ! Do I hear with my ears? What in God's footstool would you do with a ship?"

"I'd 'sail on a lusty wind.'" She hummed a line of an old song.

Stede said nothing. He stood with legs apart, looking at her gloomily. His eyes softened as he watched her move with lithe grace and take a wide flat hat, garlanded with flowers, from a hook in the ridgepole.

"Come," she said. "It's time for the meeting. Remember, Stede, firmness and boldness win, every time. Blackbeard is only a bully. You have real courage." She smiled, a dazzling smile, which showed her strong white teeth.

He caught her to him. "Tonight," he whispered, "tonight. I'll be bold enough to suit even you, my girl."

The sun went down and blazed its crimson way along the wide river of Pamticoe. It touched the sand dunes on Core Island. It spread its glory over Cape Hatteras, the long bank that bent far into the ocean to trap the storms that blew up from the Caribbean and spread the winds inland.

They found the captains seated at a long table, eight or ten of them. Worley, Fly, Harriot and Moody were seated at one end. Blackbeard was not in sight. Vane motioned for them to sit. Dressed in his sober grey, he looked more a pastor than the head of a great outlaw band. He even wore a falling band of fresh lawn over the dark collar of his coat, and his waistcoat bore no gay braiding. Nor were his knives and pistols visible. Anne knew he wore a pistol strapped beneath his armpit and a wicked Zanzibar knife in his belt, but they were covered by his coat. She wondered how long it would take him to get it out. Vane wasn't inclined to threaten with weapons, nor display them until he was ready.

Once at Green Turtle Cay she had seen him cut the ears off a man and slit his nose without raising his voice in anger. Punishment was not a matter of rage or temper with Vane.

It was justice, as he saw it, meted out with dispassionate swiftness.

Jovelike, he sat in judgement, and used his thunderbolt.

"Red at night, sailors' delight," quoted one of the captains, reaching his cup towards a lame slave who was passing down the long board table, a demijohn of rum in his black hands.

"I'll choose a red morning," Moody said. "A good stiff gale would send me northward at a spanking pace. I've a mind to catch some Virginia merchantman off Cape Henry before I go back to New York."

Vane turned at Moody's words. "You forget, sir, that there'll be no hanging off the Capes this trip. Your sphere is north, and always north. Teach has the Virginia Capes as his northern boundary, and all the waters from there to the Cape Fear Shoals."

Moody scowled. "It appears that Mr. Teach has choice pickin's. You and Teach, Captain Vane, managed to draw the prime spots for easy sailing."

Vane's granite face was without expression, but his voice had a razor edge. "Aren't you satisfied with the drawing, Moody? Why didn't you enter protest when we had the lottery?"

Moody changed his tone. "Couldn't discount a lady's drawing, Captain. Seems like such a pretty young thing couldn't draw crooked."

Vane turned away and took a seat at the far end of the table, near Worley. Anne leaned her elbows on the board. Half the captains were drunk, the others disgruntled. Stede Bonnet had left the table earlier, shortly after the drawing. He was angered because he didn't want St. Thomas for his base. He didn't like the plate route. Spanish ships were large and carried heavy ordnance. Anne knew his anger, but he would say nothing to Vane. She wanted none of his complaints later. She was tired of complaints. She wanted plans for action, not explanations and excuses.

Her attention was drawn by the mention of Roger Main-wairing's name. Worley was speaking to Captain Vane. "Two prizes did I capture on the way down. One was a sloop, the *Francis*. I overhauled her at Roanoke Inlet and shot her masts away."

"A good cargo?" Vane asked.

"Passable. Passable. Some barrels of pork and the rest in

pitch and tar. She belonged to a planter named Mainwair-ing."

Anne got up and went to a vacant seat near Worley. "What are you going to do with the *Francis?*" she asked, trying to keep her eagerness from her pale blue eyes.

Worley answered carelessly, "Don't know. Beach her, I guess, after I shift the cargo to my ship."

"I'll buy her from you," Anne said.

Vane glanced at her, a glint in his hard grey eyes.

"Or do you prefer to trade?" Anne asked.

"For what?" Worley asked, pouring himself a tot of rum.

"Oh, I don't know. What would you suggest?" Anne was wary now.

"You want her mighty bad, don't you?" Worley grinned.

"Not especially. I had an idea if you intended to beach the ship." She spread her slim hands on the table, palms upward, indifferent. Vane said nothing. Anne knew he was watching her, measuring her ability, matched against Worley. "I thought I'd do some fishing this season, when the herring is running. An Albemarle boat would suit me."

"Never said she was an Albemarle ship, Mistress. Do you know the *Francis?*"

"I never heard of her before. You said you picked her up off Roanoke Inlet. That's the entrance to Albemarle Sound, so . . ." She shrugged her shoulders and turned to Vane. "They say Governor Johnston has sent to England for help to keep the pirates away from his city of Charles Town." She smiled and drew a paper from her bag. "Stede found a copy of the letter on the *Amsterdam Merchant,* when he took that ship off Cuba. He wanted you to have it."

"Read it, please," Vane said.

Anne turned her shoulder to Worley and spread the paper on the table.

" 'Tis only a copy. The original went out on the *Dra Castle,* or so it says on the letterhead."

"Read, Mistress. Read. I've a desire to hear what the Governor has to say about our Brotherhood."

" 'Tis addressed to Lords of Trade and Plantations, in London.

" 'MY LORDS:

" 'I have written to you more than once within the year regarding the direful plight of Carolina, without any answer from your Lordships.

376

" 'The urgency of our case may be appreciated at a glance. The imminent danger threatens one of the first Proprietories, situated in a remote region, a thousand leagues across the sea. Is it not of sufficient import to disturb the distinguished repose of the Noble Lords?

" 'Once before we requested a ship-of-war of Mr. Secty. Craggs. After two months' time he brought it to your Lordships. Then it was recommended to the Board of Trade; from thence it went to the Lords of the Admiralty, who most graciously acknowledged that a ship-of-war should be sent, to put a stop to these depredations, lest the trade, not only of Carolina, but of all the English plantations in America, be totally ruined in a very short time.

" 'Of the pirates, Vane is the most villainous, for he has the effrontery to sail into our very doorways and demand, and get, enormous ransom. A gibbet is the answer for him. Stede Bonnet is a second menace. A dozen other, lesser lights follow.

" 'Now, my Lords, consider our plight. Endeavor to send us the ship-of-war, granted us over a year ago by the Admiralty.' "

Vane looked at the paper and laughed, Anne shuddered. The sound was mirthless and sinister. "Well! Well! We must turn the screws a little tighter on our good Charles Town merchants. Yes, another full turn."

Worley leaned across the table. "Madam, what have you to trade for the sloop *Francis?*" His bleary eyes took in her slim figure, the graceful curve of her breasts. "I must be persuaded."

Vane answered him. "Madam does not need your ship, Worley. There are ships here for her choosing."

Anne looked up from under her long golden lashes. "Thank you, Captain Vane."

Worley drained a cup. "She shall have the *Francis.* I swear she shall have the *Francis* in the morning. A gift. As a gift."

"Thank you, but I accept no gifts, Captain." She slipped a golden bangle from her arm. It was set with green stones. "Here. Take this for the ship. It has value. Great value. The emeralds were cut in Amsterdam, and are of rare quality."

Vane took up the bauble, weighing it in his hand. He looked closely at the stones, held against a lanthorn light. "A fair exchange, sir. Shall I make out the transfer?" he asked Worley.

The drunken captain looked from one to the other, hesitated a moment, then clutched the bangle in his stubby fingers. "Draw up the paper, Captain. Draw and I'll sign." He leaned over and peered into Anne Bonney's face. His foul

377

breath made her draw back. "You wouldn't cheat Worley, would ye now?"

Anne said, "You don't have to take the bracelet, Worley, if you're not satisfied."

Worley looked at it closely. "My missis she's fair crazy over jewels," he said, by way of an apology for giving an easy bargain. "Fair crazy. She'd rather a gimcrack than a ship, any day."

Anne nodded absently. She had a ship, a good tall ship that had once belonged to Roger Mainwairing. That pleased her, sent a warm glow through her veins. One day she'd sail up the Albemarle Sound and raze every house, every house save Queen's Gift, Roger Mainwairing's plantation.

Her thoughts were interrupted by Vane with the transfer paper. She signed, with Vane and Low called to witness.

"You're all for legality, Vane," grumbled Worley, making a clumsy mark on the paper.

Vane didn't answer. He stood for a moment watching Worley walk away, feet wide apart in the sand to keep his balance. He turned to Anne, a shadow of a smile on his thin lips. "Well, you've got your ship, Madam, a crewless ship. What will you do with it?"

Anne did not answer his question. Instead she said, "Who's the best pilot in the Brotherhood, Captain?"

A gleam of admiration shone for a moment in Vane's cold grey eyes. He considered, as if he were turning the question in his mind, going over the list of pilots. "The best pilot, all around, is David Herriot, of the *Royal James*."

"Stede's man!" Anne said slowly. "David Herriot, you say?"

"That's what I said." Vane was watching her closely, waiting for an explanation, or perhaps an appeal to him for advice.

She smiled, her teeth flashing behind her full red lips. "If David Herriot is the best pilot, then I must have David Herriot on the *Royal Anne*."

Vane laughed aloud, a great lusty laugh. "The best you must have, Mistress. By the Eternal, I believe you will always have what you want!"

"Not always, Captain." Anne let her eyes, veiled by a fringe of lashes, rest on his for a moment—a quick glance, withdrawn, secret, elusive.

Vane gave no outward sign. She moved away, out to the great fire on the beach, where the lesser pirates were roasting

378

crabs and drinking from a barrel of small beer, set on end in the sand.

Anne walked alone to the crest of a dune. From there she watched the moon rise over the Western Ocean, and break the dense shadow of Teach's Hole, where the ships lay at anchor, their masts rising from the shadowy decks.

Which ship was hers? Was it heavy and wide, like a Spaniard, or was it a tall ship, clean and slim as a hound's tooth?

Suddenly tears came to her eyes. She saw herself walking through the deep woods, the staghound, Royall, at her side. She saw his great strong limbs racing across the fields, a rabbit held gently between his strong jaws. She brushed her hand across her eyes impatiently. A woman with a ship of her own had no time for tears, or for looking into the past. Ahead of her lay the wide sea and the Golden Isles. No woman's weakness for her. A man's heart for courage, and the wiry, bending strength of a Toledo blade in her body—that was Anne Bonney of today and tomorrow. She laughed to think how she had gulled Stede about carrying his child—any man's child.

Vane gave her unspoken homage now. She had the feeling that her day was coming. She gave not a thought to Stede Bonnet, until she heard him calling, "Anne! Anne Bonney. Where are you, Anne?" She did not call an answer. She walked slowly down the dunes, bathed now in cold white moonlight. She was like the moon, shining coldly.

Stede overtook her when she was nearing her tent. He followed her in and she saw he had a small writing portfolio in his hand. He laid it on the table without explanation, and sat down in the canvas chair while she unbound her hair.

"Blackbeard got out of hand again," he said, after a long silence. "I had a bout with him on the beach, and sent his sword flying into the sea, but he had his six-man canoe waiting. They rowed him off to the Hole."

Anne made no comment. She slipped off her dress and wrapped herself in her flowered shawl. She sat down on the rug stretched on the sand in front of her tent. The moonshine was all about her, silver and cool. Stede turned so he could look into her face.

"Herriot says Coe's here," he said abruptly. "He came up from Green Turtle Cay on William Fly's *Hannah*. An expedition has been sent out searching for me." He laughed harshly. "Colonel Rhett has taken oath never to leave off till he has me hung on White Point."

Anne smiled. Rhett was not the first to swear that he would catch Stede Bonnet. There was Yardley, and Sir Nicholas Law at Jamaica, and Wintergold at Nevis. She felt a little glow of pride.

"Rhett has two vessels this time." He threw himself down beside her, lying flat on his back, looking into the night sky. "Anne," he said, after a moment, "do you never think to go back to life, to civil, decent life?"

"I never knew civil, decent life," she said shortly. "I've always been outcast."

He took her cool hand and held it against his cheek. "Sometimes I think of the old days. I've never told you, Anne. I had a house in Bermuda, a great house, looking onto the blue sea. I had slaves, bondmen and women. I lived well."

Anne did not speak. This was a mood she did not know. She would not shatter it with words.

"Lived well and had friends whom I could trust. That's a good feeling, Anne—friends to trust." What had come over Stede? Anne stirred uneasily. "Today you asked me if I were trying to ride with the hounds and hunt with the fox. I said 'Why not?' Anne, sometimes I'm homesick for another life, the life I left to go pirating. What have I gained? Wealth? I *had* wealth. Adventure? Bah! Consorting with the dregs and riffraff of the lowest prisons, men of Teach's stamp." He turned, propped up on one elbow. "Shall we leave it, Anne? Shall we find a house in Antigua, or the Southern Islands? Live as people live on the great plantations of Jamaica or St. Croix or the Virgins?"

"Are you drunk?" Anne asked, her voice low. There was something disturbing in Stede's words, something that stirred her as she did not want to be stirred.

"No, my Anne, not drunk with wine. Sane, for a moment!" He got up and went to the table. Drawing a lanthorn to it, he lighted it with his flint. He opened the writingcase and took out a paper. "Anne, I want you to listen to this letter I've written to the Governor at Charles Town."

Wonder made her speechless. She got up and walked to his side, looking over his shoulder at the closely written page. "What has come upon you?" she asked. "You are so strange tonight."

"I don't know. I think it's the way Blackbeard's eyes follow

380

you, and that grey devil Worley. They're lascivious letting their slimy eyes rest on you. They'd take you if they were not afraid of Vane. Vane is your protector, not Stede Bonnet."

The whole bitterness that had turned inward came to the surface. Anne understood now. Stede had no illusions. She felt a wave of tenderness for him, in his self-abnegation. "Don't my dear. Don't say such things. Don't think them. Vane does not protect me. Anne Bonney is her own protector and has always been."

"Think of this, Anne. You and I living in a great house in Jamaica, taking life easy. Loving and living. Let's break with this wild life. Let me take you out of this filth and slime."

"But I want ships."

"We can have ships. I have his Majesty's commission, under the law. I can sail as a privateer. Anne, you're too beautiful to live this way, with these degraded rascals."

When she made no answer, he took up the paper he had written and read it to her. It was addressed to the Governor of South Carolina.

"'HONOURED SIR:

"'I have presumed on the confidence of your eminent goodness to throw myself, after this manner, at your feet, to implore you to be graciously pleased to look upon me with tender bowels of pity and compassion, and believe me to be the most miserable man this day breathing. . . .'"

Anne interrupted him. "Stede, what ails you? Are you mad?" He went on:

"'I entreat you to let me fall a sacrifice to the envy of a few men and the ungodly rage of a few, as punishment of my sins.

"'I once more beg, for the Lord's sake, dear sir, that as you are a Christian, you will be so charitable as to have mercy and compassion upon my miserable soul, but too newly awakened from the habit of sin to entertain so confident hopes and assurance of it being received in the arms of my Blessed Jesus.

"'Now, may the God of peace, that brought again from the dead our Lord Jesus, that great shepherd of the sheep, through the blood of the everlasting covenant, make you perfect in every good work to do His will, working in you that which is well pleasing in His sight, through Jesus Christ, to whom be Glory forever and ever, is the hearty prayer of

"'Your Honour's
"'Most miserable and
"'Afflicted servant,
"'STEDE BONNET.'"

The silence which followed was profound. Far away she heard the plaintive cry of a sea-bird. The rowdy songs of the pirates were dim, under the pounding of the waves on the shore. She faced Stede, anger rising swiftly in her.

"Coward!" she said, lifting her voice. "You run to sue for pardon when you hear Rhett is coming after you."

"I wrote this before Fly told me," he said dully.

"You lie. You're afraid." Anne's voice was like a whip across his bare back. She moved away and stood looking seaward. The moon was on the water now, all shadows dispelled except the little splotches of dark from the marching dunes. She was bewildered by the turn his conversation had taken. She cried "Coward," but this was something more. He talked of God and His mercy. She had heard snivelling pirates and sailors and townsmen talk of God when they walked the plank, or fought their last fight. Did Stede Bonnet have a vision of doom ahead of him? "The Will of Allah" was a phrase often on Anne's lips.

She questioned him, her voice softened: "Have you dreamed of serpents and death, Stede? Or have you seen an animal cross your unfilled grave?"

Stede ran his hand across his eyes, as if to clear his vision. "No, no, not so. 'Tis the swaying noose that robs me of my sleep."

Anne laid her hand on his arm. "Forget what I said, Stede. My temper is quick these days. I know not why. Come, let's walk on the beach for a little, then take a long sleep. Tomorrow Vane will divide the cargoes. You know today's wrangling will increase a thousandfold."

Bonnet could not shake his low spirits. Even as they walked along the hard sand in the clear moonlight, again and again he spoke of hanging and the gibbet.

Anne said, "As to hanging, 'tis no great hardship, for were it not for that, every cowardly fellow would turn pirate and so infest the seas that men of courage would starve."

Stede laughed then and threw his arm over his shoulder. "You're a queen among women, my Anne. You always know how to get a man out of the doldrums. Come, let's go to your tent. Tomorrow we must fight for our share of cargo. For that I must have a clear head." Anne turned without protest and they walked slowly back across the dunes.

Anne rose at dawn and walked to the cove where the ships lay at anchor in Teach's Hole. A dozen men, gaily dressed in bright shirts and breeches, with sashes wound around their waists, were busy about the boats. Some wore broad black hats, others stocking caps with tassels, a few Mohammedan tarbooshes with long black tassels. An evil lot they were, but they spoke respectfully when she asked for the sloop *Francis*. One man pointed to the vessel, anchored not far offshore, a little apart from the others, towards Beacon Island. A sweet ship, built as a sloop-of-war, and mounting four guns. She was tall, graceful and smooth. Three sailors were on deck, hauling at the sails, which hung limp for drying. She was rigged with a mainsail, a club topsail, a balloon jib and a spinnaker. By the cut of her she looked a swift sailor. Anne was pleased. A ship that had belonged to Roger Mainwairing would bring her good fortune.

She heard Stede calling. She turned from contemplation of her ship and moved away in the direction of Vane's camp. Stede joined her. He was dressed in fine doeskin clothes, with a red embroidered waistcoat, and he had two red plumes trailing from his wide hat. He wore no pistols, only his Toledo sword with jewelled hilt. Her heart beat a little faster. He was straight and soldierly, with well-carried head. She thought of Calico Jack, and his rough, boisterous ways, and his foul language. She was glad she had let Rackham go to Mary Read. She wanted better things from now on. Perhaps Stede was not all wrong, with his talk of a great house in Jamaica, and sailing as a privateer under the King's ensign, instead of the Jolly Roger. These thoughts she kept within herself. Time enough.

When they got to Vane's place, all the pirates were assembled. They lounged on the sand, or sat cross-legged like Turks, before the tent of the acknowledged commander, Charles Vane.

Vane was at a table. Two clerks sat beside him with quills and papers. Anne and Stede took their places not far away, Stede on the sand, Anne seated on a canvas chair.

Vane spoke briefly. "The semiannual rendezvous is a good investment. It brings the members of the Brotherhood closer. Dividing shares of the booty is only a small part. We talk and exchange experiences. We get ideas on sailing, on manoeuvring, and ways to outwit our pursuers. Every man here has a price on his head. In spite of that, some are godly men. I wish I could think we all were. But that is neither here nor there. We are bound together by our trade and the rules of the Brotherhood. I'm glad to say the results of the past twelvemonth have been good, better than the previous.

"Captain Bonnet has paid his respects to New York and to New England and his exploits off the Charles Town bar are well known to us. He caught a Barbados sloop, a New England brigantine, as well as the *Revenge* and the *Royal James*. Others he captured, transferred cargo and burned."

Vane smiled grimly, opening his wide, thin-lipped mouth and showing scraggy teeth for an instant.

"The Charles Town paper paid Captain Bonnet the compliment of saying he has made more depredations on the coast than any man since Henry Morgan."

"Hear! Hear!" shouted some of the members. Others were silent; they did not like the praise given to Bonnet. Vane sensed the antagonism.

"Let me pass to Captain Teach. He has a long, long list of captures. The London ship, for instance, when he captured Captain Wragg and made them pay tribute. He took six thousand pounds specie on that raid. You all know how Teach has been far more useful than the capturing of vessels; he has made a friend for the pirates. The Governor of North Carolina. He goes, at will, to the Governor's summer residence at Bath Town and to his great house on the Chowan, at the head of Albemarle Sound. Charles Eden has given Teach his Majesty's Pardon."

A laugh went up from the captains.

"More than that, Teach has made friends with Tobias Knight, of Bath Town. Tobias gives us storage place for cargoes and looks the other way. Since he is Collector of the Port and sits as Vice Admiralty Judge, it gives us a friend at court. These men, Eden and Knight, know we pirates are useful. We make it possible for merchants to purchase cargo goods at low figures and sell cheaper, without paying government taxes."

Anne looked across the circle. Blackbeard was sitting on a woven mat, his men about him. He glanced from one captain to the other as Vane spoke, pulling at his long bushy beard.

One captain after another was singled out for attention. Then the clerk read the list of ships captured and the amount of cargo, and its value, and the percentage that went into the general pool. In spite of the softening process, there was fighting and bickering among the men. Worley and Fly came to grips. Fortunately, Fly's pistol failed to explode and Wor-

384

ley's life was saved, for Fly had him down and the pistol pressed against his temple. Blackbeard and Stede exchanged acrimonious words. Blackbeard threatened, but Stede held his tongue and the affair was smoothed over by Vane.

Food and drink were passed, and the division of spoils went on into the late afternoon. Some of the cargo that was still in the holds of ships was inspected.

Anne sat apart. She was bored by the talk of stinking hides and tallow, of pitch and tar; even sugar was without interest. She thought of other rendezvous at St. Thomas, or on Hispaniola, when wines and spice made the cargo, gold from the Main, and precious stones and fine goods from French and Spanish ships. This was sordid, without lustre or colour. She would take her ship south, off Jamaica and Mono Passage, lie across the trade routes. Let these low-browed devils take the leavings.

She got up and walked across the beach. Drunken men were playing dice, quarrelling and shouting obscene oaths. Black women walked among them, leering into the eyes of the pirates, rubbing against them with bare arms and thighs. It sickened her. A clean fight—to grapple a ship and board, pistol in hand—that sent the blood surging to one's veins. But not this.

When Anne returned, the business of the afternoon was over, and Vane had set up a mock court for a mock trial. They were all in place—judge, jury, solicitor for the defense and the accusers. Half the men were drunk and their tongues were loose. A great black flag with white skull hung on a pole behind Vane, the judge, who sat at a table dressed in a bright red gown, his spectacles on his nose, a bowl of punch at his elbow, a naked sword across his knees. Court officers were below him, with pikestaffs and crowbars.

A criminal was led in, in solemn procession. The attorney general, with foolscap on his head, addressed the judge: "If it please your Lordship, the fellow before you is a sad, sad dog. I humbly hope your Lordship will order him to be hanged immediately for committing piracy on the high seas.

"Sad Dog has escaped a thousand storms, and got safe ashore when the ship was cast away, which proves he was not born to be drowned. Yet, not having fear of hanging before his eyes, he went on robbing men and ravishing

385

women, and plundering ships and sinking ships as if the devil were in him." The attorney general shot out a long finger. "Worse, your Lordship, worse—he drinks small beer."

A laugh burst from the crowd. They're enjoying this childish horseplay, thought Anne, looking about her in astonishment. These were the men who lashed slaves and walked prisoners off the plank, who took women without their consent, and fought savage duels with knife and sword.

"Your Lordship knows we have no rum," the prisoner's counsel broke in, "and how should a man speak good lies that has not drunk a dram?"

"I hope your Lordship will order the fellow hanged," the attorney general said, striding up and down, his long robe flapping about his skinny shanks.

The judge leaned over the table. "Harkee! Sirrah, you lousy pitiful ill-looked Dog. What have you to say why you should not be tucked up immediately and set drying in the sun like a scarecrow? Are you guilty or not guilty?"

"Not guilty, may it please your Worship."

"Say that again," shouted Vane, "and I'll have you hanged, without trial!" The prisoner whimpered, unable to speak. His face was white, his teeth chattering. Anne leaned forward; this surpassed all acting she had ever seen.

Vane said, "I want a hanging before dinner. Gaoler, take your man."

The prisoner fell to the ground on his knees. With hands extended, he cried, "Mercy, Captain! Mercy! I did nothing wrong. I swear I'll never tell I saw you and the captains. I swear by the Virgin."

Vane rose, casting off the robe. "Take the fellow away. He annoys me. He landed on this island in a market boat to spy out our camp."

There was a sudden silence. The mock trial had become a real one. The man lay writhing at Vane's feet, his hands clasping his legs. "Mercy, Captain! Mercy!"

Worley threw off his mimic robe. "Who is the fellow? What has he done?"

Vane waved the gaoler to take the prisoner away. He moved off towards the supper table. "A market-boatman, from Bath Town. He's seen too much here to stay on this earth. Sit down, gentlemen."

386

No one spoke. Silently they moved to their places. Several of them took their rum at one gulp. Something about the quick change from comedy to tragedy got under their thick hides. Anne looked towards the beach. The gibbet already had a victim.

Chapter 27

PRELUDE TO BATTLE

Gabrielle stopped to look in on her mother before she went down to breakfast. Madam was sitting up in her bed, her breakfast tray in her lap. Her hair was arranged with a little lace cap pinned on over her curls. A soft rose shoulder cape kept her warm as she drank the chocolate Celestine had prepared. She glanced up when Gabrielle came in, and said good morning, but there was no spark of recognition behind her eyes. "Carry my clothes to the laundry room," she said sharply, looking full at Gabrielle. "You forgot them yesterday and Celestine had to carry them down." Gabrielle stood for a moment without replying, depressed and saddened.

"You . . . you . . . whatever your name is—I forget." Her mother's voice had the thin querulous quality of the confirmed invalid.

"Gabrielle," she said.

"Gabrielle, *Madam!* Has no one taught you manners?" She looked towards Celestine, who stood with folded hands on the far side of the bed. "Haven't you trained the girl? Where did you pick her up? Out of the fields?"

Gabrielle's face worked painfully. With a murmur of excuse, she left the room and hurried down the passageway that led to the main house. Every day her mother gained in physical but not in mental strength. Gabrielle had almost come to believe that she would never again be aware of the world in which she lived. She seemed content in the two rooms, with her familiar things about her and Celestine to wait on her. Celestine belonged to her old life and as such she lived in her mistress's mind, almost as though she were a reflection in a mirrored past.

The hurt in Robert Fountaine's eyes grew deeper day by day. Madam often consulted him, gave him orders about the estate, the horses and dogs. Lately she had been busy making plans for a garden. "I want a sundial with little beds all around, each bed circled with purple fleur-de-lis," she told Gabrielle one day.

Mention of the flowers brought back a poignant story of her mother's girlhood—her terror when the Dragonade, their yellow coats flying, rode down the tree-lined avenue of their home, killing servants and peasants, driving devout Huguenots to the woods to hide under hedges and in the shifting sands of the beaches. Instead of tying her clothes in a bundle as her parents had ordered, the young girl filled a sheet with purple lily bulbs. These she carried in her arms to the English ship that waited offshore to take the terrified refugees to England.

"I want to carry something of France with me," the child told her parents when they discovered what she had done. "A little of France for our new home in England."

Tears came to Gabrielle's eyes now as she watched the changing expression of her mother's face when she spoke of fleur-de-lis.

"I must have a border of purple lilies in my garden," Madam said. "It reminds me of something." She hesitated, trying to gather her vague thoughts. She turned to the maid. "Celestine, Celestine, what do the fleur-de-lis remind me of?"

Celestine's eyes met Gabrielle's. "The lilies remind Madame of France," she said, her voice soothing. "Or of next spring's garden, Madame. It is time to plant."

Gabrielle felt sad as she walked away from her mother's room. But she was grateful that she had asked Moray to pack the bulbs with the plants they were bringing to America. The lilies would grow in this New World garden as they had grown in an Irish courtyard and in a garden in England. Another season her mother would walk along a garden path bordered by purple lilies of France.

The men were seated at the breakfast table when Gabrielle entered. She kissed her father and made a curtsy to Colonel Moseley. She smiled at Edward and took her place. A moment later David Moray came in and sat down in the only chair left vacant, at her left hand. She gave him a startled look and glanced quickly at her father. He showed no surprise. Instead he was smiling.

"Good morning, David, my boy, I hope you slept well in the bachelors' house."

"Thank you. Excellently. The beds are comfortable and the meeting room cheery and bright."

"That is good. I want everyone in the settlement to be comfortable," Fountaine said to Colonel Moseley. "There are six unmarried men with us. They have common sleeping and living quarters."

"An excellent idea, sir. That is one of the chief requirements of a good settlement, to make your people content and comfortable."

"MacAlpin says I am spoiling the people. I think too much of their comfort."

Moseley smiled. "Sandy could sleep on a hard board or a corduroy road or under a tree with equal ease."

Edward said, "I tried sleeping in a pine-bough bed. It smelled pleasingly, but I must say that it irked me in several places."

"You didn't strip the boughs," David said. " 'Tis an old trick I learned long ago, with a bough bed."

Gabrielle poured the tea from the silver pot, and Barton passed the cups. She was trying to adjust herself to the change that had taken place. Everyone accepted the bondman as an equal, without question, her father among them. Was this part of the New World life? What would happen if everyone was on a plane of equality, common people sitting at the table of their betters?

She looked at Barton. There was no sign of disapproval on her face as she set the cup at the side of David's plate.

"Will you have sugar and milk, sir?" Barton was saying "sir" to a bondman! She looked up. David's eyes met hers. The corners of his mouth twitched. He was smiling.

"You find it so strange to serve a bondman?" he said in a low voice so that none might hear.

"I do not find it strange to serve my father's guest," she answered non-committally, and turned to answer Edward's question:

"We're riding down the river this morning. Will you ride with us?"

Gabrielle looked at her father, waiting for permission.

Colonel Moseley said, "I'm going downstream to the place that Maurice Moore has selected for a town site. Edward and David are going with me. They insist that they're going to carry chains for me, but I think I'll take my men Quashy and Drago, in case we have to use the brush hook."

"I'll have Barton see that there's a lunch put up for you," Robert Fountaine said.

"I'd like to go, Father." Gabrielle looked at Robert. "May I? If you don't need me?"

"I expect to be busy with Captain Bragg all day," Robert said. "If you won't be in the Colonel's way, my child."

"Indeed not. We'll be honoured."

"Then, if I may be excused, I'll change." Gabrielle rose from her place and quitted the room. As she crossed the hall, she heard her father say:

"It will be a splendid thing for us, if this project of Mr. Moore's goes through. We need more people on the river. Do you think it may develop soon?"

Moseley said, "Not at once, I'm afraid. But within a few years. There's some difficulty about land titles. South Carolina has issued patents along the river, based on the idea that the Cape Fear is their boundary from North Carolina. The Moores make claim to this river land, because Sir John Yeamans' daughter married a Moore. I hope your title is clear, Mr. Fountaine."

Robert looked up, puzzled. "I had the papers direct from Lord John Carteret and the Proprietors," he said.

"Then you're quite safe. The reason I asked is because you're located directly on the land of the Yeamans colony. The Moores are claiming all the land up the river to the Forks."

"I hope there'll be no difficulties," Robert Fountaine said.

Gabrielle moved off. One more thing for her father to worry about—land titles. She hoped that didn't mean lawsuits. She dressed quickly and was downstairs by the time the men were ready. When she went out to the mounting block, Sandy MacAlpin was putting the food Barton had prepared into his saddlebags. She was glad Sandy was back from his fortnight's trip up Far Reach. She had missed him.

Sandy went over to greet David.

"I looked at that land," he said to David. "I believe 'tis best just above here. An acreage between the two swamps— it has everything you want for a plantation."

"Thank you, Sandy. We will have it marked on Colonel Moseley's map as soon as the patents are recorded. Remember, I count on you to live with me. Two Scots should stand together."

"Aye, that I will, Mr. Moray, and the both o' us will keep an eye on the young lady and her father."

The ride was pleasant. The day was fine and clear and not too cold. Some of the bright yellow and crimson leaves still clung to sourwood and gum trees. and rowan berries were in scarlet clusters. Gabrielle rode near Edward, a little behind the others. A deer leapt across the narrow path, an old path, made by the migration of Indians from the Banks to the upper reaches of the river. Squirrels with bright curious eyes sat on hind legs, pouches fat with nuts they carried to their winter hiding places.

Sometimes they were in sight of the river, sometimes far back, as they circled a swamp. Here, in the swamp, all was dark and ancient and filled with decay of the ages. Trees closed in on them, heavy and menacing. The black water menaced, too, and the heavy intertwining vines made an impenetrable barrier. Gabrielle shuddered.

Edward asked, "Are you afraid of this wilderness, Gabrielle?"

"I don't know. Sometimes I think I never saw such beauty; again, I feel that the forest holds danger for us. Sometimes, at night, I walk to the edge of the stockade. There it is, dark and heavy, waiting to envelop us. Think of it, Edward. We have cut only a few acres out of this wilderness, a few acres, against the river. The deep wood crowds down on us, heavy and overpowering, as it is there." She waved an arm towards grotesque cypress knees, piercing the black swamp water. "Listen to the silence. It's all like this, along the river, miles and miles and miles, Sandy told me. Only half a dozen clearings lie between here and the upper river and beyond that only the red savages."

Edward replied, understanding in his honest, frank countenance, "I don't wonder that you fear this country, Gabrielle. It is so big, the forests are so vast and lonely. One has no conception of what lies beyond the edge of the forest. Sandy says the woods go on and on westward. They are so thick and close that a squirrel can travel over the tree tops to the Southern Seas. They are the western boundary—according to King Charles's charter . . . 'Westward to the Southern Seas.' It is a forbidding country. A woman must have great courage to be content here, unless she is following a man she loves." Colston looked at her sympathetically. "It will take years before the wilderness if pushed back; before this settlement is safe. Oh, Gabrielle, if you could only love me . . ." He laid his hand over hers. "No, I don't even ask you to love me. Marry me and I will take you away."

Gabrielle answered, sadness in her large expressive eyes, "I wish I could love you as you want me to, Edward. But I can't. I don't know why, when my heart is so warm and friendly toward you. But that isn't the love you deserve." She slipped her hand from under his fingers. She understooood so much she could not say to him. Love on the rebound was an old story.

"You are afraid I still love Molly?" he asked, sensitive to her thought. "I do love Molly, but not with the deep emotion I feel for you, Gabrielle. One woman may desire to be a toast to whom all men pay homage, another may find happiness in the devotion of one man. I think you are like that, my dear. I envy the man who will have your devotion."

"I'm sorry, Edward. I wish I could feel differently, but I can't. Even if I loved you with all my soul, I couldn't leave my father as long as he needs me. Surely you understand?"

"Yes, my dear, I understand. I hoped it could be different. I want so much to take you back to England."

She shook her head. "We have made our choice, Edward, the new and not the old. Please don't think of me as afraid of the wilderness. The forest doesn't always hold terror. Sometimes it is bright with sunshine and I am happy to be where it is so beautiful and so tranquil."

Gabrielle spoke to her horse and they trotted down the long aisle of pines to where Sandy MacAlpin was waiting.

"We'll turn in by the lake," Sandy told them. "The path from here on is along the bank and you can see far down the river. It is good to be able to look long distances, after you have been shut in by a forest of trees."

Gabrielle smiled. Sandy had put her thoughts into words.

She looked about her. It must have been near here that she had found the old Negro, that day not long after they had landed at Old Town. The hideout of the runaways. She started to tell Sandy of the incident, but thought better of it. Why should she betray a secret hiding place of persecuted people?

Moseley's men had cut a clearing to the river. She walked out to the point. She could see a long way, almost to the entrance. The river was broad here. The opposite shore had little timber, long stretches of sand. Beyond was Barren Head and the long narrow island that almost closed the entrance. Beyond that were the shoals.

"That is Haul Over Inlet, where the pirates hide their ships." MacAlpin pointed. "The Great Road to New Bern and Bath Town and the Albemarle will ferry just there and pick up the road that goes past Lockwood's Folly. I came that way when I marched with Barnwell and Maurice Moore from Charles Town. That was in '12, the time of the Tuscarora massacre at Bath. It was a wild country then, Miss. Wild and full of danger."

Gabrielle looked up to see if Sandy were laughing. How could there be danger in that peaceful spot? There was no laughter in his eyes or on his lips. That was the way it looked to him. Danger then, but not now. Now civilization was creeping into the wilderness he had known.

"Sit down on the log. Wait, I'll spread my saddle blanket. There's no biting bugs at this season, but it's dusty." He put the blanket on a fallen tree and Gabrielle sat down, facing the river. Sandy went off through the trees. She heard the voices of the men and the sound of falling brush as the Negroes hacked through the thickly grown vines and small bushes.

A cormorant flew past and settled on a bare tree the lightning had withered to a skeleton; black-coloured, a strange, ungainly bird, as grotesque as the cypress trees that grew in the swamp. A wedge of geese flew by, cackling and calling to the few stragglers lagging behind. Fish jumped in the water. The river was quiet, the tide running out.

She tried to envisage Mr. Moore's dream town: winding roads cut through the forest, straight little streets of a village built about a green; a chapel, a courthouse and a market place. Wharves in the little sheltered bay below her. A ferry to the other side, for travellers who would ride from Charles Town to Virginia. Ships would enter the river to repair and clean, to deliver and receive cargo. Ships . . .

She put her hand above her eyes and looked downriver. She saw a ship under slack sail near the far shore. She watched it tacking to catch the small offshore wind. She wondered what ship it could be. For a long time no ships had come up the river, now two, within as many days.

When the sun was overhead, the men came in, scratched by brambles, their clothes disarranged. Sandy came first, and one of Moseley's Negroes.

In no time a fire was built and hot water bubbling in a tin kettle ready to make tea. With Barton's meat pies and little cakes, a feast was laid.

Moseley said grace, and they all began to eat with the zest that out-of-doors work brings.

Edward sat beside Gabrielle, David across. Sandy sat on his haunches, getting up now and then to fill cups. They were

394

halfway through the meal when Gabrielle mentioned the ship.

Sandy rose at once and went out on the point. After a moment he called to Moseley. The two stood for some time looking downstream. After a time curiosity got the better of the others and they all walked down to the point.

Three ships were in sight—a large one and two smaller, sailing upriver. When Gabrielle came up, she heard Moseley say, "I don't like the look of them. I don't believe they're trading ships."

"Nor I," observed Sandy MacAlpin. "Verra like it's a pirate and two prizes."

"What will they do?" Edward Colston asked.

"Might sail upriver to Old Town Creek, to careen in a safe place, not knowing about the settlement."

Moseley nodded. "In that case it would be well for you to ride ahead and warn Mr. Fountaine."

Sandy agreed. "Just what I was thinkin', Colonel. Though it's verra little they can do with their mortars against the pirate guns."

"Take my horse," Gabrielle said to Sandy. "She's faster than yours."

"I'll ride with you." David sprang to the saddle.

The two rode off. The others mounted quickly, Gabrielle on Sandy's grey nag. The Negroes were left behind with orders to watch the progress of the ships upstream. When the ships were opposite the point, they were to ride with all speed to Old Town.

Edward said, "I'll stay with them. It might be possible that they'll anchor below here, in the mouth of the creek. In that case there'll be no danger to the settlement. If they continue upstream, we'll ride post-haste to warn you."

"Good!" Moseley said. "I feel better. My Negroes are good men, but they might lose their heads. They are terrified of pirates." He turned his horse and galloped down the narrow path.

Edward took his position behind some bushes, far out on the point. Quashy he placed fifty yards down stream, and Drago above him in a tree, where he had a long view up and down the river. The ships lay, at the moment, in line with the little rising hill on the east bank. They were moving slowly, under a light wind and against an outgoing tide. After an hour had passed, he saw they were steering directly towards the little cove below the bank where he lay—a good anchorage, this side of the spit.

Edward smiled, and a glint of excitement showed in his usually quiet eyes, to think that he, Edward Colston, merchant of Bristol, should be lying on his belly in a thicket of scrub pines, watching a pirate ship. It was beyond belief! He loosed his pistol· and looked to its priming. He laughed grimly. What good would a pistol do against the heavily armed pirates? For pirates they were; as the ship came into midstream, he saw the black flag at the mainmast. The Negroes also had seen it. They drew near to him, inching their way, so he would not notice their changed positions. The smile on his face widened. One pistol to defend the three.

Waiting to see whether or not the pirate ship would put into the cove became a task. But he must know, before he sent the men back. Another half hour passed, and into the third quarter, before he made his decision. By then he could fathom the plan. The two small ships were making for the cove. The large ship, a frigate, continued upstream. Ten deck guns were visible, and room below, in the ports, for others.

He signalled to the Negroes. "Get to your horses! Ride like the devil to the stockade. Tell your master that the larger ship is sailing upriver. It has ten guns, mayhap more. If it goes up to Old Town Creek, it will take three hours on this wind. You can make it in an hour."

"You come, Master?" Quashy asked.

"No. I'll stay here, to see why the two ships anchor."

The men lingered. "Master does not fear?"

"God, no! Get gone, both of you."

The slaves moved off silently and were lost in the thicket. They had a quarter of a mile to go to the horses; after that they would make speed. They'd be in time to give fair warning, if the lookout should happen not to see the ship because of the curving shore line and the thick fringe of trees on the bank.

The ships came slowly into the cove and dropped anchor. Edward glanced at the little beach. The tide would be out by sundown. The ships must be light draft, to venture so close in. He wriggled along on his belly until he was near the edge of the bank. Here he could look down and see the decks of both ships. Men were moving about. He could hear the rattle of chains and the squeak of windlass. He wished he had a glass, so he could see the figures more distinctly. There were several men herded at one end of the smaller sloop, while a guard walked back and forth in front of them. The smaller ship was evidently a prize, a prize with prisoners.

After a time a small boat put off for the shore, with five or six men at the oars. He heard a woman's voice, sharp and commanding. When the boat drew close to shore, he saw that the men were armed with fowling-pieces.

If they were intent on shooting game in the forest, he had little time left to make his escape. He backed away. The movement of his body, quiet as it was, disturbed the bank, and a great piece of earth rolled downward and splashed into the river.

The pirates raised their voices, shouting and cursing. Edward got to his knees. Bending low, he eased through the thicket to the open place where his horse was tethered. Mounting swiftly, he sought the path that led to the lake and the wide River Road. Once on the road he put his horse to a brisk trot. If the pirates climbed the bank at that point, they'd see the tracks of men and horses and the remainder of food, which had been left on the ground. There was a chance that they'd scale the bank farther down, and the evidence of the recent occupancy of the point escape their notice.

The stockade was crowded with settlers by the time Edward Colston got back to Old Town. Men went about taking stations on the stockade and the lookouts. Women were in the chapel and the bachelor hall. He met Moray at the door of Fountaine's house. The Scot looked troubled. Edward told him what he had seen.

"Fountaine will not let us fire on the pirate ship. He thinks it better to pay tribute than have the houses razed," David said.

"Does he realize that pirates do more than collect tribute? They carry off women and . . . Can't you convince him?"

David shrugged his wide shoulders. "I've tried. So has Moseley. But he's stubborn. Isn't it the devil how stubborn gentle people can be?"

They were walking towards the river. Edward saw that the *Delicia* was not at her anchorage.

"Where's Bragg?" he asked quickly.

"He sailed up to the Forks before daybreak."

"A pity. His guns would have saved us from being at the complete mercy of the pirates."

Moray said, "I've talked it over with MacAlpin and Moseley. They both agree that if the ship shells us, we must hide the women in the forest. MacAlpin will take them up Far Reach where there are a few mean cottages, not far up the road. You are to go with them."

"I'd rather stay here and do my share of shooting."

Moray shook his head. "Colonel Moseley is in command. He has set each man to his task. You'll have the horses at your disposal. You're to leave as soon as the ship heaves in sight. The women are gathering at the chapel. MacAlpin has told them what they're to do."

Edward walked quickly towards the chapel. He found MacAlpin and Gabrielle. The women and children were already moving through the gates. Outside, some of the men had the horses and were helping the women to mount. A few women were vocal in their disapproval.

Eunice Caslett said to him, "I don't want to go. I have my goods packed, ready to leave on the *Delicia*. My husband and my children and I are goin' to England."

MacAlpin interposed: "You'll go, Madam, if I have to bind and gag you."

Eunice's face grew red with anger. She opened her mouth to speak, but her husband motioned to her to hold her peace.

"I'll get your horse," Edward said to Gabrielle.

She moved close to him, dropping her voice so none of the women could hear her words. "I'm not going. We can't move my mother, so I must stay."

"I'll stay with you," he protested.

MacAlpin overheard him. "We need you with us, Colston. Come, it will take a little time to get this procession out of reach of the ship's guns."

Mary Treloar went up to Gabrielle. "I'd not leave my new house for any pirate, were it not for Amos saying they need me to keep the women in order."

"That we do, Mary Treloar," Sandy said. "You're as good as half a dozen men. Come. March, my girl; step out and let us fall into line, I'll go ahead, Mr. Colston. You follow and look after the stragglers. March! Forward march!"

The women moved off through the gate, the children by their sides. A pitiful little procession, walking away from a known danger, towards some unknown danger.

Gabrielle watched them move out through the gate into the forest before she went back to the house. Barton had closed and bolted all the shutters and set up settees and chairs as barricade to the front door. When she went around the side of the house, she saw four Negroes standing near the kitchen door. They were huddled together for protection, three men and a woman. They were half naked, thin and starved-looking. She had never seen them before, so she thought, until one man stepped forward. Then she recognized the old runaway slave she had seen near the swamp.

"Mistress, hide us! Hide us!" he cried. She saw he was terrified. They were all terrified, their hands shaking.

"The pirates! The pirates!They'll put us on ships and carry us away." He held out supplicating hands. "Mistress, we're your slaves. Save us."

Gabrielle was at a loss what to do. Her father would have no slaves in the settlement. He had expressed his opinion of slavery more than once.

"What's wrong?" a voice asked. "Where did these Negroes come from?"

Gabrielle turned to David Moray with quick relief. "They're runaway Negroes, from the swamp. They're afraid the pirates will find them and carry them off in their ships."

"Let me talk to them," David said. "Perhaps they have some information that will be useful."

The old Negro was reluctant to speak at first. After a consultation with the others, he said, "The big ship, she belong Bonnet, a bad man. We know him from Bermuda. The little sloop, she sail for a lady dressed lak a man. She pirate, too. Bad woman. She shoot and kill and strike with cutlash, lak a man. She name Bonney."

Moray had heard enough about Anne Bonney from the men on the *Delicia* to understand why the Africans had left their hiding place in the swamp to seek shelter at the settlement.

The old man looked at Gabrielle. "You save Annaci, Mistress. Annaci and his people serve you, yes?"

Gabrielle looked at Moray for her answer. He nodded affirmation.

"Have you had food?" she asked. The old man shook his head.

"I'll see that they get something. Then I'll let Amos put them to work, where the men are throwing up sand against the stockade for a redoubt. Don't worry," Moray said, looking at her troubled face. "We'll manage, somehow."

"I don't want to give way to any pirates' demand," she said, her chin firm and determined. "I don't think my father quite understands . . ." She stopped short, realizing her words bordered on disloyalty.

"Nor I," said David shortly.

He strode away towards the south gate, the Negroes at his heels. Gabrielle watched him with troubled eyes. His innate strength shone in his eyes and in his firm voice. She was suddenly glad he was here—someone to turn to in trouble. She moved slowly towards the house. She would sit near the door to her mother's room. If the ship fired on them, she must be near by to take whatever action was necessary.

To her repeated rapping Barton opened the door a crack. She and Celestine had barricaded it.

"We've buried the plate," she announced. "We dug a hole at the root of a big cypress tree at the edge of the swamp. I don't intend that pirates shall have your mother's nice silver pots or trays."

"Thank you, Barton. You think of everything."

She took off the little riding hat with its gay plume, and flung it on a chest. Her riding skirt was hooked up over her high boots so she could move freely.

Celestine came in breathing heavily, her fat body shaking from the effort. "Come quick! I see a sailing boat, just there, beyond the point. See, it is a beeg, beeg ship, like a Spaniard. Is it the pirate, Miss Gabrielle?"

Barton and Gabrielle followed her to the hall window. There it was, canvas spread to catch every breath of wind, sailing towards them. The departing sun splashed the great sails with gold, and the breast of the river was a gold pathway.

A puff of smoke lay on the air, above the forward deck. A moment later there was a heavy booming sound. The pirates had fired over the stockade—a single shot, a warning shot, to show that the ship came as an enemy, with evil intent.

Gabrielle ran to the door to look out. The men were along the stockade, guns in hand, peering through the peepholes. She saw her father. He stood under a great oak tree with David Moray and Amos Treloar. It seemed to her that the men were pleading with him. He was shaking his head in negation.

A second shot boomed out. This time it was lower. It tore a gap in the stockade, not far from where a watch stood.

Gabrielle went into the house and ran up the stairway to the second floor. From the doghouse window was an unobstructed view far downriver. She saw a second ship coming upstream, a smaller craft, a sloop with a tall mast.

The pirate ship was sending a longboat ashore, armed with a swivel in the bow, pointed towards the landing.

She ran down the steps to her mother's room. Celestine was sitting beside the bed, knitting quietly, as if nothing out of the ordinary routine of the day were taking place.

"I've given Madame a powder. She sleeps, but the guns disturb her. See how her hands move on the cover."

Gabrielle laid her hand on her mother's thin fingers. They moved, restlessly, in her grasp.

"What are we to do?" she asked Celestine.

"I ask the good God that question, Ma'mselle. I ask many times. Now I wait. Whatever comes comes and we must be prepared for good or bad."

"I know," Gabrielle said. "But I wish we could have moved my mother to some safe place inland."

"Madame would not like to waken and see strange things about her." Celestine lifted her knitting and began to count stitches.

Gabrielle turned away, strengthened by the woman's serenity, and took her place at the window. The ship was standing off, in the middle of the channel. The longboat had landed its men at the little wharf. She watched them moving up the path. Six men, each carrying a musket. One man walked ahead.

Her father was going out to meet him. Suddenly, in her fear for him, she ran out of the house to follow him. Halfway down the path, David overtook her. He caught her arm and held her back.

"Are you insane?" he asked angrily.

She struggled, her fingers prying at his, trying to break his hold on her arm. "I am going with my father," she cried. "Let me go!"

"You are staying here, Mistress. I don't want Stede Bonnet to see you. He covets women, and his caresses are not pleasant."

"How dare you speak to me in this manner? Let go of my arm, Moray."

"Not unless you promise to remain here," he said, his voice harsh.

"How can you let my father go alone to meet them?" she cried. "Are you all cowards?"

"Your father has given the order. I do not like to obey, nor does Colonel Moseley, but we have no choice. Don't

401

worry. He's covered by armed men in the trees and behind the stockade."

"How much good will that do, if they shoot him first?"

"That's the chance he is taking of his own wish, my child."

Gabrielle turned around. Moseley had come up without her knowledge. He, too, had a worried look in his eyes. "We protested, but your father thought his way best. He wants to deal with the pirates. He thinks they will go away satisfied, if he pays ransom money. He may be right." Moseley stopped. He watched the little group of men from the ship as they came to the gate of the stockade. He whistled softly. "Do you hear what that impudent rascal is saying?"

Gabrielle listened. "Captain Bonnet requests the leaders of this settlement to come aboard the *Royal James* for a consultation."

David said, "I'll go along."

Moseley protested. "I'd better be the one."

"No. You're in charge here. If anything happens on the ship, you're the one to take charge of the defence." He moved off swiftly and fell in step beside Fountaine.

Gabrielle caught Moseley's arm, to steady herself. "They'll be killed!" she whispered. "They'll be killed!"

"They are in the hands of God," Moseley said solemnly. He looked upstream in the direction the *Delicia* had sailed at daybreak. Gabrielle knew he hoped Captain Bragg would return in time to help them. He had guns and ammunition and there might be a chance.

She thought of her mother. She knew her place was at her side. When she got back to the house, she found the runaway Negroes near the door. The old man had a mattock in his hands and the others were armed with pitchforks and an axe.

"Master said, Stand by Miss' door and keep guard."

"Thank you," Gabrielle said gratefully. She went into the house.

Barton met her at the door. "Best that you stay inside, Mistress Gabrielle. Don't you let those vermin lay eyes on you."

Gabrielle did not answer. She took her place at the hall window again. From there she could watch the ship. No boat could come or go without passing beneath her eye.

Her father and David, what of them? Were they already prisoners in the hands of ferocious Stede Bonnet? What would pirates do with prisoners? So many tales she had heard, of blood lust and cruelty, of vicious, degenerate,

402

inhuman treatment. She covered her face with her hands; her body shook. Barton came and stood beside her; the woman's firm hand pressed Gabrielle's shoulder as she stood, tall and immovable, looking towards the river.

It was dark. Gabrielle sat before the fire in her mother's small sitting room. One candle burned on the mantel, leaving the room in shadow. An untouched cup of tea was on the small table in front of her. In spite of Barton's pleading she could not bring herself to drink it, or eat the small roll.

"You do yourself no good by starving," the woman said harshly.

"I can't, Barton. Please don't ask me. The food sticks in my throat and my stomach is opening and closing like a fish's gills." Barton went away then, mumbling to herself.

How long she sat there, Gabrielle had no idea. She heard her name spoken. David Moray stood in the open door, grave-faced, serious; he came forward slowly.

"My father?" she asked, fearing the answer.

"Bonnet has him on board his ship. Hostage, he calls it, until I come back with the specie."

"What must we do?" Gabrielle asked. "There's money in Father's escritoire. How much?"

"A great deal, I'm afraid."

"I have my jewelry, if that's not enough," she said rapidly. I'll get it."

Don't go yet. Moseley is coming in a minute. We'll talk over what must be done."

Moseley came in as he spoke. His thin face was as stern as David's.

David said, "Bonnet is not aware that you're here, Moseley. You're too well known to escape ransom, if he finds you."

Moseley laughed shortly. "That pirate Eden got to me first. I've not a cent to my name, since I put up bond."

David walked up and down a moment. "I've tried to think of ways to evade, but I see nothing but to pay what that god-damned devil asks." He turned to Gabrielle with a gesture of apology. "Your father said to ask you to get all the gold in his desk, and the little iron box with the bills of exchange on Jamaica and London."

Gabrielle took a key from a blue hawthorn jar that stood on the mantel and unlocked the desk. From a secret drawer she drew out a buckskin bag of gold coin. The iron box, with the bills of exchange, was in the drawer. She put the box and the bag into David's hands.

"What's next?" she asked. "Will they let my father go when he pays this ransom?"

"I think so. Yes, I think so." Moseley spoke reassuringly. "I've sent messages up Far Reach to MacAlpin to acquaint him with the situation. He will be able to intercept Bragg at the Forks."

David said, "If Bragg does get word he is likely to return and give fight. He must not open fire while Mr. Fountaine is aboard the *Royal James*."

Moseley looked troubled. "I should have thought of that. We will have to send a second man by canoe."

"There is a second ship in the river. I saw it before dark," Gabrielle said.

David nodded. He spoke to Moseley: "I heard them say the second ship belonged to Anne Bonney, that notorious woman pirate. They've anchored a prize, under guard, near the spot where we were this morning. Stede Bonnet won't decide about the ransom until Anne Bonney comes aboard the *Royal James*." He laughed significantly. "It seems that Anne wears the breeches in more ways than one."

He moved to the door. Gabrielle followed him into the hall. She clasped her hands about his arm. "Please, David, look after my father. Please."

"I'll do all I can."

"When will you come back?" she asked.

"I don't know. Probably not before morning."

Gabrielle's clasp tightened on his arm. "His life is very precious to us, and to all these poor people who have followed us here," she said, close to tears.

"I know," David said sadly. "I wish to God I could say something to reassure you."

He was down the hall and out of the door before she could speak. After all, what was there to say? There was nothing to do but wait . . . wait, all the night through, until morning.

Moseley looked up from his contemplation of the fire when she came in. "I asked Barton to bring you some food. You must eat, my dear, then get some sleep. There is a competent guard on watch. Each man knows what he's to do. No good is gained by worry." He rose to leave.

Gabrielle stood beside him, looking up at his kind, strong face. "I know, Colonel Moseley. But when I think of my father——" Her voice broke.

"Your father is a man of God, my child. He carries God in his heart. Have no fear."

"Thank you," she said humbly. "I'll try not to forget."

The little French clock on the table struck twelve. Gabrielle got up from the settee and lit another candle. She walked to the hall and opened the outer door. The night was crisp and cold. A north wind had risen, clearing the air. The stars shone with white brilliance. She saw shadows moving up the path that led to the wharf. A lanthorn bobbed along, darting little swords of light.

Gabrielle waited, her hand against her heart. She heard a woman's voice saying, "I'll take what I want. What do I care for an agreement made with Stede Bonnet? You'll find that Anne Bonney makes her own agreements and takes her own tribute. I'll see if these women have things worthy of my notice."

Gabrielle retreated slowly. Once inside, she locked the door that led to her mother's room. She ran across to the drawing-room, Barton close behind her. "Light the fire and the candles. Get brandy, wine and little cakes. Hurry, Barton, hurry. We must keep the woman away from my mother, whatever comes."

"I've told Celestine. She'll lock the door from inside."

"Yes, yes, that's right." She knelt before the fire, working the bellows. The hot ashes caught the fat lightwood and flamed up. In a moment the great pine knot was blazing beneath the dry oak log. Soon the logs would catch the heat and the large fireplace would be filled with the sparkle of lightwood and the acrid smells of pitch pine and oak. She heard a tap at the door, David Moray's voice.

Barton straightened her fluted cap and went to the door. She opened it and stood, erect and forbidding, holding the door wide for the pirate queen.

Anne Bonney, dressed in tight blue trousers and an open-necked shirt of white, came in slowly, her boots clicking on the polished floor. Her quick eyes encompassed the pleasant room with the bright fire, the soft myrtle candles, the young girl standing straight and immobile beside the chintz seat.

There was a moment's silence. Then Gabrielle said, "Will you come to the fire? The night is cool. The warmth will doubtless be welcome to you, Madam."

David flashed a glance of approval.

405

"You needn't be polite, miss. You'll gain nothing. I'll take what I please."

Gabrielle ignored the words. She said to Barton, "Please bring a decanter of brandy and some glasses. Perhaps the lady will do us the honour."

"Anne Bonney is my name. Mayhap you've heard it before."

A faint smile played about Gabrielle's lips, instantly gone. She bowed slightly. "Indeed yes. In England as well as in the Plantations."

Anne came forward and stood before the fire, hands spread to the blaze.

Gabrielle remained by the settee. "Please draw a chair close to the fire for Madam, David."

David slid a wing chair close to the hearth. Anne sat down. Barton returned carrying a black japanned tray; on it were two decanters, one wine, one brandy, with glasses. She pulled a small tripod table beside Anne Bonney's chair and set her glass upon it. "Will you have Madeira or brandy, Madam?" Barton was perfect—imperturbable and calm, as if she had served pirate queens every day in the year.

Anne watched her with cold, calculating eyes as she served David. Gabrielle sat down. David stood back of the settee, his glass in his hand.

"You've taken no liquor," Anne Bonney said.

"I never drink wine," Gabrielle answered, "but I'll have a glass of milk, if you have any, Barton, and bring some of your little cakes. I'm sure our guests will like some of your little currant cakes."

"I, for one," said David, sitting down across from Gabrielle.

Anne Bonney sipped her brandy slowly. Gabrielle sat looking into the fire with easy composure. Her face showed nothing of her thoughts. She might indeed have been entertaining a guest who had sought Robert Fountaine's hospitality.

Anne Bonney did not understand Gabrielle's composure. She was accustomed to fear, or cringing servility, in her captives. Her advent into this room had not caused any change in the orderly living of these people. It puzzled her. After she had finished her brandy, she remarked, "You've made yourself comfortable here in the wilderness."

"It is our home."

David said to Barton, "I'd like another cake, Barton. No one makes such excellent cakes as you."

"You're fair makin' flattery, Mr. Moray," she said. " 'Tis a way the men of Moray Firth have with them."

" 'Tis the truth, I swear, Barton."

"Pass Mr. Moray the plate, Barton," said Gabrielle. "He's been abroad all this day, and he must be starving."

Anne moved restlessly. She put the glass to her lips and finished the last drop. Barton was at her side in an instant with the decanter to pour another glass. Anne, warmed by the wine and the fire, threw off the uncertainty that had fallen upon her since she entered the room. "You stand tall, girl, almost as tall as I. Mayhap you've some fine London clothes that I can take back to my ship?"

Gabrielle hesitated, not more than a second.

"Bring the clothes out of the press in my room, Barton, the slippers, too. Don't forget the blue taffeta with the brocaded flowers. I'm sure the blue will become Madam Bonney."

Anne sat back, a puzzled look on her face. She glanced at David Moray. He got up and went to the fireplace, where he selected a long clay pipe from the rack. He bowed to Anne, then to Gabrielle. "Have I your permission, ladies?"

"I'll have one myself," Anne said promptly.

Gabrielle wondered how long she could keep this up, this play-acting. There was no chance to inquire about her father, nor could David reassure her under the wary eye of the woman. Nothing escaped her. No move, nothing.

Barton came down with a pile of clothes over her arm. Gabrielle saw that she had brought Molly's gowns, not hers. She was about to speak, but a warning look from Barton stopped her. Barton said to Anne Bonney: "There is a little room, just off, where you can try the gowns that please you."

Anne hesitated a moment, but the pile of frocks drew her. She followed Barton.

David did not move, but his low voice reached Gabrielle: "Bonnet will hold your father until the woman is ready to release him. I think he's in no immediate danger."

Gabrielle did not speak, she was trembling violently.

"Steady. Steady. You must not undo the good you've done. Let me get you a glass of milk. I think Barton forgot it."

He left the room. Anne came to the door. She was holding

407

a blue frock belonging to Molly Lepel against her body. "Strange. I'd have said you were as large as I."

Gabrielle answered carelessly, " 'Tis so hard to judge figures."

"Where's Moray?" Anne said, suddenly discovering David's absence from the room.

"He went to the buttery, to get a glass of milk for me."

"I'm so sorry. I quite forgot it, Miss Gabrielle." Barton came back into the room. She moved quietly but she had a triumphant look in her eyes.

"Go after Moray," Anne Bonney said to Barton. "I'm weary of all this. I want him to go back to my ship with me."

Gabrielle rose, as she would have risen had an honoured guest been leaving.

David came in, a glass of milk in his hand. "I'm sorry. I couldn't find the milk jug at first." He was breathing rapidly, as if he had been running. It flashed across Gabrielle's mind that he had gone to Colonel Moseley with some message.

Anne Bonney stopped in the doorway. Something of bewildered anger shone in her face. "You needn't try to bedazzle me with your fine manners, Mistress, nor think yourself above other folk. I own a ship of my own. Yes, and I've taken a prize off the shoals—a sloop, with fifteen men in it, skippered by a fine-actin' redhaired fellow. He wouldn't tell him name. Mayhap he was ashamed to be captured by a woman, but I knew him. I've seen him in the Albemarle when his uncle was governor of the province and he was courtin' the niece of Lady Mary Tower. Michael Cary he is, and I've got him safe and sound, locked up in the hold of the *Royal James*."

Gabrielle's grasp on the back of the settee tightened. Michael Cary! The man Molly wrote of so often. She met Anne Bonney's eyes. They were filled with vindictiveness.

"You know the fine Captain, Mistress," Anne stated, rather than asked.

"No, no." Gabrielle managed some degree of composure. "I don't know anyone of that name."

She glanced at David. There was a cautious, wary look on his face. She wondered what it meant.

Anne wheeled about. "Come, handsome Scot. You'll not get out of my sight. Don't forget you're hostage to Captain Stede Bonnet, you and your fine lady's father. Don't forget."

"I'm not likely to forget," David said glumly.

Anne Bonney walked from the room without further speech. Barton opened the door for her, a candle shielded in her hand to light the way. She all but dropped it when she saw two heavily armed pirates at either side of the door. One had golden rings in his long ears, the other a great scar across his nose.

"Good night," Gabrielle said, but there was no answer. She closed the door quietly. Leaning against it, she clung to the door latch to steady her hand. Her knees trembled so she thought she could not stand erect.

Barton put her arm about her. "Lean on me, Mistress. It's a fine thing you did this night. Fine and brave."

Chapter 28

THE ROYAL JAMES AND STEDE BONNET

The cabin of the *Royal James* was dim and shadowy, filled with smoke from the pirates' pipes and from one flickering candle, set on the bare table. It was silent save only for the clink of gold pieces hitting one on another, as Stede Bonnet counted the contents of the buckskin bag David Moray had brought from the house. Anne Bonney stood by Bonnet, her slim, supple body pressed against his side. Robert Fountaine sat erect in a high-backed chair, thin fingers clasping the carved arms. He was white and very weary and now and then the heavy lids dropped over his tired eyes. David looked at him anxiously. He was so frail, David wondered whether he could stand up under this excitement much longer.

Two sailing masters sat on a bench by the open door, and, outside, half a dozen of the crew, well armed, lounged within easy reach.

David allowed his eyes to drift back to Bonnet. The man looked different from his preconceived notion of a pirate captain. He had a soft face, without lines, and his mouth was petulant rather than firm. He was dressed with some degree of a gentleman's fashion. He wore a fine pearl pin in his lace cravat, and two large diamonds graced his fingers. His periwig was of the accepted chestnut brown, and his dark blue coat well tailored. His pistols lay at hand. They were mounted with pearl and olive-wood handles, overlaid with silver. From time to time he took snuff from a gold and tortoise box, and sneezed into a fine cambric handkerchief.

David thought the pirate woman was beautiful, in a cold, hard way. Two pistols were thrust through the silk girdle and an ivory-handled knife swung from her hip.

Her long hair was set in braids about her head, and she was chewing a snuff stick, making sucking noises from time to time. As she bent over Bonnet and looked at the heaps of gold Johannes, her light blue eyes lit up with avarice.

"A thousand guineas," Bonnet said, pushing the last stack

of gold pieces into the main pile. "A thousand guineas." He looked at Anne Bonney. Neither spoke. David did not know whether the amount would satisfy them or not.

"What about those?" she asked, pointing to the iron box that held the notes on Jamaica and London.

"Another thousand, but they're without value. We can't collect in London . . . or in Jamaica, with Sir Nicholas Law out searching the Caribbean for us."

Anne shut her teeth firmly on the snuff stick and looked at the pile of papers speculatively. "We can't use the London notes, but I'll engage to cash the Jamaica paper. What does it amount to?"

"Five hundred pounds."

She leaned over and took the bundle from the box. She spent some time looking through the papers. "Yes, Stede, I'll engage to cash the Jamaica notes, in spite of Sir Nicholas Law or the Jamaica Fleet." She thrust the paper into the open front of her blouse. Then she pushed the box containing the London notes towards Fountaine. "There, old man, take it. Don't say pirates are without mercy."

Fountaine opened his eyes and looked about slowly. "May I go to my family now?" he asked.

Anne's face darkened. "No. Let them worry. It will do the girl no hurt. She's a proud one. Well, let her pride hold her up while she waits."

David said, "If you let Mr. Fountaine go free, I will give you notes on Edinburgh to the amount of one hundred pounds, and be his hostage."

Anne laughed. "Give notes on hell, for all I care. The old man stays aboard tonight and mayhap tomorrow." She looked at David shrewdly. "What is it? Are you the girl's lover?"

Anger showed in his eyes, but David held himself in check. It would do no good to lose his temper.

Stede pushed Anne aside. "I'll set the ransom price and extract the punishment, my girl. The old one is a pious man. I've seen his lips murmuring prayers. I'll keep him here in my cabin. Perhaps he'll talk to me of spiritual things."

A string of oaths came from Anne Bonney's red lips. "God blast you for a mouthing hypocrite, why do you talk of spiritual things? To ease yourself into some heavenly fringe . . . when you swing?"

Bonnet shivered. "Cease such talk." He said to Herriot

411

harshly, "Take this fellow and lock him in the hold with yesterday's captives."

Anne said, "I'll take custody of Moray, since he is eager to be a hostage for the old man."

Stede looked at her. "No, you don't, my girl. I don't trust you. You'd have him in your bed before the hour's past. I'll take care of him."

"A hostage is entitled to proper treatment, by rights of war," David protested. He didn't relish the idea of being turned over to Anne Bonney.

Bonnet's face darkened. His eyes grew small in his heavy face. "We have rules of our own, fellow."

David said no more. A thought had come to him: If they put him in the hold with the other prisoners, he might find Michael Cary; perhaps the two of them could discover some way to escape. At the moment there was nothing he could do, not so long as Bonnet held Robert Fountaine hostage.

"Take him below," Bonnet said to a guard. "No, don't bind his hands. Let him see that the rules of the Brotherhood in regard to hostages is as civil as any."

The hold was dark and evil-smelling. David stumbled over inert bodies of men, trying to find his way. For this he got a kick and curses as the men turned, disturbed in their heavy slumber. He made his way to a vacant spot directly under a lanthorn, and sat down, his back against the side of the ship. He thought, If I sit in the light, Cary will see me, if he's here.

For a long time he sat without moving. Then he began to whistle softly, a little ditty the Jacobite troops sang when they marched. Finally he heard a faint echo. Someone was answering. It must be Cary. He signalled by whistling a second bar.

A harsh voice broke the quiet. "Love of Christ, quit your trilling! It's enough to drive a man crazy, whistling and singing in the night."

David did not stir. He sat with closed eyes, leaning back, as though he slept against the boards. There was nothing to do but wait. If it were really Cary, he would make some further sign. They must do nothing to arouse suspicion. He waited an hour or more, it seemed to him, in the stinking darkness of the hold. He heard quick skittering movements as the rats came out of their hiding. Men snored and stretched, cursed in their drunken slumber. He closed his eyes, unable longer to fend off sleep.

412

David wakened suddenly. Someone had touched him lightly on the arm. "Sh-h," a voice whispered. He leaned forward in the gloom, to make out the prostrate body of a man. He bent close.

"I saw your face. I remember you from Bristol's Inn of the Rose. I'm Michael Cary."

"Yes. I know. The woman Bonney boasted she had you prisoner."

"God's breath! My luck was evil the day I sailed north to hunt for pirate ships. They ran me between them, over shoals, smack into a sand bar."

David asked, "Are you tied?"

"Yes, damn them to hell! Trussed up like a fowl on a spit."

"Roll close. I'll lie down beside you. My hands are free." David eased himself until he lay full length on the floor beside Cary. Fumbling in the dark, he found the man's bound wrists and set to work. A figure eight, a hard knot to loose. He worked carefully, not to arouse the sleepers. Once a guard opened the door and flashed a lanthorn. No one moved save a man near the opening, who cursed and covered his eyes with his hand to shut out the light.

After a time Cary's hands were free. It took David longer to get himself into position to work on his leg ropes. The knots were hard, and pulled close from having been soaked in water.

Cary said, "I'm so numb I can't move. Slip your hand into my boot. There's a knife there that the devils overlooked when they stripped me of my arms."

David found the knife and passed it into Cary's hand. Lying at full length, side by side, they talked in low, cautious voices, trying to devise some way of escape. David described the creek landing and the stockade. "If you can swim ashore, go far up the creek towards the swamp before you attempt to land. You'll then be out of sight of the ships and the landing place, where the pirates have a guard. Make your way along the edge of the swamp to the River Road. Then you'll be reasonably safe."

"Will you not make the try with me?" Cary whispered.

"No, I cannot. I'm a hostage and if I break my word, they'll make reprisals on the old gentleman. I've been thinking: your best time will be before daylight. Creep near the door. When the guard swings the light may be your opportunity. Are these men prisoners or crew?"

413

"I can't be sure. Some of them may be crew. I daren't take a chance."

David followed Cary as he moved slowly towards the door. A grunt and a muttered imprecation, followed by a querulous voice crying out that he had been hit by a stone. Other voices shouted for quiet. In the confusion Cary and David took places close to the door. David made the plan. When the guard came, he'd throw his cape over the lanthorn and cover the man's head. In the darkness, Cary would strike with his knife. If he were lucky and killed the fellow without outcry, then he'd make his way to the deck and over the side. A splash would mean nothing, if there was no commotion from the hold. There were 'gators in these waters. Often they rose to the surface or splashed off a floating log.

"When you get to the stockade, ask for Miss Fountaine," David said.

"Fountaine?" Cary's voice had a strangeness in it as he repeated the name.

"Yes, Mistress Gabrielle Fountaine. Tell her you have come from the *Royal James*. She's quick-witted. She'll show you a hiding place in the swamp where you will be safe for the present."

He felt a warning pressure on his hand. Heavy footsteps sounded on the deck, moving in their direction. David rose and stood close to the door. When it opened, he threw his cloak over the lanthorn and over the man's head as well. Cary moved at the same time, striking swiftly. David felt the guard go slack against his arm. He lowered the body to the floor, then made his way quietly back to his place, having care to bring his cloak with him.

The whole incident took only a few moments. David trusted Cary would get clear of the ship and land in safety. There was nothing more he could do, so he rolled his cloak into a pillow and fell asleep. His last waking thought was that he hoped there was no blood on it for the pirates to discover on the morrow.

The boom of cannon brought David Moray to his feet. He stood swaying from his violent contact with a beam. The shot reverberated along the water and seemed to hit the distant bank.

"God's breath!" shouted someone on deck. "A guardship, upriver. To stations, men! Haul up the mains'l! Weigh anchor!"

414

Orders beat out against the wind like cracking whips. Half the men in the hold jumped up at the first call for stations, and ran towards the door. The first man sprawled over the body of the guard, which had fallen and stiffened in the passageway.

He let out a yell when he touched the cold face of the corpse. But he scrambled to his feet and ran on. The second did not even look down. He thrust the dead man out of the way with his heavy boot. The stiffened body rolled from one side of the passage to the other as the men tumbled, cursing and shouting, to their stations.

David thought, It must be Bragg, letting go with the *Delicia's* guns. The door swung back and forth on its rusty hinges. In the gloom David made out two men tied together, lying back of the door. He ran across the space and began to work on the ropes that bound them. He did not know whether they were rebellious pirates or members of Cary's crew, but they were prisoners. If there was to be a fight, they might be of use to him.

The noise and shouting above grew louder. They were dragging a heavy object across the deck. A deck gun, thought David. He finished the first man and set his hands free. "Loosen the ropes on your feet, while I get at this fellow."

"No need, Master. He's dead. All night long I've been tied to a dead man, but I durst not cry out for fear I'd be dead beside him."

"Who are you?" David asked, as he pulled the last strand through the loop and set the man free.

"I'm off a market boat out of Bath. Greening's my name, sir. We landed on Ocracock and Vane hanged my father. May his soul rot in hell!"

"Can you stand?"

"May can," the young fellow replied. He pulled himself up and moved his legs back and forth. "They'll come alive in a minute."

David turned the dead man over. He took a knife from his belt, but he did not find his pistol.

The boy spoke guardedly. "Over there behind the door I see the glint of steel."

David pushed the door. The pistol lay on the floor, near the water cask. He picked it up. A further search discovered the belt with a sack of balls and priming.

"You take the knife. What I want you to do is to keep
415

guard while I get to the cabin. There's an old man there we must find before they kill him."

He looked the man in the eye. "No private vengeance until we rescue Mr. Fountaine—understand?"

"Yes, but . . ."

David did not wait. He stepped cautiously out of the passage and up the ladder to the deck. All was thick and confusion. Stede Bonnet stood up near the charthouse, a glass held to his eyes, but it was the sailing master who gave orders. Anne Bonney was nowhere to be seen.

"Yonder goes a sloop." Greening spoke in his ear. "Running like a scared hen."

David looked over his shoulder. Anne Bonney's sloop had hoisted anchor and was under way. As she swung round, her starboard gun blazed out, aimed at the stockade. A second blazed, and the ball curved over towards a little house above the wharf. He could not see whether it had struck or not.

David held his breath, but there was no returning fire from the stockade. That was Moseley. Moseley would not let them fire on the ship while Bonnet held Fountaine.

Bragg had fired one shot only. He had apparently surmised that hostages might be held on Stede Bonnet's boat.

No one noticed David as he crossed behind the deck guns and made his way towards the cabin, Greening behind him. The cabin was unguarded. The door opened without difficulty. Fountaine rose from his chair, smiling for a moment when David entered.

"I did not know what they had done with you, David, but I prayed for you," he said simply.

"Thank you, sir. I needed prayer. We both need it, I think." He glanced around the room. He could barricade the door. The port was too small for anyone to enter, but he must close it, for fear of pistol fire. Greening did not need to be told. He closed the door and let the bar fall into place. As he did so, they heard the cannon fire begin. It rocked the deck. Over the sound of firing, they could hear the canvas whipping and the creak of windlass and rattle of anchor chains.

"They'll run for it," Greening said. "Tide's going out."

Fountaine sat down, his face calm and undisturbed. David saw his lips moving.

As the ship swung around, David looked through the porthole. A fire was burning on the hill, sending up heavy smoke. The last shot from the sloop had hit the cottage and fired it. Whose cottage was it—Treloar's or Caslett's? He couldn't remember. He saw men running along the bank; then the ship tacked and the stockade and the burning house were outside his vision.

They had caught the breeze and were running downstream. He wondered why Bonnet did not stand to fight. It must be that the channel was too narrow here and he wanted more room to manoeuvre his larger and more unwieldy ship.

Greening came to the port. "The sloop's got up her spinnaker and her flying jib. She's making headway."

Fountaine said, "I do not worry about myself. I'm old; but there are my wife and my daughter to think of. I'll not let them kill me. I must not die until my work is finished."

David wondered how he could defend himself if Bonnet took a notion to break down the door. A thought came to his mind, strangely comforting. Perhaps a man's faith was a shield, a buckler against danger.

David walked about the narrow room with growing impatience. Shut up here like a rat in a trap, unable to fight his way out, or take a chance, as Cary had done. He wondered whether Cary had gone clear, whether he was even now sitting beside the fire, with Gabrielle and Barton listening to his story as they fed him with tea and bacon and fresh-laid eggs. The thought of food was an annoyance and gave him a queer feeling in his stomach. Or was it the food? Perhaps it was the thought of Cary, with his handsome face and his bold, reckless eyes, that annoyed him.

Suddenly he broke off his pacing. A picture filled his mind: the wharf at Bristol, the handsome Michael manoeuvring Molly Lepel away from her party. A ladies' man was Cary, a bold wooer with an eye for fair women. An oath escaped him. He flexed the muscles of his strong arms and fingers.

The ship was gaining speed now. He heard the splash of water against the side, footsteps running outside the cabin, a hoarse voice shouting, "Fire, you swine! Fire!" Then came the roar of a cannon. Again the order and another burst of sound rolled through the little room. Stede Bonnet's voice: "Bring out the old man. Tie him up to the mast where they can see him."

"Stand back, sir," David said, stepping quickly in front of Fountaine. "Stand well back, behind the chest. They'll force the door. Greening, you stand opposite. Don't move until I give the order."

Fountaine said, "I'll open the door."

David pleaded with him. "Don't. We can defend ourselves in this room."

"I gave my word to make no defence," Fountaine replied.

Greening said to David, "Want I should hit him? Lay him asleep for a little so we can fight?"

David shook his head. "No, we must do as Mr. Fountaine says."

Greening's face darkened. "I've a vengeance in my heart. I must get rid of it."

Moray spoke sharply: "Your vengeance can wait. This is not the life of one man. It's the fate of a settlement. Perhaps his way is best, though for myself I don't like it." He hid his pistol in the front of his shirt and opened the door.

Stede Bonnet stood outside, a pistol in his hand. When he saw Moray, his eyes turned to gimlets.

"I thought you were in the hold."

"So I was. But the firing brought me on deck." He glanced over Bonnet's shoulder. He saw the *Delicia* under full rig, in swift pursuit. "You're running away," he said smiling insolently.

"Keep your tongue between your teeth, my fine cockalorum. You'll get your punishment when we reach our rendezvous." The hard look in his eyes deepened. "A merry time my men will have with you, fine sir, arunning the gantlet, with the rushes striking at your bare behind. Aye, and I have a man who is a fair hand at slitting proud noses and slicing off ears."

David did not answer. He did not take his eyes from Bonnet's, or erase the smile from his lips. "I'd prefer to cross blades with you, Gentleman Stede," he said. He wanted to keep the man roused at him, so he would forget Fountaine. "I wager I'd set you back on your heels."

Stede's petulant mouth hardened. "I've no time for crossin' blades with a prisoner."

David laughed derisively. "Ah, you're afraid! I've been told you were yellow-livered. You're afraid of my steel."

" 'Tis a lie, a great lie. Stede Bonnet fears no man."

"Well, a wager then. A fair fight on deck, with Fountaine's freedom for the prize."

"And your freedom?" Stede asked, a look of cunning on his face.

David shrugged his wide shoulders indifferently: "I'm your prisoner, whatever way the dice fall. Come, Bonnet, show that you have sporting blood and take a gambler's chance."

418

A sly smile came over Bonnet's lips. "If you'll put up the Edinburgh notes as well, I'll give you a bout."

"Now? Will you fight now?"

Stede glanced over his shoulder. "Why not? We're out of range of that guardship."

Moray went into the cabin to take off his coat. He slipped the pistol to Greening. "Stand where you can watch my back. I don't want anyone slipping up on me," he said, and went out to meet his opponent.

The deck was slippery from night moisture. David selected a sword from a pair Bonnet's man offered, felt its temper, bending the blade with both hands, whipping the air.

"No interference from outside," he said, nodding towards the crew, who stood gaping at them.

"Understood," Bonnet replied, taking position.

David glanced over his shoulder. Fountaine had·gone into the cabin, but Greening stood, back to the door, watching. A stout lad, with the keen eyes of a man used to the open, he made David feel easier.

The steel of Stede Bonnet's blade met David's. After a few moments spent in exploiting exchange, Bonnet's face changed; a puzzled frown came between his eyes. "Strange," he muttered. "Strange! I seem to remember someone else who used such a method of attack."

David grinned. "Perhaps it was in Nassau, on a dark and moonless night." .

"Gad! So it was. Ha, I have a deeper reason to kill you. You disarmed me that night."

David moved cautiously. An old trick, to talk and distract. He knew all the tricks. His father had taught him fencing with a broad-sword. He had cautioned him about these tricks to engage a fighter's attention, then strike.

"I was drunk that night in Nassau," Bonnet continued.

David laughed. He knew the wound to Bonnet's vanity was still open and raw. "Perhaps," he said, thrusting and withdrawing rapidly. The blade touched Bonnet's arm—a pin-prick only. "Drive your crew back. I don't like their nearness," Moray said, as the pirates crept near to them.

"Herriot, send these fellows to their stations. This is a gentleman's affair, not a matter of entertainment for the crew."

Bonnet was a swordsman. It took all of David's skill to evade his thrusts. But David, too, was sharp in swordcraft. His father had learned his skill under the great Scot swordsman, Sir William Hope. He had a trick or two in reserve. He parried and evaded Bonnet's attack; Bonnet feinted, but David was ready. A simple attack followed by a compound attack was Bonnet's style. Well, let him come. David received his sword on his own and turned it aside.

Bonnet was winded. His heavy breathing came over the clash of swords. Back of them, David saw the crew at their stations, but they watched the play from mast and rigging and gun.

The ship was under full sail now. Far back he saw the *Delicia*. She had only mainsail up. She was not pursuing. David wondered at that. Then he cleared his mind of diverting thoughts. He had all he could do to keep Bonnet from beating him down or making a touch.

"Well thrust!" A woman's voice behind him. David did not pause when Anne Bonney spoke. She moved across the deck and sat on a coil of rope, not far from the cabin where Greening kept guard.

"Go away, Anne," Bonnet said. "You divert me."

"Perhaps I'll also divert your opponent."

"No fear," laughed David. "Bonnet doesn't allow me to take my eye off him or my mind either."

"Your reach is longer and you're ten years younger, Moray," Bonnet said.

A smile came over David's lips. His opponent was feeling the strain.

Bonnet charged. He was looking for an opening. He feinted again, a cut-over, and David was safe. Lunge and parry, lunge and parry went on for some minutes. Each time David caught the blade and turned it aside.

Suddenly David brought his knee forward, lunged and thrust, his point touching Bonnet's neck, drawing a thin line of blood across the base of the throat to the chest.

"*Touché!*" Moray cried, and stepped back, his sword down.

Bonnet, enraged, thrust again. David leapt back in time.

"For shame, Stede!" cried Anne Bonney. "Have you forgotten you're duelling as a gentleman, not fighting as a pirate? For shame!"

Bonnet dropped his sword point.

"You acknowledge defeat?" David asked, staying out of range.

"I acknowledge defeat," Bonnet said, his face dark.

"What was the prize?" Anne Bonney asked, looking from one to the other.

"The freedom of the old man." Bonnet looked at Anne in doubt.

"Why not? He can do no harm, and we have his golden Jos."

Bonnet's face brightened. "Yes, we have ransom aplenty. We'll proceed downriver, pick up our prize and sail to our next objective."

Anne nodded. "Send the old man ashore, but I think I'll keep the young man for a while. I need a good swordsman as a guard. I'll take him on the *Queen Anne* when we pick up my prize at the cove."

Bonnet wheeled around. "I'll keep him on my ship," he said, glowering. "None of your tricks, Madam."

Anne shrugged her shoulders and walked off without troubling to make reply. David looked from one to the other. Who wore the breeches? He wasn't quite sure. He handed his sword to Bonnet. "My man Greening can row Mr. Fountaine ashore," he said.

Bonnet scowled. "I'll set Fountaine ashore myself, when the right time comes." He strode off in the direction Anne had taken.

Greening said, "I coulda shot him in his fat belly while you fought."

David shook his head, smiling at the boy's earnestness. "No. That wouldn't have followed the rules. Your time will come."

Robert Fountaine came to the door. His face was composed, his voice quiet. "Take no vengeance, my son. The destiny of this scoundrel is in the hands of Providence. His doom is close upon him." He spoke slowly. "The day is not far."

A feeling came to David that the godly man was speaking outside himself. He was seeing a vision as the biblical prophets had seen destruction of men and cities.

"I see ships and a long dock and crowds of people watching." Fountaine's eyes had a strange fanatical look. "I see gibbets and many men hanging by the neck, dead. Bonnet is there. I see his purple face and his protruding tongue. He dies hard. God's curse is upon him."

Bonnet and Anne Bonney came behind him. Bonnet's face was working, his eyes flashed.

"God damn you to hell!" he shouted, livid with anger at

Fountaine's words. He stepped forward and struck Fountaine on the face with the back of his hand. David and Greening sprang at the same instant, but half a dozen of the crew were upon them. Catching at them by the arms, the crewmen twisted viciously. David clenched his teeth. The pain at the shoulder was agonizing. Greening went sickly white.

Anne caught Bonnet's arm; her voice had fear in it. "Send the old man ashore, Stede. He'll bring bad fortune to us and to the ship. . . . Don't you remember your dream . . . ?"

Anne's words had a strange effect on Bonnet. His face changed. A frightened look came into his eyes.

"I had forgotten," he mumbled. "I will not listen to his curses. Send him ashore, Anne. Quick, I tell you. He will bring evil upon me."

Anne called the bo's'n. "Lower a boat!" she ordered. "Send two sailors to set this man ashore. Land him at the cove where our prize is anchored. Hold the boat until I come. I'm going aboard my sloop as soon as these prisoners are in the cabin under guard."

David made one more effort. "I'll go with Mr. Fountaine. I, too, was hostage. Since you've accepted ransom, by the rules of civilized warfare, I'm also free."

"We play no war game according to the Royal Navy rules, Moray." Anne Bonney's voice was sharp. "Take these other two to the cabin and put a guard at the door."

David resisted but his captors pushed him forward, twisting his arms until he could have screamed. He bore the pain stoically. Fountaine gave him a reassuring look as he passed.

He heard the sound of oarlocks and the ripple of water as the small boat pulled away from the ship. It didn't matter what happened to him now that Fountaine was safe ashore.

Moray stretched out on the floor. Greening placed a heavy chair against the door and sat down in it, facing the square port. He would be ready if any of the crew crept upon them. David thought they were in no immediate danger. He'd probably be carried to their rendezvous, there to have punishment meted out according to some diabolical plan Bonnet would think up. Punished he would be, for Bonnet carried the smart of two defeats by sword at his hand.

He thought of Cary. He wondered if he had escaped and found his way to the settlement. A handsome devil. Would he, in his present condition, catch the fancy of Gabrielle? Fool that he was to send Cary to her! Why hadn't he told the fellow to seek out Sandy MacAlpin or Amos Treloar?

The ship was moving downstream; the murmur of the water against the sides was soothing. After a little his eyes closed.

David was awakened suddenly by some violent shock. Greening, dozing in his chair, was thrown sprawling to the floor. The ship quivered and rocked.

"She's hit a bar," Greening said, struggling to his feet. The ship listed. David slid against the wall. He scrambled to his feet and looked out of the port. He stood silent for a moment, looking at the tall masts of two ships, their hulls hidden by the low spit. A strange place for ships to anchor, so near the river entrance. He motioned to Greening.

"What do you make of these ships?" he asked. "Is this a pirate rendezvous?"

The lad studied the position for some minutes. Then he began to laugh, a low heaving laugh that shook his whole body.

"Those ships are run aground, too—this side of Barren Head. I've been aground there myself, more'n once. If you don't ketch the river just right, she fools you. Yes, sir, she's a mighty crafty river, she is."

David stared at him. Then he laughed silently. Three ships aground, within a quarter of a mile of one another.

The boy turned to the port again. "Look ye, sir. There goes Mr. Mainwairing's sloop *Francis* and the other that lay in the cove. They're sailing right past the grounded ones."

Two puffs of smoke rose above the sand spit. After a moment the boom of cannon fire came to their ears. What could it mean—the grounded ships firing at Anne Bonney's sloop?

Moray sat down on the edge of the bed, trying to think. Something stirred in his mind, some talk he'd heard when he was at Queen's Gift. Ah, he remembered. Governor Eden. His indignation because the Governor of Virginia was sending two ships to chase down the pirates. Other talk he had heard at the same time. Ships were to be sent from South Carolina under Colonel Rhett, for the sole purpose of seeking out Stede Bonnet.

"Can't ary of them move 'fore morning tide," Greening said, his eyes gleaming with satisfaction. "They're stuck fast, so they be. Nighttime, we can try to get ashore."

Moray nodded. He put his fingers to his lips. He had heard a footstep close at hand. Someone beyond the door, listening.

423

Outside, noise rose. Ballast was being shifted and stones were dropped overboard with a splash.

"Wasting time," the boy said. "She's rammed deep into the long bar."

Dusk came. They could see nothing now from the port. It was full dark when the guard flung open the door and set a bowl of soup and two mugs on the table, and lit a candle.

David was thinking fast. If they could only find out what ships lay at the entrance. He called the guard back as he was crossing the threshold. The fellow stopped; his heavy, brutal face turned slowly. David slid a coin into his hand.

"Tell the bo's'n that this lad is a river pilot." The man hesitated a moment, then went off without speaking.

David said, "If they send you out in a boat to reconnoitre, you might warn the other ships—if they're merchantmen and not pirates."

"The masts are tall," the boy remarked. "One has three, a big fast ship."

"So I discerned. Therefore I take her for a pursuit ship. We'd do a good deed to warn them before Bonnet gets clear in the morning."

"You'd go with me, sir?"

David shook his head. "Bonnet won't let me free. He has some diabolical plan—that I know. But for you, there's a chance. We may be able to convince him that he needs a river pilot. I'm counting on that."

Greening grinned. "I'm his man," he said, catching the drift of David's thoughts.

They drank the greasy soup the guard brought them, because their stomachs were crying out, and waited. The night was heavy on the river, and there were no stars overhead.

It must have been onto nine when Bonnet flung open the door and strode into the room. "Where's the fellow who knows this damned river?"

Moray indicated Greening with a nod. "He's a market-boat pilot. He knows all the rivers and inlets behind the Banks."

"How did you know I lacked a pilot?" he asked.

Moray laughed. "You're aground, aren't you? There are two ships waiting for you, beyond the bar. Great ships, well ordnanced."

Bonnet wheeled. "You God-benighted devil you! Shut your lips or I'll have you under the lash." He strode out of the

424

cabin, Greening following behind him. The boy gave Moray a significant look as he passed. Moray knew he was shrewd and cunning. He might outwit the low-browed evil fellows that made up Bonnet's crew.

Moray got up and bolted the door. He was long enough in the entrance to see that the crew was clearing the deck, making ready for action. God's breath! If he could only get out of this stinking hole and make for the shore. But not now, when the deck swarmed with men and officers. Later, perhaps, before dawn, or in the excitement of manoeuvring the ship off the bar. He had no desire to stay aboard the *Royal James* while the guns of a merchantman or a ship-of-war pounded its decks . . . unless . . . unless . . . A thought entered his mind. He grinned with satisfaction while he paced up and down the cabin. With luck, he might do some damage to the *Royal James*. He opened the door. Instantly a guard stood in front of him.

David said, "I want fresh air to blow through this hole. Ah, an east wind. It brings the smell of the sea."

The guard pushed against him. "Get within," he growled and pricked Moray's leg with the point of his knife.

Moray clinked two coins in his hand. "I want the door left open so I can sleep."

The pirate turned to see that no one was watching. He put his hand behind his back, as he stood looking out on the deck. Moray slipped the coins into his palm.

"Blow your light," the guard said loudly. "Blow your light and lay ye down. If you try to pass through the door, I'll strew your bowels on the deck."

Moray went back into the room, blowing the candle as he passed to the couch. He lay down and faced the open door. After a time he saw a rift in the sky. A little thin streamer of moonshine slid through the clouds, making it possible to detect the movement on the deck. They were bringing up ordnance and preparing for action. At sunrise there would be a fight.

The guard changed at midnight. He shut the door with a bang. Moray got up and opened it. The guard stood back to the cabin, his hands behind him. He had been told by the first man that the prisoner had money. David laid a coin in his palm. "I'd like a drink. Rum, if you can get it."

The man nodded, and Moray went back into the cabin. This time he got a good view of the after-deck gun. It was placed just beyond his cabin. Sometime later the guard came in, set a mug on the table and went out again. David drank the raw spirits at a gulp. It burned all the way down, but it brought a pleasant glow and an illusion of strength to his body. He stretched himself on the couch again. A little rest he must have, if he were to follow his plan—one he could carry out only if Greening returned.

He lay in the dark thinking. In what a strange channel his life had run, since he rode off to war for the Pretender! If he hadn't followed the ancient pattern of his family, and come out to ride with the Stuarts and battle for their rights, he might be living now on the Firth of Moray, in the ancient seat of the Morays, drinking good whisky, riding when it pleased him, seeing his friends and neighbours at Mass and town meetings, visiting the homes of his friends, increasing his flocks and herds.

Ah, well! A man's destiny lay beyond his ken. He thought of Gabrielle Fountaine and his heart softened. Of late she had been a little kinder . . . only because he stood by her father. He smiled in the dark. Perhaps it was the destiny of the Morays to take up someone else's trouble. First the Stuarts, now Fountaine. One thing he had determined: He would buy land, just beyond Fountaine's holdings. MacAlpin told him it was good. He was pleased to have Sandy as a partner. The MacAlpins and the Morays had been friends these many centuries.

Greening spoke to him. He said, "The tall ship is commanded by a man named Rhett, from Charles Town. Two ships he has, the *Henry* and the *Sea Nymph*. I made the chance to get aboard the *Henry*. I bet the fellows in the longboat that I could climb up to the deck of the *Henry* and spy out their guns. The fools let me go."

"Good man!" said David. "Good man."

"I saw the Captain. I told him that Stede Bonnet's ship was lodged fast on the bar, her guns and number of men. Rhett's stuck, too. But the tide will float him before it floats this ship."

Moray nodded, but he didn't interrupt.

"By sunrise the tide will float the *Henry*. Then Captain Rhett will sail upriver and engage."

"Where are the other sloops?" David asked.

"The got through, and over the bar. Rhett dared not fire, for he did not know whether they were friend or foe. He did a good round of cursing when he found out that the pirate queen sailed right past his nose."

426

He slipped away, leaving David to think over the information he had brought. He would watch his time. In the confusion of righting the ship they might be able to get away unnoticed.

The tide was rising. A fresh breeze sprang up. The crew was working feverishly, shifting ballast to lighten the prow so that when the high water reached her, the ship could free herself.

Bonnet had his guns loaded and the gun crews standing by. He paced the deck, his glass trained on the masts of Rhett's ship.

He handed the glass to his boatswain, Pell, with an exclamation of disgust and anger. Rhett's two ships were off the bar. They were making for the *Royal James* with all sail.

Moray had talked over a plan with Greening. It was now almost time to put it into effect. In the excitement of the first fire, they would make for the nearest swivel, overpower the crew and fire into the sails and riddle them. If they were successful they'd go over the side and swim under water until they reached a near-by small island made up of drifted logs that had tangled together. Here they'd be concealed.

The plan pleased Greening when David explained it. He signalled to him now, loosened his knife in its sheath and prepared to move on the gun crew. As Greening sidled up to him, careful that none of the crew saw them talking together, Moray said, "We will wait until they exchange the first shots."

The *Henry* was nearing the *Royal James*, almost within gunshot, when she ran aground again. But the *Sea Nymph* manoeuvred so that Bonnet was forced out of the channel into shoal water; again the *James* rammed the long bar and stuck, this time within range of the *Henry's* guns.

Both grounded ships were now tilted in the same direction. The deck of the *James* was away from Rhett's *Henry*, leaving Rhett's deck open to the pirates' gunfire. Rhett acted instantly, and put a broadside into the hull of the *Royal James*.

This was the moment David had prayed for. While the crew was in confusion preparing to return fire, he ran from the cabin and attacked the gunner who was nearest him with an iron belaying pin. Greening knocked his man on the head and sent him overboard. David's victim sprawled on the deck, his head wobbling, his face covered with blood. Greening whirled the gun in position.

The location of the gun was in their favor. They were cut off from the rest of the ship by the deck cabin so that they had time to aim and fire before Bonnet discovered them. Luckily the gun was loaded with langrel and at the first shot the canvas was riddled.

"Over the side before they discover us!" David cried. Greening followed him to the rail. They let themselves down and dropped into the water. The stream, turgid from recent rains, befriended them. They were well away from the ship before they were discovered. They reached the floating island, bullets splashing about them.

"Our real danger will be to get to the *Henry* without having their crew shoot us in the water."

"I told Captain Rhett we would try to reach the *Henry*," Greening assured him.

David turned the water out of his jackboots. He had tied them together and hung them about his neck before they left the *Royal James*.

"Come on, let's start," he said, slipping into the river. Greening followed. They swam deep in the water, only their heads visible.

They made Rhett's ship without incident. A line was thrown over and David went up hand over hand. Greening waited until willing seamen had pulled Moray to the deck; then he followed.

Colonel Rhett was directing the firing, standing with feet broad apart to balance himself on the slanting deck.

"Damn it! Two times aground is enough to wreck a man's temper. This is the kind of luck we've had ever since we left Charles Town."

"If you will excuse a suggestion, Captain Rhett, your men are firing too high. Get them below the water line, not above."

Rhett glared at Moray. "Damn it, I'm captain here." Then he changed his mind and gave the order. "The enemy has the better of it," he said, looking at his decks strewn with wreckage of sail and guns and wounded men.

"You'll right yourself soon. The tide isn't at the full yet, sir." Greening had been looking over the side. "You'll have the edge on him then, same as you had before, for you'll float off before he can make a move."

"This man's a river pilot," Moray told Rhett.

Rhett cast a keen glance at Greening. Satisfied at the

honest look of the lad, he said, "Take over, mister. If you can get us into the channel first, I'll give you a golden Jo."

"Right, sir," said Greening as he took the wheel.

Rhett put his men to repairing damage done the rigging, for the *Royal James* had ceased firing for the moment. Moray, shivering in his wet clothes, set about mending canvas.

Five hours the ships waited, caught in the trap between shoals and bar. Five hours with intermittent firing. Then slowly the *Henry* began to right herself as the tide came in, sinking the bar under rising water.

Guns blazed now from a flat deck. Rhett got a piece of iron in his body, but he did not leave his position. While the pirates debated what course they would follow, Rhett's two ships closed in, in such a position that both were free to fire at will, while the *Royal James* remained imprisoned in the sand. A well-placed shot from the *Henry* hit the enemy below the waterline. David, standing beside Rhett, saw the confusion on the pirate ship as men crowded to her side.

Stede Bonnet's angry voice rose above the din:

"God blast him! I'll not surrender. I'll set fire to the magazine! I'll blow my ship to hell before I'll surrender to that snivelling Rhett!"

But it took more than high words to get Bonnet out of the trap in which he found himself. He was already defeated and he knew it. His men crowded about him.

"Let us make terms! Surrender!" they cried. "We're outgunned! Surrender! Surrender!"

A well-placed shot from Rhett's ship scattered the crew of the *Royal James*. It creased the deck boards and caught the main mast squarely at its base. The mast fell crashing to the deck, dragging with it a tangled mass of canvas and rigging.

Bonnet stood for a moment staring at the wreckage. With an oath he turned and strode to his cabin.

Rhett stood on the quarter-deck of the *Henry*, waiting for the arrival of the boat bearing his prisoner Stede Bonnet. His black-browed face was hard, his lips were drawn in a fine line. He had lost ten good men and two score were wounded.

He would sail into Charles Town harbour with Stede Bonnet in irons, but Blackbeard and Vane still sailed the seas ... and Anne Bonney.

The shot from Anne Bonney's sloop hit its mark, the little house on the hill where Eunice and John Caslett lived. John

429

had put off riving shakes to cover the roof and had relied on the heavy thatch to serve, the same as at home, he told Eunice when she urged him to shingle their roof as the other settlers had done. Now the thatch was afire blazing high, searing the leaves of the oak that sheltered it.

Gabrielle was attracted by the shouts of "Fire! Fire!" She looked out of her bedroom window and saw the blaze.

"Caslett's cottage is on fire!" Barton called. "I'm going."

Gabrielle ran down the steps and followed her. In the stockade men were shouting "Fire!" and running out the gate, carrying buckets and pans, anything with which to dip water. The spring was not far distant; men passed buckets from hand to hand; some beat at the side walls with wet blankets; others ran to Treloar's cottage to throw water on the roof to quench the sparks blowing in that direction.

The settlers ran in and out of the house, carrying out furniture and dishes. Eunice stood with a group of women, wringing her hands, the tears rolling down her cheeks. Recriminations burst from her lips repeated over and over.

" 'Tis John's fault. I told him not to thatch it. 'Tis John's fault."

Some of the women tried to comfort her but she pushed them aside, watching each article that the men carried out.

"My dresser! My pewter plates! My chest! My quilts! Where is my bed? John, do not let our marriage bed be given to the flames!"

John, his face blackened from smoke and grime, started into the cottage, but two men caught his arms and held him.

"Bein' crazy, man? She's fallin', can't you see?"

Eunice's shrill voice pierced through the crackle and roar of flames. "My marriage bed! My marriage bed!"

The rafters, burned through, let the blazing roof fall within the walls.

"See! You'd have been burned to death," Amos Treloar said to John. He did not hear. He was staring stupidly at the blackened walls and the flaming thatch. . . .

" 'Tis a sign," he muttered and turned away dazedly, drawing his hand across his bloodshot eyes.

The men were carrying water, trying to keep the walls intact, but with little success. The spring had gone dry. A line of men from the creek to the bank passed buckets. Gabrielle recognized Colonel Moseley and Edward Colston among them.

430

Barton said, "I'll take Eunice back with me. They can sleep in my room."

"Yes. Yes, of course." Gabrielle went to the weeping woman. "Come with us, Eunice. Barton will make a room ready for you."

Eunice drew away, her small eyes filled with hatred.

"No. I will not sleep under the roof of that old man. He told us lies. He made fine promises. Lies! Lies! All lies! He said we would have wealth and ease in his settlement. See what happens; always ill luck, ill luck." She began to weep loudly. "My marriage bed! My marriage bed." She swung away. "I hope evil comes to that old man!"

John sprang to her side. He caught her shoulder. "Quiet, woman! Do not talk rough to the kind lady."

Barton said, "Run away, Miss Gabrielle. Mary Treloar and I will take care of her."

Gabrielle was inexpressibly shocked by the vindictive words Eunice had uttered. She looked into the faces of the other women. They were expressionless; their eyes held no warmth nor sympathy. Did they also blame her father for the misfortunes that had befallen Eunice and John? The coming of pirates in the river, surely ... She turned away, her eyes blinded by tears.

John Caslett overtook her as she walked swiftly towards the forest.

"Do not be hurt, miss. Eunice is fair out of her head with grief. She's that set on her belongings, is Eunice. Pay no heed to her words. Your father is a saintly man——" He paused, embarrassed. An inarticulate man, it cost him an effort to speak.

Gabrielle tried to smile. "Thank you, John. Thank you."

She walked swiftly through the trees. She had forgotten the danger that threatened from pirates. The thought of Eunice's words and the faces of the women filled her mind. She realized suddenly how remote these people were. There was no common meeting ground between them. She did not understand them; their thoughts were closed to her. They must have talked of these things among themselves. They blamed her father for all their disappointments. They thought that he had failed them. She too had failed; she had not troubled herself to visit them, learn what they were thinking, help them. David had told her as much. David was right. She had not realized then and she had resented his words.

Face to face with herself, Gabrielle was not pleased with

what she saw. She had mistaken affection for unwavering fidelity, fearlessness for bold energy. .... A flood of tears fell from her eyes. She leaned her forehead against the rough bark of an oak and gave herself to sorrow and self-reproach.

A dead branch snapped. Gabrielle turned quickly, aroused by the noise. She saw a man standing in the path a few yards away, regarding her quietly, an amused look on his face.

"Pardon, fair Rosalind. If I had a kerchief I would be happy to offer it to you, but as you see, I am in like case, as wet as a porpoise."

The man's garments clung to him damply, his long hair hung dank and straight, plastered against his cheeks and forehead. A beaver hat, rolled to a peak, was thrust through his leathern belt, its bedraggled blue plume hanging limply against his side. He carried his boots in one hand, his bare feet were covered with swamp slime, his trousers caked with mud. His white linen shirt clung to his body, the lace sleeve ruffles torn to shreds.

She smiled. His plight was so ludicrous.

"Splendid!" he said. "Splendid! I am happy to see you smile. A woman's tears always defeat me." He removed his hat from his belt and tried to reshape it without success. He regarded the drooping brim ruefully.

"And it cost me a pretty price—four guineas, if my memory serves me."

Gabrielle said, "We make beavers in our settlement. The men will be happy to present you with a new one."

The man drew nearer. Gabrielle drew back quickly, remembering the pirate ship.

"Don't be afraid. I'm not a pirate. Instead I am a pirate's prisoner who has escaped off the *Royal James*, by swimming the river."

He clapped the sorry hat on his head, in order to remove it again, in a sweeping bow.

"Michael Cary, at your service."

At the sound of his name, Gabrielle stiffened. Molly Lepel's Michael Cary. She allowed her eye to rest on him a second. Undeniably handsome.

In spite of his condition he showed no embarrassment. His eyes were full of laughter as he watched her. When she did not reply, he said, "I am looking for Mistress Gabrielle Fountaine."

"I am Gabrielle Fountaine," she answered, relaxing a little.

Had Molly sent Michael Cary to them? She had no time to

432

ponder over this thought, for Cary said: "Moray sent me to you. He found me on the *Royal James* where the 'she pirate' Anne Bonney had left me. It was he who cut my bonds and helped me to escape. I swam to the creek. When I saw the fire and heard the commotion, I thought I had better approach the settlement from another direction." He laughed. "I didn't want the sentry to take me for a pirate and put a bullet into me."

Gabrielle said, "I'm sorry I was so inhospitable, Mr. Cary. Let us hurry to the house. I am sure we can find something for you to wear while your clothes are drying."

Cary glanced down at his sodden garments. "Thank you so much. I could be more comfortable."

"Perhaps you can give me news of my father, Mr. Cary. He is a prisoner on board the *Royal James*. We've heard nothing since they took the ransom money to the ship."

Cary regarded her with interest.

"Ah, I understand something. I couldn't for the life of me see why Moray didn't make a break when I did. Remain as hostage for the father and gain favour with the daughter."

The rising colour in Gabrielle's cheeks betrayed her. Cary did not appear to notice.

"Your father should be here by now. Moray told me that Anne Bonney would release him. I believe she was to set him ashore when she went to her sloop, the *Francis*. It is anchored below here in a small cove, with her prize—my own ship," he added ruefully.

Gabrielle's face cleared. "I know the spot. It is almost six miles from here." She began to run. "I'll send Annaci with horses to find him."

At the stockade gate they met Moseley and Edward Colston. Gabrielle mentioned Cary's name.

Moseley looked at him closely, then reached out his hand.

"I should have recognized you at once, Cary," he said cordially. "My eyes were on your clothes instead of your face! Pardon me, this is Mr. Edward Colston, of Bristol. Mr. Cary once lived in the Albemarle when his uncle was governor of the Province."

Edward Colston bowed slightly but did not offer to shake Cary's hand.

Gabrielle interrupted. "Anne Bonney has put my father ashore at the cove. It is too long a distance for him to walk. I'll send Annaci with his saddle horse."

"I will go with Annaci to meet your father," Colston said

433

eagerly, hastening after Gabrielle as she hurried towards the stable. Cary watched them, a slight smile on his lips.

Gabrielle watched Edward and the Negro enter the forest path before she went back to her guests. Cary and Moseley were walking towards the bachelors' house. She heard Moseley say:

"I'm afraid my clothes are not a fasionable cut, Michael, but they will cover you."

Michael laughed. "A drink, Colonel Moseley, a good long drink, and then we will discuss clothes."

Gabrielle stood for a moment looking after them. She wondered why Cary had not spoken of Molly, but perhaps she had not told him anything of the Fountaines. She wondered, too, about Edward—the strange expression on his face when she mentioned Cary's name. Could it be possible that Edward had seen through Molly's trickery on the Bristol dock, the day they sailed from England? Did he see her when she ran into the warehouse to meet Michael, and left him waiting? Or had he seen Molly and Michael talking, after she had left the shore boat with Madam Woodes Rogers?

One thing Gabrielle determined; she would not mention Molly's name unless Michael Cary spoke of her first. She had no wish to be involved in one of Molly's wild escapades.

She was opening the front door when she saw her father near the weaving shed. He was walking slowly, his shoulders bent, his hands behind his back.

"Father! Father!" she called, running towards him. He turned at the sound of her voice. Her heart failed her when she saw his grey, despairing face.

It is the ransom money, she thought. Bonnet has taken everything and we are left without money for the needs of the settlement.

She stopped in the path and watched him step into the weaving room and close the door. He did not need her.

She walked slowly towards the house. Upstairs in her room she stood for a long time looking out of the window towards the river. In spite of the events that had crowded in on her, Eunice's vindictive words, the arrival of Michael Cary, her father's return, her mind kept going back to David Moray. The memory of words she had spoken to him caused her painful emotion. She realized now that he had been right when he accused her of holding herself superior to the people around her.

434

Gabrielle had not meant to be superior. She had been interested in each family's problems. She had sent Barton to their homes with goodies for the children, or fresh fish and wild turkey when they had an abundance, but she remained apart, trusting Barton could meet them on common ground. That was her mistake. She knew it now from Eunice Caslett's impassioned accusations, from the uncompromising hardness in the eyes of the other women. She had failed them where she most wanted to succeed.

In London the Lords of Trade and Plantations met in Whitehall. Mr. Secretary Craggs read a report designed for his Majesty's inspection concerning trade in the Carolina Plantations.

"We daily increase in slaves, but decrease in white men. A body of white men we expect from Philadelphia, but they are at a loss to get lands. They have sent men to view the Cape Fear and they like it pretty well, but the river land is bespoke, and the land up the creeks close to the sea has likewise been taken.

"There is a certain place called Roanoke, granted to the Lords Proprietors by second charter, where Sir Walter Raleigh's cousin, Sir Richard Grenville, made first settlement. It is free and without inhabitants save the horses and cattle that run wild.

"The people who dwell in North Carolina live mostly in the three counties of Albemarle, Bath and Clarendon. They have petty courts and a supreme court, held by the government, with liberty of appeal. We are informed your Majesty's subjects in South Carolina do not enjoy this liberty of appeal.

"There are great tracts of good land, very healthy, but its situation renders it impossible of good trade, because of the vast chain of sand bars and islands, and the risks of ships crossing.

"We hope earnestly that Captain Woodes Rogers will soon rid New Providence and the Bahama Islands of the pirate hordes, so that your Majesty's trade with the southern colonies may be resumed in full effort."

Mr. Secretary Craggs laid the paper down and addressed the members:

"For this information, as well as the information regarding Sir Robert Montgomery, who is interested in leasing or buying the Carolinas from the Lords Proprietors, we are

435

indebted to Colonel Blackistone and Mr. Micajah Perry, Agents, and Mr. Joseph Boone, the South Carolina agent."

The meeting was open for discussion. There was more interest in the sale of North Carolina to Sir Robert Montgomery than in the suggestion of more settlers, or in Woodes Rogers' appeal for ships-of-war to exterminate the sea raiders.

Carolina was far away and Mr. Secretary Craggs, with the Proprietors Ashley and Danson, thought only of cash. They wanted to invest more and more guineas in the South Sea Bubble, now blown to an enormous size. So large had the venture become that some wise men were saying it could grow no larger without bursting. But others laughed at that. When the Bank of England placed its funds in a venture, the shares were as strong as the nation itself. The shares kept selling, and new shares were offered to clamouring people, money-mad, seeking wealth from the far-off shores of South America and the Summer Islands of the South Seas.

Many merchants of London and Bristol who had grown rich in trade saw their business being destroyed by lawless pirates. They combined with the masters of their vessels and petitioned the King, in Council, showing how demoralized trade had become, and prayed for relief.

But George the First had the power of the British Navy in the Baltic, to protect his little German electorate against Charles the Twelfth of Sweden, so no vessels were available for the colonies.

"Let the colonies fight their own fight. I have no ordnance to waste," the King said to the London merchants, and they were turned away.

"England is no longer England," old Edward Colston told his Bristol merchants. "Today it is a German who rules us. 'Tis a sorry, sorry day for England when she loses her trade. When she does not support her trade with the colonies, it will not be long before she loses the colonies as well."

Chapter 29

DAVID SEATS A PLANTATION

The sound of caulking hammers, axes and adzes rang against the bank and reverberated across the water, when the ship's crew and Amos Treloar's helpers began their labours to make Rhett's battle-scarred *Henry* whole and seaworthy. Rhett had engaged Amos to doctor the wounds she had received from the gunfire of the *Royal James*. This was something Amos had hoped for, a chance to show his skill as a shipwright. More than once he had talked to Mary about his dream to lay stout keels and build ships of considerable size. Up to now, he had built only one flat-bottom, for fishing upcreek and in the marshes, and had burned the centre out of a great juniper log (which Sandy MacAlpin shortened to "jumper wood") for a dugout canoe such as the Indians used.

"It's a fair, fine river for shipbuilding, with its creeks and inlets," Sandy told Amos, when he brought in the news that Rhett wanted him to take charge of the work as soon as the *Henry* was careened.

Each midday, Amos' wife Mary made her way down the narrow path, carrying a pail of hot tea and a rush basket of hot pasties. The men laid down their tools when she rang the little hand bell to announce food.

Mary and Amos sat on a log to eat their pasties and gaze at the great ship, drawn up for working over.

Mary said, "I've been over to Eunice's to help her pack up her belongings. She's not given way. She's determined to go out with Captain Bragg when he sails tomorrow."

"They'll have company," Amos said, biting into the flaky crust with the satisfaction of a man eating food to his liking. "The Storm brothers are going and several others. So I heard, last night, when I had my ale at the club room."

"You should have persuaded them to stay and give the place another trial," Mary said, pouring steaming tea into saucer. "You're a master hand at persuading, Treloar; you should have used your power on them."

Amos shook his head. He was a shrewd man who knew human nature. "No, Mary. Let them go. Such as they often disrupt a good work, with their whinin' and bellyachin' and discontent. 'Tis better far to weed out the weak at the beginnin'. Let them go back to the Old World and their cities. We want countryfolk here, used to the sound of cattle lowin' at evenin' and bird-calls at dawn. Folk who like to wet a line, and feel the tug on a hook as the fish runs, or put a bead on a wedge of geese flyin'. 'Tis they we want, Mary."

Mary was silent, surprised at Amos' lengthy speech. She knew he had been thinking all this for a long time, before he made his thoughts vocal.

"Mayhap you're right, Treloar, but ten out will leave a big gap."

"Others will come," Amos said, tapping his pipe as he leaned against the bank, his legs, in short boots and grey woollen stockings, stretched out on the sand. "Other and better will come.

"Look you at the river, Mary. See how quiet it runs below its bank, but it runs steady even in freshet time, and it finds its way to the sea. If its passage is blocked by floating trees and logs and bits of fallin' banks which block the channel, it cuts a new channel and finds the sea again."

Mary looked at Amos' thin lined face, a kind of proud wonder in her round dark eyes.

Amos did not notice her silence; his thoughts came from deep within him. "What I'm thinkin', Mary, is that a river is a roadway, and it invites men to travel. Think, now, of a ship that came from England, carryin' trade goods, made in our country and in Holland—clothes and boots, or tea from China, and fine spices for you to put in such a cake." He held up one little cake and took a slow bite, better to enjoy the rich flavour. "The ships come to the islands and along the coast," he continued. "What do they seek, Mary?"

"I cannot follow you, Treloar, when you speak deep thoughts like you be sayin' this minute."

"I'll tell you, Mary. The ships seek rivers and inlets, to bring their goods, because men always seek rivers and inlets, to plant and build and grow. 'Tis always like that: men leavin' old soil, lookin' and searchin' for deep rich soil, to plant and harvest. River bottom lands, rich, with good soil."

" 'Tis talk of a yeoman, Treloar, not of a builder of ships."

"Mayhap I be one-half farmer, Mary." He got to his feet,

438

wiped the crumbs from his lips on the back of his hand. "Thank you, my girl. A man works best when the stomach is satisfied."

The others brought their saucers to Mary. "Thanks, Mary. Amos is a man to envy," Zack Reeves said as he put his saucer on the stack. "Makes me think I'd better send me back to England for a girl."

"There's a pretty young filly up Far Reach," a companion said. "Name's Eliza Weatherby. She lives in a house near the Forks with a family named Rowan. She's a fair good-looking female."

"A bondwoman?" Reeves asked, interest showing in his face.

"No. Free woman. Owns a hundred acres."

"Must ride up Far Reach, come Sunday," Zack said. He picked up his caulking hammer and walked over to take his place on the hull.

Mary put the dishes in the basket. "You're a wise man, Amos," she said, lingering for a moment. "You think farther than me."

Amos' face did not change, but he had satisfaction. Mary had acknowledged his superiority. "Make me a suety puddin' on a Sunday," he said, "and we'll invite the bachelors in for supper."

"May can," Mary said. She took up the basket and pail and went up the path. She was proud of her man Amos. She determined to give him complete support in the venture. She would not be a drag, as Eunice Caslett was to her husband, setting her selfish whining whims before his wishes and the family's welfare. Mary also missed England and her friends and her relations, but she would not whine about it. She thought of a song she had heard the runaway Negroes singing the night before. She remembered a line or two repeated over and over:

> "I got to choose my road,
>   O Lord;
> I got to choose my road."

They had chosen this road, she and Amos. They must not falter if the way was long and hard.

The *Delicia* sailed at midday.

"We'll be back in three months' time," Captain Bragg told

Robert Fountaine. "I'll give your messages to Captain Woodes Rogers, and deliver your merchandise to the merchants you have designated in Nassau, and the packet to Mr. Ralph Izard in Charles Town."

Robert shook hands. "Don't forget to inquire about an agent to represent us in Jamaica, Captain. And if you can get the rice seed and indigo plants Gabrielle wants, we can set them this year. We'll have some of the marshland ready to seed by the time you return. I've already got men making canals to drain the marsh. I'd like to get a crop in this year, for it would be a help for next winter."

Gabrielle was standing near the rail of the ship.

She was watching the shore boats coming down the creek carrying Eunice Caslett's possessions—those that had survived the fire. The Storms were going also. Then there were the others who threatened to sail in Rhett's ship for the Charles Town settlement. One weaver was leaving. That would work a hardship on Robert Fountaine.

Eunice Caslett came on deck. She saw Gabrielle talking with Edward Colston. Her eyes became suffused with malice. She walked determinedly across the deck and stood in front of Gabrielle, her arms akimbo.

"You needn't hold your head so proud, thinking yourself better'n us common folk. You're no better'n we. Your father lies and tells us tales of this wonderful country—and what do we find? Indians and pirates and hard living with no proper chapel and no market town where a body can take her cheeses to sell."

Gabrielle opened her mouth to speak, but the woman's sharp voice silenced her.

"We're aleavin' and a many others will leave before winter comes. We've heard what's bein' said. There's a curse on the place. Indians have murdered people here. They died without the offices of the church. They'll bring evil on all who live here. You won't escape it, miss." She walked away, her heavy footfalls echoing on the deck.

Gabrielle looked at Edward. He was regarding her, his eyes full of sympathy. She looked quickly away; she did not want him to know how an angry woman's words disturbed her.

"Do not pay any attention to her, Gabrielle. She is a malicious woman."

She did not answer. She was shaken by what Eunice had said. She tried to smile but it was a poor attempt.

440

Edward glanced over his shoulder. Bragg was giving his last orders before sailing. The crew was busy running up sails, stowing last-minute cargo. Edward drew close to her.

"I don't give up readily, Gabrielle. Somehow I feel that the betrothal your father talks about will never be consummated. There's a lot of water between here and France and a man you've never seen."

Gabrielle shook her head sadly. "My father is very determined," she said. "People are always mistaking his gentleness for weakness, but he has a will of iron. I never have known him to fall back on his word, Edward."

Colston's jaw stiffened. " 'Tis a crime—a crime to give you to a man you've never seen, and whom you may loathe when you do see him."

"It's a practise common in France. It does not seem strange to my father. He has known Paul Balarand since he was an infant. His father Pierre was my father's closest friend in his youth, so you can understand."

Edward placed his hand over Gabrielle's on the rail. "It would pleasure me beyond words if you could say that you loved me, Gabrielle. I would go with a lifted heart."

Gabrielle's eyes were troubled. Her voice was low and very tender. "I wish I could say the words you wish, Edward. But I cannot. You are very dear to me, as a brother is dear, or a valued friend. But more than that, I do not know."

A cloud came over Colston's face. "Is there anyone else, Gabrielle? Any other man your heart yearns for?"

"No, Edward. There's no one who is nearer to me than you."

His face cleared. His hands dropped to his side. "I'll have to be satisfied," he said, managing to smile. "Poor consolation for a lover, but it must suffice."

She drew her cloak about her as the wind shifted to the west.

"Wind north-northwest," the lookout shouted.

The master shouted orders. A west wind behind them would speed the *Delicia* downriver.

Robert Fountaine came down the deck with Captain Michael Cary. The Captain walked with a long easy stride, his dark blue mantle billowing out. One hand was on the hilt of his sword. He swept off his wide plumed hat and bowed deferentially to Gabrielle. "Thank you, a thousandfold, for your hospitality, sweet Mistress. I shall never forget how you took a wretched wanderer under your hospitable roof." He

lifted Gabrielle's hands and kissed one, then the other—
lingering overlong, from the dark look on Edward Colston's
face.

"It was nothing," Gabrielle murmured, her cheeks blazing
at the admiration in Cary's bold eyes.

"It was everything to a man whose heart was without
hope. Know you not that a captain who has lost his ship has
lost his spirit and his soul as well?"

"You'll have your ship back, I'm sure," Gabrielle said.
Neither Edward nor her father spoke in answer to Cary's
words.

"I must fight Anne Bonney to get it," Michael said. "I
don't like to fight women. Women were made for pleasant
hours, for a man's love and protection."

Robert Fountaine said, "Come, Gabrielle. The boat is
waiting to take us ashore."

Edward walked across the deck. He drew her aside. "I've
said nothing to you of Cary, but his name is coupled with
Molly Lepel's in London. I've had letters. He has not mentioned her, nor have I. I'm not a man to carry tales, Gabrielle, but I think you should be warned in case he comes
here again. He is not a man to be trusted where women are
concerned."

She said, "I do not like Michael Cary."

Edward's face cleared. He held her hand closely. "I should
have trusted your judgement, my dear."

"Good-bye, Edward. Safe journey."

"Good-bye, dear Gabrielle. Before another year I shall
return to Carolina."

Gabrielle did not answer. She was occupied with her wide
skirts and the long step she must take to reach the flat-
bottom canoe. Strong hands caught her waist and she felt
herself lifted bodily into the boat.

She glanced up to meet David Moray's eyes. He had heard
Edward's parting words and he took no trouble to conceal his
anger.

Gabrielle turned to wave to Edward. Michael stood beside
him at the rail. He answered with a sweep of his hat.

Robert Fountaine said, "We shall be lonely without our
visitors."

"Yes," Gabrielle answered. "I shall miss Edward." She felt
her father's eyes on her. He looked puzzled and a little
apprehensive. Gabrielle thought she could read his mind. He
had overheard Edward's words. He realized that it was time

442

to speak of the betrothal to Paul Balarand, now that another man had asked her in marriage.

She sat quietly, her slim fingers trailing in the water, looking at David's back. How broad his shoulders were and how the muscles of his arms showed under his doeskin tunic! His long jaw was set and hard. When he helped her from the boat, he did not clasp his hands about her waist and swing her to the beach. Instead, he lifted her in his arms and carried her ashore. His face was so close to hers that she saw the brown flecks in his hazel eyes, now smouldering in anger.

"Let me down, Moray. I'm quite capable of walking and taking care of myself."

"As you say, Mistress," he answered with mock humility.

She followed her father up the path, walking swiftly. She thought David was behind her, but when she looked back, at the brow of the hill, he was striding along the narrow stretch of beach to where Colonel Rhett's ship was careened. She felt a little disappointment. He's scornful, she thought, and stiff-necked. Just as Barton had said: "The Scots are all stiff-necked. You must go more than halfway with them, if you want peace." David Moray was a Scot of Scots, with his high-held head. She did not object to pride but she resented his smile, as if she were the target of his secret laughter.

She hurried after her father. There were household tasks to be done. They had lost two of their guests, but Colonel Rhett would be with them for three days longer. Colonel Moseley and Sandy MacAlpin would be back by evening from the ground the Colonel was surveying for Maurice Moore.

That morning the Indian Kullu had appeared, after an absence of a month or more. He brought a great wild gobbler and a basket of fish. He would wait, he said, for MacAlpin, for he carried a message from Chief Blont of the Tuscaroras.

After the table was laid and the rooms arranged for the guests, Gabrielle walked out to look at the garden. The Negro Annaci, the old runaway, had been at work, and not only were the beds laid out and the sundial set, but he had brought low shrubs from the swamp to border the beds. He had transplanted great clusters of dogwood from the deep forest to make the hedge, which enclosed that part of the garden which surrounded her mother's rooms.

She saw that little shoots from the Holland bulbs and fleur-de-lis were pushing out of the ground. It would not be long before there would be blooms—tulips and lilies. The yellow jasmine that grew wild in the forest would bloom then, Sandy had told her, and the forest would be carpeted with wild flowers. In only a short time it would be spring, and there had been no winter. She sang a little song as she walked along the path. Somehow, she felt happier than she had for a long time. She looked up and saw her mother watching her from her sitting-room. She went quickly to the window and pointed to the sundial and the well-ordered beds, laid out in a pattern. Her mother nodded her head, slowly, as if she knew what Gabrielle wanted her to see. She smiled a little. A mocking-bird lit on the sundial and sat flirting his fantail as he pecked at some seeds Gabrielle had left on the stone. She smiled and clasped her fragile hands together and beckoned Celestine to come to see the garden and the birds. In the spring she will come back to us, thought Gabrielle. The garden and the growing things will waken her.

That night after dinner her father asked Gabrielle to come into the weaving room. She found him at the loom, his hands busy with an intricate pattern. She took a seat on a bench.

Glancing up, Fountaine said, "I asked you to come to me tonight, daughter, because I believe it is time to speak of your future."

Gabrielle listened to the words of her father with breathless attention, her eyes fixed on his.

"For some time I have thought to speak to you of your betrothed, Paul Balarand, but I have put it off." His hands fell on his knees, his eyes sought the floor.

"Balarand?" she said sadly. "Why should I be betrothed to a man I have never seen?"

An expression of surprise crossed his face. Gabrielle questioning his actions was a new experience. He answered quietly. "It is our custom to betroth our children when the time comes. I have chosen for you the son of a good man, my friend of many years. A man to whom I owe my life." He fixed his dark eyes on her, an intense gaze as though he were trying to make her envisage what was in his mind. "My child, I have told you little of those days of persecution, when we Huguenots were hunted like beasts. Thieves and murderers had more consideration than we, for they were tried before a court. We were driven from place to place, never knowing from one moment to the next what our fate would be."

He got up and walked about the room. Gabrielle did not

move. She cast a loving look at him. Her poor father. How he had suffered!

"Pierre Balarand was not of our faith, but we were friends. He helped me to escape from my prison the very night before I was to die. He united me with your mother's family and it was through his help that we all escaped to England.

"Last year he wrote me a letter. He told me his son had grown to a fine man, a barrister of note. He asked for your hand for his son, young Paul, who was enchanted with the miniature I had sent to his father."

Gabrielle stirred. "I did not know . . ." she began.

Her father raised his hand. "Let me finish, my dear." He went to his desk and opened a drawer. From it he took out a small case and put it in Gabrielle's hand. "He sent this in return."

Gabrielle glanced at the minature. A pleasant-faced young man with dark, oval eyes, a lofty forehead and a wide generous mouth looked back at her.

"Paul Balarand," her father said.

Gabrielle did not speak. She thought, I have seen his face; now he is more than a name.

"He is handsome, is he not?" her father said, smiling at her gently. "A good face. You are fortunate, my child, to have found favour with the son of my friend."

"You are really serious about this?" Gabrielle asked. "You will not force me to marry a man I have never seen!"

Fountaine's face darkened. "Surely you have listened to what I have told you, Gabrielle! I owe my life, your mother owes her life to Pierre Balarand. You understand that we owe him a debt we can never repay."

Except with my life. Gabrielle did not speak the words that trembled on her lips.

"You understand?" he persisted. Gabrielle thought, He speaks harshly; underneath his gentleness he is determined. How can I combat his will? How can I say what is in my heart?

"I do not want to leave you or my mother. Please, Father, do not ask me to marry."

Fountaine's face cleared. "If that is your reason, we will put it aside. I was afraid . . ." He broke off abruptly.

Gabrielle understood now the puzzled apprehensive look on his face when he heard Edward's farewell words.

He rose and put his hands on her shoulders. "You are a

good daughter and you will make a faithful wife. Good night, my dear. I am expecting MacAlpin. We are going to work on my Tuscarora vocabulary tonight."

She went away, her feet dragging. She felt weary. An expression of profound discouragement showed in her dark eyes and on her face as she walked slowly across the garden to the house.

Captain Rhett's ship was repaired and sailed away, carrying Stede Bonnet to face his doom in Charles Town. The days were longer now, and the migrating birds were in the forest and in the marsh. Ducks and geese winged their way northward, wedges of dark lines in the sky.

In spite of the loss of men, the little settlement had begun to take on the appearance of permanency, as leaves budded on the tulip and the gum trees and oaks were showing little pink bud-rolls. Sap had begun to run. The earth was stirring, strong and fertile, redolent with new life, waiting for the first warm, life-giving sun of spring.

Kitchen gardens were put in order; fields were ploughed and seeded. The men who had undertaken to select the turpntine trees—Amos Treloar and John Hawkins and Mark Akim—went each morning to the forest and did not return until sundown. They took two of the Negro runaways with them, for they were forest men who had worked cutting timber and boxing turpentine trees and making charcoal. Since Robert Fountaine would allow no slaves in Old Town, they were paid a wage out of the common fund and were given a small field to work as their own.

The woman Cissy helped Mary Treloar on washing and cleaning days and cooked for the bachelors.

One morning Gabrielle wakened to the sound of birds singing. The windows were wide, and a soft breeze waved the long streamers of moss in the great oaks. Squirrels darted up the bark of the hickory tree, and twigs and branches had a greenish cast that foretold the bursting green of early spring. She got out of her warm bed and dressed quickly. It was a morning for a canter. She would ride up the River Road. She had a curiosity to see the tract of land MacAlpin and David Moray were seating.

She ate a hurried breakfast, alone. Barton told her her father had ridden off early, with Amos, to the turpentine woods and would not be back until after dinner. "I thought today we were to settle the room next to yours, in case Miss Molly should come, unexpected."

Gabrielle spread the scone with a slab of unsalted butter: "We'll do that tomorrow, Barton. I want to ride because the day is so fine. Tomorrow it may rain, and then we can work in the house."

"That's what you've been saying for a fortnight, Mistress. Always tomorrow may rain, but it doesn't."

"Well, it will, because the rain frogs sang last night, and that brings rain. Annaci told me it meant rain in twenty-four hours."

Barton sniffed. "I don't hold with such," she said primly.

"Annaci said we were not to plant in the east wind, or the bugs would eat the plants, and we must watch all our seeding for the right time of the moon."

Barton poured a second cup of tea for Gabrielle. "I don't know why you pick up these things. We've been planting a long time, in Scotland, and we don't talk about east winds."

Gabrielle got up from the table. "I'm going to take Annaci with me for a guide. He knows the paths through the swamp and all the short cuts."

The woman cleared the dishes from the table. "I can't think you're safe, riding around these dismals, nor do I hold with trusting black men and redskins. I told Sandy MacAlpin he should not let you shank yoursel' awa', with only a red Indian Kullu or a runaway slave to guide you. I told him that, I did. But he laughed and said 'twas far safer here than in the streets of Glasgow or Edinburgh."

Gabrielle threw her arm about Barton, causing the dishes she held in her hands to tilt dangerously.

"Go awa' with ye. You'll be breaking the china if you don't be more careful. Go to your riding, but I hope you carry a pistol in your pocket."

Gabrielle tied the ribands of her plumed riding hat under the tight bun at the nape of her neck. "I'll carry a loaded riding whip. That's enough protection—that and my mare's hoofs."

Annaci was waiting for her at the block with the bay mare. Gabrielle mounted. The Negro swung himself astride a long-legged mule.

"Lead the way, Annaci. Let's ride through the turpentine woods. I want to go as far as the mill site, if we have time."

"Yas, Mistress. There's time if we cut through the 'cosin."

They trotted along the edge of the swamp along a narrow

447

track that might have been made by animals or by the bare feet of countless Indians passing through the forest to the ocean. The black water was choked with swamp lilies and water hyacinths. Osiers grew thick and tall along the edges. White cranes rose as they came near and flew out to the river, their long legs dangling, their thin necks outstretched. A water moccasin slithered from under her horse's hoofs. An alligator crawled awkwardly over the bank and flopped into the water with a splash. A grey heron flapped its strong wings as it stood deep in the water prepared for instant flight, its head, with its long grotesque bill, turned towards her. Cardinals darted through the trees, bright splashes of red against the dark green of the trees, and a hermit thrush balanced itself on a bending twig.

"Byn 'n' bye they all make pretty songs," Annaci said, his black face beaming. "The woods will be full of cheeping and bird-calls."

They rode out of the swamp and into the open woods. The turpentine pines grew straight and slim here, tall as the masts of ships. There was little underbrush. The sun cast long shafts of light through the trees and splashed the path with light.

They came to a clearing where the men had been at work. Here the trees had been raked and boxed, to catch the precious sap which would bring them wealth.

"Men gone up Far Reach, Mistress, up where dey makin' charcoal."

They left the pines and rode through a thicket of poplars and hardwood. Dogwood bloomed along the fringes of the forest in waxen white beauty. Yellow jasmine and coral honeysuckle grew in profusion, climbing up tree trunks and spreading over low bushes in a mass of bloom. Bees hummed drowsily, drawing the sweet essence, and gold and black and sea-blue butterflies floated through the air like petals of tropical flowers.

The track they followed led them to an opening where a field had been cleared and burned over. A trench, cut by a plough, encircled the field, and long straight furrows of fresh-turned earth made a rectangular carpet of brown.

Gabrielle pulled up her horse. The scene before her eyes was one of incredible beauty. The field looked towards the river, hemmed in by the forest on three sides, a wide tongue of land between the cypress swamps. Beyond the high bank lay the marsh land. The silvery reeds and osiers swayed gently as a field of grain ripples under a soft wind.

448

She saw a house, long and low, almost hidden in the shade of a group of giant oaks. Long streamers of silver-grey moss swayed from the branches in unison with the rippling marsh grass.

"What place is this?" she called over her shoulder to Annaci.

"Plantation, he belong to Master Moray."

So that was the land Sandy had talked about so enthusiastically! She did not wonder. She thought it more pleasantly located than the spot where their settlement was. She wondered why her father had not examined the country along the river before he settled. It occurred to her now that her father had never shown interest in the surrounding country; never once had he explored the forest beyond the stockade. From the house to the weaving room, day after day—that was the extent of his interest.

Annaci pointed his gnarled black hand towards the river.

"They make canals now, rice fields. I bring my black boys from Green Swamp to dig, bye 'n' bye, dig big ditch so ship can come right to they door."

Gabrielle looked towards the marsh where a dozen Negroes were digging.

Moray, mounted on a sorrel horse, was riding slowly across the field towards the house.

She was turning away when he saw her and trotted across the field.

"Please don't ride away! Sandy will be desolated if you don't stop to see our house and the improvements he has made. Sandy is very proud of his handiwork."

The sound of his voice, the look of pleasure in his face brought an answering smile. Why was it whenever she saw David her heart beat so furiously? Even when she said unkind things to him, something kept telling her that it brought joy to see him. She thought again how bronzed and strong he was, as though he had drawn strength from the forest and the sun and the river.

"Do come. It would pleasure us to have you drink tea in our home."

"Thank you. I'd love a cup of tea."

David glanced at Annaci. "Perhaps you'd like to see how your men are getting on."

A broad smile spread over the man's face. "They know they got good master. They work hard to please him."

When Gabrielle and David turned to the house, Annaci rode to the marsh.

Sandy MacAlpin stood in the doorway. When he saw Gabrielle a smile lighted his stern face. "Welcome to the plantation." He came out towards the block to help her dismount, but David was there before him.

He lifted her from the saddle. For a moment she was against the length of his body. There was a curious light in the depths of his eyes that made the blood rush to her cheeks, a secret, triumphant look that drew her irresistibly.

"Put me down," she said faintly. "Please put me down." He did not heed, but held her, looking deep into her eyes.

"Your chin is adorable," he said.

When Sandy came around the horse, she was straightening her little plumed hat. Gabrielle managed a smile but her heart was beating violently.

Sandy's hearty voice steadied her. "Mistress Gabrielle, I was about to brew our morning tea. Now we shall have company, delightful company."

Gabrielle looked. One big room, with a great fireplace made of ballast stones. Two chairs of crossed boards with laced leather seats; two long benches, also with leather seats lashed to the sides with thongs—each with blankets, neatly rolled; one with a cover made from the fur of a cinnamon bear. Bear and deer skins on the floor. A long table near the centre of the room. A few books and several copies of the *Spectator* on a low stool near the fire.

"You're comfortable," she said. "I didn't know you had built a house."

"I haven't. I only roofed the cabin. I took over from Rowan, who moved farther up the stream, near the mouth of Swampy Creek. Colonel Moseley is arranging the patent for me."

He put tea, from a black-jappaned canister, into an earthenpot, poured the boiling water and set the pot on the hearth to steep. "I'm sorry we have no cakes to offer," he said as he poured the tea into a blue and white cup. "But neither Sandy nor I have learned to make cakes."

"Barton will make you some tea cakes," Gabrielle said. She sat down near the fire and took the cup Moray offered her. A thought struck her. "Why don't you take Tom and his wife Cissy to do for you? We really don't need them at the settlement."

"They're runaways, aren't they?"

450

"Yes. They came here from South Carolina. We don't know who their owners are. My father pays them wages. Cissy is an excellent cook."

"What about the bachelors?" MacAlpin asked. "They would raise hell—beggin' your pardon, Mistress—if we took their good cook."

"They have a good man. He can cook and he's almost through boxing the turpentine trees. Annaci is doing my gardening work. . . ." She paused, her cheeks reddening.

"Is he as good a gardener as your bondman David Moray?" he asked, his eyes twinkling, knowing the reason of her confusion.

"I'm sorry I was so stupid. I didn't mean to sound priggish."

"I want to be praised. I really had a model garden at Meg's Lane. So if you get in a tight place, I'll come over and do my best."

Gabrielle laughed. "Don't offer. I'm quite likely to call for help. You see, my mother loves gardens. I hope by the time the fleur-de-lis blooms, she'll be able to walk out of doors and enjoy her flowers."

David's face was grave. "Your father told me the story of your mother and the lilies. I hope they do well here, so that she may enjoy them."

Sandy was not attending. He sat with his head cocked on one side. "Did you hear a hoot owl?" he asked, getting up and going to the door.

Gabrielle and David listened. The call was clear, as if it came from the grove of cypress trees near the marsh.

Sandy picked up his gun and went out. Gabrielle looked at Moray inquiringly.

"Sandy is like that. He appears and disappears without rhyme or reason." He stirred his tea as though it was his only interest.

Gabrielle wished Sandy had not gone and left them alone. She wished her heart would not beat so violently.

David got up and looked out of the door.

"Sandy is getting into the canoe with Annaci. They are going to the lower canal."

He came back into the room and stood towering above her. He reached for her hand and drew her to her feet. For a moment they stood facing each other.

The look in his darkening eyes frightened her, yet she did not draw away. With her free hand she pushed the little

451

tendrils of hair from her forehead. She could not draw back. She wanted to move forward, closer to him, closer to his strong, taut body, but she did not stir. She waited, watching the passion deepen in his eyes.

He drew her to him slowly, as though he could not bear to shatter the warm throbbing silence.

"You are so beautiful, so desirable!"

His arms closed about her. All sense of time left her. It was so new, so radiant an emotion that she closed her eyes against the blinding light. His lips pressed hers, drawing her deeper into the world of his passion.

Gabrielle drew away slowly, dazed for the moment by the strength of her own emotion. David dropped his arms to his side, but his eyes did not leave her. Silence flooded the room. The song of a bird came through the open door, a wild joyous song that found an echo in her heart. She watched the little pulsating veins in his temple, the long line from his mouth to his nose, the flat brown planes of his cheeks. She wanted to touch him, to draw her fingers across his forehead. In his arms she had the deep sense of hidden violence in him, but he could be gentle too. . . . Her world was breaking all about her. She felt a passion of gratitude towards him, for carrying her into the unknown.

"I love you!" His voice was harsh, as though it were a struggle for him to speak. She felt all the old opposition falling away from her, leaving her free. She did not speak, fearing to lose the ecstasy of the moment. The perfume of jasmine was in the air, and a rapturous song of the thrush.

They walked out towards the canal, and sat on a log watching the paddles flashing in the water as Sandy brought the canoe up the stream.

David sat looking at his hands loosely clasped over his knees.

"You cannot marry Colston. You love me." He spoke roughly.

Gabrielle paled. In the joy of the moment she had forgotten there was anyone in the world but David.

Her expression alarmed him. He grasped her hand.

"Gabrielle!" he cried, a ring of uneasiness in his voice.

She shook her head. "I am not going to marry Edward. I had forgotten—you made me forget that I am betrothed to Paul Balarand."

"Balarand?" He was incredulous, angry.

"My father told me, only a short time ago."

452

The dark look passed. "Oh. A marriage of convenience. I think less than nothing of such marriages. Doesn't your father know that such arrangements are demoded? Of course you will refuse to go through with such a silly contract."

Gabrielle shook her head dispiritedly. "You do not know my father. His will is iron . . ."

"I, too, have a strong will." David's jaw closed firmly.

"You do not understand, David. My father owes his life to Paul's father."

"So he sacrifices you! No. That is something I can never understand."

He got to his feet. Sandy was walking up from the canal, the dripping paddles over his shoulder.

Gabrielle rose. "I must be going on," she said, her voice low. "Oh, David, try to understand."

There was no time for his answer. Sandy was close beside them, his face wreathed in smiles.

"They've run the long ditch clean to the river," he said to David. "By the time Bragg brings the rice on his next trip, we'll be ready."

"Splendid," David said, "Splendid. I hope you told the Negroes that they were to have an extra pannikin of rum tonight."

"Surely I did. They'll work the harder, knowing they've got it coming at the end of the day."

He turned to Gabrielle. "Going so soon? Didn't David ask you to dinner? Stay and help us settle an argument about a name for the plantation. I'm for Scots Hall, but David, he's holding out for Clarendon, same as they used to call the river."

Gabrielle shook her head. "I don't want to settle a dispute. . . . Both names are nice but . . ."

"But you like Clarendon best?" Sandy finished the sentence for her. "I was afraid you would. 'Tis a grand-sounding name, but . . ." He shrugged his shoulders. "It should be a great house setting there instead of a log cabin."

"Perhaps there will be a great house one day," she answered.

David helped her mount. His lips were firmly set and his eyes gloomy when he told her good-bye.

She took a moment to adjust her knee over the horn and settle her skirt before she took the reins. Sandy stood close by.

David said, "I will ride over tomorrow, if we don't plough the new field. I want to speak to Mr. Fountaine."

"Please do," she said, equally formal.

Sandy said, "Wait a minute. I'll get my horse—I think I'll ride with you. I've just remembered I want to speak to Amos Treloar about making us a canoe."

When they reached the compound they found the settlement in a state of excitement. A ship had come in, a big ship from Virginia. Gabrielle and Sandy dismounted at the barn and walked to the bank where the people were waiting.

Sandy said, "I'm glad I got my fox skins bundled and ready to ship. This will get them off a month earlier than if I sent them out by Bragg." After a moment he said, "I think I'll go aboard to see if they have any Copenhagen snuff."

Gabrielle was drawn into the excitement of watching the ship come to anchor. A ship on the river brought them something of their old life—new faces, letters and packets, merchandise that had been ordered from England. She saw her father on the wharf, and most of the men of the settlement.

The boats neared the creek. Two young boys, dressed in the round collars and dark suits of schoolboys, stood up, ready to make the first landing as the boat reached the wharf. Gabrielle picked up her skirts and sped down the path.

"Etienne! René!" she cried. . . . When they leapt ashore she saw that there was another passenger, a young woman wrapped in a dark cloak, a little bonnet with a gay flower on her blonde hair.

"Molly!" she cried. "Molly!"

Chapter 30

MOLLY COMES TO OLD TOWN

The Fountaine house was buzzing with activity. The boys had come home, René and Etienne, tall fellows with pleasant, shy manners, rising respectfully when their elders came into the room, listening politely to the conversation. Molly had changed to a green house dress, full skirted, with little bows of bronze velvet from skirt hem to breast, her soft hair in becoming curls. She wandered about looking at everything, with little cries of approbation at the comfortable rooms, at the view of the river and the garden. She shivered delicately at the deep forest and spoke of danger lurking there.

Robert Fountaine stood by the fire, talking to Roger Mainwairing, who had come down on the *Phoebus*, and to Maurice Moore, who accompanied him. Moore had brought a dozen men to clear the forest, where he proposed to lay out his town, and Roger planned to go upriver, above the Forks, where Moseley had located land for him before riding on to Charles Town.

Robert poured drinks for the men and offered the boys each a glass of Madeira, which they accepted politely, lifting the glasses to their noses to enjoy the bouquet, in true connoisseur style.

Gabrielle went back and forth from kitchen wing to the dining-room, to see that all was well. The table was laid for nine, at her father's suggestion. She did not know who the extra guests were to be, until the door opened and Sandy MacAlpin and David Moray walked in.

Molly came in from the garden at the same time that David walked in from the hall. She stood quite still for a moment, gazing at the tall, bronzed Scot. A look of surprise passed to one of extreme pleasure. She spread her skirts and made a deep curtsey, as Robert Fountaine, forgetful of David's earlier acquaintance with her in Meg's Lane, introduced David Moray and Mr. MacAlpin. She walked demurely to the dining-room between the two, flashing Gabrielle a questioning look as she took her place at the table beside David Moray.

Molly dominated the table. Her sprightly conversation, little bursts of laughter, her wit, kept all the men amused and entertained. Her eyes sparkled; her cheeks were the soft pink of a damask rose. Even Robert Fountaine smiled at her sallies, and affection showed in his sad eyes.

As the meal progressed, the talk became more concerned with the problems of the colony, as it always did when a few planters got together. They talked of tobacco and the high duties, the necessity of having new laws to protect their forests and conserve their trees. Roger Mainwairing said, "We are progressing amazingly with our trade. This year I've shipped twice the tobacco I sold last year, and a third more pork and hides. But the wealth of this province is in its forests. Naval stores will be our principal export for many years, and we must not waste our God-given wealth."

Maurice Moore agreed. "I want to set up a mill in here, as soon as I can get the machinery from England. I plan to install it on the creek directly west of the site I've chosen for my town, so that when our settlers come from South Carolina and the Albermarle, we'll have lumber ready and there'll be no delay in building their houses."

Fountaine asked about brick. He thought there was no permanence without brick buildings. All the men agreed to this. Moore said that his brother Roger had already ordered brick from England. It took several years before they could get enough brick over to build a house of any dimensions, since they brought it in small lots as ballast, and much of it went to the bottom of the sea when the pirates sank their ships.

René leaned forward and spoke to his father. "We saw a pirate when we were coming down from Virginia. It was horrible . . . beastly."

Robert said, "What are you talking about, René?"

"I saw the head of a pirate, stuck on the bowspirit of a ship, sir. A fearsome sight, with open, staring eyes, and a long black beard. The captain of our ship told us it was Blackbeard, a notorious pirate who had been taken prisoner by Lieutenant Maynard, of his Majesty's Navy, after a great fight in Pamticoe Sound."

His brother broke in: "It was as horrible as the time when we saw a highwayman drawn and quartered at the Tower, his head carried on a pikestaff so that all the people could take warning not to break the laws."

Robert addressed Roger Mainwairing: "This is news to us here. That means two of the greatest obstacles to our trade are out of the way—Blackbeard dead and Stede Bonnet captured. This will please Captain Woodes Rogers."

"It's good news to everyone in the province," Maurice Moore observed. "The scandalous part of it is that we had to rely on Virginia's Governor to do our dirty work for us, instead of our own Governor taking action."

"What happened?" asked David Moray. "There was a great deal of talk when I was in the Albemarle about the collusion of Governor Eden and Tobias Knight, with Blackbeard the pirate. Has there been any new development in the case?"

"Enough to implicate Knight," Maurice Moore answered. "He'll have to put up a good case in the autumn term of High Court, or he'll be sent to England, under the charge of high treason. When Lieutenant Maynard had his successful fight with Blackbeard, another Virginia ship sailed up to Bath Town and discovered that a cargo of sugar, from a ship of Blackbeard's, had been stored in one of Knight's barns. The Virginia captain loaded the sugar in his ship and carried it off to his province. Now Eden is making a wrathful protest to Governor Spottswood for its return to North Carolina."

A laugh went up from the men.

"Where was Governor Eden when all this excitement was going on at Bath Town?" David Moray asked.

Maurice Moore lifted his wineglass to his lips and returned the glass to the table before he answered. "Our Governor always manages to be in the clear. He was safe in Eden House, on the Chowan River, when the capture took place and when Blackbeard was killed. Some say he fled from his Bath Town residence in the dark of the night, and rode post-haste up the Governor's Road to Eden House as though all the devils in hell were after him." Moore's face hardened; his strong jaw was thrust forward. "But we found enough evidence, Moseley and I, so that his Excellency will have to stand trial for conspiracy. We haven't much chance of convicting him. No matter what the verdict is here, the final trial will have to be held in England, and the Lords Proprietors will never convict one of their own governors."

Gabrielle looked about the table. It was borne in on her with increasing consciousness that this was a masculine world, and the problems that faced them were not only the problems of the fight to conquer the wilderness, but of a stern and terrible justice, justice to high and low alike, so that there would be equality for all the people. She glanced at Molly. She was looking from one man to another in bewilderment. She had never in her life been so close to realities. The bright, frivolous world of gay, casual talk and barbed satire based on trivialities gave her no background of experience. She knew only the fringes of the pleasant, placid stream. She was unprepared for the deep current that flowed about her. She was timid and frightened by the iron strength behind the men's words. She did not understand justice for everyone. Justice was for the few priviliged people in high places.

The boys were leaning forward, listening eagerly. They were of such tender years, Gabrielle wondered what it would do to them. Suddenly she was afraid of the harsh, stark cruelty of the New World.

While the others talked, Sandy MacAlpin said nothing. He went on eating Barton's well-cooked food with gusty relish. Now he laid his knife and fork down. "We stand to lose this country if we don't have strong government," he said forthrightly. "We must have strength, and strong people—not only to establish our villages and plantations, but to keep the Indians subject. When we're weak, the Indians know it. They take advantage and prey on us. Don't imagine because Chief Blont has signed a treaty, that we've the redskins in the palm of our hands. I've followed the Cape Fear and all its tributaries, through the Indian country to the western mountains, and I know."

This was a long speech for Sandy. When he had finished, he picked up his knife and fork and attacked the second helping of venison that Barton placed before him.

Roger Mainwairing nodded his approbation. "No one knows better than you, Sandy, that we have danger behind us as well as in front of us. The Indians press from the forest, and the pirates from the sea; and there must be unity among the few of us who are here, if we wish our land to grow strong and prosper."

David leaned forward. His shoulder brushed against Gabrielle's arm as he engaged Roger Mainwairing's attention. "Have you any way of recovering on the loss of your ship that Anne Bonney captured, Mainwairing?"

Roger laughed. "I've written it off. I've lost only one ship in the last three years, so I don't complain."

"There's a smart woman, even if she is a pirate," MacAlpin said with reluctant admiration. "She sailed right out over Frying Pan Shoals under Rhett's guns, while her partner Stede Bonnet dangled a white flag and cried surrender. Aye, and she took a prize with her. Captain Michael Cary was stomping around, cursing himself black in the face at the loss of his ship; but if it hadn't been for David, here, she would have had Cary captive, as well as his ship."

Gabrielle looked quickly at Molly. She was gazing at Sandy, white-faced. She endeavoured to put the glass, which she held in her hand, on the table. It struck against her plate, and the wine spilled—a great red splotch on the white cloth. Gabrielle rose. To her surprise, her voice was quite steady. "Let's leave the gentlemen to their port, Molly." Her quiet words covered Molly's confusion.

"I'm so sorry," Molly said to Robert. "I hope Barton won't punish me, as she used to when I was little."

It was a pitiful attempt; her voice was high and unnatural. Gabrielle hoped no one suspected the real cause of Molly's embarrassment. Then she caught David Moray's eye. She knew he was aware that it was Michael Cary's name, and not the wine on the tablecloth, that had made Molly's lips pale and her hand tremble.

The moment the door closed after them, Molly caught Gabrielle's arm. She gave a little forced laugh, with her head thrown back. "So Captain Michael Cary was here!" She tried to speak casually but the look in her eyes betrayed her.

"Yes, Molly, he was here. The pirates captured him and his ship, but David Moray helped him escape. He was with us three days. That was last month."

"Where did he go?" Molly lost all pretence of indifference. "Oh, Gabrielle, to think I've missed him by so little. Tell me, how did he look? Did you speak of me?"

Gabrielle shook her head. "I said nothing about you, Molly. In truth, I spoke little to him, and never alone. We were in great distress at the time. A home was burned; several people were injured. My mother was almost beside herself from the cannon. We had all we could do to quiet her."

Molly moved about the room, touching a chair or a table. "To think he was here—here in this room!" she murmured. A smile rose to her lips, a delicate, subtle smile that suggested some cherished remembrance. "How could you see him without loving him, Gabrielle? Can't you see how noble he is? Noble and brave, a man who rises above all others."

Gabrielle listened to her, an incredulous look in her deep brown eyes. "Have you lost your head, Molly Lepel?"

"Perhaps more than my head," Molly answered. Her eyes seemed larger and deeper than Gabrielle remembered; but there were small lines of discontent at the corners of her mouth, a look of disillusionment, almost fear. "Don't say it, Gaby. I know he's married. He has never let me forget that. But I don't care, I'd go with him, anywhere." She sat down, her hands loosely in her lap. "I mean to follow him—Nassau, Jamaica, the Southern Isles. Wherever he goes, I shall go too."

Gabrielle noticed the strength of her small jaw, set in stubborn lines. Molly threw her arms wide. "Oh, Gabrielle, pray the good God that you will never love as I love Michael Cary! The memory of him drives me to complete despair."

Gabrielle heard the men talking. They were getting up from the table. She heard her Father say, "I've been thinking about the Indians. There must be some way to bring them closer to God." In a moment the men would be in the room.

"Control yourself, my dear. Quick, run upstairs and wash your eyes."

Molly jumped to her feet. She snatched up a lighted candle from the shelf near the hall door. Her skirts swayed and fluttered as she ran from the room. A trace of rare scent rose from her garments. When she came back a few minutes later, there was no trace of melancholy in her lovely face. Roger Mainwairing asked her for a song of his fancy. She sat down at Gabrielle's harp and sang a sad song in a sprightly manner.

> "Lay a garland on my hearse
>   Of dismal yew.
> Maidens, willow branches bear.
>   Say I died true;
> My love was false, but I was firm
>   From my hour of birth.
> Upon my buried body lie
>   Lightly, gentle earth."

Gabrielle poured brandy from the glass decanter. David stepped to her side. "Let me assist you," he said. He took the tray of glasses and passed the brandy. When he finished, he returned and took a seat beside her. Under cover of the

460

general conversation, he said, "I trust Miss Molly doesn't put too much faith in Captain Cary."

She looked at him, trying to read, in his hazel eyes, just what his words conveyed. She must not betray Molly. She tried to keep her voice casual. "Molly has many enthusiasms, and Captain Cary is attractive."

David's brow darkened. "I suppose he is attractive to women."

Gabrielle smiled. "Yes. I fancy most women like a man of elegant manners, one who constantly pays them the compliment of being interested in them." She felt the satisfaction of a little revenge, when his brow grew even more clouded.

"I suppose Cary is all that. But just the same, if I were Mistress Molly, I'd have a care."

"Do you know something to Captain Cary's discredit?" Gabrielle asked. Moray was silent. He had said all he intended to say. A warning and no more.

Gabrielle felt an increasing uneasiness. Her own distrust of the man; Molly's wild words; now David Moray's warning following Edward Colston's.

"Since Captain Cary is not here and probably will never be here again, I presume we need not worry about his morals." She looked directly at David. "I suppose it is the Captain's morals . . . ?"

They were back on the old footing of opposition. It hurt Gabrielle deeply. They talked as two people in a play. Could he have forgotten so soon? Did he take every woman in his arms?

"Damn Captain Cary's morals!" David muttered under his breath. "Any subject would do for a disagreement between us." He rose, bowed elegantly and crossed the room to join Maurice Moore and Roger Mainwairing, who were talking to Molly.

Gabrielle glanced about the room. Her father and the boys had disappeared. Sandy MacAlpin had left immediately after supper. She noticed that the knob of the door which led to the wing where her mother lived was turning from the other side. The door opened slowly; her mother stood in the doorway. Gabrielle saw Celestine's frightened face directly behind her. She rose and walked quickly across to her mother's side and made a low curtsy before her.

Madam Fountaine looked from one to the other. A delicate, hesitant confusion seemed to hover about her.

"Good evening, gentlemen," she said, nodding carelessly to Gabrielle. "I wish to make my guests welcome."

No one spoke. Gabrielle took her mother's hand and led her to the elbow chair by the fireplace. "Madam, will you be seated so that I may present your guests."

Madam sat down and spread her blue silk skirts about her, so that only the points of her little satin shoes showed beneath the ruffled petticoat. She straightened the lace of her fichu, and laid her thin white hands on the arm of the chair. Her hair, in the candlelight, had the colour of pale gold.

Gabrielle said, "Madam, may I present Mr. Maurice Moore, of the Albemarle?"

Madam Fountaine extended her hand. Maurice raised it to his lips. "I am honoured," he said.

"Mr. Roger Mainwairing, of Queen's Gift, Madam, and Mr. David Moray." The men, each in turn, bowed and kissed Madam's hand, answered her murmured words of greeting.

Molly swept a great curtsy, and sat on a footstool at Madam's right.

Gabrielle motioned to Celestine, who came quickly across the room to stand beside her mistress. Her face was troubled. She said in a low aside, "She heard voices. She would come, in spite of all I could do to prevent."

Gabrielle felt the cold sweat in the palms of her hands and on her forehead. Her stomach contracted in fear. What would happen? One thing: they must not oppose her now. So much was at stake. Perhaps this was the beginning of a return to normal.

"I thought I heard music," Madam said, looking from one strange face to the other. "Someone was singing."

Molly, too, was puzzled, but she answered without hesitation, "It was my poor voice you heard, Madam."

"A sweet voice, but a trifle thin, my dear. When you have had a little experience, it will fill out." She turned to Gabrielle, a slight note of displeasure in her voice. "Gabrielle, why have you not had the card tables set up, and some refreshment and drink? I will not have my guests think we lack in hospitality."

"Yes, Madam. I will get the tables at once." She went to the door and spoke to Barton, who stood wide-eyed with astonishment. "Bring card tables and playing decks, Barton."

Roger Mainwairing sat down beside Madam Fountaine's chair. "I am sure you sing, Madam," he said quietly. Ga-

462

brielle loved him for his acceptance of the situation, treating it as if it were, in every way, normal.

"Yes. Once my voice was good. But not now." She put her delicate fingers to her head. "I've been ill," she said vaguely, "quite ill."

David Moray brought her a glass. "Madam, this is a delicious port. Will you not try it? It is strength-giving."

Madam smiled up at the tall young Scot, a dazzling smile, her crimson lips opening over her small white teeth. "You are very good, sir. I'm afraid I don't remember your name."

"David, Madam. David Moray."

"Of course. Gabrielle just mentioned it. Please sit near me.

"It is so nice to have guests once more. It has been so long ..." She passed her hand across her eyes. "Ah! There is Robert. Come in, Robert. You want to see me about the garden? I am sure these gentlemen and this sweet young girl will not mind if we talk about my garden."

Robert Fountaine did not move from the doorway. Surprise, apprehension, anguish, followed each other over his expressive face. His eyes questioned Gabrielle. She nodded. "Madam has planned a beautiful garden with the Holland bulbs, bordered with fleur-de-lis."

Madam nodded her beautifully coiffed head, a look of pleasure on her face. "You remembered about the lilies," she said to Gabrielle. "That is a good girl." She glanced from one face to another. "You know I love the lilies of France. We have always had them in our garden. I can't imagine a garden without rich purple lilies." She broke off and put her hand to her eyes, as if to brush away something unpleasant. "They trampled our garden. The soldiers ..." She began to tremble. Her eyes grew incredibly large and dark. "Heavy, coarse boots on ..."

Celestine touched her arm. "Come, Madame. It is time for your rest. You must not overtax your strength."

Madam looked at Roger Mainwairing. "Do not think me discourteous, if I make my duties and leave you gentlemen to your games." She rose and leaned on Celestine's arm for a moment. Then she drew herself erect. With a slight, gracious bow to the gentlemen present, she moved slowly across the room and out the door. Robert Fountaine followed her.

Gabrielle realized that she had gripped the back of a chair until her knuckles whitened.

Molly said, "She is very thin, but she is so much better."

Gabrielle breathed easier. Molly had not realized the true

situation. The pattern of life her mother had known years ago was so deeply engrained she had not deviated a hair's breadth from it.

Gabrielle took up where Molly left off. "It's the first time Mother has seen any guests since her illness began. I'm so happy that you were here, all of you, our few friends, who have grown so dear to us."

She laid her hand, for a moment, on Roger Mainwairing's arm. He felt it tremble against his sleeve. He was the only one who realized the truth. He said, "Madam Fountaine is vastly improved since I saw her on the journey over, last summer. Vastly."

Gabrielle thanked him with her eyes. No one appeared to notice that her mother regarded her as a servant, her husband as her steward. It had all passed them by.

"I'm certain," David Moray said, "that Madam Fountaine will improve even more when she can get out into the garden."

Maurice Moore took up the cards, shuffled them deliberately. "A little game of piquet, Mainwairing?"

"If you don't play too late. You know I'm riding on to Charles Town tomorrow." Roger patted Gabrielle's hand and crossed to the table.

"Is it too cold to look at the stars?" Molly asked David, looking up into his face with a little inviting glance. "I wonder if the stars in Carolina are different from the stars in England."

"Quite! They're much more potent. I'll get a wrap for you," Moray said with alacrity.

Gabrielle felt suddenly very tired. She left the room to find her father. He had gone from Madame's room, Celestine told her. Madame was resting, no worse, she thought, for her excursion. Celestine's eyes were red. She had been weeping. Gabrielle put her arm about her and snuggled her face against the faithful woman's plump neck.

"She whispered, "Oh, Celestine, I was so frightened when I saw her. I did not want anyone to know."

Celestine's words were reassuring. "No one surmised. No one except Mr. Mainwairing, and he already knew from the ship. Have no fear, Ma'm'slle."

Gabrielle dabbed at her eyes with a thin linen handkerchief. "I must find my father," she said, and left the room.

Robert Fountaine was in the weaving shed when Gabrielle found him. She opened the door quietly. He did not see her.

He was sitting at the loom, his long thin fingers flying back and forth, back and forth. Deep shadows fell upon him, cut by the flicker of the wood fire on the hearth. She opened her mouth to speak, but thought better of it. Solitude was Robert Fountaine's comfort and the source of his strength. She closed the door softly and started for the house.

The night was clear. The stars seemed almost within reach of her hand, little flecks of light in the velvet blackness of the sky. She moved across the space between the weaving shed and the house. She saw the blurred figures of a man and a woman walking along the bank, above the river. They moved slowly, close together. A surge of loneliness came over her. Her feet dragged as she walked towards the open door. She felt lonely and a little afraid of what lay before her.

The boys were in their beds, sound asleep, when Gabrielle went in. She spread an extra quilt on each bed, for the night was cold, and touched René's cheek gently. He moved a little and murmured something. She caught the words "pirates," and "long black beards." It was not good for young boys to be thinking of criminals. She would talk to her father. The boys must go to school, either to William and Mary College, in Williamsburg, or to King William's School, at Annapolis in Maryland. Perhaps there was a good one in Charles Town. She would ask Mr. Mainwairing about schools.

She took up the bed candle and went to her room. Molly was still outside, looking at the stars with David Moray. Gabrielle was strangely annoyed. She remembered how often at Meg's Lane Molly had made excuses to run out to the garden to see the handsome bondman. She remembered also what Molly had said, this evening, when they had gone into the great room—that she had always known David Moray was a gentleman. She was never fooled, not for a moment, as Gabrielle had been. "Why were you always so distant and superior when you spoke to David? You were never like that with your other servants." She thought of the tall, lean-faced man, with his long jaw, hawk nose and firm mouth, which even the pointed beard did not conceal. She should have recognized the soldierlike bearing as quickly as Molly. But how could she, when he was always bent over a flower-bed, his body concealed by the blue gardener's smock?

She blew out the candle and opened the window towards the river. She saw again the shadowy forms of Molly and

David. They were standing still, facing the river where the riding lights of the ship were visible in the darkness.

The front door opened and Gabrielle heard the voice of Colonel Moore. "I plan to make my camp near the site where Moseley had laid out our new town of Brunswick. I figure it will take a week for my men to slash the lines and outline the square and the market place and run a road down to the river landing."

Roger said, "You sound as though you were going to auction town lots next month."

Moore laughed. He had a strong, full-bodied laugh, with humour to it. "I wish that were true. I'd like nothing so well as to get out of the Albemarle, if Eden is going to remain governor. But my brother Roger writes me he cannot arrange his affairs to leave South Carolina under three or four years. Roger's the constructive member of our family. The success of this settlement will rest on his shoulders. They tell me I'm only a dreamer, that I don't see things through."

The conversation was interrupted by the arrival of MacAlpin and a tall Negro, carrying a lanthorn.

"Excuse me for interrupting you, gentlemen," Sandy said, "but your man Metephele and I have been out to the River Road investigating. There have been three war parties, of about twenty-five each, pass by the bridge on Old Town Creek. I think they're headed for the Great Road, on their way to South Carolina. I don't like the look of it. I was about to say, Mr. Ma'n'ring, I wouldn't care to be ridin' horseback down that road, at this time. 'Twouldn't be safe."

"Do you think there's going to be more Indian trouble between here and Charles Town?"

"Might be, and might not, sir. But if 'twas my party, I'd take ship instead of roadway."

"They've been expecting trouble in the south, for some time," Maurice Moore said. "This may be it."

Gabrielle leaned against the window sill. She had no thought of eavesdropping. This was something that concerned them all. She heard Mainwairing say:

"Thank you, MacAlpin. I'll take your advice and continue the journey by ship. Metephele, will you get my boxes from the bachelors' house? We'll go on board tonight."

"That's good. There's no need of walking wide-eyed into Indian trouble."

"Will you look after my horses until I come back, Sandy?"

"That I will. We've plenty of pasturage on Moray's plantation."

They moved off, and Gabrielle heard no more; but it was enough to make the old feeling of the danger lurking in the forest come back to her. She shivered and crept into the warmth of the feathers, and pulled the blankets up to her chin. For a long time she lay sleepless in the dark, staring at the ceiling. She heard Molly's footsteps coming quietly up the stairs. They paused at her open door. The glow from the candle she held in her hand made a flickering shadow on the counterpane. Gabrielle did not speak, and, after a time Molly tiptoed down the hall to her room, where Gabrielle heard her moving about, humming a little song. She could never understand Molly Lepel. A few hours ago she was passionately declaring her deathless love for Michael Cary; and now . . . Gabrielle put her hand over her eyes. She wanted to shut out the image of Molly and David Moray, standing side by side in the shadow.

She was half asleep when she heard Sandy MacAlpin say, "I've talked to Treloar, and he's putting on extra sentries at night. Kullu tells it is the season for the Indians to camp on the beaches at the mouth of the river." His words faded and became part of a restless dream, a succession of pictures, in which she stood at the watch tower, a musket in her hand, looking into the deep green isles of the forest. Then she was running through the trees, in the night, with no light but the flash of the fireflies, deeper and deeper into the great swamp, splashing in the black water, the heavy earth clinging to her, sucking her into the horrible slime. She cried aloud for help. No one came. The tears ran down her cheeks. She knew fear, stark terror. Then a hand caught her shoulder, a strong firm hand, dragging her out of the heavy, clinging mud.

"Wake up! Wake up! You're crying out fit to wake the dead."

Gabrielle opened her eyes. Barton stood over her, her hard, bony fingers grasping her shoulder. Two skimpy braids hung over her flannel gown, and she looked frightened. "You've been riding a night horse clear into the sky," Barton went on, sourly. "Looks like a body gets no sleep around here any more."

She took up her candle and walked off. Gabrielle sat up and looked out of the east window. A rim of gold cut the dark horizon. She heard the rattle of anchor chain, and the voices of the sailors. The ship was moving slowly down stream.

The rains were late. All February and into March, the earth was saturated and the water lay in pools on the surface. In the swamp, the growth was rank, an unearthly yellow green that made the forest look as if the sun were shining. The ground was covered with tender green and the first sunshine of April brought a carpet of flowers. Yellow azaleas sprang up out of the burnt-over areas, hiding the charred and blackened remnants of the autumn fires.

In April, Madam's garden was in full bloom. Holland bulbs nodded gaily in the beds. The leaves were out in the bushes Annaci had transplanted to make a hedge around the garden and cut it off from the kitchen wing.

Every fair day Madam walked in the garden, watching the flowers opening to full bloom. Some days she was strong enough to dig with a small trowel, loosening the earth around the green leaves of the daffodils, or pausing to tie up a wild jasmine vine, now a blanket of yellow bloom. She spoke little, but often hummed some gay French song.

More than once Gabrielle had seen her father standing in the door of the weaving shed, watching his wife, his face white with poignant sorrow. Madam had received the boys so easily. Sometimes she walked with them, her white hands on the arm of each, talking of the flowers, the birds and the beauty of the river. They had accepted her loss of memory with the ready ease of youth, adapting themselves to whatever situation arose. Molly knew, now. She spent long hours singing or talking with Madam. Gabrielle saw that her mother was growing fond of Molly. She smiled when the girl's infectious laughter rang out. Molly was like an April day, all smiles or all tears. Sometimes, for hours, she sat in her room, writing. Writing letters home, she said, but Gabrielle knew better. She had broken completely with her Aunt Lepel and her cousin Mary. It was over Lord Hervey, in reality, though the reason they gave for banishing Molly from their *ménage* was her conduct with Michael Cary.

Half the women of fashion went to hear Mr. Handel's music or drink a cup of China tea in the East India warehouse. Molly could not see why Aunt Lepel had made a fuss; she always wore a vizard when she went to meet Michael, like any woman of fashion. It was not as if she had gone to his rooms, though sometimes she wished she had.

468

Gabrielle said nothing to this. She was weary of hearing Molly talk of London, of Mr. Addison and Dean Swift and young Henry Fielding. She was weary of the ladies of Mapledurham and Mr. Alexander Pope, and quite worn out with Lord Fanny, as Molly called Hervey, and his mad infatuation for Lady Mary Montagu. The real reason Aunt Lepel hated her, Molly told Gabrielle more than once, was that she had caught Lord Hervey kissing Molly's hand in much too lingering a manner to suit her ideas of the conventions. A lovely young girl about was too dangerous to her plan of marrying her daughter to Lord Hervey.

Gabrielle was interested only in things that belonged to the New World: how Edward Moseley's and Maurice Moore's trial would come out; whether there would be enough evidence, when Christopher Gale appeared before the Lords Proprietors to ask for the removal of Governor Eden; whether Stede Bonnet had been hanged in Charleston, on Execution Wharf; how much profit her father would make on the first shipment of worsteds he had sent to Woodes Rogers' colony; and how long could they hold Sandy MacAlpin in their settlement, now that winter had passed.

The fields were green. The river teemed with shad and herring, leaping out of the water at dusk or daybreak. Birds were singing. The mockers were tuning up, rehearsing for the full song of late spring. The indigo plants were two inches high and growing. The men had cut canals in the marsh and rice had been planted. Dear Lord, here was the beginning of a dream, long desired!

All this was in Gabrielle's mind as she rode down the track that led to the lakes. She had forgotten the heavy suffocation of the swamps and the Indians moving stealthily along the forest paths. She had forgotten the pirates and Stede Bonnet's attack on their homes.

The day was warm, the breeze against her cheek was soft, the long streamers of moss on the oaks moved with the gentle wind. "Lord, Lord, I thank Thee for our blessing."

She spoke the words aloud. They seemed to skim across the dark waters of the lake and reverberate among the rushes that grew at the water's edge.

At the charcoal-burners' hut, a few miles up Far Reach, a half-dozen Indians from some wandering band waited behind the trees. When dusk fell, they closed in silently. With terrible shouting and whooping and brandishing of sharpened knives, they attacked the two defenceless men working at the kiln.

Sandy MacAlpin found their mutilated bodies: Marius Akim and Zack Reeves, who, scarcely a month ago, had married the Weatherby girl and set up housekeeping just beyond the stockade.

He stood looking down in anger and despair at the bloody, scalped bodies, stiff and grotesque. This colony would go as the earlier ones had gone. The forest would close in on them. The forest would not let them encroach on its ancient fastness.

Chapter 31

A VIZARD AND A SWORD

Roger Mainwairing stood at the rail of the *Phoebus*, as the ship passed Sullivan Island on its journey into the river. By the time it docked they could see crowds of people waiting on the shore, as if something out of the ordinary were expected.

People stood aside respectfully when Roger passed down the wharf. He made a fine figure, in his dark blue coat, his fine doeskin riding breeches and his high boots, varnished by Metephele until they reflected the glint of sword and spurs. The day was warm. The women passing along the ·cobbled streets in their carriages wore cotton garments and wide hats. Their gay sunshades formed a pattern of bright colors as they made slow progress along the waterfront streets.

Roger walked down to the market place. His Charles Town agents, Samuel Deane and Edward Brailsford, had their counting house off Market Place, and he wanted to talk over the cargo of the *Francis*, lost when it was captured by Anne Bonney some months previous.

He found Brailsford in his office. A short, rotund man with a ruddy face, Brailsford had a quickness and energy not often seen in the indolent climate of Charles Town. He greeted Roger with heart-warming cordiality. He shouted to a slave to bring him his white linen coat, which hung behind the door on a peg. The slave held it while his master arranged the ruffles of his fine cambric shirt before he slipped his arms into the sleeves.

"Your arrival is most timely, Mainwairing," Brailsford said. "I'm meeting some friends at the Exchange for a little refreshment and a glass of fishhouse punch."

They crossed the square and went into a ground-floor room in the Exchange, where merchants and planters met to talk over matters of shipping and trade.

Half a dozen men had already arrived, some of whom Roger knew: Ralph Izard and Arthur Middleton; Rutledge, from the Santee district. Brailsford introduced Roger to

Colonel Thomas Broughton, Speaker of the lower house of the Assembly, a tall man well over six feet, with broad shoulders and a quiet, reserved manner. The Colonel spoke of his friends in the Albemarle, Maurice Moore and Edward Moseley. He had recently come back from the upper river country, he told Roger. There was Indian trouble there. The Indians were carrying off cattle and hogs. There had been no killing of the white settlers yet, but the situation was not good.

"We hear nothing of red Indians in Charles Town," the Colonel observed. He accepted a glass of fish-house punch from the ancient slave who presided over the enormous silver punch bowl, and the two sat down on a window seat.

"Charles Town is too engrossed in pirates to think of anything else," Roger said. "We've been in like case, but Blackbeard is dead, and since he was our greatest menace, we have time to turn to something else."

"Eden's complicity?" Broughton asked, raising his heavy eyebrows. "I suppose you'll never really know how far Eden went in encouraging the pirates. Roger Moore tells me that Tobias Knight is sure to be convicted."

"So I think," Roger said, answering the second statement. Broughton's eyes turned to a newcomer, wearing the uniform of a Captain of his Majesty's Navy.

"Will you pardon me, Mr. Mainwairing? I must speak to the Honourable Captain Thomas Howard, of his Majesty's ship *Shoreham*. The Captain has been sent here, on special commission from England, on matters concerning the pirate trials," he added by way of explanation.

Roger was joined by Samuel Deane and Brailsford. Brailsford wanted to point out the ship models that were displayed in another room.

From there they went to the dinner room, where Brailsford had reserved a table near a window that looked beyond a garden, now in luxuriant bloom of tropical brilliance, to the harbour and ships at anchor below the island.

A dozen men stopped at their table to speak with the merchants. There was but one topic of comment—Stede Bonnet, the arch pirate, or "archipirato," as Judge Trott, of the Admiralty Court, titled him. From all these sources, Brailsford gave Roger the full story.

It seems that Rhett had captured Stede Bonnet and his ship, the *Royal James*, in the Cape Fear, in October, and brought him to Charles Town to stand trial. With him were two of his men, Herriot and Ignatius Pell, as wicked and brutal a pair as could be found in all the Caribbean. The town went wild when Rhett's ships and their prize sailed in. Merchants thought that with the capture of Stede their troubles would be over.

"We didn't dream that it was only the beginning of our troubles." Brailsford lifted his glass to his lips. He began stripping the backbone from a large section of sea trout. Sam Deane took up the story. He was a sombre-faced man, always gloomy and despondent over the prospects of successful trade; yet he had amassed a fortune and had a fine house on the point.

"I told Brailsford it would be this way. All the pirates in the Caribbean are sailing our waters, waiting for a chance to dash in to rescue their leader. Can you imagine it? The pirate hordes have boldly defied the merchants; yea, and the officers of his Majesty's Navy. They've thrown the black flag to the winds of every sea. They inhabit our islands, Edisto, Johns, and Sullivan. They sail boldly up creeks and inlets and up the Ashley River, to prey on settlements and plantations."

He turned his gloomy eyes on Roger. "It's the fault of North Carolina. You've given the vandals, the desperate, evil vandals, the protection of your government. What can we do, as long as they can sail for sanctuary behind the North Carolina Banks, and hide in the deep water of the Cape Fear River?"

Roger had no time to say a word in defence. When Deane stopped for breath, Brailsford took up the story:

"We've petitioned the King, the Lords Proprietors, the Lords of Trade and Plantations. They do nothing. Nothing. The only help we've had was from Woodes Rogers, who sends us a guardship now and then. But he has all he can do to keep the beasts out of New Providence Island. Why, we've lost six ships and six English cargoes this year. We will all be bankrupt if this continues."

Brailsford stopped long enough to take a generous portion of baked chicken the Negro waiter put before him.

Roger said, "With Blackbeard disposed of and Stede Bonnet in gaol, surely you can look for some improvement."

"Gaol? Gaol did you say?" Deane and Brailsford spoke together. "We have no gaol strong enough to hold a child."

"Then where in God's name have you got Stede Bonnet?" Roger exclaimed.

Deane leaned forward and dropped his voice so that the

men seated at near-by tables might not overhear. He said bitterly, "You'd scarce believe it, but Bonnet's at the home of the Marshal, in his custody. Because he was once a gentleman! All they do is place two sentinels about the house every evening at sunset."

Brailsford handed over his empty plate, his ruffles dragging in his teacup. "Our harbour is practically blockaded, Mainwairing. A sloop from Jamaica got in yesterday only by a trick of sailing. Her captain told me that he saw half a dozen sail carrying the black flag, standing off the entrance, waiting to prey on shipping. More than that, some folk believe that Vane and Worley and Rackham—aye, and that despicable Anne Bonney—are waiting their time to come in and rescue their brother-in-piracy Bonnet."

His round eyes swept the room, contempt openly displayed in his face. "It's hard to believe it, sir, but we have men, merchants and planters, some of them seated in this very room, who are ready to befriend these vile fellows, even Stede Bonnet. I say to the shame of Charles Town that such a fact is true. Friends he has, numerous and strong enough to be a very effective force in thwarting the officers of the law in the discharge of their duty."

Brailsford's voice rose in indignation. "Yes, a considerable number who want to deal with pirates and freebooters, because of the gold it brings them."

A sudden silence followed. A man at a nearby table rose and came across the room, a spare man with a sandy complexion and a long, thin-bridged nose. His lips were narrow and turned back over discoloured teeth. "Do you name names, Mr. Brailsford? Or do you take refuge in vague generalities?" he said, towering over the table.

Brailsford sprang to his feet. "I'll name names, since you ask for names. Yours, Mr. James Trigg. Yours and that rascally son of yours. You've made money, in trade, with your ship, while honest merchants see their cargoes sunk or held ransom."

Roger rose, too, and backed away to give Brailsford a free space to draw.

Deane said, "This is a matter for private discussion, not public."

"The charge was public. Let us fight it out in public," said Trigg. He swung with his clenched fist. Brailsford, who expected a challenge, sent in proper and dignified manner according to a gentleman's code, was taken unaware. The

474

blow landed on his jaw. It sent him reeling against the wall and then in a crash to the floor. His wig fell off, exposing his pink, shaven poll.

"For shame!" came from a dozen voices.

"No brawling within this room!" A white-haired man of dignified bearing pushed his way forward. "No hitting with fists. If you want to duel, do it in the regular way."

Deane, who was bending over his partner, looked up. "Get a doctor, someone. He's scarce breathing."

"I request you to leave this room, Mr. Trigg," the white-haired man said in a tone of authority.

Roger helped stretch Mr. Brailsford out on the floor. Someone opened a window to let in fresh air. A black waiter placed a screen around the stricken man. Roger heard nothing but words of contempt for Trigg:

"What can you expect of a bounder, and a man of low origin, who fights with fists?"

"The governors should bar him from the Exchange."

A man seated at the next table laughed unpleasingly. "Bar him from the Exchange? Why, half the merchants in Carolina are in Trigg's debt."

"Brailsford's a fool, but he has courage. It's time for someone to speak out about the scandalous performances that go on here."

"Fancy, allowing Bonnet to roam the town at will. They say, 'He's given his word!' Hah! What does a pirate's oath mean? I ask you!"

The doctor came. He leaned over Brailsford to listen to his heart beat, shook his head and called for the waiters to carry him to the antechamber, where he could attend to him properly.

"His heart's not too good," the doctor said to Deane. "A shock, after a full meal, and he's like to have a stroke. We must get him home and into his bed as soon as possible. I think the fellow smashed his jaw."

Roger stayed with Deane until a vehicle came to carry the injured man to his house on the Ashley. Brailsford was conscious when they lifted him into the carriage. "I thought I'd force him to swords," he whispered. "But the damned low scoundrel fought like a gutter man."

"Don't exert yourself," Deane said with more solicitude than Roger thought him capable of.

Brailsford pressed Roger's hand. "Sorry, Mr. Mainwairing.

Don't misunderstand us South Carolinians. We don't always brawl."

Roger walked up the street towards St. Philip's. He had sent Metephele, with his boxes, to the house of his friend, Colonel Alexander Paris, where he usually stayed while he was in Charles Town.

Paris had a house on White Point also, as well as his plantation on the river. He would probably find his host at the Parsonage House, where some of the Assembly members were having a private meeting.

As he walked along the street, he could scarcely suppress his wonder at the growth of the settlement. It was far beyond Edenton; on a par with Williamsburg in volume of business.

At the parsonage House gate, he saw Michael Cary. He recognized him at once, although it had been several years since Cary had quitted the Albemarle. The Captain was dressed in elegant style, wearing a sword and carrying his wide hat under his arm, his long chestnut hair in curls down his back. Cary was coming out of the garden of a fine house with a fashionably-dressed woman wearing a large hat, tied with a crimson tissue veil. Roger thought there was something familiar about her, but he could not see her face. In addition to her drooping hat brim, she wore a black silk vizard, such as the London women wore, and only her chin was visible, and the suggestion of full, red lips under the black chantilly lace that fringed the vizard.

Roger paused to watch them walk down towards the sea wall, still puzzled over the suggestion of familiarity in the woman's easy grace. Another thing occurred to him: was it not strange for a fashionable woman to be strolling at this time of day, when all Charles Town was indoors taking its siesta?

He gave a coin to the old Negro who sat on the carriage block in front of the Parsonage House with his basket of bright yellow daffodils. He refused the bunch the old man extended in his black, palsied hand.

"Keep them, good uncle, and sell them to a young man, to take when he makes his call on some beautiful young woman." The old man thanked him and put the flowers back in the moss-lined basket. "Do you know the name of the lady who just passed by with the gentleman?"

"Ah expects you be foreign, Marster. Every ge'm'n in Charles Town know that lady is Madam Delphine Latour."

Roger put another coin in the ready black hand.

"Yes, sah. Thankee, sah. Madam, she live in the big house down on the point, d'rekly next to Co'n'l Alexander Paris' house. She come here not so long ago—two, three months maybe, excusin' one."

Mainwairing was halfway up to the Parsonage door when a thought struck him, and he turned back. "On second thought, I'll buy all of your flowers, uncle, if you'll take them to the lady's house, and have them there so you can give them to her just as she's entering her door."

The old man got to his feet with surprising alacrity. "Yes, Marster. Thank you, Marster." Grinning broadly, he pocketed the generous purchase money. "Shall I say who sent them, sah?"

"No, uncle. No name. Just say, 'A foreigner.' "

Mainwairing had his hand on the knocker when Metephele opened the door and said to him, "Colonel Paris man he out there with carriage. Colonel Paris he depart Nassau last week, but he's man say ever'thing ready for the Master."

Roger noticed that his giant *capita* had not only changed to a fresh white garment, but he had added his short red Zanzibar jacket, embroidered in gold thread. His red tarboosh was set sidewise over one eye, and the long black tassel hung to his shoulder.

A dozen small black boys stood by the carriage block, open-mouthed at such splendour. Roger smiled. Metephele always had a dramatic touch about his dress. He wanted the people of Charles Town to know that his master was a man of consequence. The *capita* opened the carriage door. After he had closed it, he walked around and took a seat beside the coachman, who looked almost a dwarf by the immense size of the Angoni warrior. Metephele folded his arms across his chest, and the carriage drove on, followed by an ever-increasing procession of chattering picanin's. They had never before, in all their lives, seen such magnificence in a black man, and they voiced their approval by exuberant cries of delight.

The noise made by Metephele's followers brought older people to their doors. Jalousie louvres moved, as unseen eyes of the womenfolk followed their progress. Roger found it hard to maintain his dignity and live up to the standard of elegance that Metephele had established. It reminded him of London, where crowds had always followed the black warrior wherever he went.

The bedroom that Colonel Paris' slave had assigned Roger

faced the water. It was a cool, high-ceilinged room, with windows on three sides. A great canopied bed, with a mosquito net, occupied the fourth wall. A French door opened onto the double gallery, on the garden side of the house. The garden was enclosed in a brick wall, and Roger, standing at the window, noticed that the flowers were much advanced over those of his own garden. The little summer-house near the water was covered by a jasmine vine in full flower. The lower end of the garden was shaded by a group of giant oaks, from which the Spanish moss trailed almost to the turf.

He crossed the room and looked out the opposite window. Beyond the brick wall was a large, rambling house with double galleries on three sides, set in a lovely garden. It was the last house on the point. It must be the home of Madam Delphine Latour. He smiled slightly and wondered whether his flowers had arrived in time to cause Captain Michael Cary a little embarrassment. He did not often harbour prejudices, but he had never fancied Michael and he liked him less after he had carried off innocent little Marita Tower, and married her without the consent of her guardian. Lady Mary had never acknowledged the marriage performed by the daft Quaker preacher, and she had taken the girl off to London.

This was all past history. He had the feeling that something of more vital interest lay in the present. Across the street was the Marshal's house, where Stede Bonnet was held, with freedom all the daylight hours, and only two sentries to guard him at night. All three houses were close to the water. Very close.

Metephele woke his master by pulling gently at the sheets at the bottom of the bed. He had slept all the afternoon. The sun was low, lighting the upper reaches of the river.

"Bath laid, Master. The bathing room is down the hall."

Roger took up his towels and left the room. Metephele had laid out the shaving brushes and honed the razor to a fine edge.

"The pirate captain lives there," he told Roger as he lathered his face. "He walks in his garden and people ride out from Charles Town to call on him. His men, they lay in the gaol, and some are chained to the wall; but the Captain, he walks around like a master. It is not good. I will sleep, this night, outside the master's door."

The soap stiffened Roger's face so that he could not smile.

478

The idea of danger, because they were close to the house where Stede Bonnet was confined, amused him.

While he was still at supper, a slave announced Mr. Roger Moore. Moore came into the dining-room and accepted a glass of brandy. He resembled his brother very little. He was darker in colouring, almost swarthy, and he moved quickly, whereas Maurice was deliberate. He had dark, piercing eyes that seemed to take in every detail at a glance. Maurice's eyes were deep-set and heavy-lidded, and given to dreams.

Moore at once plunged into political talk. Since they were alone, he could speak freely. The men of Charles Town were considering a break with the Lords Proprietors. They thought North Carolina should do the same. "We will do much better under the Crown," he said, moving nervously about the room. "Look at Virginia. As a Crown Colony she has a fine, stable government and a splendid governor. Look at the governors the Lords send us: a poor, indifferent lot of meagre intellects, with no thought but to make a fortune out of our trade, so that they can return to England. We want men to build our country—build and develop, not mulct dry of its resources. I tell you we must make a change . . ."

Moore stopped abruptly. In the distance a bell was ringing. They heard the slave going across the hall to the door.

Three or four men entered the hall, asking for Mr. Mainwairing. Roger rose from the table. "I think we may as well go into the drawing-room," he said to Moore.

Metephele came in and handed his master a twisted paper, placed in the exact centre of a small silver tray.

"Pardon," Roger murmured, but Moore had already left the room. Roger pulled the candle close to look at the note. It bore no name, just a few lines written in a large bold hand:

"To attempt to thank you for the wealth of flowers would seem futile. Yet I will make the attempt. Suppose we say, in my garden, after your guests have departed. The door in the garden wall, beyond the summerhouse. I will see that it is unlocked."

Roger smiled and slipped the note into the pocket of his embroidered waistcoat. There was an intriguing quality about it that interested him. "Bring the decanter to the drawing-room," he said to Metephele, who was eyeing him askance.

"Strange ships come in the nighttime, Cato says. Strange

ships and strange people." He moved his head in the direction of Madam Latour's house.

Roger found Deane and two of his merchant colleagues in the drawing-room. Moore after a few minutes went away. Metephele passed the glasses of port. Deane said that Brailsford was resting easily, but his jaw was broken. "I've sent a challenge to Trigg. I'm no pistol man, but I'll do my best for the honour of my firm."

"Trigg won't fight like a gentleman," one of the men said. "You may as well save your paper and wax."

They made themselves comfortable and began to talk of ships and shipping; of cargo sent to Jamaica and the Virgins; of sugar from Antigua, and spices from the Southern Islands. Trade was always increasing. They talked in figures and cargo-pounds, the ships needed and the problems of the planters along the river.

Deane waved his hand towards the Marshal's house. "You have a notorious neighbour, Mainwairing," he said with a laugh. "Have a care you aren't robbed in the night."

One of the merchants turned from the window where he had been standing. "It's the neighbour on this side who's the most devastating," he said. Filling his glass, he bowed to the unseen Madam Latour: "To beauty and mystery."

"I'll join you in that." Roger raised his glass.

Deane said, "I feel lucky tonight. Let's have a dice table. I'll throw you three hands that your ship doesn't run the pirate blockade, Izard."

"Done," said Izard.

The dicing went on until well after midnight. The passing watch called, "One o'clock, and moon at the full."

Roger stood at the open door and saw his guests walk down the path to their waiting carriages. The Marshal's house was in darkness. When he went back to the drawing room, Metephele had closed the dicing table and put the glasses on a tray.

"You need not wait up for me, Metephele," Roger told his servant. "I shall not go to bed for a little."

"I will wait for Master," the man said, lifting up the tray.

"No. I shan't need you. Go to bed at once." Roger spoke irritably.

"*Ndawo*, Master," the *capita* said, and left the room.

Roger glanced at the Sèvres clock on the mantel. Quarter past the hour. Damn the fellows, staying so late. One couldn't go about entering doors in garden walls at this late hour, even though the lock was turned. Better go upstairs to bed, he said to himself. But instead of following his common sense, he walked across the room and out onto the gallery. A ship lay off the point, not far from shore, its masts straight and tall.

The moon was high, the pattern of the garden outlined in silver splashes of light. Along the wall the shadows lay deep and fragrant. He walked down the path towards the river, and stood looking at the house next door. There was no sign of light. The wall was too high to see into the garden. He felt his pulse stir. I'm too old for moon madness, he thought. But still—there was the wall, and a door, half hidden under a vine covered with flowers that sent off a cloying sweet perfume, a heady intoxicating perfume. His hand found the latch. He raised it gently. The gate swung open without a sound, on oiled hinges.

He heard a faint movement and stepped back, his hand on the hilt of his sword.

A woman stood in the shadow at the open door. A woman's husky voice spoke quietly. "Your guests stayed overlate, Mr. Roger Mainwairing. I am weary of waiting."

"But you did wait, Madam Latour. For that I thank you." He bowed over the woman's hand. In the moonlight, her hand and arm were as white and cool as alabaster. She indicated a seat. Roger sat down. The chair was in the moonlight. She sat in the shadow. He saw that she wore a vizard, not a full mask with lace concealing her chin, but a small one that left her mouth and chin uncovered.

" 'Tis after twelve," he said with a laugh. "All dancers unmask at twelve. 'Tis tradition."

"I never follow tradition." Her voice was deep and husky. It had vibrations that made Roger think of a viola, and something more. Where had he heard that voice?

She shifted her chair. The faint perfume of amber came to him as she moved. Again the sensation of familiarity swept over him, gone in an instant. He tried to fix his mind, to bring back the vague recollection.

Madam was saying, "I must tell you how you pleasured me by the basket of flowers. The old man stood at my door, his gay basket held out before him. 'Madam,' he told me, 'Madam, 'tis the present of the handsome foreigner.' "

Roger Mainwairing laughed. Madam Latour went on: "I knew instantly who it was. I had seen you as we passed the gate of the Parsonage House."

"You did not look at me. I was desolated." This time it was the woman who laughed, a deep, throaty laugh that vibrated warmly.

"A vizard has its advantages, I assure you."

"Your escort did not glance my way. He was too intent, looking at his fair companion. A handsome fellow."

"Michael Cary?" She shrugged her shoulders. "Well enough, I suppose, but variable. A weathervane, blowing north and south, east and west." She paused. Roger had the feeling that she was laughing silently. *"Monsieur le Capitaine* did not approve of your great basket of flowers. He said a single flower, perfect and well chosen, denoted love. A great mass meant only the impulse of the moment."

"The impulse of the moment may be very pleasant." Roger got up and sat on the bench beside her. He, too, was in shadow, the warm pulsating shadow.

The fragrance of jasmine mingled with the clean essence of amber. Amber made him think of Egypt and the Near East, and a balcony of carved marble screens, and veiled women whose eyes flashed and invited behind the yashmak. Perhaps it was the garden or the moonlight, or the scent of amber that went to his head. He found himself taking the woman in his arms, pressing his mouth against her fragrant lips.

For a moment she was taken by surprise. Then her lips responded to his. Deep kisses. Her lips remained cold under his, but her arms were about him, and her body pressed close to him; a cold, hard passion, without warmth. Cold, cruel, yet strangely attractive. She drew him, yet at the same time repelled him.

"You are as cold as Luna," he whispered against her cheek.

"I am Luna. I am the moon's own daughter." She disengaged herself from his arms and got to her feet.

He rose too and stood in the doorway. "If you are Luna's daughter, come walk in her light."

She hesitated a moment, then followed Roger into the garden. He led the way down towards the water, moving in the moon-splashed path near the garden wall.

He noticed the ship again. "It must be sailing tonight," he said, as he watched the sail being hauled into place. "I wonder where it is bound."

"To the island of Martinique perhaps," she said dreamily. "My beloved island."

For the first time Roger noticed the slight trace of accent.

482

He thought he heard the sound of muffled oars come over the water.

Madam Latour shivered a little. She laid her hand on his arm. "Let us walk back to the summer-house." She walked close to him. He noticed she was tall and moved with easy, almost feline grace. She wore some soft, clinging robe that showed the movement of her limbs and the curve of her breasts. A woman to intoxicate a man's senses, thought Roger; better beware. He said, "So lovely a woman must have had an eventful life."

She shrugged her shoulder. "Not too eventful. I have had two husbands, but . . ." She paused as if she were listening, half turned towards the water. "Two husbands. Each time I thought I had found a man of power; a strong man, who could hold himself high among other men. Each time I was wrong." She spoke with intense bitterness, as though the words came from a deep resentment.

"Perhaps you are the one who has strength." He said it idly, just to say something. He too was listening. It seemed to him that suddenly the garden was alive.

"Strong enough to despise weak men," she said scornfully. She thrust her hand under his arm and walked more swiftly. "Come. The night wind is cool. I feel the need of brandy."

Inside the summer-house, she made her way to the table. Roger heard the gurgle of liquor.

"I am a cat. I can see in the dark," she commented. "Come, let me guide you."

Her fingers were cool in his as she led him to the bench. She touched her glass against his. He drank slowly. It was growing more shadowy, as though a cloud had crossed the moon. She took his empty glass and set it on the table. She moved closer to him.

"Your sword," she whispered. "It rubs against me." Roger loosened the buckle. The sword clanked to the floor.

"I'll trade a sword for a cowrie belt," she whispered, her cheek close to his. Roger's pulse leaped. A bold woman, without hesitation. He knew the meaning well enough. The cowrie shell girdle, which the African virgins wore about their waists.

Her arms were about him, her body close.

"Luna's daughter has more to give than the daughters of the sun."

Roger heard her words from a long distance. His head was light, his throat constricted. The brandy, on top of all he had drunk earlier. He tried to move, but he could not. He was sinking deep, deep into a profound and eternal darkness, where not even the moon gave light. The heavy perfume of amber was all about him, suffocating him. He thought he heard voices . . . far out over the water. He felt himself lifted, without effort of his own, moving through space, a harsh voice saying:

"I thought you would never give him the brandy. Were you up to tricks, my sweet Delphine?"

Then darkness came again, deep pulsating darkness.

Roger opened his eyes slowly. His head was splitting. He tried to move, but his arms and legs ached. Fever? Was it . . . Or had he drunk too much? He drew himself up on one elbow. He was in his own bed. At the same time, Metephele drew back the net and raised it into place. He offered Roger a drink of brandy, without comment. Roger put his hand to the back of his head, and drew it away quickly. A great welt shot pains through him at a touch.

He looked at the table beside him. In plain sight, where Metephele had placed them to catch his waking eye, were a woman's vizard and his own sword.

"No cowrie girdle?" he murmured wryly, remembering too vividly.

Metephele did not hear. He stood very tall and erect, looking down at Roger. "Master, strange things go on in the moon of last night."

Roger made no reply. Strange things indeed . . . he could not remember how strange.

"Last night a ship comes in the harbour and rests in the water, there." He indicated the spot where Roger had seen the ship the night before. "Today the ship is no more, nor either is the pirate captain, Bonnet. He take he wings and fly away in the moonlight. He make a *Mankwala*, and he fly."

Roger lay quiet in the great bed. Magic! He wondered how much was magic and how much was careful planning by Luna's daughter. Delphine Latour . . . Luna's daughter . . . More likely Satan's daughter. He noticed Metephele was still looking at him.

"The lady, she takes she wings and fly away . . . just like the pirate man; she make magic, and take she wings."

Roger drank his morning tea. His mind became clear. He seemed to hear a man's voice: "Up to tricks, Delphine?" The way he emphasized "Delphine" meant something. . . . What?

Metephele gave him the answer as he waited for Roger to eat his breakfast. "The lady . . . maybe she sometimes walk in the forest at Queen's Gift, with great dog by her. Maybe she sometimes sail on a ship, wearing clothes like a man!"

Roger laid his fork on the plate, his eyes fixed on his black servant. What a fool he had been not to be more suspicious! Anne, Anne Bonney. He should have recognized her voice even in disguise. But how could he, her blonde hair covered, her figure concealed under her flowing gown . . . her face half hidden under the Spanish mask? He knew he had not really tried to penetrate her disguise. He was looking for a little adventure, an interlude . . . and a charming woman gave him the opportunity. He had so readily fallen into Anne Bonney's little trap! She must have laughed at his stupidity. But the thought did not disturb him greatly. A blow on the head was better than being run through with a sword.

Roger Mainwairing went to the Exchange with Deane. From there he walked to the water front. The dock was packed with men, waving arms and talking in loud excited tones. The responsible men of Charles Town were horrified that Bonnet should escape three days before the date set for his trial. Ignacius Pell told the examiners how pirate gold had tempted the sentinels, so that Bonnet and Herriot had both escaped on a ship that boldly sailed into the harbour, her guns masked. No doubt corruption went farther than the sentinels. Roger saw the Laurents, and the Hugers, the Gaillard brothers and Grandfather Ravenel, and talked with De Gaudin. They were all indignant at the escape of the notorious Bonnet.

Governor Johnston strode up and down the wharf, shaking his gold-headed cane and offering seven hundred pounds reward for the capture of Bonnet and Herriot. The fair reputation of the city was at stake, he declared.

Printing presses had worked, and placards were already posted bearing the amount of the reward in black letters, under the banner of Hue and Cry and Express by Land and Water. Ships had been sent out to scour the coast from north to south. But Bonnet, with his rescuers, had a good start, and he was well on his way to Ocracock.

Colonel Rhett had again come forward. His ships were outfitted. He had a company of picked men, put himself at the service of the Governor, in spite of the bad feeling that existed between them.

Roger and Deane joined a group of merchants who were discussing the escape.

"They say the woman Latour had a hand in it," someone remarked as they came up. "It was an excellent time—moon, no one to see them go out to the point to embark with Paris away."

Deane gave Mainwairing a quick glance, but Roger's face showed nothing. After a little they went back to the office in East Bay to go over the estimates of Roger's losses on the *Francis.* They worked until siesta time when Roger returned to the house. His head was splitting. It was more than evident that he was in the way of the conspirators. They had counted on an empty house. Instead he was there, with his friends. Then Anne Bonney had stepped in.

That night a heavy storm came up. It lasted the next day and the next. The sky was overcast and the wind blew ceaselessly. On the third day the alarm bells rang and crowds gathered on the docks, as they did in time of disaster.

The Governor rode into Market Place, his horse dripping with sweat and lather. Stede Bonnet was on Sullivan Island, at the entrance to the harbour. Word had come by a lone fishing boat that the pirate's ship had been driven back by the storm.

The Governor called for volunteers. Colonel Rhett was first to step forward.

After nightfall, the party set forth, hoping under cover of darkness to capture Bonnet and bring him back. The people were demanding a trial. They wanted to see pirates swing from the gibbets. They wanted them hung in chains until their blackened corpses dried and fell into pieces, from the sun and the wind and the rain.

The second day the victorious Rhett returned to Charles Town. He had Stede Bonnet alive and in chains. Herriot's body was displayed so that the people could see. And the crew was in irons.

Roger Mainwairing was at the wharf when the ship lay off waiting for the Governor's arrival. All Charles Town was on the water front. Bells were ringing in church steeples. Men of the Trade Board were drinking to the health of the gallant Rhett, and damnation to the pirate crew. Rhett himself had nothing to say. He had done his task, and all he wanted was bed and a long sleep.

No word was said of the capture of Anne Bonney. Roger did not ask questions. He did not want Deane to know he had any interest in that direction. He sent Metephele to mingle with the blacks of the fishing boats and the docks.

When he got back to the house, his servant was packing his boxes. "Boat sail early tomorrow for James River," he announced.

"That is good," Roger answered.

Metephele went on folding clothes and laying them carefully in the leather travelling box. After a time he came over near the chair where Roger was sitting. "The woman she say, 'Let us run swiftly, and see who reaches the water first.' The man say, 'Wait. I have a desire to kill.' Woman she say, 'No kill. Do not a fool be.' Man wait behind take out pistol."

Roger listened. Metephele was telling him in his own indirect way what had happened the night of Bonnet's escape.

"Then I myself I step out from garden wall and make loud call, like *kudu* horn blast. They run, very fast then, to the boat. But woman run faster than anyone, they got in boat and row out to ship."

Roger knew what had happened from there on. Metephele had picked him up and brought him to the house.

"What of the woman?" he asked.

"I have sat at a cooking fire on the beach. It is said that the woman go out in a different ship, a big ship that lay off the entrance. The ship she belong to a very big captain name Vane——

"Ngoka akam wambia! Twah Wewe Hii Juhari"
"The snake said to him, take yourself this jewel."

The Angoni bowed and left the room. He had made his report to his master. The snake said to him, "Take yourself this jewel." By that he meant that Anne Bonney had put herself in the hands of Vane. Even now they were sailing north to rendezvous at the Carolina Banks.

Roger's eyes fell on the vizard and his sword, and he smiled.

Chapter 32

MY SONS

The spring flowers blossomed and faded under the heat of early summer. The settlement at Old Town had fallen into a routine of labour, such as yeomen knew. It was familiar with the heavy earth after the rains, when the plough moved heavily in the clinging soil. It knew the backbreaking season of planting corn and millet. In the rice fields, newly drained, they laboured valiantly. This was a new crop to them. But Annaci knew. He was a rice-field worker and he showed them how to cut the small canals and set the low marshland ready for planting and flooding, as he had at Moray's plantation.

The colony was losing in numbers. Two weavers had gone to Charles Town. They left without warning, stowing away in the *Phoebus.* Zack Reeves and Akim were dead. Caslett had taken eight with him.

Gabrielle sat in her father's office in the weaving shed. It was early May and the day was warm and sultry. She was showing René how to do the accounts. He was struggling with unaccustomed figures, trying to make the columns add up correctly. His square-cut brown hair hung over his brow, and from time to time he mopped the perspiration from his smooth forehead. Gabrielle checked the list of their people with a feeling of distinct discouragement. Twenty families it was in the beginning, now it had dwindled to fourteen. She sat looking out of the small-paned window towards the river. She noticed a number of Negroes working in the marsh. She got up and went to the door, counting eight or nine. She wondered who they were and where they came from. She must ask Annaci.

René called her. "Please look at these figures, Gaby. I've counted them over half a dozen times and they always add up differently." He took out his silk handkerchief and mopped his forehead.

"I'll check them for you, René. Why don't you take my horse and ride for an hour or so?"

The lad got off the high stool with alacrity. "I'd love to ride, but," he added as an afterthought, "I didn't want to leave you with my work to do."

"It won't take me a moment. I'm used to the work. It comes easy after a time."

"I hope so," the boy muttered.

Gabrielle called after him, "Perhaps Molly would like to go with you. Be sure to take Annaci; he knows all the paths."

"Shall I take my pistol?"

He was looking at her eagerly. He wanted to go armed, to be a man. She read his thought. "Of course, your pistol. You must have your pistol. Tell Annaci to take a fowling-piece; you may blow up a wild turkey."

Gabrielle settled down to the task ahead of her. Dear René! He was so anxious to do his share, yet he wanted to be out riding and fishing. Etienne had no thought of labour of any kind. He was off at daybreak with the men who were fishing; or he was in the turpentine woods; or riding to the Black Lakes. She was glad the boys were not lonely here; but she must persuade her father to send them to King William's School at Annapolis in September. They could have the summer here, at least. She sighed as she climbed up on the high bench. It was so nice, having the boys. They brought new life into the house. She wrinkled her forehead and dug her pen into the well. She loathed long columns of figures.

Robrt Fountaine came in and sank wearily into a hard board chair. "The last wool is very poor. It breaks easily and knots. This whole lot of cloth is inferior."

"Why don't we bring over some Merino sheep, Father? We don't want to send out any inferior yardage."

"No. Certainly not." He took out his handkerchief and wiped his face. "The air is heavy. There must be a storm brewing. Where is René?" He looked about the room. "I thought he was to take care of the manifests and the lists."

"He's worked all morning. I sent him for a ride."

Robert looked at his daughter with affectionate eyes. "So you do his work. I'm afraid we are all leaning on you, my child. I am equally culpable. I find myself constantly turning to you."

Gabrielle went over and knelt beside him. "Dear Father, you make me very happy. Why shouldn't you turn to me?"

"You are too young for such heavy responsibility," he murmured, stroking her soft brown hair from her damp forehead. "Much too young. Sometimes I wonder whether I chose the right road, coming here. It is different, so different from what I thought it would be."

Gabrielle's heart chilled. It was the first time her father had ever voiced discouragement. "I must get back to my weaving," she said lightly. "I miss it so much. Now that Molly's here, she wants a share in the duties of the house."

Fountaine's face brightened. "Good! Very good! Your weaving is far superior to that of any man I have now."

"I'll begin in the morning," she answered him. "I'm sure I can handle the thread. . . . Maybe Barton could find time to help out."

Fountaine rose. His care-worn look had dropped away. He kissed Gabrielle lightly and patted her shoulder. "I must go to your mother. She has asked me to sit with her this afternoon."

Gabrielle said, "Mother is stronger now, much stronger."

"Yes. Sometimes I think she knows me. Really knows me." He took up his hat and walked towards the house. He stooped a little, leaning on his cane.

Suddenly she saw him, leaning on a staff, walking alone in a forest of trees. She drew her hand before her eyes. Of course it was nothing, nothing. But the thought recurred, all the long afternoon: a pilgrim, walking his weary way along a thorny road.

Molly and René came in at suppertime. Molly was flushed and bright-eyed. They stopped at Gabrielle's door to tell her about their ride. Annaci had brought a huge wild turkey—they had killed a poisonous water-moccasin crossing the swamp. Molly went to her room.

René said, "Mr. Moray told us it was the largest snake he'd seen since he'd been here, a disgusting stumpy-tailed snake with eyes that gave one the shivers. Molly was terrified." René laughed. "It took Moray some time to quiet her."

Gabrielle steadied her voice. "Did you go to the plantation?"

"Yes. Molly suggested it. She said it was a nice ride through the woods. She spent most of her time drinking tea with Moray. Why don't you call him Captain, Gaby? He's a real captain in a Highland regiment. He's been in real war."

Gabrielle didn't answer. Every word René uttered gave her pain. She had not seen David alone since Molly came. He had not sought her out.

"Mr. MacAlpin showed me around," René went on. "They're building a big canal, from the river right to their front door, so ships can sail up to their dock."

Gabrielle said, "Yes?" Her voice was muffled.

The lad looked at her closely. "What's the matter, Gaby? Do you feel ill? You look so strange." The boy's bright eyes scrutinized her face. "You're pale as anything. . . . Have you got a chill?"

"No. Just tired," she said, and sent him along to change for supper.

Molly did not come in after dressing, as she usually did, to talk over some happening of the day. She heard her moving about her room, humming a tune. It made Gabrielle wonder. Was Molly bored by the quiet dull life of the plantation and turning to David Moray for the excitement so necessary to her happiness?

She sat looking at her own reflection in the glass as she brushed her dark hair into curls and bound it in place with a crimson riband.

She must talk to her father again about Paul Balarand. She did not want to marry a man she had never seen. She did not want to marry anyone. She wanted to stay right here with her family and make a success of the plantation. But how could she go contrary to her father's wishes? Never in her life had she disobeyed him.

A light tap at the door announced Molly. She did not come in. Gabrielle noticed she had changed to one of her lovely silk frocks, corn-coloured over a blue petticoat. The yellow was the colour of her pale blonde hair and the blue matched her eyes.

"Did you have a nice ride?" Gabrielle asked.

"Very. René is really an excellent horseman, and his conversation is quite grown-up."

The gong sounded through the house. "There's the dinner gong," Molly said. Catching up her skirts, she started down the stairs. "You know Uncle Robert always wants us to be on time."

Gabrielle followed the bright figure. She felt quite drab and nunlike, in her pale grey gown with no touch of colour save the knot of crimson riband in her hair, and the cream-white ruffles at her square-cut neck and her short sleeves. She felt dull, and a strange unrest settled upon her, impossible to throw off.

They found her father and the boys waiting in the great

room. They talked for a few moments. Robert Fountaine kept his eyes fixed on the closed door that led to Madam's quarters. The little French clock had ticked off five minutes, when the door opened and Madam Fountaine came out. She stood in the entrance looking about her, a sweet, vague smile on her lips. She inclined her head gently when Robert offered his arm, and answered the boys' greetings by extending her hand to be kissed. She nodded graciously to Gabrielle and Molly.

"Have I detained you?" she asked politely. "I am so sorry. A hostess should never keep her guests waiting."

The dinner was almost gay. The boys chattered about their activities. Molly told about her ride. Quite casually she said they had taken a new path through the turpentine woods and, to their great surprise, came out on Captain Moray's plantation.

"Has David returned?" Robert Fountaine asked, rousing himself from his preoccupation at the sound of Moray's name. "Did you see Sandy? I rather expected him over, yesterday or today." He looked about the table. "Sandy is teaching me the Tuscarora language. I'm getting along famously. It is really very simple."

"Why, Father," the boys said together. "Why didn't you tell us? We want to learn to speak Indian."

Robert's face darkened. "No. No. You do not need Indian. Stick to your French, with Molly, and your Latin. You should improve your Latin." He sat for a moment, looking down at his plate. "Yes. Latin is important. I must write this week and enter you both at King William's School, for the autumn term."

René said, "Do we have to go away again, sir? We love being here with you."

Etienne was not so tactful. He said, bluntly, that he didn't want to go to Annapolis. He had had enough of school. He liked to hunt and fish and drive deer.

"If I'm going to be a planter, why should I worry over Latin conjugation?" he asked forthrightly. He looked at his father. "I am going to be a planter, aren't I?"

"Yes, yes, of course, but planters in Carolina are not ignorant folk. They are men of education and culture." Robert's eyes were on Etienne, but Gabrielle had a feeling his thoughts were far away.

Madam spoke. "I do not wonder that these young boys are bored with Latin. My governess tries so hard to induce me to

492

become interested in Latin, but——" she laughed; her sweet, light laughter made the tears rush to Gabrille's eyes— "dancing is more to my pleasure."

They were having their port in the great room when David Moray came to the door. Behind him was Sandy MacAlpin. Robert rose and asked them to come in. Sandy declined. He wanted a word with Robert, he said.

"If Madam will excuse me," Robert said. She bowed graciously. She sat on a little settee, René and Etienne on either side.

"You are adorable young boys," she said, touching René's cheek. "If I had sons of my own, I would want them to be as near like you as could be."

There was a silence. Robert stopped as he was going out of the room. Gabrielle's hand went to her throat. Molly turned her startled eyes towards the boys.

The silence lasted only a moment. Etienne lifted Madam's hand to his lips. But it was René who said the words that caught at Gabrielle's heart. "Madam, you are so kind. Could we not pretend you are our own mother? It would make Etienne and me so happy. So very happy."

There was poignancy in his voice. Madam's eyes clouded, her hands fluttered to her lips, then pressed against her forehead.

It seemed to Gabrielle that the silence was interminable. Then Madam said, "Dear, dear lad, of course we will pretend." She turned to Robert, who was immovable in the doorway. "Is it not wonderful? I now have two beautiful sons."

"Quite wonderful," he said.

Molly came forward. "May we not have some music, Madam? I have a new song, if Gabrielle will accompany me on her harp."

"Yes. That will be delightful." Madam leaned against the back of the settee.

Robert and Sandy went away. David's eyes met Gabrielle's. They had in them something that stirred her deeply, something kind and protective and understanding.

She got up and busied herself removing the cover from her harp; running her hands across the strings. Molly ran upstairs for her music.

David set up the music rack. He said to Gabrielle, his voice very low, "When may I talk to you, alone?"

She looked up, startled by his words, and met the serious

look in his eyes. She heard Molly's footsteps on the stairs. She said hurriedly, "Later. When my mother has retired."

"I shall ask you to walk out in the garden," he said, and turned away as Molly came into the room. She looked quickly from Gabrielle to David. Gabrielle was pulling up strings that were out of tune.

Molly's clear young voice filled the room:

"Go, lovely rose!
Tell her that wastes her time and me . . ."

Madam listened, humming a little, a smile on her lips. Gabrielle watched the changing expression in her face. She's happy, she thought. I must not spoil her happy thoughts by my fear for her.

"How sweet and fair she seems to be. . . ."

Molly's voice died out. She moved across the room and sat down near David. Nor would she repeat. A song, once sung, should remain so. Let it become a memory that is treasured, not a repetition to satiate.

Madam shivered, drawing her scarf closer. "I am cold. I think there must be a mistral blowing." She rose. The boys walked with her to the door, where Celestine waited.

"Good night, my sons. Rest well." She kissed each boy lightly. Smiling, she said, "Good night. Good night. The good God have you in His keeping."

Gabrielle's hand fell on the strings of her harp. They gave out a wild discordant sound. Etienne went hurriedly out of the room without saying good night. She heard him walk slowly upstairs to his room. René crossed over and took a seat beside her. His eyes were luminous with tears.

"Let's walk out in the garden," he said. "Come, dearest Gabrielle."

She covered the harp and they went out. Molly had pulled out the loo-table, and was rummaging in the drawer for the little fish counters. "Hurry back, and we'll have a game," she called to Gabrielle. "We need you and René."

Gabrielle waved assent, and followed her brother out of doors. The night was mild; a half moon shone in the east, rising over the river.

"I could weep, if it were not unmanly," René said, holding Gabrielle's arm close to his side. "I could weep for saying

494

the wrong thing. Oh, Gabrielle, how could I have been so unthoughtful?"

"My dear, you spoke from your heart. Whatever comes from the heart is always right. Dear René, you gave our mother great pleasure. You gave her something to fill her empty heart. A new thought. Who knows? Perhaps out of this pretended world, a rare new world will come to her."

He gave her arm a squeeze. "Dear, dear Gabrielle! What would we do without you? I'm young, I know, but I notice we all lean on you. You're so wise, and so serene."

Serene? Was she serene, with her heart in turmoil? She kept her silence, touching René's hand lightly, to show that she was pleased.

"Perhaps we'd better go in," René suggested; after a moment, "I say. Do you think Molly is going after Captain Moray? All she could talk about when we were crossing was Michael Cary—some fabulous person, as great a sailor as Sir Walter, or Sir Richard Grenville."

Gabrielle laughed. "You must make allowances for Molly's enthusiasms."

"Of course. I understand. Molly's life has been so empty that she has to dream up exciting things."

Gabrielle thought, René is grown up; he has more than a child's wisdom. She suddenly knew that she did not have to carry all the weight of the settlement alone. René, tall and young, stood beside her. He was showing her, by his words, that he was no longer a boy.

"Dear René," she said, "I'm so glad you're here."

They walked past the weaving shed on their way back. She saw, by the light, that her father and Sandy were still there. She heard her father say, "I'm sure they would receive the Lord's words. Receive and be helped."

Sandy's voice was dry as dust. "I never thought to proselyte, Mr. Fountaine. Indians have their religion and I have mine. I don't want interference, nor do I interfere."

Robert Fountaine's reply came to her clearly: " 'Go into the highways and preach the Gospel'—do you remember those words, Sandy?"

"Yes I remember. But I don't feel a call to go about preaching the Gospel to Indians. I'm a trader, Mr. Fountaine."

René whispered, "What is our father talking about?"

"Nothing that concerns us, René," Gabrielle replied. But

she was troubled. "Come," she said, determinedly cheerful. "The loo players will be waiting. Let's go into the house."

The time passed slowly. Gabrielle failed to win tricks and her forfeits piled up. After a time René suggested tea, and carried Molly off with him. As soon as they were out of the room, David got up. "Shall we go now? Before they return?"

She followed him into the garden.

They followed the path that led to the little latticed summer-house. Gabrielle sat down on the bench. David remained at the door. He looked very tall and dark against the faint light of the moon. She waited for him to speak, trying to still the tumult within her.

"MacAlpin and I were deer driving today. While we were down near the black lakes we saw a large company of Indians go by, going towards the ocean. We counted over a hundred, not Tuscaroras."

Her heart sank. Was this danger, which during the past months had become obscure, to rise again?

David's voice broke in on her thoughts. "Sandy spoke to Amos about an extra sentry, as long as this band of Indians is passing this way."

"Do you think there is danger?"

"I don't think so, but it is well to be prepared. It may be only an annual migration from the western mountains to the coast." He hesitated a moment, then continued. "We have had word that there has been some disturbance in South Carolina, but that does not mean that it will spread."

He came over and sat down beside her. In the half light she noticed that he folded his arms over his chest. She felt his nearness but she did not move. They were seated so close to each other that she heard his breathing, yet he was remote, far from her. She could not reach him. He was so still. The night sounds rose, a bird twittering in the overhanging branch of a tree, cicadas, the rising chorus of frogs in the marsh. She too was still, without thought, without desire.

David broke the silence. "I spoke to your father. I told him I loved you. Did he tell you?"

She was startled by his words. After a moment's silence she replied, "No. He said nothing. I . . ." She was trembling. She felt his eyes on her, but she waited for him to go on. She could not ask the question on her lips. She knew the answer, yet while the words were unspoken she allowed herself to hope.

"He told me his reasons for promising you to Balarand. I

496

am afraid I spoke my mind too freely. ... I know what you mean when you say he has a will of iron."

They were both silent now.

"I told him that I was determined to marry you, that it was something between us. If you love me, I am content to wait. Perhaps he will change."

"My father will not change," she said sadly.

He touched her cheek. "Long ago in Bristol, I determined that I was going to marry you. I have not changed my mind. After this let us not waste time quarrelling. Love by opposition is not love at its highest, my dear."

They heard René calling. Gabrielle got to her feet. "We must go," she said.

"A moment more. Gabrielle, I promised your father I would not press you for an answer—that I would be content to be friends. ... I will keep my word, but it will be hard not to tell you I love you, to take you in my arms ... to feel your warm lips."

"David!" she cried. "It is unjust. I ..."

René called again. "Gaby, where are you?"

David said, "I won't go into the house again. I don't want to talk of inconsequential things or see anyone now. Good night, my dear." He raised her hands to his lips and went away. Gabrielle waited for a moment, watching his shadowy figure until he was lost in the darkness. Then she walked slowly to the house. She pulled herself up sharply. When she entered the room, there was nothing in her face to show anything but the pleased anticipation of a cup of hot tea and one of Barton's honey cakes.

Gabrielle could not sleep. She got up from her bed and went to the window. It was very still; only the long-drawn-out hoot of a screech owl, far off in the forest. Was it a bird or a signal? The moon cast a half light, bathing the garden and the stockade in a luminous haze. She saw the sentry moving near the forest gate. The clock in the hall chimed two, and was still.

She put on her shoes and stockings and felt in the cupboard for a dark dress, which she put on, without petticoats. She would slip downstairs and walk around, to see that all the windows and doors were bolted. The great room was dark, with the heavy darkness of a close curtained room. As she crossed the room to the window near the garden, she thought she heard the sash moved cautiously.

She was standing near the fireplace. She reached for the heavy iron tongs. Silently she advanced towards the window. Standing to one side she moved the curtain away from the window a small crack. She saw the naked shoulders and torso of an Indian outlined. He was holding the window up with one hand; the other hand was on the sill. She did not stop to think that there might be others behind him. Her only thought was to prevent the red man from entering the house.

Silently she lifted the heavy tongs and brought them down, smashing the hand that grasped the window sill. The tongs wrapped in the curtain and tore it from the hooks. She heard groaning, as the Indian's grasp on the window gave way. She saw him running across the garden towards the stockade. She flew to the door. The key seemed to be frozen in the lock. She dared not cry out for fear of disturbing her mother. She struggled with the key. When she finally got the door open, the Indian was scaling the stockade on the river side. She saw the figure of the sentry running towards her.

"No! No! The stockade. Indian!"

The sentry pursued, but it was too late. The Indian disappeared in the heavy brush of the bank. The sentry fired into the shadow, but there was no sound save the far-off hoot of an owl.

Gabrielle turned back to the house. At the door she met Sandy MacAlpin. He must have been on guard, for he was fully dressed. She told him what had happened.

"You shouldn't'a' done that," Sandy said. "What if the savage hada' got within the house? Lord love us! A fine thing! A wee sma' girrl attackin' a savage with a pair of wood-tongs."

He spoke roughly, but Gabrielle knew he was worried.

"I won't tell anyone," she said quickly.

"Better not. Just you had a little scare."

But she need not have worried. She thought she had screamed at the top of her voice, but no one in the house had heard her, only the near-by sentry and Sandy. They went off and left her standing in the doorway. A moment later David Moray came around the side of the house. He was out of breath from swift running.

"What was it?" he asked Gabrielle. "I heard a shot."

Gabrielle hesitated a moment, then she said, "I hit an Indian with the wood-tongs. I think I broke his hand." With that she began to sob. "I heard the bones crunch. It was frightening."

498

"Here, don't do that," David said sternly. "You're not going to faint, or anything, I hope. Sit down. I'm going after the fellow."

"Sandy's gone already, and the sentry." She managed to pull herself together.

"I'll take you inside." The entry was dark. She groped for the candle, but there was none on the table.

"Wait. I'll get a candle," she said. She found one in the great room, near the door, and lighted it from the coals in the fireplace with a sliver of lightwood.

David caught up the candle and strode to the window. The curtains were in a tangled heap on the floor. He moved the light along the sill. A dark stain marked the white paint, where the tongs had cut, as well as crushed. He turned around and set the candle on the table. It cast a feeble glow in the shadows of the long room.

"You little fool. You silly little fool," he said gruffly. "Don't you know you might have been scalped?" He lifted her long braids above her head. "I shouldn't like you to be scalped." He was leaning over her; his voice was low. "You silly little lionhearted fool."

She felt her body trembling as though she would fall. David's hands slid from her shoulders down to her waist. His arms closed about her.

"I shall not have a scalped wife," he said, his lips close to hers.

Somehow it was easy to creep into the shelter of his strong arms. The horrible face of the Indian faded from her thought. "I was afraid, David. Awfully afraid."

His arms dropped to his sides. "I forgot that I have given my word to your father." He left her abruptly and went out into the darkness.

When Gabrielle came down in the morning, the family had breakfasted and gone from the room. Barton served her in silence, glancing at her now and then, words on the tip of her tongue. Finally she could stand it no longer.

"A fule is soon killed," she remarked. "Sandy MacAlpin told me that you went running after a stray Indian, hitting at him with our good fire tongs. The curtains are in a mess, and a great spot of fire ash on them. I've a notion to turn you over my knee."

Gabrielle looked at the woman's face. She was trying to hide the tears in her eyes and the fear in her heart behind her harsh words. She got up from the table and threw her arms about Barton. "Do. Do. I think I need a paddling. I was awfully frightened afterwards. Really frightened."

"Should be! I hope you don't go tellin' the guid mon about all this. No need worritin' him."

"No indeed, I'll not tell my father, or Molly or the boys."

Barton wiped the tears out of her eyes with the corner of her apron. A smile came to her lips. "You needn' atrouble about Mistress Molly. A sloop came up the river early this morning. Treloar told me it belonged to Captain Michael Cary, and he had black slaves aboard, hoping Mr. Moray would be buying some."

Gabrielle ran to the door. There was no sign of a sloop on the river.

"Needn't be lookin', Mistress Gabrielle. She sailed upriver early, while you were still sleepin'."

"Where's Miss Molly? Does she know Captain Cary is here?"

"That she does! She ordered her horse and went off early, riding through the woods in that direction." She waved her hand towards Moray's plantation.

Gabrielle went about her work quietly, but she was troubled. She did not like the idea that Michael Cary had come back, now that Molly was at Old Town. She finished her housework and went over to Mary Treloar's house. Mary was busy making bread, her sleeves rolled up, her strong round arms deep in dough.

"Amos is fair daft this day," she told Gabrielle. "He be sent for to come to the Albemarle, to build a big sailing ship for Mr. Mainwairing."

Gabrielle said, "Oh! That's very nice. Amos wanted to build a big ship."

Mary wiped her floury arms with a whole flour sack. "Yes, Mistress, 'tis what every Devon man is dreamin' of, to build and sail a ship."

"What will you do when he's gone, Mary?"

Mary glanced away. "I think I'll be going along with my man, Mistress. Treloar would never be strong to build a big ship, without I stay by and have his pasties and his tea and his cakes ready for him."

Gabrielle sat down on the bench. It seemed as if her knees had given way. "Oh, Mary. What will Old Town do without you and Amos?"

Mary pulled up a chair and sat down, something she

500

seldom did when Gabrielle came to see her. "I know my manners," she would say, and remain standing, unless Gabrielle insisted.

"I thought mayhap we should not go. Treloar thought the same way, so he went to Master Fountaine, and laid the thing before him. Master Fountaine he says 'Go, Amos, 'tis a fine chance for you to build your tall ship'; and so we do be going."

"When?" Gabrielle asked.

Mary looked towards the river. "The *Delicia*, with Captain Bragg, will be in within a fortnight. Amos says we will be ready to go when she sails north."

"What will you do with all this—your nice house?"

A cloud came over Mary's round face. " 'Tis a pity, a terrible pity, but we be packin' everything, all our furniture. They say there be good houses aplenty up there, and this house it will not run away in seven or eight months."

"But the harvest . . . and your cattle?" Gabrielle cried.

"The boys'll look after them and store the grain for us. 'We must go now,' Treloar says, if he's to finish the ship by next winter. I don't like to be on the move. I told Treloar we're not good folk any more, moving and moving. More like Gipsies we are these days."

"Of course you must go, Mary. Only I'll miss you so much. It always felt so safe to know you were here."

Tears came to Mary Treloar's eyes. She brushed them away impatiently with the back of her hand. "I wish I could say I was astayin' behind. But I cannot. My duty is with Treloar."

"Of course. I know that. I'm being selfish. After all, Albemarle is not so far away."

Gabrielle walked out of the gate and into the open ground beyond the stockade. The corn was tasselled and beginning to brown; in a little time it would be ripe. Already the kitchen garden had given them peas and young beans.

A snake with a bright red belly slid along the path and sank its writhing body in a nest of dried leaves. She thought of Annaci. Annaci would not walk a path where a snake had crossed.

"Turn back. Turn back," he had told her once. "Take another road. This path belongs to evil things this day."

Now she stood still, hesitating. Remembering last night, she knew she should not walk far into the forest. In the sunlight, the fears of the dark hours of the night seemed of no moment. Probably it was a lone straggling Indian, who had dropped behind the war party, and was set on pilfering, not on killing. She felt rather ashamed that she had struck at the marauder. She walked toward the creek. She heard movements in the forest. A mocker started to sing and stopped, its lovely song incomplete. A rabbit scudded along the path, and a fox, crossing, turned bright impudent eyes at her.

It seemed to Gabrielle that she heard voices, faint voices, as from far away, the words vague and unformed. She stood listening. She turned her head; Annaci was walking behind her, his long forked snake-stick in his hand, his hunting knife in his belt. She wondered how long the Negro had been following her.

She waited for him to come up. As she waited the voices seemed to grow louder, to speak a warning to her. She turned to Annaci. "It sounds as though there were people talking, off that way, a number of people." She looked at him questioningly.

A wonderment spread over his countenance and shone in his liquid eyes. "You hear them, Mistress? You?"

The sense of unreality deepened. She dropped her voice. "What is it?"

"Spirit Voices, Mistress. The great, great dead, who live all about us. They speak to their children."

Gabrielle drew a deep, shivering breath. "Let us go home," she said.

"Yes, Mistress." The man stepped aside to let her pass, and fell in behind her.

The great, great dead. That was the Negroes' belief. What if it were true. . . . What if all those dead of the forgotten colonies lived again in the earth, and the trees? Spoke through the winds in the pines and the faint ripple of water of the incoming tide? She quickened her step. When she came in sight of the stockade gate, she realized she was almost running. She slowed down her stride. It would never do to get into a panic because she had heard the wind soughing in the pines.

Molly had been in a despondent mood for some days, and her short periods of gaiety were forced and unreal. Now she was gay, gay to the point of hysteria.

Gabrielle watched her that evening, when she came in from her ride. Her eyes were bright, her lips curved in a faint smile. She ran up and put her arms about Gabrielle: "He's here! Michael's here! I've asked Uncle Robert to have him with us while the ship is in the river."

"Of course," Gabrielle said. "I'll send word to Annaci to see that a room is put in order in the men's quarters."

Molly opened her mouth to speak, then closed it. The shadow in her eyes spoke her thought. She wanted Michael in the main house, not in the bachelors' house. Gabrielle left her and went out to the weaving shed. She found her father reading a letter. Beside him were other packets that had come in on Michael Cary's ship.

Robert laid down the sheet of paper and greeted his daughter. "I am disturbed," he said, picking up the letter. "Very disturbed, Gabrielle. There is a difference of opinion as to whether the South Carolina government, or the Lords Proprietors have the right to give out titles of land on the Cape Fear River. It seems there is an old grant to some Landgrave ... I do not quite understand." He looked tired and disturbed, and very helpless.

Gabrielle took the letter from him and folded it. "Do not bother about it now. I understand there's a discussion about the boundary between North and South Carolina, which hasn't been settled. I heard Mr. Mainwaring talking about it. He says it will be adjusted. Have no fear, Father. You have your land from Lord Carteret himself, and he'll protect your interest."

Robert Fountaine's face brightened. "So he will. I had forgotten for the moment. Come, let us go to the house. It is time for me to go to your mother. Lately, she has come to enjoy the verses of François Villon that I read to her. She remains very quiet, listening, always listening." He paused. "But sometimes I wonder whether she is really listening to me. She seems to turn so often to the forest, as if she were listening . . ." He broke off and put his hand on Gabrielle's arm, leaning on her as they walked. "I must not let troubled thoughts cloud my faith. In God's time!" he said. He walked quickly in the direction of the garden. He had forgotten Gabrielle.

Chapter 33

THE GREAT, GREAT DEAD

René and Etienne came on the old graveyard by chance. They found it early one morning, when they were out setting a bear trap near the turn in the creek below the bridge. The tides had worn away the bank, and the box containing the bones of a woman with a child laid across her breast had slipped over the bank and broken, so that the skeletons were plainly visible.

The boys scrambled up the bank. Under a tangle of berry brambles and grape vines, they found the outline of a brick tomb. No name was to be seen, and they were afraid to investigate further on account of the snakes in such over-grown spots.

Gabrielle heard them planning another trip to the spot, and accepted eagerly when she was asked to accompany them. They were taking Annaci with them, and one of the new group of runaways, who had lately attached themselves to the colony. The Negroes had left their hiding place in the swamp, near the lakes, because they were in deadly fear of the Indians. Amos had put them to work in the rice fields and they were living in a quarters line, a few yards outside the stockade.

The boys found the place again without trouble. It was no more than half a mile from the fields. Annaci and his companion cleared the overgrown path with a brush hook. Then they burned the tall weeds, and set about grubbing out scrub pine. There were some small gravestones, only a few, the cutting almost gone. One name they made out—Vassels; but the Christian names under it were blurred. The stone evidently marked the burial place of settlers of the first Venture. A date was visible on the only flat stone, a very small stone: 1667. That was the year Sir John Yeamans' people gave up and left the colony at Old Town deserted. Gabrielle and the boys imagined they could make out twenty-five or thirty mounds. A rough cross of cypress had fallen over and lay across a mound, the two arms broken.

504

While René and the Negroes hacked away at the heavy brush, Gabrielle walked among the old graves. She tried to envisage those early people, their struggle, their loneliness, and their futile effort to establish a colony.

The wind stirred the leaves in a great tulip tree. A hermit thrush gave its sweet clear call. A flashing cardinal skimmed across the path in front of her, and everywhere the sounds of the forest, crickets and tree frogs, the humming bees. Suddenly she became conscious of another sound—the low murmur of many voices. Were they speaking, answering, across the years? She was near to them here, those who had gone before. She remembered Annaci's belief that spirits of the Great, Great Dead lived forever in the leaves of the trees, the flowers, the wind and the rippling water. Were the spirit voices speaking to her, giving her their laughter and their love and their tears? She bent forward, listening. If she could only hear their words. . . .

She noticed that the boys had ceased work and were leaning on mattock and shovel; they, too, were listening. The Negroes paused, their lips moving. Annaci touched a charm he wore about his neck. But soon they took up their work. The sounds were faint for them and far away; not close and encompassing, as they were for her. Here they lay, the long dead in the rich, yielding earth. Quiet and still, for they had fulfilled their destiny.

René came up. Sweat dripped from his forehead and made a line across his upper lip, where the first light down had begun to show. He had taken off his coat and his thin linen shirt clung to his back.

"Thirty mounds or more," he said, taking out his kerchief. "For a small settlement, isn't that quite a large number of graves?"

Gabrielle showed him the stones. "I think this must have been the burial ground for both settlements."

Etienne's voice broke in: "Come here, Gabrielle. See what we've found—a skull that has been cleft, and an Indian tomahawk and some arrowheads." He was digging about in the earth.

"Have care, young Master!" Before the words were out of Annaci's mouth, he had sprung forward and smashed the head of a moccasin that was sliding out of the tangle of vines, almost under Etienne's feet.

Etienne turned white. "Candle, book and bell!" he muttered. He turned away while the Negro crushed the wicked

505

head with the mattock. "I'm sick," the boy said, hurrying away down the path.

"*Mankwala*," Annaci said, under his breath. "The great snake untie the bag so that all make escape and crawl. Let us go, Mistress. Let us go quickly, lest evil befall."

A feeling of unreality pressed down upon her. She was near to panic again. "Yes," she answered. "Let us go."

They walked back over the new-made path, Annaci behind her, the other Negro in front of the boys. He, too, carried a long forked stick, to beat the brush. He sang a little song, to warn the snakes that they were coming:

> "We come as friends,
> Not as enemies,
> O animal with tails.
> See the sky is clouded over.
> Do not come out of your hole,
> If there are not gleams of sunshine."

Annaci translated for Gabrielle. After they were clear of the forest, he said, "It is well if the Mistress has a care. Danger moves swiftly out of the forest. Mungulu, the Great, Great Dead, speaks loudly today, out of many tongues."

Gabrielle said firmly, "It was not voices I heard; it is only the wind shaking the leaves of the tulip tree."

Annaci said no more. They walked swiftly, in deep silence. Only when she saw the men at work in the fields, and the open gate of the stockade, did Gabrielle breathe normally.

Michael Cary did not come that afternoon. Molly made no effort to hide her disappointment. She kept looking out of the window and going to the door. The sun set in a blaze of red. Red reflected on the great bank of clouds that hung in the western horizon, until it seemed that the dome of the heavens was aflame. The air was heavy and humid, as though a storm were gathering.

After supper Gabrielle walked out in the garden to see that the chairs under the little bush tent, where her mother sat every day, were turned over. She thought the garden had never been so lovely. There had been just enough rain to give the plants heavy growth. Larkspur and poppies, dusty miller and Canterbury bells grew in profusion. A wild rose vine twined up the pole supports of the pine boughs that made the roof of the tent. It was covered with waxen-white bloom, as clear and lovely as early dogwood. The frogs in the marsh

506

had tuned up for their evening concert; shrill small voices and strong-bellowed bullfrogs sang in unison. The marsh birds fluttered about with sweet, delicate cries. Beyond the rice fields, white cranes stood deep in swamp water. A great blue heron rose, followed by a second, their heavy wings beating to gain speed for their flight along the river. An alligator flopped clumsily from the bank to the water with a heavy splash. The forest creatures made their evening calls: the bark of a fox, the crash of brush breaking beyond the stockade where the forest took over.

Gabrielle watched the sun go down behind the pines and the crimson afterglow cover the world of forest and of stream.

She heard the faint tapping of a drum and the sound of voices. The Negroes were singing, sitting in front of their little huts. She had no idea how many there were—eight or ten maybe that Annaci had shepherded out of the swamp to the safe haven of the settlement. Women and a child, she had seen that morning. Nothing was ever said about their arrival. She noticed Barton had put some of the newcomers to work, in the kitchen and the milk-house, where butter was churned and cheese made.

The beauty of the night drove out the uneasy thoughts that had hung heavily upon her of late. Was she overly anxious? Was the danger only of her imagination? When she looked on the river, she had no fear. It flowed quietly, peacefully, towards the sea; but when she turned towards the swamp and the deep forest, the old fear came back. She heard René talking to Etienne. They had been down to the wharf, watching the fishermen mending their rust-brown nets.

René said, "Cary's ship is careened upriver in a little creek, near Captain Moray's plantation. A good thing. It stinks from black men he's been hauling between decks. I shouldn't like to be a slaver. It's foul business."

Etienne's answer was distinct: "Oh, I don't know. There's many a golden guinea to be made slaving. I've been talking to Cary about triangular trade, as he calls it: England to Africa to the Caribbean, and back over the route. Sometimes it's New England ports to Africa, with trade goods; slaves from Africa to Jamaica; and cargo of rum and sugar from there to Boston."

"I wouldn't like it," René said emphatically. "Our father says slaving is wicked, and none but wicked men sail slave ships."

"Oh, well. You know our father, René. He's a saint. But I'm an earthly man. I want to make a pile of golden doubloons. Perhaps I'll sail a slaving ship myself. It's legal—a slaver won't swing on a gibbet like Jack Sheppard, the highwayman!"

"Hush, Etienne! Don't let Father hear you. You should be laid by the heels for talking that way."

Etienne laughed boisterously. "Well, slaving is better than piracy or highway robbery. Many a good man is a slaving captain in the Africa Company."

They moved away and Gabrielle heard no more. The little conversation gave her another anxiety. The boys were growing so fast, thinking men's thoughts. Yes, they must be sent to school in September. She would have her father write the letter to be sent up on the *Delicia*, on her next sailing to Virginia.

Molly was playing on her zither as Gabrielle entered. The great room was in shadow. Gabrielle went about lighting the candelabrum and the wall sconces. Molly did not speak. She looked as though she had been crying.

"Shall we play a game of piquet?" Gabrielle asked. "Or maybe the boys would like a round of loo."

Molly shook her head. "No. I have a bursting head. I don't want to play games, Gabrielle." She laid the zither on the table and crossed the room. "I think I'll take a little walk. It's so ghastly hot inside."

Gabrielle wanted to say something to her, some comforting word. She knew Molly was upset because Captain Cary had not come. But, unless Molly said something first, she could not force her confidence. "Don't go outside the gate, Molly," she cautioned.

Molly did not answer. She left the room quickly, letting the door close noisily. Gabrielle knew she would not go far, for the moon was not up, and Molly was timid.

It was hot; but she could not open windows since the air was clouded with little whirling gnats and numerous insects that bit and stung. "Merrylegs," Sandy called them. She walked about the room, snuffing a candle, setting a chair to rights. She was as restless as Molly, with no reason.

Barton came in carrying a tray with glasses of water. "I've been to the spring. I thought you'd be wanting a little cool water, Mistress Gabrielle."

"Thank you, Barton." She lifted the glass to her lips. "It's so refreshing."

508

"So it be. Adam's ale is a finer drink than any man made. MacAlpin's here with the Master. He's had a wee drap hisself, and is in a laughing mood. 'Twas only that he had laced his ale with brandy, he told me. He says the strange captain, he's up at their place, very well disguised with liquor at this moment." She stood looking at Gabrielle, disapproval in every feature. "MacAlpin says Cary was all for coming here, to see the Master and Mistress Lepel, but Captain Moray overpowered him and laid him on the bed, to sleep it away. A pretty fellow to come courtin' a wee sweet girl, now isn't he?" Barton did not wait for Gabrielle's answer. She was hot with her indignation. "Such should be catched and gibbeted; carrying poor black people away from their homes and families, I say." She picked up the tray. "Do you mind if I spend the evening with Mary Treloar? She has need of help, apackin' up her pewter and her earthenware in the barrels Amos coopered for her."

"Of course not, Barton. Do go and help Mary." She picked up the snuffers and trimmed a candlewick. "We will miss them, Barton."

"Aye, that we will. I think Amos he will perish if he does not get on with building a tall ship. It's so firm in his mind that he thinks of nothing else, night or day. I'll leave a glass for Mistress Molly." Barton put a glass of water on the candle stand and went out, carrying the tray.

So that was it. Michael Cary did not come because he was "disguised with liquor." She wondered about David. Was that the way they spent lonely evenings, drinking ale laced with brandy?

Michael Cary did not come to the plantation the next day. Molly roamed around the place like a lost soul. She sat in the great room looking into space most of the time, or got up to walk as far as the west gate. Gabrielle was deeply concerned. Molly was slipping away from her. The old sisterly relation was lost and nothing had come to take its place. She did not know what to do about it. She dared not offer the wilful girl gratuitous advice. She would only drive her farther away. She devotedly wished Michael Cary had never shown his handsome face in the Cape Fear. He was a stormy petrel, who brought only trouble in his wake.

All these things ran through Gabrielle's mind as she sat at her loom, her facile fingers weaving the intricate pattern on the cloth the Governor of Jamaica had ordered. When she had finished her daily stint, she went to the stable, thinking that a canter would clear her mind and offer some solution to the problem of Molly. She was glad the *Delicia* would soon be in the river. She could talk with Captain Zeb. He was both wise and discreet.

Annaci did not answer when she called. A black man who was piling firewood into the high-wheeled cart told her that he had gone with the lady and the young master. They had ordered the saddle-horses and ridden off in the direction of the turpentine woods. Gabrielle knew at once that they had gone to Moray's plantation. Her first thought was to follow them, but there was no way. The horses were all in the field, where the men were cultivating corn.

The Negro said, "Fixin' for a storm, Mistress. Rain frogs singin' las' night, and a great ring wound hisself round the moon."

Gabrielle glanced at the cloudless sky. She didn't dispute his prophecy. She had found the Negroes right so many times, with their signs and symbols and their curious awareness of the variable moods of Nature. She turned back to the weaving room. As she passed her father's office, she saw him seated at his desk writing, while René stood at a tall desk reading off figures. So it was Etienne who had accompanied Molly. Remembering the way he had talked about slaving ships a few nights before, she was disturbed.

The afternoon advanced. The air grew more sultry. She thought she heard the roll of thunder in the far distance. She hoped it did not foretell a heavy storm; wind and rain would be bad for the crops, so near harvest time. The regular movement of the pedal and the rhythm of the shuttle cast a soothing spell over her troubled mind and she forgot everything but the completion of the pattern under her hand.

A heavy peal of thunder almost overhead brought Gabrielle back to a sense of the outside world. The wind had risen sharply. She jumped from her seat to close the narrow windows. She locked the door behind her and ran to the house; there were windows and shutters to be closed.

The sky was black and there were flashes of lightning.

She found Celestine struggling with the storm shutters. The French woman was muttering imprecations because the boards would not go together. "My poor Madame! She is so terrified. Always she thinks she must run away and hide when she hears such great noise."

"Go in, Celestine. I'll shut them," Gabrielle said. She put her shoulder against the shutter and brought it into place.

510

The wind was increasing. Trees bent before the blast. It grew darker as the black clouds rushed across the sky from the west and from the east. Only a small strip of blue remained overhead. The thunder in the west rumbled, growing in intensity. Small branches of trees fell in all directions. Towels from Barton's kitchen line, lying flat, sailed through the air as a kite sails in a strong gale.

Barton ran out to help Gabrielle with the shutters. "Old Nick's riding across the treetops in his chaise. Listen! Don't you hear his horses' hoofs and the crack of his long whip? The devil is ripping around this night."

Gabrielle was too busy to answer. Her skirts blew this way and that; the wind loosened her braids and flung them over her face. The air was heavy. Perspiration dripped from her forehead with her exertions.

"Where's Father? Where's René?" She had to shout to make herself heard.

"The Master is with Madam. The young master is upstairs, closing the house," Barton shrieked back.

The garden chairs tumbled over with a crash.

Gabrielle finished one side. "I wonder if the men have housed the animals," she cried in Barton's ear. "I'll go . . ."

She ran to the barn. She found some of the men herding the frightened sheep into the fold. She saw two men driving in from the fields, the chains clanking as they slapped the horses' rumps with the reins to make them trot faster. Little Gwen Akim escaped from her mother and ran out, whirling and dancing with her small arms extended, hands uplifted to feel the rain. Gabrielle had the same inclination. A storm excited her; she wanted to run with flying hair and billowing skirts before the wind.

A small drum sounded, down at the quarters line. The Africans were making *Mankwala* to keep off the demon of the storm. Old Nick rode in the bending treetops, for Barton; a greater monster rode in the winds, for the Negroes. They must keep drumming to hold him at bay.

Lightning tore a great jagged hole in the black clouds overhead and sent a pointed sword of flame into the forest. Thunder broke with terrific impact, directly over Gabrielle's head. The shock threw her staggering against the barn. The sentries were running to close the gates, as if closing the gates would keep out the storm! She saw Amos Treloar and his men tie a great canvas over the hull of his boat. The wind

511

caught and tore it into shreds. The loose ends slapped against the sides with a sharp crackling noise of canvas ripping.

She ran for the house, her wide skirt turned over her head. She saw the bush tent in Madam's garden lifted high. It whirled, then sailed out across the river. A limb off the great oak fell with a crash on the ground in front of her. A branch scraped her cheek and shoulder. She leaned against the wind, making slow headway. Once she raised her eyes; Barton was at the door, holding it open. She struggled towards it. She seemed unable to move against the pressure of the wind.

The lightning was almost continuous now. Thunder followed each flash, long roll upon long roll, breaking and vibrating against the low clouds.

The rain came before she reached the door, a deluge that beat against her slender body, whipped and stung against her face.

Barton ran to meet her, clutching Gabrielle's arms, forcing her through the door. It took both of them to close and bar it. They were both drenched to the skin. Gabrielle fell panting into a chair.

"Go upstairs and change at once, or you'll be chillin' and having ague." Barton shook the rain from her skirts. "Come, lass, hurry."

Gabrielle ran towards the stairs, Barton following close behind. "Has Miss Molly come in?"

"No, Mistress, nor the young Master."

"Oh, Barton, I hope they're not in the woods in this storm. They'll be so frightened."

"Don't worry. They'll find shelter." Barton's lips were drawn to a thin line. "They're safe enough."

"But the horses. I hope they'll think about my horses."

Barton did not answer. She was peeling the soggy muslin dress over Gabrielle's head. "Strip to the skin and I'll give you a good rub with a Turkey towel."

Before Gabrielle knew it she was rubbed and dried and bounced into bed and told to stay there, while Barton went to make a good hot drink to keep her from chilling.

The roar of the storm was steady. Crash after crash of thunder. It vibrated through the house, rattling the windows, shaking the roof. The lightning flashes penetrated the cracks of the closed shutters.

René came into the room and sat on Gabrielle's bed. His dark eyes were wide and excited. "Is it a hurricane?" he cried.

512

"No. A summer thunderstorm. The wind isn't high enough to be a gale, yet."

The boy laughed aloud. "I want to see a hurricane." He shouted to be heard. His voice was flattened, lost in the roar. "A hurricane must be wonderful, if it's worse than this."

Barton came up with the hot tea, "Drink it all at once, and stay there in the feathers. It's safer," she ordered, stamping off.

The wind rattled in the chimney. The limbs of the great oaks scraped and rustled against the roof—great clutching hands dragging one way and another.

René opened a shutter to look out. The wind came in with a rush, pushing him against the bed. Gabrielle sprang up. Both of them struggled to get the bar back into place. The room was a wreck—everything blown from dressing table and chest; bottles and vases in fragments on the floor; Gabrielle's clothes blown from the chair into the hall; pictures blown from the walls.

René ran about, picking up garments and bits of glass. He kept saying, "Oh, Gabrielle. I'm so sorry, so sorry," over and over.

It was after nine that night before the storm abated. The thunder died down into an intermittent roll and the lightning retreated to the distant horizon, though the rain kept up a steady downpour.

Gabrielle and René ate a cold supper. It was impossible to keep a fire going, for the wind, which had lessened, was still strong enough to drive the smoke down the chimney into the room. Robert came in when they had almost finished. He sat down near by and drank a glass of milk. Barton hovered over him, pressing him to eat liver sausage and cheese, but he shook his head.

"Your mother suffers so much when there's thunder," he said to Gabrielle. "The noise seems to bring back all the scenes of horror through which she has lived in the past. It is pitiful to see the terror in her eyes."

"Is she quiet now, sir?" René asked, his young face grave.

"Yes, when the rain came she quieted down." He looked about. "Where is Molly? And Etienne? Have they had their supper?"

"They went out for a ride and have not come back," Gabrielle said.

Robert pushed back his chair. "We must send for them. Where do you think they have gone, Gabrielle?"

"Annaci is with them. He'll surely find shelter for them. I've been worried, but I trust Annaci."

Robert paced the floor nervously. "I'm afraid I haven't watched after my children as I should have. There is something about this wilderness that defeats me." He ran his thin hand across his forehead.

Barton said, " 'Tis the forest, sir. 'Tis this rank growing. 'Tis all wild, wild as the wind in the Highlands! 'Tis green enough, but a strangling greenness, like to suffocate one. And today I heard the devil ariding the treetops. There's a spell, a heavy spell. Some dead ha' left a curse upon this place. That's what it is."

"Hist, woman," Robert said quickly. " 'Tis no way to speak. God watches over the forest and the river. We are God's creatures, under His care."

Barton gathered up the dishes and went out, mumbling to herself. Gabrielle watched her go. She wondered if Barton had heard voices.

She tried to read an old *Spectator*, but her eyes followed her father's nervous pacing. René threw himself on a settee and closed his eyes.

Etienne came in shortly after the hall clock struck eleven. He was windblown, his clothes drenched. "Your horse is all right, Gabrielle. He brought me home safely," he said, after he had greeted his father.

"Where is Molly?" She and her father spoke at once.

Etienne looked from one to the other. "Didn't she come home? I haven't seen her since morning. I went up Far Reach. She wanted to ride to Moray's plantation, so we separated. Annaci rode with her."

No one spoke. Etienne continued, "I stayed in a charcoal-burner's hut during the storm. Then I helped our men with the cattle. The wind levelled all the shelters and the cattle were terrified." He went to the door. "Barton, may I have something to eat? I'm starved."

Robert Fountaine looked at Gabrielle. "I suppose she is safe from the storm, at Moray's."

"I'm sure she is," Gabrielle hastened to assure her father. "She'll be quite safe."

Robert looked at René, who was sleeping soundly. "MacAlpin told me that Captain Cary has brought slaves into the river. I do not like that, Gabrielle. We do not want slaves here."

"David Moray bought slaves of Cary." Etienne came back

514

into the room, a glass of milk in his hand. "Cary's going to be an out and out slaver. He says there's money to be made . . ."

Robert's eyes flashed. "Evil money," he said angrily. "Let us hear no more about it." He went out of the room.

Etienne looked after him. "I didn't know . . ."

"Father doesn't believe in traffic in human beings," René said flatly.

Gabrielle went to the door. It was still raining but there was a break in the sky overhead, and the faint suggestion of moonshine behind the clouds.

"I wish Molly would come," she said.

René came out to join her. "Don't worry, Gaby. Molly will be all right. She's like a fluffy kitten—she knows how to find a warm nest near the stove." He kissed her cheek. Yawning, he took up a bed candle and lighted it. "I'm going to follow Etienne to bed," he said. "Don't sit up waiting for Molly Lepel."

Molly came into the great room shortly after daybreak. Her habit was streaked with mud and pitch and she was ready to drop with fatigue. She sank wearily into a chair and pulled at her riding boots, sticky and covered to the instep with swamp mud. She did not see Gabrielle on the settee until she had taken up the filthy boots, preparatory to dropping them in the passageway before she went upstairs to her room. When she saw her, she stopped short. Her face hardened as though she were buckling on her armour to withstand an onslaught.

"You need not have waited up for me," she said coldly.

"Oh, Molly, I'm so glad you're back! We, my father and I, were so worried about you."

"I had Annaci to look after me. We were caught in the storm. I stayed in the charcoal-burners' hut, up Far Reach." Her light blue eyes flicked as she said the words. Gabrielle knew it was not the truth. Etienne had taken refuge at the charcoal-burners'; for an instant it was on the point of her tongue to tell Molly that, but she thought better of it. Instead she got up from the settee.

"I'll have Barton bring your tea upstairs, Molly. I know you must want a rest." She smiled a little. "I knew you would be terrified of the lightning. That's why I worried for you."

A faint colour crept into Molly's pale cheeks, a strange light came in her eyes. "I *was* terrified," she whispered. "I cannot tell you how terrified I was." She went upstairs without another word.

Gabrielle went in search of Barton. She found her preparing breakfast, with the help of a Negro boy. "Please take tea to Mistress Molly, Barton," she said.

Barton looked furious. She rattled copper kettles and pans, to show her displeasure. "I told Master Moray it was ill conceived of him to let a wee girl go skylarking around the wild woods of a nighttime, in a storm, too."

"What has Captain Moray to do with Mistress Molly?" she said.

Barton gave her a quick glance. " 'Twas he fetched her home this morning," she said shortly. She lifted a kettle from the fire and poured hot water into an earthen pot that contained the tea leaves. She closed the lid, put the cozy over the pot to steep, and set up the tray. "A poor, weak, befuddled girl, havin' no better sense than a child. I told him what I thought, no fear. I said more than befitten for a woman to say to her betters." She stalked out of the room, carrying the tray before her, muttering to herself.

Gabrielle went up to her room. For a long time she stood at the window looking out over the clearing that lay beyond the stockade. The corn was flat, as if a giant had mowed it down with a great scythe. The cattle shelter was destroyed. She changed and went out to see what other damage the storm had done. Her heart failed her when she saw the wreck of fowl-run and sheepfold; half the roof was gone from the cow barn, as well as the shelter. Men were in the field, trying to straighten the corn by bracing it with a lacing of young reeds and saplings. The stable boy was rubbing down the horses. Her mare, which Molly had ridden, limped a little. "A thorn in her foot," the boy explained. "Annaci gone to make poultice."

It was the church that had suffered most. The roof, not quite finished, had blown away, and lay a wreck in a small clump of pine trees near the north gate. A group of women stood around, talking and gesticulating. Mary Treloar was trying to quiet them. "It is God's will," Gabrielle heard her say.

"God's will! More like the devil's." Gabrielle recognized the wife of the farrier. "I told Tom 'twas a sign, breaking down the Lord's chapel, a sign that it was not meant for folk to worship in the wilderness." She began to cry. The little girl tugging at her skirts began to wail loudly.

516

Mary said, "Nonsense, woman. Wind blows all over everywhere. The roof wasn't yet pegged on tight. Come, let's go within and see if there's damage to the Lord's altar."

Gabrielle followed them in and stood near the door. The wind had disturbed nothing. The altar remained as it had been, the cross standing, the candlesticks in place. Only the altar cloth was streaked and wet by rain. The Bible was closed in its tin box.

" 'Tis a miracle," Mary exclaimed, and fell on her knees in front of the altar. The other women followed. In the back of the chapel Gabrielle knelt to say a little prayer of thanksgiving.

She slipped away without the women seeing her, and walked slowly back to the house. She was despondent, not alone over the wreck of the storm, but Molly . . . Molly had lied to her. She had been remote and hard, as though Gabrielle were her enemy, instead of a friend who loved her.

She went to find Celestine. She, too, showed the effect of the storm in her bloodshot eyes and lined face. "Madame is resting. She slept so little. She lay awake holding the Master's hand half the night."

"Can't you rest now, Celestine? I'll sit with my mother."

"There is no need. Master René is with her. She is quiet for him."

"Where is my father?" Gabrielle asked.

"In the weaving room. He said he wished not to be disturbed."

She went to her room. She heard Molly moving about, but her door was closed. She took off her dress and put on her wrapper. She must rest a little. A few minutes' sleep and she would feel refreshed. She moved restlessly, turning from one side to the other. Why didn't Molly say she was storm-bound, and stayed at David Moray's plantation? Why did she lie? Why did he ride over with her and not come in?

After a time, sleep came, the deep sleep of a weary body and tired mind.

The sun was low when she woke. Barton was standing beside the bed. There was something in her expression that filled Gabrielle's with alarm. She sat up, pushing her hair back off her face. "What is it, Barton?" she cried.

"Captain David Moray is below. He asks to speak with you, at once."

Gabrielle slid off the high bed, her feet deep in the shag rug.

"My clothes, Barton, quick! The blue dress, no the yellow."

Barton went to the press and took out a Holland riding skirt and underbreeches. "Better wear these," she said grimly. Gabrielle started to question her, but thought better of it.

She found David standing by the window. He turned when he heard her footstep and walked quickly towards her. "Please sit down," he said, leading her to a chair. He did not sit, but stood looking down at her, his face grave. "I've thought of a dozen ways to say what I must say, so that it will be easy for you. But I cannot find the words to soften the truth. Molly Lepel has gone away with Cary."

Gabrielle sprang to her feet. "No! That's not true! Molly's here. I spoke to her. She is upstairs in her room, resting." She started for the stairs.

David detained her. "Don't go. You'll not find her. She went this afternoon, while you were sleeping."

"Oh, no, no. Molly would not be so unkind. She . . ." Her hands trembled as she raised them to her eyes.

David took her hands and led her to the settee. "My dear, I'm sorry to be the one to bring you this news. I know it will hurt you. Hurt you in your dear, loyal heart. But remember Molly is in love, and lovers are ofttimes selfish, thinking only of themselves."

"But how? Where?" Gabrielle looked at him, bewilderment in her dark eyes. "Gone! We must go after her, bring her back to us. Is there some way?"

"If I had known earlier, I would have killed the fellow rather than let this happen. Only a small chance. But worth trying. I've talked to Barton. She'll keep it from your father till we come back." He led the way out of the room. Barton was in the hall, with Gabrielle's riding hat in her hand. She saw two saddle-horses at the block.

"If you find the villain, I hope you give him Moses' law, excusin' one, Captain Moray. He don't deserve gentleman's sword."

"Where are we going?" Gabrielle asked, as he swung her onto her horse.

"We'll ride down to the cove, where Moore surveyed his town site. I think that's where she went to meet him. I've made inquiry. His ship did not put in here for sweet water, and he must get it somewhere before he sails. I think he will

518

get it at the cove. He must have told Molly to meet him. Molly ordered a horse and rode off by herself. She told Annaci she didn't need him. She was going only a short way. But he noticed the saddlebags were packed."

"Wouldn't a boat be surer?" she asked.

Moray's smile was grim. "Not a boat here without leaks, or damaged sail. The storm played havoc. The only thing we can do is to try to make it through the forest by the lakes."

He swung his long leg over the horse's back. Gabrielle fell in behind him as he led the way, trotting swiftly. There was no time to lose if they were to get to the cove before Michael Cary's ship lifted sail and put off down the river to the open seas.

As they rode through the trees, Moray told her Molly had come riding over the day before. He was busy on the plantation and she had walked down the bank of a new canal to Cary's ship, which was being readied to sail. Then the storm came. David was too busy getting the animals housed and the house closed to think of Molly Lepel. When he remembered, he ran out to look for the ship, but Cary had put it out of the canal, into midstream, to keep the ship from blowing ashore. Molly must be aboard the ship, and there was nothing he could do about it. They must have made plans then, for when the wind stopped, Cary brought her to the house. It was almost morning by that time. David had his man make tea and prepare food. At daylight Cary left, saying he was going to sail within the hour. David insisted on riding over with Molly, who seemed in a great rush to be home.

"I'm afraid Gaby will be worried," she had told David. He was back at his plantation when the thought came to him that Molly had not been in the least sad about Cary's leaving. That was strange, very strange, for she had not tried to conceal her feelings for him. He rode back in all haste. Barton went upstairs and found Molly had gone. Some clothes were missing, the rest were scattered about, as though she had packed with great haste.

Gabrielle listened to David's words. She remembered the look on Molly's face when she came in—how cold and remote she had been. She had hardened herself against Gabrielle. She did not want to talk for fear she would betray her secret plans.

Gabrielle's heart sank. "I'll never see Molly again," she said. Tears gathered in her eyes and fell unheeded down her cheeks. "It is cruel. Cruel. It will hurt my father so. He loved

519

Molly. We all loved Molly. She used to be so gay, so loving."

Six miles through the forest, then they came to Maurice Moore's clearing; a short distance farther and they were in sight of the water.

A ship, with slack sails, was anchored in the cove.

"Stay here!" David said sharply. He dismounted, unstrapped his sword from his saddle and disappeared into the thicket of pines that grew along the bank of the river.

Chapter 34

"LIGHTLY, GENTLE EARTH"

It seemed to Gabrielle that she waited hours for David to return. She tried to follow him, but there was no path, and her riding skirt caught in brambles and held her fast. She was a long time freeing herself. When she scrambled back to the level, cutover land, she found that her horse had pulled the reins free and got away. She spent some time trying to follow, but the hoof-marks, plainly visible in the clearing, were lost in the weeds and grass.

She was without hope that David Moray would succeed in bringing Molly to her senses. She should have gone herself. She looked to see that David's horse was securely tied, and started off, this time from the opposite side of the point of land. The way was hard. The pine needles under her feet were slippery. More than once she found herself flat on the ground. Brambles and thorny vines caught and held. Her arms and hands were scratched and bleeding, but that did not matter if she could only get to the little narrow sand strip in time.

Halfway down the steep bank, she came to an open place in the bush. She could see the water. She drew her breath sharply. Michael Cary's ship, under full sail, was already in midstream. Across the small ravine she saw David climbing the bank. He was alone. She turned around and began the long climb upward.

When she finally reached the top, David was calling her. She thought she discerned a note of alarm in his voice. She answered quickly. Suppose he did not hear her! Suppose he went on without her! She ran, breathing rapidly, calling, "David. David. David."

Then she heard him crashing through the brush. A moment later she reached the edge of the clearing. He was coming towards her, an expression of anxiety on the dark, thin face, which changed when he saw her.

"I thought you'd gone. Your horse . . . Where were you?" he asked, looking at her dishevelled habit.

"I tried to get to the beach, but it was too late."

"Yes, it was too late, months too late," he said, half under his breath. He set about brushing her skirt and taking out the burrs.

"Don't bother," she said. She was anxious now to go home. She wanted nothing so much as to get to her own room, to be alone. She did not have voice to speak without betraying her grief.

"You'll have to ride my horse," David said in a matter-of-fact tone.

"What will you do?"

"Walk. Why not? Six miles or eight miles is nothing to a Highlander." He smiled a little.

"I can't have you do that. It was my stupidity. I'll wait here while you go for a horse ... or perhaps you'll overtake mine along the path."

"No. You can't stay here alone."

"Why not? I'm not afraid."

He walked over to the remnants of a fire and kicked at the charred wood. "That is why. Indians camped here—recently. Since the rain."

He led his horse to a fallen tree. Gabrielle stepped on the log and mounted. "You'll have to manage cross-saddle," he said.

She unhooked her skirt at the knee and slid over. "Won't the horse hold both of us?" she asked timidly.

He did not answer. He walked beside her, his hand on the horse's mane. They were both silent as the horse made its way the length of the clearing, where Maurice Moore had surveyed and set the stakes for his town of Brunswick.

"I talked to Molly. But it was no use. She was set to go. She told me to tell you she loves you." He lingered a little over the words. Gabrielle felt her pulse quicken. But he did not glance at her. "I would have fought Cary, if it would have done any good. She made the decision."

He did not repeat Molly's words spoken through her tears: "I will go with Michael ... or I'll die." Wild words spoken by a wilful, emotional woman.

After a time Gabrielle said, "My father will be sad. He loved Molly." She choked a little and turned her head so that he might not see the hot, stinging tears that filled her eyes. David was not looking at her. He was leaning forward, looking at the path. Gabrielle saw the same quick, alert intensity of gaze that she had noticed in Annaci when he was following an animal trail.

She looked down, but saw nothing. Perhaps he saw the track of a bear, or a panther. She saw him lay his hand on his pistol holster, but he did not speak. A moment later he straightened his body and strode on ahead, for the path was narrow under the heavy overhanging trees.

After a time they came to the Lower Lake. He said, "Wait here a moment. I want to see where this path leads. Don't move from where you are."

He disappeared at once, walking swiftly along the path that led into the rushes. White lilies lay in green pads, in the mirror of the lake, and blue water hyacinths grew thick at the rim, pushing their bloom above the dark water. It was very still. Suddenly a dozen white egrets rose from the reeds; they flew low over the surface of the water, flapping their great wings.

What had disturbed the birds? Not Moray, for he was on the other side of the lake from the birds. Gabrielle peered into the gloom of the deep woods. She thought she saw a shadow glide from one tree to another. She shivered. Could it be Indians again? It had been weeks since there had been any sign of them, on the river or near the settlement.

David came back. He said, "I believe I'll ride for a while. Do you think you can hold on?"

"Yes. Certainly." She slid back. David mounted.

"Put your arms about my waist." When she hesitated, he insisted: "Do as I say, please." She clasped her hands over the heavy buckle of his leather belt. "Hold on!" He put the horse to a trot. She felt herself slipping. Her arms closed tightly. "That's right. Hold hard! We're going to gallop."

He spoke a word to his horse. She felt his thighs move as he touched the spurs to the horse's flanks. She pressed her face against his leather jerkin. Her head came as high as his shoulder.

"I thought I saw an Indian among the trees," she said. He turned his head. His cheek touched hers. It was hard and firm against her face.

"They camped by the lake this morning." The horse was galloping along the hard path that encircled the swamp.

"Are you afraid?" he asked, after a time. There was a laugh in his voice. She thought he was one who always welcomed danger.

"No. Not really," she answered. "But I think I'm slipping off."

He pulled up. "Wait. I've thought of something better." He dismounted hurriedly. "Slide into the saddle. I'll ride behind. It will be easier for you." Before he ceased talking, he was up behind her, his arm about her now.

Her heart beat violently. Was it danger, or the nearness of his strong, firm body pressed against her?

They were crossing the bridge at Old Town Creek when they saw the Indians, six of them. They were moving through the reeds near the water, silently, one by one, downstream. Not until the horse's hoofs touched the bridge timber were they aware. In an instant they had vanished. Gabrielle, for a moment, wondered whether she had really seen them, or whether it was imagination, heightened by danger.

"Six, I saw. More may be following." David's lips were close to her ear. "They wore war feathers."

Gabrielle's knees dug into the horse's sides. They had come to the outer clearing, when an arrow flew past them. Grazing the horse's neck, it buried itself into the ground ahead.

"Ah," David said. She felt his body turn as he lifted out a pistol from the holster.

The horse did not break, but galloped on down the road. They were in sight of the stockade now. Men were ploughing in the field; in the gardens half a dozen women were chopping weeds, singing as they walked down the long rows.

"I'll get down here," David said. "Go on in. No need to disturb your people yet. I think I see MacAlpin over yonder in the field."

"You will come to the house?" she said.

"After I've seen Sandy. He must warn his men." He slipped from the horse and walked across the field.

Gabrielle dismounted and gave the horse over to the stable boy. "Rub him down well. Captain Moray may want him soon."

"Your mare—he came in by heself."

Gabrielle nodded. She had forgotten the mare.

"He have arrow through he blanket."

"Was she struck?" she asked anxiously.

"No, Mistress. Annaci say he tremble lak a quivering leaf, he so scared. Annaci he go look for the Mistress."

"Has Annaci come back?"

"Yes, Mistress, he over there." The boy waved his hand in the direction of the field. He led the horse away to the stable.

Gabrielle went to the house. If the Indians were near, the men would know and take the necessary measures. A small party of six, even a war party, meant no particular danger, yet Moray had felt the urgency of putting the long stretch of deep forest behind him.

She slipped off her dishevelled habit and threw a light cotton wrapper about her. When she walked across the room to the dressing table, to brush her long dark hair, she saw a letter addressed in Molly's thin fine hand.

She broke the seal, her hands trembling.

"MY DEAREST GABY:

When a woman makes up her mind to run away with a man, it means she loves him, and cannot live without him. You, who have a free and untouched heart, may never understand the suffering I have experienced. Before I took this step, Michael spoke to your father.

"His marriage to that girl—it was never a marriage, performed by one unsanctioned. But Michael held it to be . . . but now he loves me.

"Your father refused to talk with Michael or listen to his explanation after he discovered that Michael was captain of a slave ship. I would go with Michael if I knew he were the most desperate pirate and had as many wives as a Turk.

"I will always love you . . . all of you, because you have given me the only home I have ever known. I am sick with fear. Forgive my instability.

"Pray for your
"MOLLY."

Gabrielle read the letter through. She folded it back into shape and put it in her desk, under a bundle of old letters. The agony of mind left her. Her resolution was taken. She would put Molly out of her thoughts. The humiliation and alarms were gone. She remembered words David Moray had spoken in his effort to comfort her: "Lovers are always selfish." His words were no comfort. They were a warning. She felt curiously dispassionate and remote, but she was determined not to allow herself to grieve for Molly.

The murmur of conversation greeted her when she walked down the stairs. Her father stood at the open door, talking to David and Sandy MacAlpin. The men were evidently on the point of departure.

Sandy said, "There's nothing we can do about it, sir. Amos has given orders to all the folk who live outside to sleep within the stockade tonight. The cattle and the sheep they've driven into the inner fold for safety."

"I can't think of the red men as savages," Robert said. "Poor misguided people who do not know the Lord's words!"

She saw a look of impatience on David's face.

"Sir, that may be true. But we are dealing with savages, not enlightened Indians, *now*. There may be no trouble. Perhaps it will turn out to be only a stray party. But they did shoot their arrows."

Gabrielle looked at her father. His eyes were troubled.

"We are in the Lord's hands. I cannot help thinking that the Indians, also, are God's children."

David said, "We are riding back to the plantation. We have our Negroes to take care of. If you wish, we will come back here for the night."

Fountaine thought it wasn't necessary, unless they wanted the protection. Gabrielle watched them go across the compound. David, tall and straight, moved easily with his long stride. Sandy, shorter by a head, stooped a little, walking with a sort of swinging lope that covered the ground as easily as a long stride.

The table was set for six. After Robert had said grace, he spoke to Barton: "Madam will have supper in her room. She is very restless and uneasy tonight." His dark, fathomless eyes fell on Molly's empty chair. "Barton, you may put Miss Lepel's serviette ring away. It will not be necessary to place it on the table in the future." His voice was flat.

Barton gathered up the silver and the napkin ring, and went towards the side table. She made a queer sound as she moved away, as if she had choked back a sob. René and Etienne looked at each other quickly, then down at their plates. Gabrielle sat with her hands folded in her lap. She had tried to eat, but it was no use. The meal was finished in silence.

René was waiting for Gabrielle in the hall. Together they walked out in the garden. There was a strong east wind and no insects to annoy them. The night was warm and fragrant; the storm had washed away dust and dirt from the garden, leaving the fragrance of the crushed flowers. Annaci had straightened the bushes, and set the beaten-down flowers erect with little twigs to hold them. He and his men had made a new bush shelter, and the fresh-cut pine boughs sent off a clean, resinous odour. The young sickle moon shone over the river, and the stars were thick in the sky.

526

"It's a shame, a horrid mean shame, for Molly to act so," René burst out. "But she was always selfish."

"Women in love are selfish," she found herself saying.

"Don't ever fall in love then, Gaby. We want you with us, just as you are, Etienne and I. We were talking tonight. You've made us such a comfortable, tranquil home." He put his arm over her shoulder, giving it a little squeeze. She noticed he was taller than she. A man almost, sixteen.

She felt the tears come to her eyes. They did need her. Her father needed her, although he did not know it. Little things escaped his notice. She took great pains to lift the burden from him. It was she who carried the weavers' work. René helped with the books, now that he was getting the hang. Etienne had no time. He was fishing, in the turpentine woods, or helping the men with the boats. But he had interest, too, in the cattle and the crops. It was well; between them they could make the plantation a success. She wanted that so much.

They walked in silence. The trees rustled overhead, and the night birds called. She looked towards the forest. She wondered again if danger lurked unseen in the heavy pulsating darkness of swamp and forest.

"I must go in now, René," she said. "I'll say good night to Mother, and then to bed."

René kissed her forehead. "I'm going to stand watch at the forest gate tonight."

"Oh, no, René. You're too young. There are enough men. If we had needed more, Sandy would have stayed."

He lifted her hand from his arm. "I'm old enough to help protect my womenfolk and my home."

There was something new in his voice, something deep and strong and manly.

"Dear René, of course you are old enough. I keep forgetting . . ." She kissed him lightly on the cheek, and walked across the garden to the side entrance that led to her mother's sitting-room.

Celestine opened the door. Her round face was troubled; anxiety looked out of her eyes. "Madame is so restless tonight," she said. Following Gabrielle into the sitting-room, she pulled a chair for her and lighted the candelabrum on the little onyx-topped table. "I don't understand," she went on. "She has never before been so, so uneasy. She walks about her room, talking always of voices that speak to her." Celestine twisted her small fluted apron with her short, stubby fingers. "Oh Ma'm'selle, I'm frightened. Ver' frightened."

Voices. Her mother spoke of voices. A thin edge of fear cut into her. She answered mechanically, "It is only the heat, Celestine; nothing to worry about. 'Tis the wind in the trees. I've often fancied I heard voices."

Celestine shook her head. "No. It is not that, Ma'm'selle. Something above the natural."

"Perhaps she misses Molly."

"Non. It is something . . . something . . ." She put her apron to her face.

Gabrielle spoke energetically. "Nonsense, Celestine. Nonsense. Don't give way. I count on you. You're the only one . . ."

Celestine wiped her eyes. "Yes, that is true. I must not give way. . . . But oh, Ma'm'selle, I wish this night was over."

"Nonsense!" Gabrielle repeated, almost too strongly. "It's a beautiful night. A new moon brings good luck. You know that."

She went into her mother's bedroom. Madam was sitting up in bed. The candles were lighted, and her blue eyes looked almost black in her white face. She wore a light mull jacket over her gown, and her long hair was in two plaits over her shoulder.

"Gabrielle," she said, "surely you know they are coming tonight. Is everything ready?"

"Who is coming, Madam?" She tried to keep the quaver out of her voice.

"Sir John and his friends. He promised to bring them all tonight. Sir John used to live here, in this house. . . ." She paused and looked into Gabrielle's eyes, with the wide, clear look of a child. "Sir John is a man of parts; we must receive him suitably. Tell Robert, please." She leaned back on her pillows and closed her eyes. "I must rest," she said. Gabrielle looked across the bed at Celestine. The serving woman nodded.

Suddenly Madam sat up and caught Celestine's hand in both of hers. "Don't let the others come," she whispered, terror in her eyes. "Keep them away—the evil ones that hide in the forest."

Before Celestine could speak, Madam had dropped back to the pillow. The anxious lines smoothed from her face. She breathed quietly.

Neither Gabrielle nor Celestine had dared to move. Now

they stole from the room. Gabrielle struggled to shake off the terror she felt.

Celestine said, "You observe? She speaks of the dead as though they were living. I'm afraid."

"I don't think it is anything to cause alarm," Gabrielle replied. She spoke calmly. She did not want Celestine to know how her mother's words frightened her. "I'll have Barton make up a cot for me in there."

"Thank you. You ease my mind. . . . Sometimes folk like Madame see deeply, with eyes not given to others."

Gabrielle wakened and sat up. Celestine stood beside her. She was holding a candle.

"Will you come? I can do nothing with Madame. She insists on being dressed. She wants the peach-coloured silk with the raised pattern you wove for her. She says her guests are very near. She can hear their voices and the wheels of the coach. Please call your father, Ma'm'selle. I am afraid to leave her for a moment."

Gabrielle jumped quickly from the cot. "Do what she wants, Celestine. Don't cross her. I'll call my father."

"She says it's a large company of people. She asks if we have wine and other refreshment ready."

"Tell her yes. Yes, everything is ready. Keep her as tranquil as you can."

Gabrielle ran across the hall and upstairs to her father's room. He was lying asleep on the couch, fully dressed. She touched his shoulder.

He opened his eyes and sprang up.

"Come quickly, Father! Celestine wants you to come quickly!"

"What is wrong?" he asked.

"I don't know. Mother thinks a great company of people are coming. She wants to be dressed to receive them."

"Strange," he said, walking beside her. "She is sensitive. Can it be that she sees beyond us?"

Gabrielle repeated her words—the evil in the forest . . .

"Yes, yes, danger is a presence. She may feel it about her. Come, let us hurry."

Gabrielle paced the little sitting-room. The door to her mother's chamber remained closed. She had sent Gabrielle from the room to prepare food for the guests—chicken and truffles . . . a good wine, *that* she would leave to Robert.

Gabrielle waited, afraid of some intangible unseen thing that was visible to her mother. Gabrielle heard voices, but no more. She was shivering though the night was warm. Hour after hour passed.

Celestine came out with a cup of tea. She shook her head mournfully and wiped her eyes with the corner of her apron.

"I am afraid," she kept repeating. "I am afraid."

She turned and was gone, leaving Gabrielle in the midst of intense, terrifying silence.

The attack came before dawn. A bright flame leapt up, higher than the stockade. Almost at once she heard shouting and the cry of "Fire! Fire! Fire!"

The door opened and her father came out. "See what it is, Gabrielle. Run quickly. I dare not leave your mother."

As she ran, she saw Madam, fully dressed, standing in the middle of the room, her hands tightly clasped, a look of terror on her white face.

Gabrielle met Barton at the stairs. She had thrown a shawl over her gown and her sleeping cap was awry. "Where is it?" she cried. "Where is the fire?"

"I think it's one of the cottages outside the stockade," Gabrielle answered.

They ran through the dark house, bumping against chairs and tables. From the kitchen they saw not one, but two blazes, leaping skyward; the flames were spreading. They heard the crackling of the fire.

"Look over there." The quarters line too was flaming.

"Indians! Indians!" The shouting was close, as men ran to the western gate.

Gunfire was steady. They heard answering cries and shouts from the forest. Etienne ran by with a musket in his hand. "Go back! Go back!" he shouted to Gabrielle, and disappeared around the corner of the house. Men were running to and fro, their figures silhouetted in the light of the flames. Cattle were bellowing, horses neighing. They were driving the cattle away from the stockade.

She ran back to her father. As she came to the garden, she saw a great blazing knot of fatwood come hurtling over the high poles and fall not far from the weaving room. "I must get the cloth out," she called to her father, and ran down the path. It was easy to see her way. Half a dozen cabins had been fired now. If they could only keep the Indians outside the stockade.

René overtook her; they ran silently, hand in hand. They reached the weaving room. The door was locked. René hurled a stick of wood through a window and climbed in. The flame of the pine knot was still blazing within a few yards of where they stood. Gabrielle's breath came painfully as she lifted the rolls of cloth René pushed from the window, and staggered to the oak tree. Here she laid them on the ground on a strip of canvas he had thrown out.

Back and forth she went, carrying bundles. Annaci came up and took a roll of woollens from her arms. "Better to rest now," he said.

Another pine knot blazed through the air. It fell closer to the shed.

"Break down the door. Get the looms out," she cried to Annaci. He threw his weight against the door, but it did not give. He caught up a log from the woodpile and hammered at the lock. It gave, and the door flew open.

She saw them drag the loom towards the door. She ran inside to aid. She knew where to unpeg the pedals and the arms.

They heard crackling of flames overhead. The Indians had found the target. They pulled and tugged and got the loom out the door, section by section.

"The records, the books!" she called to René. He ran to the small office. Two men with muskets came out of the darkness. One took aim at a savage who had reached the top of the stockade.

René called, "Everything out." A moment later a section of roof fell in.

"Get back! Get back!" one of the men shouted. "The damned savages can see you in this light."

Gabrielle ran to the shelter of the trees. There was nothing more to be done there, so she ran to the house. By the time she got as far as the door the Indians were holding torches against the west gate. It would not take long for the dry, resinous pine to catch and blaze.

She heard women talking excitedly. They had run to the house for shelter, crowding up near the kitchen. She called to Barton to open the door so they could come inside. She led the crying children into the great room. Barton had set her Negro helpers to making tea.

"It's all gone! My wedding dress and all," a woman wept.

"And my baby's cradle that my man made for the wee tot," another lamented.

Mary Treloar came in the room. Gabrielle took comfort in her calm presence. She said, "Shall we put the children to bed? I don't think the Indians can reach this house with their firebrands."

Mary nodded. "I doubt even the children will sleep, but we can try. 'Tis a fair hard blow to us poor folk, if the red men burn the corn in the stalks and kill the cattle."

"Are the men all safe?" Gabrielle asked anxiously.

"Near as I know. But if the gate gives and the devil's get within . . ."

Gabrielle said, "Keep the storm shutters closed and barricade the door. I'll be back. Barton knows where the light muskets are. Have the women keep them loaded."

She ran to the garden. It was light as day now. Shadowy forms of men ran about. She saw the sentry moving his musket. . . .

That was her father's voice, quiet and commanding. "Watch the gate, Amos. Watch the gate."

There was no target for the men to fire at. The Indians kept behind the shelter of the stout gate, against which they piled the brands. René was climbing a tree, his firearm strapped over his shoulder. "God watch over him!" she whispered. "Watch over them all." There was a break in the stockade near the gate. She saw the tonsured head of an Indian pushed through. A man in the watch tower lifted his musket. The Indian fell. But there were others behind, pushing their way through the gap.

Gabrielle, terrified by what she had seen, ran to her mother's room. The door was wide open. "Celestine! Celestine!" she cried. There was no answer. Her heart beat to suffocation. Where were they? The door to the great room was closed and locked. She ran around the house and entered by the front door. In the hall she met her father and Celestine.

His voice shook with anxiety. "Have you seen your mother? She slipped away while Celestine was closing the shutters. We cannot find her."

Celestine covered her head with her white apron. She was crying.

Fountaine spoke sharply. "Do not cry, Celestine. No one blames you."

Gabrielle ran after the boys. "Tell the men to watch for her," her father called. She ran into the garden. When she turned the corner of the house she saw her mother, walking quietly towards the west gate, her skirts upheld daintily. She was moving directly towards the flaming stockade.

Two Indians, bows in hand, slid through the opening in the stockade. They stood motionless, watching. Dear God, what must she do? If she cried out, her mother would be frightened. She was oblivious to the danger that stood in her path.

Gabrielle moved forward cautiously, keeping in line with the oak trees, out of sight of the Indians. If she could reach her mother in time to shield her with her own body. . . . There was no sentry in sight. She dared not call for help, she could only pray.

She heard her mother's voice: "You are welcome, sirs, very welcome indeed. We are so delighted to have guests."

Gabrielle's heart beat to suffocation. Her mother was speaking words of greeting to the savages, holding out her hands in welcome. . . . The Indians did not move. They watched Madam come towards them, with eyes hard and expressionless as obsidian. She spread her skirts of primrose silk and bent her knees in a low curtsy, reserved for distinguished guests.

Then it happened. In the distance a shot was fired. A death scream followed. Gabrielle rushed from behind the sheltering tree and ran forward. But she was too late. Her mother wavered, threw up her arms with a cry of terror and ran through the gate. The forest beyond was alive with hidden foes.

Gabrielle sped after her, crying, "Mother! Mother!"

She saw a red body and the gleam of a knife in an upraised hand . . . heard her mother's voice echoing through the trees, "Robert! Robert! My husband, Robert!"

Gabrielle caught her as she fell, her thin fingers clutching at her throat. Gabrielle felt her knees give way . . . dizziness engulfed her. She sank to the ground, her mother's frail body clasped in her arms.

From a great distance she heard savage screams . . . David's voice: "This way! Throw your firebrands!" . . . a rush of feet, and the shouts of their people as they beat back the Indians with axes and pikes and musket butts. Savagery met savagery almost over her prone body.

She felt herself lifted in strong arms . . . word spoken softly in her ears: "My brave girl. My brave girl" . . . David's voice. Then blackness closed down upon her.

When she awoke she was lying on her bed. Barton sat beside her, bathing her forehead.

"They drove them off. Deep into the forest. Our men are patrolling the river road."

"Mother," Gabrielle whispered.

"It was your father who carried her home. He closed her eyes . . . now he keeps vigil alone."

Gabrielle buried her face in the pillow. Barton touched her hand. Her voice was gentle.

"God's way is best. . . . Did you not hear her call out 'Robert, my husband'? He heard her crying aloud for him . . . that will be his comfort."

They laid Madam Fountaine under an oak tree in the old burying ground beside the stream. Amos Treloar had pegged cypress boards into a strong coffin. Celestine and Mary Treloar lined it with a length of the white cloth which the Governor of Jamaica had ordered for his lady. Their people came to say a last farewell to the woman they had never spoken to and had seen only at a distance. The settlers from up Far Reach waited at the open grave, and their barefoot children, with yellow hair and clean cotton dresses. They all were sad, except the little ones, who watched a cardinal hopping from bush to bush, and a white crane flying along the dark water of the creek.

Gabrielle stood, erect and steady, between her two brothers. Barton and Celestine were close to her. Through the mist she saw the people on the opposite side of the grave. It was all unreal. The sun shone brightly. A gentle breeze stirred the long grey moss on the great oak trees. She saw Sandy's rugged, lined face, David Moray near him. David was looking at her, his face solemn, his eyes filled with tender sympathy. She looked away quickly. René's hand pressed hers. His young lips were trembling. . . . She thought she again heard the voices whispering in the trees. Were *they* those others who had gone, welcoming her mother to their august company?

She raised her eyes to the river. A ship was sailing upstream, moving slowly under a light breeze. Resentment came over her. Why should it come now, when it was too late? When the cottages were ashes, when her mother . . .

She closed her eyes. Robert Fountaine's voice, quiet, even, without expression, read the Service for the Dead.

Chapter 35

TRANSITION

The months that followed Madam Fountaine's tragic death brought desolation to the settlers. The feeling that a doom was upon them grew stronger. They were like people lost in swamps, struggling to reach solid ground. Gabrielle watched the breaking up of the settlement with aching heart. As she looked back she saw that the disintegration was inevitable. Only a few of the men and women her father had brought out had the stamina to stand up to the hardships.

The first seasons they had been swept along by building and planting and gathering the fruits of their industry. As the first excitement waned, their spirits drooped. They were not all antagonistic as Eunice Caslett had been, but they dropped into a lethargy that was more devastating than active hatred of the country.

They made less effort. The heavy fertility of the land played its part. Things grew easily and luxuriantly. There was no struggle, such as a man has on a small strip of land that has been planted for hundreds of years. The virgin land yielded a hundredfold. Its fecundity killed their energy and effort.

The dwindling colony, the apathetic attitude of her father, roused Gabrielle to a more determined effort. Her days were full. Each morning she made her rounds—the turpentine woods, the fields outside the stockade and those near the River Road. In the afternoons she had Annaci or one of his men take her out in the flat-bottomed bateau to inspect the rice fields, through the cross ditches and canals. Annaci had worked long in rice fields and she relied on him to oversee the work. Edward Colston had sent her rice seed from Charles Town. When he arrived at Jamaica at Tom Chapman's plantation, he had interested Tom in her venture and they had sent her not only Madagascar seed, but a hundred young indigo plants as well. Indigo brought wealth in Antigua and Jamaica.

Edward wrote:

"Tom thinks the climate will be suitable for raising indigo. If it is successful you will have another commercial product. If not, you can certainly raise enough for your own dye."

The plants had been set out. With the exception of a small number that had not rooted, they were thriving.

Edward had given her some items of news in his letter.

"Tom heard that Michael Cary was living on the island of Nevis, with a woman he introduced as his wife. Cary now captains a Royal African Company's slaver, on the 'Triangular' run. Whether Molly sails with him or not, he had not heard. There is money in the slave trade and Cary will make a fortune. I would not worry about Molly. She chose the man she wants.

"One other thing of interest—Anne Bonney has been seen in King's Town more than once. She now commands a large barkentine. Word has been received here that she has been raiding the French portion of Hispaniola, where her crew landed, seized cattle and some French prisoners. On their way back to Jamaica they overtook two sloops which they fired upon and boarded, and got tackle and apparel valued at over a thousand pounds. But all this is small stuff for Anne Bonney. In October she sailed into Porta Maria Bay, on the coast of Jamaica, and took tobacco and pimento, which were in casks ready for shipment. This was a rich haul, and Sir Nicholas Law, the governor here, sent out Captain Jonathan Barnet, a stout barque man, to follow her. Late one evening he overtook her ship, which was Cuba bound, demanded she strike colours to the King of England. It was Rackham's voice that answered through the darkness. He shouted that he would 'strike no strikes.' Captain Barnet told me he fired a broadside but the ship outsailed him in the darkness.

"He swears he heard Anne Bonney's voice shouting to Rackham, urging him not to surrender.

"Sir Nicholas has sent a report to the Lords of Trade and Plantations, giving them all the details. He swears he will have Rackham on the gibbet, with his woman Bonney swinging beside him.

"My grandfather's factor here had a letter for me from Bristol. My grandfather writes that he is feeble and he wants me with him. So I will not return to the Cape Fear as I had planned. When I think that I will not see you again I am desolate. A convoy is leaving tomorrow and my boxes are aboard a stout ship, the *Holland Venture*. I wish you were sailing with me, Gabrielle. When you receive this I will be halfway across the Western Ocean, the distance between us growing greater each day. But my thought of you does not change, my dear."

Captain Bragg gave her the letter when he brought the seed rice and the young plants, some time past. "I missed Mr. Colston by a week," he told her, "and I missed that pirate Anne Bonney by an hour in St. Thomas harbour, in the Virgins. It's getting so an honest ship daren't sail into a' harbour in the Caribbean without running into Anne Bonney. The woman is roaring up and down the seas from Hispaniola to the Spanish Main, sinking ships and sacking towns. She's like to be as great a menace as old Henry Morgan."

Gabrielle thought of Edward's letter now, as she sat in the stern of the bateau. Annaci was poling up the creek into the heart of the swamp, under the low-hanging branches of cypress and the tangle of grapevines that covered the bushes. It was late autumn and the trees were ablaze with crimson and scarlet and gold. "Indian summer" Sandy called it. It had been weeks since she had seen Sandy and she missed him sadly. He must have gone away on a trading trip to the Indian country.

David Moray was away too. He left the plantation in early September, to go to Charles Town. He rode over, the night before he left. He talked with her father in his office for an hour, before he came into the great room to say good-bye to her. She remembered the look on his face even now, weeks later. The lines had deepened, his eyes were grave and there was no laughter on his lips.

He made no reference to the conversation; instead he talked of his journey to Charles Town. It would take four days' riding with nights spent at Lockwood's Folly and on the Santee, along the Great Road.

He intended to hire an overlooker, a man who knew both rice culture and tobacco culture.

"I'll bring you a fine gown, Gabrielle, rose-coloured silk with flowers, like the one you used to wear at Meg's Lane." The colour came to her face. She was pleased that he remembered.

"You won't find one like it," she answered. "I wove it myself, from silk thread that was sent to Father from Lyons."

"Then I'll bring skeins of silk thread from Charles Town. I have heard that the mulberry trees are well grown and the silk worms very active."

He left soon after. Only at the last as she stood at the front stoop did he make any reference to his conversation with Robert Fountaine.

"I cannot make your father see reason, Gabrielle. I tried again tonight. I asked him to release me from my promise not to speak to you of love or marriage, but he refused. I am in honour bound to keep my word." His tone was bitter.

"I gave my word too, David." Her voice was low. "Often I have to remind myself that my duty to him is greater than it ever was. Since the boys went to King William's School he has no one but me."

"I know, but that doesn't make it easier. But I will not give up. Balarand isn't here. . . . As long as he stays in France I have hope, and . . ." He laid his hand on her shoulder for a second. He leaned over her, his lips close to hers, but he drew back.

"Sometimes I've thought if he does come I'll challenge him and kill him, before I let him have you."

She felt the violence that racked him. He was strong-willed, arrogant in his strength. She looked upwards in the darkness. His face was white and luminous. She reached up to him in a passion of fear. She clung to him, touching his firm strong face, his eyes, his lips. "David . . ."

She could not think of the moment, even now weeks later, without a return of the emotion that his anger had kindled . . . to kill for her. . . . She shuddered.

More than once since then, she had been near rebellion, determined to go to her father, tell him she would not marry Paul, but her courage failed her.

"Parents know what is best for their children." René had said when she spoke to him about Paul. "Of course you'll marry the man your father has selected for you. He has wisdom. What does a woman know of such matters? I'm surprised that you even consider going against Father's wishes. It must be this new country which gives you such strange ideas."

Annaci's soft spoken words recalled her from her disturbing thoughts. "We are at the place, Mistress."

"Wait here, Annaci." She got out of the bateau and walked up the bank to the burial-ground of those others, those earlier ones who had dared so much, only to lose. She walked

538

slowly, careful not to step on the uneven elevations, to her mother's grave.

The grass had grown, covering the naked earth, carpeting the mound. A few late wild asters and a sheaf of crimson leaves lay on the ground. Bricks and ballast stones were piled near by. When there were enough, a tomb would be built to hold the flat slab of granite her father had ordered from England.

She stood for a moment, looking down. The futility of her mother's life rose before her, stark and tragic. Her bright gay youth sacrificed, to what?

She dared not dwell on the past. The present was all she had to hold to. She must cleanse her soul of her rebellious thoughts. She leaned against the great oak with its sheltering arms. The land, the slow growth of the trees ... the never-ending repetition of rich earth, the young tender sprouts ... the full growth ... back to the earth to enrich the soil. ... In some intangible way she felt her future was linked with this slow growth of the forest.

Annaci watched her as he stood in the stern of the bateau, poling his way skilfully among the lily pads. The black water gave back a reflection of swaying boughs and softly waving streamers of moss. After a time he said, "Mistress, our people say 'Wa-fetsa, kwache ku-li maliro'—he has died, there is mourning at his village, 'Mwezi wa-fa'—the moon has died, the month is finished. And sometimes we say 'Njira i-fa-ku-pita umo, koma i-kula ndi i-terepa'—the road passes just here, but if it grows over it just does the same."

Annaci's words sank into her heart and comforted her. The road passes ... even if it grows over, it is still there.

The following Sunday, Robert Fountaine held service in the little chapel. The small handful of worshippers sat close to the chancel—the unmarried yeomen, two families from up Far Reach, and Sandy MacAlpin. It was a comfort to her that Sandy was back again. In the back benches were a dozen Negroes, under the watchful eyes of Annaci. They knelt, their dark wondering eyes on the pastor. Gabrielle noticed new faces among them. She never questioned Annaci. He had given refuge to many runaway slaves, feeding them, sending them on to their ultimate destination. Some, she knew, found their way to Moray's plantation and remained to work in the rice fields.

Celestine sat near Barton, her mournful eyes fixed on her

book of prayer. Gabrielle had asked her more than once whether she did not want to go to Charles Town to the Huguenot colony, but each time she refused.

"I will stay," she repeated. "You will need me. Who will make your ruffled petticoats and tuck your underbodies? Who will weave the fine linens? Who but Celestine?" So she stayed on, growing more sorrowful each day.

Her father walked in, his black robe sweeping the boards. His face was dark and thin above the white falling bands; streaks of white showed in his black locks. His eyes, which used to hold such tenderness, were fixed on something far away. Today he looked thin to emaciation, and his voice when he read the prayers had lost its vibrance and life.

He opened the Bible, turning the leaves slowly. Gabrielle raised her eyes and saw the Indians, while she knelt in prayer. Kullu had slipped into the chapel, with him a woman and two round-eyed children. They stood quietly back of the benches, Kullu a step in advance of the woman.

Her father spoke and she turned her face towards the pulpit. Robert Fountaine stood very straight, his shoulders back, the long black robe of his office adding to his height. His voice deepened as he spoke.

"The gospel of St. Matthew, the third chapter," he read, "Repent ye, for the kingdom of heaven is at hand ..." His black dilated eyes were upon her as he leaned forward. The compulsion of his words, the hidden meaning beat down upon her, until the pressure was unendurable. ... "The voice of one crying in the wilderness, Prepare ye the way of the Lord, make his paths straight ... and John had his raiment of camel's hair, and a leathern girdle about his loins; and his meat was locusts and wild honey ... and were baptized of him in Jordan, confessing their sins."

When he completed these words he raised his arm. There was a slight stir in the congregation; a yeoman turned his head. Gabrielle saw Kullu and the woman and children walk forward towards the chancel.

Gabrielle turned cold. She recoiled as from a blow. She lost all sense of reality as her father moved to the crude wooden baptismal font. She heard whispering and faint rustling as the people stirred uneasily on the benches.

"And now also the axe is laid unto the root of the trees: therefore every tree which bringeth not forth good fruit is hewn down, and cast into the fire."

He motioned to the Indians. They advanced towards him,

540

the children close to the him of his robe. He dipped his fingers into the basin.

"I indeed baptize you ... with the Holy Ghost and with fire."

The words sank deep into her soul—with fire ... baptized with fire ... She closed her eyes; the rest of the words were lost.

She seemed to be rushing down a dark stagnant swamp with no light, trembling, unable to check her advance towards some unknown disaster. She slipped to her knees and laid her forehead against the rail of the bench before her.

Barton touched her hand. "Rise up, Mistress," she said. "The sprinkling is over; the people are gone. 'Twill do you no good to stay on your knees on the bare floor."

They walked towards the stockade. The sky was covered with heavy dark clouds. She shivered and looked back over her shoulder towards the forest. It was dark and menacing.

The fields which had been lying fallow took on a faint tinge of green. Migrating birds appeared and duck wedges were often in the sky, flying north to their summer feeding grounds. The months of winter had gone, the naked brown of the trees was giving way to new growth.

To Barton the season brought new energy testified by her desire to brush away the old dust of winter and make ready for spring. She attacked the great room first, with two of Annaci's runaways to do the heavy lifting. Chairs and tables and benches were set out of doors, pictures came down from the walls, vases and candle sconces were carefully moved to a safe place. A Negro with heavy woollen cloth bound around his feet polished the wide floor boards with myrtle wax, left over from candles of Barton's candle-moulding. Two small picaninnies sat on the lawn polishing brass fenders and fire-irons and candlesticks. Birds were starting up the first faint trills, their first liquid notes.

Gabrielle came down for breakfast dressed in her habit. She intended to ride as far as Brunswick that morning. Although there were no houses erected in Maurice Moore's new town, half a dozen hardy settlers had put up temporary dwellings. Sandy MacAlpin had built a log house and outfitted it with a small supply of trade goods; in charge was an old Indian trader, crippled in the foot by an Indian arrow.

His name was MacDermot, and he had the craggy features of his native hills, and the toughness of seasoned hickory.

Gabrielle put her head into the dining-room. Barton had her mob-cap pulled down to her ears so that no hair was showing. She had pinned her skirt back over her quilted petticoat and was engaged in washing the crystal prisms of the gilt candlesticks. The dining-table was covered with vases and candlesticks and small objects she had removed from mantel and tables. She paused when she saw Gabrielle and wiped her reddened hands on the cloth.

"I've set up a tray out under a tree. The porridge is made. It's a fair fine morning and it will do you good to sit in the sun. I've some bannocks baking on the griddle and I made your tea and set it to steep when I heard you stirring from your bed."

"Thank you, Barton." She went outdoors where Barton had placed the table under an oak. A white cloth, a little silver mug of cream and a silver box for the precious sugar. A few minutes later Barton came out carrying the tray. After she arranged the food on the table and poured the thick cream over the porridge, she lingered, rearranging cutlery, lifting the lid of the covered butter dish.

"As soon as you finish your porridge I'll bring the bannock," she said. While Gabrielle was eating, Barton told her the gossip of the settlement. With only two familes and the six unmarried men, as a rule there was little to tell. This morning it was different.

"Sandy MacAlpin has been," she announced. "He visited Edenton on his way home from the Rapids. Mr. Roger Mainwairing sent a message that he would be down within the fortnight, in a new sloop Amos Treloar built for him. Mr. Moseley was coming also. The Governor had set a pretty fine on him and he could not hold office or practise his law for three years. Mr. Moseley might start building a house by the Forks, or he might go to the Jamaica plantations. He had not resolved what he would do during the three years. The same as banishment, to sentence a man not to hold his office of Surveyor General, or to appear in court for his clients! It caused a mess of words among Edenton folk, and Squire Pollock and Mr. Moseley like to've fought with swords on the green, but Mr. Mainwairing stopped it."

"Sandy seems to have gathered a quantity of news," Gabrielle said, when Barton paused for breath.

"I had enough trouble getting it from him. Sandy's no mon

to tattle. A good mon." She hesitated. "Sandy's for marrying me, but I told him I'd never marry a hawker."

Gabrielle raised her eyes in surprise at Barton's statement.

"Yes, it's God's truth, Mistress. I told him he could leave off his Indian trading ... now he's got him that trading shop in the woods." She pointed in the direction of the lower river.

Gabrielle watched Barton. There was a faint triumph in her face and she moved briskly.

"Are you going to marry MacAlpin?" she asked, putting her teacup into the saucer.

Barton gave her a sharp look. She motioned to the small Negro who was polishing the brass fender. He came obediently, his dark face, his eager eyes turned to her.

"Get a branch from the tree," she told him, "and keep these flies away." The boy broke a long bough from an evergreen and stood behind Gabrielle, moving it unhurriedly above the table.

"You don't answer, Barton," Gabrielle persisted.

Barton's mouth twitched. She did not speak for a moment, then she said, "I told him I'd marry nae man so long as my mistress goes unwed."

A slow blush crept over Gabrielle's face. . . . Was there a faint accusation in Barton's words?

"Oh, Barton!" she cried. "You must not give up Sandy because of ..."

"There, there. I'm not in a mood to marry Sandy MacAlpin until I see how he settles. I've no want of a man who's always thinking of putting his foot in the road. That I don't. So no use bringing tears to your eyes, this early of the day."

Gabrielle touched her eyes with her kerchief and tucked it into the little pocket of her habit.

"Sandy says Captain Bragg'll be here before long, a-sailing Mr. Mainwairing's new sloop."

Gabrielle said absently. "How nice." She got up from the table when Annaci brought her mare to the block.

"One of the boys can go with me. I don't want to take you from the field today," she told him.

Annaci took off his peaked hat and held it in his hands until she had finished giving her orders. She rode out the gate and through the field. The blue smocks of the men ploughing made a note of colour against the overturned earth, as the slow white oxen moved down the long rows.

They crossed the creek over the log bridge and turned into

the grove of oaks that grew, heavy and dark, along the bank of the river, the Negro boy riding bareback on Annaci's mule. Gabrielle welcomed the solitude of the woods. She was troubled. The long ride to Brunswick would give her time to think without interruption. Her father's behaviour the past months gave her grave concern. He was withdrawing more and more from their life and the life of the dwindling settlement. Even before the boys had gone away, he sat night after night at the supper table without speaking. When she made an effort to attract his attention, he would look at her as though he were called back from some world in which she had no part. If she consulted him about the affairs of the plantation or the crops, he was impatient.

"I know nothing of such matters. Talk to Sandy or Annaci. . . . I will attend to the weaving."

At first Gabrielle thought it was grief for her mother that had made the change in him. Now she knew it was something new, some strange antagonistic thing that stood between them. It hurt her deeply. In her heart she had only love and loyalty for the lonely man. Sometimes she felt a passionate nostalgia for England—for Ireland. Perhaps the dissolution of the colony had gone deeper than she realized. All the more reason why they should redouble their efforts to have the few succeed in their fight against the forest.

She would make every effort to win her father back to the old way of living, to make a success of the plantation. Surely that would give him back his confidence and assurance that he had chosen the right way.

A deer crashed out of the forest and paused in the path, its large startled eyes fixed on her for a moment before it bounded away, lost in the woods. A fox barked in the distance and the raucous cry of a bluejay cut through the profound stillness.

Heavy gloom bore down upon her. The green of the deep wood was shadowless and sombre. Overhead the interlaced crowns of trees resisted the sunshine. She touched spur to her horse. She must get beyond the green gloom of the trees. Was she, in her isolation, caught by some inflexible fate?

They came out of the forest into a clearing; in the distance was MacAlpin's log house. There were a dozen horses at the hitching rack—jaded horses that had been ridden hard and far. She saw a group of men standing near the river bank. Their backs were towards her. Wide hats hid their faces, but their clothes bore the marks of travel. They were watching a ship that lay in the middle of the river, its sails slack.

She rode up to the front of the house. Sandy came out. His face brightened when he saw her.

"Great day in the morning!" he exclaimed.

She smiled at his greeting. "You have visiters?" she asked, as he helped her to dismount.

"Yes indeed, distinguished visiters—Mr. Rutherford and Mr. Ashe and Mr. Davis. They've come with Mr. Roger Moore, to inspect the river bottom land, with a view of taking out patents themselves." He closed one eye with an amused, sly glance. "If there's anything left on the river after the Moores get through! The other, the stocky fellow in the buff coat, is Ancrum. Moray's brought him up to give us advice about rice and indigo planting."

Gabrielle stood still at the door of the cabin. Did he speak of David? Was David there by the river bank, only a hundred yards from her? She leaned against the doorway, her heart pounding.

"Step inside, Miss Gabrielle; see our little stock of goods."

The few men loafing on the bench watched her with curious eyes. Two Indians stood immobile, leaning against the wall. MacDermot came forward, a smile on his craggy face. 'Twas not often they had a *leddy* to view their stock. He dusted off a bench for her, while Sandy motioned the Indians out of the place. Sandy set about boiling the water for a cup of tea.

Gabrielle leaned back against the wall; through the open door she could see the ship on the river. The men were walking towards the log house. David lingered behind, looking towards the river.

She got up and slipped out a side door, avoiding the strangers. She walked across the rough ground towards the bank. A large clearing had been cut. Trees were lying on the ground, ready to be sawed into lengths. The smell of newly cut pine wood and resin was in the air, a fresh clean smell that cleared the nostrils.

Gabrielle stepped on a dry twig which snapped loudly. David whirled around. When he saw Gabrielle his lean brown face changed. His eyes met hers.

"Gabrielle!" he said. "Gabrielle." He lifted her hand to his lips. "I had not hoped for such good fortune." He still held her hand. "Have you missed me?"

545

"You have been gone a long time, David," she answered, withdrawing her hand.

"Almost four months. Too long, far too long."

Sandy joined them. "Tea is ready, Mistress." He stood for a moment watching the ship. "I'm nae positive but she looks for all the world like Mr. Mainwairing's new sloop." They turned towards the log house.

Gabrielle drank her tea, listening to the talk of the South Carolina men. They were to meet Moseley at the Forks, they told her, where he and Maurice Moore would be waiting.

Gabrielle finished her tea and prepared to leave. "My father will be pleased to have you break your ride and stay overnight with us at Old Town," she told Roger Moore.

Moore demurred. "There are too many of us. We had better ride on to Moray's place."

She smiled. "I can recommend our housekeeper's cooking and there is room at the guest house."

"Thank you, Mistress Fountaine. We will be delighted." He bowed in his courtly fashion. She liked Roger Moore, a man of purpose and decision. Perhaps the visit of these men would stir her father into renewed interest.

When they came out of the log house the sky was overcast.

"A storm is brewing," David said. "I hope it won't break before you get home."

She placed her foot in his clasped hands and vaulted easily into the saddle.

"I wish I were riding with you," he said, "but Moore must ride along each creek and inlet, smelling the soil." He smiled. "Moore is thorough in everything he does. His coming to the Cape Fear will be the guarantee of a successful colony."

A gust of wind came from the river. She saw the slack sails lift and fill. With this wind the sloop would be at Old Town almost as soon as she could ride the distance by road.

By the time Gabrielle reached the lakes the sky was black. She put her horse to a gallop, the little Negro boy shouting to his mule. Soon after they passed the lakes the first drops of rain spattered against her face, followed by a gust of wind that tore her little hat from her head. She felt the gay plume graze her cheek as it floated to the ground.

"Don't stop!" she shouted over her shoulder to the boy. His thin cotton shirt stuck to his shoulders, his black face glistened.

The heavens opened and a deluge of water descended. She

urged her horse on, unmindful of flying twigs and branches. The forest was almost as black as night. Now and then a flash of lightning illuminated the path. Her horse quivered with each roll of thunder.

By the time she reached the stockade she was wet to the skin. She jumped from her horse; head bent she ran for the kitchen door. Barton met her there.

"Praise be to God!" she exclaimed as Gabrielle pulled the door open. The Negro women ran forward to help her strip off her soggy skirt and coat. She stood in her breeches and boots, shivering. Barton pushed her out of the room.

"Run, rub yourself with a Turkey towel and jump into bed. I'll be up in a jiffy, as soon as I make some jasmine root tea. I'm not going to have you shaking with the ague this night." She put an arm over Gabrielle's shoulder, hurrying her along the hall.

"Wait, wait!" Gabrielle cried. "There will be men here for supper."

"How many?"

"Six or eight, I don't know—Mr. Moore and some others."

"No matter. We've a good big ham in the oven and I baked a spice cake today. I'll send Cissy out to make the beds.

Gabrielle lay shivering in bed. Even hot jasmine root tea and the extra blanket Barton brought did not warm her. Chills ran up her back and her limbs were numb. After a time she fell into a fitful slumber and dreamed of snow and cold winds.

When she awoke Barton was standing beside the bed, a cup of steaming liquid in her hand. With the other she touched Gabrielle's forehead.

"You got yourself a fever," she said accusingly, "just when all the company's here. Mr. Mainwairing's sloop and Mr. Moore's men."

"I'll get up," Gabrielle said. She sat up, her head was aching and her mouth parched. Instead of shivering she now was burning up. "I'll get dressed so I can help you with the table."

"No need. I've already had Annaci put the two falling leaf tables together and hooked on the end table. Cissy is cooking the grits and yams, and Mr. Mainwairing has brought us a square of guava jelly that came from Jamaica; so we'll do well enough."

"Where is Father?" Gabrielle got out of bed and went to her dressing-table.

"With the gentlemen, last I saw him, when I took in drinks." She bustled away intent on her duties.

Gabrielle's bones ached to her fingertips. Her face was flushed—as red as a barmaid's, she thought, as she struggled with the long dark mass of her hair. She was ready to go down when her father came into the room and closed the door. For a moment he stood looking at her.

"Sit down, my child. I have something to say to you."

She put her hands behind her, clutching the hard surface of the table, her knees trembling. Something in his voice frightened her. The sudden stillness beat down upon her, the beat of rain against the window. . . . She stiffened, ready for the blow when it fell.

"I am going away at once. I have thought it out. I do not want you to try to dissuade me. I am going to the Indian country. The Lord has called me to go forth into the wilderness to bring the gospel to all the people." He paused a moment, the pupils of his dark eyes dilated. She thought of the waters of a dark lake that reflected nothing.

She struggled to speak but he held up his thin hand.

"Wait. I've talked with Mainwairing. He will take you home with him. His wife will be happy to have you until you arrange to go to England. I have written Balarand that you will come this autumn."

"Father, why must you go? Let someone else . . ."

"There is no one. I've learned the language. I feel that I am now prepared."

"How long?" She managed to say the words. His eyes were dreamy.

"How long? I don't know, on and on, following the rivers . . ." Before she could speak, he left the room, closing the door gently.

She sank down into a chair, her hands before her eyes.

The door opened and Barton came in. "I heard him," she said. "I think he is bewitched by those Indian devils." She stared at Gabrielle, her lips tight. "Bewitched is what he is, to go away in a canoe following the rivers. Bewitched."

"Don't," Gabrielle said faintly. "Help me. I must put on another dress. Not this; it is too dull—something bright, bright—the crimson silk with the quilted petticoat."

"Your cheeks are too red. The fever's got you."

"Don't mind, dress me quickly. I must go down to our

548

guests. I must ..." She buried her face against Barton's shoulder.

"There, there, now. Wipe your forehead and your wrists with cologne water and freshen yourself. I've been fearful of this ever since he baptized those red devils ... with fire he said, aye, with fire."

Gabrielle sat at one end of the long table, her father at the other. On her right hand Roger Moore, on her left Roger Mainwairing, Maurice Moore and Edward Moseley; Mr. Rutherford, Mr. Davis, Captain Bragg. Midway, where her eyes could rest on him over the low centrepiece of wild azaleas, sat David Moray.

She sat back in her chair and tried to attend to what Roger Mainwairing was saying, but she found it difficult. Her head ached. Pain shot behind her eyelids; she was burning. Her food remained untouched on her plate; from time to time she moistened her parched lips with a little wine. She felt David watching her with anxious eyes ... she was numb, her heart without feeling . . . Mainwairing's voice came dimly:

"The Albemarle is a granary for Virginia . . . we've long been her butcher pen all because we have no proper harbour. For that reason the Cape Fear must succeed. . . ."

"Already we have two thousand tithables in the north. That means nine thousand souls, white and black." Maurice Moore was speaking. "Now with proper government . . ."

"That's your trouble," Roger Moore's resonant voice interrupted. "If you will follow South Carolina and throw off the Lords Proprietors' government you will have a chance. The Lords Proprietors have not the favour of the Crown, nor of the merchants of England."

The voices faded, then became loud again. She swallowed some of the wine. Warmth flowed through her veins.

A chair scraped. She saw her father rise to his feet, his glass in his hand. "A toast!" he said. His voice was harsh and unnatural, a stranger's voice. The men rose, their faces turned toward him, waiting. Gabrielle lifted her glass.

"To my daughter Gabrielle and her betrothal!"

Her shaking hands grasped the rim of the table. She tried to speak but her dry lips gave forth no sound.

"No. No." She felt the world slipping away from her, the faces turned to her, blurred.

"My daughter is going home with Mr. Mainwairing, from

there to England to marry Paul Balarand, the son of my old friend."

The glass fell from Gabrielle's fingers. It shattered and left a little river of crimson on the white cloth.

"No!" Her voice came from her dry lips, hard and decisive. "No. I will not go. I will stay here. I have made up my mind."

Her father's eyes met hers. There was no tenderness in them, only determination. They faced each other across the long table. She did not see the others. Something broke in her. Words came rushing from her lips.

"I will not go," she repeated. "Our settlement shall not fail."

"I am offering the land to Mr. Moore." Her father's voice came from a long distance.

"Mr. Moore cannot have the plantation!" she cried. "If you go away, the land is mine. I will plant and harvest. I have made up my mind . . . you cannot drive me away."

She felt the horrible blackness bearing down on her. Her father's commanding voice: "Gabrielle, are you mad?"

"I think she is the sane one!" David's angry voice came from far away. She heard Barton's anxious voice:

" 'Tis the fever speaking. Look at her glittering eyes and the red on her cheeks . . ."

She tried to loosen her fingers from the table, but she had not the will nor the strength. She saw Mainwairing push back his chair, but it was David Moray who lifted her in his arms and carried her from the room. Robert Fountaine followed, a look of astonished wonder on his face. Barton closed the door and ran ahead, up the stair.

Roger Mainwairing turned to his friends who were still standing, glasses in hand. Admiration shone in their eyes.

"Gentlemen, let us not be deprived of our toast!" He lifted his glass, and bowed to the empty chair.

"To Gabrielle!" he said.

Chapter 36

OLD TIMOTHY

Within the hour, the Lords Proprietors of the Carolinas would assemble in their meeting room at St. James Palace, in the City of London. At their invitation, the Lords of Trade and Plantations would attend.

The room was silent save for the crackling of the wood fire in the huge fireplace, and the scraping of old Timothy Whitechurch's quill as it slid over the ledger which held the transactions of Carolina government and record of the meetings.

Of late, the meetings had been ill attended. Sometimes no more than two of the honourable Gentlemen came to lend ear or to offer advice concerning the welfare of the growing colonies that bordered the Western Ocean. Always, Lord John Carteret was present. More astute, more diplomatic than before, he was moving slowly into a place of power behind the throne. It was he who insisted on the meeting with the Lords of Trade and Plantations. It was he who still believed that wealth for the Proprietors lay in the development of the Carolinas.

"Strong colonies spell a strong Britain," he said more than once in meeting. But the others did not follow his lead. With two members of the board minors, it cut down interest. Ashley and Danson still talked outright sale, now to the Crown, instead of a lease to Sir Robert Montgomery.

Timothy laid down his quill, put his papers in order. He had little to report. The Lords of Trade and Plantations would have the bulk of the business. There would be new faces on that committee. Mr. Secretary Craggs was dead—grieved himself to death, gossip had it, because his father, old Craggs, had killed himself when the South Sea Bubble burst . . . a good thing, Timothy thought, well rid.

He got down from his stool and went over to the fire. He stood with his back to the blaze, his thin, gnarled hands clasped under his long coattails. He glanced around the walls. The portraits of the original eight Lords Proprietors looked

551

down on him. He shook his head sadly; the great had passed, only the lesser remained. He had outlived them all—he and his dreams of the day he would visit the far Plantations of Carolina. Year after year he had written the story of their growth and development, written and dreamed.

He was glad that Ashley and Danson had not had their way and sold out that great empire for shares in the South Sea Bubble. He thought of the meeting when only Lord John had stood against that sale. Strong and firm as the iron men of Cromwell's army. He would not barter good rich soil for a slip of paper, no matter how well printed and illuminated the shares might be; after all, a share was no more than a bit of paper. Trade with South America and the South Seas remained only a bubble. Trade with Carolina was tangible. Timothy wrote it often enough in his books. Tar, pitch, and turpentine, tobacco, hides; masts, timber, staves and shingles; pork and tobacco. This was Carolina.

Timothy smiled when he thought of the biting irony that rolled from Lord John's lips the day he foiled the sale of Carolina. That day the shares of the Bubble were steady at 1,000 pounds. Why, the South Seas Company had even offered to take over the national debt, and Craggs had induced King George to become a director! By September a change came, shares were quoted at 770, by November 210.

That autumn the *Broker Stock Jobber* was the successful farce of the London stage season. People laughed at their losses at first, not when thousands were ruined. The climax came when old Craggs killed himself. Every day men killed themselves, and women pawned jewels and family plate to make up losses.

Well, that was done and good honest Robin was firm in the saddle as First Lord of the Treasury and Chancellor of the Exchequer. It was good to have Walpole in again. He had always spoken sharply against Bubbles.

Today the Lords would not speak of Bubbles or the trade with the South Seas. Instead they would talk of trade with the American Plantations, and bring reports of success in clearing the seas of pirates. From Jamaica to Virginia, no longer would it be necessary to send merchantmen out under convoy.

Timothy stepped to the window. The yellowed leaves of the plane tree fluttered in the wind. A gentle rain beat against the leaded windows, flattening leaves against the glass in an irregular pattern.

552

The Lords of Trade and Plantations and the Lords Propri-etors of the Carolinas drifted in to the meeting room. There was the usual clatter of swords as their owners unbuckled and dropped them on settees and padded window seats; beavers were piled on tables—a large cockade, in the new fashion, stood out among them, laced in silver with paste buckles. Damp capes were thrown over chairs near the fire, where they gave off the acrid odour of steaming wool. Some arrivals nodded carelessly to Timothy Whitechurch as they crowded to the fire and called for punch or raw brandy. Footmen came in hurriedly and put trays and decanters and glasses on the side tables, on either side of the chimney breast. Timothy retired to his desk at the far side of the room, near the leaded windows. From where he sat he could look out of the leaded windows and see the movement of coaches and carriages of the great, and lesser folk drawing their damp cloaks about them to keep out the wind and the rain. November was a chill month, and foretold the coming of dread winter.

Inconsequential talk drifted to his ears. . . . Was the Secre-tary of State, Mr. Addison, really married to Lady Warwick? . . . Mr. Pope's vicious satire about Lady Mary Montagu. "Blood in her veins as cold as a turtle" . . . "Cargo of muscavadas, sugar, rum, mahogany slabs, wet sweetmeats, and green parakeets" . . . "Put my blood in a flame" . . . "Never draw a sword in front of a woman" . . . "Sir John Blount languishes in custody, as he should, for his part in wrecking the country with his Bubble. Was he not guilty of other fallacies: wanting to bring pure water to London, from the country?"

Voices rose and fell and beat about Timothy's old ears. He felt tired. That night he would take a tonic of Peru bark and camomile tea . . . "I had to run like Holy Anthony" . . . "I said to her, 'Take off your mask, there's a healing virtue in your eyes' " . . . She blushed when I exposed her garter . . . "Young nabobs, from the Indies, with a touch of the tar-brush" . . . "A close old fox, but I unkennelled him" . . . "A hasty lover is an abomination" . . .

Timothy got up and moved his chair a trifle. . . . The wind that sucked in from the chimney chilled him to the marrow of his old bones. A new-comer joined the group at the fireplace. "His Majesty has issued a proclamation of a fast against the plague, on next fifteenth of December. Humilia-tion and prayer to avert severe judgement of plague, both

553

here and to our colonies across the sea." . . . Another voice broke in: "Pour me a glass. A chill goes over me at the thought of the plague." . . .

There was a movement towards the sideboard, and the clink of glasses. In the silence that followed, Whitechurch heard someone in the entryway, close at hand. A strong resonant voice said: "We've withstood many a tough gale, an abundance of hard blows; now we pray for a peaceful wind."

The door was thrown open. A footman announced: "Gentlemen, The Honourable Palatine, John, Lord Carteret, and His Excellency the Governor of the Bahamas, Captain Woodes Rogers." The gentlemen rose for the Palatine, and bowed to the Governor.

"Pray be seated, gentlemen," Lord Carteret said. He laid his hat, with sweeping plume on a table, and allowed a footman to remove his cloak. "I presume you all know Captain Woodes Rogers." He spoke to each man in turn, in his easy, gracious manner. "Mr. Chetwynd, I salute you. . . . Mr. Docminique, it is some time since I have had the pleasure. Mr. Pitt, this is your first visit with us. I bid you welcome." Bowing, he said, "Mr. Cardonnel, and Mr. Adams."

Lord John was dressed, today, in sober plum-coloured brocade, with fine Holland lace at his sleeves and cravat. He wore all his orders. Timothy knew he would repair from here directly to his Majesty. Lord Carteret crossed the room. "Timothy, good day. I hope I see you in the very best of health."

Timothy bowed deeply: "Thank you, my Lord. Never better; please God for His mercies."

Carteret laid his hand on Timothy's shoulder, a gesture of familiar affection. He turned to the Governor. "Your Excellency, Timothy Whitechurch is worth all the Proprietors thrown into one. He has been here since the beginning, seeing Lords Proprietors die and inheritors take their place, Governors come and go, but he still keeps watch and weal over the carolinas."

Woodes Rogers grasped Timothy's bony hand warmly. "I remember you excellently well, sir. You were here the last time I appeared before the Lords—three, or was it four years ago? Time goes so swiftly."

The Palatine took his seat at the head of the long table, and indicated chairs for the guests. Timothy stepped to the door of the antechamber to call in his clerks Bates and

Wilde, who were to keep the record. He found that it was a little difficult for him to discern all the voices around the long table—not that he was hard of hearing, but it was an effort. He sat down a little to one side of the Palatine, in case he might be wanted for some bit of information or reference during the meeting. Sitting thus, he faced the portrait of the great Shaftesbury, looking straight down at him from the mellow panelled wall. He thought there was an answering smile from his great patron, but perhaps it was the flickering light from the fire that fell on the deeply indented corners of the Earl's lips.

Timothy was pleased at Lord Carteret's praise. He felt warm within himself. They had worked well together. He hoped it would be always so. The thought came to him that he might not live out the period of the Lords Proprietors. . . . South Carolina was gone, turned to the Crown through James Moore's revolt. North Carolina stayed loyal. It had been all but lost when Eden quarrelled with Moseley and Maurice Moore over the pirate Blackbeard. A noxious business. One that did evil to the prestige of the Lords Proprietors' government. Thomas Pollock had smoothed things out for the time. Eden was dead now. He wondered how the new Governor, Mr. Burrington, would manage to rule those strong, hotheaded Carolinians.

They were talking commerce at the long table. Timothy could not follow them. When they spoke of ships, he thought of great rivers, pressing their way into the fertile land, making great roadways on which to foster trade. When they itemized produce, he thought of men with bent backs, working the rich land. "Timber" summoned up the dark green of the deep woods. He brought himself back by a strong effort. He must not let his mind wander. Captain Rogers was talking.

"The seas are being swept free of freebooters and pirates. I came in a ship without convoy, gentlemen. And you know what that means. Any seaman of stout knowledge and wisdom will tell you that *he who commands the sea, commands trade*. I am here to arrange for more ships. We have not enough bottoms to take care of our trade on the Western Ocean."

Mr. Ashley asked a question: "Are all the pirates gone from the Caribbean?"

"Not all, but most of the leaders have been captured and

555

put to death. Others have settled down to a less adventurous life. Blackbirding, for instance."

Mr. Chetwynd said, "I've read Law's report on the capture of the pirate Rackham's ship, off Jamaica. That *was* a battle."

"It wasn't Calico Jack Rackham that gave battle," the Governor reminded him. "It was Anne Bonney, who kept the men fighting until half of the pirate crew lay dead on the deck. Mr. Chetwynd, you say *that was a battle*. I say *there was a woman*. She had more courage than any pirate captain, and more sagacity, unless you wish to except Charles Vane. One of my lieutenants was in the fight. He said she was a Fury and a Medusa, rolled into one. She stood on the deck of her ship, dressed like a man, her long yellow hair blowing in the wind, driving her men to battle. For all her delicate look, she had the strength to wield a cutlass with the hardiest man." A slow smile came over his firm lips, a smile that lightened his dark features and made the stern face young, almost boyish. "I lay you a hundred to one that Anne's beautiful body will never swing from the gallows."

Carteret raised an eyebrow and looked down his long, aristocratic nose. "Taken," he said. "You mean a hundred pounds to one?" He brought out his tortoise-shell betting book, and held the gold pencil poised above it.

"Long odds," Ashley observed, a touch of sarcasm in his voice. "The Governor must have information that is not available to the rest of us."

"No, Mr. Ashley, I know nothing more than you know, save one thing: I've seen the lady in question."

"Ah, then she really *is* the queen of the Caribbean." Ashley laughed pointedly.

"Without a doubt," said Woodes Rogers.

There was a stir about the table. Several voices spoke in unison. Chetwynd said, "Tell us more about this mysterious creature."

Mr. Pitt, with a twinkle in his eyes, said, "Yes, I think we, as the Lords of Trade, should know. Doesn't she come under the head of interference with his Majesty's trade?"

There was a chorus of "Hear, hear."

Woodes Rogers' smile deepened, but he did not heed his interrogators. He addressed the Palatine: "My Lord, I will go even farther. I wager you that good Sir Nicholas Law, the Governor of Jamaica, will hang Calico Jack Rackham as high as Haman. He will quarter him and put him on the city

556

gates, with all his evil pirate crew. He may put Queen Anne, of the Caribbean, in gaol. She will fare not too badly there, and after a time she will disappear. You and I and the world will hear no more about her."

"Taken," Carteret said, and wrote industriously in his little book. Six other gentlemen said "Taken," and made notations in their betting books.

The two clerks were also writing. Their feather quills scratched.

Carteret turned to Timothy. "A motion has been made that this information be stricken from the minutes. Would you mind telling the gentlemen what record you will make of today's meeting, Mr. Whitechurch?"

Timothy thought he sensed what was wanted. The light touch. He rose. With the utmost solemnity he said, "On November 15, 1725, the Lords Proprietors of Carolina held joint session with the Lords of Trade and Plantations, at St. James's Palace, Whitehall. Matters of importance concerning the advancement and welfare of trade in his Majesty's American Plantations were under intensive scrutiny."

Laugher and cries of "Hear, hear" followed his words.

Ashley leaned across the table. "The honourable Secretary of State, Mr. Addison, has asked me to give him a report on the matter of sale of North Carolina to the Crown. A tentative offer of twenty-five thousand pounds has been suggested by his Majesty."

Carteret's face hardened. The arrogant expression, for which he was noted, took the place of laughter. He drew his jewelled watch, with dangling golden seals, from his broidered waistcoat pocket. "I shall be seeing Mr. Addison, within the half hour, at his Majesty's Council. I shall make it clear to him that the Granville shares of King Charles the Second's grant to the Lords Proprietors are not for sale. Gentlemen, the meeting is dismissed."

Carteret lingered a moment after the others had gone. "If it isn't too much trouble, I should like to have the list of which we were speaking last meeting," he said to Timothy. "I would like to have the names of the holders of grants and patents along the Cape Fear River. His Majesty has asked for it. Perhaps it should be alphabetical. Could you have it by tomorrow?"

"Yes, my Lord. Certainly, I can have it by tomorrow readily."

"Splendid. I can always count on you, Timothy. I wish that

all his Majesty's servants were as faithful and loyal as you have been through the years." He smiled his rare, warm smile, and went away.

Timothy dismissed his clerks. It was early, but they had earned a little holiday. They were young, and youth needed its play as well as its work.

A servant came in and put another log on the fire. He too went away and Timothy was left alone. He took down a ledger and spread it on the long table, found fresh quills and filled the inkwell. He moved his chair so that the light would fall over his shoulder. He found writing his fine copperplate hand more difficult each passing month, in spite of his spectacles. He spread the clear parchment sheet in front of him and began to write.

The rain had stopped. The low sun laid a pattern of triangles on the polished floor. Little rainbows of light, reflection from the leaded glass, flickered on the paper in front of him. He leaned against the high back of his chair. A log burned through. It fell from the irons, scattering sparks. The pleasant smell of wood smoke drifted through the room. He must mend the fire. But he had no inclination to move. His tired eyes rested on the painting of Shaftesbury. He thought, as he had thought a thousand times before, that it was a speaking likeness of his great patron.

Timothy had no sense of passing time. Something strange was happening. The painting took on life and colour. It was no longer a flat surface of oil and canvas and paint. The well-remembered voice seemed to fill the shadowy room: "Young Timothy, isn't it time that we went to the Carolinas, together?"

There was no strangeness. It was right that his old friend should speak to him. He leaned forward so that he could hear more clearly and put his hand behind his ear, a gesture that he had found himself using of late. "They are going to banish me from England, young Timothy. Shall we seek sanctuary in the green forests of Carolina?"

Timothy sought to rise, but he had no strength. His head dropped. His chin sunk to his thin breast. The hand that he held to his ear fell to the table. The ink ran in dark rivers across the parchment. Only the last column of names of those who held the land along the Cape Fear River stood clear and bold on the white surface—Fountaine, Etienne, Gabrielle, René; Hassel, James; Lillington, Alexander; Mac-

Alpin, Alexander; Mainwairing, Roger; Moore, Nathaniel, James, Maurice, Roger; Moray, David; Moseley, Edward; Treloar, Amos . . .

The log blazed up and burned itself out. The quiet of evening filled the room.

Chapter 37

" ... THE NOBLE UNDERTAKING"

David and Gabrielle walked down the path that led to the canal. A sail-boat lay anchored, and a long canoe was pulled up on the shore. Behind them the new home was almost completed, a large spreading house, room enough for the children that would come. He spoke of them now. "David and Angus, and the twins, Donald and Dougall—four boys we will have, four fine good Scots who love their land enough to stay on it, and not wander off to new worlds." David put his arm over his wife's shoulder. "Don't be growing so red, my girl. There's nothing wrong in a man wanting fine bra' sons, is there?"

Gabrielle laughed. "A girl or two might be welcome, David. Remember French women love land, too."

David grew grave. "Do I know it! I remember well how you faced us all, that night when you would not give up the land or the New World. A fine trim slip of a girl, putting your will against all the men in the room. You were beautiful then, my Gabrielle, with your eyes bright with fine purpose, and the colour in your cheeks. . . . 'I have never gone against your wishes, Father,' you said very low, 'but this time I will do as I want.' "

"I think it hurt my father," Gabrielle said slowly. "It hurt me in my heart, to speak as I did that day. I am glad he forgave me before he went away into the forest."

"You were right, my brave girl. I well remember that we stood tongue-tied, not daring to speak. But my heart was bursting with pride at the iron in you. It was your father's will against yours. It was his that broke first, and why not? Had he not already made his plan to go off to convert the Indians and make them Christians? And leave you with strangers?"

"Do you recall, David, how Barton rose up next morning, and said her mind? 'I'm staying along with my mistress, and to make it decent for two lone females to live among so many men, I'll have the banns said. I'll marry with Sandy MacAlpin, God willin'.' "

David's laugh rang out. "Can I forget the look on Sandy's face?"

They walked through the new garden towards the field. "I'm glad we came here to live, David," Gabrielle said. "The old place is weighted heavy with sorrow and sad memories. Perhaps Sandy was right. Perhaps a doom lay on the ground. Annaci too—he says that white man will not live there." Gabrielle looked off in the direction of the old settlement, her eyes full of sadness and yearning. "But when I go there now and hear the voices they are benign. They no longer bring sadness."

David's arm tightened around his wife's slender waist. "No regrets, my sweet girl. It took me long to win you. I'll have no time wasted looking back on ill-omened days. Look beyond, my dear. Think of the river, as it is today: Maurice Moore's new town rising from the floor of the forest; the walls of Roger Moore's fine house; their brothers laying out fields and fencing pastures; the others, from the Albemarle, sending their men to clear and seat the land above the Forks. Soon it will be too crowded on the river."

Gabrielle looked at him quickly, anxiety in her eyes. "You are not thinking of following the river to its source, David?"

"No, my sweet. We'll stay here. Let our sons and our sons' sons follow the river, to seek new rich bottom lands. We'll stay as we are."

They walked to the edge of the woods that surrounded the north field. The sun was setting, sending slanting yellow light through the tall pines. A dog barked in the distance and cattle lowed—sounds that come at twilight, to ease a man's heart.

The plantation bell sounded, calling the slaves to their supper.

"Etienne should come home this next year," Gabrielle said thoughtfully as they turned homeward. "It's time he took some of the burden from René."

They walked awhile in silence. Then David said, "My dear, we Scots are fighting folk, if need be. We take up our claymores and our swords and march off out of our glens, following the pipes. But when the fighting is done, we hurry back to our homes, for we love the land."

Gabrielle went into the house. David walked to the canal, his eyes on the river. It was given to some men to follow rivers to their beginnings; others sailed brave ships into unknown waters. He had chosen the way of men who tilled the land and loaded the waists of ships with cargoes for ports beyond the seas.

In his mind he saw ships passing on the amber breast of the river: long canoes of the Indian warriors, falling down to the sea; the Elizabethan captains' high-waisted ships; Sir Richard Grenville bringing his colony to settle Roanoke Island for his cousin, Raleigh ... seeking safe harbour in the river before he sailed north to be battered by the storms off Hatteras; their own tall ships, built on their own river at Amos Treloar's shipyard.

He tried to look into the future, to bring his imagination to bear on the ships his sons' sons would build, but the vision eluded him.

The plaintive sound of the ricebirds fell on his ears, tender and poignant. An eagle planed above the trees and rose to the darkness of the sky. In the fields, Annaci and his men were driving home the oxen, the day's work over. He heard laughter and the faint tinkling of music from the quarters line where the Negroes lived. Good sounds from happy, carefree hearts.

David remembered something Woodes Rogers had said, when he talked of the great part the Merchants of Bristol played in extending known boundaries for the world of trade: "Necessity has more than once sent simple, private men on a noble undertaking."

Perhaps that was what this whole New World was: the noble undertaking of simple, private men.

BRING ROMANCE INTO YOUR LIFE

With these bestsellers from your favorite Bantam authors

Barbara Cartland

☐	13827	BRIDE TO THE KING	$1.75
☐	13910	PUNISHED WITH LOVE	$1.75
☐	13830	THE DAWN OF LOVE	$1.75
☐	13579	FREE FROM FEAR	$1.75

Catherine Cookson

☐	13279	THE DWELLING PLACE	$1.95
☐	14187	THE GIRL	$2.25
☐	13170	KATIE MULHOLLAND	$1.95

Georgette Heyer

☐	13239	THE BLACK MOTH	$1.95
☐	11249	PISTOLS FOR TWO	$1.95

Emilie Loring

☐	12946	FOLLOW YOUR HEART	$1.75
☐	12947	WHERE BEAUTY DWELLS	$1.75
☐	12948	RAINBOW AT DUSK	$1.75
☐	13668	WITH BANNERS	$1.75
☐	13757	HILLTOPS CLEAR	$1.75

Eugenia Price

☐	13682	BELOVED INVADER	$2.25
☐	14195	LIGHTHOUSE	$2.50
☐	14406	NEW MOON RISING	$2.50

Buy them at your local bookstore or use this handy coupon for ordering:

Bantam Books, Inc., Dept. RO, 414 East Golf Road, Des Plaines, Ill. 60016

Please send me the books I have checked above. I am enclosing $_____
(please add $1.00 to cover postage and handling). Send check or money order
—no cash or C.O.D.'s please.

Mr/Mrs/Miss_____

Address_____

City_____State/Zip_____

RO—10/80
Please allow four to six weeks for delivery. This offer expires 4/81.

THE LATEST BOOKS IN THE BANTAM BESTSELLING TRADITION

☐	12998	**THE FAR PAVILIONS** M. M. Kaye	$3.50
☐	13752	**SHADOW OF THE MOON** M. M. Kaye	$3.95
☐	13545	**SOPHIE'S CHOICE** William Styron	$3.50
☐	14115	**INDEPENDENCE!** Dana Fuller Ross	$2.75
☐	14070	**NEBRASKA!** Dana Fuller Ross	$2.75
☐	14325	**WYOMING!** Dana Fuller Ross	$2.75
☐	14045	**WHITE INDIAN** Donald Clayton Porter	$2.75
☐	13559	**THE RENEGADE** Donald Clayton Porter	$2.50
☐	13452	**THE HAWK AND THE DOVE** Leigh Franklin James	$2.75
☐	12271	**LOVESWEPT** Lynn Lowery	$2.50
☐	12961	**LARISSA** Lynn Lowery	$2.50
☐	12958	**THE CINNAMON GARDENS** Jeanette Rebuth	$2.50
☐	14026	**A WORLD FULL OF STRANGERS** Cynthia Freeman	$2.95
☐	13641	**PORTRAITS** Cynthia Freeman	$3.50
☐	13463	**BLUE ROSES** Joyce Selznick	$2.50
☐	14064	**DAYS OF WINTER** Cynthia Freeman	$2.95
☐	14063	**FAIRYTALES** Cynthia Freeman	$2.95
☐	14033	**ICE!** Arnold Federbush	$2.50
☐	11820	**FIREFOX** Craig Thomas	$2.50

Buy them at your local bookstore or use this handy coupon:

Bantam Books, Inc., Dept. FBS, 414 East Golf Road, Des Plaines, Ill. 60016

Please send me the books I have checked above. I am enclosing $_____ (please add $1.00 to cover postage and handling). Send check or money order —no cash or C.O.D.'s please.

Mr/Mrs/Miss _____

Address _____

City_____ State/Zip_____

FBS—10/80

Please allow four to six weeks for delivery. This offer expires 4/81.